INI

FROM CURZON TO NEHRU
AND AFTER

INDIA
FROM CURZON TO NEHRU
& AFTER

DURGA DAS

with a Foreword by the President of India
Zakir Husain

RUPA

Published by
Rupa Publications India Pvt. Ltd 1969, 1981
7/16, Ansari Road, Daryaganj
New Delhi 110002

Sales centres:
Allahabad Bengaluru Chennai
Hyderabad Jaipur Kathmandu
Kolkata Mumbai

ISBN: 978-81-716-7591-3

Sixth impression 2015

10 9 8 7 6

Printed at Rekha Printers, New Delhi

This book, inspired by the ideal of
One World, is dedicated to :

my wife, Ratan Devi, and my children,
Savitri Uggersain, Inder Jit, Vikrama Jit,
Satya Jit, Brahma Jeet, Rani Tarneja,

whose love and forbearance made it
possible for me to savour both the
tears and joys of journalism to the full.

CONTENTS

Foreword, 13

Introduction, 15

BOOK I
1900–21
Political Awakening

BOOK II
1921–39
The Gandhian Revolution

BOOK III
1939–47
Independence Dawns

BOOK IV
1947–64
The Nehru Era

ILLUSTRATIONS

MAPS

FOREWORD

Perhaps no period of Indian history has been so packed with significant and exciting events and outstanding personalities as the sixty-eight years of the twentieth century. This period has seen the end of an empire as well as of an epoch—colonialism—after a political struggle whose repercussions were felt far beyond India's shores and which acted as a beacon for the aspirations of other nations in Asia and Africa and Latin America under foreign rule.

It is this historical panorama, spreading from the fledgling years of the freedom movement beginning with Curzon and embracing the succeeding pro-consuls of Britain on the one hand and the torch-bearers of the freedom movement—from Tilak to Gandhi and Nehru on the other—and the years that followed 15th August, 1947, the great watershed of Indian history, that is chronicled in this volume of personal memoirs.

It is fitting that this chronicle should come from the pen of my friend Durga Das, whom I first met in 1921. We are contemporaries and I have been intensely interested in the period the memoirs cover, although I was most of the time outside the current of politics. To mention only two reasons: he was born in the first year of the century and he therefore grew up along with the movement which culminated in freedom; from 1918, when his journalistic career began, onward he was at the centre of things, as it were. During his fifty years of journalism, he has held key positions—first as Editor of the Associated Press of India (the forerunner of the Press Trust of India) in New Delhi and Simla, subsequently as the first Indian Special Representative of the *Statesman* with the Government of India, then as Chief Editor of the *Hindustan Times* and, finally, as the founder and Editor-in-Chief of India News and Feature Alliance. Scarcely anything of political importance took place in Delhi or Simla, the twin seats of the British Raj, and later in Nehru's Delhi without his being a close and discerning observer, reporter and interpreter of them.

In those days of struggle for freedom, journalism was a sacred mission, not a mundane profession. Educated young Indians took to it not for monetary inducements, which were very meagre or practically non-existent, but with the fervour of patriots. What others achieved on the political platform and with the spoken word, they did with the written word in newspapers which took the message of freedom to every village.

Journalism played a very big role in those stirring times, being no less than a complement to, and an inspirer of, political action. One of the most ardent crusaders in the cause of freedom among the scribes of Delhi was Durga Das. This book bears testimony to the service he rendered the nation, first as one of its spokesmen against its alien masters and later as the stern and impartial critic of the flaws he saw in the new India that was taking shape after independence. His weekly political column has marked him out as a penetrating and shrewd analyst who foresaw events and had the courage to state his convictions.

I have watched Durga Das's activities closely from the time I became Vice-President. I count the frequent dialogues I have had with him among the most rewarding and relaxing experiences. His art of establishing rapport with others and making stimulating talk have lent weight and colour to the story he has unfolded.

Here is Indian history seen from the inside, combined with personal judgments and at the same time presented clearly and objectively. With his wide travels and intimate knowledge of the men and women who made the history of these times in India and around the world, Durga Das has been able to interpret events in the light of what happened behind the scenes and the interplay of powerful and often strongly conflicting personalities. The result is a fascinating narrative that is as valuable to the serious student of Indian politics of the modern era as to the lay reader.

The memoirs, I cautioned him, when he sought my advice, should make an organic whole. He has certainly succeeded in that task. He has recounted what he gathered and how he reacted to significant men and events. One can differ with his conclusions, but this narrative of the most convulsive period in India's history makes absorbing reading. He has discharged honourably the debt he owes the nation of telling the story of a working journalist's life, lived intensely and dedicated to the service of his country and the promotion of international understanding.

Rashtrapati Bhavan   ZAKIR HUSAIN
New Delhi   *President of India*
20 March, 1969

INTRODUCTION

Curiously, the decision that I write my memoirs was taken in the West Indies late in 1965 by my eldest son, Inder Jit, and some old friends. Jit, Director-Editor of INFA, had gone there to attend the quinquennial Commonwealth Press Conference as one of the two delegates from India.

When he returned home he had a surprise for me. He said: "Your friends at the Conference missed you a lot. They said you should write your memoirs. Gandhi had brought his autobiography up to 1920 and Nehru's account of his life and the 'Discovery of India' had taken the narrative up to the thirties. But very little had been written about the most dynamic period of their lives. They said you had observed the scene at close quarters and had had an equation with the top men who played a significant part in the history of modern India."

The material was there. I had written some twenty million words constituting straight reporting, features, analyses and comments for almost half a century. I had kept half a million words in the form of notes in shorthand or scribbled in longhand. I had written and received thousands of letters which, too, had been preserved. A part of this material had been eaten by termites, but most of it remained in good shape.

My wife, Ratan Devi, a stickler for tidiness, often remonstrated that a whole room was being wasted and would say: "Do you wish to build a new pyramid?" I would reply: "Keep it. Jit may find in the material a glimpse of what India was like and what his father did—or he will burn it." Clippings of all I had written were there, and also of articles by men of significance. Suddenly, in 1957, soon after my wife and I returned from a world tour, I found her solicitous about carefully stacking the material I had brought back.

Why this sudden change in her attitude? An astrologer from Ludhiana, the industrial hub of Punjab, she said, had drawn up a chart about the future. "He says you will write a book, which will bring 'fame'. I now realise what you had in mind in preserving all that stuff." She, like most Indian women, had great faith in the *patriwala* (astrologer). As was wont with men of my generation who considered themselves modern, I laughed away what she said.

Perhaps the seed of the idea of writing memoirs was unconsciously sown then. So what Jit said on his return from the West Indies registered. But the professional code stood in the way of revealing what I had gathered in off-the-record talks while the principal actors of the contemporary drama were alive. With the death of Nehru, the last of the national heroes of the Gandhian era, the remaining hurdle was removed.

Not long afterwards, N. J. Nanporia, then Editor of the *Times of India*, joined Jit and me for lunch during one of his periodic visits to New Delhi from Bombay. We were reminiscing about the pre-independence era when suddenly Nanporia said: "You ought to write your memoirs some day. All this unrivalled information must be shared. You must."

One doubt remained. Could I do full justice to either the theme or the period without bringing my knowledge of India and its role in the larger world context up to date? This meant another global tour since the last was undertaken in 1959. John Grigg (formerly Lord Altrincham), with whom I struck up a lasting friendship at the Ottawa session of the Imperial Press Conference in 1950, happily arrived on a visit to India in January 1967 accompanied by his charming wife Patsy. John had not only welcomed the project but had sold the idea to Collins. I now sounded him about undertaking another world tour, mentioning that it might delay the book. "Oh, that will provide a grand finale to the memoirs," he said.

I sought the advice of our philosopher-President, Dr. Radhakrishnan. He welcomed my decision and said the book should centre on me if it was to be real memoirs. Dr. Zakir Husain, then Vice-President and subsequently President of the Republic, said that memoirs, to be of value, should unfold a story in such a way as to make it an organic whole.

Since the twenties, I had covered the doings of our Central Legislature, the annual sessions of the Indian National Congress, of the All-India Muslim League and of other political organisations and of commercial and industrial bodies functioning in the sub-continent. I had toured the country with the Lee Commission on Civil Services in India and the Simon Commission on Constitutional Reforms. Further, I had visited Europe and London in the summer of 1931 and thereafter toured abroad fourteen times. These travels included four trips covering the two hemispheres, a tour of the Middle East and Europe as a war correspondent early in 1945 and again at the end of the war, and a visit to London when the Attlee Cabinet was deeply involved in devising a formula for the transfer of power in India.

It was my business to make contacts with, and seek the confidence of all who made politics and held the levers of power—the Viceroys from Lord Chelmsford to Lord Mountbatten; politicians from Tilak and Gandhi to Jinnah, Nehru, Shastri and Indira; top civil servants of the "steel frame" who symbolised the bureaucracy that ruled India, and leaders of the business community, both European and Indian. Besides, I had the opportunity of holding dialogues with top world personalities, among them five British Prime Ministers, three U.S. Presidents, three Prime Ministers of Japan, two Chancellors of West Germany, two Chairmen of the Soviet Union and Presidents Tito and Nasser.

I rarely put set questions. It was a give-and-take dialogue. Whatever I put down after off-the-record talks was in a sense a test of memory, a paraphrase adhering as much as possible to the actual words used, at least the meaningful ones. Often the persons I interviewed emphasised their own part in an event and played down that of the others. Therefore, I made it a point to get a cross-section of opinion on whatever subject I was pursuing and to check and double check on the facts and conclusions gathered from various sources.

The memoirs are divided into five books which, politically, mark distinct periods of India's evolution from a colonial dependency to a democratic republic. They tell the story of the British Raj at its height, of its gradual decline and dissolution, of the growth and triumph of nationalism, the rise and fall of free India's credit in world counsels and of the challenges that face our young democracy and the question marks that hang over its future. Curzon's regime at the turn of the century represented the high-water mark of British authority, symbolised by peace and contentment in the land. The Nehru era reached its peak in the mid-fifties, when he bestrode the stage like a colossus. The half-century dividing these two men of destiny saw the emergence of Gandhi as the leader of a non-violent revolution, the exit of the British with the creation of the two independent and separate dominions of India and Pakistan and the evolution of a new polity in the sub-continent.

Book One (1900–1921) covers the period which constituted unadulterated British Raj and marked the rise of the Indian National Congress as the main challenger to the imperial power. How did this happen when Curzon had reported to London soon after assuming the viceroyalty that he would see the demise of the Congress? These two decades also saw the recognition of the Muslim community as a separate political entity, the outbreak of World War I and the formulation by Whitehall under the compulsion of circumstances of its policy of granting responsible government to

Indians by stages. Tilak's slogan of "Home Rule is my birthright" had infected the mind of the newly educated elite when Gandhi, sensing the national mood, introduced the weapon of protest he had tried in South Africa. By the end of 1920 he had succeeded in making the Congress reject the constitutional reforms enacted by the British Parliament and swing to the extreme course of non-violent non-cooperation.

Book Two (1921–1939) deals with the period of British-cum-Indian rule flowing from the first instalment of constitutional reforms, the ups and downs of the Gandhian movement and the sharpening of religious animosities. The Prince of Wales' tour failed in its missions. So also the Parliamentary Commission, headed by John Simon and including Clement Attlee. They only helped to add fuel to the nationalist fire. Peace seemed to dawn with the Gandhi–Irwin Pact. But the proceedings of the Round Table Conference and debates on the Government of India Bill of 1935 caused a fresh political stir and blew up the bridge the pact attempted to build. The struggle for power, which was bipolar until then, now became pentangular.

Book Three (1939–1947) deals with the most momentous period in Indo–British history. World War II caused a breach between the British and the Congress because of differences over war aims, and the Raj, consequently, assumed absolute authority to mobilise India's resources. But the fortunes of the war combined with American pressure made London respond favourably to the Congress demand for the transfer of power. The Muslim League, under Jinnah's leadership, proved a major roadblock because of an assurance given by the Viceroy in August 1940 to neutralise Congress intransigence. The intriguing drama ended with Britain deciding to cut its losses. Who was the winner and who the loser in this "Divide and Quit" operation?

Book Four (1947–1964) covers the Nehru era—its challenges, successes and failures. It describes the blood bath that accompanied partition, Gandhi's assassination, the framing of the Constitution, Pakistan's attack on Kashmir, the integration of the Princely States with the Union and the clash behind the scenes, first between Nehru and Sardar Patel and later between Nehru and Rajendra Prasad. After the Sardar passed away in December 1950 and until his death in 1964, Nehru was India and one witnessed both his rise to un-rivalled heights and his fall after the Chinese aggression of 1962. In between, Nehru groomed his daughter Indira Gandhi for public life—and brought forward the ingenious Kamaraj Plan.

Book Five (1964–1969) deals with the post-Nehru period, the

drama of the succession of Shastri to the prime ministership, the Indo–Pakistani war of 1965 and the Tashkent meet where Shastri died after signing the historic agreement. The most significant aspect of this deal is the role that Kosygin played to establish Soviet interest in the affairs of the sub-continent. The narrative unfolds the behind-the-scene story of Mrs. Gandhi's appointment as Prime Minister, the break-up in 1967 of the Congress Party's monolithic twenty-year rule since independence and the emergence of new challenges—Communist and revivalist. It spotlights the growing malaise in Indian politics, and ventures an assessment of how Indian polity is evolving and where India and humanity might stand by the end of the century.

The tour of fourteen world capitals in 1967 enabled a fresh assessment of India's image abroad and role in Asia and in the balance of power between the Big Powers. Australia's elder statesman, Robert Menzies, summed up the situation aptly on the occasion of the visit of Prime Minister Indira Gandhi to Melbourne University in May 1968. Menzies, who took over as head of the university after a record term as Prime Minister, said: "The measure of India's success is the measure of the success of the future world." But a question that will haunt thinkers and observers of the Indian scene for a long time is: Will India break through or will it break up?

This is not a documented history of the time; only an assortment of incidents symbolising our age in an ever-changing world. It is an attempt to portray men and events in an effort to help the evaluation of Indian political affairs of yesterday, today and tomorrow. The centre from which I operated was New Delhi—and India. The wide world was the sounding board from which I judged the evolution of international politics and its reaction on India. What follows are personal impressions about distinguished men and women, some self-effacing, others seekers after glory, some with a profound philosophical outlook, others playing the game on the chessboard of power with ruthless determination. The purpose is not to praise or censure, but to help throw some light on a few dark corners of history.

2 *Tolstoy Lane,*   DURGA DAS
New Delhi
April 7, 1969

Book I

1900–21

POLITICAL AWAKENING

(1) CHILDHOOD IN A PUNJAB VILLAGE

Plague—that scourge which ravaged the country in the early years of the century! I was hardly two when it struck me down. The family priest muttered prayers and incantations as I hovered between life and death. The village soothsayer dipped into my horoscope and solemnly assured my parents that I would not succumb. Indeed, he forecast for me "crossings of the seven seas." I was snatched from the brink, but the terror of plague lingered on for years; every time the disease appeared in the neighbourhood, I was packed off to Simla, that salubrious hill station where my uncle and elder brother were running a business establishment. It was during such a visit in 1918 that I was to meet the man whose stimulating words were to mould my future. Fifty years of unending thrills in journalism—I owe them to plague.

Immunity from this dread visitation was to be purchased only through inoculation; but in those distant days the operation was so crude and its after-effects so excruciating that few villagers would submit to it. One of my earliest recollections is of a boy screaming that the inoculators were on the prowl in the village and of scores of little children running helter-skelter for asylum. I recall vividly how I hid in a godown, while my mother, Uttam Devi, went round frantically looking for me. It was only as the darkness of night descended on the village that I crept out of concealment. My mother then told me, between laughter and tears, that it had been a false alarm. To soothe my fears, she added that having once suffered the affliction I now enjoyed immunity and that, in any case, I had already been inoculated. But all through early boyhood the inoculator was to remain my bogy-man.

Plague, as I have said, brought me good luck. But to the family of my wife-to-be, Ratan Devi, it spelt disaster. Their mansion in Garhshankar town was perched on an eminence in keeping with the distinction that belonged to the Kanungos (pundits in law) that the menfolk had the right to carry arms. The head of the family firmly believed that the inoculator was a greater scourge than the plague itself, and one day, in an uncontrollable fit of indignation, he got his gun out and shot one of the "accursed breed." The townsfolk acclaimed him a hero, of course, but the law took a different view. He had to pay for his crime with his life, and for a whole generation the family fortunes suffered eclipse.

(2) VILLAGE FESTIVITIES

The scene of my childhood and that of my future wife was the Doaba, the land encompassed by two rivers, the Sutlej and the Beas. The districts of Jullundur and Hoshiarpur were deservedly re-nowned, for their soil was fertile and the peasants hardy and adventurous.

The area represented the heart of the Punjab. Largely dependent on well irrigation, its light-brown soil yielded excellent varieties of wheat, maize, gram and sugarcane. In the season for fruits, mangoes, melons and berries were plentiful.

Most of the villagers lived in mud-walled houses with flat roofs. But the well-to-do among them owned brick structures whose height was in a sense the measure of the family's affluence.

It was a self-sufficient tract, but, compared with other districts, overpopulated. Little wonder that the more enterprising sought fresh pastures far and near. Many families migrated to the Crown colony in West Punjab, where the canal irrigation system introduced by the British had opened up a land of great promise. This irrigation system was indeed the largest of its kind in the world and a monu-ment to the beneficence of the Raj. Crown lands in this rich tract came in handy as gifts for loyal service to the Government.

In my village of Aur were families some of whose members had migrated to Australia and Canada, and some performed regular *safars* (journeyings) as far afield as Burma, Java, Sumatra and Penang. Thus in the small cocoon we inhabited we often heard whispers from wondrous realms far beyond our ken. Our fancies roamed the wide world when my father, Ishwar Das (headmaster-cum-postmaster), distributed remittances from abroad or read out letters received from overseas.

Ours was a village of considerable size and was therefore known as Qasbah. Its importance was emphasised by the fact that it had a school, a post office and a hospital. Its shops served the needs of a score of surrounding villages. As the hub of social and cultural life, it attracted hundreds of peasants from the countryside all round for the big festivals of Dussehra, Moharrum, Divali, Lohri and Holi.

Peace and harmony prevailed on all these festive occasions. Only

Dussehra (to celebrate Lord Rama's victory over the Demon King Ravana) sometimes proved an exception, for it was then that long-simmering village feuds erupted. Yet the Dussehra committee of the Khatris of Aur managed without police assistance. If heads were broken or someone got killed, the matter was duly reported to the police station at Rahon, seven miles away. No more was said about it—the combatants themselves would patch up and forget their wounds or would bide their time until Dussehra came round again to even the score.

Another festival children looked forward to was Moharrum. The Shia and Sunni Muslims would vie with each other in turning out *tazias* for the ritual procession. Both sides decked these emblems in gilt and shining baubles. It was a labour of love in which Hindu boys would readily lend a helping hand. This was a gesture that was reciprocated during Dussehra, for then young Muslims would join their Hindu brethren in setting up the gigantic cane-and-bamboo effigies of the King of Lanka, Ravana, and Meghnath. Moharrum at Aur was a joyous affair, far removed from the traditional day of mourning; there was no beating of the breasts or wailing. The Muslims went round in procession attired in their holiday finery, intermingling with Hindus no less gaudily dressed. In the country-side this kind of fraternisation was not unusual, though in the towns British officials professed to be concerned about communal clashes.

Divali, the festival of lights, was celebrated with great éclat at Aur, as everywhere else in India. The cynosure of all eyes was the Qila Ihata, the elevated site of the ruins of an ancient Sikh fortress, with the school over which my father presided sitting atop. There, tier upon tier, twinkled several thousands of little earthen lamps, each with its cotton wick floating in mustard oil. It was a magnificent spectacle that gladdened one's heart.

The Qila Ihata school was the focus, too, of Lohri, the festival that marks the end of winter's rigours and the shy advent of spring. For a bonfire, the villagers built a pile of cowdung cakes towering to a height of twenty-five feet, and into the flames licking it they thrust sugarcane to roast. The delights of chewing on the succulence of the roasted cane were only a small part of the general merriment that lasted late into the night.

Holi marked the coming of spring, a very joyous occasion when all rules of normal behaviour were suspended in the gay abandon of throwing coloured water on anyone and everyone who came one's way.

Chapter 2

(1) THE SOCIAL AND RELIGIOUS MILIEU
BLESSINGS OF THE RAJ

One's memories of childhood are often nostalgic, invested with an illusory romance. But, viewing things objectively, the very early years of the twentieth century formed the golden period of the British Raj. People enjoyed peace and contentment in a climate of social security. To the intelligent and adventurous, opportunity beckoned with open arms. Anyway, I cannot recall a single reason for being dissatisfied with the conditions of my childhood.

My father's standing in the village was high. In the schoolroom, he often spelled out the blessings of the Raj. My grandmother appeared to hold the alien ruler in the same high regard. Many of her bedtime stories revolved round *Sikha Shahi* (Sikh misrule) and the Mutiny, of which we now speak as the First War of Independence. She was all praise for the Ram Raj of Malka, Queen Victoria.

Grandma had, however, what we would now describe as superstitious taboos. She would caution me, for instance, against all social contacts with the *farangi* (foreigner)—he was an untouchable who ate beef. If I were ever to shake hands with a white man, I must cleanse myself of the pollution seven times over. Never eat in a Brahmin's house, she would say with a warning shake of her old finger; a Khatri (Kshatriya) must not partake of food given away in charity, never eat with a Jat (a peasant cultivator) either, for he does not conform to the strict code of cleanliness enjoined upon the higher castes. As for the Muslim or the lowly Chamar or sweeper, the eatables that he touched must be thrown away.

Despite the seemingly senseless rigours of such injunctions, life flowed smoothly in the village. The various castes understood the taboos and respected them. My father was no slave to these social barriers. His relations with Muslim families were cordial; on feast days he would send them cooked food, and they would reciprocate on their Id day or other festive occasion by instructing Hindu shopkeepers to supply us with grain and sweets. At his house Hindus and Muslims would squat on the same carpet, the latter withdrawing discreetly for a moment when a Hindu wanted a drink of water. My father had no scruples, either, about visiting an untouchable's house to persuade him to send his children to school.

In these troubled days, my thoughts often flash back to a vivid picture of the Hindu–Muslim harmony of long years ago. Arrayed on two sides are long-bearded Muslim divines engaged in hot disputation over the precise interpretation of an injunction in the Holy Koran. The arbiter seated at the head of the assemblage is a Hindu. The arguments go backward and forward, and at the end my father pronounces the verdict. Nodding their heads in amiable agreement, the divines depart, each with a reverential salaam.

Incidents like this underscore the mutual respect and understanding that nourished a climate of tolerance and harmony in rural India over the decades.

The basic tenet of the British Raj was not to interfere with the customs and traditions of the people, and the people for their part regarded the alien Government as the source of security and the guarantor of freedom for each to pursue his individual vocation.

(2) BELIEFS AND SUPERSTITIONS

If the elders were to call down a benediction upon a boy, they would invariably say: "May God make you a Thanedar or a Patwari"— the embodiment of power and authority. The Thanedar was the sub-inspector of police, a local potentate, and the Patwari wielded great influence as the village revenue accountant. Even the words of reproof were significant. If someone was fractious or arrogant, the villagers would remark acidly that he was becoming a Lat Sahib or Nawab. The Lat Sahib was the Governor of the province and the ultimate repository of governmental authority, and the Nawab the highest symbol of feudal grandeur.

All this defined the horizons of the villager's thinking. In addition, there was the vast body of beliefs that you would dismiss today as quaint. I recall vividly a noisy bazaar brawl over a clean-shaven youth. He had, Curzon fashion, lopped off what in the Punjab countryside was reckoned the very mark of manhood and virility. Without a well-groomed moustache, smartly curled upward at the ends, he was effeminate, an object of ridicule. Lord Curzon was the first Viceroy to discard this hirsute adornment; and in rural Punjab he was for that reason the butt of many irreverent jokes. I was to learn later that in the towns local bards had composed lampoons on "Cur-zon," with the barbed accent on *zon* (woman).

Not dissimilar was the superstition that clung to the turban—

the headgear native to the Punjabi. The turban is just the kind of protection that the most sensitive part of one's anatomy needs against the severity of the Punjab weather. But in those far-off days there was more to it. To go about bareheaded was to proclaim oneself bereft of all shame, to show brazen disrespect to your elders. The turban was the mark of dignity and honour. There was no personal insult more unpardonable than to dislodge it from your opponent's head; an adversary who threatened to snatch your turban off was obviously intent on humiliating you. By the turn of the century, however, imported caps had invaded the countryside, and boys were permitted to wear these in place of the more cumbersome headgear. But the taboo on uncovered heads was not to vanish for a long time.

I call to mind what occasioned a sensation while I was a boarder at the middle school at Rahon a few years later. Word was passed round in whispers among the boys that a Bengali adult who went about bareheaded was in town. Stirred by curiosity, we flocked to his house. He was not only bareheaded; he ate eggs—in our eyes a sin—and spoke in English. That he was a Bengali was in itself intriguing enough. Except as a province marked in the atlas, what did Bengal mean to us then?

The Bengali who lisped in English had his precursor in my village in the person of a boy who spoke Hindustani. This lad, whose father was employed at Dehra Dun, was fluent in a language that we had to master laboriously through text-books. We were taught Urdu in the first and second primary classes and Persian from the third. The spoken language was a dialect of Punjabi, which varied from one part of the province to another. Hindustani, spoken in the neighbouring United Provinces of Agra and Oudh, was to us an enviable acquisition.

It was a narrow world we lived in. Contact outside our own small region was restricted. All marriages, for instance, were contracted within a radius of ten to twenty miles. Seldom would one look for a match across the nearby river. If that was done, it was suspected that there was some blemish the parties sought to hide from the critical scrutiny of their neighbours.

For all that, the concept of India as our home and motherland was implanted in our minds and nourished by the two epics, Ramayana and Mahabharata, and by the tales of pilgrims who had devoutly journeyed to the four corners of the country—Hardwar in the north, Rameshwaram and Kanya Kumari (Cape Comorin) at the southern tip of the peninsula, Dwarka to the west and Puri and Kashi (Banaras) far to the east.

(3) LEARNING THE RUDIMENTS OF DHARMA

Long before I entered my teens I was to absorb the rudimentary principles of Dharma at the knees of my parents. Dharma (inadequately rendered into English as the right path and righteousness) embraced, in the child's comprehension, religion and its prescribed ritual, a code of conduct, of which cleanliness was an inescapable part, and a certain basic philosophy.

First came personal hygiene and self-discipline. We were to cast off our footwear before we crossed the threshold of the house. The daily ablutions were carefully laid down and enforced. The teeth had to be brushed with the twigs of certain trees, and the ritual of washing and bathing was exacting. Food was invested with a measure of sanctity, and so was the kitchen where it was prepared and served.

Discipline was instilled into our minds through elementary lessons in the law of Karma (reward based on deeds). If things went wrong, one was paying for wrongs done in a past life. If one prospered, one was reaping the fruits of good deeds performed previously. My mother was my early mentor in these mysteries. Tell a lie or steal, and you will be born to poor parents in your next life. If you are cruel to animals, you might be born into the animal kingdom yourself. Discharge your duty and act righteously and you will be rewarded in this life and in the next as well.

Better than precept was the example the elders set. My father, for instance, would never fail to throw crumbs to pariah dogs or cast a morsel on the roof for the birds. My mother would invariably set apart a piece of *chapati* (baked flat bread) for the cow before she sat down to her meal. Charity and kindliness to all life around us is part of the obligation we owe the Creator. Trees too are sentient beings, my father said, and must be treated with solicitude. Never disturb a tree after nightfall, he cautioned me; it is asleep.

Religion, where it was a matter of ritual, was largely the preserve of the priests, who officiated at all festivities and ceremonies. But the teaching of it was principally in the hands of pious women well-versed in scriptural lore, often widows whose austerity of life was a byword among us, or of itinerant monks who roamed for alms from door to door, chanting sacred songs. There was little distinction between the holy books of the Hindus and the Sikhs. In fact, the first texts I heard intoned as I sat in my mother's lap were from the Guru Granth Sahib, the Holy Book of the Sikhs. Muslim mendicants and *pirs* (saints) were held in no less esteem. Sufism was, in fact, closely akin to Hindu philosophy.

Much of what we thus imbibed was, of course, beyond our understanding. Our acceptance of it was instinctive, but it did affect our minds. The law of Karma gave one the feeling that yesterday is linked with today, even as today with tomorrow, in a never-ending cycle. One sensed, too, the underlying oneness of all God's infinite creation. And all around one noticed how this spiritual outlook tempered the rigours of the caste system and leavened social life with humaneness.

Caste consciousness can be a great evil; but in those ancient days people had learnt to accept life without resentment. It was not merely fatalism. In some degree at least it was rooted in a spirituality one cannot pin down in precise words. Take the case of the untouchable sweeper woman of the village. She called from door to door at midday, collecting the food set apart for her as religiously as it was laid aside for the cow. The lowly outcast thus experienced a sense of participation in the good things of life.

Chapter 3

FIRST CONTACT WITH THE WHITE MAN

The social milieu in which life jogged along in the village was tradition-bound. But under the surface one sensed the slow swell of change. Take the scale of values in the world into which I was born. Of all vocations agriculture was reckoned the most rewarding, next came trade, and Government service about last. This derived from the feudal economy of the times and determined one's worth in the marriage market. The British rulers felt, however, that the agriculturist was the underdog, deserving preferential treatment. Thus students were enrolled on the school register as agriculturist or non-agriculturist, the former being exempted from payment of fees and, in addition, having a goodly share of the scholarship awards set apart for them. Curiously enough, agricultural labourers, the real have-nots, were not entitled to these concessions. Maybe, the Raj respected the taboos in respect of the lowly in the caste hierarchy.

At the turn of the century, however, a new order of social precedence was taking shape. The yardstick was one's eligibility as a prospective son-in-law. Formerly, a youth's status was determined by the landed possessions of his family, but now the Government servant stood on a higher rung of the ladder. Women's gossip turned invariably on the question of how much the bridegroom-elect earned. The accent was not on his salary so much as on the *buksheesh* (tips) that came his way. With pride the prospective mother-in-law would proclaim that the boy made as much in perquisites as in pay. No stigma attached to such additional gains.

The Punjab has for long been deservedly famous for its martial traditions. And the British took care to invest soldiering with many attractions. The young Punjabi peasant was sturdy and adventurous by nature and *bharti* (recruitment to the armed forces) therefore exercised an irresistible appeal on him. Here was release from the drudgery of rural existence, a uniform that would stir the heart of the village maiden and, best of all, a handsome wage that would help swell the family's cash resources. My father, for his part, would point out to them the economic security that soldiering promised, and no less the social advantages. The widow of a person killed in military service would, besides getting a small pension, be taken for wife by one of his brothers by convention in certain castes and thus be well provided for.

In this placid pool of village life, my first glimpse of an Englishman was in the person of the Deputy Commissioner of the district. Astride a horse, he halted before the school for a bare five minutes. The village headman and my father, as headmaster, were there to welcome him attired in white garments, for they were *sufaid posh*, of the ones entitled to appear before the ruling élite in the regulation white. My own reaction was perhaps governed more by instinct and emotion than reason. I was charmed by his personality, so handsome and well-groomed, the very embodiment of the Raj. Soon, in a sudden fit of hostile reaction, I was asking myself: "Why is he here?" All that had been hammered into my mind about the blessings of the British Raj had mysteriously evaporated. Was this due to the childhood prejudice against the beef-eating *farangi* (foreigner) or the faint stirring of that spirit which was to find expression in the years to come in the Gandhian revolution?

The next contact with the white man occurred two years later. I was then reading in the seventh class of the Anglo–Vernacular Middle School at Rahon, not far from my native Aur. It was the District Inspector of Schools visiting our institution—a tall, egg-headed Briton. He addressed the headmaster, whom we held in great awe and veneration, rudely. At the same time, he gave us a taste of the white man's authority. There was a cloudburst while he was on his rounds, and water dripped from a leak in the roof on to his bald crown. The boys could hardly suppress a giggle, and the representative of the Raj shouted that the offending roof must be pulled down. I recall the sequel vividly—not only was the roof redone but the entire boarding house was built anew.

Just across the boundary wall of our school lay the Dak bungalow, and here one saw, not infrequently, English officers out on a duck shoot in the local *jheel* (low-lying area that the rains convert into a lake.) Up and down the steep, cobbled lane below my window, the sahibs strode with their womenfolk, whose thin waspish waists filled the boarders with puzzled admiration. Our own concept of affluence and good living was associated with a thick waistline, an ample corporation and well-upholstered limbs.

These shikaris were a community apart. They were of the privileged ruling class, aloof and overbearing. Not the white man alone, but also the Anglo–Indians and the westernised Indian Christians who often came with them. All sahibs, from whom we recoiled instinctively.

Life at Rahon brought me in touch with Muslims too. Here they were among the bigger landlords, Chaudhries (the elect), not the peasants and artisans one encountered at Aur. But the two communities lived in peace and harmony. The Muslim chaudhry was often a spendthrift and deep in debt to the Hindu moneylender. But contact between Hindu and Muslim went further than money transactions. Every Friday Hindus and Muslims alike would light little lamps as offerings at the tomb of the Muslim *pir*. This tomb was close to our boarding house, and many of the boys prayed at its side for success in examination, and when their prayers were answered they spent their pocket money on votive gifts.

Chapter 4

(1) SCHOOL DAYS – COMMUNAL RIVALRIES ARYA SAMAJ AND THE REFORM FERMENT

From the Middle School at Rahon to the High School at Jullundur, the district headquarters, was a big step. At 14, I enrolled myself at the Sain Das Anglo-Sanskrit High School, an Arya Samaj institution.

This was my first introduction to a world of communal rivalries. The city's high schools, I quickly discovered, were organised on communal lines. Hindus, Muslims and Christians had separate institutions. The Sikhs were regarded at that time as a section of the Hindu community; they were not enumerated as a separate community until the Census of 1911. True, the doors of such schools were open to all communities, but in each the dominant element belonged to the denominational group financing it. Inter-school competitions, whether in sport or scholarship, acquired a keen communal edge.

Arya Samaj, a movement launched by Swami Dayananda, who hailed from Gujarat, had quickly swept large sections of the Hindu intelligentsia in the Punjab off their feet, and by the turn of the century it had become a dynamic social and religious phenomenon. Being in a sense a revolt against the established order, it seemed to offer an outlet for the younger generation's mood of rebellious questioning. The crusaders' standard of the movement was borne by the galaxy of orators it threw up, outstanding figures like Lala Lajpat Rai, Swami Shraddhanand and Mahatma Hans Raj. It is not surprising that most of them were to be found in the van of the Gandhian revolution later. That was the natural culmination of the spirit of dissent inculcated by the early missionary adventure.

Arya Samaj preachers in Jullundur had several targets for attack—orthodox Hinduism going under the name of Sanatan Dharma (ageless religion), the rival Arya Samaj which ran the Doaba High School and the Christian missionaries striving to win converts to their Church. They accepted the Sikhs, however, as brothers-in-faith, and the Muslims as part of the pattern of social life.

The Arya Samaj leaders were careful during the first two decades of the century to steer clear of politics. They were afraid lest they be suspected of nurturing seditionists under their wing. The Government had banned a history of India written by Bhai Parmanand, a stalwart of the Samaj who was later to become life President of the All-India Hindu Mahasabha. The stories woven round the exploits of Bhai Parmanand and Lala Lajpat Rai were legion, and I still remember how they stirred my imagination as a fresher at high school. The former was then in detention, and the latter had gone to America to escape the unwelcome attention of the Government. We believed the most fantastic tales then afloat about these legendary heroes, even the one that told how Lala Lajpat Rai had been offered the presidentship of the United States but had declined the honour because he could not bring himself to forswear the undying loyalty he owed his motherland.

I recall how I used up my pocket money to buy Bhai Parmanand's

proscribed history of India. But hardly had I browsed through the
first chapter when the superintendent of the boarding house pounced
on me. "If the British should come to hear of a boarder in possession
of this book," he shouted, "they will have me arrested and put in
prison and order the school to be closed down." This stormy incident
came to my mind years later when as a journalist I happened to
meet Bhai Parmanand. To my intense surprise, I discovered that the
fulminations of my boyhood idol were turned more against Gandhi
than the British.

But for all that the main impact of the Arya Samaj was as a
dynamic movement combating superstition, challenging the caste
system as taught and practised by the orthodox Hindu, championing
the cause of women's uplift through education, urging inter-caste
marriages and meals and the removal of untouchability, and
upholding the ideal of simple living and high thinking.

The daily morning prayers in the temple were intended to introduce the element of congregational worship, from which Christianity
and Islam derive the strength of their appeal. The Christian ideal
of the brotherhood of all mankind and the Islamic concept of a
classless society were, as the Arya Samajists had perceived, nourished
and sustained by such congregational prayers. The Arya Samaj also
stood for proselytisation, especially of those who had once been
Hindus. It was indeed trying to copy the methods of the rival
religions in an effort to protect Hinduism.

The prejudice against women's education was a long time
adying. The strength of the taboo was determined by the environment. Where the Muslims formed the élite, strict *purdah* was observed
even among the Hindus. My father did start a school for girls, but
he employed a woman to teach the pupils, and the classes were held
in the privacy of his own residence. Things were wholly different
with the family of my future wife. Living on terms of social intimacy
with aristocratic Muslim Rajput families in Garhshankar, a sub-
division of Hoshiarpur district, they themselves observed *satar*,
seclusion of the womenfolk. Imagine then the furore when her
mother surreptitiously sent her to a private woman teacher. Her
grandfather discovered the trespass and threatened to chop the poor
girl's legs off should she ever venture again to step across the
threshold. That was the end of her schooling. Even as late as the
twenties, Sir Malcolm Hailey, Governor of the province, was to
observe that hardly one Punjabi among a hundred could expect to
have an educated wife.

Against this social background, one can readily understand the
sensation caused by the opening of a girls' institute, a Kanya

Mahavidyalaya, at Jullundur. As the girls in uniform, yellow sari after the fashion in Vedic times, trundled along in *tongas* (horse carts) past our high school, the boys ran to the roadside to gape at the spectacle. On the occasion of an anniversary, a chorus of girls draped in saris appeared on the platform to sing a religious song. How indeed could the orthodox put up with the indignity of girls from respectable families being exposed to the public gaze? Stones and shoes came hurtling on to the stage.

The principal protagonist of women's education at Jullundur was a scion of the Sondhi family. His heterodoxy caused many pious eyebrows to be raised. But his younger brother, Bhagat Ram, seemed to give even greater offence, for he had the temerity to employ a Muslim cook. Their caste-conscious minds outraged, the high school boys went about saying he had turned Muslim. He enjoyed a formidable reputation, though, as the top lawyer of the district. In the villages around men audaciously proclaimed that they could commit murder and get away with it so long as Bhagat Ram was available to take up their defence. His fee was fifty rupees— an exorbitant sum in those early days—but one was safe in his hands, such was his skill in advocacy and cross-examination. In fact, he became an idol of mine, the more so since I had once overheard my father and uncle say that I should be sent to England to qualify for the Bar.

(2) NEW VALUES EMERGE

One fine day, the students of the high school were marched to the railway station to welcome lawyer Bhagat Ram—the Lat Sahib (Governor) had just conferred upon him the much-coveted distinction of nomination to the Punjab Legislative Council. The town's élite too were all there to pay him tribute. Soon after, Bhagat Ram was invited to preside at the anniversary of our high school. That put the finishing touch to the rehabilitation of his image.

Even our suspicion and resentment of the Englishman came to be softened. The school authorities had purchased an extensive tract of land for a college and new boarding house. The scheme was jeopardised by the proposed alignment of a railway running from Jullundur to Kapurthala, the capital of one of the most-travelled Maharajas of India. Our principal made a frantic representation to the British official in charge. The potentate took kindly to his plea and ordered a change in alignment. What a hero's welcome the school gave this representative of the Raj.

Our concepts of sartorial fashions too underwent a slow transformation. A boy from an affluent Indian Christian family enrolled
in our school appeared in our midst clad in an English suit and sola
topi. He was for some time an object of goggle-eyed curiosity and
not a little envy. When I was up in Simla for a summer holiday, I
prevailed upon my brother to buy me a similar suit. On my return
to school, my stature went up quite a few inches.

The world around us was indeed becoming larger. We heard one
day that the son of a flourishing lawyer in town was returning from
England after qualifying as a barrister. The whole of Jullundur, it
seemed, turned up in a fleet of cars to welcome him with garlands.
For the desk-tied students of the tenth standard it was too exciting
a show to miss. We ran out of the classroom to a bungalow across
the road to have a look at the hero. We were all soundly caned for
this disorderly conduct. But our imaginations had been set on fire.
What more splendid prize could life offer than a barristership?

To me, more painful than the flogging for breaking class was the
sense of frustration the incident momentarily revived. I recalled
how my uncle, who had tasted affluence in Simla, had said to my
father that I should be sent to England to become a barrister. All
that was needed to win that distinction, he had learned, was to
attend a certain number of dinners and to acquire British ways. But
my father, in his practical wisdom, had ruled otherwise, and as the
head of the family his verdict was final. Said he: "If we were to send
him to London now he would be lost to us; he will have acquired
habits and tastes that will not fit in with our way of life. Besides, he
will have learnt wrong money values. Let him go abroad with money
earned by the sweat of his brow when he is well settled in life. Now
he will throw away a pound as if it were a shilling, then he will spend
a shilling as if it were a pound." Wise words, as I was to realise
when I undertook my first voyage to England some eighteen years
later. But at that moment, why, I kept asking myself, should my
father perversely turn down a suggestion that would have opened to
me the very gates of heaven?

Chapter 5

MOMENT OF DESTINY: JOURNALISM
BECKONS

From the Sain Das High School at Jullundar, students naturally gravitated to the Dayanand Anglo–Vedic College in Lahore, run by the same section of the Arya Samaj. The dividing line between the two factions of the Arya Samaj was that one looked upon meat-eating as sinful while the other was more tolerant. In Jullundur they ran two rival high schools. For higher education, the meat-eating wing believing in a modern system of instruction, had established the Lahore D.A.V. College, and the other group Gurukul Ashram (like a Catholic seminary) at Hardwar. Students at the latter, upon whom celibacy was enjoined until the age of 25, devoted themselves to Sanskrit and Vedic lore in an environment of rigid austerity. Prominent among the college group were Lala Lajpat Rai, who was later to attain great renown as a leader of the revolutionary national movement, and Mahatma Hans Raj. At the head of the Gurukul faction was Mahatma Munshi Ram, who in after years came to be known as Swami Shraddhanand and was assassinated in Delhi by a Muslim fanatic.

College days in Lahore were memorable. First, there were the fiery religious disputations conducted on public platforms. The orators of the Arya Samaj, fired by the spirit of revivalism, had in the past two decades engaged the champions of Sanatan Dharma (orthodox Hinduism) in debate, and succeeded in weaning the educated young away from idolatry and superstition. Now they were taking on the Muslim divines. The exchanges were lively and each side of the mixed audience would cheer its spokesman lustily when he scored a debating point. True, no heads were broken, but such confrontations sowed the seeds of separateness and hostility. The Christian missionaries, however, prudently declined to be drawn into such religious debate; their attention was concentrated on the depressed classes, among whom they were winning converts by the hundreds.

Then there were the political lectures at Bradlaugh Hall, to which students were attracted as iron filings to a magnet. Here was the voice of that passionate nationalism whose flame was being kindled in countless Indian hearts. Of all the stirring speeches that I listened to in those impressionable years the one that left the most enduring mark was by Mrs. Sarojini Naidu, the "Nightingale of India." Words rolled off her tongue in a torrent of poesy. "Self-expression," "self-realisation," "self-determination," she said many times over, and to us they became a political *mantra* (words invested with sanctity). Our pulses astir, we talked for weeks thereafter as if freedom was already dawning on the horizon.

This was awakening into a new world, the stormy realm of politics. Avidly next morning, I pored over the account of Mrs. Naidu's speech in the *Tribune*, to become aware of a new impulse. I resolved to invest my pocket allowance on a subscription to this daily newspaper. To my friends at the hostel this was as much an extravagance as that of another boarder who had gone in for a bicycle. My proctor was not pleased, either; he warned me solemnly against neglecting my studies.

Then came the moment of destiny. I happened to be at Simla on vacation, having passed the university examination and been sent there to be out of the way of an epidemic of plague that was again ravaging our district. It had already taken a toll of three lives in our family of five brothers and five sisters. There, at the family shop, a thin, darkish, well-dressed man had pulled up with the bluff greeting: "Lalaji, how's business?" Next moment he had caught sight of me and was asking who I was. The question that followed was addressed to me: "What do you intend to do in life, my lad?" Little realising that I was speaking to K. C. Roy, the well-known newspaperman, my words tumbled out: "I want to work in a newspaper." The response had been instinctive, born out of long months of poring over the columns of the *Tribune*.

Roy's immediate response was an incredulous guffaw at a Punjabi wanting to turn a journalist. But he was soon saying: "Go and learn typing and shorthand, my boy. When you can type 40 words a minute and take down 120 words a minute in shorthand, I will make a journalist of you. You see," he added, "a journalist must express himself in simple and direct English, within the grasp of the meanest intelligence. At the moment, you are raw, and I can mould you for the profession." Roy himself had run away from high school in Faridpur, now in East Pakistan, and was a self-taught man. "How many editors and distinguished reporters in England have ever passed through the portals of a university?" I often heard him remark. In any event, this was a view shared by many journalists of his generation.

I was now seeing visions of a career in journalism. But not so long before, in Lahore, politics and public life had been the height of my ambition; further back, at Jullundur, the legal profession had seemed the passport to El Dorado; and earlier still, under the spell of my father's example in my home village, I had thought nothing could be nobler than teaching. These others had been just calf love.

* * *

To gain a measure of competence in stenography one needed practice. For this I needed a job. The vast wartime expansion of the administrative machinery and the setting up of new bodies like the Munitions Board had opened up countless avenues to the job-seeker. All that one required was a patron, and in the social dispensation of the time to sponsor one's kith and kin for a vacancy was not nepotism but a moral obligation. The entire character of the Secretariat, too, was in the process of transformation. The British of course, occupied the higher posts, and Anglo–Indians those next in importance. But all junior berths were until then filled by Bengalis, for Calcutta was up to 1911 the capital of the country. Now Punjabis were storming into this Bengali preserve in a flood, though the new entrants' intellectual rating in the eyes of the Bengali was low.

It was in this climate that I took up a temporary job. The war had entered the decisive phase; an Allied victory seemed just round the corner. Gone were the days of despondency when all over the country people spoke under their breath of the 'invincible" German armies advancing relentlessly on the battlefields.

Life at my desk was not all drab routine. My seat commanded a grandstand view of the bridge over which the Commander-in-Chief and top Army Brass strode into the building on alighting from their magnificent mounts. One of the greatest thrills I experienced was when I beheld in the midst of one of these imposing processions the Nepalese Prime Minister, more resplendent in his General's uniform and plumes than any British officer, a man bearing a Hindu name comporting himself with impressive dignity. The Gurkhas had covered themselves with glory on the war fronts and he was there to receive the gratitude and honour due to a gallant and loyal ally.

The old Bengali despatcher who stood at my elbow as I gazed spellbound on the scene refused, however, to be carried off his feet. He recalled how that very bridge had trembled as Lord Kitchener stamped across it. Kitchener, he exclaimed, was a true Mahavir (the legendary Hanuman, the embodiment of physical prowess). Did he not consume dozens of eggs at one sitting and spend five hours daily in the gymnasium? More, had he not threatened to throw the puissant Lord Curzon himself out of the window after a wordy duel? And at the mention of Lord Curzon, he whispered: "A curse be on Curzon; he partitioned our beloved Bengal."

Chapter 6

WITH API UNDER K. C. ROY

Came the armistice. While I was employed I applied many hours to improving my shorthand and kept in touch with Roy. On his advice I attended the sessions of the Imperial Legislative Council in Delhi. The liveliest debate that I listened to revolved round the controversial Rowlatt Bills. Breaking all past records, the exercise spilled over into an after-dinner sitting. Among the participants were the political giants of the day, not the least of them Mohammed Ali Jinnah, who was destined to make history by fathering the plan for the partition of India. At that time, he was a member of the Congress, and his words breathed the fire of ardent nationalism.

My father had to be reconciled to the idea of my embracing so precarious a profession as journalism. Government service was different; it promised security and considerable rewards, and was an invaluable asset in the marriage market as well. Moreover, the family business in Simla was in the doldrums. When I first broached the subject, my father turned a puzzled look upon me. "I have never heard of this profession," he said. But then he relented. "If you must become a journalist, though," he adjured me gently, "choose a guru (teacher) and become his shadow." A meeting with the "boss" served to reassure him.

Having been formally enrolled as a parliamentary reporter about the time of the Punjab disturbances, I set out earnestly to become my guru's shadow. Roy himself had come up the hard way. The headquarters of the Government of India were then the monopoly of British newspapermen. These representatives of the British-owned dailies of the country enjoyed almost the same status as their editors; in fact, they did a stint of special correspondentship and editorial writing on Government affairs as preparation for succession to the editorial chair. These journalists acted, in addition, as stringers for the leading dailies of London, sending despatches with an antinationalist slant. Roy was the first Indian to storm this citadel of privilege.

Those were the days of a primitive system of news purveying and dissemination. Press releases and Press conferences were unknown. The Government depended solely on the weekly Gazette of India to make its decisions known to the public, and newsmen therefore took the greatest pains to secure for themselves a proof copy of the Gazette from the Government Press from which to make stories. After Lord Curzon's famous *obiter dictum* that "India's budget is a gamble on the monsoon," they looked upon the daily weather bulletin issued by the Simla Meteorological Office as another must. The break of the monsoon was one of the most important news items and was issued as a flash all over India and the world. All this notwithstanding, news by and large depended on the individual's contacts with the high-ups in the administration, members of the Viceroy's Executive Council and Secretaries and Deputy Secretaries to Government departments.

Roy had launched on his career as a special correspondent in Simla of a number of Indian-owned newspapers about the time Curzon became Viceroy. The idea that news could thus be syndicated and supplied cheap fired his imagination. The fact that many of the papers defaulted on payment of the meagre fee charged for the service failed to damp his ardour. He organised a news agency operating from Simla and the presidency towns of Bombay, Calcutta and Madras, and called it (after the Associated Press of America) the Associated Press of India.

To begin with, he relied a great deal on his Bengali friends to put him on the scent of events in the various Government departments. With the appointment of Sir Satyendra (later Lord) Sinha as the first Indian member of the Viceroy's Executive Council, however, he gained a contact in high quarters that gave him an advantage over his compeers. Everard Coates, who was running the Indian News Agency, was quick to perceive the new star; it was not long before he had bought Roy's interest in the Associated Press and was running an efficient joint enterprise.

The Indian News Agency (INA) had been started by Coates at the instance of the Finance Member of the Viceroy's Council, who had been greatly chagrined by the snail's pace at which news travelled in India. A bank failure in Madras had come to his knowledge a full week after it had occurred. Means must be found to keep officials posted with crucial happenings all over the country. Coates had thus been persuaded to set up a news service, the Government providing financial backing by buying its news on behalf of all the Executive Councillors, Secretaries, heads of departments, Commissioners, Political Agents and chiefs of Army commands and the various branches of Army Headquarters.

The INA service had proved its utility to the ruling circles. But Roy's rival agency had exposed one of its major weaknesses—its failure to report on the feelings and activities of the people. The amalgamation of the two ushered into being the first organised domestic news agency.

The alliance was, however, shortlived. The two fell out over Coates' refusal to accept Usha Nath Sen, whom he considered Roy's "personal assistant," into the fold of ranking journalists. The break was the signal for Roy to set up a Press News Bureau of his own in competition with API and INA. To build this up into an independent agency, he tried desperately with the assistance of Surendranath Bannerjea to raise funds, but to no purpose. What made matters worse was that many Indian papers, far from rushing to Roy's help, exploited the competition; they claimed they were doing a favour to Roy by using his items at all. Coates suffered heavy financial loss, too, and sold his interest in his venture to Reuter. Roy, as badly hit, closed down his News Bureau, sold his house in Simla and threw in his lot with the Reuter outfit, the Eastern News Agency Ltd., the new owner of both API and INA as an employee. The news service was entrusted to Roy, while the British head conducted managerial operations. Associated with Roy as a colleague in the top echelons of the Simla–Delhi set-up was Edward Buck, Reuter's correspondent in Simla and stringer for *The Englishman* of Calcutta.

Thus when I first joined API, it was Reuter-owned and well on the road to broadening its base to meet the challenge of the post-war era with its mounting political overtones. A passionate nationalist ferment was erupting to the surface. The Rowlatt Bills, aimed at curbing "sedition" and "terrorism," had been passed into law, and the country seethed with indignation. Was this the reward promised for the invaluable help India had rendered in the prosecution of the war? The joint report on constitutional reforms submitted by Edwin Montagu, Secretary of State for India, and Lord Chelmsford, the Viceroy, which had just been published, had given rise to a bitter political controversy. A new star had appeared on the horizon—Mohandas Karamchand Gandhi. Even the great "seditionist," Bal Gangadhar Tilak, had receded into the background. India was resolved to follow Gandhi's lead—to *Swaraj* or perdition.

Chapter 7

(1) THE CURZON LEGACY

Having satisfied himself that I had the required zeal for the profession, Roy outlined in his informal intimate style the chores I would have to do to become an efficient reporter. He laid down three courses of study. I must daily read the editorials of all newspapers—about two score—for six months. I must study the book *Nation Builders* to get acquainted with the life and doings of nationalist leaders. I must read up the reports of the proceedings of the Imperial Legislative Council beginning with Curzon's viceroyalty, and, in particular, the speeches made by Curzon and Gopal Krishna Gokhale inside and outside the Legislature and writings and political activity of Bal Gangadhar Tilak. These three, in his view, had made a mark on the history of the time.

I pored over the editorials sitting up well past midnight. This laborious study developed my capacity to weigh the pros and cons of every issue of topical interest, for one thing, and for another the art of expressing oneself with force, clarity and precision. The editorials in *The Englishman* (which was later absorbed in *The Statesman* after it had been published for about 104 years) impressed me most. But those in *The Hindu* of Madras and the *Amrita Bazar Patrika* of Calcutta gave emotional satisfaction, the first with its ponderous style and the other with its homely invective.

The records of the Imperial Legislative Council opened a vast vista of information and gave me an insight into the politics of the time and the role played by prominent personalities. The study brought about a sudden transformation in me. In school and college I studied just enough to pass the annual examinations comfortably; my passion was for outdoor games. Now thirst for knowledge became insatiable. A new unsuspected world had opened to feed a restless spirit.

Finding I had done the chores he had laid down, Roy now passed on to me every week three British dailies—*The Times*, the *Daily Telegraph* and the *Daily Mail* and an American daily, the *Chicago Sun*. They came in a weekly packet by sea. The editorials in *The Times* and the *Telegraph*, the feature article—the centre piece—

on the editorial page of the *Mail* and news reporting in the *Sun* attracted me. I felt the American style of reporting was more objective and human although I was puzzled by the constant reference to prominent political figures in the United States as the "owl" of the party. In Indian idiom it meant a fool, while in the U.S. it denoted wisdom. When and how this term went out of favour I cannot say, but I did not come across it after the thirties.

The Indian scene, as grasped from a study of editorials in the nationalist Press, was oversimplified in my mind. India has been bled white by British exploiters; the defence forces are an army of occupation and a standing army for imperial exploits; the inflated military budget has starved nation-building activities; the British Civil Service is the highest paid bureaucracy in the world, governing the poorest people on earth; there is racial discrimination in every sphere of life, administrative, social and economic. Indians are treated as helots in the British Empire. Home Rule is India's birthright, and until it is achieved the people's misery will not end; the British rulers have cunningly devised the system of communal electorates for Muslims to divide and rule the country; they are driving a wedge between the agricultural and non-agricultural classes to further weaken the national struggle; the Press Act is a Draconian measure against freedom of the Press. The Queen's Proclamation, while assuming direct governance of the country, has been dishonoured and all professions of the rulers regarding the association of Indians with the government of their own country are insincere and dishonest. Was there a solid basis for this indictment?

All this was an indispensable study and orientation for my profession. But what I valued most were the qualities cultivated through close association with my mentor. He surpassed his rivals in his gift for picking brains and ferreting out news, his capacity for inspiring confidence and establishing rapport with the persons he talked to.

Delving into the history of India since the advent of Curzon by way of preparation for the arduous duties of parliamentary reporter and political analyst, I was immediately impressed by the fact that with his viceroyalty dawned the period of glorification of the British Raj. Curzon's own concept of his responsibilities on the eve of assumption of office only went to confirm the nationalist charge when he declared:

"India is the pivot of Empire, by which I mean that outside the British Isles we could, I believe, lose any portion of the Dominions of the Queen and yet survive as an Empire; while if we lost India, I maintain that our sun would sink to its setting."

Curzon's one aim therefore was to buttress the foundations of the Indian Empire. The obligations imposed by this vision were clear. India must be welded into an abiding unity; she must be given a strong and progressive administration; the basic requirements of her internal stability must be fulfilled. Curzon made a start by bringing the Governors of the three Presidencies, accustomed in the past to function like independent mandarins, under effective Central control. As for the administration, district officials wont to behave like petty nabobs were likewise made to bow to Central authority under the integrated pattern of the all-India public services.

To ensure a smooth-running administrative machine, Curzon compiled a Note running into some 10,000 words to serve as the Civil Servant's Bible. This he penned barely five months after assuming office; he would not put it off, "lest, like previous would-be reformers, my senses become dulled by the routine of everyday contact, and I end up by being merely an additional cog in the machine itself." Some in the younger set of officials in the Secretariat mouthed its purple passages with derisory gusto; but there were others who strove conscientiously to model themselves after its dictates. What Curzon had to say was notable for its imaginative grasp of essentials.

The measures Curzon introduced to reform university education and promote technical training bear the stamp of a courageous vision, although they confirmed his anti-Indian bias by excluding Indian intellectuals from membership of the commission on university education. No less enlightened was his concept of railway development on commercial rather than departmental lines. And most significant was his stress on irrigation as the only answer to the recurring threat of famine. He had seen for himself the devastation wrought by one of the worst famines of the past century. If one could use just two per cent of the colossal waste of river waters flowing idly into the sea, he felt, one could hope to sustain millions of lives in a country where rain does not always fall where it is most needed.

He was disturbed by the fact that Indian news that hit the world headlines invariably concerned famine. (This was so even in 1967.) Early in his career, famine took a toll of some 750,000 lives. His only satisfaction was that over a century earlier, in 1770, famine mortality had been much more frightening—a third of the entire population. Under his regime, six million people were given relief, though he himself had laid down the dictum that the financial position of the government must not be imperilled by prodigal philanthropy and that "any government which, by indiscriminate alms-giving, weakened the fibre and demoralised the self-reliance of the population would be guilty of a public crime."

An outstanding achievement was his organisation of the All–India Archaeological Department for the preservation of ancient monuments, priceless heirlooms from a rich cultural past. There were cynics, of course, who sneered at this effort to "restore old dynasties to the throne." That was their way of looking at the rehabilitation of the Mughal palaces at Agra and King Thibaw's Throne Room and Audience Hall in Mandalay, which a Philistine officialdom had converted into a garrison church. Curzon was responsible, too, for the construction of the Victoria Memorial in Calcutta, which he intended as the finest structure raised since the days of the Mughals and equally as an appropriate memorial to the British Raj.

It was Curzon, again, who initiated the move to secure Nepal's permission for assaults on Mount Everest. He did not live to see his dream fulfilled, but his spirit must have rejoiced when Edmund Hillary and Tenzing first set foot on that snowy pinnacle, exulted too when an exclusively Indian team of mountaineers later surpassed others in their exploits.

Curzon looked down with disdain on the Indian National Congress. "It is tottering to its fall," he once observed loftily, "and one of my ambitions while in India is to assist it to a peaceful demise." His mind was warped by his concept of the British Raj as a dispensation from heaven.

I was struck by the clear confirmation of the nationalist charge that the army in India played a pivotal role in empire-building when I came upon this passage in a speech made by Curzon to the Imperial Legislative Council in October 1900: "It was the prompt despatch of a contingent of the Indian army a year ago that saved the colony of Natal. They were Indian regiments who accomplished the rescue of the Legations at Peking. . . . If our arm reaches as far as China in the east and South Africa in the west, who can doubt the range of our influence, or the share of India in Imperial destinies?"

It was at Curzon's suggestion, again, that Lord Kitchener was appointed Commander-in-Chief and was assigned the task of creating that base on which the subsequent massive expansion of the Indian Army for the two World Wars was carried out. Even his stand in the quarrel with Kitchener, over which he petulantly tendered his resignation, is significant. The Army Chief insisted that he himself should be the Army Member of the Viceroy's Executive Council; Curzon, on the contrary, would have a Military Adviser in his Council as a second arrow to his bow. Curzon quit office, but he had succeeded in maintaining the supremacy of the civil authority over the Army by laying down a definite schedule of cases which the Secretary to the Army Department would submit to the Viceroy for orders and securing for it the approval of the home Government.

To the large body of Curzonian lore I may add what Edward Buck, Reuter's agent in Simla, recounted to me with glowing pride. I had no sooner been introduced to him than he pulled out a book that he himself had produced, *Simla, Past and Present*. Curzon, he said, had not only persuaded him to write it but had personally helped in revising and enlarging the manuscript. Buck showed me the carefully-preserved document, with amendations and additions in Curzon's own hand.

(2) CURZON AND NEHRU

In the process of growing up as a journalist, I was to arrive at a true appreciation of Curzon's role as one of the principal architects of modern India. As the representative of the Raj, he was to give a new meaning and content to that office. He had two objectives in view: first, to convert the soulless bureaucracy manning the administration into a benevolent autocracy; second, to assert the India Government's autonomy in the face of the Mughal the Secretary of State at the India Office in London. The irony of it was that the Mughal thought that Curzon wanted him to function as his Ambassador at the court of St. James's.

As a corollary, Curzon sought to arouse Indians to the consciousness that the country's geographical situation was pushing it willy nilly into the vortex of world politics. Of course, his main concern was safeguarding the strategic frontiers of this pivot of Empire. In a real sense, nevertheless, Curzon was the midwife of India's emergence on the world scene. What Curzon set in motion was, decades later, to find consummation at the hands of Jawaharlal Nehru who, as independent India's first Prime Minister and Minister for External Affairs, made a dramatic début on the world stage. But Curzon was in truth the first Foreign Minister of the Government; the traditions he helped build up were to persuade Whitehall to look to the Foreign and Political Services in India as the main instruments of the British Foreign Office in its dealings

with Tibet, Afghanistan and the countries bordering the Persian
Gulf.

"Lord Curzon was the first of the Viceroys of India, Nehru was
the last of the glittering tribe." This cliche has been employed by
Nehru's admirers, likewise by his detractors. Yet it embodies a
substantial truth.

Both were patrician intellectuals endowed with an abundance of
gifts—prepossessing features, great personal charm, brilliance of
mind, the capacity for tireless work and, above all, eternal boyish-
ness. They brought to their appointed tasks a sense of dedication,
for both looked upon themselves as men of destiny. Both began work
after an early breakfast and carried on indefatigably, often into the
small hours of the morning. Curzon was an adept at cutting the
Gordian knots into which ponderous files had tied a problem over
the years. There were few administrative problems he would not
himself tackle, zealously and with conspicuous success. Nehru, on
the other hand, was more concerned with enunciating doctrines;
he had little patience with the details of administration. When confronted with the need for a decision, he would skirt round, weighing
the pros and cons, tormented, as it were, by the spirit of self-
questioning. Nehru's genius lay in romanticising politics, not in the
sphere of administration. With Curzon it was the other way about.

In one respect, however, they closely resembled each other.
Sensitive and highly strung, neither believed in delegating authority.
Each was convinced that there was no better draftsman than himself. Curzon is reported to have himself drafted all the 150 odd
resolutions adopted at an educational conference held at Simla over
a fortnight. It was Nehru's habit to dictate communiqués, or *aides
mémoire* or resolutions after meetings with foreign dignitaries,
Cabinet meetings and sessions of the Congress Working Committee.

Curzon, like Nehru, felt called upon to address himself to the
issue of provincial boundaries. His aim, though, was to reduce the
units to dimensions more easily administered by a single Governor.
These measures included the detachment of misgoverned Berar
from the dominions of the Nizam of Hyderabad and its incorporation
into the Central Provinces. The partition of Bengal, with its explosive
political consequences, was in reality the brain-child of British
officials who had begun to treat the Muslims as the favourite of two
wives. Curzon adopted the plan in keeping with his policy of making
the provinces more sensitive to Central guidance and direction.

Nehru's reorganisation of states, on the other hand, owed little
to administrative exigencies; it was a concession to a sub-nationalism
that sought identity through language. But, though he yielded to

Curzon in his robes of office

Gandhi calling on Ramsay MacDonald at 10 Downing Street

ABOVE Left to right: Radhakrishnan, Nehru and Shastri

BELOW Jinnah speaking into the microphone at a reception given at India House
In December 1946. Nehru, wearing the European dress for which
he had been criticised, is second from jinnah's right

The turning-point came with the massive political agitation and the wave of terrorism that followed on the heels of the partition of Bengal. The British bureaucrat's first move to counter the menace was the "All–India Muhammedan Deputation" that waited on Minto at Simla on 1st October, 1906. Its leader was His Highness the Aga Khan "of Bombay." On him had been conferred the status of "leader of the Muslims in India." (He figured in this role on many a crucial occasion in later years. About the time the Raj came to an end, he forswore Indian citizenship and vanished from the Indian political scene, although fifty million of his co-religionists remained in this country after Pakistan had been carved out.)

The deputation itself was a collection of individuals, hand-picked for the purpose, in disregard of the fact that the All–India Muslim League was the recognised forum of politically minded Muslims in the country.

The cardinal point of the address was a plea for separate electorates for the Muslims in any scheme of political reform on the ground that they were loth to place "our national interests at the mercy of an unsympathetic majority." At the same time, it asked for a due share for them in "the gazetted and the subordinate and ministerial service." The idea that the Muslims were not just a minority was further reinforced by the demand that their representatives in the Imperial Legislative Council "should never be an ineffective minority."

What was left unsaid in the address was underscored in the reply of Lord Minto. "I am grateful to you," he declared, "for the opportunity you are affording me of expressing my appreciation of the just aims of the followers of Islam and their determination to share in the political history of our Empire." The Viceroy went on to dot the i's and cross the t's of the Muslim claims. "The pith of your address," he said, is a demand "that in any system of representation, whether it affects a municipality, a district board, or a legislative council, in which it is proposed to introduce or increase an electoral organisation, the Muhammedan community should be represented as a community." He expressed the firm conviction that "any electoral representation in India would be doomed to mischievous failure which aimed at granting a personal enfranchisement regardless of the beliefs and traditions of the communities composing-the population of this continent."

The comment in a nationalist newspaper was caustic. Said the *Amrita Bazar Patrika* of Calcutta: "The whole thing appears to be a got-up affair, and fully engineered by interested officials . . . So the

All–India Muhammedan Deputation is neither all–India, nor all–Muhammedan, nor even a deputation so-called."

Congressmen felt deep resentment at Minto's reference to India as "this continent" and to its people as so many nations, each with its own traditions. More partisan was Minto's allusion to the Muslims as "the descendants of a conquering and ruling race," for in fact the overwhelming majority of Indian Muslims are converts from Hinduism, not descended from the Turks, Persians, Pathans or Mughals who once held sway over the country. Those who can trace their ancestry today to these conquering races are but a drop in the ocean of Indian humanity.

If the Establishment in India was responsible for Minto's excursion into communal politics, it was equally to blame for planting another kind of harvest which concerned the entire social and political milieu of the times. By the close of the nineteenth century the Civil Service had begun to attract the best talent from the British middle class. No longer was the administration manned by the soldiers of fortune of the earlier days, who in their sudden affluence were not wholly averse to taking Indian wives and adopting "native" ways, down to smoking a hookah.

But with the advent of the steamship the official hierarchy began to assume a very different complexion. Englishwomen came to India in larger numbers and there grew up a new ruling caste, exclusive as in the home country and governed by the same rigid middle class morality. Financially secure and socially exclusive, the Civil Servant and his wife set about behaving as barons and big landlords did at home, a battalion of domestics to carry out their slightest behest, the club to preserve their social prerogatives and the executive authority to buttress their eminence.

A privileged and strongly entrenched ruling class would resist anything suggesting change. The British civilians in the earlier stages opposed, for instance, the establishment of the Imperial Legislative Council. When they were reconciled to it, they attended its sessions in formal morning-coats and behaved much like British M.P.s. But nationalism, whatever its shade or temper, was anathema to them.

Much of the impulse behind the early political upheaval stemmed from the popular revulsion against this particular edifice. The middle class Indian who spearheaded the agitation against the Raj represented the sector of the community ousted from power; he was now battling the alien usurper. Only, the original urge had been overlaid by a burning sense of nationalism; it had been given a more meaningful direction by a pride in the past awakened under the impact of several reform movements and of a religious and cultural renaissance.

(2) A BREATH OF LIBERALISM

Lord Hardinge, who succeeded Minto, had been just over a year in office when he was catapulted into the imperial pomp and pageantry of King George V's Coronation Durbar. The dazzling ceremony took place in Delhi, "the ancient seat of civilisation and Empire" to which the imperial capital of India was moved from the modern metropolis of Calcutta. To mark the occasion, His Imperial Majesty announced the unsettling of the "settled fact" of the partition of Bengal.

Things seemed to be shaping well for the new Viceroy. The grievous hurt to the pride of the articulate Bengali had been healed; the transfer of the capital too appeared a good augury. But the fates had a cruel blow in store for Hardinge. Riding an elephant at the head of a resplendent procession entering the new capital in state on 23rd December, 1912, a year after the Coronation, he was severely wounded by a bomb hurled at him. His attendant was killed instantly in this "terrorist" outrage. Edward Buck was to claim proudly at my first meeting with him that he had scooped the world with this sensational news, leaving the India Office in London confounded that it had had to depend on an agency for the earliest report on the incident.

This abortive attempt on his life did not affect the Viceroy's liberalism. There was an indication in his address to the Imperial Legislative Council as early as 17th September, 1913, that he was guided by Curzonian concepts in foreign affairs. Significantly, he referred to the country's northern and north-eastern borders. Said he: "In Tibet the situation has been of constant anxiety. The Chinese Government have been in conflict with the Tibetans, who have succeeded in expelling the Chinese from Lhasa. At the same time there has been a good deal of fighting between Chinese and Tibetans on the northern and eastern frontiers of Tibet. A conference has been summoned at Simla, where accredited representatives of the Governments of China and Tibet will meet the representatives of the Government of India to discuss the future status and limits of Tibet. (It was at this conference that the MacMahon Line was agreed to.) In the north-east, we have established posts on our administrative frontier and have thus removed any cause of future conflict with China." A vain hope, as Nehru was to realise in 1962.

Such pronouncements had little impact on the vast mass of

Indians and only confirmed the politician's charge against the British of imperialist expansionism. But what Hardinge said in support of the struggle Gandhi was waging in South Africa instantly captured the heart of nationalist India. Replying to an address presented to him at Madras only some ten weeks later, he said: "Recently your compatriots in South Africa have taken matters into their own hands by organising what is called passive resistance to laws which they consider invidious and unjust, an opinion which we who watch their struggles from afar cannot but share. They have violated, as they intended to violate, those laws with full knowledge of the penalties involved, and ready with all courage and patience to endure those penalties. In all this they have the sympathy of India—deep and burning—and not only of India but of all those who, like myself without being Indians themselves, have feelings of sympathy for the people of this country.

"But the most recent developments have taken a very serious turn and we have seen the widest publicity given to allegations that this movement of passive resistance has been dealt with by measures which would not for a moment be tolerated in any country that claims to call itself civilised."

This bold stand of the Viceroy did not come as a surprise to those behind the scenes. Roy told me that Hardinge treated Sir Ali Imam, the only Indian member of the Executive Council, as a sounding board for Indian opinion about the Raj. In fact, the British members even carried tales to London alleging that Sir Ali was exercising undue influence on the Viceroy. This practice was continued by him when Sir Sankaran Nair succeeded Sir Ali. Sir Sankaran was in office when I joined the profession. I learned that Hardinge sent his speeches to Nair for his comment as he wished to avoid anything unpalatable to Indians. In the atmosphere of close co-operation at the time such a gesture by the head of the Government made considerable impact on the Indian intelligentsia.

In his farewell address to the 1915–16 session of the Legislative Council at Delhi, Hardinge seemed to take his courage in both hands to reveal the depth of his understanding of Indian aspirations. "I do not for a moment wish to discountenance self-government for India as a national ideal," he said. In the official climate of the day it was a bold stroke of statesmanship on the part of the Viceroy to visualise the distant goal.

Roy told me the interesting background to this pronouncement. Gokhale submitted a memorandum in March 1915 demanding provincial autonomy. The Congress session at Bombay that year carried a resolution demanding home rule. Hardinge, in response to the Congress demand, submitted a memorandum on reforms, but his tenure ended before he could pursue the matter.

The Bombay session gained special significance because for the first time representatives of the Muslim League attended the Congress in a body. The occasion was even marked by a joint Hindu–Muslim dinner organised by the younger elements, who wore a badge combining the crescent and the lotus. This was hailed as the realisation of the great Akbar's dream.

Jinnah wanted the time-limit for the grant of self-rule to be laid down in the statute and not be left to the will of any party, so that "automatically, the one step we propose in the scheme of reforms will lead to the next step till complete responsible government is established by the statute itself."

The eminent lawyer and newly emerging leader from Bengal, Chittaranjan Das, on the other hand, did not wish to rely on the dictum of politicians but on his natural right. "I do not care what the Constitution of England or the Constitution of Switzerland or that of Australia is. I want to build my own Constitution in a way which is suited to this country, and which afterwards will be referred to as the great Indian Constitution."

Chapter 9

GOKHALE: TOWERING PARLIAMENTARIAN

My study of the book *Nation Builders* showed that among the first leaders to fire my generation's youthful imagination were Dadabhai Naoroji, the Grand Old Man of India, who was elected to the British Parliament with the help of pro-India intellectuals and Labour leaders and the thesis of whose impassioned voice was that his country had been bled white by the imperial exploiter; Gopal Krishna Gokhale, the idol of the members of the Imperial Legislative Council; Surendranath Bannerjea, the fiery orator of Bengal; and, towering over them all, Bal Gangadhar Tilak, the embodiment of the revolutionary nationalist sentiment of the times.

Gokhale's intellectual gifts were as phenomenal as was the rectitude of his personal life. His very first speech in the Legislative Council on the Indian Budget in 1902-3 created a profound impression. Curzon, speaking in the House of Lords after Gokhale's death, said of him that he had never met "a man of any nationality more gifted in parliamentary capacities."

Gokhale's politics were not of the kind calculated to make him a leader of the masses; but there were few among the intelligentsia who were not inspired by the principle cardinal to his faith—that morality must govern not only private life but public activity as well. Indeed, he touched the spiritual chord in India's heart by organising the Servants of India Society, whose members virtually pledged themselves to a life of poverty by agreeing to serve all their life on a monthly allowance which barely kept body and soul together. It was in tune with the Indian ideals of renunciation, simple living and high thinking. In politics he was a protagonist of moderation; though he held that passive resistance as preached by Gandhi was a legitimate political weapon, he himself sought to bring about constitutional progress through the pressure of public opinion.

The central theme at which Gokhale hammered away in the Legislative Council was the "deep and deepening" poverty of the people. His main target of attack was the Army, maintained on a war footing even in times of peace and consuming a disproportionate share of the Indian revenues.

But the British view of the role of the Indian Army remained as it had been defined in 1904 by Sir Edmund Elles, Military Member of Curzon's Council. He put it thus: "Are we to be safe whilst the absorption of Asian kingdoms is steadily in progress? It is, I think, undoubted that the Indian Army in the future must be a main factor in the balance of power in Asia; it is impossible to regard it any longer as a local militia for purely local defence and maintenance of order." Curzon himself, concurring with this view, had added: "This is the secret of the whole position in Arabia, Afghanistan, Tibet and as far eastward as Siam. And the whole of our policy during the past five years has been directed towards maintaining our predominant influence and preventing the extension of hostile agencies in this area which I have described."

Few today would argue that Curzon and his military adviser were wrong in their formulation of the interests of Indian security. But at that time Indians firmly held the conviction that what the British Raj maintained on their soil was an army of occupation, an instrument for the defence and expansion of the Empire. This natural resentment was exacerbated by the cost of the Army's upkeep, which starved nation-building activities like education.

Mass education was another cause that Gokhale pursued with a crusader's zeal. The Compulsory Education Bill Gokhale introduced in the Imperial Legislative Council in March 1911 received more overwhelming public support than any earlier measure, but it was thrown out a year later by the British-dominated legislature. Frustrated at heart, Gokhale confessed to Roy that he was convinced the British looked upon the measure as a danger to the Raj as it would make the masses politically conscious.

Yet another cause that attracted Gokhale's passionate championship was the Indianisation of the public services. In this long-drawn battle he challenged Curzon himself, who in 1904 had airily proclaimed that in the matter of the public services Indians had been treated "with a liberality unexampled in the history of the world." It was easy for Gokhale to prove that very few Indians held posts carrying a monthly salary of Rs. 500 or more. The appointment of the Islington Commission was the crowning reward of his labours, and though he passed away before it had concluded its inquiry some of the ideas he had expounded were embodied in a note appended to its report by Abdur Rahim, a judge of Madras High Court and a member of the Commission.

While serving on the Islington Commission, Gokhale used to have intimate private talks with Roy, who confided to me afterwards that the great Moderate leader, notwithstanding the reverses he had sustained, held firmly to the faith that the movement for political emancipation would gain rapid momentum and be crowned with ultimate success in twenty-five years.

Gokhale was truly a giant in his own right; but part at least of the esteem he still enjoys derives from Gandhi's constant references to him as "my mentor and political guru." It was Gokhale, as Gandhi often admitted, who had counselled him against active participation in politics until he had thoroughly studied India and its multitudinous problems.

Chapter 10

CHELMSFORD: PLEDGE OF REFORMS

Lord Chelmsford was serving in a British regiment in India when he was chosen for the high office. The appointment caused foreboding, and he had not been long in the Viceregal Lodge before the Indians, with their uncanny instinct for appraising human character, sized him up as the voice of the reactionaries headed by the Home Member, Sir Reginald Craddock.

Chelmsford's first act was to send a despatch to Whitehall whittling down Hardinge's proposal envisaging the goal of self-government by asserting that "the rate of progress towards the goal must depend upon the improvement and wide diffusion of education, the softening of racial and religious differences and the acquisition of political experience."

Chelmsford's treatment of Nair, the only Indian member of his Executive Council, was cold and distant. Nair wrote a minute of dissent to Chelmsford's despatch. The Viceroy made a British member cajole and then threaten Nair to make him withdraw it or not to attach it to the despatch. He was further told that in urging reforms not on the strength of India's loyalty during the war but on the universal discontent of the people he was only corroborating the German propaganda that India was seething with discontent.

Nair not only did not yield but suggested to Bhupendra Nath Basu, a former Congress President who was staying with him, that he back his stand. Basu and Narasimha Sarma (who later succeeded Nair), prepared a memorandum at the Simla residence of Nair. They took it to Jinnah, and after his approval got the other elected members of the Imperial Legislative Council, in all nineteen, to endorse it. The memorandum, while conceding the principle of communal electorates, demanded a substantial majority of elected members in all legislatures, power over money bills, fiscal autonomy, an equal number of Europeans and Indians in all the Executive Councils and the abolition of the Secretary of State's India Council. This memorandum formed the basis of the Lucknow Pact between the Congress and the League in 1917.

Chelmsford considered Nair's conduct improper and to his mortification, when the despatch reached the India Office, Sir Austen Chamberlain remarked that he must take account of public opinion in India and accepted the principle underlying Nair's note of dissent. He proceeded to draw up a declaration of policy. But before Chamberlain could get it passed by the Cabinet he resigned over the disastrous Mesopotamia campaign in the First World War. The politically minded Indian felt that the reshuffle of the British Cabinet elevating Edwin Montagu to the Secretaryship of State could make the voice of liberalism prevail over the woodenness of the bureaucracy.

Chelmsford's heavy hand was soon apparent, though. An address protesting against the repressive Press Act of 1910 was presented to him by a deputation of the Press Association of India in Delhi on

5th March, 1917. It was led by B. G. Horniman, Editor of the *Bombay Chronicle*, and among its members were Pandit Madan Mohan Malaviya, C. Y. Chintamani, Editor of the *Leader*, Allahabad, and Sacchidananda Sinha, Editor of *Hindustan Review*. Chelmsford's answer seeking to justify the continuance of a measure severely curtailing the liberties of the Press was characteristic. Said he: "For so long as there are papers in India, as there still are, that in pursuit of their own ends think it right to magnify the ills from which she suffers—to harp upon plague, famine, malaria and poverty and ascribe them all to the curse of an alien government; so long as there are papers that play upon the weaknesses of impressionable boys and encourage that lack of discipline and of respect for all authority that has done so much to swell the ranks of secret revolution; so long as it is considered legitimate to stir up hatred and contempt in order to foster discontent, I feel that any relaxation of the existing law would be followed, as surely as night follows day, by a gradual increase of violence until we should come back to the conditions that prevailed before the passing of the Act."

Indian opinion was reinforced in its assessment of Chelmsford's role by the allusion in his opening address to the Delhi session of the Legislative Council on 7th February, 1917, to the Lucknow Pact, arrived at between the Indian National Congress and the Muslim League. The Viceroy brushed aside the pact, whose acceptance would have cemented the Congress–League entente. (The succeeding forty years were to witness the Congress and the British outbidding each other in concessions to communalism to win the Muslims to their side.)

Then came a development of great moment—the Declaration of 17th August, 1917, by Montagu mentioning the goal towards which the Raj was pledged to lead India. It stated that "the policy of His Majesty's Government is that of the increasing association of Indians in every branch of administration and the gradual development of self-governing institutions with a view to the progressive realisation of responsible government in India as an integral part of the British Empire."

For an official pronouncement it was of revolutionary import. Montagu's own inspiration was transparent; but in Simla and Delhi the knowledgeable were aware that Curzon had played a crucial role in winning the Conservatives over to making this gesture in response to the political aspirations of the Indian people at a time when the fortunes of war were in a state of stalemate. The Declaration was not put in cold storage; close on its heels Montagu visited

India and, in consultation with the Viceroy, formulated proposals for the first instalment of constitutional reforms, which came to be known as the Montford Report.

Minto's regime had seen the seeds of Muslim separatism being sown. Chelmsford's viceroyalty marked the mobilisation of the Princely States as a counterpoise to the nationalist upsurge. Chelmsford announced at the second Conference of Princes and Chiefs held in Delhi on 5th November, 1917, that he contemplated the early establishment of a Council of Princes. This was later to become the Chamber of Princes, which embraced most members of the princely order eligible for membership. The Nizam of Hyderabad, however, stood apart under the grandiloquent title of His Exalted Highness and Faithful Ally of the British Power.

The original memorandum placed before the Princes at the previous session of the conference had stated that "every succession (to the throne) requires the approval and sanction of government." In the light of the new relationship being forged, the harsh rigidity of "approval and sanction" was softened by way of appeasement to "recognition and confirmation."

The new status accorded to the Princes as the third side of the Indian power triangle only needed to be dramatised. This was achieved at India's début at the Imperial War Conference, to which the Maharaja of Bikaner was nominated alongside Sir Satyendra Sinha and Sir James Meston (of the Indian Civil Service) to represent the country.

The policy of divide and rule was given a new dimension because while Muslim separatism could take care of the situation in the Indo-Gangetic plain, the regions below the Vindhyas had to be tackled differently. Here a beginning was made with the sponsoring of a non-Brahmin movement. This was followed by a subtle attempt to drive a wedge between the Dravidian and the Aryan. Their cultures, it was claimed on the basis of zealous research on the part of a Christian missionary, were distinct and apart; Tamil was an older language than Sanskrit and its literature far richer.

The final bid to split the Hindu community was even more ingenious; the untouchables were encouraged to claim they were a sub-nation entitled to separate electorates. These moves were perhaps not part of an overall conspiracy but merely local or regional manifestations of the bureaucracy's strategy of self-defence.

There is an element of irony in the fact that almost on the morrow of the Montagu Declaration the Government should have announced the appointment of a Revolutionary Conspiracies Inquiry Committee under the chairmanship of Mr. Justice Rowlatt. The one was a gesture calculated to enthuse Indian public opinion, the other the forerunner of a policy of repression.

From Britain's point of view, however, there was no contradiction. The pledge of reforms was compatible with the move to meet the challenge of terrorism. The Rowlatt inquiry was professedly directed towards the growing threat posed by the activities of one wing of the nationalist movement. This had erupted to the surface after the partition of Bengal and was slowly spreading to other provinces. The terrorists of Bengal derived their inspiration from similar organisations in Europe, the Nihilists of Czarist Russia and more particularly the Sinn Feiners of the Irish revolutionary struggle.

The terrorists were in a minority, but their activities were truly disturbing to the rulers. Side by side were the sober elements in Indian politics. The intellectuals in the Congress, who had drunk deep at the fountain of the Italian Risorgimento and imbibed the teachings of Mazzini, lent no countenance to terrorist violence. Neither did the Moderates, who in fact stood for orderly evolution towards self-government through the pressure of public opinion. Their approach was patterned on that of the great Egyptian national leader, Zaghloul Pasha.

Montagu's pledge was Britain's response to the aspirations of the Moderates and the more reasonable sections of the Congress leadership. The Black Acts, which seemed to make a mockery of this pledge, were the official reaction to a secret movement that jeopardised the safety of the Raj. It is another matter that with Gandhi's ascendancy the terrorist movement suffered a decline and in time disappeared altogether. In those early days, it was powerful enough to stampede the British Government into the very measures that were to serve as a fillip to the forces ultimately destined to encompass the freedom of the country. Indeed, the Acts provided a starting point for the Gandhian revolution, for they shook the people's faith in British professions. Without their stimulus Gandhi might not have shot to the forefront of Indian politics, eclipsing every other leader of the nationalist movement.

The Congress held its first ever special session in Bombay at the end of August 1918 to consider the reforms scheme adumbrated in the Montagu-Chelmsford report. The session was presided over by Hasan Imam, a leading lawyer of Bihar and brother of Sir Ali Imam. He said: "Let the motherland be first in your affections, your province, second, and your community wherever thereafter you choose to put it."

His nimble mind dissected the Governor-General's position under the Montford Reforms and described it as "sole responsibility, special responsibility, discretionary responsibility, exclusive responsibility, general responsibility, and on the top of it all the 'veto'. It is autocracy *par excellence*, autocracy with a vengeance."

The Congress session described the reforms as "disappointing and unsatisfactory," asked for the adoption of the Congress–League scheme for communal representation and for a statutory guarantee that full responsible government would be established in fifteen years. Significantly, the Congress resolved at the session that women should have the same franchise as men, which was not even the case in Britain at the time.

Tilak was elected President of the Delhi session in 1918, but as he was in London Pandit Madan Mohan Malaviya took his place. Since the war was over, the session demanded the application of the principle of self-determination to India as formulated in President Wilson's Fourteen Points and appointed Tilak, Gandhi and Hasan Imam to represent India at the Peace Conference in Paris.

Chapter 11

TILAK: HOME RULE IS MY BIRTHRIGHT

Bal Gangadhar Tilak—his was a name to conjure with in those distant days. Lokamanya they called him in a spontaneous surge of affection and reverence—"the beloved of the people," "universally venerated," a tribute of the nation, as it were. Tilak's appeal to our generation born at the turn of the century was matchless; he was the very personification of uncompromising nationalism and his method of agitation marked the end of arm-chair politics. His political mantra, "Home Rule is my birthright, and I will have it," was on the lips of most articulate Indians; it appeared frequently in the editorial columns of the nationalist Press. As Gandhi wrote in the *Young India* of 4th August, 1920: "No man of our times had the hold on the masses that Tilak had. . . . No man preached the gospel of *Swaraj* with the consistency and insistence of Lokamanya."

Sri Aurobindo, the revolutionary who sought political asylum in the French possession of Pondicherry and thereafter trod the path of spiritual self-illumination, described Tilak "as a born leader of the sub-nation to which he belongs," and added that a leader's standing in India would depend on "living work and influence in his own sub-race or province." (This thesis may have had little application to the lives of Gandhi and Nehru, but it acquired fresh validity in the politics of the post-Nehru era.)

What set Tilak in a class apart from other intellectual giants who had so far bestrode the Congress stage was the fact that he was as much a revolutionary as a scholar. Two works of abiding interest bear witness to his vast erudition and his passion for research—one a commentary on the philosophy of the Gita, and the other an abstruse treatise seeking to establish the Arctic regions as the home of the Vedas, the primordial Hindu scriptures.

Tilak was the first to use religious fervour to buttress political agitation. To give a spiritual orientation to the nationalist impulse, Tilak revived the Ganesh festival, sacred to the elephant-headed deity popular in the Deccan, and side by side the cult of Shivaji, the brave Maratha chieftain who fought the Mughal power and carved out a kingdom in the Western Ghats. Through the former he sought to inject social and political content into a purely religious cele-bration. The latter served as a rallying cry for nationalism. A staunch champion of Hindu orthodoxy, he was in the forefront of the agitation against the Age of Consent Bill, contending that it interfered with the people's religious beliefs. Official anti-plague measures in Poona too he considered an outrage on the religious susceptibilities of Indians. So violent indeed was this antipathy of his that he even suffered eighteen months' imprisonment for alleged-ly inciting the murder of two Englishmen engaged in combating an outbreak of plague in Poona district.

Tilak fervently believed that a national language was a vital concomitant of nationalism. He therefore advocated the adoption of Hindi as the national language. His disciple Savarkar, who cham-pioned the same cause, had gone to the length of proposing a resolution on Swaraj at a gathering in London, not in English, but in Hindi, "India's lingua franca." Gandhi paid Tilak a very hand-some tribute when he said it was a treat to listen to the Maharashtrian leader's calm discourse in the Calcutta Congress on the claims of Hindi to become the national language.

In the light of happenings in post-independence India, among the most impressive aspects of Tilak's many-sided genius is, to my mind, the modernity of his thinking. I wonder sometimes whether his penetrating vision did not see far into the future. In those early days he envisaged a Constituent Assembly to frame a constitution for the country; universal adult franchise; the division of India provinces on the basis of language; the introduction of nationwide prohibition; the protection of labour through a guaranteed minimum wage; and the development of a public sector for key industries. Here indeed was a gigantic intellect unafraid of looking decades ahead and discerning the imperatives of freedom.

Tilak shared the belief of the pioneers of the nationalist movement that the Press offered the most effective instrument for the propagation of their message. Nationalist leaders who took to journalism were aware of the risks they were running under the law against "seditious" writings. They often tended to hover over the dividing line; when they transgressed the limits they endured the penalties cheerfully. Tilak founded the Marathi daily, *Kesari*, his most powerful instrument. His English weekly, the *Mahratta*, was a subsidiary, but a must for study. Both were issued from Poona, the intellectual and spiritual capital of Maharashtra.

To us journalists particularly, the most appealing part of Tilak's variegated activity was the stubborn, though unavailing, fight he waged in a libel suit against Sir Valentine Chirol, of *The Times*, in a British court of law. Sir Valentine had written a book entitled *Indian Unrest*, which Indians felt was intended to persuade the British public that bureaucratic repression in India was more than justified. Tilak's grounds for action were the "defamatory" observations in the volume.

Sir Valentine's analysis of the nationalist movement was hurtful to Indian sentiment since it sought to show that its principal aim was to overthrow the British Raj and to re-establish Brahmin supremacy through a Hindu revival. Of its creed he wrote thus: "Hinduism for Hindus, or as they preferred to put it, Arya for the Aryans, was the war cry of zealots, half fanatics, half patriots, whose mysticism found in the sacred story of the *Bhagavad Gita* not only the charter of Indian independence, but the sanctification of the most violent means for the overthrow of an alien rule."

Chapter 12

PASSING OF THE TILAK ERA

Gandhi's emergence on the Indian political scene began with his leadership of a nationwide agitation against the Rowlatt Act in 1919. Under this draconian legislation a person could be detained anywhere, arrested without a warrant and his house searched.

Certain offences could be tried *in camera* and the accused was not entitled to engage counsel. There was no right of appeal from the orders of the special tribunals. In short, the authority of the executive was substituted for that of the judiciary so far as security of property and safety of persons were concerned. The Act was a direct negation of the rule of law, which the Raj claimed to be the most striking feature of its system of administration.

I first saw Gandhi from a distance when he sat in the public gallery of the Imperial Legislative Council during the debate on the Rowlatt Bills in the 1918–19 winter session in Delhi. He wore a long loose coat and a turban awkwardly tied. He was hardly noticed as he was still an unknown political quantity. My attention was drawn to him by a colleague under whom I was apprenticing. As it turned out, the debate on the Bills left an indelible mark on Gandhi's mind and gave an idea of the issue on which he could mount a nationwide agitation.

Indians coined a slogan which truly characterised the new law as "No vakil (lawyer), no daleel (argument), no appeal." The agitation spread like wildfire when Gandhi introduced the new weapon of *hartal* (closure of shops and markets) against the "Black Acts." Riots broke out as Gandhi was prevented from entering Delhi and the Punjab and the searing tragedy of the Jallianwala Bagh massacre at Amritsar, resulting in several hundreds dead and injured, the crowning humiliation of the order forcing Indians to crawl on their bellies in expiation of the murder of two British women and the aerial bombardment of civilians in another town, Gujranwala.

Gandhi's meteoric rise to unrivalled leadership received a powerful impetus from the popular fervour at the resignation of Sir Sankaran Nair from the Viceroy's Executive Council and Rabindranath Tagore's renunciation of his knighthood as a protest against the Jallianwala Bagh massacre. Nair's action marked the culmination of disagreement with the Viceroy over constitutional and administrative issues. When I met Sir Sankaran in Delhi along with Roy after his resignation, he said Chelmsford's regime was a disaster. The elevation of this military man to the position of Viceroy, I gathered later, was the fault of Asquith, who as Prime Minister had chosen him because he had married into a well-known Liberal family.

To stem the tide of popular unrest and to reinforce his programme of rallying the Moderates, Montagu saw to it that Press censorship was abolished, martial law withdrawn and a Royal Commission headed by Lord Hunter appointed to inquire into the Punjab

ABOVE Gandhi Day demonstrations in Delhi in 1922. Note the giant
spinning-wheel
BELOW The Rich and the Poor: Gandhi meets the Aga Khan at the
Ritz Hotel in London

ABOVE The author (centre) with Dr. M.A. Ansari, Gandhi host in Delhi, and Mrs. Sarojini Naidu, former Congress President, at a tea party to celebrate the Gandhi-Irwin Pact in March 1931. The author scooped the world press and his despatch was the first agency message to be printed by *The Times* on its main news page

BELOW Gandhi, surrounded by enthusiastic admirers on his arrival in Canning Town to meet Charlie Chanlin. in September 1931 disturbances. This acted as a balm and revived faith in the Secretary of State's liberal outlook.

While I and my colleagues in Simla were coping with the flood of news about the aftermath of Gandhi's challenge, our attention was suddenly diverted to a major development, which in the eyes of the rulers was a bigger immediate threat than the Indian unrest. The story broke of the murder of Amir Habibullah of Afghanistan in February 1919, Amanullah, who succeeded him, took advantage of the unrest in India to launch the Third Afghan War. This first military initiative by the Afghans against the British was repulsed, but Britain in a treaty abandoned the right to control Afghan foreign policy. Amanullah assumed the title of King. Afghanistan won its fuller freedom as an indirect consequence of the banner of revolt raised by Gandhi.

The battle against bureaucratic ruthlessness now shifted to the Imperial Legislative Council at its summer session in Simla. I deputised for a senior reporter who had suddenly taken up work elsewhere. The proceedings were stormy, for on the agenda was the Indemnity Bill, seeking to give Government officials immunity from prosecution for their actions during the Punjab disturbances and the martial law regime. I had already reported the proceedings of the Hunter Commission. To the thrill of listening to Titans like C. R. Das, Motilal Nehru and Madan Mohan Malaviya, top counsel for the Congress, was added the fascination of watching Sir Chimanlal Setalvad, who as a member of the Commission subjected General Dyer to a gruelling cross-examination and extorted from him an admission—more in the spirit of bravado—that he had intended not merely to restore order but to terrorise the inhabitants of the Punjab. Pinned down by skilful questioning, the general admitted to his men having fired 1,605 rounds and mustered armoured cars which could, if they had passed through the narrow alleys of the locality, have wrought great carnage. To Sir Chimanlal therefore goes much of the credit for exposing in its gruesome nakedness the Amritsar tragedy. Indeed, the Minute of Dissent he signed with Jagat Narain Mulla virtually nullified the Hunter Commission's report.

I retain vivid memories of this session. There were, for instance, Malaviya's sharp exchanges with Sir George Lowndes, Law Member-who often relieved Chelmsford in the Chair, and the smooth flow of his marathon eloquence that no interruption could ruffle. I remember too how Surendranath Bannerjea, then reckoned India's greatest orator, sounded mechanical. What, however, impressed me was his colossal memory. Malcolm Hailey, then Chief Commissioner of Delhi, won plaudits on making his début on the floor of the House. But to me, unaccustomed to an Englishman's accent, he was unintelligible; I had to look surreptitiously over Buck's shoulder for my copy. The official reporters who at the time shared the Press Room with a half-dozen occupants of the Press Gallery were also helpful.

An incident occurred when Lowndes pulled up Sachidananda Sinha, a lawyer from Patna, for a slip of the tongue. When Chelmsford condoned the slip, Sinha remarked that his excuse was that he was speaking a foreign language. The remedy, he said, was that the proceedings of the provincial councils should be conducted in the provincial languages and those at the Centre in Hindustani, "a resultant of Hindi and Urdu."

One of the clichés current in newspaper columns at the time was that India was Britain's pagoda tree. I made some research and traced it to what Lord Pentland, Governor of Madras, had told the Prince of Arcot in expressing displeasure at his having signed a memorandum prepared by the Mohammedan Association in support of Constitutional reforms. Pentland said: "Prince, we have shaken the pagoda tree long enough and we may well leave. But the Muslims will have to look after themselves and will suffer."

The proceedings of the Council hardly soothed public feelings. Gandhi pressed home his advantage and proposed non-cooperation with the Government to right the wrong done to the Ottoman Empire, which represented the Khilafat, the Papacy of the Muslim world, and as a protest against the terrorist regime in the Punjab.

My first direct contact with Gandhi occurred when he attended a meeting of the Khilafat Conference in Delhi on 24th November, 1919. At it, he made an initial attempt to speak in Hindustani and apologised for his *tooti phooti* (broken Urdu). His words touched the hearts of his audience but I could sense that he was struggling hard to be precise and intelligible. He urged the people to withhold co-operation from the Government until the Khilafat wrong was righted, and as he faltered for the appropriate word to express his thoughts in Hindustani he coined the expression "non-cooperation" and said it in English. I came away impressed with his zeal and sincerity, but little did I then visualise him emerging as India's man of destiny.

Accompanied by Roy, I called on Gandhi at the house of Principal Rudra of St. Stephen's College, who was his Delhi host. The Rudra–Gandhi friendship had been forged through the Rev. Charles Andrews, who had espoused the cause of Indians in South Africa and had been a professor at the college.

Gandhi explained to us the background to the new movement he was inaugurating. He said he had decided in July 1917 that *satyagraha* was the only weapon India could use to win freedom. Indeed, a *satyagraha* manifesto had been drawn up and B. G. Horniman topped the list of signatories. Then came the August Declaration defining the British policy of gradual development of responsible government. Gandhi held back the plan for passive resistance to guage public feeling.

There was general discontent. The peasants and workers were hit by rising prices. Hundreds of thousands of demobilised soldiers and employees of war supply agencies were disgruntled. On top of this came the Rowlatt Bills, introduced in the Central Legislature on 6th February, 1919.

Gandhi read them in Ahmedabad and took counsel with Vallabhabhai Patel, who was nursing him for a heart ailment. Both agreed that the measure could be blocked if the Government was forewarned that its enactment would be met by *satyagraha*. (It is an amazing coincidence that in the last hour before his death on 30th January, 1948, Gandhi was similarly closeted with Patel. Again he was taking counsel on "what shall we do now?")

A pledge was drafted in Ahmedabad and signed by a small group, which included Patel, Sarojini Naidu and Umar Sobhani, a well-known Muslim leader of Bombay. It was later signed by more than a thousand people in Bombay. To show that they meant business, the *satyagrahis* decided to begin by breaking the laws regarding proscribed literature and the publication of newspapers. They publicly sold *Hind Swaraj* by Gandhi and the biography and addresses of Mustafa Kemal Pasha. They also started a hand-written paper called *Satyagraha*.

Gandhi further recalled that he went to Madras in response to a call from Kasturi Ranga Iyengar, Publisher–Editor of *The Hindu*, and stayed with C. Rajagopalachari. He told his host that as the Rowlatt Bills had been opposed by every non-official Indian member of the Imperial Legislative Council the hour for a nationwide protest had struck. He thought of adopting the traditional method of passive protest, which the religious lore of India had sanctified. He proposed a day of fast and prayer accompanied by a *hartal* and he announced his plan at a mammoth meeting held on the Madras beach. "You know what followed," he added.

Gandhi set up his own press in Ahmedabad and brought out *Navajivan* in Gujarati on 7th October and *Young India* the following day. These two organs, so quietly and unceremoniously born, became the greatest instruments of the Gandhian revolution and may be said to have a unique place along with their successor, *Harijan*, in modern journalistic history.

Then dawned the day to which I always look back as the turning-point in my life. I was deputed to join the API team chosen to cover the proceedings of the Congress session in Amritsar in December 1919. I had attended the previous session in Delhi as an apprentice reporter. But this was something infinitely more exciting. For one thing, the venue itself promised a great deal. The choice of Amritsar had been made in a supreme gesture of defiance. It was an attempt, besides, to rally to the standard of revolt a province then more loyal to the Raj than any other, whose people moreover were regarded as less politically minded than Indians elsewhere.

Even more significant, Gandhi was to attend the session, he who had already captured the hearts of the masses and was being hailed as Mahatma (Great Soul). Besides, presiding over the momentous deliberations was Motilal Nehru, who had thrown away a princely lawyer's income in protest against the Rowlatt Act and the Punjab atrocities. Swami Shraddhanand, chairman of the Reception Committee, too was a legendary figure. Head of the Gurukul (Seminary) section of the Arya Samaj, he had laughed at mortal danger, bared his chest and defied the British and Gurkha soldiers barring a procession he was leading in Chandni Chowk, Delhi's main bazzar, to shoot him down.

Amritsar had just had its winter rains, which generally occurred around Christmas. The huge circus-like pandal in which more than 50,000 delegates, distinguished guests, visitors and newsmen were packed was a sea of slush. Most of them had found seats on benches but the rest had to stand ankle-deep in mud. Yet the atmosphere was so emotionally charged that all alike underwent the discomfort uncomplainingly and repeatedly cheered the electrifying speeches of the participants in the session. This may have been due to a spontaneous desire to seek an outlet for the feelings suppressed under martial law in the province. It was undoubtedly the most thrilling gathering of the Congress I have ever attended.

The Punjabis were accustomed to the prevailing weather and took the bitter cold in their stride, but not so the delegates from South India and other warm regions, to whom it was a terrible ordeal. They lacked woollen clothing and padded cotton quilts to keep them warm in bed. It was as a result of this unpleasant experience that it was decided not to hold subsequent Congress sessions in the North in winter.

The session was to pronounce judgment on the Reforms Act, on which the British Parliament had set its seal of approval. A resolution was to be moved demanding the recall of Chelmsford, at whose door had been placed the ultimate responsibility for the gruesome tragedy enacted in the Punjab. And to crown it all, word went round that a clash among the giants was imminent. Tilak, the hero of our youth, would, it was reported, plead for responsive co-operation, C. R. Das urge total rejection of the Reforms Act, and Gandhi·advocate a middle path.

Released from internment under the general amnesty granted by the King's Proclamation heralding the new Reforms Act, the Ali brothers made a dramatic entry into the Congress pandal. Indeed, they stole the show, judging by the way in which they were cheered when they appeared on the dais with fez-shaped caps bearing a crescent and in dark suits which gave them the look of militant Young Turks. Since the Khilafat's future was one of the twin battle cries raised by Gandhi, these two symbolised its meaning. While Mohammed Ali was the prodigal come home, the more emotional big brother Shaukat Ali was to associate himself closely with Gandhi.

My two API colleagues covering the session were South Indians from our Bombay office. Neither knew shorthand, and it fell to me to report extensively the important speeches in English and all the speeches in Hindi. One of them, a newcomer, would get so emotionally charged that he would sob and forget to take notes. There were no microphones and loudspeakers. In oratory the Bengalis stole the thunder, especially Bipin Chandra Pal. His stentorian voice would reach out to the farthest corners of the pandal. The orations of Gandhi and Tilak were mild. Gandhi, the new star on the horizon, won hearty applause; the delegates were content with his *darshan* (sight of a venerated person) even if they could not hear him.

After the daily session, the leaders relaxed in their camps. I persuaded the senior colleague from our Bombay office, who knew Tilak well, to take me to him. Tilak looked impressive, wearing his Mahratta turban and his face had the glow of a determined crusader. I had felt disappointed at the moderate stand taken by the hero of my college days at the open session. But what he said to us in simple language was convincing and prophetic. He explained why he had advocated a moderate line.

Tilak believed that through the policy of responsive co-operation Indians could hasten the achievement of Home Rule. "I may not live to see it, but the next generation will if we work hard and apply our mind to the new task. I recognise, however, that the Punjab disturbances, the martial law regime and the Jallianwala massacre, which have made men like Sir Sankaran Nair and poet Tagore throw up their jobs and honours, have charged the political atmosphere with a spirit of revolt, of which Gandhi is the new symbol. I will not stand in his way, even though I feel that responsive cooperation will yield the maximum benefit."

Tilak did not disguise his fear that the British bureaucracy, which had already undone the good achieved by the Lucknow Pact, might intensify its efforts to separate the Muslims and the backward classes from the main current of the national movement. Anyway, he added, he would do nothing to create a division in the ranks of the Congress Party. He did not think that Motilal Nehru or C. R. Das or any other leader had Gandhi's mass appeal. "These brilliant lawyers," he added, "will rue the day they took up an extreme position to defeat my resolution. They will retrace their steps one day, but by then Gandhi would have grown too powerful for them. I have done my duty.

"My faith in responsive co-operation is based on my belief that Montagu means well by India. We can strengthen his hands to get a time-limit fixed for self-government, say fifteen years. It is because of this feeling that on my way to Amritsar I sent a cable to the King promising responsive co-operation as a reply to his appeal for co-operation in working the Act which became law on 24th December. I have faith in the Labour Party helping us achieve our goal.

"Well, a compromise resolution sponsored by Gandhi and Malaviya has been passed, declaring that the Reforms Act is 'inadequate, unsatisfactory and disappointing'. The session has also demanded the recall of Chelmsford, the removal of General Dyer from his command and of O'Dwyer from membership of the Esher Committee.

"Mr. B. N. Sarma's was the only voice raised against the resolution for the recall of Lord Chelmsford. I expect he will be duly rewarded." (Sarma was later made a member of the Viceroy's Executive Council in preference to Sir Chimanlal Setalvad. The custom at the time was that the outgoing member recommended his successor. Sir George Lowndes had originally proposed Sir Chimanlal Setalvad, but when the latter signed a minute of dissent to the Hunter Report on the Punjab disturbances, he fell from grace, and the Viceroy agreed to Sarma's being rewarded for his "courageous act.")

The off-the-record talk in which the great Tilak was in an introspective mood, left on me the impression that his head was not with Gandhi but that his heart was affected by the scenes he had witnessed of the new leader being lionised. He made one more effort to turn the tide. In April 1920, he organised the Congress Democratic Party to fight the coming elections. It envisaged a federation of India fashioned by Indians themselves. It stood for religious toleration, a minimum wage, promotion of national unity by such means as a link language for all India, betterment of inter-communal relations and readjustment of the provinces on a linguistic basis. But time was not on his side. Gandhi had enunciated his programme of non-violent non-cooperation to right the wrongs of the Khilafat and the Punjab. He had indeed promised *Swaraj* within a year if the country carried out his programme and raised a Tilak Swaraj Fund of Rs. 10 million, enrolled 10 million members for the Congress and introduced 2.5 million spinning wheels in villages to make the boycott of foreign cloth effective.

Later, Press reporters called on Gandhi to get his assessment of the Amritsar session. The only comment he made to us was that from an observer he had become an active Congressman and that "Plassey laid the foundation of the British Empire, Amritsar has shaken it."

Gandhi visited Delhi on 18th January, 1920, and conferred with a Khilafat deputation that was to wait on the Viceroy. The outcome of the meeting with Chelmsford was disappointing and he advised a nationwide protest. Nineteenth March was observed as Khilafat Day and its significance was dramatised by the announcement that Hakim Ajmal Khan, a renowned practitioner of the Unani system of medicine, had returned to the Viceroy the Kaiser-i-Hind gold medal awarded to him for high public service.

Gandhi published on 25th March the report of the committee appointed by the Congress to investigate the Punjab disturbances. It forestalled the Hunter Commission's report and demanded punishment of the guilty, including General Dyer and Sir Michael O'Dwyer. As a propaganda technique, it paid high dividends, for the Hunter Report, published later in May, lost its value in Indian eyes. Moreover, it was not unanimous. The majority report characterised the officials' conduct as an "error of judgment" while the minority report by the Indian members tended more towards the conclusions reached by the Congress committee. The indictment in the Congress report provided a great impetus to the enthusiastic nationwide observance of 6th to 13th April as National Week.

Gandhi knew it would not be easy to capture the Congress and bend it to his will. This became apparent to him when the meeting of the All–India Congress Committee (AICC) at Banaras in May did not entertain a proposal for adopting a policy of non-cooperation and decided to call a special session of the Congress to consider Gandhi's programme.

The peace terms offered to Turkey were published on 14th May.

These provoked the Khilafat Committee to decide at a meeting in Bombay on 28th May that non-cooperation was the only course left to the Muslims of India. This was the first shot in Gandhi's campaign to sell his programme to the people, especially Congressmen.

He received fortuitous help from the debate on the Punjab disturbances in the British Parliament. To assuage Indian feelings Montagu had characterised Dyer's action as Prussianism, but it was Churchill's indictment that proved most handy to Indian agitators for condemning the Chelmsford regime. The House of Lords, however, exonerated Dyer on 20th July, and this nullified the effect of the vote in the Commons, where the Lloyd George Government was barely saved from defeat. Churchill's remarks during the debate were now broadcast from scores of platforms in India. "One tremendous fact stands out," he had said. "I mean the slaughter of nearly 400 persons and the wounding of probably three or four times as many at Jallianwala Bagh on the 13th April. That is an episode which appears to me to be without precedent or parallel in the modern history of the British Empire. It is an event of entirely different order from any of those tragic occurrences which take place when troops are brought into collision with the civil population. It is an extraordinary event, a monstrous event, an event which stands in singular and sinister isolation."

Charging Dyer with "frightfulness," Churchill added: "What I mean by frightfulness is inflicting of great slaughter or massacre upon a particular crowd of people with the intention of terrorising not merely the rest of the crowd but the whole district or the whole country. Frightfulness is not a remedy known to the British pharmacopoeia."

In an atmosphere so charged with emotion, Gandhi scored a propaganda victory over the Viceroy and at the same time forced the pace of advance towards the inauguration of his form of rebellion by announcing that the non-cooperation movement would begin on 1st August, 1920.

In a letter addressed to Chelmsford, he stated that he was returning the Kaiser-i-Hind Gold medal, the Zulu War Medal and Boer War Medal conferred on him by the British Government. He explained his action thus: "Events have happened during the past month which have confirmed me in the opinion that the Imperial Government have acted in the Khilafat matter in an unscrupulous, immoral and unjust manner and have been moving from wrong to wrong to defend their immorality. I can retain neither respect nor affection for such a government."

Fanaticism over the Khilafat reached such a pitch that thousands of Indian Muslims began to migrate to Afghanistan. But King Amanullah persuaded their leaders to give up the movement and the majority returned to India disillusioned and penniless.

Tilak fell ill on 23rd July and died on 1st August. His funeral, and the enthusiasm roused by Gandhi's movement, brought together the largest gathering ever witnessed on Chowpatty Sands in Bombay. The people said: "Here we ring the death knell of the Angrezi Raj (British rule)." That Tilak should have died on the day fixed by Gandhi to launch his programme was significant. It marked the end of one era and the beginning of another.

The Treaty of Sèvres was signed on 10th August, 1920. It inflamed the Muslims. Gandhi struck while the iron was hot and held at the end of August a Gujarat Political Conference under an influential Muslim leader, Abbas Tyabji. The conference, a constituent of the Congress, passed a resolution favouring non-cooperation. Ahmedabad was Gandhi's home base and he could go to the coming special session of the Congress in Calcutta with this mandate instead of as an individual speaking for himself. This was the second shot in his campaign.

Gandhi's movement led some of the Congress leaders to have second thoughts. A special session of the Congress had been called at Calcutta from 6th to 9th September to consider the findings of the Hunter Commission, the Khilafat wrongs and the final attitude to the question of political reforms in view of the impending elections.

Lajpat Rai, known as the "Lion of Punjab," presided over the session. He had recently returned from America where he had sought asylum during the First World War. While he was shocked at the atrocities of the martial law regime, he did not feel convinced that the Gandhian policy was the right answer.

The session was marked by the usual scenes of enthusiasm. I found much tension in the delegates' camp. It was said that C. R. Das had mobilised his strength and that a strong contingent had come from Maharashtra to defeat Gandhi's attempt to get endorsement of the non-violent non-cooperation campaign he had launched on 1st August. Lala Lajpat Rai, the Congress President, and Jinnah were also with them.

Motilal Nehru wanted the demand for *Swaraj* to be included in the main resolution. This goal was to be obtained within the Empire if possible, or outside it, if necessary. This was agreed to, although Malaviya and Jinnah wanted to confine it to "within the Empire."

C. R. Das and B. C. Pal attempted to sidetrack the main issue and proposed that a mission be sent to England to get an authoritative statement of British policy. Meanwhile, the elections should be fought and not boycotted. They failed in this move.

Gandhi reaffirmed that if there was sufficient response to his programme *Swaraj* could be had in a year. He had the backing of Motilal Nehru, the delegates from the South and the Muslim delegates. In fact, all the Muslim members of the Subjects Committee except Jinnah supported the main resolution. The hour came for counting of heads. The President asked all the visitors to leave the pandal and personally supervised the registering of votes. The tenseness of the proceedings made me feel emotionally involved. My head was with Lajpat Rai and C. R. Das; my heart with Gandhi. At the end of the count Gandhi won by 1,855 votes to 873. When Press representatives gathered round him, we did not find him quite happy. He wanted a clear directive and effective action, he said, but these had not been forthcoming. Anyway, this was the thin end of the wedge.

The Muslim League also met in Calcutta on 7th September. Finding it difficult to swim against the tide of popular opinion, Jinnah conceded that there was no course open except to support non-cooperation. But he added that he did not necessarily approve Gandhi's programme. The resolution adopted by the League supported non-cooperation.

The Congress resolution wanted a beginning to be made by the social classes which had hitherto moulded and represented public opinion. It called for the surrender of titles and honorary offices, a boycott of official functions, a gradual withdrawal of children from schools and colleges aided or controlled by the Government, a gradual boycott of British courts, a refusal to enlist for service in Mesopotamia, and a boycott of the elections to the reformed legislatures as well as of foreign cloth. This was the blueprint of the revolution which was to convulse India shortly.

Chelmsford and the Civil Service hierarchy often referred to Gandhi as a charlatan in talks in the lobbies of the Legislative Council, and no wonder Chelmsford said in his address to the Legislature on 10th August, 1920: "The common sense of the people and the opposition of all moderate men will erect an insuperable bar to the further progress of this most foolish of all foolish schemes." (I could sense from the Press Gallery a feeling of resentment among the Indian members at this abusive indictment.) Gandhi retorted by saying that "unfortunately for His Excellency the movement is likely to grow with ridicule, as it is certain to flourish on repression."

Gandhi's star was on the ascendant. The country echoed with the cry of "Mahatma Gandhi ki jai (victory to the Great Soul)." It was apparent that the regular session of the Congress due to be held after three months in Nagpur would be dominated by Gandhi.

Chelmsford, as was customary with an outgoing Viceroy, was given a farewell banquet at the United Service Club, Simla on 11th October, 1920. I accompanied Edward Buck to report the speeches of Sir William Marris, who proposed the toast, and the Viceroy's reply. The post-prandial oration was a studied attempt on Chelmsford's part at retrospection and introspection. Two remarks struck me deeply. "We are passing through anxious times and pessimistic rumours of the deepest dye come over the Reuters to us in India. (No, Mr. Buck is not to blame.) But I think some of us are responsible. I fear that some of us do write home in such a gloomy strain about the situation in India that those at home without a closer view seem to think that things are very bad indeed. I would stigmatise this attitude as wanting in foresight and in perspective."

But what the Viceroy told us informally after the dinner was even more eloquent than the oration. "Well, Buckie," he said, "I have fallen between two stools. The Services think I sold the pass, meekly submitting to Montagu. Indians consider me a reactionary, a tool in the hands of the Services. Well, history will judge."

Chapter 13

THE NEW CHALLENGE OF NON-COOPERATION

The Nagpur session of the Indian National Congress in December 1920 turned its back on constitutional methods of agitation and handed over the reins of the freedom struggle to Gandhi.

Gandhi, dressed in loin cloth and carrying a handspun toga, presented an odd figure amidst the élite in formal costumes. With complete self-confidence and sense of purpose, however, he carried all before him. He persuaded the Congress to adopt a new constitution, which declared the attainment of *Swaraj* (self-rule) by "peaceful and legitimate" (replacing the word "constitutional") means as the aim of the Congress, and spelled out his programme of non-violent non-cooperation.

The President of the session, Mr. Vijayaraghavacharya, known as the Grand Old Man of the Congress, pleaded in vain for a

conciliatory gesture to strengthen Montagu's hands. The voice of
dissent was silenced; even C. R. Das changed his stand and gave
full support to the non-cooperation movement. The only one who
had the courage to oppose Gandhi was Jinnah. "With great respect
for Gandhi and those who think with him," he declared, "I make
bold to say in this Assembly that you will never get your independence without bloodshed."

The session urged boycott of the Duke of Connaught's visit to
India for the inauguration of the reformed legislature. This was the
first occasion on which royalty was dragged into politics. It also
passed a resolution paying homage to the memory of Terence
MacSweeney, the Mayor of Cork, who died after fasting seventy-four
days for Irish independence. This was as much a gesture to Irish
patriotism as to the anti-British elements in the United States.

Since the Sikhs, who constituted an important segment of the
Indian Army, were being built up by the British rulers as a separate
communal force, the Congress adopted a resolution assuring them
the same protection in any scheme of *Swaraj* as was provided for
the Muslims and other minorities. Thus the Congress, forestalling
the British, gave the Sikhs a political identity.

Gandhi's leadership was reinforced by the appointment of Pandit
Motilal Nehru, the outgoing President, Dr. M. A. Ansari, of Delhi,
and Mr. C. Rajagopalachari, of Madras, as the General Secretaries
of the Congress.

The session marked a watershed in the history of the Congress and
of the freedom struggle. Whereas at former sessions the Congress
President was the first among equals, Gandhi emerged as the
supreme rebel leader. Secondly, the constitution he drew up created
a mass base and an infrastructure. Its provincial units were realigned
linguistically to make it possible to communicate with the inert
rural masses. Thirdly, he took up in earnest the plea made at the
session by the Chairman of the Reception Committee, Jamnalal
Bajaj, that Hindi–Hindustani, a mixture of Sanskritised Hindi and
Persianised Urdu written in the Devanagari script, be made the
rashtrabhasha, the national language.

Intrigued by Jinnah's defiant demeanour at the session, I interviewed him after the day's sitting. "Well, young man," he remarked,
"I will have nothing to do with this pseudo-religious approach to
politics. I part company with the Congress and Gandhi. I do
not believe in working up mob hysteria. Politics is a gentleman's
game."

Jinnah talked more in sorrow than in anger. He was not prepared
to engage in a fight with the Congress; he would honour its mandate

and abstain from contesting the coming elections for the reformed legislatures. But he expressed the hope that before long the Gandhian magic would lose its potency and the Congress revert to the path of constitutional agitation.

Jinnah particularly deplored the Khilafat agitation, which had brought the reactionary mullah element to the surface. He was amazed, he said, that the Hindu leaders had not realised that this movement would encourage the Pan-islamic sentiment that the Sultan of Turkey was encouraging to buttress his tottering empire and dilute the nationalism of the Indian Muslim. He recalled how Tilak and he had laboured to produce the Lucknow Pact and bring the Congress and the League together on a common political platform. The British, he added, were playing a nefarious game in by-passing the pact and making it appear that the Muslim could always hope for a better deal from them than from the Congress. "Well," he concluded, "I shall wait and watch developments, but as matters stand I have no place in Gandhi's Congress."

Another person whose attitude baffled me was Lala Lajpat Rai. He privately expressed his diffidence about the Gandhian programme, but he would not go against the current. "Do you realise," he said, "that in our effort to carry the Muslims with us we have adopted the Khilafat programme which, if successful, will make them more fanatical? I have this conflict in mind. We have to get rid of the British; we have to carry the Muslims with us. Maybe this gamble of the Mahatma will pay off. I shall watch and decide my course of action later. For the present, I go with Gandhi. To the extent it will strengthen the nationalist movement and revive faith in our own culture, I will back it."

The atmosphere in the country was surcharged with excitement. The common people thought God had sent a saintly man to lead them to freedom and followed him with blind faith. India was in the throes of a mass upsurge, a revolt that spread even to the remotest village. Lawyers suspended practice in their hundreds. Along with the sacrifices made by Motilal Nehru and C. R. Das, all this added up to a great moral victory for Gandhi.

The whole land seemed astir. Boys left school by the thousands. Two particular targets of attack were Banaras Hindu University and Aligarh Muslim University, which represented the highest seats of learning for the two communities. Both universities refused to disaffiliate themselves from the State educational system and survived the challenge. Many of their students, however, went over to national institutions. The highest positions in the land were later to be filled by students or teachers of such institutions.

Notable among them were Lal Bahadur Shastri, who succeeded
Nehru as Prime Minister in 1964, and Zakir Husain, who became
third President of the Indian Republic in 1967.

Lal Bahadur passed the Shastri examination from Banaras
Vidyapeeth, set up against the Hindu University, and this degree
was later affixed to his name. Husain was one of the founders of
Jamia Millia, the national college, in Delhi. At the time of Gandhi's
call for boycott, he was in the final year of the law course at Aligarh.
He happened to visit Dr. Ansari at Delhi for a medical consultation
and learned of Gandhi's arrival at Aligarh. Husain, a former Vice-
President of the Students' Association, immediately returned to
Aligarh. His group, defying detractors, arranged a hearing for
Gandhi, whose speech touched his heart and that of many others.

Recalling this incident, Dr. Husain later told me: "That one
decision changed the whole tenor of my life. I forgot all about
career and about law practice, about everything in fact. The die
was cast. I met Dr. Ansari, Hakim Ajmal Khan and the Ali brothers.
The greatest influence on my life was that of Hakim Ajmal Khan
and Gandhiji. I got my instructions from them. We started the
Jamia Millia. Mohammed Ali was its first Principal. Two others
followed. Then I became the Principal."

Chapter 14

DYARCHY IN ACTION

Montagu made a last bid to rally the Moderates. He assured those
in his confidence that the promised inquiry in ten years into the
working of the Constitution was really the penultimate stage towards
the establishment of full responsible government. This did have an
effect, and several men of talent and patriotism decided to work the
new Constitution.

The scheme of reforms, known as dyarchy, had, like all British
institutions, its checks and balances. The Government in the provinces was divided into the reserved half and the transferred half.
Law and order and finance constituted the former, and the so-called
nation-building departments—among them education and health—
the latter. Irremovable Executive Councillors held the reserved
portfolios, while Ministers took up the transferred subjects, owing

responsibility to the provincial legislature with a majority of elected members.

There was no transfer of power at the Centre, but the majority of members of the Lower House, the Legislative Assembly, were elected under a franchise which covered about three per cent of the population. An Upper House, the Council of State, had been created, with a safe majority for the Government, as a check on the activities of the Lower House. Only power over money Bills was conferred on the latter, but the Viceroy was armed with the power to veto any action of the legislature and make laws by ordinance. Thus, the Central Legislature was a pale shadow of the Westminster Parliament. It had all the forms of authority but not the substance.

Elaborate preparations were made for the inauguration of the reformed legislature by the Duke of Connaught, the King's uncle. Unruffled by the *hartals* which marked the royal visitor's landing in Madras and arrival in Delhi, Montagu used the occasion of the Duke's inaugural address to touch the hearts of the Indian people. A copy of the speech was given to Roy in advance. I felt a thrill as I read it and put it on the wires. The Duke referred to the shadow of Amritsar (the Jallianwala Bagh massacre) having lengthened over the fair face of India, and read out the King's message declaring that in the reforms they had "the beginnings of *Swaraj* within the Empire." This was the first use of the word *Swaraj* in a royal message, and from the Press Gallery I watched an emotional wave rise from the Indian section of the House.

The Duke said: "With the current constitutional reforms, the conception of the British Government as a benevolent despotism has been finally abandoned, and in its place has been substituted that of a guiding authority whose role it will be to assist the steps of India along the road that in the fullness of time will lead to self-government within the Empire. For the first time the principle of autocracy, which had not been wholly discarded in all earlier reforms, has been definitely abandoned."

This certainly was the great divide. But everything depended on how each party would play its role and on whether the people would trust the British promise or go over to swell the ranks of the non-cooperators.

The Executive Council of the Viceroy had been enlarged; with the advent of the reforms it now had three Indians (instead of one)— Tej Bahadur Sapru of Allahabad, Mian Mohammed Shafi of Lahore and B. Narasimha Sarma of Madras, all drawn from the legal profession.

I first met Dr. Sapru when he called on Roy in his room at

Maiden's Hotel, Delhi, soon after becoming the Law Member of the Viceroy's Executive Council. Sapru referred to his talks with Montagu. Lord Reading, whose appointment as Viceroy had just been announced, would bring to his task the spirit and outlook of Montagu, he said. He felt, too, that Reading, having been Ambassador to the U.S. during the war, was aware of the anti-colonial sentiment in that country and would be keen to help India go forward on the road to self-rule. Sapru referred also to his project for bringing the Viceroy and Gandhi together. Sapru played this role of mediator, for though he was often a bitter critic of Gandhi and of the Nehrus he was at heart a Congress fellow-traveller.

The Opposition, too, had several men of talent, although few of them were familiar with parliamentary procedure. The general spirit in the first session was reflected in the attempt of the elected Indians to mirror public sentiment and seek redress for longstanding grievances—the top-heavy administration, the crushing military budget and the scandal of both executive and judicial functions being vested in the magistracy. They also demanded the repeal of repressive laws, the Indianisation of the services, the opening of the commissioned ranks of the Army to suitable Indians of all classes, and the immediate grant of provincial autonomy and dyarchy at the Centre.

The first session ended amidst scenes of general goodwill, and the people's attention moved to Simla, where Reading was to take office imbued with the desire to work the reforms in the spirit of Montagu's assurances. The appointment of Lord Sinha, first as Under-Secretary of State for India in London and then as the first Indian Governor of a Province (Bihar), was another striking indication of the change in London's outlook on the future pattern of the Raj.

This was the political atmosphere in Delhi; but the Provinces were reacting differently, as I discovered from a tour of provincial capitals. For the first time, senior British officials worked under Indian politicians and took orders from them. That seemed galling to some, but they were too disciplined to show it. While financial resources were inadequate to promote education, health and social services, there was scope for distributing loaves and fishes and for obliging legislators and their friends. This aspect of ministerial activity was magnified into communal or caste preferment as largesse began to be distributed. The average legislator, too, realised that Ministers depended on their vote to retain office and began to seek favours in return.

British bureaucrats as Governors, Executive Councillors and Secretaries to various Departments too used their powers to encourage elements loyal to the Raj and buttress the claims of the backward classes and rural interests against the noisy and troublesome agitators drawn from the legal and other professions in the towns.

The Presidency of Madras alone had the distinction of returning a single party, the anti-Brahmin Justice Party, with a clear majority. Brahmins constituted only three per cent of the Presidency's population, but had a virtual monopoly of Government jobs and the white-collar professions. It was the defeat of a leading non-Brahmin, Dr. T. M. Nair, by a Brahmin, in a municipal election that made him start the anti-Brahmin movement. He founded a daily, *Justice*, and as the paper espoused the cause of non-Brahmins the Nair party came to be known as the Justice Party. Since the Congress boycotted the election, this party had no rival. (It held sway until 1936, when the Congress Party triumphed in the elections that year and dominated Madras politics for the next thirty years.)

Lord Willingdon alone among the provincial Governors tried to make the two wings of the dyarchical Government work as a joint Cabinet, as the non-Brahmin party had won a clear majority at the polls. Elsewhere, the scheme of dyarchy was rigidly observed. Since the brunt of fighting the Gandhian movement had to be borne by the local administration, the reaction of district officers and the executive heads in the provincial capitals was different from that of the Centre.

For the first time, district officials saw fraternisation between Hindus and Muslims brought about by the Khilafat agitation. They saw, too, successive *hartals*, resulting in the stoppage of all business, and shopkeepers refusing to sell goods to Government officials. Alarmed by these developments, they set about planning their counter-strategy.

In the Punjab, the Government supported the party which represented the propertied rural classes among the Muslims, Hindus and Sikh Jats and Rajputs. The bureaucracy's tactics in the Punjab envisaged a division on economic lines—rural *versus* urban interests.

In Bombay and Madras, the non-Brahmins and the depressed classes were encouraged to demand separate representation and a reserved share in the services. This moral posture of the British as the guardians of the masses created a stir among the have-nots. In the United Provinces, Sir Harcourt Butler (Rab Butler's uncle) succeeded in creating a favourable political climate by making friends with the landed aristocracy and legal luminaries of the Province.

But, while the dyarchial regimes were functioning smoothly so far as the legislative forum was concerned, the country was seething with discontent. Gandhi's name had become a household word. His charm extended particularly to the rural areas. Whereas formerly wearing *khadi* (hand-spun and hand-woven cloth) was the badge of poverty, it now became in Jawaharlal Nehru's poetic words the "livery of freedom." Since Gandhi had issued a call for enrolling 10 million Congress volunteers in a year, every village was astir.

Gandhi's appeal proved particularly strong to the villagers because they had unbounded reverence for a holy man. Even the urban intelligentsia of the time was sucked into the vortex of the Gandhian movement, for it hugged mid-Victorian values and was under the spell of such religious reformers as Swami Vivekananda and Swami Dayananda who had preached simple living and high thinking as the ideal of good life. Indeed, Bengal had in Curzon's time begun the *Swadeshi* movement and the boycott of British goods and had familiarised the intelligentsia with these weapons.

Thus two parallel forces were at work: the call of politics, with its lure of loaves and fishes, and the call of patriotism involving sacrifices. The two conflicting impulses were beginning to affect the Congress Party and dividing it into No-changers and Pro-changers.

But the Gandhian charisma was too strong to make these forces come into the open while he rode the high horse as the chief rebel, the dictator of the Congress, the new messiah.

It was an India in ferment, with its soul in revolt, that Chelmsford left as a legacy to his successor.

Book II

1921–39

THE GANDHIAN REVOLUTION

INDIA

BEFORE THE TRANSFER OF POWER

1 British India

2 Princely States

3 Princely States which did not accede to either India or Pakistan

JAMMU and KASHMIR
Srinagar
N.W.F.P.
Rawalpindi
PUNJAB
Lahore
BALUCHISTAN
INDUS
UNITED PROVINCE
SIKKIM
BHUTAN
ASSAM
Shillong
Karachi
RAJPUTANA
Lucknow
Patna
BIHAR
BENGAL
Calcutta
Junagadh
GENTRAL
Nagpur
PROVINCES
ORISSA
Cuttack
Bombay
BOMBAY
HYDERABAD
Hyderabad
MADRAS
MYSORE
Bangalore
Madras
LACCADIVE IS.
ANDAMAN IS.
TRAVANCORE
Trivandrum
CEYLON
NICOBAR IS.

Chapter 1

SIMLA–DELHI EXODUS

Until the outbreak of World War II, the normal routine for the Government of India was to spend the winter in Delhi and move up to Simla for the six summer months. This annual exodus was the cause of much chagrin to the people of the plains, and also to those white bureaucrats who had to send their wives and children to the hill stations and rough it out themselves in the sweltering heat while their more favoured colleagues basked on the Olympian heights, ignorant of or indifferent to the life of the people. The disgruntled bureaucrats attributed to this remoteness the failure of Gorton Castle (where the Imperial Secretariat was lodged) to respond promptly and realistically to the references sent up to it.

As far back as 1890, Pherozeshah Mehta stated in his presidential address at the annual Congress session: "The air of Simla necessitates a more than ordinary long period of gestation to perfect even counsels of perfection." In 1920, Gandhi, declining to travel in a class higher than third, said: "I can no more effectively deliver my message to millions by travelling first class than the Viceroy can rule over the hearts of India's millions from his unapproachable Simla heights."

This charge of remoteness was equally applicable to the provincial Governments which moved up to their own hill stations and "camp" offices for a spell in summer. Simla gained extra significance because, apart from its being the summer capital of the Government of India, its suburb, Chhota Simla, happened to be the hot-weather seat of the Government of the Punjab. The Governments of the other provinces were jealous of this proximity of Punjab civilians to the Central Secretariat.

One of the hardy annuals for debate in the Central and provincial legislatures at the time was the demand for abandoning this shift, and the Government's resistance to this was used by agitators as continuing proof of the unresponsiveness of the rulers to popular sentiment and insensitiveness to popular sufferings.

This exodus to Simla was manageable because the total strength of officers, both civil and military, up to 1937 did not exceed 500, and that of the ministerial establishment 3,400. But it was given up when the war had brought intờ being a colossal bureaucratic machine of over 5,000 officers and 40,000 subordinates.

Life in Simla before the bicameral legislature was established revolved round the needs of its white population. The Mall was a special European preserve; most of its shops were run by white men. No load-carrying porter was permitted to use it, nor any ill-dressed Indian either. The rule was relaxed only at night, when middle class Indians strolled along the Mall, gazing admiringly at the show-windows of the European shops on their way to the Kali temple where the goddess Durga was worshipped. My first recollection as a child is of being carried on the shoulders of my brother and setting the temple bell clanging.

Indians lived in the lower bazaar. Thus there was practically a dividing line between the whites living in bungalows on the high-lands and the Indians occupying crowded tenements in the lower areas. The only Indians who mixed socially with the Europeans were those who lived in the Western style in bungalows with a retinue of domestic servants and owned rickshaws pulled by four or five liveried coolies or those who stayed in hotels run by whites.

The advent of the Montford Reforms made the first dent in the privileged position of the white man. Now Indian Executive Coun-cillors and Ministers of the Punjab Government went about in rickshaws with the same dignity and poise as Englishmen. Larger numbers of Indian holiday visitors too came to stay in European hotels. The Indian Princes, however, avoided Simla, since they did not want the Viceroy and the Political Secretary to witness their gay living. Their favourite haunt was Mussoorie.

Middle class Indians penetrated the Mall in 1920 and opened shops for drapery and general merchandise which became the even-ing rendezvous of the new middle class. In Simla's purdah-ridden world, Mian Muhammad Shafi, a member of the Viceroy's Execu-tive Council, set a new pattern by bringing his wife and daughters out of their seclusion. The middle class slowly began to follow suit.

I had married in 1919, but my wife, having been brought up in strict purdah and out of deference to my orthodox mother, took a decade to give up the veil. In a way this suited me, for I had an 18-hour job on hand. I would accompany Roy on his morning and evening walks, which generally yielded rich dividends as we met some of those in authority and obtained clues to good news stories. During the sittings of the legislature I could not get home until after midnight. My wife would wait up for me, since custom prohibited her eating before her husband.

I really lived three lives daily. When I was doing my rounds as a journalist, I breathed in the atmosphere in which the high and mighty moved. In the evening I would consort with my middle-class friends at Scandal Point on the Mall. Back at my flat in the bazaar, I lived in the traditional fashion. It was a rich and varied experience, flitting between the ruler and the ruled, the upper class and the middle, the Mall and the bazaar.

I had a stimulating excursion into Simla's civic administration. Elected to the Municipal Committee in 1927 with popular support and backed by letters of commendation from Sapru, Jinnah and Lajpat Rai, I achieved some measure of success in the Indian community's fight against racial discrimination by getting the municipal-owned Gaiety Theatre on the Mall thrown open to Indian amateur dramatic clubs. For the porter and the rickshaw-puller I was able to secure a better deal—by way of higher wages, uniforms, rest platforms, and shelters against rain. This was a rewarding five-year experience of public life.. But I had to give it up when the growing pressure of civic responsibility began to impinge on my professional obligations.

* * *

Old Delhi, inside the fortified wall, had its own corporate life, not much affected by the advent or departure of the Government of India's Secretariat. This was because all the officials lived in Civil Lines, where there were branches of the shops in Simla, while the clerical establishment lived in Government quarters built in the outlying areas or in rented tenements in the old city.

The temporary Secretariat and Council Chamber was enlarged to accommodate the Central Assembly, and Metcalfe House was renovated to house the Council of State. The Duke of Connaught inaugurated the reforms in the Assembly Chamber in February 1921. Here there were separate toilets marked for Europeans and non-Europeans—a segregation abolished only in 1925 when Vithalbhai Patel was elected the first Indian President of the reformed Assembly.

New Delhi had not yet been born. World War I had halted its construction when only the foundations had been laid for the new Secretariat on the elevated site. It was all a vast wasteland. Jantar Mantar, an ancient observatory, was accessible only by a footpath winding through dense shrubbery. The area was still called Raisina, after the village which had been uprooted. It was only when construction was well advanced in the twenties that it was named New Delhi with King George's approval.

Everyone believed New Delhi would be a white elephant, that it would never become a town in its own right. The circular shopping centre called Connaught Place was almost untenanted in the summer months and only partly occupied in winter until the outbreak of the Second World War. The commodious house I built in 1936 near it on Keeling (renamed Tolstoy) Lane stood in isolation for nearly three years. Jackals were our only companions by night. Today, it is in the heart of the metropolis, an area so crowded that it could almost be described as a high-class slum.

So dispirited were the members of the Central Legislature about the prospect of New Delhi ever becoming a normal town that resolutions were repeatedly moved for the transfer of the capital to a more central place with a salubrious climate. Members from Bengal, indignant at the dethronement of Calcutta in 1911, were the most vociferous advocates of change. Only, they could not agree on an alternative, and the fact that British royalty had raised Delhi to the dignity of the capital stood in the way of rethinking on the issue. (But the war, partition and the consequent influx of refugees and the diplomatic importance of Delhi in the first decade of India's independence gave such an impetus to its growth that its population has now multiplied tenfold, and the housing of its three and a half million inhabitants has necessitated constructions covering all the seven capitals that Delhi has housed since the days of the epic *Mahabharata*.)

The Delhiwala was very proud of his language, Hindustani, and of his way of life, developed on the basis of mutual respect for religious and social taboos and practices. For instance, no eating shop which served meat or eggs, or even used onions, could be opened in Chandni Chowk, the main shopping centre in the old city. The Mughal emperors had agreed to this ban out of regard for the religious susceptibilities of orthodox Hindu shopkeepers. A customer had to talk in Hindustani and Punjabi was taboo, for the shopkeeper was not expected to learn the dialect of village folk.

The well-to-do Hindu or Muslim had customarily one or more mistresses, and these were maintained in separate mansions or in gardens to which he repaired every evening for relaxation along with his friends. At this level, as they shared drinks and watched nautch girls sing and dance, there was complete social cohesion between Hindus and Muslims. The lower strata would visit the professional singers' dwellings in Chauri Bazar, each one contributing to the evening's charges.

The people of Delhi hardly bothered about their imperial rulers or about the politicians. Asaf Ali, Independent India's first Ambassador to the U.S., was a recent convert to Congress politics. Immaculate in Western clothes, he would hold forth against British rule in

Queen's Garden. Maulana Abul Kalam Azad, a young and hand-some sedition-preaching Muslim divine of Calcutta, made his début as a Congressman at a local theatre. If Asaf Ali's oratory was empty thunder which roused the emotions, Azad's was the voice that touched the deeper chord of patriotism. Swami Shraddhanand introduced the oratory characteristic of the preachers of the Arya Samaj. In 1920, the activities of the politicians hardly caused a ripple in the placid life of the Delhiwala.

Chapter 2

READING AS VICEROY

Lord Reading assumed the viceroyalty in April 1921 and im-mediately plunged into a study of the Indian scene. He reverted to Lord Hardinge's technique of using the Indian Councillor as a sounding board and made Sapru his political confidant. He created a favourable impression by increasing the compensation allowed to victims of the Jallianwala Bagh massacre and their families and by bringing a fresh outlook to bear even on small matters which in those colonial days assumed exaggerated importance in the eyes of Indians as a subtle change of spirit.

Viceregal Lodge was always looked after by a British engineer. Once, when this officer went on leave, Lady Reading wanted his Indian junior to act for him. The Chief Engineer of the Public Works Department pointed out, however, to the Viceroy that according to an injunction laid down by Lord Curzon no Indian should be appointed Executive Engineer of the Lodge as the personal safety of His Majesty's representative in India was involved. Reading firmly overruled him declaring that if Curzon could lay down one rule he for his part could lay down another. That an Indian should assume this role in the holy of holies was a blow to the concept of the white man's superiority.

A sensation was caused in the Secretariat dovecotes when the first Indian Accountant General put up a note proposing an inventory of all the furniture, paintings, carpets and valuables in Viceregal Lodge as a precaution against misappropriation of Government property in future. This was an implied reflection on the integrity of the white man who, it was alleged, helped himself lavishly with mementos when viceroyalty changed. Simla, especially the bureaucrats, tensely awaited the Viceroy's reaction. They felt shaken when Reading not only readily agreed to the suggestion, but went to the length of reprimanding an officer who resisted its implementation. Such incidents strengthened the people's expectations of fair play.

I remember the warm handshake Girija Shankar Bajpai gave me as I broke to him the news that Sarma had succeeded in persuading Reading to appoint him to the Central Secretariat. I derived some personal satisfaction as I had pleaded with Sarma to make history by bringing into the white man's preserve an Indian member of the ICS. The news, when published in the Gazette of India, caused quite a stir. It was an age when every move towards Indianisation of services fed the national ego. (After independence, Bajpai became the first Secretary-General in the Ministry of External Affairs under Nehru.)

It was customary to look on the reactions of the solitary Indian Executive Councillor as the barometer of the political climate of the time. Now there were three and they made a notable contribution to life in Simla. Sapru, who had been at the top of the legal profession in Allahabad, was lavish in hospitality. His house was the hub of politics, for he did not relish small talk. He was the most erudite and eloquent of the three. Muhammad Shafi owed his position to his pro-British leanings; he had fathered the Punjab's revolt against the Lucknow (Hindu–Muslim) Pact. In Simla, however, he laid communal politics aside, and despite his pro-British bias in the inner counsels of the Government, set about promoting social intercourse between Europeans and Indians. His home became the centre of a cosmopolitan culture and of a gracious social life.

Narasimha Sarma was the very antithesis of his two colleagues. A lawyer of modest ability, he had little aptitude for anglicised social ways. At the fortnightly dinners at the homes of the Executive Councillors in rotation, he was ill at ease. An orthodox Brahmin, he would call on the services of a European caterer when his own turn to entertain came. Making a pretence of eating at the common table, he would settle down to a South Indian meal all by himself after the guests had left.

Sarma earned some notoriety through the studied insolence of his manner of greeting Europeans. Having once suffered a grievous affront at the house of a European Collector, where he had been reprimanded by the Sahib's valet for sitting on a bench while awaiting an interview he was resolved to get his own back. He made it a habit, therefore, merely to raise his walking-stick by way of acknowledgment of a white man's salutation. There is a story of how he responded in this fashion to Lady Reading's courtly greeting on Simla's Mall. The incident passed off, however, with just a polite remonstrance communicated through his personal assistant.

He further flouted tradition by visiting the Princely State of Udaipur. No Indian member of the Viceroy's Executive Council had dared enter this white man's preserve. The British Resident strove to prevent his meeting the Maharana. But Sarma ran into the ruler while on a stroll, and had the unexpected thrill of listening to the latter's whispered remark, "Rid the country of these devils," before the Resident could catch up with them.

Simla experienced its first major stir when Gandhi came to meet the Viceroy on 13th May. The crowds that followed him to the gates of the Viceregal Lodge raised·cries of *"Betaj Badshah ki jai* (victory to the uncrowned king)." The Viceroy's main purpose on seeing Gandhi was to create an atmosphere for a warm welcome for the Prince of Wales. This, he felt, would strengthen his hands in enlarging the sphere of provincial autonomy. At the same time, he made an attempt to understand Gandhi's ideas on *Swaraj* and non-violence.

On learning that Sapru was disappointed with the meeting he had taken great pains to bring about, I sought Gandhi's own reactions. He said a positive gain was that a dialogue had begun with the King's representative, and added: "But I see no change of heart." The Viceroy was only keen to win his support for a welcome to the Prince. Gandhi said he could not agree to this in the absence of a political settlement, which was not, however, in the Viceroy's power to bring about. He told the Viceroy frankly that he must overcome the bureaucratic system if he wished to succeed, or the system would swallow him.

Reading gave a different complexion to the meeting. During the dialogue on the creed of non-violence, the Viceroy drove home the point that the Ali brothers had preached violence and extra-territorial loyalty in their speeches at the Khilafat Conference in Karachi. Gandhi the lawyer concurred with the interpretation of Reading, who was a former Chief Justice of England, and agreed to make the Alis recant publicly.

Speaking at a banquet in Simla on 30th May, 1921, the Viceroy dramatised the Ali brothers' apology as though it was the main outcome of his 12-hour dialogue with Gandhi spread over six sittings. As Reading concluded his speech, I rushed to Roy and said: "H.E. has let the old man down." Roy went up to Sapru to get his reactions and asked me to sound Sarma. Sapru was unhappy but Sarma said: "What else did you expect? Don't you see he has failed to pull off a deal with Gandhi? He is a Jew. He does not want it to be said that he parleyed with a rebel and made things difficult for the Prince of Wales's visit. He had to show that it was Gandhi who had sought an interview and that he had scored over Gandhi by remarking that the interview was not entirely fruitless."

This sounded plausible. Anyway, the viceregal utterance embarrassed Gandhi and caused a break which widened when, with Gandhi's return to the plains, the non-cooperation movement received a fresh impetus. His followers believed that if only they intensified their anti-Government activity his promise of *Swaraj* "within a year" might yet be fulfilled.

But a shock was in store for those who were working for Hindu Muslim fraternisation. The Government issued a resolution on non-cooperation on 6th November, 1920, enunciating its policy towards this novel movement, which it did not know how to handle. The resolution called on the people to reject as "visionary and chimerical" a movement which "could only result in widespread disorder." This appeal fell on deaf ears, but the Government's fears proved real.

The worst of the disorders that followed in the wake of the agitation was the Moplah rebellion of August 1921. A large number of demobilised soldiers, many of them Muslims, had returned to their homes on the Malabar coast from Mesopotamia. Mohammed Ali's speeches in South India, it was alleged, had inflamed the religious passions of the Muslims. Besides, reports of the non-cooperation and Khilafat movements had incited the Moplahs of Malabar, the descendants of Arab traders. The worst victims of their fanaticism were Hindus, who suffered rape, loot, conversion and murder. This incident had nationwide repercussions in that it poisoned the good relations between the Hindus and the Muslims.

Gandhi knew after his meetings with Reading that the fight was on. He told me before leaving Simla that he would move from one end of the country to the other raising money for the Tilak Swaraj Fund and carrying his message to the people. He travelled as far east as Dibrugarh, in the north-eastern province of Assam, and as far south as Tinnevelly, in Madras Presidency. His visit to Bombay was dramatised by a huge bonfire of foreign cloth.

On 21st September, when he was at the pilgrim centre of Madurai, in Madras, Gandhi had his head shaved and, discarding his ordinary wear, donned only a loincloth, a dress which led to his being described later by Churchill as a "half-naked fakir."

Reading on his part made desperate efforts to see that at least Muslim feelings about the Khilafat were soothed. A deputation of loyal Punjab Muslims waited on 'him in Simla on 21st October, 1921. I was taken aback when suddenly, after reading the written text he had with him, Reading began to speak extempore. He wanted to speak to the deputationists as man to man and to drive home the point that the prosecution of those who had participated in the Khilafat Conference in Karachi was not an attack on Islam. Without directly telling them that he was a Jew, he said: "My very presence here as the Viceroy appointed by the King Emperor is itself a proof of the religious freedom under him."

Since I had to transcribe this part of the speech for his approval before its release to the Press, I stayed back and took the opportunity to inquire whether he thought that Gandhi would avoid a boycott of the royal visit. Reading replied: "Sapru and Malaviya are hopeful. I tell you, if India honours the Prince, *Swaraj* is within your grasp. The Prince would make his visit memorable."

Gandhi, now on the warpath, announced that civil disobedience would begin on 17th November, when the Prince was due to land in Bombay. He would start it, he added, in Bardoli *taluka* (sub-district) in Surat district of Bombay Presidency. Once the flag of *Swaraj* flew victoriously over Bardoli, the movement would be extended district by district throughout the country. He acknowledged that a Punjabi Congress leader, Raizada Hansraj, had suggested that the Congress tricolour should have a *charkha* (spinning wheel) at the centre, thus making it the ideal ensign of freedom. Gandhi also struck a note of warning: if the movement did not observe absolute non-violence, he would call it off.

Chapter 3

THE PRINCE OF WALES'S TOUR

The Reading–Gandhi parleys having failed, however, the non-cooperation movement gathered momentum, and the Prince's landing in Bombay was marked by a *hartal* and riots which led to many deaths through police firing. The human touch in the first speech the Prince made on Indian soil—"I want you to know me, I want to know you"—was lost in the din of the affray.

Gandhi reacted to this violence by putting off civil disobedience and going on fast on 19th November, remarking: "The *Swaraj* I have witnessed during the last two days has stunk in my nostrils." When he broke his fast on 22nd November, he vowed he would observe a 24-hour fast every Monday until *Swaraj* had been attained. He explained to me later that this was meant to reassure the people that he would never waver in his pledge to achieve *Swaraj* by non-violent means.

The Viceroy made a bid to retrieve the situation at least in Calcutta. Addressing a deputation of "Pressmen and Indian gentlemen" there on 7th December, he urged them to give the Prince an enthusiastic reception. Those who held different views could "abstain from the celebrations." Since the Prince's arrival in Calcutta coincided with the day chosen for a settlement between Britain and the Sinn Fein movement for Irish independence, Reading drew a lesson from the fact that the King's speech at Belfast had given an auspicious start to the negotiations. If India desired *Swaraj*, this was the time to show loyalty to the Crown, when the eyes of the Empire were riveted on the country.

Since *hartals* became the pattern in other towns too, the Government arrested in the first ten days of December 1921 the top leaders of the non-cooperation movement—C. R. Das, Motilal Nehru, Lajpat Rai and Azad. In a final bid to retrieve the situation, Sapru prevailed upon Pandit Madan Mohan Malaviya to wait on the Viceroy and urge the release of all political prisoners, numbering over 10,000, and the withdrawal of notifications under the Special Criminal Law. This formal meeting had been preceded by secret *pourparlers* for a political settlement. As these proved fruitless, the Viceroy, in his formal reply, regretted that he could not grant an amnesty without a formal assurance that the agitation would be withdrawn. Privately, he promised to grant provincial autonomy if the Congress would agree to welcome the Prince.

Reading was very keen on exploiting the occasion to secure further constitutional advance within the ambit of the Government of India Act. He felt it was possible to introduce provincial autonomy without amending the Act. Sapru, a constitutional lawyer, endorsed this view. I learned later from Sapru that the British Cabinet had been shocked by the Viceroy's offer.

Seeking to unravel happenings behind the scenes, I gathered that Das and Azad were in favour of calling off the *hartal*, but that Motilal Nehru opposed it. The result was that the Prince's visit to Calcutta on 24th December was marked by hostile demonstrations;

a *hartal* dampened the city's accustomed Christmas Eve gaiety and transformed it into a semi-dark, dismal place.

The Pressmen who covered the Prince's tour agreed that he maintained a dignified bearing throughout the strenuous programme he had to fulfil. He was visibly moved when he declared open the Victoria Memorial in Calcutta, which Curzon had conceived as a monument to the British Raj comparable with the Taj Mahal.

The highlight of the Prince's visit to the capital, Delhi, where a similar boycott greeted him, was his address to the Indian rulers gathered under the umbrella of the newly created Chamber of Princes (Narendra Mandal). This move was aimed at building up additional support for the Raj.

Buck and I were given a preview of the annexe built to house the Prince in the grounds of Viceregal Lodge in Civil Lines, Old Delhi, now the location of Delhi University. The Duke of Connaught, who visited Delhi the previous year, had been accommodated in a large, silk-lined, double-roofed tent. But it was decided to build the annexe for the Prince to eliminate the danger of fire through an electric short circuit. The building was elegantly furnished, and I learned later that the Prince felt more at home in it than in the gaudy chambers in which he lived and enjoyed the lavish hospitality of various Indian rulers. Thanking the Indian engineer in charge of the arrangements in the annexe, the Prince later remarked that he felt at home among plain carpets and he showed him a scratch on his foot caused by a carpet with gold and silver embroidery in a ruler's palace.

The hostility shown by Congress-led demonstrators towards the Prince had the effect of strengthening the anti-reform lobby in London and the diehard element in the ICS. Prime Minister Lloyd George's disappointment found expression in a speech in the House of Commons on 2nd August in which he said "that he could see no period when they can dispense with the guidance and assistance of a small nucleus of British Civil Servants and British officials in India." The British Civil Servants, he added, were "the steel frame of the whole structure" and he did not care "what you build on or of it; if you take that steel frame out, the fabric will collapse."

The sensation the speech caused was apparent from the flood of news despatches that poured into our office from all parts of the country denouncing it in the bitterest terms. The Civil Servants, however, felt elated in general, and one of them remarked: "What else did you expect after the way Congressmen behaved towards the Prince?"

Sarma sent for me as his house was besieged by politicians who
urged him to resign in protest. Sapru and he took counsel with
Reading, and it was decided that a deputation of public figures,
mostly persons well-known for their loyalty to the Raj, wait on the
Viceroy. Reading received 29 deputationists on 19th August and
assured them, on the authority of the British Government, that
Lloyd George's speech did not represent a going back on the
pledges made previously but was really a warning to the Swarajists
to desist from their professed tactics of gaining control of the
legislatures to wreck them from within.

Sapru felt depressed and told me he would seek an early opportunity to quit the Government, though Reading had tried to
assuage his feelings by assuring that Lloyd George's remarks were
more an oratorical flourish than a statement of policy and that he
had uttered them to counter Tory dissatisfaction with him. Thereafter, the Civil Service was known in India as the "steel frame",
more in derision than as a compliment, particularly in political
speeches.

Chapter 4

GANDHI'S TRIUMPH AND RETREAT

Gandhi was riding the crest of the revolutionary wave when the
Congress session was held in December 1921 in Ahmedabad, where
he had his ashram at Sabarmati, on the outskirts of the city. C. R.
Das, elected to preside over the session, was in jail and was replaced
by Hakim Ajmal Khan. This meeting set the seal on Gandhi's
mastery over the Congress. The party took on a new look and
adopted a new idiom. It broke with the tradition of providing
chairs and benches for delegates, who now squatted on the floor.
The venue of the session was significantly named *Khadi Nagar*, and
handspun worth Rs. 350,000 had been used for the pandal and as
carpeting. Since most of the delegates and visitors also wore *khadi*,
the atmosphere was that of a gathering of village folk, a *panchayat*
(village council) on a national scale.

The session was brief and very businesslike. Patel's speech as
chairman of the Reception Committee was delivered in Hindi and
took only fifteen minutes. The presidential address was equally brief.

G. V. Mavalankar, later Speaker of the Central Legislative Assembly, and of the Lok Sabha (House of the People) after independence, was Patel's principal aide during the session.

Malaviya's attempt to commit the session to a demand for a round table conference to solve the political deadlock found little support. So did the more extreme view of Maulana Hasrat Mohani of Kanpur to change the Congress credo to complete independence. Gandhi's view that the issue of dominion status be kept open received overwhelming support on the other hand.

I remember describing Patel as a "man of action" who disdained harangues. Gandhi meant business, and so did his lieutenants. *Satyagraha* (non-violent non-cooperation) was described in the main resolution as "the only civilised and effective substitute for armed rebellion." It advised Congressmen and others to organise individual and mass civil disobedience.

But Hasrat Mohani was not to be deterred. As President-elect of the Muslim League, which had for some years held its sessions along with those of the Congress, he advocated violent methods, including guerrilla warfare, to win independence. This speech caused little public stir in *Khadi Nagar* or the adjacent meeting place of the League, *Muslim Nagar*, but on paper it made fearful reading for the ruling class. He had handed the only English version of the speech to me, and I wired its text to newspapers subscribing to API's special service. The document was later seized by the police from the telegraph office and employed as evidence on which Mohani was convicted of sedition and sentenced to three years' jail. Thereafter, the League became dormant and remained in a state of suspended animation for a few years.

Gandhi had been given the powers of a virtual dictator. I found his face and body aglow with the revolutionary fervour surging within him as he declared he would ride roughshod if necessary over the Congress constitution to carry out the session's mandate. My colleague and I established a special relationship with Gandhi, as he agreed to admit us to the hitherto closed-door meetings of the Subjects Committee on the understanding that our reports would be submitted to him for vetting to ensure their accuracy. We also undertook to report for the Congress record the speeches delivered in English at the open session. The reporter for Hindi speeches was Algurai Shastri, who ended his career as a Minister in U.P., his home province.

Mavalankar, through whose good offices these arrangements were made, saw to it that I met Gandhi to get his approval of our report of the proceedings. It did not take Gandhi long to do so. My meeting with him provided an opportunity to gather his views on the criticism levelled at his policies by Dr. Besant and Jinnah. The former had said: "*Swaraj* was to arrive by 30th September: it is as far off as ever." Gandhi explained to me that his tour of the country had convinced him that *Swaraj* had dawned, in that the minds of the masses had been freed from the chains which had bound them. Had he not fixed a deadline, the upsurge which attended his nationwide tour would not have taken place.

I asked Gandhi how he would counter Jinnah's charge that his was a pseudo-religious movement likely to lead to a reactionary revivalism. Gandhi replied that his own idiom was the only one that the masses could grasp. The villagers responded to his call, for they lived nearer to God than did the townsfolk, and understood his message as a call for self-abnegation and self-purification.

As for revivalism, Gandhi said he certainly wished to see among the Hindus a revival of the spirit of resistance to evil and a shedding of their cowardice. How could the nation become strong if the majority of its population was timid? Anyway, Hindu–Muslim unity was to him an article of faith, and he could never be so foolish as to inaugurate a movement likely to harm this cause. Gandhi added that there was a fundamental difference in his approach to the issue of freedom from that of Jinnah and others who wanted to build the movement for it from the top. He, on the other hand, wanted to build from below. The Muslim masses instinctively understood the religious issue and would feel brotherly towards non-Muslims who espoused their cause. He had only to tell them that while they earned two annas a day the Viceroy's salary was Rs. 700 a day to make them realise the tyranny of the system and join hands with the rest of the nation in demanding *Swaraj*.

"But Mahatmaji," I said, "your programme is village-oriented. It makes little appeal to the intelligentsia. They are not with you at heart. They will revolt one day." Gandhi replied: "The movement is gathering momentum among the masses. I will be ever on the move, creating the only sanction the Government will respect. I do not think the intelligentsia have any weapon in their armoury that will bend the mighty British to their will. The people are intelligent. They bow before authority, but they revere those who stand for God and truth. Hindus and Muslims are blood brothers. The untouchables are also flesh of our flesh. I want them all to feel a common urge for regeneration through breaking their chains of slavery. These chains are as much social and economic as political. I have much faith in our people that as long as I tread the path of truth and non-violence the masses will not betray me. The intelligentsia will have to change their thinking if they want to achieve *Swaraj*. This exploitation of the villager must end. There must be a two-way traffic between the rural and the urban in ideas, goods and services. The revolution has begun and *Swaraj* will come, come what may."

Gandhi perceived every problem with the shrewdness of a *bania* (trader). He used his legal talent to sell his creed and programme. He was convinced that the British were in India for material gain, and that if the economic ties between India and Britain were weakened or sundered they would cut their losses and depart. Lancashire textiles being the most important British export to India, he decided to concentrate his fire on them. He advocated spinning and weaving by hand with the dual purpose of helping unemployed villagers supplement their meagre earnings and of loosening Britain's grip on India. Moreover, it would foster a sense of affinity between the town and the village.

As Gandhi explained this to me at Ahmedabad, my thoughts went back to my student days at Rahon. My grandmother and mother used to spin fine yarn and the village weaver would turn it into cloth for the family to wear. But I gave up wearing *khadi* when I found my schoolmates looked down on it as the badge of the village poor. The townsfolk wore longcloth and other fabrics imported from Lancashire.

By one stroke Gandhi changed this mentality and taught the people of the towns to feel at one with the countryfolk. Since India lived in her villages, this identification made for unity and harmony. But whereas the townsfolk followed Gandhi's mandate, they let him do the thinking and arguing.

From the time I heard Gandhi at the Amritsar Congress and had a dialogue with him at Ahmedabad, I felt charmed by his expression and his power of persuasion. Every word he spoke or wrote in English was carefully chiselled and meaningful. His speeches and writings were transparently sincere and devoid of semantic jugglery.

The intellectuals in the freedom movement felt paralysed by the new agitational approach adopted by Gandhi and understandably sought escape in the legislative forum. By and large the teenagers who joined the movement abandoned their studies and shut the chambers of their minds to knowledge and blindly followed the leader, sowing dissatisfaction among the masses with their inflammatory charges and going in and out of jail. (This ill-educated element reached the top echelons of the various political parties in the mid-sixties, with deplorable consequences.)

The war drums sounded at Ahmedabad caused Malaviya and

Jinnah to decide to take steps to avert the threatened upheaval. They called an all-parties conference in Bombay on 14th January, 1922, which was attended by about 300 delegates. Sankaran Nair, who was elected to the chair, left in a huff when he heard Gandhi lay down his conditions for a settlement with the British. The conference adopted Jinnah's proposal urging the desirability of a round table conference on conditions acceptable to Gandhi and the Government in order to prevent the crisis from deepening.

The Congress Working Committee responded by putting off civil disobedience until 31st January. The Viceroy rejected the mediators' suggestion and the people of Bardoli, numbering 87,000, decided to launch civil disobedience under Vallabhbhai Patel's leadership. Gandhi wrote on 7th February that the people were all agog at the idea.

The following day, the police tried to halt a procession of demonstrators at Chauri Chaura, in the United Provinces of Agra and Oudh, and in the clash that followed they opened fire. Their ammunition exhausted, the police withdrew to their station. The mob pursued them and set the building on fire, burning 22 policemen alive. I remember the flurry caused in Government circles. The Home Secretary said: "A police post is the symbol of Raj. This is rebellion." Gandhi characterised the tragedy as an "index finger," and, calling the civil disobedience movement off, fasted for five days as penance for the violence. He said he had ignored three previous warnings, and then God had spoken to him clearly through Chauri Chaura. The Working Committee approved of his action, but Motilal and Jawaharlal Nehru, writing from jail, strongly opposed it. They asked Gandhi to isolate Chauri Chaura and go on with the disobedience movement, individual as well as mass. Gandhi maintained, however, that the cause would prosper by this retreat.

This was Gandhi's finest hour. He rose to supreme moral heights, though it marked an anti-climax politically, causing a setback to the national movement whose effects lasted a decade. This suspension came as a shock to most Congress leaders and workers, who thought that the rebellion was gaining strength and that Gandhi had blundered in arresting its momentum. There was much questioning and demoralisation in the ranks of the party, and the rulers were quick to seize the initiative.

In London, the calling-off of the agitation in Bardoli made Montagu declare that if demands were made "in the very mistaken belief that we contemplate retreat from India—then India would not challenge with success the most determined people in the world, who would once again answer the challenge with all the vigour and determination at its command.". Speaking for the Tories, Lord Birkenhead reminded Indians of Britain's "hard fibre."

Gandhi reacted equally forcefully in an article entitled *Shaking the Manes*, which was included in the evidence produced later in prosecuting him on a charge of sedition. He wrote: "The rice-eating puny millions of India seem to have resolved upon achieving their own destiny without any further tutelage and without arms. In Lokmanya's language, it is their 'birthright' and they will have it, in spite of the 'hard fibre' and in spite of the vigour and determination with which it may be administered. India cannot and will not answer this insolence with insolence, but if she remains true to her pledge, her prayers to God to be delivered from such a scourge will certainly not go in vain. No empire intoxicated with the red wine of power and plunder of weaker races has yet lived long in this world, and this British Empire, which is based upon organised exploitation of physically weaker races of the earth and upon a continuous exhibition of brute force, cannot live if there is a just God ruling the universe. Little do these so-called representatives of the British nation realise that India has already given many of her best sons to be dealt with by the British 'hard fibre'. Had Chauri Chaura not interrupted the even course of the national sacrifice, there would have been still greater and more delectable offerings placed before the lion, but God has willed it otherwise. There is nothing to prevent all these representatives in Downing Street and Whitehall from doing their worst."

A fortnight after he had penned these words in *Young India*, Gandhi was arrested and sentenced to six years' imprisonment. His statement admitting his guilt and asking for the maximum penalty and the British magistrate's judgment have passed into the realms of political literature.

This was the beginning of the rift between Gandhi and the intellectuals in his camp. They now began to think of a way of rescuing themselves and the Congress from the frustration caused by the suspension of the civil disobedience movement. Gandhi on his part believed that the country should use the period of abeyance to push forward his constructive programme of promoting manual spinning and weaving, Hindu–Muslim unity, uplift of the depressed classes and other social activity.

This programme had no appeal for the intellectuals, but it made the masses feel at one with Gandhi. Indeed, the programme demanded little in the way of intellectual equipment or exercise and therefore suited the Congress worker at the grassroots, who had little education and no interest in intellectual pursuits. Many of the Congress leaders in urban areas felt, however, that the working of the reforms had revealed possibilities both of embarrassing the Raj and of providing material benefits to the politicians and their followers.

Chapter 5

INDIANISATION OF THE SERVICES

In the climate engendered by the Reforms Act of 1919, it was inevitable that the popular clamour for the Indianisation of the Civil Service and the commissioned ranks of the Army should take on a keener edge. The first Central Assembly, striving to reflect national aspirations, thus put the issue squarely in the forefront of its programme and scored an early victory. A commission on the public services was appointed in 1922 under the chairmanship of Lord Lee of Farnham, well known in England for his gift of Chequers as a week-end resort for Britain's Prime Ministers.

I was deputed to cover the public sittings of the Lee Commission. My first talk with Lord Lee revealed that the main task of the Commission was to lay down the rate of Indianisation of the services and, at the same time, suggest measures to make them more attractive to the white man. British recruitment had virtually stopped during World War I and fresh recruits were reluctant to come forward for fear that, in the context of the reforms, they would have to work under Indian political masters. In fact, several British officers had retired on proportionate pensions rather than accept such a position.

Lee, however, created a favourable impression by displaying a sense of fair play; every witness examined by the Commission was given the utmost latitude in expounding and substantiating his views. I was the only Press representative to accompany the Commission on its tour of the country, and I recall the sympathy and understanding with which Lee listened to what I had to say in informal conversations. He even went to the length of inviting me to submit a note on the subject. I advocated total stoppage of British recruitment as the only means of ensuring the devolution of power to Indians in my generation. It was truly satisfying to discover these views substantially endorsed by Gopalaswami Ayyangar, who led a deputation of the Provincial Civil Service Association of Madras. (He rose to be a member of Nehru's Cabinet.)

This was my first visit to Madras. Here was the India of Vedic lore—simple living and high thinking. Even High Court judges walked barefoot. Life centred on the temples, and sustenance was cheap. The people one met were very intelligent and patriotic, and in contrast to the North, ate and dressed alike, whether they were Hindus, Muslims or Christians. This to my mind was Indian India.

The educated devoured their newspapers. While papers elsewhere were content to carry my 4,000-word summary of the day's evidence before the Commission, the Madras dailies supplemented this with verbatim reports of questions and answers filling twenty columns. Besides enjoying South Indian meals served on plantain leaves at the homes of Gopalaswami Ayyangar and Gandhi's Madras host, G. A. Natesan, I had the benefit of talks with leaders of the anti-Brahmin movement and with Annie Besant. In the peaceful surroundings of her mansion at Adyar, headquarters of the Theosophists, she exploded against Gandhi and almost endorsed Sankaran Nair's view that the Mahatma was leading the country to anarchy.

The Commission's report, which appeared soon after the Labour Party assumed office in Britain, was denigrated in the Indian Press as well as in the legislature as "Lee loot" because of the generous concessions accorded to the services in respect of home leave, free passages, family pensions and the like. Yet, in fact, the recommendations of the Commission did mark a break with the past in proposing virtual Indianisation of all the services except the two connected with security, the Indian Civil Service and the Indian Police. By almost a stroke of the pen, a wide range of new careers had been opened for the youth of the country. Even for the ICS, it was proposed to hold comparable competitive examinations in India as well as in Britain and to add a fifth of the complement by way of promotions from the provincial services.

(The pace of Indianisation gained further momentum during World War II, so that when independence dawned in 1947 the Indian element in both the ICS and the IP was strong enough to maintain the stability and efficiency of the administration.)

The Army, exclusively officered by Britons, was as much a target of attack, whether on public platforms or in legislative debates, as the ICS—the preserve of the "heavenborn" as it was derisively called. The military budget itself came in for violent criticism on the ground that it bled the country white. A committee presided over by Lord Inchcape in 1923 trimmed this expenditure somewhat. Departmental heads were wont to remark flippantly that their schemes had foundered on the "Inchcape Rock," and its labours gave Indian opinion very little comfort.

The demand for the grant of King's Commissions to Indians had always come up against stout resistance, especially after the "Mutiny" of 1857. The kernel of the British argument against Indianisation was summed up by Curzon when he said: "Great stress has been laid on the military danger of reawakening a martial spirit that is now dormant among the higher ranks of Indian society, and of creating trained military leaders who, in times of emergency, might turn their experience acquired in British schools to the detriment of British interests."

Curzon, nevertheless, relaxed the ban and set up the Imperial Cadet Corps, to which a few Indians carefully selected from among the Princes and the loyal landed aristocracy were admitted. This toehold was converted into a foothold during the time of Montagu, who saw the fulfilment of the promise to throw open King's Commissions to Indians as a concomitant of the declaration of August 1917. But the British India authorities ensured that the trainees at Sandhurst belonged only to families of proven loyalty.

The next limping step forward was the announcement amidst a great fanfare on 17th February, 1923, of Commander-in-Chief Lord Rawlinson's scheme under which eight units of infantry or cavalry would be officered by Indians. Simultaneously, Indian officers would continue to be posted to other units. No sooner was this scheme announced than I was interviewing legislators in the lobby along with my colleague Iyengar. We were able to put out a strong condemnation of a "blacklisting" plan intended to prove Indian unfitness for leadership, a scheme moreover vitiated by an insidious racialism inasmuch as it would prevent Indians from holding command over British officers.

The Central Assembly witnessed a stormy protest against the Rawlinson scheme of segregation. But the Commander-in-Chief, defending himself in the House, was outspoken. It was impossible, he declared, to envisage a self-governing India without an Indianised army. And such an army was unthinkable in the absence of an urge for the hardships of a military career and of "a definitely Indian patriotism." This sounded like a plea to postpone the transfer of power to the Greek Kalends, and the indignant protest aroused by it led Reading to set up the Indian Sandhurst Committee, on which Motilal Nehru and Jinnah were invited to sit. This body whose public sittings provided a stimulating experience, recommended the increased admission of Indians to Sandhurst and also the establishment by 1933 of an institution of the same pattern in India. On the basis of Rawlinson's thesis, this was tantamount to postponing self-government until after 1952. But Sir Sivaswamy Aiyar, the stoutest champion of army Indianisation, demolished Rawlinson's argument. Self-government, he contended, had been granted to the white dominions even before they had acquired the capacity to defend themselves, Britain herself assuming responsibility for overall defence, particularly in the naval sphere.

What really knocked the bottom out of the theory of Indian unfitness for a military career was the phenomenal expansion of the Indian Army on the outbreak of World War II and the grant of commissions to hundreds of Indians, many of whom won distinction for gallantry on the field of battle. But for all that, no Indian had attained a rank higher than that of brigadier when the country became independent.

Chapter 6

THREE REVOLUTIONS

With Gandhi and his principal aides behind bars, students of politics could perceive the beginnings of three revolutions, one obvious and the other two latent. The first was the Gandhian revolution, which swept like a gale through the countryside as well as the towns. The second was the "ballot box" revolution, whose seed was sown by enfranchising directly about three per cent of the adult population under the Montford reforms, and the third the administrative revolution under which the all-powerful bureaucracy became answerable to a Government responsible to or under the scrutiny of the elected representatives of the people.

The most immediate impact of the August Declaration, which promised to associate Indians increasingly with the governance of the country, was in the administrative sphere, for this meant a hand in making appointments and other forms of patronage. Since getting a Government job was the height of every young Indian's ambition at the time, the fight for such posts gained greater significance as responsible government gradually developed. The Punjab and Madras, two provinces which had popular Ministries backed by solid majorities, attracted public scrutiny because of the manner in which the Ministers in the Punjab favoured the backward rural communities, chiefly the Muslims, and those in Madras favoured non-Brahmins, who constituted 97 per cent of the population of Madras but found that the services were virtually a closed preserve of the Brahmins. But the tussle for the loaves and fishes of office was also present in the other provinces. For instance, in the U.P., the Muslims, forming only 14 per cent of the population, filled 60 per cent of the posts in the subordinate services and preponderated in the police force.

The fight in the provinces was between communities, castes and sects, but at the Centre it was between the Indian and the Britain. Thus the Central Legislative Assembly spotlighted the racial inequalities based on the white man's supremacy in trade and commerce and near-monopoly of key Government posts. This helped to present the image of a united national front against an alien bureaucracy clinging to power and foreign capital insisting on its pound of flesh.

Emboldened by Lloyd George's combative speech on the "steel frame" of India, the bureaucracy shed its earlier attitude of responsive co-operation and began to show the mailed fist. The Central Budget for 1922–23 provided for doubling the salt tax. This impost, of a kind only reserved for grave emergencies, sparked off an agitation whose echoes were heard in the remotest parts of the country. The Central Assembly threw out the budget clause relating to the tax, but the Viceroy certified it as essential, thus exposing the hollowness of the claim that India enjoyed fiscal autonomy under the reforms.

Two incidents outside the legislatures helped to break the stalemate on the "battle front" and stoke the fires of the freedom struggle. First, the Congress flag hoisted on Government buildings at Nagpur and Jabalpur, in the Central Provinces, on the occasion of a countrywide *hartal* to observe Gandhi Day, was not only pulled down, but was trampled underfoot by the police.

Secondly, a head-on collision between two Liberal Ministers in the U.P. Cabinet and their resignation over what was considered a wrong exercise of Governor's powers. A British official was given permission to file a libel suit against a Liberal politician without consulting the Minister concerned. Congressmen dramatised these incidents and proclaimed: "The emptiness of the reforms has been established; let us now destroy the legislatures from within."

While Gandhi was in jail, no one in the party's top echelons came forward to bear the Cross. Most of them were lukewarm towards his techniques of political warfare. In fact, they carried their fight against Gandhi's programme to the annual Congress session at Gaya. The rival factions came to be known as No-changers and Pro-changers. C. R. Das, Motilal Nehru, Ajmal Khan and Vithalbhai Patel were Pro-changers who proposed carrying the war into the legislatures by capturing them at the next elections. "Destroy from within" was their battle cry.

With Gandhi behind the prison walls, it seemed a foregone conclusion that the Pro-changers comprising the Congress giants would carry the day. But a major surprise was in store for them. They were worsted both in debate and in the voting by the delegates. The battle for the No-changers was won by C. Rajagopalachari (also referred to as C. R. or Rajaji) and Rajendra Prasad. Rajaji was then a relatively unknown lawyer whose razor-sharp intellect proved a match for the giants. Rajendra Prasad, acknowledged as the most Gandhian of the Mahatma's followers, carried conviction with the rank and file. (C. R. succeeded Lord Mountbatten as the first Indian Governor-General and Rajendra Prasad was elected the first President of the Republic of India.)

The defeat of the Pro-changers at Gaya indicated clearly to Das and Motilal Nehru that Gandhi was the idol of the masses and also of the lower middle class which now largely constituted the Congress rank and file. They now adopted the tactic of seeking permission to pursue the Congress programme for ending the Constitution "from within." Their most telling argument was that the myth that the British governed India with the consent of her elected representatives had to be destroyed.

Das was so shaken by his defeat at Gaya that he resigned from the Congress presidentship. About the turn of the year, Azad was released from jail. He set about finding a compromise, so that the Pro-changers, who had now named their group the Swaraj Party, could be given permission to enter the legislatures. His efforts succeeded, partly because of the growing sentiment among the intellectuals in favour of council entry, and partly because of the disillusionment of the Moderates with the working of the reforms. A special session of the Congress held in Delhi under Azad's presidentship set its seal on the compromise.

Chapter 7

SERVING THE NATIONALIST PRESS

Working for the Associated Press of India, I was in large measure responsible for covering the proceedings of the Central Legislative Assembly. Side by side, A. S. Iyengar, also an API staffer, and I ran a Special Correspondent service for the benefit of a dozen leading nationalist newspapers in the country, including *The Hindu* of Madras and *The Tribune* of Lahore. None of these papers could then afford the cost of a whole-time staffer. Roy, who helped us to make contacts with editors, killed two birds with one stone. He filled a gap in the nationalist Press coverage and ensured a virtual monopoly in this field of reporting. Called the Siamese Twins, we supplied our clients with a daily analytical sketch of the Assembly and other political news, with a nationalist slant.

Apart from this activity, we even prepared questions, resolutions and adjournment motions on behalf of members. This was not only a means of serving the national cause but professionally a rewarding business, for it put us ahead of our rivals in regard to happenings in the lobbies.

Our role as political commentators soon attracted official attention, and the Home Member received clippings of our writings with a note suggesting that the API be pulled up for encouraging such political propaganda. Roy was sent for. His explanation was ingenious. "I am keeping the wolves away," he said to Sir William Vincent, meaning that if we were not permitted to function the newspapers would employ staffers, who would assuredly be more unbridled in their comments. Besides, he argued, the arrangement was intended to keep his key men ("my general staff," he called us) contented.

Sir William, on his part, took it all sportingly. "Frankly, Roy," he answered, "your boys serve my purpose too. Their comments keep me in touch with what the Opposition is up to. And to be forewarned is to be forearmed."

The matter was taken up again by certain officials with Sir Roderick Jones, Chairman of Reuters, when he visited India in 1924, but he too was content to let the arrangement stand.

The non-cooperation movement, meanwhile, began influencing the pattern of the Press. The well-established nationalist newspapers, though they supported Gandhi's challenge to the Raj, were luke-warm to certain aspects of his programme. So it was that Motilal Nehru started his own daily, the *Independent*, in Allahabad, C. R. Das *Forward* in Calcutta and T. Prakasam *Swarajya* in Madras. The new journals were, however, unable to survive the fierce competition of the time.

Odd as it might appear, Delhi, the capital, was without a nationalist daily worth the name until September 1924, when funds allegedly provided by the *Ghaddar* (Revolution) men in San Francisco helped the setting up of the *Hindustan Times*. (This was the paper that I joined in 1944 as Joint Editor and from which I retired in 1960 as Editor-in-Chief.)

One of my recollections of these early days was of a casual meeting with Jawaharlal Nehru, then fretting as a barrister in his home town of Allahabad. I was strolling with Roy towards the dining-hall of his Delhi hotel when Jawaharlal, as he was then called, greeted my boss. Roy asked him how he was faring in his profession, and he replied somewhat ruefully that he could not put his heart into it. "I would rather be a journalist, Roy," he added before we parted. He wore a fur cap and a closed-collar coat. He was handsome but struck me as one musing over his fate. Roy observed to me at lunch that Jawaharlal was critical of the way top lawyers amassed wealth—an attitude, he added, that was typical of the intellectual brought up in luxury.

There was an interesting sequel to this incident that Mohammed Ali, the Editor of the weekly *Comrade* and President of the Congress, narrated to me. Motilal Nehru, riled by his son's indifference to the practice of law, said he must fend for himself and not enjoy a care-free life on his father's money. Jawaharlal reacted sharply, stopped eating at his father's table and started living on roasted gram, the poor man's diet. He also stopped ordering new clothes and made do with whatever he had. Sometimes he appeared in public in darned and patched *khadi* garments. He even went to the extent of making his wife follow his example. Shaken to the depths by this unexpected spirit of rebellion, Motilal unburdened his feelings to a young follower, Mahavir Tyagi who happened to drop in and found him greatly depressed. Motilal told Tyagi (who later became Minister of Defence Organisation in the Nehru Cabinet) that it was bad enough that Jawaharlal was behaving as he was. But what made the situation unbearable was that Jawaharlal had imposed the same way of living on his wife for no fault of her own.

Fortunately, Mohammed Ali, who was a guest at Motilal's house, Anand Bhavan, in Allahabad, was then taking a walk in the garden. Tyagi rushed to him and sought his help in assuaging Motilal's feelings. As Tyagi himself confirmed later, Mohammed Ali went into action instantly. In a stentorian voice, he summoned Jawaharlal into his presence and ordered him to beg his father's forgiveness. Overawed, Jawaharlal complied, and Motilal, tears streaming down his cheeks, embraced his son. That was the end of the misunderstanding. For young Jawaharlal it meant liberation from the grind of earning his living, but it did not satisfy his soul. He wanted to stand on his own feet.

Gandhi told me in Belgaum in December 1924, when I mentioned the incident to him, that Jawaharlal was very sensitive about living on his father's bounty. Jawaharlal had written to him about this, and Gandhi had offered to get him a job as a newspaper correspondent or a professorship or even an executive post in a business house. He added that he could have a wholetime job as Working Secretary of the AICC with Gandhi as President. He would be paid from public funds, or if that was not acceptable he should not mind being financially dependent on his father as he was performing a public service as a fighter for freedom. This advice reconciled Jawaharlal to the existing state of things.

Chapter 8

THE RISE OF COMMUNALISM

My eyes were opened to the realities of Indian politics by my countrywide tour with the Lee Commission and study of the massive volume of evidence submitted to it and the oral examination of individuals and deputations. Although Congress and League sessions and the debates in the Central Legislature had made me wise to the political and constitutional aspects of Indian politics, the overriding importance of the services in that context was now apparent. Indeed, the tour revealed that employment under the Government was the main yardstick of a person's or community's or caste's degree of advance and of social justice. Here was a feudal impulse magnified tenfold, a bar to the development of a healthy democratic system of government. One of the ironies was that the Punjab, whose ordeal under the O'Dwyer regime gave a great impetus to the movement for freedom and brought Gandhi on the national scene, also gave birth to communalism, which culminated in the country's partition and had a sequel in the further division of the truncated Punjab which remained in the Indian Union.

This process began with Mian Fazli Husain's resignation from the Congress in 1920 and his zeal to work the Montford reforms in a constructive spirit. He and other Punjab Congressmen had frustrated O'Dwyer's move not to introduce the reforms in this province on the plea that it did not have a legislative council and even the experience of working the Minto–Morley reforms. The Punjab was kept politically backward and administered ruthlessly by British officials. O'Dwyer had even refused to recommend Fazli, then leader of the Lahore Bar, for appointment as a judge of the Chief Court because of his political views.

But on account of the pressure exerted by Congressmen and others the Punjab was placed on an equal footing politically with the other provinces. Sir Edward Maclagan, who followed O'Dwyer as Governor, selected as his Ministers Fazli Husain and Lala Harkishan Lal to manage the transferred departments. Both were former Congressmen and Lal had been condemned to death under the martial law regime and later given a reprieve. Fazli took advantage of the fact that the Muslim members of the Legislative Assembly, who were generally returned from rural constituencies, and the Hindu members from similar areas formed a majority to establish a new party representing the landowning interests. He took pride in the fact that this grouping, which was named the Rural Party, was non-communal, and his motive in forming it was to elevate socially the backward villagers through education and better medical attention and showing them preference in filling posts in the administration in order to give them their share of employment. But, since the chief beneficiaries of these policies were Muslims, every measure he took and every appointment he made assumed a communal tinge.

The Punjab Government spent six months of the year in Simla and I got several opportunities of questioning Mian Sahib, as Fazli was generally called in conversation by his Indian friends, on his policies and actions, which were frequently the subject of bitter controversy in the provincial Press. Patiently and in soft tones, he explained that his family had been converted to Islam from Hinduism several generations earlier, and yet it was so much under the influence of Hindu culture and traditions that when he was due to marry a pundit was called in to examine his horoscope and fix the auspicious hour. He was married both according to the Muslim law by a *qazi* (priest) and according to Hindu rites.

Fazli recalled that he set up the first district Congress Committee in the Punjab early in 1917 and presided over the first provincial (Congress) conference the following October. Harkishan Lal was the chairman of the reception committee, and the conference endorsed the scheme of legislative reforms jointly sponsored by the Congress and the League. Fazli assured me he sincerely believed in the unity of the Hindus and the Muslims, but he did not consider he would be honest in saying that he was an Indian first and a Muslim next. He was an Indian and a Muslim at the same time. He would champion separate electorates and special treatment for the backward groups of the population until the gap between them and the advanced sections was bridged, or at least narrowed. I cannot say I was disappointed with these talks, but I had the feeling that Mian Sahib had, in spite of his patriotic profession, sown the seed of communal disharmony.

The national spotlight in the early twenties was on the Akali movement in the Punjab. Originating as a puritanical upsurge, it soon clashed with the Raj and revived the drooping spirits of the non-cooperators elsewhere in the country. The Sikhs, welded into a militant community under the leadership of their gurus in the 17th and 18th centuries, had stubbornly resisted Muslim oppression. In the 19th century, they established hegemony over the Punjab under Maharaja Ranjit Singh. Now they were aroused to a sense of separateness by the development of communal consciousness among the Muslims in response to Fazli's policies.

The champions of the new Sikh upsurge were the Akalis, the followers of the Eternal Faith. One group based its strategy on the capture of the *gurdwaras* (shrines), for they enjoyed incomes then running to over Rs. 2 million a year and offered besides a platform for congregational prayers through which Sikh political revivalism could be propagated unhindered by the State.

The Akalis succeeded in pushing out the *mahant* (head priest) of the Golden Temple at Amritsar. But, when they attempted a similar tactic at the rich Nankana Saheb Gurdwara at the birthplace of Guru Nanak, the founder of the faith, they met with fierce resistance from the Pathan guards employed by its *mahant* and were thrown back with the loss of 130 lives.

This reverse was the signal for the adoption by the Akalis of the Gandhian technique of *satyagraha* (passive resistance). The demonstrations that followed at Guru Ka Bagh led to hundreds of non-violent Akalis being injured in baton charges by the police. Gandhi acclaimed the movement as demonstrating his thesis that civil disobedience was a weapon for the brave and not for the cowardly. Fazli told me that the *mahants* had been let down by the Hindus because Gandhi had blessed the *satyagraha*. He himself had put through a Gurdwara Act providing legal remedies and fair compensation, but it had been rejected by the Akalis.

The Akali revolt, Sir Malcolm Hailey, Governor of the Punjab, felt, was undermining the morale of the Sikhs in the armed forces. The danger signals could not be ignored after the titled Sikh Deputy President of the provincial Legislative Council had resigned in protest and given the movement a fresh fillip. Sir Malcolm's answer was the promulgation of the Gurdwara Act. Framed on the lines of the religious endowments measure in Madras, it threw crumbs to the Akalis, over which they started fighting among themselves. Nevertheless, the movement had succeeded in giving the Sikhs the kind of political identity that was to obstruct efforts for a communal settlement in the Punjab in the years to come.

On the eve of the second general election under the Montford reforms, Fazli, in combination with Chhotu Ram, who represented the Hindu rural interests in East Punjab and had been a Congressman from 1917 to 1920, formed the Punjab Nationalist Unionist Party. The election manifesto of this new grouping virtually pitted the rural classes against the trading classes of the towns. The elections resulted in a majority for the party, in the provincial Legislative Assembly. Fazli and Chhotu Ram were appointed Ministers.

I asked Fazli why he had not attempted to form a coalition with the Swarajists, who had a programme similar to his, or with the Mahasabhaites to create confidence among the Punjab's Hindu minority. Fazli replied that he could work only with those who shared his political faith, a point of view resembling what Jawaharlal Nehru took when he turned down Jinnah's plea for a coalition with the Muslim League in 1937. Fazli's decision was as fateful as Nehru's, as they gave the wheel of fortune a turn in Jinnah's favour.

Sir Malcolm became Governor of the Punjab on 31st May, 1924. He had come to perceive, as Home Member and Leader of the Central Assembly, that the Swarajists and the Hindus were the main political forces the British Raj had to contend with and that it must wean away a sizeable section of the Hindus from the Congress in order to retain its hold on India.

So Hailey decided to end Fazli's dominance in Punjab politics. He vetoed the Moneylenders Regulation Bill and created difficulties in the passage of the Land Revenue Bill, both measures backed by the Unionists. He got an opportunity to execute his political aims in

1926, at the time of the third general election. He persuaded Fazli to become the Revenue Member of the Governor's Executive Council and formed a non-party Ministry, with the Governor holding the balance between the three major communities of the Punjab on the ground that communalism had increased since the introduction of the Montford reforms.

Chapter 9

THE QUESTION OF COUNCIL ENTRY

The Council entry programme evoked a large measure of enthusiasm. The Swarajists entered the electoral battle in November and scored several spectacular victories. Under the leadership of C. R. Das, they captured the majority of elective seats in Bengal, defeating giants like Surendranath Bannerjea and S. R. Das, the Advocate-General. In the Central Provinces, too, they were triumphant, and in the Central Assembly they constituted the largest single group.

In this atmosphere, the annual session of the Congress held at Cocanada, in the South, under the presidentship of Mohammed Ali strove to impart new vigour to the cry for Hindu–Muslim unity by endorsing the national pact conceding to Muslims 25 per cent of the share in the all–India services. It refused, however, to countenance the Bengal pact sponsored by C. R. Das for fear of country-wide repercussions. The pact generously gave a 60 per cent share to the Muslims of that province in recruitment to the public services, which was higher than their population ratio. Das was furious, and when I broached the matter with him he said he would wash his hands of all–India politics and confine his activity to Bengal to recover the lost ground. The Congress decision led, however, to the same kind of estrangement between the Hindus and Muslims in Bengal as had been witnessed in the Punjab.

The second all–India Legislative Assembly had 45 Swarajist members. As the only organised party, they assumed the role of Opposition under the leadership of Motilal Nehru and were assigned seats facing the Treasury benches. Jinnah formed the Independent Party consisting of those who won in the elections without a party label. The new party was without a formal constitution or rules to govern its activity. This group, however, occupied a crucial position, inasmuch as the Swarajists had to depend on its support for the success of their resolutions, like those urging a round table Conference to determine the future constitution of India and the annulment of all repressive measures.

Jinnah, egged on by his deputy, Sir Purshotamdas Thakurdas, a Bombay businessman who had gained fame for the stand he took in favour of State management of the railways as a member of the Acworth Committee, concentrated his fire on two issues—reduction of the military budget and rapid Indianisation of the higher ranks of the Army. The appointment of the Indian Sandhurst Committee, under General Skeen, Chief of Staff, was due mainly to his passionate advocacy in the Assembly.

The balance sheet for the first three months of 1924 was most encouraging from the Swarajist viewpoint. A virtual deadlock had been created both in Bengal and the Central Provinces, and at the Centre too the struggle to "destroy the reforms from within" was gaining momentum. But Gandhi's unconditional release from jail on 5th February, 1924, after an operation at Poona for appendicitis revived the controversy over Council entry. Convalescing at Bombay's seaside suburb of Juhu, Gandhi rebuffed a desperate attempt by Motilal Nehru and Das to secure his blessings for their programme of entry. "There is an honest and fundamental difference," he declared at the conclusion of the talks. "I retain the opinion that Council entry is inconsistent with non-cooperation as I conceive it."

Gandhi's attitude must be viewed against the background of happenings in the Central Assembly. Replying to the debate on Motilal's motion for a round table conference to consider a scheme for self-government, Sir Malcolm Hailey had in February not only propounded the thesis that responsible government did not imply dominion status but declared somewhat categorically that in no event was a change in the form of government contemplated before 1929—that is, before the expiry of the ten-year period stipulated in the Reforms Act of 1919. The Swarajists' position had thus been considerably weakened.

While the top Congress leadership was engrossed in political debate a serious Hindu–Muslim riot occurred in Kohat, in the North-West Frontier Province causing a grave setback to their efforts at promoting communal harmony. According to official estimates 155 people were killed and Hindu temples and property destroyed in the carnage allegedly sparked by a virulently anti-Islamic poem circulated by *agents provocateurs*. Gandhi went on a

21-day fast at the residence of Mohammed Ali in Delhi on 18th
September to make his people feel ashamed of the tragedy. Motilal
Nehru called a conference on communal unity, the first of its kind
to include two Britons, a clergyman and a journalist, but the various
groups represented at the conference tried to bargain among themselves rather than produce a plan for ending religious antagonisms.
After his fast, Gandhi wished to visit Kohat, but the authorities in
Delhi refused his request. Incidentally, during his fast, Gandhi
studied the constitution of the Soviet Union and told me that he had
been struck by the provision "no work, no vote."

Not long after, Das, convalescing from an illness at Mashobra, a
suburb of Simla, revealed to me his sense of desperation. Gandhi,
he felt, was leading the country away from the path of constitutional
struggle into the wilderness of sterile political agitation. It was so
difficult, though, to counter his overwhelming popularity. "How can
we get rid of the Mahatma," he exclaimed, "and put the people
back on the road to the capture of power, now within our grasp?"
The same feeling of bewilderment and frustration was expressed to
me on other occasions by Motilal Nehru and Vithalbhai Patel.
Gandhi, they seemed convinced then, was rendering it impossible
to fight the British with weapons they understood and respected;
his own way of civil disobedience would take the nation nowhere.

The estrangement between Gandhi and Das was clearly growing
and the bureaucracy decided to take advantage of the situation,
to strike a blow at the extremist element in the Swaraj Party.
Accordingly, the Bengal Government arrested Subhas Chandra
Bose, at that time Chief Executive Officer of Calcutta Corporation,
and others on a charge of encouraging terrorism. Gandhi saw
through the game and decided not to allow the Raj to take advantage
of the differences among them. He hurried to Calcutta, where
Motilal and Das joined him soon after, and there entered into a pact
with the two, under which he suspended non-cooperation while they
agreed to continue the boycott of foreign cloth, wear *khadi* and spin
yarn in payment of the membership fee of the Congress Party. This
deal was a conscious surrender on Gandhi's part and put the No-
changers and Pro-changers on an equal footing. Gandhi had been
chosen to preside over the annual Congress session at Belgaum on
26th December, 1924. The session put the seal of approval on the
pact.

But, while Gandhi stooped to conquer, his presidential address
was a forceful assertion of his faith in the triple boycott. Indeed, his
contention that constructive work even by itself would ensure
Swaraj was received with acclamation. To gain a tactical advantage

Gandhi shrewdly picked Jawaharlal Nehru to be his principal aide as General Secretary of the Congress. Jawaharlal was thereby promoted over the heads of senior party men, and his elevation served to neutralise his father's dissent from the Gandhian approach to the fight for freedom.

Gandhi dropped from his Working Committee his principal lieutenants, Vallabhbhai Patel and Rajagopalachari, and put two followers of Tilak in their place. Once again he undertook a tour of the country to enthuse the masses for his programme. Meanwhile, the short-lived Labour Government had been ousted in Britain and a long-range flirtation began between Birkenhead, the new Secretary of State, and C. R. Das.

In a memorable speech at Faridpur, now in East Pakistan, on 1st May, 1925, Das, a sick man nearing his end, had declared in a feeble voice that he was prepared to negotiate, provided the Government divested itself of its discretionary powers of constraint and followed this up by proclaiming a general amnesty for all political prisoners. If the efforts at a reconciliation failed, the Congress would have to resort to civil disobedience by implementing Gandhi's constructive programme, he added.

A day earlier, Gandhi addressed a meeting in Calcutta in which he declared that he preferred to put through his programme instead of entering into diplomatic relations with "matchless" diplomats from England. He knew nothing about Das's negotiations with Birkenhead, he said.

Das died in Darjeeling on 16th June, 1925, and Gandhi, who was in Khulna, rushed to Calcutta for his funeral. Gandhi won the hearts of the Bengalis by remarking that he had never doubted the usefulness of Council entry for the purpose of embarrassing the Government and putting it in the wrong. The emotional Bengalis warmly responded by deciding that the funds raised to erect a memorial to Das be dedicated to propagating the wearing of hand-made *khadi* and spinning.

Gandhi had made up his mind to hand over the Congress completely to the Swarajists, and he got the A.I.C.C. session at Patna in September to ratify this. He brought into being at the same time the All-India Spinners Association, which, although under the auspices of the Congress, would not participate in politics. He felt that the association would, however, create a strong mass base for future political struggles.

I asked Gandhi after the Patna meeting whether he was planning a break with the Swarajists. He replied: "I am giving them a long rope. They will get nothing from Reading and Birkenhead. When they return crestfallen, Bapu (the term of address affectionately used for Gandhi) will be ready to succour them. I must go set the country afire meanwhile by constructive work."

The Swarajists, on their part, could point to their victory in the election of the Speaker of the Assembly. Vithalbhai Patel, their deputy leader, won in a close contest with the official nominee. Motilal later confided in the lobbies that through this successful manoeuvre he had rid himself of a lieutenant whom he looked upon as a thorn in his side.

The protagonists of Council entry, however, had really little else to show as the fruit of their policy. Reading, inaugurating the autumn session of the Central Legislature in 1925, had poured cold water on nationalist aspirations. To settle accounts with the Viceroy, the Opposition successfully sponsored a motion in the name of Motilal characterising dyarchy as a "fraud" and the system of government as "treason against God's law."

The Kanpur session of the Congress, held in December 1925 and presided over by Mrs. Sarojini Naidu, the first Indian woman to hold this exalted position, voiced the popular frustration in un-mistakable terms. It was at this session that Hindustani was recom-mended as the language for Congress sessions. Early in 1926, therefore, when the All–India Congress Committee called upon the Swarajists to withdraw from the legislatures, they were in no mood to resist. They walked out of the Central Assembly on 7th March after a symbolic rejection of the first demand for budget grants. Jinnah's group was too weak to carry on as an effective opposition, and the parliamentary experiment went into a state of suspended animation.

Chapter 10

READING'S SUCCESSES AND FAILURES

Lord Reading's viceroyalty, which had begun auspiciously with the dawning hope of an amicable settlement of the conflict between Indian nationalism and the British Raj, closed in April 1926 in an atmosphere vitiated by mutual suspicion and recrimination. Typical of this was Motilal Nehru's withdrawal with his supporters from the Central Assembly in protest against the Government's failure to respond to his party's national demand, declaring as he left the Chamber that he had no use for these "sham institutions." Nevertheless, the elder Nehru's denunciation of Reading's stewardship did not take note of the element of dynamism that had been injected into the economy and the administration in these crucial years for the future of India. With the Swarajists walking out from the provincial assemblies as well, the attenuated legislatures forfeited much of their meaning and purpose. But the lessons the Indian political leaders gleaned from their shortlived but exhilarating parliamentary experience was not without profound value, as later years, particularly those following independence, were to reveal.

Sir Frederic Whyte, the first President of the Central Assembly, gave this body its stamp of authority as a legislative forum. He summoned the first conference of Speakers—an exercise that today makes for uniformity in legislative practice at the Centre and in the States and contributes not a little to nourishing the concept of Indian unity. The foundations he helped lay in those formative years, the traditions he was responsible for fostering and which his successors—Vithalbhai Patel, Abdur Rahim and Mavalankar— enlarged, endured the vicissitudes of the struggle for freedom. When the time came to establish independent India's Parliament, there was already a solid base to build upon.

Sir Frederic received many farewell parties, ending with a banquet at Viceregal Lodge. In a frank assessment of the Indian political scene, he told me in a private talk that Lord Morley's enlarged councils provided an effective forum for debate and for nationalist propaganda and the new legislature had multiplied that opportunity tenfold. He was struck by the fact that although Hindu–Muslim differences and the struggle between Brahmins and non-Brahmins intensified occasionally, the proceedings in the Central Assembly had largely underlined the racial cleavage between Indians and Europeans.

India, he felt, was trying to work a modern constitution through a people still mentally in the Middle Ages. The Central Assembly could stand comparison with any other body of its kind for the standard of its debates and the talent of its members. But would India produce a governing class that would give it national cohesion?

I attended a farewell dinner to Reading given by "leading Indian gentlemen" of Simla on 6th October, 1925. Shafi proposed a toast to the departing Viceroy and said that "the non-cooperation programme with its five boycotts adopted at the special Congress held in September 1920 is now absolutely dead" and paid a special tribute to the help the Viceroy had rendered in Indianising the

Imperial Services and the commissioned ranks of the Indian Army and in promoting financial solvency and industrial development.

In reply, Reading said that the credit for solvency belonged to "divine Providence, who gave us the monsoons." He regretted that the Swarajists had not responded to Birkenhead's gesture. The Secretary of State had said to them: "Give us evidence of sincere co-operation and India and you will not find England a niggardly bargainer."

Roy and I went up to the Viceroy and asked whether he agreed with Shafi that non-cooperation was dead. "Oh, no," he replied, "you cannot count out Gandhi. He has a hypnotic influence over the masses. I hope Lord Irwin will have better luck with him. We have lost the chance of reconciliation with C. R. Das's death."

I asked the Viceroy what he felt was his greatest contribution to India. He replied unhesitatingly: "Justice between man and man." Racial discrimination in favour of Europeans in judicial trials and the excise duty on Indian cotton, imposed in the interests of Lancashire, were abolished in Reading's regency. The steel industry received protection and a Tariff Board was set up to examine the need to protect other nascent Indian industries. The management of the Indian railways was taken away from British companies. He added: "India will have her own Reserve Bank and Blackett's (Sir Basil Blackett, Finance Member) post office cash certificate scheme has given a great fillip to national savings. I hope the Royal Commission on Agriculture will make proposals to look after the interests of the poorest of the poor."

Was he taking any regrets with him? I asked. The Viceroy replied he had, instead, the feeling that he had carried out the mandate Montagu had given him to guide the working of the scheme of reforms. Through Indianisation of the services and the abolition of repressive laws, including the Rowlatt Act which he had never used, he had laid a sound foundation for responsible self-government. His one regret was that communal differences had sharpened.

Reading was fortunate in the men he had in his Executive Council. But with the exit of Sapru he was left without an Indian Councillor who could assist in a correct appreciation of Indian opinion. Sapru's successor, S. R. Das, was a great lawyer and the revision of the Transfer of Property Act is a monument to his legal talent, but he was so much an admirer of British character and ways that he failed to reflect Indian sentiment. He used his official position, however, to found Doon School, the Eton of India, at Dehra Dun as a permanent memorial to the values in character and education he wanted to inculcate in his countrymen.

Reading's last act as Viceroy was of historic significance in the light of later developments. This was the rebuff he administered to the Nizam of Hyderabad's plea for the restoration of Berar, which Curzon had taken on perpetual lease on the ground that it was misgoverned. The Nizam thought that in the pro-Muslim climate of the time in Delhi he could claim back this area with success. His advisers made him write a letter to Reading, giving the impression that Berar was a point of dispute between two sovereign authorities. No Indian ruler, the Viceroy retorted sternly, could claim to negotiate on equal terms with the British Government. "Paramountcy is truly paramount," he said. This snub dampened the ambitions of the Princes, who had hoped to carve out independent states with the decline of the imperial power in India. Muslim sentiment was, however, appeased by permitting the Nizam to call his heir apparent the Prince of Berar.

Chapter 11

IRWIN'S BID TO EASE TENSION

With the departure of Reading, the period of constitutional agitation virtually came to an end. Though the legislatures functioned and passed much useful legislation, the preoccupation during this period was the power struggle between the rulers and the ruled. The Government now concentrated its attention on the creation of allies, and the Congress on weakening the strength and morale of the Raj. In this fight no holds were barred. The Government had at its disposal unlimited power and patronage, the Opposition the emotional upsurge among its followers.

The advent of the new Viceroy, Lord Irwin, in the summer of 1926, seemed to relax tension. The story went round that he was a humble, godly man who fasted and knelt down to pray every Sunday. It was also said that he would walk down to the tennis court carrying his canvas shoes and play with members of his staff in the full gaze of passers-by. These very human qualities endeared him to Indian opinion, and it was natural that he himself should draw closer to Gandhi. Symbolic of the new spirit was the decision of the Government to neutralise the recurring agitation in Lahore by changing the inscription under the Lawrence statue on the city's

Mall from "Will you be governed by pen or sword?" to "With sword and pen I served you."

Irwin soon made it clear that he was not out to exploit communal animosities for political ends. He declared at a welcome dinner at a local club that the reforms had been introduced to create harmony among the various communities. He amplified this view when he told a deputation of Muslims of Bombay Presidency that "if communal representation comes to be regarded as an end in itself, what was designed to promote the cause of unity may quickly become the seed bed of division." (And so it did.)

Addressing the Central Legislature in August, 1927, Irwin reinforced this view when he said that "national self-government must be founded upon the self-government and self-control of individuals. Where private citizens do not possess these qualities, political self-government of a nation is an empty name, and merely serves to disguise under an honourable title continuance of something perilously akin to civil war."

With Gandhi's exit from the active leadership of the Congress after the Belgaum session, the Swaraj Party began to crumble. This process had three causes. Srinivasa Iyengar, its Deputy Leader, was firstly in revolt. He told me Motilal's "magistracy and arrogance" were unbearable. Secondly, some Swarajists began to see the prospect of material advancement through official patronage. Thirdly, the Maharashtrians felt that after the failure of non-cooperation they should give a sincere trial to Tilak's credo of responsive co-operation, and Jayakar, Leader of the Swaraj Party in Bombay Legislative Council, felt that its members should accept ministerial office. Hearing this, Motilal dashed to Bombay "to crush this revolt," he told me, of Jayakar who had resigned from the All-India Swaraj Party Executive. The dissidents met at Akola and formed the Responsivist Party with Jayakar as President.

Motilal now tried to revive public interest in his party's programme by resorting to a dramatic move. He and his followers walked out of the Assembly Chamber after refusing funds for the Executive Council. Motilal said on the occasion: "We will try to devise those sanctions which alone can compel any government to grant the demands of the nation." This gesture was as much a protest as an attempt to create a good impression on voters in the impending general election. Bereft of Gandhi's protection, Motilal faced a more serious revolt when Lajpat Rai and Malaviya formed the Indian National Party on 3rd April, 1926, to fight for *Swaraj* of the dominion type.

At this critical juncture in the life of the Swaraj Party, Gandhi, who had concentrated on building up the Spinners Association, came to Motilal's rescue and effected a settlement between him and the Maharashtrians under which Motilal agreed that the Government's response to the national demand would be considered acceptable "if, in the provinces, the power, responsibility and initiative necessary for the effective discharge of their duties are secured to ministers." In effect, this meant harking back to C. R. Das's offer of political settlement made before his death.

But Malaviya and Lajpat Rai were not to be deflected from the course of action they had decided on, and they formed the Independent Congress group on 7th August, 1926, to contest the elections. This was a veiled attempt to pursue the policies of the Hindu Mahasabha in the name of the Congress. Gandhi reacted characteristically to this situation. "Lalaji sees no escape from communalism," he wrote. "Panditji cannot brook even the thought of it. I must hold myself in reserve till the storm is over."

The result of the rift in the Swarajist camp was disastrous to it. Motilal's candidates did not capture a single Muslim or non-Muslim seat in the U.P. legislature, and Motilal alone secured election because he was not contested. When I met Motilal after the elections, he confessed that his nominees had been worsted because the question of cow slaughter had been dragged into the campaign by the rival parties and he himself had been denounced as a beef-eater. He added by way of explanation that he had once been served beef at a restaurant, but on learning of this he had immediately felt sick and rushed to the toilet, where he had expelled it. The Swarajists scored heavily, however, in Madras and also did well in some other provinces.

A year earlier, Gandhi had given a prophetic explanation of this development. He did so after meeting Fazli Husain, Lajpat Rai and Bhai Parmanand at Cecil Hotel, Simla, in an attempt to help solve the communal tangle in the Punjab. Gandhi said Fazli had made out a convincing case to the effect that his policies were really not pro-Muslim, and therefore communal, but aimed at helping all the socially and economically backward strata of the province. The truth of the matter was, Gandhi explained to me after his unsuccessful attempt at mediation, that all the parties were preparing for a share of the power they believed would result from "our non-violent revolution."

To Gandhi, the apostle of communal harmony, this Hindu–Muslim–Sikh tension caused the deepest pain. On the several occasions on which I met him during those years, he expressed his inmost thoughts on the problem. What he found most baffling was that communalism had become inextricably mixed up with politics. For his own part, he had diagnosed the causes of Hindu–Muslim tension and suggested what he deemed to be excellent remedies. But he confessed that neither he nor his colleagues, Ajmal Khan, Ansari and Azad, had made a worthwhile impact on the Muslims. That, he said to me, was mainly because the British were continuously dangling before the Muslims a carrot in the shape of greater privileges and concessions.

Ironically, this was a feeling Jinnah then shared. He was frustrated, on the one hand, by the fanatical attitude of the pro-British Muslims and, on the other, by the failure of the Congress to make common cause with him for fear of driving the Hindus into the arms of the Hindu Mahasabha, which was progressively copying the technique of self-seeking pro-British Muslim politicians.

The annual session of the Congress at Gauhati on 26th December, 1926, was marred by the assassination of Swami Shraddhanand in Delhi by a Muslim fanatic who, on the pretext of paying his respects to the ailing swami, had shot him dead. His slaying was the outcome of a fanatical outburst against the publication of a book maligning the Prophet. Its author had been cleared in judicial proceedings, but a Muslim had murdered him in Lahore.

The Gauhati session stiffened the Congress mandate by calling on the Swarajists not to accept office and to paralyse the legislatures. Gandhi undertook another tour of the country, starting with Bengal. The dual theme of the message he preached was that India could not get *Swaraj* without accepting the gospel of *khadi* in theory and practice and that he felt humiliated to speak in English and therefore wanted every Indian to learn Hindustani. He even went further and advocated the adoption of the Devanagari script for all the Indian languages. Once again, he found South India most enthusiastic in its response to him, and he addressed about two dozen public meetings in Madras city alone. The tour ended abruptly in October 1927 when Irwin called him to Delhi.

Chapter 12

DIVIDE AND RULE

After meeting the Viceroy, Gandhi felt very disappointed. "I have been dragged all the way up to receive this document," he said with ill-concealed contempt. "I expected better from the man of God." The Nehrus were away in Europe and also visited Moscow, where they had gone to attend the anniversary celebrations of the October Revolution. When they came the father told me he found Soviet life unutterably drab, but the idealism of Lenin had fired his son's imagination. On their return, Motilal wanted Jawaharlal to be the next Congress President, but finding Dr. Ansari in the field he did not press his son's claim.

Irwin had blundered in accepting an all-white parliamentary commission to report on India's fitness for another instalment of constitutional reforms. Congressmen, Liberals and Jinnah's followers combined to boycott it. Indian antipathy to the Commission, headed by Sir John Simon, was evident from the fact that the very announcement of its appointment was the signal for a countrywide *hartal*. When the commission began its tour of the major cities, it had to face a massive boycott, accompanied by angry demonstrations. At Lahore, Lajpat Rai, leading the demonstrators, was among the victims of a police assault and sustained injuries and a severe shock which, as was stated in the Central Assembly later, hastened his death on 17th November, 1928. At Lucknow, Jawaharlal and Govind Ballabh Pant, who later became Chief Minister of Uttar Pradesh and subsequently Home Minister of the Indian Union, were among those hurt in the police attack. Pant was so badly shaken that he bore the marks of nervous damage all his life.

Hostility to the Raj was exacerbated in 1927 by the bitter controversy over the exchange rate of the rupee. Sir Purshotamdas Thakurdas, in a minute of dissent to the report of the Currency Commission, had suggested 1s 4d to the rupee, while the majority stood for 1s 6d. The minority recommendation became a battle cry which resounded all over the country from political platforms and gatherings of Indian commercial interests. The manner in which Sir Basil Blackett, the Finance Member, secured a narrow majority in the Central Assembly for the less favourable rate strengthened the suspicion that this had been engineered in the sole interests of Britain.

Katherine Mayo's *Mother India*, published in August 1927, aroused a storm of indignation throughout the country, particularly because Reading's Government, it was suspected, had had something to do with inducing her to malign India in the same way as she had earlier denigrated the Filipinos. Gandhi described the book as a "drain inspector's report." (Dr. H. N. Kunzru, a veteran legislator, told me several years later he was shocked to see this book with cadets at West Point, the U.S. military academy, when he visited it in the forties.)

The winter session of the Central Assembly in 1928 was noteworthy for the adoption of Jinnah's motion censuring the Government for whittling down the Indian Sandhurst Committee's recommendation on speeding up the Indianisation of the officer ranks of the Army and for passing Motilal's motion refusing funds for the Simon Commission.

Now that the country was again in a ferment, Gandhi scored a great victory at Bardoli independently of the Congress. Gandhi had declared after his release from jail in 1924 that he was morally bound to abstain from active politics until March, 1928, when the six-year sentence of imprisonment imposed on him would have expired. About this time, unrest surfaced in Bardoli over higher land revenue assessments. Vallabhbhai Patel organised a civil disobedience and no-tax campaign which paralysed the administration in the area in April. The people named him Sardar (born leader). Indian and foreign correspondents reported that Patel's writ ran throughout the sub-district. The movement ended four months later, on 6th August, when the Bombay Government agreed to appoint a committee to revise the revenue rates.

The campaign had been so well organised and was so peaceful and successful that it opened the eyes of the Viceroy to the possibility of a similar defiance on a larger scale. Patel won nationwide plaudits and was hailed everywhere as a hero and various provincial committees proposed him for the Congress crown at the coming session in Calcutta.

The period 1927–28 provided the most interesting prelude to the development of political alignments which were to shape inexorably the future course of Indian politics. It was a struggle concerning as much the personal fortunes of the major actors on the political scene as of the sectional interests they represented. Gandhi stayed in the wings, letting his lieutenants fight among themselves, keeping himself in readiness to take command of the movement for freedom when these men turned to him in frustration for guidance.

Motilal, Jinnah and Sapru were making Herculean efforts to bring about a national identity of views on the pattern of self-government and the adjustment of communal claims through an all-party convention. The outcome of their labours was the Nehru report. Fazli Husain, on the other hand, was campaigning for the acceptance of his own political beliefs, and Bhim Rao Ambedkar, who had emerged as a powerful spokesman of the depressed classes, walked the stage as a latter-day Moses striving to free his people from bondage. The Raj, on its side, was aiming at exposing the weakness of the Indian case for self-rule through the probing eye of the Simon Commission. Finally, there was the rivalry between Srinivasa Iyengar and Motilal, the upshot of which was that the former plumped for complete independence at the Congress session held in Madras in December 1927. Subhas Bose and Jawaharlal, rivals for the future leadership of the Congress, joined the Independence League that Iyengar set up as its secretaries.

The Raj, looking for ways of driving a wedge into the national movement, hit on the strategy of giving sustenance to the group of Muslim politicians ranged behind Fazli and to Ambedkar's demand for special safeguards for the untouchables. The aim of the bureaucracy was to neutralise the caste Hindus, who it felt was the major political force antagonistic to the continuance of British rule. At this stage, the conflict was brought to a head by two closely connected events—the publication of the Nehru report on constitutional reforms in August 1928 and the arrival of Simon and his colleagues for public hearings in October 1928.

The salient points of the report of the Motilal Nehru Committee, constituted in answer to Birkenhead's challenge to produce a blueprint for India's constitution, were:

"All power of Government and all authority, legislative, executive and judicial, are derived from the people and the same shall be exercised in the Commonwealth of India through organisations established by, or under, and in accord with, this Constitution."

"There shall be no state religion; men and women shall have equal rights as citizens."

"Separate electorates shall be abolished. Every person of the age of 21 shall have the vote."

"A Supreme Court shall be set up."

"The redistribution of provinces shall take place on a linguistic basis on the demand of the majority of the area concerned, subject to financial and administrative considerations."

The report, having recommended adult franchise, attempted to appease communal sentiment by proposing a "balance" between the Hindu-majority and Muslim-majority provinces. It recommended the advancement of the North-West Frontier to full provincial status and the separation of Sind from Bombay Presidency.

The All–Parties Convention at Calcutta adopted the report, disregarding the plea of the Muslim extremists for the retention of separate electorates, the reservation of a third of the seats in the Central Assembly for Muslims and for a federal, rather than unitary, constitution, with the provinces holding residuary powers. The modifications suggested by Jinnah were also voted down, even though Sapru pleaded for a gesture to the League leader.

The question who should preside over the next Congress session had assumed special importance. Writing to Gandhi on 11th July, 1928, Motilal said: "I am quite clear that the hero of the hour is Vallabhbhai, and the least we can do to appreciate his public services is to offer him the crown. Failing him, I think that under all the circumstances Jawahar would be the best choice." Gandhi solved the dilemma by proposing that Motilal himself become President. By this gesture, he won over the Nehrus and at the same time gave his blessing to the Nehru report.

There were unprecedented scenes of enthusiasm when Motilal, as President-elect of the Calcutta Congress in December 1928, was taken round in a procession led by Subhas Chandra Bose, who was in the smart uniform of the commander of the party's volunteer force, a rehearsal, it might appear, for the role he was to perform as Commander of the Indian National Army of the Azad Hind Government in Singapore during World War II. The presidential chariot was drawn by graceful white horses, and Motilal stood upright in this resplendent vehicle like a Roman consul as the crowds lining the route smothered him with garlands of jasmine.

The session was a triumph for Motilal, for it went back on the resolution on complete independence adopted at the previous session and endorsed the constitutional scheme, based on dominion status, embodied in the Nehru report and endorsed by the All-Parties Convention. Gandhi wanted to give the Raj two years to meet the demand, but reduced the period by half under pressure from Jawaharlal. Subhas Bose was not reconciled to this policy, but his demand that the Nehru report be rejected was defeated by 1,350 votes to 973. I asked Subhas why he stood out against it, and he replied: "I do not like Gandhiji's appeasement of the Nehrus. We in Bengal represent the real revolutionary force. Jawahar only talks. We act."

The Muslim League, at its session in Calcutta, split on the Nehru report; one section supported it, another opposed it, and a third favoured a compromise. Meanwhile, the supporters of the Raj, headed by the Aga Khan, had prepared plans to by-pass the League and held a meeting of the All-Parties Muslim Conference in Delhi on 1st January, 1929.

One of its resolutions pleaded that a federal system, with complete autonomy and residuary powers vested in the constituent states, should be the basis of the new constitution. Among its other demands were that separate electorates must be continued; that 33 per cent of the seats in the Central Legislature must be reserved for Muslims; that Sind be constituted as a separate province and the N.W.F.P. given reforms; that no change in the Constitution should be made without the concurrence of all the states constituting the Indian Federation and, finally, that "no constitution, by whomsoever proposed or devised, will be acceptable to Indian Musalmans unless it conforms with the principles embodied in this resolution."

A significant development was that Shaukat Ali spoke at the conference, and this marked the break of the Ali brothers with the Congress.

Chapter 13

THE SIMON INQUIRY

The next scene opens with the public sittings of the Simon Commission. To placate Indian opinion, the Viceroy had appointed an Indian Central Committee with Sir Sankaran Nair as Chairman to work in close association with the commission, whose all-white composition had aroused nationwide resentment.

Sir John Simon paid a preliminary visit to Delhi to discuss with the authorities the arrangements he had in mind for the inquiry. Roy saw Simon and I was deputed to cover the proceedings for the special service A.P.I. had organised for reporting the Commission's public proceedings. I gathered from Sir John in a private talk that he would concern himself largely with the manner in which the

Constitution had been worked and with the question whether the country was fit for provincial autonomy. The problem at the Centre, he hinted, was too complex, and his commission would occupy itself with an analysis of the various political forces operating in India to arrive at conclusions on the future process of transferring power to Indian hands.

The Commission arrived in India in the autumn of 1928 to record public evidence and held its first sittings in Poona in October. The day before the sittings began, I learnt something about the procedure it intended to follow. All the witnesses would be first examined by the Commission and thereafter by the Indian committee. Each body would come to its own conclusions and report to the authority to which it was responsible. As to the memoranda received by the Commission, the most important in Sir John's view were the ones embodying the opinions of provincial Governments and of Muslim organisations and associations representing the depressed classes.

From this preliminary investigation, I came away with the impression that the Commission did not really intend to deal seriously with the national demand formulated by the Central Assembly for the early achievement of a system of responsible government on the model of the dominions.

The first few public sittings revealed the true character of the inquiry. Sir John subjected every witness to a very thorough examination, and his loaded questions gave a clear indication of how his mind worked. The other members of the Commission seemed to take their cue from him and contributed little of their own to the inquiry. This really meant that Sir John intended to provide the leadership and the brain-power. Sir Sankaran was an extinct volcano, while some of the representatives of the Muslims and the depressed classes on his committee only served to buttress the views Sir John himself was trying to project.

I was entrusted with the responsibility of feeding the Indian newspapers and the British Press through Reuter, with a brief objective account of the daily proceedings. After reporting the opening week's sittings, I felt a sudden urge to give my Indian readers a peep behind the scenes. Accordingly, one afternoon when the commission was not sitting, I produced a sketch of about 2,000 words conveying my impressions of its functioning for the benefit of the newspapers which subscribed to my political commentary.

No sooner had the exposure appeared in *The Hindu* of Madras than the *Times of India* splashed across its main news page extracts from my despatch with a banner headline: "Anti-Simon Commission Propaganda through Associated Press." The paper laid a grave charge at my door. Representing "a semi-official news agency heavily subsidised by the Government," I was alleged to have not only been accorded special privileges, including travel in the Commission's special train, but also to have enjoyed the confidence of every one of its members. The paper contended that I had abused these privileges and had fed the nationalist Press with stories manifestly calculated to hold the entire inquiry up to ridicule. The attack was overdone, for at no stage had I disclosed anything said to me in confidence. The impugned despatch merely set out my candid personal impressions.

Though the *Times of India*'s broadside impaired my relations with Simon the result of this peep behind the scenes was that the newspaper-reading public and politicians throughout India were confirmed in their suspicion that nothing of substantial benefit was to be expected from the inquiry. I worked with the Commission for another two months, before a stroke of malaria compelled me to withdraw. As we travelled from one place to another, I had the opportunity of exchanging views informally with its members. In particular with Burnham, proprietor of *The Daily Telegraph*, and Clement Attlee under whose Prime Ministership India became independent in 1947.

Major Attlee, as he was then called, frankly admitted that the more he studied the situation the more puzzled he became. India seemed to him too big a country to be brought under the British system of parliamentary democracy. The terms of reference ruled out the projection of schemes like the presidential system in the U.S. as being more suited to Indian conditions. Further, it was very difficult, he said, to see how hundreds of states, big and small, could remain islands of autocracy in a country with parliamentary institutions. He confessed to me that the inquiry had raised more question marks than it had found answers to. I can hardly say that I was impressed either by his personality or his intellect. I certainly did not imagine that I was exchanging informal confidences with one who would blossom into a Prime Minister, and, what is more, be the instrument to transfer power to India. My interest in him was to see how far a Labour spokesman could be worked up to back the Indian case for self-government.

Chapter 14

THE WORSENING CRISIS

The Central Assembly met early in 1929 in an atmosphere of tension. The Government had brought forward a Public Safety Bill to deal with terrorist crimes. On 8th April, Vithalbhai Patel got up to deliver his ruling on whether the bill was in order. Before he could do so, a bomb was hurled on to the Assembly floor and a couple of shots rang out. I rushed out of the correspondents' gallery into the Press room and immediately dictated a message which I asked the A.P.I. news desk to flash to Reuter in London and all over India. Before I had time to give details, the telephone line was cut. The police authorities closed the doors of the Council House in order to search visitors and arrested Bhagat Singh and Batukeshwar Dutt.

The message I transmitted became a scoop, as journalists had not anticipated this blockage. Now they could neither get out of the Council House nor establish telephonic contact with their offices. Reuter's London office was puzzled by the absence of a follow-up for well over three hours. The bomb fell near the Finance Member. Fortunately, he and others escaped injury. Most Members rushed out. Some took cover under benches. The Speaker, standing amidst the smoke engulfing the chamber adjourned the House immediately after the incident.

Vithalbhai ruled three days later that the Bill was out of order. The issues it raised, he said, were *sub judice* in the Meerut conspiracy case against certain Communists. A debate on the Bill would therefore be prejudicial to a fair trial. The Viceroy did not agree with this view and issued an ordinance enacting the measure. Later, when he addressed the Assembly in September, he referred to these happenings. The Speaker wrote to the Viceroy pointing out that no one could question his ruling within the precincts of the House. The Viceroy wrote back to say that he had not meant to question the ruling and expressed regret for his remarks.

The Simon report was published on 5th September, 1929. As was expected, it aroused bitter disappointment in every segment of Indian opinion. The Commission relegated to the distant future the establishment of an all–India federation. It failed to make even a passing reference to dominion status. Indeed, the report expressed scepticism about the suitability of the parliamentary system for India and threw out a hint that the provinces might develop different constitutional practices later on.

The Viceroy realised that the political situation was getting out of hand and that, on the expiry of the Congress ultimatum that the national demand embodied in the Nehru report and endorsed by the Calcutta session of the Congress be accepted within a year, the nation would resort to civil disobedience. Irwin accordingly visited London and succeeded in persuading the British Government to announce that a round table conference to determine India's future would be held there the following year. This was accompanied by the statement that dominion status was the natural issue of India's constitutional progress.

To stir public opinion in India came Ramsay MacDonald's declaration in a speech just before becoming Prime Minister: "I hope that within a period of months rather than years there will be a new dominion added to the Commonwealth of our nations, a dominion of another race, a dominion which will find self-respect as an equal within the Commonwealth. I refer to India." Unfortunately, however, to allay the uproar among the British Conservatives and a few Liberals against these remarks, Wedgwood Benn, the new Secretary of State for India, offered an explanation that detracted a great deal from the favourable impact of the announcement of a conference.

Gandhi toured the U.P. extensively and declared in his speeches that only constructive work would bring *Swaraj*. He dismissed Irwin's promise of dominion status as "undated and undefined." Vithalbhai Patel, who had been helping to build a bridge between the Viceroy and Gandhi, called a leaders' conference at his house and succeeded in persuading Gandhi to modify his stand. The conference resulted in a statement signed by Gandhi, Malaviya, Motilal, Sapru, Ansari, Jawaharlal and Mrs. Besant conceding the sincerity underlying the declaration and the desire of the British Government to satisfy Indian opinion.

The statement proceeded to lay down certain conditions for negotiations, including the demands that all discussions should be on the basis of dominion status and that the Congress should have majority representation at the proposed conference. Subhas Bose declined to sign the document and thus stood out as an uncompromising champion of full independence on the eve of the Congress session to be held at Lahore.

In a final bid to resolve the differences, Irwin invited Gandhi and other leaders to meet him on 23rd December. The terrorists, apparently apprehending an understanding between them, placed a bomb on the track of the train bringing Irwin to Delhi. The bomb damaged a bogie but the Viceroy's compartment fortunately escaped the blast. The talks that followed failed to bring about an understanding. Irwin maintained that it was impossible to prejudge the action of the conference or restrict the liberty of Parliament, while Gandhi insisted that the conference draw up a constitution based on dominion status which should become immediately operative. Vithalbhai Patel felt greatly dispirited and said to me: "You can lead a horse to water but cannot make it drink." He added: "I wash my hands of all this."

It was now clear that the Congress session at Lahore would be crucial. The provincial committees had recommended Gandhi and Sardar Vallabhbhai Patel for the presidentship of the Congress. Gandhi, who had resumed the party's active leadership at the previous session, was expected to welcome the nomination of the hero of Bardoli, his most dependable lieutenant. When Gandhi announced his preference for Jawaharlal, the general body of Congressmen, especially the senior leaders who felt they had been superseded, were astonished. For one thing, it was considered odd that a son should succeed his father to the Congress throne, and for another there was regret that Sardar Patel's outstanding services had been overlooked.

Having learnt from private inquiries that Gandhi had succumbed to pressure from Motilal, I sought Gandhi's version. The Mahatma pointed out that Motilal had repeated with greater emphasis the argument put forward in his letter of July 1928 that Jawaharlal represented youth and dynamism. He had agreed with Motilal, and the choice was particularly appropriate when the Congress was about to launch a fresh struggle. He added that Sardar Patel would be with him in any case and that he was strengthening the movement by bringing Jawaharlal in as an active leader. The Sardar would be the obvious choice for the next session.

It is certain that Gandhi's decision marked a turning-point in the history of modern India. A dying man, Motilal was naturally eager to see Jawaharlal Congress President in his own lifetime. Azad expressed to me the feeling that "Jawahar would make a great appeal to Muslim youth." But the effect of Gandhi's decision was to identify the Nehru family with the nation. There is little doubt that this identification was a factor in the choice of Nehru as the first Prime Minister of free India and of his daughter Indira as the third.

Enthusiasm at the Lahore session reached a climax when Gandhi moved a resolution declaring that *Swaraj* meant complete independence and that, as the year's notice to the Government to accept the national demand had been ignored, the scheme embodied in the Nehru report had lapsed. They were no longer interested in dominion status and would fight for complete independence. A call was issued to the Swarajists to resign their seats in the legislatures. As this resolution was bound to evoke worldwide interest, I slipped out of the pandal a few minutes before the debate had concluded and waited at the Congress Camp telegraph office to catch the echoes of the applause that was bound to signal its adoption. As soon as the welcome sound reached my ears, I put the message I had already prepared on the wires. This simple device enabled me to convey the news to India and London ahead of my rivals.

The most moving scene of the session was enacted not in the pandal but on the banks of the Ravi River at midnight on 31st December, when the banner of independence was unfurled in pursuance of the resolution, and the Declaration of Independence read. Both Motilal and Jawaharlal attended the ceremony, symbolising as it were the transfer of the torch of freedom from the older generation to the younger. The most striking document of the *Swaraj* movement was the Declaration of Independence adopted at the session and ceremoniously read out as a pledge all over the country on 26th January, 1930. This document declared that the people of India had the inalienable right to freedom, which they required to promote the opportunities of growth. It affirmed that there was no liberty without equality, and that universal adult franchise would ensure such equality.

The resolution adopted at the Lahore session split the party and gave birth to the Congress Democratic Party, whose members did not respond to the call issued to Congress members of the legislatures to resign their seats. Jayakar led this revolt and assumed the role of Leader of the Opposition in the Central Assembly.

An interesting sidelight of the session for me was a meeting with Khan Abdul Ghaffar Khan, later known as the Frontier Gandhi. This was the first time he and his followers had attended a Congress conference. They were organised as Khudai Khidmatgars (Servants of God) and popularly known as Red Shirts. Ghaffar Khan was so impressed by the Lahore deliberations and by his talks with Gandhi that he decided to join the Congress and become a votary of non-violent non-cooperation.

The fact that the Congress had voted for independence had an interesting reaction in the U.S., where within a week of its adoption a resolution was tabled in the Senate urging the American Government to recognise this Indian aspiration. An important offshoot of the resolution was that 26th January was designated Independence Day, to be celebrated annually with all Congressmen renewing the independence pledge. (When India became a republic, the new constitution was brought into force on this day, now observed as Republic Day.)

The Lahore Congress had authorised the A.I.C.C. to launch civil disobedience whenever it deemed the time ripe. With an unerring instinct for a simple and at the same time dramatic effect, Gandhi chose to inaugurate his *satyagraha* campaign with a march to the sea at Dandi, in Gujarat, to break the salt laws. Law Member Brojendra Mitter revealed to me how his legal advice had helped Irwin resist pressure to arrest Gandhi. He told the Viceroy: "The crime is still in the intention. It has not been committed; who knows, the intention may change. There is no law to arrest a person unless he commits a crime." Irwin accepted this advice.

Ridicule was poured on this particular form of civil disobedience in Government circles, but it received extraordinary publicity not only all over India but in the U.S. as well. The Government's intelligence service sent out daily reports on Gandhi's health during the march, some of them so alarming that Mitter one day told me with obvious trepidation that Gandhi was not expected to survive the ordeal. Gandhi belied this assessment and reached Dandi on 5th April after marching 241 miles in 24 days, broke the salt laws and sparked off a nationwide movement for similar defiance of authority.

Gandhi had issued a 36-hour ultimatum to the Government before setting out from his ashram at Ahmedabad with the slogan "Victory or Death." As the movement created a ferment all over the country, the Government countered it by unleashing a ruthless campaign of repression, and wholesale arrests took place. Gandhi was arrested on 4th May and taken to Yeravada jail. Eight days later, the Viceroy announced the personnel of the delegation to the round table conference. Gandhi then assured a correspondent of the *Daily Herald* of London that civil disobedience would be suspended if the terms of reference of the conference included framing a constitution giving India the substance of independence. Irwin responded by assuring the Central Legislature on 9th July that the pledge of dominion status would be honoured.

A new chapter in political history opened when Fazli Husain joined the Viceroy's Executive Council on 1st April, 1930. He had already acquired national fame as the champion of Muslim interests in the Punjab. He now proceeded to operate with the entire country as his ambit. Since the League was moribund, Fazli revived the

All–India Muslim Conference to follow up the demands formulated at the All–Parties Muslim Conference held under the Aga Khan's chairmanship in Delhi on 1st January, 1929. He got funds from the Nizam of Hyderabad and the Aga Khan to finance the secretarial and propaganda work of the conference.

Fazli's Simla residence, The Retreat, was a stone's throw from my office and I became a frequent visitor to it. He was not in favour of a round table conference because he believed like Gandhi that the communal issue should be resolved first in India. Now that the conference was to take place, he set about ensuring that only those who supported the demands formulated by the All–Parties Muslim Conference found a place in the Muslim delegation and that the Government of India's despatch on the Simon Commission's report and the White Paper related to it should support the safeguards the conference sought.

What happened in the Executive Council was revealed to me by Mitter. One morning, when I called on him, he said: "The devil has won his point. He threatened to resign and lead an anti-Government agitation if our despatch did not back his demands. What is worse, he has succeeded in making the Viceroy nominate Muslim delegates to the Round Table Conference who would only echo Fazli's views."

The Conference was opened by King George in London early in November 1930. In the first flush of enthusiasm some leading delegates, including Jinnah, Shafi, and Malaviya, worked out a formula for a community-wise division of seats in the legislatures. Since this was projected by Press reports as a "communal" settlement, I called on Fazli to get his reaction. He counted, said Fazli, on the Aga Khan to repudiate the settlement. He had already got many organisations and individuals to send telegrams to the Aga Khan about this. Soon the majority of Muslim delegates repudiated the offer made by Jinnah and Shafi to the Hindu and Sikh delegates. It was clear Fazli had pulled strings from Delhi successfully.

The proceedings of the first Round Table Conference, however, underscored the impression that no solution could be found unless the Congress was a party to it. Accordingly, Irwin decided to do what Lloyd George had done in the case of Ireland. He lifted the ban on the Congress Working Committee and invited Gandhi for talks.

Chapter 15

GANDHI–IRWIN PACT

The news of the invitation thrilled the whole country. The Mahatma in his loincloth had parleyed with a Viceroy before but this particular dialogue held out promise of immense potentialities. Political India expectantly awaited its outcome, for Irwin was in some degree akin in spirit to Gandhi, and in popular imagination the understanding between them extended beyond politics. The talks attracted world-wide attention. Professional competition was severe, and a score of correspondents, mainly British and including James Mills of the Associated Press of America, were in Delhi to chase the story.

Roy was determined that we must outdo all rivals and this is how he deployed the forces at his command. Seshadri Iyengar was stationed at Ansari's residence, where Gandhi was staying, and Usha Nath Sen commissioned to keep in touch with the "peacemakers," Sapru and M. R. Jayakar. I was assigned to cover the Viceregal Lodge where the momentous talks were being held. Roy himself was to correlate news from these three "battle stations." For two days excitement was at fever pitch. Then, as the talks intermittently crawled along at the pace of a tortoise, a sense of dullness pervaded the scene.

I idled in the A.D.C.'s room at Viceregal Lodge as the minutes ticked away. The atmosphere in the room was irksome. The young British members of the Viceroy's staff who frequented it made no effort to conceal their annoyance at the parleys, and they mockingly referred to this "meeting of saints" which had interfered with their normal routine and escorting dignitaries who called on their master and exchanged pleasantries with the aides.

I was offered a drink but declined. The A.D.C. who made the offer said: "Don't be abstemious. We have a gentleman Viceroy." I ordered coffee instead. The aide's remark recalled an incident narrated to me by Sir Bhupendra Mitra, a member of the Viceroy's Executive Council who had risen from the ranks. Reading had asked him to select an Indian officer of the Audit and Accounts Service to scrutinise his household accounts. "I am the highest-paid official in the world," Reading told Mitra, "and yet I had to draw on my savings from England. I must live on my salary and sumptuary allowance." The auditor discovered that, according to the accounts furnished, each guest ate and drank at a meal as much as would suffice him for some weeks. This led to drastic action, including the dismissal of household staff. The A.D.C. was implying there was a difference between the former Jewish Viceroy and his English successor. To meet the high cost of entertainment, Irwin received an allowance from his father to supplement his official emoluments.

To add to the depression in the A.D.C.'s chamber, Herbert Emerson, the Home Secretary, who helped draw up the agreement, would walk in daily exhibiting much irritation at the manner in which Gandhi dotted the i's and crossed the t's in his drafts. But one day he came in and remarked: "Well, I'll say this to Gandhi's credit. He is a very good draftsman. Instead of preparing a draft, I now ask him to dictate."

The only official who kept his smile and sense of humour was George Cunningham, the Viceroy's Private Secretary. He was a supporter of the parleys, and he wanted them to succeed. But he kept his lips tightly shut. To relieve my boredom, I loitered in the corridor leading to the chamber where Irwin was parleying with the "rebel" leader behind closed doors. I heard the chatter of a huddle of peons to whom the head peon was holding forth on what he had seen and heard in the Viceroy's room, in and out of which he flitted in the discharge of his duties.

A platoon of peons in smart uniforms bowed low as Gandhi entered the conference room, and this ritual was repeated when he left. In between, they lapped up the gossip that their chief retailed. Discreetly eavesdropping on their conversation, I heard lively accounts of how the parties to the dialogue were seated, of how they had laughingly stoked the logs in the fireplace, of how Mira Behn had served Gandhi with his frugal meal in the Viceroy's presence. The gossip told of an atmosphere of relaxed good humour. True, the peon, ignorant of English, could hardly say what was happening; but an Indian, however low-placed, is sensitive to atmosphere.

I fed the Press with stories of human interest. Ensued the inevitable howl of protest from my foreign rivals. Cunningham strove to pacify them with the assurance that there had been no leak of any kind, that the Viceroy himself had assured him that not a soul had been permitted to intrude on the privacy of the dialogue. I was sent for and questioned. The despatches were based on "intelligent surmise," I said, feeling certain that the official mind would not guess I had gleaned all these sidelights from the lips of illiterate "menials."

The dull moments were enlivened by the broadsides fired by

Churchill from London. He declared it "nauseating to see Gandhi striding half-naked up the steps of the viceregal palace while he is still organising and conducting a defiant campaign of civil disobedience on equal terms with the representative of the King Emperor."

When the talks appeared to be moving towards a settlement, Churchill fumed: "The loss of India would be final and fatal to us. It could not fail to be part of a process that would reduce us to the scale of a minor power." (And he was not far wrong.) His outbursts increased the zeal of the participants in the talks to make them fruitful.

But as day followed weary day, a depression settled on me. One afternoon, I went over to the residence of Sir Joseph Bhore, a member of the Viceroy's Executive, and poured out my tale of suffering—hanging about Viceregal Lodge for hours on end without a square meal. Lady Bhore promptly sent for a cup of coffee. Sir Joseph himself murmured that it would all be over soon. Surely, then, something big was cooking. I rushed back to Viceregal Lodge. The move paid off. No sooner had I taken cover than Fazli Husain arrived. On his heels followed the other Councillors in their cars. An emergency meeting of the Council had been summoned. I clung to my position in the courtyard until the last Councillor departed two hours later.

Time to go home for dinner, I thought, and what should happen but Gandhi himself alighted from a car. Back to pacing the deserted courtyard. The British sentry on duty, imagining maybe that I was an intelligence officer in mufti, ignored my presence. It was a long vigil. All I could see was Emerson toiling up and down the stairs, maintaining contact with his staff summoned for night duty. The hour of midnight had struck long since when I beheld Gandhi coming down the stairs leaning on the Viceroy's arm. From the smiles wreathing their faces I guessed the pact was through.

As Gandhi, seen off by the Viceroy, boarded the car, I dashed to his side and asked: "Mahatmaji, will you issue a statement about the agreement?" Gandhi perhaps mistook me in the dark for a member of the Viceroy's staff and answered: "Ask the Private Secretary." I now addressed Irwin as he was about to walk back to his office room. "What are you doing here at this hour?" he asked me, surprised. "At the post of duty, Your Excellency, even as you are," I said, adding: "Is a communiqué on the agreement being issued tonight?" His first response was a puzzled frown, then a smile as he said: "You will know tomorrow."

Driving straight to the Central Telegraph Office, I flashed a message announcing the news that Gandhi and Irwin had reached agreement and that the pact now only awaited ratification by the Congress Working Committee. A message of this kind takes barely a minute to get to London, and another five to reach New York. *The Times* (London) gave it top display on the main news page, with the credit line to Reuter.

Many hours after my flash had girdled the globe, the official communiqué stilled the tumult caused in the Press corps by a scoop which some of them airily tried to explain away as "intelligent anticipation."

Gandhi and Irwin signed the agreement at noon on 5th March. I asked Gandhi later how the ceremony went off. He told me Irwin and he had joked about Churchill's broadsides and jibes and had drunk to each other's health, Irwin in tea and Gandhi in *nimbu pani* (lime juice) flavoured with a pinch of salt he had manufactured illegally. While they drank, Gandhi had joked that the occasion reminded him of the Boston Tea Party.

What hurt Britain most during these years was the publicity the Gandhian movement was receiving in the U.S. James Mills had told me that the genesis of the Gandhi–Irwin talks was Whitehall's anxiety to make Gandhi take part in the Round Table Conference and by exposing the differences among the Indian participants devalue him as the national leader of rebellion.

I gathered from Mills that Dr. J. Haynes Holmes of the Community Church of New York, who attended the Congress session at Kanpur in 1925, regarded Gandhi as Christ reborn and was the most powerful American advocate of the cause of Indian freedom. Louis Fischer was for a time a favourite American commentator on Indian affairs and he did much to sell the freedom movement in the U.S. and the West generally by interpreting the phenomenon that was Gandhi and the new star on the Indian horizon, Jawahallal Nehru. Among Indians, Syud Husain did more than anyone else to sell India and Gandhi to Americans. Placed by popular polls among the three top platform speakers in the U.S. he demolished the British case at every public debate in which he participated. He was reported to have challenged Katherine Mayo, the author of *Mother India*, to a debate, but that worthy lady flinched from the encounter. A Briton who took Syud Hussain up on her behalf was easily worsted.

The British had miscalculated, however, the effect of Gandhi's failure to make an impression at the Round Table Conference. His activities received wide publicity in the U.S., and the British Establishment was blamed for sending Gandhi back empty handed.

Chapter 16

(1) GIANTS OF THE CENTRAL LEGISLATURE

Outstanding among the legislators of the time was Vithalbhai Patel, the first Indian to become Speaker of the Central Assembly. He was an impressive figure with his flowing grey beard, and he was often mistaken for a Muslim in the Turkish cap he affected in the pre-reform days. "That is symbolic of Hindu–Muslim unity," he explained to me with a twinkle in his eye when I asked him why he wore it. I mentioned this to Gandhi when he visited Simla to meet Reading, and he confessed he too had taken him for a Muslim and Ali Imam for a Hindu. This only showed, he said, that Hindus and Muslims were one people.

As an upholder of the dignity and independence of his office, Vithalbhai asserted his right to occupy a seat beside the Viceroy when the latter attended the House for the formal opening of the legislative session. But Sir Abdur Rahim, his successor, deferred to Lord Willingdon and was content to occupy a seat on the floor of the House facing the Viceroy. It was left to G. V. Mavalankar to reassert the Speaker's prerogative in the matter as the "host."

Vithalbhai's mental equipment was formidable; there was not the smallest detail of British parliamentary lore he had not mastered. Distrusting the bureaucratic advice of the British Secretary of the Legislative Department, he demanded an independent secretariat for the Assembly. Irwin, with whom he took up the issue, was prevailed upon to ensure for the Speaker, as master of the House, a large degree of independence by making the Assembly Secretariat his own portfolio.

Vithalbhai's sympathies were with the nationalist Opposition, and he used every opportunity available to enlarge its influence in the legislature. Although he was known to confer frequently with Motilal Nehru on political questions, his rulings could not be challenged on the score of partisanship.

Of Vithalbhai's championship of his rights as Speaker many stories went the rounds. Once, when he was apprised of a whispering campaign in the lobby impugning his impartiality, he lodged a protest with the Viceroy, and the Home Member had to apologise in the House. Even more sensational was his snub to the Commander-in-Chief, Sir William Birdwood, for absence from the House when a question arising from a speech of his had to be answered. His exalted status in the official hierarchy notwithstanding, the Army chief was obliged to make amends on the floor of the legislature. But from then the Commander-in-Chief was made a member of the Upper House to save him from a future brush with the Speaker of the popular Chamber. No less significant was Vithalbhai's insistence that security control in the Chamber be vested in the Speaker's Watch and Ward. During a crisis over his right to control admissions to the Assembly galleries, he ordered them to be closed until he won his point.

The years when Indian members of the Executive Council could be depended upon to reflect national views in the inner council were over, and Irwin therefore valued Vithalbhai as a link between him and the Congress High Command. For this reason, he gave Vithalbhai much support and agreed to make the separated Assembly Department his portfolio by delinking it from the bureaucracy-ridden Legislative Department. But Irwin also administered a couple of snubs to the Speaker. The day the Swarajists, led by Motilal Nehru, walked out of the House in response to the Congress mandate, Patel ordered an adjournment, declaring that it had become unrepresentative. Irwin conveyed his displeasure at this procedure, and Vithalbhai expressed regret for this action. On another occasion, Vithalbhai refused to allow the Public Safety Bill to be introduced on the ground that it was unconstitutional. Irwin had the rules amended to ensure that the Speaker could not throw out a Bill as being unconstitutional, an authority which only the judiciary was empowered with.

Motilal Nehru, the leader of the Opposition, was a striking personality. Tall and handsome, he looked as imposing in his homespun *dhoti* and *kurta* (long shirt) as he had in the elegant Western attire of his princely lawyer days at Allahabad. The shawl he affected was draped round his shoulders much like a Roman toga. The senior Nehru was intolerant of opposition. He could not keep peace with his Deputy Leaders, Vithalbhai Patel and Srinivasa Iyengar, a former Advocate-General of Madras, who considered themselves possessed of sharper intellects than he had and believed in aggressive opposition. He was also responsible for the resignation of Jayakar and his lieutenants from his party. "They are a diseased limb, and I have amputated it," he remarked to me when he had got rid of Maharashtrian leaders. To Jayakar's erudite Sanskrit quotations, he had been wont to retort with fragments from Persian scholars. Jayakar on his part resented as he often complained to me in the lobby Motilal's "insufferable arrogance."

For all his allegiance to Gandhian principles, Motilal retained much of his aristocratic way of life. He would not completely abjure alcohol, nor would he deny himself the luxury of rich food. One day, in the Assembly lobby, when I pointed out to him that the European Members spoke of his habit of drinking with Sir Alexander Muddiman, the Leader of the House, he protested that he took of alcohol strictly on medical grounds. C. R. Das, he added by way of explanation, was hastening his death by giving up the kind of food and drink he had been accustomed to as a lawyer with a flourishing practice. In deference to Motilal's "weakness," Sir Harcourt Butler, who once visited him in jail, is said to have taken him aside, expressed sympathy at the privations his friend of thirty years' standing was being subjected to and promised to send him whisky and champagne. According to Mahavir Tyagi, a fellow prisoner, whether or not the promise was redeemed, the liquor never reached Motilal.

Jinnah, the leader of the Independent group, tall and lean, always appeared immaculate in European dress. His skill as a debater owed much to his gift for picking on the weaknesses of his opponent. He spoke "basic" English, mostly monosyllabic words, but his gestures were dramatic. He drove home his points with a finger jabbing eloquently, and reinforced them with a brief reference to his notes, which he read elegantly, using a monocle. Of his astuteness as a politician, I recall vividly an incident outside the legislature. The Government's success in organising the Muslim Conference had led him to revise his stand, and when I met him to discuss the programme he was to submit to the Muslim League Council that day, he spiritedly remarked: "Durga, I want your help urgently. Please use your journalistic talent to enunciate our stand by amalgamating our resolutions with the demands made by the All-Parties Muslim Conference. We must appear before the Muslims as the best protectors of their interests."

Jinnah being always friendly and communicative, I gladly responded and scrutinised the resolutions of the League and of the Conference and reduced them to thirteen points. After a quick glance at my effort, Jinnah exclaimed; "Good, but let us make them fourteen—like Wilson's fourteen points." The idea came to him in a flash. "Let me go one better than the Conference," he said, and forthwith added the following point: "No Cabinet, either provincial or Central, should be formed without their being a proportion of at least one-third Muslim Ministers." Jinnah was not thinking in terms of demands but of tactics, of keeping himself afloat as a political leader. His last point was thus motivated by the desire to champion the cause of the Muslims in areas where they were a minority. His main support at the time was in Bombay and the U.P., and this provision was meant to strengthen his hold on these provinces.

I accompanied Jinnah to the meeting of the League Council at a cinema hall in Old Delhi. The Opposition had mobilised rowdies to break up the meeting, and they did succeed in their design. But Jinnah adroitly outmanoeuvred them by announcing amidst din and confusion that his fourteen points had been adopted. By now chairs were flying and Jinnah rushed out and drove back to Western Court, the residential block for legislators. From that day the fourteen points, dramatised in Press reports, became famous. Compared with the demands of the All–Parties Muslim Conference, Jinnah was conciliatory only to the extent that he kept the issue of separate electorates open to negotiation, leaving it to the community concerned to abandon them at any time in favour of joint electorates.

The "licensed jester" of the House in those years was Kabiruddin Ahmed from East Bengal. I recall how he halted the floodtide of Motilal's fiery oratory when he was speaking on his resolution embodying the national demand. As the Swarajist leader, presenting his case for freedom, was declaiming that he would fight for self-government day and night without respite, Ahmed interjected: "When, then, will you spin?" The House dissolved in laughter. Motilal had only recently accepted the obligation to perform ritual spinning every day in return for Gandhi s approval of the Council entry programme.

Sir Malcolm Hailey, the most brilliant I.C.S. man of the time, was given another term as Governor and moved over from the Punjab to the U.P. This was a novel experience for him, for while the Swarajist influence in the Punjab was insignificant, Congressmen constituted the main political force in the province to which he was transferred. The landlords of the U.P. had formed a non-communal Agriculturists Party on the advice of Fazli Husain. I visited Lucknow and called on Hailey at the Secretariat, which he attended. I wanted an accurate picture of provincial politics. Remarking that he was running a much bigger province with a smaller Secretariat, Hailey suggested that I lunch with him at Government House, where we could have a quiet talk.

In the privacy of the library, where no A.D.C. was present, he satisfied my curiosity. This province, he said, was very different from the Punjab, where the landed classes were aware of their

interests and had leaders of intelligence. His main task in Lahore
had thus been to hold the communal balance and provide the
Ministers with guidance. In the U.P., the talukdars and zamindars
had formed a party, it was true, but they had done so at Government prodding, not out of their own conviction. The talukdars, he
said, were an effete lot with neither strength of character nor even
the intelligence to realise their own interests.

The only well-organised political party in the U.P. was the Congress, he frankly admitted, imbued as it was with faith in its ideals
and prepared to make sacrifices for the cause. Only those with
strength of character could hold the reins of government, and it was
the Congress that could boast of men of such character. He had
little doubt in his mind that, when the British quit, they would have
to pass the responsibility of government on to the Congress.

In the final analysis, the British could not deny to India institutions
they had developed in their own land. The bureaucracy, Sir
Malcolm realised, was fighting a rearguard action. It was not
possible, however, to stop the onward march of the forces championing self-government; at best, they could only be held up for a decade
or two.

(2) IRWIN'S DEPARTURE

The annual session of the Congress was scheduled to be held in
Karachi at the end of March. Gandhi met Irwin on 19th March
and pleaded for the reprieve of Bhagat Singh and his two colleagues
from the death sentences to which they had been condemned. He
reinforced this oral request with a powerful appeal to the charity of
a "great Christian" in *Young India*. Irwin took the public into
confidence on his reasons for rejecting Gandhi's appeal. Irwin's
farewell speech on 26th March, 1931, at a local club in New Delhi
was very forthright and a sort of political stocktaking.

In the course of the speech Irwin remarked: "As I listened the
other day to Mr. Gandhi putting the case for commutation formally
before me, I reflected first on what significance it surely was that
the apostle of non-violence should so earnestly be pleading the cause
of devotees of a creed fundamentally opposed to his own, but I
should regard it as wholly wrong to allow my judgment on these
matters to be influenced or deflected by purely political considerations. I could imagine no case in which under the law the penalty
had been more directly deserved."

I told Roy: "He too has given a parting kick to the old man."

When we went over to speak to the Viceroy later, he explained he had been caught between two stools. He said: "There are extremists who would condone violence. I have saved Gandhi from falling from his own moral standard." Then there was the book entitled *Lost Dominion* published at the time by an anonymous author, reflecting the views of those who believed in a paternal administration, with India a reserved market for British goods. The champions of these views in England had spoiled the favourable atmosphere he had created in India by his announcement on dominion status. "They call me a defeatist. They do not realise that we are up against rising nationalism and not just the growls of the intelligentsia."

I asked Irwin to name the outstanding events during his tenure of office besides the pact with Gandhi. He replied he was deeply moved when he opened Council (now Parliament) House and thereby inaugurated the new centre of government in Delhi. (This was on 18th January, 1927. and I remember being greatly struck by his description of the circular edifice as "the emblem of permanence, of eternity.") What troubled Irwin most was the growing estrangement of the Hindus and the Muslims. He added: "I wonder whether I have not missed an opportunity to bring Gandhi and Fazli together."

Gandhi's failure to save the life of Bhagat Singh caused much indignation in Congress circles. Gandhi tried to pacify Irwin's critics by stating that commutation of the sentences was no part of the Gandhi–Irwin Pact. "We may not accuse them of breach of settlement." On 23rd March, the three young men were hanged in jail and their bodies cremated on the banks of the Sutlej. Two days later, Sir Abdur Rahim, Leader of the Opposition, and Sir Cowasji Jehangir, Deputy Leader of the Independents, walked out of the Central Assembly as a protest against the executions, showing that the non-Congress parties were equally indignant. Jawaharlal Nehru declared that "the corpse of Bhagat Singh shall stand between us and England."

Subhas Bose's protest took a more extreme form. His group, named the Nawajawan Sabha (Youth Association) waved black flags with the legend "Gandhi go back" as the Mahatma arrived at Karachi railway station for the Congress session. Later, waiting in deputation on Gandhi, they demanded a workers and peasants Free Republic of India.

The Congress session, presided over by Sardar Patel, marked another departure from earlier practice. It was held in March instead of December, the month formerly chosen to suit lawyer-members, as the courts recessed during this time. Secondly, the Karachi audience being large, the session was held in an open stadium, a practice which has been followed since then.

Subhas Bose attempted to raise some controversial issues, but the session endorsed the Gandhi–Irwin pact without much ado and authorised the Working Committee to appoint delegates to attend the Round Table Conference under Gandhi's leadership. It conceded to the people of Burma the right to separate from India or to remain an autonomous partner, with the right to secede whenever they wanted.

Jawaharlal countered Bose's bid to outshine him by getting the session to adopt a resolution on fundamental rights which admitted that political freedom would include economic freedom. It also provided for halving the military budget and fixing the Viceroy's salary at Rs. 500 a month.

It was apparent that the road to London for the second Round Table Conference was not without roadblocks. In an attempt to reach a Hindu–Muslim settlement, Gandhi went to Delhi, where the All–India Muslim Conference was in session. Since the main plank of its political platform was opposition to the Congress, he found little scope for a settlement. I asked Gandhi what dress he would wear in London, adding that I myself was about to leave for England: "It will not be European, nor even that of the polished Nehrus," he replied.

Gandhi now made a dash to Bombay to bid farewell to Lord and Lady Irwin on 18th April. This was his way of underscoring his faith in the Viceroy's sincerity in trying to further a peaceful and honourable settlement between Indian nationalism and Britain. It was not, however, apparent at the time that with Irwin's departure had ended the chapter of bipolar politics, the contenders being the Raj and the Congress.

But administratively and economically India had made great strides in the decade which closed with Irwin. Curzon found the country with narrow, impassable pathways, to put it metaphorically. He gave it a metre-gauge track on which traffic could move fairly quickly and efficiently. From the twenties, with the introduction of political reforms, began the process of broadening the old track to enable expresses to roar along. Progress was accelerated many times over. Among its manifestations were the railways, air services, commercial and industrial establishments, an expanding banking system, an irrigation complex, broadcasting and beam wireless and an ever-proliferating administrative machine. On this base, free India could project herself into the jet age.

Chapter 17

VOYAGE TO LONDON

It was in the summer of 1931 that I first left the shores of India. My destination was London, the focal point of the Empire and the world's major political centre. The time was propitious for my journey, for the conclusion of the Gandhi–Irwin Pact and Gandhi's acceptance of the invitation to attend the second Round Table Conference seemed to have transformed Indo–British relations. There were many aspects of European life, besides, that I wanted to observe at first hand, chief among them the ferment of new forces coming to the surface all over the Continent and the working of parliamentary institutions.

Embarking on a Lloyd Triestino boat at Bombay, I got off at Suez to travel to Cairo by road, and thence back to catch the steamer at Port Said. This diversion enabled me to meet some Egyptian leaders and view political developments in a country whose struggle for freedom had for years inspired our own nationalist movement. Zaghloul Pasha was a household name among the politically minded in India, and the Wafd was the equivalent of the Indian National Congress.

During my talks with Nahas Pasha and his colleagues, my eyes were opened for the first time to the key to the politics of the entire Middle East. The countries of this region, they pointed out, were like pegs to hold down the imperial tent that was India. Their liberation therefore depended primarily on India's success in winning her freedom. If the British quit India, they declared, they would lose all interest in holding down the Arab world. Suez, Aden and the Persian Gulf would then cease to be strategically important. This brief Egyptian interlude imparted a new dimension to the problem of Indian freedom.

In Italy, my next stopping place, more than the much-vaunted sights of Naples, the magnificence of the Vatican, the ancient monuments of Rome and the dainty, fairyland loveliness of the Venetian canals and waterfront held my mind in thrall. All around me I beheld manifestations of the Fascist upsurge under Mussolini.

Vienna, where we stopped next, was a very different world—of gaiety, enchantment and romance. Its citizens were happy-go-lucky, pleasant-mannered, without a trace of colour consciousness and passionately fond of music and dancing. Vienna was at the same time the Mecca of the medical world. My companion, who had an attack of lumbago while in Rome, went into a sanatorium here. One day, at his bedside, I casually referred to the occasional bouts of writer's cramp from which I suffered. The attending physician promptly whisked me off to a room, had me wrapped up in a wet sheet and covered with blankets. I emerged from this treatment cured for good.

The most rewarding of the encounters with which I filled my hours in Vienna while my companion convalesced were those with Vithalbhai Patel, who too was lying ill in a sanatorium in the city. He was in a reminiscent mood and recalled with a touch of asperity how, though he had brought Gandhi and Irwin together, he had not been asked to accompany Gandhi to the Round Table Conference. He was best fitted, he said, to deal with the wily diplomatic manoeuvrings of the British. Further, he had been cheated of the coveted distinction of presiding over the Karachi session of the Congress. Gandhi had secured the election of his younger brother Vallabhbhai instead.

At a touching farewell in Vienna—I little realised then that this was to be our last meeting—Vithalbhai urged me to write my reminiscences of the Central Legislative Assembly and, remarking that freedom was round the corner, urged me to enter parliamentary life in free India.

A municipal councillor in Simla, I visited Vienna's Socialist Corporation, the first of the kind anywhere in Europe. It had brought tram fares within reach of the poorest citizen, built multi-storied flats for the workers and opened crèches for their children. This was a preview of the Socialist heaven that its crusaders in the Austrian capital promised their followers.

Next on my itinerary was Berlin, then struggling out of the twilight of the years after World War I towards the sinister shadows of the Nazi upheaval. It was one of the cleanest of all European cities, and the most orderly too. Traffic was regulated by light signals and signs of the traditional German regimentation were abundant. Berlin lacked, however, Vienna's human touch.

The charm and elegance of Paris was marred, unlike Berlin, by patches of unmitigated ugliness. What I witnessed at the *Folies Bergeres* was unforgettable. During the intermission, whom should I run into but a former member of the Viceroy's Executive Council, Narasimha Sarma, an austere Brahmin at home. He remarked with a twinkle in his eye: "Well, my friend, you have to come to Paris to learn that nudity is an art." I agreed wholeheartedly. When I dropped into the Lido, in the course of an organised tour of Parisian night life, I found the then Prime Minister of Hyderabad State engaged in a lively tête-à-tête with a young woman in a ravishing costume. This dignitary gave me a warm smile and wished me luck.

One thing struck me during these journeyings. Neither the European Press nor its politicians took much notice of India. They had all heard, of course, of Gandhi the rebel, but of little else. Europe seemed to be free from colour consciousness, Paris and Vienna strikingly so. An individual's worth was judged not by his colour but by the money he spent, the pleasures he bought.

On the last lap of a long adventure, there was the boisterous Channel crossing, and the short train journey to London. With every moment the feeling grew upon me that I was entering a familiar milieu. All round me people spoke English, and the Englishman was no stranger. I knew how he behaved and comported himself. Only, in the past all whites had been Europeans with little to set Englishmen apart from the French, the Irish, the Germans or the Italians.

Chapter 18

(1) THE INDIAN PROBLEM: BRITISH VIEW

London was not the world's "swingingest" city it is reputed to be today. Yet, at the height of summer, the sprawling metropolis had much to fascinate a visitor from abroad. A large part of my time was absorbed, however, in exploring Whitehall's thinking on the Indian question. I was armed with introductions from Sapru to the Marquess of Zetland and Evelyn Wrench, Director of the Overseas League, which gave me access to those at the very hub of things.

I met the Labour Prime Minister, Ramsay MacDonald, at the House of Commons. He told me he would be guided by the conclusions reached at the forthcoming conference, and that, though he was all for dominion status for India, progress towards this goal would, however, depend hereafter more on the Indians than on the British. This was a far cry from the days when he had been chosen

President of the Indian National Congress but had been prevented by his wife's illness from accepting the honour.

In Attlee, with whom I was renewing contacts forged during his association with the Simon Inquiry, I discovered a refreshing change. He had had time to study the Nehru report and to digest the conclusions of the Simon Commission and the proceedings of the first Round Table parleys. Over a cup of tea on the House of Commons terrace, he revealed a broader vision and spoke with self-confidence. The Tories, he feared, would exploit the second round of talks to set up obstacles to India's advance towards self-rule. They would play up the grievances of the Muslims and the depressed classes in their bid to thwart the Congress. The Muslims, he disclosed, were the Tories' Crescent Card much as Ulster had served as their Orange Card in Ireland. They were planning to drag the Princes as well into the cockpit to delay, if not to sabotage, the transfer of responsibility at the Centre. How he wished the Congress had struck a deal with Labour while it was in power. The party that mattered in India, he readily admitted, was the Congress.

Wedgwood Benn, Secretary of State for India, was frankly pessimistic about the outcome of Gandhi's participation in the conference. A talk with Zetland, though more congenial, did not hold out the prospect of a political deal with Gandhi.

Turning to those who had held viceregal office in India, I first met Reading in his London apartment. Wistfully, he recalled how Gandhi's obduracy over the Prince of Wales's visit had shut the door to his own offer of provincial autonomy. In collaboration with Sapru, he said he had formulated a scheme of federation embracing the Princes as the only means of hastening the advent of dominion status. If Gandhi were to abide by Sapru's counsel, the forthcoming talks would open a new chapter in Indo–British relations.

Irwin, whom I also met in his apartment in London, had not deviated from his stand on India. Gandhi, he declared, was seeking evidence of a change of heart among the British. But would he find it in such a big conclave as the Round Table Conference? He added: "I shall, however, continue to hope for the best, for there is nothing I desire more than peace and contentment in India." He did not disguise his fear that opposition to the grant of dominion status represented the hard core of Tory thinking. But he placed his hope in Baldwin to overcome it.

(2) ADVICE FROM BALDWIN

My desire to meet Baldwin had been whetted by the discovery that the Tory leader had supported Irwin's statement on dominion status in defiance of the diehards in his own party. Besides, I had been assured by Attlee that on the Indian issue Baldwin was "at heart with Labour."

It was not without a lively sense of anticipation that I called on Britain's former Prime Minister on receiving the following letter from his Secretary from 24 Old Queen Street, Westminster, dated 27th July, 1931: "I am desired by Mr. Stanley Baldwin to acknowledge receipt of your letter of the 25th July enclosing a letter of introduction from Lord Zetland. Mr. Baldwin would be very glad to see you in his room at the House of Commons at 4.00 p.m. on Wednesday next. If you will come to the Ladies' Gallery Entrance in Speakers' Court, you will be brought up to his room."

I was pleasantly surprised to find Lord Linlithgow waiting in the corridor. He greeted me warmly and said he would see Baldwin after I had had my interview. I had met him in India when he presided over the Royal Commission on Agriculture.

Baldwin sat impassive, gazing at me as I proceeded to give him my analysis of political affairs in India and suggestions on how Whitehall could deal with them. Not the flicker of an eyelid nor a twitch of his facial muscles revealed his feelings. My talk with MacDonald, I told Baldwin, had given me the feeling that he had not the strength to put through a deal with Gandhi during the latter's visit to London. Why, indeed, did the British, as newspaper writings here seemed to indicate, look upon Gandhi as a joke? Warming up to my thesis, I argued that the Congress was the only body with which Whitehall could enter into a profitable dialogue. In that way alone could Britain strengthen the vast reservoir of goodwill in India, against which the tide of disaffection was now perilously lapping. "If Britain fails, it will be the failure of the West to befriend the East," I said.

At long last, Baldwin broke into what had virtually become a fifteen-minute monologue. MacDonald's misgivings about the outcome of the London parleys, he remarked, were not unjustified. He had to reckon with the hard-core Tories. Baldwin traced the hostile climate to the hurt inflicted on Lancashire's textile industry by the Congress through its boycott of British goods. The financial crisis precipitated in Britain by World War I had been aggravated by this boycott. The burden of Empire, he admitted candidly, was becoming more and more oppressive. It was more than likely that before long Britain would be compelled by sheer necessity to cut her losses.

India, Baldwin declared reflectively, might secure self-government much earlier than anybody now thought possible. (In August 1947, I was to wonder whether Baldwin had then been peering into a prophet's glass.) He himself was convinced of the need for a meaningful dialogue with the Congress. He would urge the Indian leaders to employ to the maximum advantage whatever instruments were available to them now and whatever others were placed at their disposal under the coming reforms. Only thus could they strengthen the hands of those Britons whose broad sympathies were with them.

Did the key to Indian freedom then lie in India itself? No, in Whitehall, Baldwin answered. But settle with the Muslims for a start, he said, for Muslim intransigence, real or imaginary, was the weapon the British opponents of Indian self-rule would use to delay advance.

Baldwin gave me a piece of salutary advice to round off what had been a rewarding forty-minute talk. It would be a great help, he said, if I propagated my views in the British publications such as the *Spectator*. Accordingly, I wrote an article for the *Spectator*, reputed to be close to the Establishment, on "Goodwill in India" and one for the Liberal *News Chronicle* entitled "Gandhi is not a joke." The *Spectator* published my piece in its issue of 15th August, 1931, with this introduction: "The writer is a well-known Indian publicist, holding a detached, non-political position as Editor of the Associated Press of India at New Delhi."

(3) JINNAH IN LONDON

The opportunity for a chat with Jinnah in London was one I could not pass up. Among newspapermen in Delhi, I had been closest to him over a long period. I called at his chambers, and he took me to lunch at Simpson's, close to the Savoy.

Over an excellent meal, the talk revolved mostly round politics. Jinnah confessed he was not enamoured of his legal practice in London; what he coveted professionally was a seat on the Judicial Committee of the Privy Council. Or he might try to enter Parliament. Did that mean he intended to retire from Indian politics for good? I asked. "No, Durga," he replied, "I came away to London because I did not wish to meet that wretched Viceroy. (Willingdon, with whom he had quarrelled when the former was Governor of Bombay.) I was hurt, besides, when my very reasonable proposals at the Calcutta All–Parties Convention were turned down by Motilal Nehru and his lot. I seem to have reached a dead end. The Congress will not come to terms with me because my following is very small. The Muslims do not accept my views, for·they take their orders from the Deputy Commissioner (district authority)."

What did he think of the prospects of the forthcoming conferences? His answer came pat: "What can you expect from a jamboree of this kind? The British will only make an exhibition of our differences." Jinnah was forthright in expressing his opinion on Gandhi's decision to participate in the London parleys. "They (the British) will make a fool of him, and he will make a fool of them," he remarked caustically. "Where is the Congress claim that it represents the Muslims as well? Gandhi has failed to get Ansari nominated. Frankly, Durga, I expect nothing to come out of this conference."

But he could get together with Gandhi, Sapru and others, I suggested, and work for a communal settlement in the favourable climate engendered by the patriotic impulse of every Indian delegate. "Suppose I do succeed," was Jinnah's comment, "they have this fellow, the Aga Khan, and Fazli's dogs." Before I took leave of him, I told him in all sincerity that I missed him in Delhi. "I may come back for good," he replied, and, with a shrug of his shoulders, added: "You never can tell."

(4) MEETING THE IRISH GREAT

I did not expect George Bernard Shaw to find time for me as he was known to shun our tribe. It was therefore with a feeling of excitement that I called at his flat in Whitehall Court as fixed by him in response to a letter from Evelyn Wrench. As I thanked him for giving me an interview, he remarked: "I am a selfish fellow. I thought you might help me understand a bit about India." Seeing me puzzled, he explained to my pleasant surprise that he had read my article in Headway, entitled "How West Meets East—The Spirit of India and the League" and felt that I wrote the language he understood. (Headway was the organ of the British branch of the League of Nations' Union.) When I remarked that he might do this at a meeting with Mahatma Gandhi when the latter arrived a month later for the Second Round Table Conference, he replied with a mischievous smile: "I am a minor Mahatma myself. I have enough experience of India's learned men to know that what they say goes over my head."

Now began a dialogue which lasted over two hours, provoked by his question: The civilisation of Babylon, Egypt, Greece and Rome had passed into oblivion after a few hundred years. What had given the social order in India its permanence and its strength to defy the ravages of time? What was the secret of Indian survival?

Ours was a system of social security, I explained. In modern idiom it guaranteed employment, the incentive to work and the exchange of services, adequate provision for the aged, the widow and the orphan and a sort of insurance against natural disasters. The State as such did not come into the picture. In fact, the system was rooted in the assumption that the State did not exist, or was an abstraction, or at best to be identified, if need be, with the person of the ruler.

After a detailed exposition in which he pulled me up whenever I digressed, I concluded with the observation that the turn of the century had found the country's population balanced by its economic growth. But the expansion of population since then had far outstripped the economic gains. This imbalance had not been appreciated by the rulers, for the joint family cushion had absorbed its shocks. But the cushion was wearing thin, and, should economic development be delayed, India would break up and dissolve under the weight of its mounting population and the lag in economic growth, if British rule continued for another fifteen years or so.

There was a smile on Shaw's face as he remarked that imperialism was on the way out. Shaw insisted on coming down in the lift to see me into the car the Indian High Commissioner had lent me for the occasion.

My visit to Ireland coincided with the Horse Show in Dublin, which attracted large crowds from England and the Continent as well. I met there Eamon de Valera, A. E. (George Russell), William Butler Yeats and several newspaper editors. De Valera was positive that the roadblock to Indian progress was the India Office and that India must attack where it hurt most, namely through a boycott of British goods.

The bearded A.E. was known in his own country as a *rishi* (inspired sage). He talked of India's spiritual wealth and of how he had been fascinated by the depth of the Indian comprehension of the universe. India was the world's teacher, and he had no doubt that the revolt of the Indian soul Gandhi had sparked off would lead to early freedom.

Yeats, who entertained me to tea at his home, surprisingly asked about the City of London's economic stranglehold on India. I referred to the precipitous fall in the price of silver, which had ruined the Indian peasant, who invested his meagre savings in ornaments of this metal. The poet expressed confidence that India would win freedom under Gandhi's unique leadership and said he looked forward to her contribution to world thought.

I recounted how I had felt at home in southern Italy and in southern Ireland, where people treated strangers warmly as did the Indians. I told him of a visit to a village fifty miles out of Dublin and of how the first shopkeeper I approached, unshaven and unkempt like his Indian counterpart, had left his shop and taken me round to the parish church and the local creamery. He had insisted on giving me lunch at the eating house and seeing me off at the railway station. I discovered to my surprise that he had heard of India. Yeats ascribed this to the publicity given in the Sinn Fein newspapers to the Indian struggle for freedom.

Chapter 19

(1) BRITISH PRESS AND INDIA OFFICE

My visit to Reuter's London office proved a rewarding experience. Sir Roderick Jones, the Managing Director, impressed by the fact that my piece had been published by the *Spectator*, discussed the Indian situation with me for over an hour.

The new Editor-in-Chief, Rickatson-Hatt, took me to lunch at the Press Club. I was shown round the club and left it convinced that India must have one like it to give journalists an identity of their own. True, it had a boiled-shirt atmosphere, but what impressed me was that the Prime Minister was the chief guest at the club's annual function (And twenty-six years later, when we were able to found the Press Club of India, I was its president during its first three teething years.)

There was apparently a tacit agreement under which Fleet Street looked at India through the eyes of the India Office. In fact, I learned while lunching at the Reform Club with Wilson-Harris, Editor of the *Spectator*, that it was the normal practice of the leader writers of *The Times* to meet men from the Foreign Office or the India Office over lunch at the club and exchange notes before writing editorials.

I paid several visits to the House of Commons. The informality of the atmosphere amidst all the solemn formality of behaviour struck me. I was overawed by the imposing building, the lobbies and the labyrinth of corridors and rooms. The Press Gallery people, with a sector of their own run by a committee gave me the inspiration for a similar set-up in Delhi. Although we succeeded in getting a Press Gallery Committee started when Sir Shanmukham Chetty was Speaker in 1933, the Press failed to get a sector of its own and to create an esprit de corps among gallerymen.

Perhaps the most important part of my discovery of London was the understanding I gained of the way the India Office functioned. I owe much of this to what Sir Bhupendra Mitra, the High Commissioner, told me over lunch at the National Liberal Club. If anybody understood the bureaucratic machine thoroughly, he did. Another person with authority who threw light on the subject was Sir Findlater Stewart, head of the India Office Secretariat.

I learned that the India Office had a complete replica of the entire administration in India, down to the district level. Nothing, however trivial, happened in India which was not recorded and assessed. Policy was formulated at the India Office and directions were sent from there in relation to every sphere—financial, administrative, economic and commercial. Even the Viceroy got an occasional glimpse of high policy in his private correspondence with the Secretary of State.

The policy cell at the India Office had its links with the Foreign Office, the Treasury, the Board of Trade and the City. Thus India was governed from the India Office, and the Viceroy and the Civil Service were in truth the agents of the home Government. The theory of the "man on the spot" applied merely to administrative acts in pursuance of general policy directives.

Tilak was right, therefore, in maintaining that the key to freedom lay in London and that political pressure in Parliament would help a lot. But Gandhi had diagnosed the situation even more astutely. The British, a nation of shopkeepers, would react to a blow struck where it hurt most. It would take ages to work on the British conscience alone.

(2) THE PASSING OF ROY

I left the shores of England about the time the delegates to the second Round Table Conference were landing at Marseilles *en route* to London. At Port Said, I picked up an Egyptian paper published in English and read the shocking news of the death of K. C. Roy in Simla from a stroke while addressing the Central Assembly, to which he had been nominated by the Viceroy as a distinguished journalist.

Roy, in my view, was not only one of the pioneers of the syndication of news and political commentaries but also helped to mould political events both as a publicist and as the friend and adviser of leading Indian politicians and Britons.

While he maintained that news must be objective, he was equally convinced that it must serve political, economic and social ends. He believed that a journalist's IQ must be very high to pick brains, and that news often broke unexpectedly and fell into the lap of those always on the *qui vive*.

Roy was very human. When I joined him, he was a bachelor with two ambitions—to become a legislator, and to marry and have children. Both were fulfilled. He told me his first romance with Amrit Kaur (then known as Bibi) did not fructify because her mother insisted (as she had done with her own husband) on Roy's embracing Christianity before he could marry. Roy married on his own terms when he visited London in 1928 as a member of the Indian delegation to discuss with the Colonial Office the treatment of Indians in Kenya and East Africa. His wife was a widow. Roy brought up his stepson Sunil with great affection. Sunil later entered the Indian Foreign Service and won considerable popularity in the sixties as India's Consul-General in New York. Roy's own children, a daughter and son, were brought up by their mother in London and are now happily settled.

The chief's death marked the end of an era and the change in the agency's perspective coincided with the advent of a political climate in which to the Briton "those who are not with us are against us."

Chapter 20

WILLINGDON–CIVIL DISOBEDIENCE RESUMED

I came back home to discover that the political climate had deteriorated considerably. Facing heavier responsibilities after Roy's death, I got in touch with the Indian members of the Viceroy's Executive Council, particularly Sir Fazli Husain and Sir Brojendra Mitter. I was picking up the threads of political developments, and this also entailed meetings with the new Viceroy, Lord Willingdon, who had assumed office in April 1931, and his Private Secretary.

The two Councillors apprised me of Willingdon's open hostility to Gandhi. He had lost little time in proclaiming Gandhi a "humbug" to whom he was determined to give no quarter. Mitter told me that while I was in London Fazli had queered the pitch for Gandhi. The Nawab of Bhopal, he said, had brought together representatives of the Muslim Conference and the nationalist Muslims and they had reached an agreement. But Fazli got it disowned by the Muslim Conference executive. He next persuaded Willingdon to disown Irwin's commitment that Gandhi could take Ansari and Ali Imam, or at least Ansari, with him as Congress delegates to London. Thus Gandhi's plan to show that the nationalist Muslims did not agree with the Aga Khan–Fazli group had been frustrated. "I pity Gandhi," Mitter added. "This Fazli is a devil and the Viceroy dances to his tune. Willingdon too acted cleverly. At their meetings in May and July, he was non-committal and almost charged Gandhi with breach of faith by pointing out that the main purpose of the Gandhi–Irwin Pact was to enable Gandhi to participate in the Round Table Conference. When they met again in August, Willingdon took advantage of the Congress Working Committee's keenness to see Gandhi proceed to London and firmly turned down the proposal that Ansari join him as a delegate. Thus Fazli won hands down."

Fazli's version was equally intriguing. He said the effort to find a communal settlement failed because Gandhi wanted the Muslims to present a common demand. This, in his opinion, was like the

British wanting the Hindus and the Muslims to prepare an agreed constitution or at least a communal settlement. One dissenting Jinnah was bad enough, and he did not want the Muslims to speak in different voices at the London conference.

I learnt that the Viceroy, despite his antipathy to the Mahatma, was prevailed upon by Whitehall to meet him. Lady Willingdon herself came out to escort him to her husband's presence. She urged him to bring his wife with him when he next visited the Lodge. Gandhi complied, and Kasturba accompanied her husband soon after, carrying for her a gift of *khadi* dyed in mauve, the Vicereine's favourite colour. Lady Willingdon, touched by the gesture, used the fabric as a curtain for her living-room.

Authenticating this story later, Gandhi revealed too that Lady Willingdon's courtesy was not reflected in the Viceroy's own unbending stance. I met Ansari and he confirmed that the talks had yielded nothing of substance. But Gandhi would nevertheless not go back on his decision to participate in the London parleys. He was resolved not to violate the spirit of his pact with Irwin.

Disillusionment came to Gandhi early, when the provisional agreement reached with some Muslim delegates in the first week of October was disowned by the others under the influence, according to Jinnah, of the Aga Khan and of remote control by Sir Fazli. The effort of a settlement had been trumped with the Crescent Card. Gandhi realised too that besides playing the Crescent Card the British were out to split the Hindus into caste Hindus and the Depressed Classes.

The Congress lobby in New Delhi was shocked when Ramsay MacDonald announced on 13th November that the previous evening an agreed formula embodying the demands of the minorities had been formally presented to him by the Aga Khan and that he would give a Communal Award on his own should the Indian delegates fail to agree by a given date. Gandhi's response was challenging. On 30th November, he claimed that "the Congress alone represents the whole of India, all interests," thereby questioning the minority leaders' claim that their charter of demands drawn up in London was a reflection of the will of their people. MacDonald's final address to the conference was ominously worded, for, besides promising an award on communal representation, he said his Government would also make provision to protect the minorities from an "unrestricted and tyrannical use of the democratic principle expressing itself solely through majority power."

Of Gandhi's sojourn in England, one of his British followers, Miss Christine Slade, who adopted the name Mira Behn, revealed certain interesting sidelights. She told me how Gandhi had been advised by Sir Samuel Hoare to convert the City if he wanted radical reforms and how his attempt to do so had proved unavailing. Against that failure was set the impact he made on the common people of Lancashire. They gave him a welcome, she said, exceeding in fervour what they accorded even to royalty. Mothers brought their children for him to touch and bless. It was a demonstration of affection, she added, that moved Gandhi profoundly. He had inspired the severest boycott of Lancashire textiles, yet to the average Lancastrian he was not to be hated on that account but to be honoured as a saint.

Meanwhile, the Congress Working Committee, reacting to the virtual collapse of the London parleys, had urged Gandhi to withdraw and return to India. Jawaharlal Nehru went a step further and precipitated a crisis on 18th November by announcing a fresh passive resistance campaign without awaiting Gandhi's homecoming.

Willingdon was only too ready to accept the Congress challenge. Thus, within three weeks of Gandhi's landing in Bombay on 28th December, 1931, the Congress was banned and its leaders were arrested in thousands. Besides Gandhi and Patel, some 35,000 civil disobedience volunteers were imprisoned. These included "dictators" and members of fifty-two "war councils." The largest number of arrests was made in connection with the protest against the export of gold to pay for imports, largely of British goods. This was the time Britain was facing a financial crisis and a drain of gold. The funds of the Congress were sequestrated, its offices sealed and its publicity media choked.

The campaign, resumed after a lull created by the expectation of a political deal in London, was volcanic. Towns became centres of a throbbing new life and women came out of the seclusion of their homes to offer *satyagraha*. It was a massive upsurge. Watching scenes of such confrontation in the company of James Mills, I quickly realised that the police did not know how to handle women volunteers and, faced with the new technique of resistance, clubbed them indiscriminately. Mills sent out harrowing reports of wanton police assaults to the U.S. The effect of these stories was to jolt the British out of the belief that provincial autonomy for India would appease American opinion.

Women "dictators" were the order of the day. The two most prominent were Hansa Mehta of Bombay (daughter of the Dewan of Baroda and wife of Jivraj Mehta, who rose to be Chief Minister of Gujarat and India's High Commissioner in London in the sixties) and Mrs. Krishandas Kohli, wife of the Manager of the *Hindustan Times*.

To attract the widest publicity in the world, and especially in the U.S., Congressmen planned to hold their annual session in Delhi in defiance of the ban on their party. Underground workers organised a surprise march on the square around the clock tower in Delhi's main shopping centre, Chandni Chowk, on the opening day of the session in April 1932. I had been informed of this plan by an emissary to make sure the demonstration got a good Press. The suddenness of the gathering took the police unawares, and before it could be dispersed a resolution had been passed reiterating the demand for complete independence. About a thousand participants, including the Congress President, the veteran Malaviya, were arrested.

The Third Round Table Conference in November 1932 was somewhat of a farce as neither the Congress nor the British Labour Party nor the Princes joined it. As expected, those who attended the Conference failed to reach any conclusion and by arrangement Ramsay MacDonald gave his Communal Award to put an end to the Hindu–Muslim controversy. The award not only upheld separate electorates and other safeguards for the Muslims but categorised the Depressed Classes as a separate political entity and allotted them a specified percentage of seats in the legislatures.

Nationalist India reacted sharply and Gandhi, then in Yeravada jail, began a fast up to death on 20th September, 1932. Gandhi had earlier told me that he would stake his life to prevent the bifurcation of the Hindu community. He said that if this move succeeded it would be the end of the community and of nationalism as well.

The fast caused worldwide sensation and Mitter confided to me that even Willingdon felt panicky as Gandhi had numerous admirers in the West, especially in the U.S. Hindu leaders from all parts of the country rushed to Poona to persuade Gandhi to abandon the fast, and in a bid to save his life orthodox Hindus threw open many temples to the untouchables on 26th September. Gandhi gave up the fast the following day after he and Ambedkar entered into the Poona Pact. Under it, the Depressed Classes remained a part of the general electorate but were given a larger share of seats and the right to choose through electoral colleges their candidates for the seats reserved for them in the total quota for Hindus. The Government on their part accepted the pact and its implication, that Gandhi should be free to propagate its acceptance by the Hindu community and the removal of the social disabilities of the Harijans.

The White Paper on reforms issued in March the same year

proved a damp squib. Even the Indian Liberal Federation referred to it as a document aimed more at emphasising safeguards for imperial interests than concessions to the Indian demands. The All–India National Trade Union Federation condemned the scheme as "a double roller, capitalism and communalism, to crush socialism and nationalism."

Chapter 21

(1) COUNCIL ENTRY–REFORMS ACT

The advent of 1934 saw a marked change in the attitude of top Congressmen to constitutional questions. A conference of leaders, among whom were Ansari, Bidhan Chander Roy, later Chief Minister of Bengal, and Bhulabhai Desai, former Advocate-General of Bombay, held in Delhi on 2nd April, 1934, decided to revive the Swaraj Party and to contest the general election the coming winter.

They met Gandhi on 4th April, and he agreed to call off the civil disobedience movement but reserved the right to civil resistance for himself. This, he told them, would retain for them a sanction when, after experimenting with the parliamentary programme, they were again with their backs to the wall. Gandhi wrote to bless this move: "I have made an independent study of the Council entry question. It appears to me there has always been a party within the Congress wedded to the idea of Council entry. The reins of the Congress should be in the hands of that group, and that group alone needs the name of Congress. They will also boycott the legislatures whenever they deem it necessary."

Since this looked like a *volte face* by Gandhi, I took an early opportunity to meet him. The talk made me conclude that Gandhi had realised that, whereas formerly the Swarajists counted on his movement as a sanction for their fight within the legislatures, hereafter the constructive programme for which he stood could receive an impetus through the power that the coming Reforms Act would place in the hands of popularly chosen Ministers in the provinces.

This change in tactics, endorsing Council entry, induced the Government to lift the ban on the Congress. A meeting of the

A.I.C.C. was held at Patna on 16th May to get the new programme ratified. Gandhi attended it. This body set up a Parliamentary Board of twenty-five with Ansari as Chairman to fight the coming elections. Later, the Working Committee declared its neutrality on the Communal Award, and that led to the resignation of Malaviya and his lieutenants who wanted the Congress to disown the Award. But this was not possible because Azad and other nationalist Muslims favoured the Award.

On 17th September, 1934, Gandhi announced his retirement from the Congress. He was disappointed at the failure of even his trusted lieutenants to offer individual civil disobedience according to the code laid down. Publicly, in his spirit of self-effacement, he merely said: "I am a hindrance to the growth of the Congress." The separation was not without a pang, as he confided to Vallabhbhai, the outgoing President, in a letter. He felt that in quitting the party he was being less than true to Rajendra Prasad, the new President, "who, unlike Jawaharlal, shares most of my ideals and whose sacrifice for the nation, judged whether in quality or quantity, is not to be excelled."

The Congress held its next session in Bombay under the presidentship of Rajendra Prasad and Gandhi attended it briefly to bid farewell. I vividly recall the moving scene when Gandhi entered the packed pandal and the entire audience to a man stood up to give him a loud ovation, a powerful expression of full confidence in his leadership against the backdrop of his earlier announcement of severance of formal membership of the party. Before finally withdrawing Gandhi got the session to authorise J. C. Kumarappa, a member of his inner circle, to form an All–India Village Industries Association. Not many among the delegates or in the top echelon realised that thereby Gandhi had forged another weapon as much to win the heart of the rural masses and weaken their allegiance to their alien rulers as to keep the parliamentary wing of the party on an invisible leash.

The session endorsed the decision of the A.I.C.C. to participate in parliamentary activity and form a board to pick party candidates for the impending elections as well as for those under the Government of India Act, which was expected to come into force in 1936. It also resolved to lay down the policy and programme for Congress candidates. Willingdon was therefore right in a way when he told the Secretary of State for India that he expected the Congress to work the Constitution once it was passed.

Gandhi's exit from the Congress did not, however, dim his popularity with the masses and the rank and file Congressmen, as was shown by the countrywide tour he undertook before the Congress session. The tour caused a stir and created the goodwill on which Congress candidates cashed in in the elections of 1934–35. The party became the main opposition in the Central Assembly, with Bhulabhai Desai as leader and Govind Ballabh Pant as his deputy. The rejection of the Government's annual budget and its restoration through the use of the Viceroy's special powers became a regular ritual, and Desai's orations on constitutional matters and Pant's devastating criticism of financial policies received wide publicity and much acclaim. Jinnah, who had been persuaded by Liaquat Ali Khan and others to return to India, was elected to the Assembly and resumed his role of holding the balance between Government and Congress.

Nationalist propaganda had a new cause to feed on with the publication of the Reforms Bill towards the end of 1934 and its enactment by the British Parliament in the summer of 1935. The electoral provisions of the Act were to come into force on 3rd July, 1936, and the Act in its totality on 1st April, 1937. Although the part relating to federation was not to become operative until a given number of Princely States had consented to it, the provinces gained a separate legal entity and their own financial resources, and the Central Government's powers of direction and control were limited to specific spheres.

To garner views on what was happening in the Government's inner councils, I had a talk with Mitter, who analysed the situation thus: Irwin recognised the Congress as a vital force and signed an agreement with Gandhi. But the British Government, after 1931, began to whittle down their pledges. They thought that if they could promote communal clashes they could retain control of the country. They had begun for the first time to think of the Muslim question in terms of their own safety.

Fazli had now thrown up another idea, Mitter said almost in panic. Not content with securing separate electorate and a fixed number of seats in the legislatures, Fazli had talked in the Executive Council of creating Muslim majority zones as a counterpoise to Hindu-majority areas. He sensed that the British were now building up a new power triangle designed to retain their hold in India. They were planning to divide the country into Hindu, Muslim and princely domains in the belief that the pro-British Muslims and Princes would outvote the nationalist Hindus in a federal set-up. He added: "The whole attempt of the new plan is to break the back of the Congress for fifteen to twenty years. Hoare and Willingdon are foolish to think so, but I keep silent in the Council. I do not want to reveal my inner feelings to them. I do not agree with these Congress fellows, but I find that the conspiracy is to weaken the Hindu community and forge an Anglo–Muslim alliance to hold the Hindu down."

But this was not how farseeing Britons viewed the prospect. Hailey, Governor of the U.P., who was made a peer on retiring from the I.C.S., speaking at a farewell dinner given by members of the civil service at the Chhattar Manzil Club in Lucknow in 1934, when the Congress movement had been virtually paralysed by repression, said in effect: "It is impossible to suppress a nationalist movement. We have tried to suppress it with all the force at our disposal, but even so you cannot be sure that the Congress will not come up again. There is no safeguard for the Civil Service in a democracy, except that trained officials will be necessary to execute ministerial policy and not merely deal with law and order. The future Government of India would be largely socialistic."

A senior I.C.S. officer, C. S. Venkatachar, who retired later as High Commissioner for India in Canada, gave me this account of the dinner and commented: "Hailey had read the signs of the times."

(2) BRITISH AIMS AND ATTITUDES

I was then in touch with developments in London through my friend Chuni Lal Katial, a medical practitioner, who was in close contact with the Labour leaders and had personal relations with William Whiteley, who later became the Party's Chief Whip and occupied No. 12 Downing Street when Attlee became Prime Minister. It was at Katial's house that Charlie Chaplin met Gandhi in 1931.

The information I received from London confirmed what I had learnt from Attlee, that the transfer of responsibility at the Centre would be made conditional on the Princes joining the federation. This proposal had emanated from Sir John Simon, who had argued that the Princes would not agree to come into it and that what would come into effective operation would therefore be only provincial autonomy.

Only two speeches attracted special attention in India when the Reforms Bill was given the second and final readings in the House of Commons in 1935. Attlee was very outspoken, and so was Churchill. My attention was drawn to them by Sir Nripendra Sircar, Law Member and the new Leader of the Central Legislative Assembly.

Speaking on 4th June, 1935, Attlee said: "My first objection to this Bill is that I think it is deliberately framed so as to exclude as far as possible the Congress Party from effective powers in the new Constitution. But all the way through the Government have yielded time after time to the states and time after time to minority communities, but have always stood strongly up against any yielding to Congress or the nationalists. Hence we stress the need for making a far stronger provision than there is in the Bill for the transference of the reserved subjects, and particularly of defence. The result of anyone reading through this Bill is that he is struck not by what is conceded but by what is withheld. That will have an extraordinarily bad effect on our future relationships. . . . Finally, is the Bill going to be accepted and worked by the people of India? I do not think so."

Churchill's speech, during the second reading of the Bill, on 11th February, 1935, put his contrasting point of view in a nutshell: "We have as good a right to be in India as anyone there except, perhaps, the Depressed Classes, who are the original stock. Our Government is not an irresponsible government. It is a government responsible to the Crown and to Parliament. It is incomparably the best Government that India has ever seen or ever will see. It is not true to say that the Indians, whatever their creed, would not rather have their affairs dealt with in many cases by British courts and British officers than by their own people, especially their own people of the opposite religion." Seeing the widely divergent interpretations put on it by Labour and Tory spokesmen, politicians in India naturally found it difficult to assess the true worth of the Reforms Act.

After the Congress session, Gandhi once again traversed the country. Before he left Bombay, he told me that although he would work with special zeal on the plan for making a success of the newly formed Village Industries Association, he would continue his crusade urging everyone to learn simple Hindi. "We must give up English as an inter-provincial language and introduce into Hindi–Hindustani words from other provincial languages. A common Devanagari script would help as a common script had helped the development of the European languages."

Back in New Delhi I had a talk with the Home Member, Sir Henry Craik, and was convinced that he was more concerned with Gandhi's village programme than with the wordy bouts in the legislatures. This was confirmed by what I gathered of his talk with "friendly" Pressmen, to whom he had mentioned that he had sent a confidential letter to the provincial Governments that Gandhi's new move was meant to cause disaffection among the masses and subvert authority. To counter it, the Finance Minister, Sir James Grigg, included in his budget Rs. 20 million for a two-year drive for rural improvement. I met Gandhi when he later visited Delhi. He welcomed the Government move and hoped it would really help in ending idleness and improving living conditions in the rural areas.

Chapter 22

THE SEEDS OF PAKISTAN: FAZLI'S VIEWS

I owe to Sir Fazli much of the inside information on the slowly widening rift between the two major political forces in India. I had for long been puzzled by the apparent contradiction in his political attitudes. A communalist where Muslim interests were concerned, he displayed a strong sense of nationalism at Simla–Delhi so far as general problems went.

Meeting him soon after the Congress had adopted the parliamentary programme, I discovered behind his dissection of the Hindu–Muslim question a penetrating and analytical mind and remarkable clarity of vision. Most Muslims of today, he said to me, belonged to families that were Hindu not so long ago. Two generations back, the forebears of Sir Muhammad Iqbal, the poet, were Saprus—Kashmiri Brahmins—and Jinnah's ancestors not so far removed either were also Hindus. In his self-interest, the Muslim was inclined to flatter the British by protestations of loyalty.

Fazli threw considerable light on the plan for Pakistan, then insidiously germinating in certain minds, non-Muslim as well as Muslim. Those who fathered the idea in the early thirties had been financed by British intelligence in London, he said. But their brainchild had evoked no interest at all in India. Sir Mohammed Zafrullah Khan, who echoed Fazli's views before the Consultative Committee set up in London to consider the White Paper on proposed reforms, had, for instance, dismissed it as chimerical. The Aga Khan had, however, made a vague allusion to Pakistan in a letter to Fazli as a means of safeguarding Muslim interests under a democratic regime in India. The Aga Khan was providing funds at that time to the Unionist Party in the Punjab, the All-India Muslim Conference and the Praja Krishak Party of Khwaja

Nazimuddin and Fazlul Haque in Bengal. Fazli had published the letter only after expunging this reference.

In politics, Fazli told me he steered his course by two fundamental propositions. First, that democracy would be ill-balanced if progress in the rural areas did not keep pace with that in the towns. Secondly, that it would be inadvisable for the Muslims to organise an All–India political party of their own. What one could at best attempt was a balance between the Hindu-majority and Muslim-majority provinces, as the Nehru report suggested. Until adult franchise was introduced, he would continue to favour separate electorates. He stood for a United States of India in which both Hindu and Muslim states would contribute to a composite culture.

The best way to protect the interests of the minorities, according to Fazli, was for them to form provincial parties which could join hands with other parties to improve economic conditions. Communal differences, he added, were not based on religion but on sharing political power and the meagre economic resources of the country. He had a poor opinion of Jinnah, whom he considered an arm-chair politician. He thought Jinnah stood for joint electorates with reservation of seats merely to earn kudos from the Congress and Moderate leaders. Jinnah's main contribution to the national movement, he said, was his consistent advocacy of Indianisation of the commissioned ranks in the Army.

Fazli spoke of the agreement he had negotiated in Capetown on his visit to South Africa as a member of an Indian delegation. At his instance, Gandhi had permitted Mrs. Sarojini Naidu to accompany him on the mission. He told me that on seeing what Gandhi had done for the Indians his respect for him had gone up. Indeed, he was nearer Gandhi than most other politicians. He added: "Gandhi wants the maximum monthly salary to be fixed at Rs. 500. I receive twelve times that figure. The way I live, however, is not one that our economy can afford for a long, long time. I hold we shall have to devise an Indian standard of living lower than the Western but higher than the traditional one here. I am all for a way of life that the urban and rural people can share. It would be a tragedy if our cities go Western while the people in our villages remain backward. Some day, when our political troubles are over, we shall have to do something on Gandhian lines."

On 31st March, 1935, Fazli's membership of the Viceroy Executive Council ended. Four days earlier, I had a long talk with him to ascertain his future plans and get his assessment of the political forces in the country, and in the Punjab in particular. After this interview, he sent me an autographed photograph.

I began the talk by mentioning that Jinnah had revived the League and resumed its leadership and that Sir Sikander Hayat Khan, an influential landlord of West Punjab and Revenue Member of the Provincial Government, had come to an understanding with the Hindu and Sikh leaders of the Punjab on communal differences. Fazli replied that his first task was to restore self-respect among the Ministers in Punjab. Because of Hailey's tactics, which were being continued by his successors, the Ministers had become glorified *tahsildars* (subordinate revenue officials). Secondly, he would revive the Unionist Party. He told me what he said was a four-year-old secret. He had sent a message to the Secretary of State for India through Irwin in December 1930 that it was unfair to the Muslims, who had kept away from Gandhi's civil disobedience movement, to make them accept what the Nehru report had offered them. He had coupled the message with the threat that if the Muslim demands were not conceded before the reforms were introduced he and his followers would throw in their lot with the Congress in its political struggle against the Government. This threat worked, he added, and ultimately resulted in the Communal Award, because meanwhile there had been a change of government in Britain and the Tories became the dominant force.

Reverting to the current situation, he said that as matters stood he was agreeable to the formula devised by Sir Sikander for joint electorates, provided the Muslims were given the seats allotted to them under the Communal Award and the size of the three communities was correctly reflected in the electoral register. He said the Sikh leaders had backed out because, though thirteen per cent of the population, they formed twenty-four per cent of the electorate. The Hindu proportion was fair, but the Muslims, who constituted fifty-six per cent of the population, formed only forty-four per cent of the electorate. He said the Punjab Muslims could not work the reforms without Hindu support. He proposed to reorganise the Unionist Party on the basis of the advance of the backward classes and open it to all the communities. "I do not want Punjab to be the Ulster of India," he added.

Fazli expressed total opposition to Jinnah's plan to fight the elections through a communal party, the League. He would see to it, he said, that Muslims everywhere joined non-communal parties. He was surprised that Jinnah was taken seriously by anybody. He recalled that Jinnah had written to the *Times of India* on 3rd October, 1925, decrying the charge that the Congress was a Hindu body. Speaking in the Legislative Assembly, he had declared: "I am a nationalist first, a nationalist second and a nationalist last." He wanted the Assembly to become a "real nationalist Parliament." He joined the boycott of the Simon Commission in 1928 and split the League. He did not co-operate with the Muslim delegates at the R.T.C. in London. "His League is on paper. It has no organisation. He only wants kudos, however he may get it," he concluded his indictment. His final words were: "If God gives me two years, I shall have completed my service to the Punjab and to India. Now that the Communal Award has given the necessary safeguards, we can work for the early achievement of *Swaraj*."

Fazli reached Lahore on 1st April, 1935. Ten months later, he got the Aga Khan to attend a meeting of the Executive Board of the All-India Muslim Conference in Delhi in February 1936 and made it declare "that the Muslims put India first, being as much their motherland as of other races who inhabit India." The Aga Khan also gave funds to help counter the propaganda of Jinnah's League, which received financial support from the Hindu millowners of Bombay because of its tacit alliance with the Congress in the coming elections.

In a bid to capture all-India leadership of the Muslims, Jinnah prepared a purely communal programme and invited Fazli to preside over the next session of the League. Fazli turned down the offer and asked his followers not to meet Jinnah when he visited Lahore. Jinnah in anger retorted: "I shall smash Fazli." He set up a central Parliamentary Board of the Muslim League on the pattern of the Congress. Fazli told me he did not approve of an inter-provincial organisation as it would fetter provincial initiative in settling communal issues and was contrary to the spirit of provincial autonomy.

On 1st April, 1936, Fazli reorganised the Unionist Party under his own chairmanship. He drew up a manifesto which proposed a reduction in the emoluments of Government servants (the Gandhian touch) and declared that community of economic interests was the true basis of political parties. He proposed to remove economic inequities and dramatised his programme by remarking that the average income of a Punjabi was less than the expense of the clothing and feeding of a prisoner in a Punjab jail.

After surveying the situation in the Punjab, within a fortnight Fazli wrote me the following letter:

39 Empress Road,
Lahore, 16th April, 1936.

Dear Durga Das,

I have not heard from you for some time. Who is your

representative (meaning A.P.I.) in Lahore? He seems to be a good deal different from you or people at the headquarters. Perhaps he takes his own position to be analogous to that of a bureaucrat, and that those desiring publication of news should be asking him for his favour, to be so good as to do it. This is not very helpful.

At Lucknow (where the Congress session had just concluded under Nehru's presidentship and had decided to fight the elections), though not as clear as one would have desired the decisions to be, they are probably much better than one had reason to expect them likely to be. In actual practice, the work Jawaharlal wants done in the provinces is more or less the same as the programme the Unionists have set before themselves to execute. I doubt whether he will get workers outside the range of the Unionists to carry out his programme in the Punjab.

The new Viceroy will be approaching Delhi.

Yours sincerely,
Fazli Husain

Here was a tragic situation. Fazli, a communalist-turned-nationalist, envisaged co-operation with the Congress on the economic plane and Jinnah, a nationalist-turned-communalist, sought a coalition with the Congress on a communal basis. But fate frustrated Fazli's plans at this point. He fell ill on 1st July and died on 9th July. A huge crowd demanded that he be buried in Badshahi Masjid (King's Mosque) in Lahore, but Fazli's wishes were that he be buried in his family graveyard in Batala. His remains lie in India's Punjab, his motherland. It is one of the ifs of history whether, had Fazli lived another two years, politics would have taken a different turn.

The idea of partitioning the country took root among the Muslims only after Fazli's death. Apparently, none of his instruments— Zafrullah Khan and Noon among them—had imbibed the true spirit of patriotism of their mentor.

Chapter 23

NON-COOPERATION ENDS

A new chapter in India's political and constitutional history began in the opening days of 1936. Gandhi had withdrawn from the active leadership of the Congress and was pushing ahead with his Village Industries Association. The annual Congress session held at Lucknow in the middle of April under the presidentship of Jawaharlal Nehru finally gave up the policy of boycott of legislatures, and decided to fight elections to capture power in the provinces.

Nehru was personally opposed to working provincial autonomy and in his presidential address characterised the Reforms Act of 1935 as a "charter of slavery." I watched his discomfiture when the session rejected by 487 votes to 255 a Socialist motion favouring wrecking the Constitution and refusal of ministerial responsibility. Wondering whether Nehru would treat this as a vote of no-confidence, I approached him for his views. He said he had had his way on the larger issue. The session had agreed to his proposal demanding a constituent assembly to draw up a constitution. It had further endorsed his plea for mass contact among the Muslims.

An interesting sidelight of the session was the manner in which Nehru quickly took the lesson of the rebuff. In his presidential address, Nehru had pleaded for the infusion of younger elements into the top echelons of the party. Everyone therefore waited to see what Nehru would do in exercising his prerogative of nominating his "Cabinet," the Working Committee—whether he would make peace with the old guard or carry the fight forward. Surprisingly, Nehru sought the help of Vallabhbhai Patel and Rajendra Prasad in selecting his team. They asked him to choose his general secretary first. When Nehru replied, "Of course Kripalani," they understood he was not prepared to break with the old guard and the crisis blew over.

Jinnah almost simultaneously staged a session of the League in Bombay. It opposed the federal part of the Act but favoured contesting the elections to the provincial legislatures.

A welcome note was introduced into the political scene with the arrival of Lord Linlithgow in succession to Willingdon. Taking advantage of the rapport I had established with the new Viceroy when he came out to India as Chairman of the Royal Commission on Agriculture, and also the brief talk I had with him after meeting Baldwin in London in 1931, I approached him with a request for a gift of an acre of land near the Council House for a Press Club of India, which he readily conceded. I also took the occasion to discuss the prospect of federation as envisaged in the Act of 1935. He was enthusiastic about provincial autonomy and said they had a long way to go in getting the federal part into operation. He expressed doubt whether the Princes would co-operate.

I got the impression that he was anxious to push on with rural welfare schemes because of the uncertainty of the federal scheme. Apparently, Gandhi and he operated on a common wavelength in this sphere, while Jinnah, sophisticated urbanite, made little appeal to the Viceroy. Linlithgow also told me he would try to make friends with the Congress, for it was the only political body which stood for nationalism and promoted self-respect. He was happy at the stand against Socialism taken by Patel, Rajendra Prasad and C.R. He expected Gandhi's co-operation for a programme to improve rural conditions.

Meanwhile, the country was getting ready for the electoral battle, having digested the significance of the reforms. Patel and Prasad inaugurated the election campaign in Bombay on 7th July, 1936, and the A.I.C.C. met on 22nd August to adopt its election manifesto. Significantly, the Congress gave up its neutral attitude to the Communal Award with an eye to neutralising the Hindu Mahasabha's appeal to the Hindu electorate. The Congress election manifesto stated that the party would seek to wreck the Reforms Act, while the League promised to work provincial autonomy for all it was worth and, although favouring a "new social edifice," opposed "any movement that aims at expropriation of private property."

The selection of the President for the next annual session again assumed political significance in view of the differences between Nehru and Patel on the issue of socialism. Patel and Nehru had been proposed by Provincial Congress Committees; the former had a majority backing. Gandhi, however, decided that Nehru be given another term and persuaded Patel to withdraw in his favour. Gandhi's object was to avoid a split in the party against the background of the vote in the previous session at Lucknow in which Nehru's group had been trounced. Patel bowed to Gandhi's wishes, but made it clear that he did not accept Nehru's ideas on socialism nor agreed with him that the reforms be wrecked. He had an open mind on acceptance of ministerships in the provinces under the new Reforms Act.

The session, the first in a rural setting, was held at Faizpur in the middle of January 1937. The camp, constructed of bamboo, was named Tilak Nagar, and the session attracted more than a hundred thousand people. It marked a compromise. Nehru conceded in his presidential address that the Congress stood for a democratic state and not socialism while the issue of office acceptance was put off until the results of the poll were known. The session reaffirmed the decision to fight the elections, but called for a *hartal* on 1st April "to mark the country's protest against the imposition of the new Constitution" on that day. Actually, this was the first shot in the Congress election campaign, and another was a resolution asking the people to boycott the ceremonies connected with the coronation of King George VI following the abdication of King Edward VIII.

Jinnah too was in a belligerent anti-British mood. He told me he was looking forward to co-operation with the Congress in fighting the elections under the Reforms Act. With the death of Fazli the field was clear, he said, for imparting new life to the League. He undertook an extensive tour of the provincial capitals—a novel experience for an "arm-chair" politician.

The election results took even Congressmen by surprise, for, despite the franchise being limited to a bare twenty-seven per cent of the adult population, they won clear majorities in six of the eleven provinces, namely Bombay, Bihar, the Central Provinces, Madras, Orissa and the United Provinces, and emerged as the single largest party in Assam. Their most outstanding success was in Madras, where the Non-Brahmin Party, which had ruled uninterruptedly since 1921, was routed, securing only twenty-one seats in the Lower House of provincial legislature against 159 for the Congress.

Gandhi kept totally aloof from the election campaign, whereas Jawaharlal threw himself heart and soul into it. It was in this campaign that he arrived politically. He drew crowds everywhere and became the idol of the masses, not in the sense Gandhi was but as his glamorous and noble disciple. When I congratulated Nehru on his triumphant tour, he said: "Make no mistake. I was greeted everywhere with 'Mahatma Gandhi ki jai'. It is Bapu's spell that gave us their vote."

The League did well only in the U.P. and Bombay and made little impact on the Muslim-majority provinces. Fazli's plan had succeeded even though he was no more, for the League candidates did not poll more than four and a half per cent of the total Muslim vote.

Now that the Congress had triumphed in most of the provinces, the acceptance of office became a live issue. A session of the A.I.C.C. held at the end of March 1937 in Delhi found Nehru and Subhas Bose opposing ministerial responsibility but Gandhi's compromise formula favouring acceptance on certain conditions was carried.

During a brief talk, I found Gandhi doubtful whether the Congress had elected men who would be true to its pledge. He feared that most of them would succumb to the temptations of office and material gain. When I asked him whether he would seek an interview with the Viceroy, he replied that he would be free to re-enter the political field only after 17th July, 1937, when his remitted sentence of imprisonment would end.

Gandhi met Linlithgow in Simla early in August and their talk related to animal husbandry, village industries and rural improvement in general but not politics. Nevertheless, the meeting established a rapport which made Gandhi feel drawn towards Linlithgow even more than he had been to Irwin.

Chapter 24

GRIGG–BREAK WITH REUTER AND API

In 1937, I severed my link with Reuter and Associated Press of India, for which I had worked for eighteen years. The story of my break with the two agencies throws light on the political strains and stresses of the time. The Briton's wholesome respect for the Fourth Estate was being overlaid by the urge to make the journalist a sort of public relations man for the Raj.

Sir James Grigg, the new Finance Member, unlike his two predecessors in that office, was not from the City. He had been with the Treasury in London, a Civil Servant at the head of the Inland Revenue set-up. Of his talents there can be little doubt; and after his retirement from India he was to become Britain's Minister for War under Winston Churchill. He was something of an *enfant terrible* in the eyes of both the Establishment and spectators of the parliamentary scene, a curious amalgam of bluffness and intellectual refinement. There was nothing that pleased him more than to cross swords with "Supplemurthi," as he had nicknamed S. Satyamurthi, who fired supplementary questions at the Treasury benches with the rattle of a machine-gun. Grigg respected genuine talent, though. His instructions to the Chief Whip were precise, that he himself should be promptly sent for whenever Pandit Pant, Deputy Leader of the Opposition, was on his legs to speak on economic and financial issues.

Grigg was suspicious of the Press and had few friends in the Fourth Estate. He even had a brush with the representative of *The Statesman*, Malcolm Muggeridge, who later gained world fame as author and commentator. Malcolm was unconventional and his informality, which brought a whiff of fresh air to the closed corporation atmosphere of the ruling élite in Simla, was frowned upon by the traditional Blimps. A Civil Servant, Grigg tried to play politics, for which he was neither trained nor temperamentally suited. That his close friends found him warmhearted was another matter. What Grigg dreaded most was the risk of budget leakages. He therefore set out to devise a new "foolproof" system for handling the budget. He divided the budget statement into two distinct parts, the first a general review of the economic and financial operations of the year, and the second embodying specific fiscal proposals. The latter was revealed to the Executive Council a couple of hours before its presentation and was released to the Press at the precise moment he unfolded it on the floor of the Legislative Assembly. That wrote finis to the era when A.P.I. was permitted to handle the proposals in advance.

Grigg, eager to counteract Gandhi's move to spread his revolutionary gospel in the countryside through his Village Industries Association, allotted Rs. twenty million for a two-year Government-sponsored programme of rural uplift. An annual report on the use of the fund by provincial Governments was to be placed on the table of the Central Legislature.

Contrary to established practice in regard to official documents, the Finance Minister did not send an advance copy of the first annual report to A.P.I. for putting out its own summary. Instead, the Information Bureau prepared a summary and had it endorsed by Grigg. No sooner had the Finance Minister placed the report on the table of the House than the Bureau Chief slipped into the seat next to mine in the Press Gallery and handed over his own summary with a polite request that it be used exactly as it stood.

With a smile, I picked up an address slip, scribbled a dozen-word introduction, signed the message and passed it on to my assistant for despatch to the telegraph office. The official gave me a friendly grin, as much as to say: "I shall tell the boss that you obliged." Next morning, however, the fat was in the fire. The "intro" proclaimed that the summary of the White Paper had been supplied officially. Grigg exploded: "We have been—— (the oath was vivid, but unprintable)." Since the A.P.I. disowned responsibility for the summary, it lost a great part of its value.

Grigg was thereafter on the warpath. Fortunately for us, we were well insulated against local dangers. We had access to the Viceroy and maintained excellent relations with the Home Member and the Leader of the Assembly. Grigg therefore mounted an attack on us in London while back home on mid-term leave. He complained against our using the agency network to put out nationalist propaganda and allegedly threatened to withdraw the Government subscription unless the "twins" (Iyengar and myself) were packed off from our Simla–Delhi preserve. Not long afterwards, Reuter's General Manager in Bombay put forward a scheme under which both of us were to be moved out of Delhi—one to be posted in Bombay and the other in London to reinforce Reuter's India desk. Meanwhile, the Company's Chief Accountant was sent from Bombay to Delhi to fill the newly created post of Deputy General Manager, presumably to ensure British supervision even while we functioned at the headquarters.

We had strong roots in Delhi and Simla and could not think of pulling out of the centre of political warfare. Roy's advice to me strengthened our resolve. He had said: "This is not a job. It is a forum of self-expression. Quit if it ceases to be one." Iyengar and I conveyed our decision to Usha Nath Sen and, as a life-long associate of Roy, he said he would quit with us, and that the three of us could then pool our resources and share the rewards. That evening Sen rang up the General Manager to acquaint him with the developments. Presumably fearful of the political consequences of the exit of three senior Indian members of his staff, the General Manager prevailed upon Sen to stay on, giving him charge of the Delhi outfit and a directorship on the local board set up in India. Next morning Sen told us he had slept over our proposition and was reluctant to be an encumbrance to us. But we were not to be deflected from our resolve.

From New Year's Day of 1937, when the General Manager handed to us the terms of our "re-engagement" in a sealed cover, to 20th January, when we finally took the plunge, was a period of intense personal drama. Both of us were then earning higher emoluments than any Indian editor and many perquisites, including a free first class railway pass. I had six children, the eldest only 15. Our refusal to compromise won appreciation in nationalist circles. "Never put money above honour," Jinnah exhorted us. Sir Chimanlal Setalvad's support was qualified by a characteristic warning: "Don't fall into Congress hands either." Satyamurthi's "congratulations on your stand" was also a morale booster. An agreement annulling the previous contract was signed. We were on our own from 1st April, 1937.

That finished my plan for the second overseas trip, which this time included Japan and the U.S. and was to take me to London for the King's coronation. I had gathered from the leader of the Japanese delegation which concluded the first Indo-Japan Cotton Agreement in 1934 that the motive force in Japan was economic development to match that in the West. I was keen on studying this process. I had also been thrilled to learn from the Assistant Finance Editor of the *Mainichi* of Osaka, who accompanied the delegation that when he was a child his grandmother used to tell him about the wonderful country called Tenjiku (paradise), an old Japanese name for India. I wanted to see whether that spiritual bond still existed between India and Japan. Further, I wanted to assess the depth of American interest in our freedom struggle.

First April, 1937, a red letter day in India's political calendar because it marked the inception of provincial autonomy, also marked a turning-point in my career. Iyengar and I quickly organised a news-cum-feature service on the model of the special material we had been supplying to various newspapers. My own plan was to develop this ultimately into the kind of all-India organisation I was to embark upon some twenty-three years later.

Arthur Moore, Editor of *The Statesman*, who was anxious to popularise his paper among Indians, particularly in the North, by publishing material written from the Congress viewpoint, invited me to join his staff as the first Indian special representative. My effort to get the offer diverted to my colleague was unsuccessful. Iyengar pressed me to accept it. I succeeded, however, in deferring the decision for six months, during which *The Statesman* agreed to publish our material as emanating from a special correspondent. This Delhi–Simla interlude enabled me not only to strengthen Iyengar's hands in running the service we had launched independently but also to help build up *Roy's Weekly*, a periodical we set up in collaboration with Sen as a memorial to K. C. Roy. It was a period of adventure.

I tore myself away at the end of six months from the exhilaration of the Delhi–Simla round to take up *The Statesman* assignment in Lucknow. What awaited me in the new milieu was a rich experience, a grandstand view of provincial autonomy at work—indeed a preview of *Swaraj*.

Chapter 25

JINNAH - BREAK WITH THE CONGRESS

If Punjab gave birth to communalism which vitiated the working of the Montford Reforms, the U.P. sparked off a controversy which culminated in the country's partition.

Rafi Ahmed Kidwai was the operator of the party machine in the U.P. He had been Motilal Nehru's private secretary and one of the Swarajist Whips in the Central Assembly under him. After the elder Nehru's death, he became the son's principal aide. Known to his friends as Rafi, he organised the Congress campaign for elections to the U.P. legislature in 1937. It was not easy to divine how Muslim electors would vote and they formed an influential section in a majority of urban constituencies. The Muslim League, too, was not sure if its appeal could outdo the feudal influence of the powerful landed aristocracy, which had a party of its own and which consisted of both Hindus and Muslims.

Rafi as a matter of electoral tactics persuaded Chaudhuri Khaliq-uz-Zaman and Nawab Mohammed Ismail and other Muslim Congressmen to contest the elections on the ticket of the Muslim League. The Congress, unsure of sweeping the polls, was willing to go into partnership with Congress-minded Leaguers. But the overwhelming Congress electoral victory in U.P. and six other provinces altered the picture radically as the Congress Party suddenly found that it could form Ministries without the aid of the Leaguers. Jawaharlal Nehru was the Congress President for the year and political interest centred on the lead the U.P. would give in the matter. Gandhi, Patel, Azad and Pant were agreeable to enlisting the League's co-operation in a coalition as envisaged originally.

Rafi made Nehru parley with Khaliq-uz-Zaman and his followers and suggest that they rejoin the Congress or at least endorse the Congress election platform. Jinnah was counting on establishing the League's identity by a Congress-League coalition in U.P. and Bombay. He quickly sensed that the Rafi–Nehru move would leave him high and dry and launched a bitter attack on Nehru. Interviewed on 26th July, 1937 he said: "What can I say to the busybody

President of the Congress? He (Nehru) seems to carry the responsibility of the whole world on his shoulders and must poke his nose
into everything except minding his own business." Nehru reacted
equally sharply and opposed a coalition with the League.

The terms proposed by Rafi were acceptable to Khaliq-uz-Zaman
but not to Jinnah who considered them an affront to his prestige.
The opportunity for a Congress–League entente was thrown to the
winds. Rafi made matters worse by encouraging defections from the
ranks of the League. (This was an evil precedent, as the defection-
ridden politics of the late sixties was to show.) The Congress
Ministry was formed and the League assumed the role of a militant
opposition in combination with the party of the landlords.

I was still in Simla preparing for the move to Lucknow for my
new assignment. Jinnah told me: "This is war to the knife." The
break thus caused by Nehru's impetuosity and Jinnah's arrogance
was never repaired. I watched the drama of the widening breach
first in Simla–Delhi and then in Lucknow.

In the autumn of 1937, Jinnah proclaimed that his enemy was
the Congress, and his words implied that his enemy's enemy was
his friend. He fired the first shot of his campaign at the Lucknow
session of the League in October, declaring that the Congress was
a Hindu body championing the cause of "Hindustan for Hindus"
and that it called for the liquidation of the League as the price of
collective responsibility. This broadside concluded with a reminder
that the blank cheque Gandhi had earlier offered to write on Jinnah's
terms for a Hindu–Muslim settlement had remained unsigned.

The controversy was embittered by the Jinnah–Nehru correspondence in April 1938. Nehru spoke of Congress willingness, in
the light of the critical international situation, to work with any
organisation or individual in furtherance of its policy of attaining
independence. But, to Jinnah's mortification, he characterised the
League as "an important communal organisation," not as "the one
and only organisation of Indian Muslims."

Jinnah's reply marked the final break with the Congress. Nehru's
mind, "obsessed with the international situation," he said, was
entirely divorced "from the realities which face us in India." He
resented Nehru's "arrogance and militancy of spirit." He urged the
Congress not to act as if it were the "sovereign power" but to deal
with the League on a footing of complete equality.

Now on the warpath, in his presidential address to the League
session in December 1938, Jinnah challenged Nehru's theory that
there were only two forces at play, the British and the Congress.
He said there were four: the British Raj, the Princes, the Hindus

and the Muslims. He inveighed against the Wardha scheme of education and the Nai Talim Sangh (New Education Organisation) set up to implement it as "worked out behind the back of the Muslims," as "Hindi–Hindustani" intended "to stifle and suppress Urdu." He called the Congress fascist and its executive a "fascist Grand Council." When I found Britons in glee over such denunciation of their principal enemy, I met Jinnah and remonstrated with him that this attack would hurt Gandhi and stiffen the attitude of the Congress. He agitatedly replied: "Durga, this is the only language Gandhi understands."

As for the charge about the Wardha scheme, I told him that it was unfair and recalled what Madam Cram Cook, an American who had lived in Gandhi's ashram had told me when she came with James Mills of A.P.A. to our office in New Delhi. She had spoken to me in Hindustani which, she said, she had learned at the ashram. According to her, "Gandhi above all wants to make use of what India's own life has evolved for the language. He feels Hindustani has come to fill a need and indeed told me over and over again: 'Learn Hindustani as the Muslims speak it if you want to be understood from end to end of India'. Gandhiji considers Hindustani a uniting element, and in the bargain a tonic to the Muslims, a way of utilising all they have done in art, in eclecticism, in culture for the unity of India in the greater sense. The wonderful scientific vocabulary being developed in Hindi is the gift of Sanskrit, and every Indian language can have the same. Gandhiji told me he longed to have the right Muslim emerge to be the President of free India." This plea left Jinnah cold. I further mentioned that Dr. Zakir Husain was the Chairman of the Committee which had prepared the Wardha scheme. But he emphatically asserted he knew one thing: Gandhi stood for Hindu revivalism.

Chapter 26

PROVINCIAL AUTONOMY AT WORK

Of the various Ministries formed by the Congress, three in particular attracted much attention. The one in the U.P. represented the cream of party talent. Madras had as its Chief Minister C. Rajagopalachari, the only member of the Congress High Command to take up this role. The Ministry in Bombay was the symbol of collective leadership. The Central Parliamentary Board under Sardar Patel's leadership was to keep a watch on the functioning of the Ministries. This "superintendence, direction and control" of an extra-constitutional character detracted from the democratic freedom of the provinces, but it was meant to assure adherence to Congress ideology and implementation of its programme.

I was happy at the opportunity of having a glimpse of *Swaraj*. I had cordial personal relations with the Governor of U.P., Sir Harry Haig, and with Chief Minister Pant, with whom I had established rapport in Delhi. I was able to rent a new house facing the official residence of the Chief Minister in Lucknow. The close proximity and our daily meeting over a cup of tea in the morning made me an insider. Indeed, not long after I had begun to function in Lucknow, *The Pioneer* and the *Leader*, one mirroring the landlords' point of view and the other that of the Liberals, characterised *The Statesman* as the "Congress organ." My professional experience helped, and Pant capped it by setting up a Press Consultative Committee and inviting me to be its Chairman. Composed of editors of leading dailies of the province, the Committee was the first of its kind in India.

Pant told me one day of how his Ministry came to be formed. Purushottamdas Tandon was senior to Pant but was dedicated to the cause of Indian *sanskriti* (culture) which appeared to Nehru and Rafi a reactionary outlook. Tandon was senior to Nehru too, and in fact was among the few who called him by his first name. Rafi manoeuvred to get Tandon to accept the Speakership of the U.P. Assembly and thus cleared the way for Pant, who had been the leader of the Swaraj Party in the defunct provincial legislature, to take over as Chief Minister. Rafi, for his part, told me how he had helped to insulate the Pant Ministry against "the irritable criticism and interference of the unpredictable Nehru." Pant and he waited on Nehru at his residence in Allahabad and sought his blessings for the inclusion of Mrs. Vijayalakshmi Pandit in the Ministry. Nehru, who doted on his younger sister, readily agreed. This plan did succeed to a very large extent, but still Nehru could not help an occasional outburst.

I was present at a public meeting at which he noticed Pant's peon in his gold-embroidered red uniform. Nehru shouted against this exhibition of authority and asked why the liveried *Jamadar* (head peon) was there. He thus ridiculed Pant and drew cheers from the vast crowd. The incident caused quite a stir at the gathering, where it was interpreted as a calculated rebuff to the Chief Minister, who was known to be Patel's lieutenant in U.P. just as Rafi was Nehru's. Pant himself suffered a psychological shock. Anyway, Nehru made it obvious to the people who was boss. Commenting on the incident, Mrs. Pandit told me: "Bhai (brother) went off the deep end. I never travel without Ahmed (her liveried peon). The common people know me to be a Minister because Ahmed is with me. They *salaam* 'Ahmed's livery.' " (Nehru himself realised this well enough when he became the Prime Minister and had a retinue of peons and security staff—several times the size any Viceroy had had—when he moved among the people.)

Not long after assuming office, Pant clashed with the Governor when he received a peremptory directive from the High Command to secure release of the remaining political prisoners and, failing that, to tender the resignation of his Cabinet. This directive was issued a few days before the annual Congress session at Haripura to avoid criticism from the Leftists who had opposed acceptance of office. Pant felt helpless and told me that the Chief Minister of Bihar was in a similar predicament. He drew up his letter of resignation, but for fear it might give undue offence to the Governor he asked me to vet it. His anxiety was not to make an issue of the incident but to avoid a crisis. Suitably phrased, the communication was approved by the Council of Ministers and sent to the Governor.

Pant was keen on breaking the deadlock. But as he and his colleagues were leaving Lucknow to attend the Congress session he urged me to stay behind to persuade the Governor against accepting the resignation in haste and to find a way out of the crisis on the lines we had discussed earlier. Gandhi came to the rescue by adopting what sounded to me like Pant's formula. He suggested that the crisis could be ended if the Chief Ministers gave an assurance, after talking with the Governors, that the misunderstandings about interference with their sphere had been removed. Haig was equally anxious for a settlement. I was at the railway station to greet Pant on his return to Lucknow. Little time was lost thereafter in ratifying the agreement that gave the Ministry a fresh lease of life.

I cannot say that the preview of *Swaraj* gave me a thrill. The Pant team was undoubtedly talented. But each Minister ran his Ministry as his or her special preserve. Pant loved to wrestle with files, his appetite for notes and memoranda was insatiable. He prided himself on the fact that his own notes were longer, better written and meatier than those of the civilians. Pant was apparently seeking to establish his authority by proving himself a super Civil Servant. Ridiculing Pant's methods, Rafi said to me in those early days: "I have to give decisions, not to write notes to convince myself. I read notes put up by the Secretariat, weigh issues in my mind and write orders."

The Government front bench was more than a match for the Opposition in parliamentary skill. Pant was of course the outstanding parliamentarian. Dr. Kailash Nath Katju, who rose to be the Defence Minister and later Home Minister in the Nehru Government at the Centre, was an efficient administrator and skilful debater. Hafiz Mohammed Ibrahim, who resigned from the Muslim League to join the Pant Cabinet and successfully contested a by-election on the Congress ticket, represented the enlightened social conscience of his community. Mrs. Pandit made her mark as a Minister who had a mind of her own, was articulate and had a gift for the rough and tumble of parliamentary life. Lal Bahadur Shastri was then Parliamentary Secretary to Pant and Ajit Prasad Jain to Rafi. Shastri was hardly noticed since he concentrated on handling unobtrusively numerous petitioners and party men who sought the Chief Minister's intervention—a role that endeared him later to Nehru.

The Governor, Sir Harry Haig, and British Civil Servants observed the obligations imposed by the Constitution. Haig with whom I had established cordial relations in Simla–Delhi complimented the Ministers on their zeal and fair play but felt that Pant, in tackling the problems of law and order, had displayed a lack of perspective ("his action almost touched off a police mutiny at one place") and rather meddled in the appointment, transfer and promotion of Civil Servants. The Indian officers of the service laboured sincerely to help the Congress Ministers implement their programme despite the British civilians' scepticism about their practicability. There thus grew slowly and invisibly a wall between the Indian and British Civil Servants, the latter in private talk accusing the former of going over to the "rebels."

One rewarding aspect of my duties as *The Statesman*'s representative in Lucknow was the opportunity to tour various parts of the province. I discovered that the Muslims enjoyed a special position and represented a vital force. There was communal tension in the western districts of the province, it is true, but there was some kind of fusion of the Hindu and Muslim cultures in the towns, where the spoken language was Hindustani intermixed with Persian. The peasantry had been indifferent to politics before the advent of Gandhi. The Muslim masses had hardly been touched by Islamic fervour until the Khilafat movement awakened them. It was in the interests of both Hindu and Muslim landlords to see that communal harmony was preserved in the countryside. Communalism was an urban excrescence.

The district administration in the U.P. was highly centralised. The landlords kept peace in the countryside. The British encouraged Muslims of talent and sixty per cent of the junior executive posts under the Raj were held by Muslims although they constituted only fourteen per cent of the population. Young Hindus, who were denied opportunities for employment in Government service, were drawn towards the Congress movement. So also were the millions of tenants to whom the Congress held out the promise of hereditary tenancy and abolition of feudal landlordism. Indeed, it was this platform which contributed largely to the Congress success at the polls.

The Pant Ministry's outlook was genuinely secular. However, in fulfilling its pledge to the tenantry it unwittingly drove a further wedge between the Congress and the Muslims. Rafi's Tenancy Reforms Bill encountered stiff resistance from the League landlords, the only propertied class among the Muslims. In a bitterly fought passage through the Assembly, the Bill was described as destructive of the culture of the minority community, sustained by the patronage of the Muslim landed aristocracy. Nawabaza Liaquat Ali Khan (who became the first Prime Minister of Pakistan), was the chief exponent of this charge as a spokesman of the Opposition. The Nawabaza was of course playing politics. Nevertheless the fact is that the Congress regime did make the urban Muslim feel that he had lost the pre-eminence he had enjoyed under the Nawabs and their British successors.

In a piece I wrote for *The Statesman* headed "U.P. in Travail" and published on 5th May, 1939, I summed up the situation at the end of two years of Congress rule thus: The Congress Party, on assuming office, proceeded to translate its pledges into legislative and administrative acts. At once rose the cry: "This is revolution." The intellectual classes found themselves put on the shelf. The stake-holders asked themselves whether they had supported and financed the Congress for the purpose of promoting their own ruin. The masses inquired if the Congress really intended to play a revolutionary role. The public servants wondered whether the administration would be run on idealistic lines and at the same time avert chaos. Legislators rubbed their eyes at the disregard shown to the "non-official" opinion voiced by them. The spokesman of the minorities complained that they had asked for liberty, not communal raj. The Ministers were overworked. Unemployed Congress legislators were getting on the nerves of the Ministers and a desperate Opposition

sacrifices for party exigencies the larger issues of a constitutional
and financial nature which should be above party politics.

On his retirement towards the end of 1939, Governor Haig wrote
to me: "I have always enjoyed and profited from our talks, for I
know no one who can analyse a political situation so acutely. I
have been particularly glad that you have been in Lucknow during
these difficult times. Before you came, the exaggerated stories
current in Delhi were an embarrassment. (The reference is to the
Grigg episode.) You have been able to present U.P. conditions
fairly, yet with a benevolent attitude towards the Congress, which
was of real value, and you have helped a great deal to a clearer
understanding of our conditions."

I visited Bombay and Madras to make a study of the Congress
regime in these provinces. The Bombay Ministry improved the
administration and won laurels for the efficient way K. M. Munshi,
the Home Minister, handled a Hindu–Muslim riot within three
months of assumption of office. C. Rajagopalachari, who headed the
Congress Ministry in Madras, was so dominant a figure that his
Ministry came to be known as a one-man show. Madras was fortunate in possessing a cadre of experienced civilians, both British
and Indians who served the Ministers with conspicuous loyalty and
co-operation.

The three Ministries, indeed, set separate patterns of political
management. In the U.P. the Cabinet responsibility was a façade.
Each Ministry worked as a separate empire, subject to the overriding vigilance of the Chief Minister. The Bombay set-up was an
example of collective responsibility and cohesive team work. While
Ministers were encouraged to express their view frankly at a Cabinet
meeting, they backed the final decision both in their public statements and private talk. Madras set the pattern for a compact
Ministry under a father figure whose word was law.

Book III

1939-47

INDEPENDENCE DAWNS

Chapter 1

WORLD WAR II

(a) JINNAH GETS THE VETO

The outbreak of World War II in September 1939 marks a watershed in the political history of India. This global catastrophy, more than any human design or the interplay of domestic political forces, hastened the liquidation of the British Raj in India and, side by side, the partition of the country.

To comprehend the drama that unfolded itself, it is relevant to recall certain broad facts that influenced the course of events. Minto put a brake on the nationalist movement by launching on a policy of divide and rule through the grant of separate electorates to the Muslims. Consequently, the political controversy from 1910 till 1935 centred on separate electorates versus joint electorates. Jinnah was then the protagonist of joint electorates with reservation of seats and the Aga Khan and Fazli Husain of separate electorates. The separatists won the day when Prime Minister Ramsay MacDonald gave the Communal Award, which conceded to the Muslims a share in power through legislators chosen by the Muslim electorate. The award was later embodied in the Government of India Act of 1935. But the Act did not affect the basic political situation, namely that the main forces contending for power were still the Raj and the Congress.

The elections of 1937 for the reformed legislatures brought the Congress sweeping victories in the Hindu-majority provinces. The League suffered a major reverse in the Muslim-majority provinces, but many of its candidates in U.P. and Bombay, who were mainly former Congressmen, won. Jinnah now expected the Congress to reward his nationalism by forming a coalition with the League in these two provinces and thereby give his party a national identity. When the Congress insisted that the Leaguers should first endorse the Congress platform, Jinnah's prestige suffered a major blow and he started attacking the Congress virulently as a Hindu–fascist body.

Jinnah now proceeded to gather evidence of the "atrocities" committed on the Muslims under Congress rule in the U.P. He set up a committee under a Muslim landlord, the Raja of Pirpur, to prove the matter. The committee produced a report which came in handy to Jinnah and all those who wanted to blast the Congress as an "oppressive Hindu tyrant." The report raised many questions, including one about the Governor's role. I asked Sir Harry Haig, a highly conscientious civilian, whether he had failed to exercise his overriding powers as Governor to protect the minorities as alleged. He categorically denied the charges levelled against the Congress in the report. That, however, made little difference to Jinnah when I mentioned this to him. A skilful lawyer, he went ahead to use the Pirpur report to strike a new note. The safeguards provided in the Act of 1935, he contended, had proved inadequate in protecting the interests of the Muslims.

The situation on the Congress front at the time was not altogether satisfactory. Two succeeding sessions at Haripura and Tripura in 1938 and 1939 respectively had brought into the open the struggle between Subhas Bose and Jawaharlal Nehru for leadership and created a major crisis. Having presided over the Haripura session, Bose offered himself for re-election on the precedent established by Nehru's presidentship of two successive terms. Gandhi opposed Bose's candidature and put up Pattabhi Sitaramayya, a veteran Congressman, as his candidate. Bose triumphed and Gandhi proclaimed the victory of the young leader from Bengal as his own defeat. The High Command, however, promptly neutralised Bose by getting the session to pass a resolution directing the new President to form his "Cabinet" in consultation with Gandhi. Bose took the resolution as a vote of no-confidence and resigned. Prasad stepped into the breach.

The outbreak of the war tended for a while to revive the struggle between Nehru and Bose. Nehru was then on his way back from Chungking after a visit to Generalissimo Chiang Kai-shek. Interviewed by Press correspondents in Rangoon, he declared: "This is not the time to bargain. We are against the rising imperialism of Germany, Italy and Japan and for the decaying imperialisms of Europe." Bose quickly seized the opportunity provided by Nehru's Press statement to embarrass his rival and score over him. When Nehru arrived in Calcutta, he was confronted with a demonstration organised by Bose displaying placards demanding firm action against Britain and proclaiming: "British adversity is India's opportunity." Gandhi again came to Nehru's rescue and nipped the controversy in the bud by demanding a definition of Britain's war aims and ruling that the Congress would finalise its stand in regard to the hostilities only thereafter. Nehru promptly accepted Gandhi's line and into the bargain not only played safe but enabled the Congress to speak with one voice.

In the meantime, the Viceroy, anxious to mobilise the support of all sections of the Indian people for the war effort, invited Gandhi, Jinnah and the Chancellor of the Chamber of Princes for talks and sought their co-operation. While the League asked for further discussions and clarifications, the Congress Working Committee took strong exception to the failure of the British Government to include India's freedom among its war aims and called upon the Ministries to resign in protest. This the Congress Ministries did in October, and Jinnah imaginatively used this psychological moment for a call to the Muslims to observe "Deliverance Day." He cleverly fixed this demonstration for Friday (2nd December, 1939), when the Muslims normally close their businesses and hold congregational prayers in their mosques. He could now assert that 10,000 meetings had been held all over the country to celebrate the deliverance from "Hindu tyranny." Incidentally, for Britons too the exit of the Congress Ministries was a deliverance from the handicap of subjection to popular Ministers. They could now go full steam ahead in organising the war effort.

Linlithgow's action in inviting not only Gandhi (as was the case in the past) but also Jinnah and the Chancellor of the Chamber of Princes had the effect of greatly inflating Jinnah's stature politically. The League leader had been equated with Gandhi for the first time and, what is more, the Viceroy's decision eloquently confirmed the basic contention made by Jinnah in his correspondence with Nehru that the power struggle in India was between four parties, namely the British, the Hindus, the Muslims and the Princes, and not between the British and the Congress only as Nehru asserted. The fact of the matter was that the invitation to Jinnah was not extended without reason. Over the preceding two years he had emerged as the tallest among the Muslim politicians and as an uncompromising critic of the Congress. In doing so, he created a favourable impression both on the Princes and on the British bureaucracy.

But Jinnah was still a nationalist at heart. He tried to cash in on his new status and made another effort in January, 1940, to persuade the Congress to accept him as the sole spokesman of the Muslims. "That is all that I seek," he told me. But he was again rebuffed. He took further offence when the Congress elected Azad as its President for their annual session in March at Ramgarh to demonstrate to the world that Jinnah was not the sole spokesman of the Muslims. "They have now added insult to injury by selecting that showboy," he bitterly remarked. I pleaded with him that the moment the Congress recognised the League as the sole Muslim spokesman the British would organise another Aga Khan show as a challenge. But he was in no mood to argue. "No, Durga," he replied, "if only Gandhi would join hands with me, the British game of divide and rule would be frustrated."

Linlithgow made another effort to persuade the Congress to co-operate in the war effort and invited Gandhi in February for talks. He assured him that a new constitution would be drawn up after the war in consultation with the Indian leaders. But the deadlock continued, and the Viceroy thereupon decided to seek the League's co-operation both to counter the Congress and fight the war. Jinnah was invited for a talk on 13th March, and he used the occasion to assure the Viceroy that the Muslims would not retard the war effort if an undertaking was given to them that no political settlement would be reached with the Congress without the previous consent of the Muslims. The Viceroy, according to Jinnah, reacted favourably and said he would communicate his views to London.

Gandhi was quick to sense the significance of the Viceroy's move and realised that the British were now boosting Jinnah to create a roadblock to ride out the period of the war. He therefore decided to counter the British move and, at the pressing request of Nehru and Azad, agreed to attend the party's annual session at Ramgarh in March 1940. Addressing the Subjects Committee and the delegates after a gap of six years, he put forward ·the proposal for a Constituent Assembly as a solution to the Hindu–Muslim problem. Under his proposal, as Gandhi explained to me earlier, the eighty million Muslims of India would be conceded the right of self-determination provided their representatives were elected to the Constituent Assembly on adult franchise. They could then decide whether they wanted independence for India as a joint family, with the right to claim a division if they wanted. Gandhi, as I wrote in my despatch of 20th March in *The Statesman*, "still hopes by this move to get into the pocket of Mr. Jinnah."

At the same time, the Congress passed a resolution at the session reaffirming that "nothing short of complete independence" was acceptable and calling for the setting up of a Constituent Assembly on the basis of adult suffrage to determine the future. It stated that the Congress would make every effort to secure communal harmony by agreement or by arbitration. The resolution declared that the withdrawal of Ministries was only a preliminary step and would be followed by civil disobedience. Gandhi was authorised to launch the movement at an opportune time.

Jinnah, now after a bigger prize, was unmoved and four days later, at the League session at Lahore, he made his next shrewd move in the wartime game of political chess in India. He got the session to declare in a resolution that no constitutional plan would be acceptable to the Muslims unless designed on the following basic principle, "that geographically contiguous units are demarcated into regions which should be so constituted with such territorial adjustments as may be necessary that the areas in which the Muslims are numerically in a majority as in the north-western and eastern zones of India, should be grouped to constitute 'independent States' in which the constituent units shall be autonomous and sovereign." The session further authorised the League Executive "to frame a scheme of constitution in accordance with these basic principles, providing for the assumption finally by the respective regions of all powers such as defence, external affairs, communications, customs and such other matters as may be necessary." Significantly, the resolution made no reference to the issue of war, and by implication left the Muslims free to support the war effort.

The resolution did not employ the word Pakistan, although in his presidential speech Jinnah specifically asserted that the Hindus and the Muslims represented different and distinct social orders and could not therefore evolve a common nationality. A Hindu correspondent asked him whether the resolution "meant a demand for Pakistan?" Jinnah still avoided using the word Pakistan and replied that it was open to him to think so and that he was prepared to accept his interpretation. (The resolution was eventually publicised as demanding Pakistan.) When I met Jinnah after the session and pointed out that Sikander Hayat Khan had categorically told me that the resolution was essentially a bargaining counter, Jinnah replied: "A bargain, my friend, is struck between two parties. Let the Congress first accept the League as the other party."

Now that the two parties had made their pronouncements, it was clear that the Congress was on the warpath and that the League would co-operate at a price in fighting the war, made grim by the blitzkrieg Hitler suddenly launched to end months of phoney confrontation. The Viceroy accordingly invited Jinnah to another talk on 27th June, and this proved most rewarding to the League leader. In a statement on 8th August, 1940, Linlithgow placed in the hands of Jinnah a veto on constitutional progress by declaring that the British Government could not contemplate the transfer of power "to any system of government whose authority is directly denied by large and powerful elements in India's national life. Nor could they be parties to the coercion of such elements into sub-

mission to such a government." Jinnah was on top, and when I
saw him he disclosed in confidence that the League owed this
concession to Leopold Amery, the Secretary of State. (The India
Office had once again played the Crescent Card.) Jinnah was
remarkably relaxed and, leaning back in his chair, added: "All I
have to do now is to wait for the next Congress move and to counter
it. I have no doubt that Nehru will play into my hands."

(b) SAPRU ON NATIONALISM

As the situation was getting desperate, some of us felt a determined effort should be made to avert the crisis. I discussed certain
ideas with Pant and Rafi, who reflected the views of the High
Command, and finding them react favourably, wrote in *The
Statesman* in June 1940 two articles headed: "India at Bay; Way to
Avoid Disaster." In these articles I suggested the formula of a
national government comprising nominees of the provincial administrations. If an announcement of this kind was made, I felt the Congress would return to ministerial responsibility. I drew the attention
of Sapru to my articles in the hope that if he supported the plan it
would gain weight.
Sapru was then holidaying in Kashmir and sent me a very
interesting reply:

"There is a good deal in your articles with which I am in
agreement. With the concluding portion in which you say that
'a self-governing India would need to spend 300 crores of rupees,
not forty-five crores, annually (one crore means ten million), to
keep herself in a state of preparedness to meet a possible attack by
a major power', I am in complete agreement. I regret that I do
not share the optimism of some of your distinguished Congress
leaders, who have been saying recently in their speeches that
there is no apprehension of a foreign invasion, and that if one
takes place they will be able to face it. The foreign invasion may
never—and I hope will never—take place, but I should not like
to be put off my guard and it is extremely dangerous and unwise
to lull people into a false sense of security. It is mainly because
of this that I think that in matters of defence it is an advantage to
remain a member of the Commonwealth. In fact, no country
can afford to be completely independent of another in the altered
state of the world.
"I should have thought that the immediate question before us

was to get self-government and not the domination of any particular school of thought. You say Gandhi's socialist state will evolve round the village economy. To improve the economic condition of our villages is undoubtedly a vital necessity and I regret that it has been neglected so far, but I doubt whether you are justified in using the phrase 'Gandhi's socialist state.' His 'socialism' is more akin to humanitarianism than to a political creed, and it is so elastic that the orthodox socialist and the combative Marxist may well claim standing room under his canopy.

"You then say that the leftist conception is of a Marxist brand. For one thing, if the leftists adopt the Marxist brand, they cannot be nationalists; for another you cannot avoid class struggle. All this will be fatal to the establishment, or at any rate continuance of self-government. Class struggle must also be strengthened by the forces of communalism.

"Nationalism in the case of India is, and must be, very different from the territorial nationalism of Europe, which is the result of the Treaty of Vienna made more than 100 years ago and which has been accentuated in Europe by trade rivalries. Nationalism in India must aim, for a long time to come, at reducing the internal points of conflict to a minimum, multiplying the points of contact and fostering a sense of community of interests. This will require very conscious and continued effort.

"Personally speaking, I see very little evidence of such nationalism in India. Each party is using democratic phrases and slogans really for the establishment of its own supremacy. When you express the hope that the Viceroy may cut the Gordian knot by ignoring the claims of both the Congress and the League to represent the will of the Indian people and of the Muslims respectively and calling upon the autonomous provincial units to nominate their representatives to form a provincial federal Government, I share that hope with you, though I realise that such a step on the part of the Viceroy will, at the start, meet with the strongest possible opposition both from the Congress and the League.

"The recent pronouncement of the Mahatma that it is no use calling an all-parties conference, as other parties do not share the point of view of the Congress, has filled me with despair. Bluntly put, it is the very essence of totalitarianism, and it does not matter that his totalitarianism is different from other brands of totalitarianism in that it is based on non-violence. The result is the same. There is no toleration for difference of opinion.

"I am most unwilling to express my opinion on these questions at present and if I have written to you this *personal* letter (*not for publication*), it is only out of my regard for you."

(c) DELHI–LUCKNOW INTERLUDE

At the turn of the year, I came to Delhi for the Budget session of 1941 to act for a British colleague and probed political developments in the capital since the outbreak of the war. During the period, I met the Viceroy and his high officials, the members of the Congress High Command and Jinnah to get the last picture of the developments that had brought about a political deadlock. What I saw and heard held out little hope of a breakthrough. In fact, the scene was being complicated by an additional factor—the Princes. Nehru had gone ahead and helped promote the States People Conference (despite Gandhi's lukewarmness) and the rulers were now reacting. "They are now more inclined towards the League," Jinnah gleefully claimed.

Surprisingly, I found the bureaucrats quite unperturbed by the new Congress campaign. In fact, they seemed quite complacent and full of confidence. Symbolic of the general feeling was the Secretary of the War Supplies Department's remark to me: "As a bureaucrat, I do not see why we need a national Government. We are getting all the supplies we need for our war effort." The credit for this situation mainly went to Sir Jeremy Raisman, the Finance Member and the only member of the I.C.S. to be given charge of this portfolio since 1922. I consider Sir Jeremy one of the architects of the Allied victory. It was primarily this design that provided the manpower and goods worth hundreds of millions of pounds which brought the British their victory at El Alamein in North Africa.

Sir Jeremy confided to me he knew that unlike in World War I, when India voted £100 million as her gift towards the war expenses, the Central Legislative Assembly this time would not make any contribution. He, therefore, devised an ingenious plan under which he was not only able to get all that he wanted for the war effort but created such a powerful profit motive that even Gandhi-capped businessmen came forward to provide supplies. He achieved this by adopting the simple device under which Britain would not pay India for the goods and services in gold but in sterling and, what is more, the rupee reserve would be held in paper currency and not in metal. India, no doubt, built up a huge sterling balance but the country suffered considerable inflation. Insofar as Whitehall was concerned, it was convinced that a national government was not necessary to mobilise India for the war effort. The Americans, however, thought otherwise, the more so when Japan began to knock at India's gates.

Back in Lucknow in the summer of 1941, I found Governor's rule functioning effectively and the British bureaucracy confident that this time it would see the demise of the Congress. The civil disobedience movement did not excite much public interest and was at a low ebb by the end of the year. Life moved at a dull pace even as the Government stepped up its repressive measures. I had the arduous task of repeatedly coming to the rescue of the *National Herald* (founded by Jawaharlal Nehru) against repressive action. As President of the U.P. Press Consultative Committee, I maintained that the comments objected to did not amount to a breach of the Defence of India Rules, nor of the code adopted by the All–India Newspaper Editors' Conference. After I left Lucknow the paper closed down for over a year and most of its meagre editorial staff was absorbed by the *Hindustan Times*. This gesture somewhat mollified Nehru, who was bitter against Devadas Gandhi for refusing to help the *Herald* out when it fell short of newsprint and for treating it as a rival. When I mentioned this incident to Mahatma Gandhi in Delhi after I joined the *Hindustan Times*, he remarked: "Devadas is a finished diplomat."

An event at the end of April gains significance in the light of later developments. I had watched Indira Gandhi attend the yearly sessions of the Congress and recalled seeing her for the first time as a little girl at an A.I.C.C. meeting seated on the lap of her grandfather. She looked so frail and sickly that I felt sorry for Jawaharlal that his only child did not have a more robust constitution.

She first attracted public attention in her own right when she addressed the Lucknow Students' Federation on 29th April, 1941, in Ganga Prasad Memorial Hall. What she said haltingly was not important, for she merely wanted Indian students to follow the example of those of Spain and China, an echo of her father's ideas. But whoever drafted the Federation's address to her was politically inspired. It stated: "Having lived in the very storm centre, you must have noted the duel between the old and the new and seen that revolution is a more grim affair than many of us in this country realise. If you can utilise the experience in decisions that you will be called upon to make in this country, you will be a worthy political heir to your illustrious father." (She took a long time to arrive politically, but the speech writer planted a seed which flowered twenty-five years later.)

Chapter 2

THE CRIPPS MISSION

Although the Viceroy and the bureaucracy were satisfied that India was putting in the maximum war effort, Whitehall, concerned about American criticism, authorised Linlithgow to enlarge his Executive Council in a bid to win popular support. Eight Indians and four Britons were appointed to the new Council, the "natives" outnumbering the whites for the first time. But the gesture was lost when Churchill dashed all the hopes roused by the Atlantic Charter with his statement in the Commons that the Charter did not apply to India. Nationalist India reacted angrily and Gandhi firmly refused to approve an earlier proposal by a section of the Congress leaders, who had come out of jail at the end of their term, that they should resume ministerial responsibility. Gandhi told me he opposed the move any way because of his fear that Congressmen would get enmeshed in the power and corruption rackets which had sprung up round war supplies, especially when no political gain would accrue in the existing conditions.

The Japanese attack on Pearl Harbour on 6th December, 1941, brought the U.S. into the war and quickened the pace of political developments. New Delhi suddenly became a focal point for the war effort in Asia and *The Statesman* decided to shift me to the capital. Even though the Congress leaders were in jail and the political scene dull, I felt a wrench, for I had developed abiding friendship with leading politicians and Civil Servants in Lucknow. Among the public figures were Pant, Rafi Ahmed Kidwai, Kailash Nath Katju, Mrs. Pandit, Lal Bahadur Shastri, Mahavir Tyagi, Ajit Prasad Jain and Keshodev Malaviya, all of whom (except Mrs. Pandit, who took up a diplomatic career) later played an important role as Ministers in the Nehru Cabinet. What equally paid me deferred dividends was the rapport I established with civilians then on the middle rungs of the ladder. They too filled top roles in the Union Government after independence. Wajahat Hussain became Deputy Governor of the Reserve Bank of India, Vishnu Sahay Cabinet Secretary, Bhola Nath Jha Secretary, Ministry of Home

Affairs, C. S. Venkatachar Secretary to the President, Shankar Prasad Secretary for Kashmir Affairs, Bhagwan Sahay Ambassador in Nepal and later Governor of Jammu and Kashmir, S. Ranganathan Comptroller and Auditor General of India and V. Vishwanathan Governor of Kerala.

By the beginning of 1942, I was posted to Delhi permanently as *The Statesman's* first Indian representative at the Centre with the status of a Senior Assistant Editor. In addition, I also functioned as the Special Representative of the *Times of India* (whose own correspondent had been drafted for war duty) and wrote editorials for both papers on topics of interest concerning the Government of India, besides providing news and features. My return to the capital was professionally timely and a few days later Chiang Kai-shek and his wife visited India in February to urge the Indian leaders to support the war effort against Japan. They met Gandhi in Calcutta and at the end of the visit Chiang issued a statement supporting the Indian demand for independence. (I well remember the furore caused when Chiang's statement came through. It was not released for broadcast until the Viceroy had been sounded and had agreed to allow its publication.) Madame Chiang, whom I met in Delhi, assured me that the Americans were fully behind the Indian demand and that their visit would strengthen the hands of President Roosevelt in putting pressure on Churchill to change his attitude on India. She added that Lord Halifax was exerting pressure from Washington and that Churchill would have to yield.

Not long after the Japanese entered Singapore and Rangoon had fallen, the British Government decided to send the Cripps Mission to India, thereby rousing great expectations. Roosevelt wanted to make sure that the mission was handled properly and therefore sent his personal envoy, Col. Louis Johnson, to Delhi in April 1942. The Cripps proposals envisaged setting up a constitution-making body at the end of the war and the creation of a new Indian Union as a dominion. Provision was to be made for the participation of the Indian States and the constitution so framed was to be accepted by Britain subject to a treaty for the protection of racial and religions minorities and subject also to the right of any province to stay out of the Union. Britain, meanwhile, was to retain control and direction of the defence of India as part of their world war effort "but the task of organising the full military, moral and material resources of India" was to be "the responsibility of the Government of India with the co-operation of the peoples of India."

Cripps believed that his personal relations with Nehru would help him win the approval of the Congress Working Committee for his

plan. He was reinforced in this faith by the powerful support given
to his proposals by Rajagopalachari. But Gandhi told me that the
Cripps proposals had all the bad points of the federation plan of the
1935 Reforms Act and had further introduced the evil principle
of partition of India to be decided by people chosen on a very
limited franchise. He had told Cripps that his proposals at best
offered "an undated cheque on a crashing bank" and was leaving
all power in the hands of the Viceroy and the India Office to govern
India while the war lasted. One day, soon after the Congress Working
Committee had dispersed after meeting at Birla House, I broke in
on confabulations between Gandhi, Patel and Azad. I asked them
whether they had drafted their resolution on the proposals. Patel
replied: "We are waiting for our Englishman to finalise it." Gandhi
laughed, and Azad added: "Han, bhai" (this is so, brother).

Gandhi left Delhi in disgust before the resolution was passed.
He held the view that if the Japanese invasion was to be met the
British must immediately transfer power so that an Indian government could take command of the instruments of administration,
attune them to its purpose and direct the masses how to conduct
themselves. I gathered that Gandhi expected the Japanese to land
in India and he did not wish the British to leave a vacuum which the
invader would fill with a puppet regime.

Besides Gandhi's opposition, the reason for Cripps's failure was
Churchill's refusal to back the assurance he had given Azad that
the Viceroy's Executive Council would function as a Cabinet and
that the defence portfolio would be entrusted to an Indian. Wavell,
then Commander-in-Chief, according to some insiders, was agreeable to this arrangement.

Johnson was functioning behind the scenes and an accidental
scoop on a secret meeting between him and Nehru enabled me to
get the low-down on his role. I was in touch with Johnson and
keeping a track of his movements. Turning up at his residence one
day, I sensed excitement among the chauffeurs clustered about the
house. I soon learnt that Nehru was closeted with Johnson. To watch
Nehru depart from a vantage point and to run a story about the
mysterious parleys was just routine. I had not bargained, however,
for the sensation it would cause.

Linlithgow took offence at Johnson's diplomatic *faux pas*. Johnson
himself, when I called on him after these developments, was impeni-
tent. The handshake he greeted me with almost crushed my fingers
—he was powerfully built—but it was one of the warmest I remember. "You are a guy after my own heart," he exclaimed, adding
that his doors were open to me at all times. As rewarding were

certain confidences he shared with me about the pressure he had put on Sir Stafford and also on London through his cables to Roosevelt on how the deadlock over the defence portfolio could be easily resolved, if only Churchill would relent.

The situation on the war fronts was now becoming increasingly desperate. Japanese warships appeared in the Bay of Bengal. The Government, fearing an invasion was impending, destroyed installations in Madras harbour and took other measures in pursuance of its "scorched earth" policy. The British Parliament had already passed an Act providing that in the event of a complete breakdown of communications with Britain the Viceroy would exercise the powers of the Secretary of State. The Congress High Command was advised by the Madras Congress Committee to authorise it to function in the name of the party in case of a breakdown in communication.

Rajagopalachari and Kamaraj toured Madras and Mira Behn went to Orissa to urge the people to keep calm and refuse to cooperate with the invader. The Madras leaders were of the opinion that the British power should be replaced by the Congress organisation so that when the Japanese landed they would find a national government functioning. The Congress members of the Madras legislature, led by C.R., passed a resolution recommending that the League's claim for separation be accepted and negotiations with it for a national government started. The Andhra Pradesh Committee passed a resolution opposing the stand taken by the Madras legislators. Within a week, the A.I.C.C. met at Allahabad and discountenanced the Madras resolution by a large majority. Instead, it passed one of its own, emphasising the unity of India and calling for non-cooperation with and non-violent resistance to the invader. Rajagopalachari, thus disowned, soon resigned from the Congress. By this time, however, the danger of a Japanese invasion receded and the perspective considerably altered.

Chapter 3

DO OR DIE

The failure of the Cripps Mission, curious as it might seem, did not gladden the hearts of the Tory diehards. Relief that no interim national government was possible in India was temporary, and was quickly swamped by the conviction that this "jewel of the British Empire" was lost. Striking evidence of the feeling then prevalent in the ruling circle in Britain is afforded by a note in the diary of King George VI recorded after one of his Tuesday luncheons with Churchill in July 1942:

> "He amazed me by saying that his colleagues and both, or all three, parties in Parliament were quite prepared to give up India to the Indians after the war. He felt they had already been talked into giving up India. Cripps, the Press and U.S. public opinion have all contributed to make their minds up that our rule in India is wrong, and has always been wrong for India. I disagree and have always said India has got to be governed, and this will have to be our policy." (From *King George VI—His Life and Reign*, by John W. Wheeler-Bennett.)

True, both Churchill and the authorities in India held firmly to the belief that the war effort would be gravely impeded were popular governments to be established in the country. But they had to reckon with increasing pressure from Roosevelt. William Phillips, who had succeeded Johnson as the President's personal representative in Delhi, was a suave diplomat, but his reports to Washington on the Indian situation were forthright. During our frequent tête-à-têtes, Phillips confided to me that few Americans believed that adequate mass support could be mobilised in India for the Allied cause in the absence of a popular government. American opinion was particularly exercised over the grim prospect of a Japanese invasion of India and the possible need to organise a resistance movement.

The deadlock in India, however, persisted. The India Office and the Viceroy were now agreed on building up Jinnah as their Crescent Card to neutralise the Congress challenge. This was manifest from Sikander Hayat Khan's disclosure to me that the Viceroy, on instructions from the Secretary of State, had enjoined upon him and Fazlul Haque not to undermine Jinnah's position as "leader of the Muslim community." This happened towards the end of 1939, when Jinnah had taken up an uncompromising attitude and the Muslim Premiers of Punjab and Bengal were under pressure from some of their followers "to disown Jinnah or cut him down to size."

The political situation was clearly developing into a triangular contest. The Congress still laboured under the sincere belief that it could cope with Jinnah's intransigence if it succeeded in striking a deal with the British. The Cripps proposals had conceded the principle of partition and Gandhi therefore left Delhi in a fit of disgust. The Congress Working Committee adopted a resolution expressing regret that the proposals "gravely imperil the development of a free and united national government and the establishment of a democratic state."

"Nevertheless," the resolution went on to say, "the Committee cannot think in terms of compelling the people of any territorial unit to remain in the Indian Union against their declared and established will." This resolution, drafted by Nehru, ironically, introduced the novel principle of yielding to the provinces the right not to accede to the federation if they so chose.

Jinnah exultingly told me that he had won his battle, for he considered this a surrender to the concept of partition. (The validity of his contention was borne out by a statement issued from 10 Downing Street on 6th December, 1946, at the end of talks with Nehru, Jinnah, Liaquat Ali and Baldev Singh. The statement concluded as follows: "Should a Constitution be framed by a constituent assembly in which a large section of the Indian population had not been represented, His Majesty's Government could not contemplate—as the Congress have stated they would not contemplate—forcing such a Constitution upon any unwilling parts of the country.")

Kripalani, confronted with this interpretation, denied that the principle of partition had been conceded. The sentence relating to secession, it was explained, was a concession to men like Asaf Ali who had suggested that the committee should endorse the principle of self-determination. Had that been done, according to Kripalani, any village could have asked for independence.

The League executive almost simultaneously passed a resolution expressing "gratification that the possibility of Pakistan is recognised by implication by providing for the establishment of two or more unions in India" and rejecting the Cripps proposals for the reason that they were not open to modification.

Reluctant to alienate American sympathy, however, the Congress adopted another resolution on 14th July, 1942, stating that it would "change the present ill-will against Britain into goodwill and make India a willing partner in a joint enterprise of securing freedom for the nations and people of the world" and that this was only possible "if India feels the glow of freedom." It added: "The Congress is, therefore, agreeable to the stationing of the armed forces of the Allies in India, should they so desire, in order to ward off and resist Japanese or other aggression and to protect and help China."

Britain having spurned this significant gesture, the Congress chiefs persuaded Gandhi to resume active leadership of the party and give a call to the people in the manner he alone could. It was thus that the Congress embarked on the Quit India campaign on 8th August, 1942. Meeting in Bombay on that day, the A.I.C.C. adopted a resolution authorising Gandhi to lead a mass struggle on non-violent lines on the widest possible scale "so that the country might utilise all the non-violent strength it had gathered during the last twenty-two years of peaceful struggle" in the fight for liberation. Gandhi, addressing the gathering, called it open rebellion— the "do or die" struggle to compel the British to depart.

Linlithgow's Government had anticipated the move and had made its plan to deal with it a couple of months in advance. In a resolute bid to nip the rebellion in the bud, it arrested Gandhi and all the other leaders on the morning of 9th August and incarcerated them in Ahmednagar Fort in Bombay Presidency. The Congress organisation was outlawed throughout British India.

Bereft of effective leadership, the agitation was carried on by underground workers and quickly turned into a chaotic battle with authority. The eruption into the ranks of the non-violent freedom fighters of extremists and terrorists on one hand and anti-social elements on the other led to alarming disturbances all over the country. Communications were disrupted, much public property was destroyed indiscriminately and the war effort was impeded considerably. The situation in Bihar and the eastern regions of the U.P. was particularly grim. Communications with Bengal and Assam were paralysed and the supply of war material to the forces defending India on the Burma border was placed in great jeopardy.

The Quit India movement then degenerated into an ill-organised mass upheaval, lit up as much by acts of surprising individual ingenuity and heroism as by crude outbursts of incendiarism and looting. Anti-social elements and the Communists indulged in violence and destruction. Among the many who went underground was Yashwantrao Chavan, who later became Chief Minister of his State, Maharashtra entered the Union Cabinet in 1962 as Defence Minister and thereafter became Home Minister. Another was Aruna Asaf Ali, who once took shelter with a tenant in my house. (After independence, she became the first woman Mayor of Delhi and won the Lenin Peace Prize.)

But the back of the struggle had been broken by the end of September. The Raj, employing all the instruments of suppression at its command, had imposed on the country, a sullen, frustrated quiet.

The political stalemate induced by the arrest and imprisonment of the Congress leaders and the ruthless quelling of the revolt was marked, however, by feverish activity at the India Office in London, where a cell had been set up to work on a new formula for the future governance of the country. Sir Reginald Coupland, a professor of Oxford University who had spent the winter of 1941-42 in India and was attached to the Cripps Mission as an unofficial adviser, had come out with a report which contained a memorandum prepared by an "expert" showing that Pakistan was financially viable.

The Coupland plan was an ingenious amalgam of various other schemes then in the air. It sought to resolve the problem by dividing the country into four broad geographical regions: the Indus basin, the Gangetic basin, the delta of the Brahmaputra, and the Deccan. Two of these regions would have a Muslim majority, and the Hindus would predominate in the other two, and this would result in a balance of power at the Centre. For the princely States, he suggested either a single separate dominion or several dominions where viable units were feasible. It is interesting to note that Coupland wanted a statutory guarantee for the continuance of the work of the Christian missions in the hill tracts of Assam. (This lends weight to the suspicion that the present-day movement for independence among a section of the Nagas and Mizos on the Assam borders is inspired by missionaries.)

The pressure of the war and of political happenings in the country, however, thrust the Coupland plan into the background. But Jinnah seemed to go from strength to strength. Back from a League session in April 1943, glowing with pride, he told me that now indeed his claim that the League was the sole representative of the Muslims in India had been vindicated, for three Muslim-majority provinces were being governed by League Ministries. I asked Jinnah why he had not responded to Gandhi's request for a definition of his demands. His reply was illuminating. "You see, Congressmen are dying to get back to power. My men are in power. It is for Congressmen therefore to state what they are prepared to concede. The ball is in their court. I am in the happy position of being able to extract the best terms, as they want power and the British do not want to part with it." Jinnah's parting shot was almost prophetic: "You can depend on Rajagopalachari to use his sharp wits to define Pakistan for me."

Wavell took over as Viceroy in October 1943. This change, Phillips confided to me, had been hastened by Roosevelt's advice to London that Linlithgow should be replaced by someone who could handle the Indian constitutional deadlock with greater imagination. A week before his departure, Linlithgow provided me in an interview with an insight into his thinking. With apparent sincerity he expressed the belief that India could not hope to become free for another fifty years. This country, he declared blandly, was new to parliamentary institutions and would require a large leavening of British officials and Europeans to ensure their successful functioning. With the advent of air-conditioning, it was now possible for Britons to settle down in India permanently in areas like Dehra Dun, and when there were some six million of them to buttress a democratic administration India might expect to make substantial progress towards self-government.

Soon after Wavell's assumption of office, the League decided to establish a Committee of Action to combat a unitary constitution. This was intended to intimidate the Viceroy who, it was said, had arrived with a new mandate from Whitehall. Ignoring the threat, Wavell proclaimed in his address to a joint session of the Central Legislature on 17th February, 1944, that India was a "natural unit."

Wavell made an auspicious start. Early in February 1944, he toured vast areas of Bengal ravaged by one of the most devastating famines of the century during the closing months of his predecessor's regime. He also ordered the release of Gandhi on medical grounds and received from him a letter offering withdrawal of civil disobedience and full co-operation in the war effort should a declaration of Indian independence be forthcoming. The steady Japanese advance was underlining the need for an immediate ending of the political deadlock.

Nothing came of this bold overture. Yet, though only a few were conscious of it, freedom was "round the corner."

Chapter 4

OVER TO THE *HINDUSTAN TIMES*

My six-year association with the British-owned *Statesman* had been as pleasant as it had been rewarding. But always in the secret recesses of my heart I had nursed the ambition to edit a nationalist newspaper. This was fulfilled when I accepted the post of Joint Editor of the *Hindustan Times* of Delhi on 1st April, 1944. It was not without a pang of regret that I bade farewell to *The Statesman*, which had provided me with six years of exhilarating journalistic activity. But I had not been wholly happy after Moore had relinquished the editorship of that paper. He belonged to that genre of great editors the like of whom are hard to find today. There were occasions when he acted inexplicably and perversely, but by and large he displayed a remarkable sympathy for Indian aspirations.

Ian Stephens, who succeeded Moore, was cast in a different mould. He was courteous and considerate in conversation, but his face often betrayed his inner annoyance and fretfulness. Economy in the use of words was Stephen's besetting passion. Not infrequently, he rubbed his colleagues up the wrong way by rewriting what others had produced in conformity with his own particular style and way of thinking. His approach to Indian politics was very different from Moore's. When I joined the *Hindustan Times*, Prem Bhatia took over from me on behalf of *The Statesman* and Frank Moraes as the special representative of the *Times of India* in New Delhi. It was pleasing to know that both papers would be represented by Indians, an implicit acknowledgment by the British owners of these publications that Indian talent was now competent enough to handle assignments hitherto the exclusive privilege of Britons.

The financial control of the *Hindustan Times* had passed into the hands of G. D. Birla, one of the most enterprising Indian industrialists; Devadas Gandhi, the youngest son of the Mahatma and son-in-law of C. Rajagopalachari, was its Managing Editor. Politically, its heyday was the period when Pothan Joseph regaled the ruling hierarchy and the intelligentsia with his wit and subtle daily commentary, *Over a Cup of Tea*. The editorials made little impact, but Shankar, one of India's top political cartoonists, produced "seditious" cartoons. He not only got away with them because of the Briton's healthy respect for cartoonists' fancies but many of the targets of attack, especially James Grigg, bought the originals. Linlithgow indeed helped him to visit England on a study tour to improve his technique. The paper's editorial staff consisted of seven persons whose total emoluments did not even add up to the salary of the Editor of the *Statesman*. The daily had tided over its lean period and was by now firmly established, but the Managing Director's mandate to me was to make the *Hindustan Times* hold its own against the British-owned *Times of India* and *The Statesman*.

Thus began a sixteen-year association with a newspaper that was to reach a position of pre-eminence not only in Delhi but all over North India. The pleasurable part of this experience was the close understanding and the spirit of comradeship with Devadas Gandhi. As Managing Editor, he brought to the handling of the affairs of the paper a penny-pinching astuteness and a flair for administration. I enjoyed a large degree of freedom in editorial matters and he rarely turned down my proposals regarding new offices, employment of staff and promotions and transfers. Until death snatched him away in 1957, Devadas worked zealously to strengthen the institution.

I began to pursue political developments with redoubled enthusiasm in my new assignment. Jinnah was hostile to the *Hindustan Times* and would not admit its representatives to his Press briefings. The ban, happily, became inoperative after I joined the paper because of the cordiality of our relations. Jinnah was now riding the high horse, and not without reason. Events seemed to be shaping exactly as he wanted. Early in April 1944, Rajagopalachari embarked on negotiations with him on the basis of a formula for which he said he had secured the general support of Gandhi, who was confined in the Aga Khan's palace, an isolated and old-fashioned mansion which lay in disuse at Poona, after his arrest in Bombay in August 1942. The formula was a subtle attempt to reduce the League's Lahore resolution to concrete and intelligible terms.

Jinnah had not been wrong in expecting C.R. to perform this useful job for him. But he would not foreclose on the deal despite the assurance that it had received Gandhi's blessings. He argued that C.R. lacked the credentials to speak on behalf of the Congress. Gandhi was released unconditionally on 6th May, 1944. In a Press interview, Gandhi said in July that what he asked at that time was different from what he wanted in 1942. He would now be satisfied with nothing less than a national government in full control of the civil administration. Such a government would be composed of persons chosen by the elected members of the Central Assembly. This would mean a declaration of independence, qualified by the fact that a war was on. He said: "The national government will let the military have the facilities they require. But the control will be that of the national government. Ordinance rule would give place to normal administration by the national government."

Asked whether the Viceroy would continue in this set-up, Gandhi replied: "Yes, but he will be like the King, guided by responsible ministers. Popular government will be restored in all the provinces so that both the provincial and Central Governments will be responsible to the people of India. So far as military operations are concerned, the Viceroy and the Commander-in-Chief will have complete control. . . . The Allied forces would be allowed to carry on their operations on Indian soil. I realise that they cannot defeat Japan without that."

A couple of days after this interview was published, I wrote in the *Hindustan Times* a piece entitled: "Conspiracy Between British Diehards and Jinnah." This was based on a talk with a top Briton who said to me: "Mr. Jinnah will never come to an agreement during the war. While he is intransigent, he is on top; the moment he settles with the Congress, the latter will be on top. Once he agrees to a transitional arrangement, the League will get merged in the nationalist movement and will never be able to dictate terms to the Congress. Mr. Jinnah's intransigence suits us, and if he maintains his attitude and keeps his hands off the Punjab, which is our special preserve, he will deserve some support at the end of the war."

Despairing of getting justice from Britain and its representatives in New Delhi, the Indian leaders now pinned their hopes on Roosevelt exerting pressure on Churchill to meet their demands. In the middle of 1944, a confidential report on India submitted by William Phillips to Roosevelt created a big stir in New Delhi, London and Washington. Parts of the report were published in the American Press by Drew Pearson though authentic versions of it were not available in India. Phillips pointed out that the Indian people were at war only in a legal sense, as they had no say in their own government and cynically regarded the fighting as a clash between fascism and imperialism, between which there was nothing to choose. It also said that the Chinese, who regarded the Anglo–American bloc with distrust, might feel differently if India was liberated.

Roosevelt had brought about two meetings between Churchill and his special envoy before the report was published, but they had proved unfruitful. Phillips left India a disappointed man and was appointed political adviser to General Eisenhower, supreme head of the Allied forces in Europe. When Phillips's findings found their way into print, the British Government was vastly annoyed and made that known to Washington. Thereupon, a member of the U.S. House of Representatives moved that Sir Ronald Campbell and Sir Girja Shankar Bajpai, who had been sent to Washington to "mould" public opinion to accept the British point of view on Indian independence, be in turn declared unacceptable to the U.S. Administration and asked to quit the country.

While Gandhi's attention was concentrated on countering the anti-Indian propaganda in the U.S., Devadas and I decided to run a column in the *Hindustan Times* exposing this vicious campaign. The U.S. President's Special Representative in New Delhi told us he would see that the contents of this column were brought to the notice of Washington and other centres interested in the question of India's freedom. The column was titled "I accuse" and Devadas suggested that I write it under the pen-name Insaf, inspired by Mahatma Gandhi's definition of Ram Raj as Insaf Raj. These articles identified and exposed the outfit that was providing a cloak for the official propaganda machine, accused the Government of India of misrepresenting this country in the Soviet Union, China and the Middle East and of spending Indian money abroad to popularise British rule.

We next ran a series of four articles in February on the "British Propaganda Racket in the U.S." which were attributed to a special correspondent. The material for this series came from friendly American sources.

One of the most telling ripostes to the British propaganda was delivered at a time when Churchill was in Washington for one of his frequent consultations with Roosevelt. Some Indians and their American sympathisers booked a full-page advertisement in the *Washington Post*. Churchill was breakfasting with his host at the White House when the *Post* was brought in. Roosevelt was unaware that the paper contained the ad, which had been prepared by Syud Hussain, Chairman of the Committee for Indian Freedom, and was a biting indictment of British rule in India. He passed the paper to Churchill, who opened it and saw the ad, captioned "What About India?" Churchill threw the paper down angrily. On learning the cause of his ire, Roosevelt calmly observed that the ad had obviously been paid for, and buying newspaper space for propaganda purposes was not unusual in the U.S.

While Indian politicians were pinning hopes on intervention by the U.S. President, C.R. convinced Gandhi that he should take up the threads of the negotiations with Jinnah where C.R. had left them. The Gandhi–Jinnah talks in Bombay in September lasted well over a fortnight, but the two parted as distant as ever. Jinnah poured scorn on Gandhi's formula, which envisaged an all-India central authority. "What I am being offered is a truncated and moth-eaten Pakistan," he exclaimed indignantly.

When I met Gandhi in Bombay, he emphatically denied he had countenanced the vivisection of India. Jinnah, on the contrary, was jubilant when I saw him in Delhi soon after the luckless parleys. "You see, Gandhi has defined Pakistan for me," he said. "Gandhi asked me whether it would be a state whose policy on defence and external affairs could be in conflict with India's. I had only to answer 'yes'."

As the effort to bring about a communal rapprochement dragged on wearily, Jinnah's intransigence seemed to acquire a sharper edge. In November, a non-party conference organised by Sapru set up a standing committee to examine the communal and minorities questions. Jinnah disdainfully refused to recognise it; he would not unbend even to meet Sapru.

Chapter 5

PAKISTAN ON A PLATTER

Bhulabhai Desai approached the Viceroy on 20th January, 1945, in an effort to break the political deadlock. He suggested complete Indianisation of the Executive Council, giving the Congress and the League groups in the Central Assembly forty per cent each of the seats in the Council and the remaining twenty per cent to the minorities. Desai put forward this proposal with the assurance that Liaquat Ali and he had agreed to it and that it had Gandhi's approval. This was a bold move to end the Congress–League wrangle, and Wavell welcomed it as an opportunity to play his desired role as a conciliator. He had been looking for such an opening since his conference with the provincial Governors in August 1944, when it was felt that a positive move was essential to redeem the British Government's promises to India. But Jinnah upset the apple cart by stating in February that he had no knowledge of the pact between Desai and Liaquat Ali.

Meanwhile, the political landscape underwent a change with the Congress assuming power in the North-West Frontier Province, the formation of a Congress–League coalition in Assam and the imposition of Governor's rule in Bengal as no stable ministry could be formed in that communally strife-ridden province. In the Central Assembly the Congress inflicted a series of defeats on the Government, partly with the help of the League, whose main spokesman was Liaquat Ali.

In an imaginative and statesmanlike move to lift the clouds darkening the political horizon, Wavell proceeded to London on 23rd March for consultations with Whitehall. He returned on 4th June and made his fateful announcement ten days later on reconstituting his Executive Council.

Unfortunately, two developments almost checkmated the Desai–Liaquat initiative. Nehru, Patel and the other Congress leaders, fretting impatiently in Ahmednagar fort, where they were detained, as they watched the turn of events in distant New Delhi, got the impression that Desai was keen on levering himself into the Executive Council and seeing that its first act after its reconstitution was to announce the release of political prisoners. They also felt that the pact tacitly endorsed the two-nation theory of Jinnah, which was anathema to them.

Unaccustomed to the subtleties of the political game, Wavell was misled into converting the formula of equal representation for the Congress and the League into an equation between the caste Hindus and the Muslims. His statement of 14th June said "It is proposed that the Executive Council should be reconstituted and that the Viceroy should in future make his selection for nomination to the Crown for appointment to his Executive from amongst leaders of Indian political life at the Centre and in the provinces, in a proportion which would give a balanced representation of the main communities, including an equal proportion of Muslims and caste Hindus."

The very next day, to create the right climate for the impending talks on the new formula, he ordered the release of the Congress leaders in detention. But no sooner had Wavell made his announcement on the Executive Council than Gandhi disowned it, saying he had never thought in terms of equating the caste Hindus and the Muslims when he blessed the Desai–Liaquat pact.

The Wavell proposals represented, however, a considerable advance on the road to self-rule, and the Working Committee decided to join the conference the Viceroy had summoned. Patel was, however, so incensed at what he regarded as Desai's manoeuvres that he insisted on writing him off as a political liability, and that meant the eclipse of the Leader of the Congress Party in the Central Assembly.

Another incident also weighed against Desai. Rajkumari Amrit Kaur had reported to Gandhi that she had seen Desai drunk at a party. Mahadev Desai, Gandhi's secretary, wrote to Bhulabhai at Gandhi's instance inquiring whether he drank. Bhulabhai did not reply. Gandhi mentioned the Rajkumari's charge in the Working Committee, which was considering the panel of Congress names for the Executive Council. He next turned to Azad and asked him pointedly whether he drank. The flustered Maulana falteringly confessed that he used to. When did he give it up? Before he could answer, Nehru intervened and said: "I took sherry last evening. Why pursue this matter?" Gandhi kept silent, but Desai's goose was cooked.

The Simla Conference opened on 25th June, a day after Wavell met and talked with Gandhi, Jinnah and Azad separately. In these talks, the caste complexion of Hindu representation in the Executive Council was removed and it was agreed that the composite Central Cabinet would comprise fourteen Indian Councillors, five each to be selected by the Congress and the League and four viceregal nominees. Among the last group would be a Sikh, two Harijans and Sir Khizr Hayat Khan, leader of the Unionist Party of the Punjab.

The Congress proposed at the conference that its panel consist of two Hindus, a Muslim, a Christian and a Parsee. As the League had already been accorded parity with the Congress, this should have pleased Jinnah. Further, the fact that seven of the fourteen Councillors would be Muslims should have won him over completely. The League Council favoured acceptance of the Wavell plan, and the Congress Working Committee got down to the task of preparing a panel of names for the Viceroy's approval.

But on 11th July, to the amazement and disappointment of all who had set great store by these proposals to end the political deadlock, Wavell announced that his private confabulations with Jinnah had failed. Three days later, the world was told that the conference had foundered on the rock of Jinnah's insistence that all the Muslim Councillors be nominated exclusively by the League. This was a condition the Congress would under no circumstances accept, for it would have reduced it to the status of a body representing only the Hindus and the smaller minorities while subscribing to Jinnah's claim that the League was the sole spokesman of the Muslims.

Why, in the hour of the League's triumph, having won parity

with the Congress, should Jinnah have dragged it back from the threshold of power? On the face of it, his recalcitrance seemed pointless. But his real aim was known to a few insiders. He was expected to announce his final decision on the Viceroy's proposals to the Press at his hotel lounge. A few moments earlier, he had, however, received a message from the "cell" of British Civil Servants in Simla, which was in tune with the diehards in London that if Jinnah stepped out of the talks he would be rewarded with Pakistan.

As Jinnah emerged from his meeting with the Press and entered the lift to go upstairs to his suite, I joined him. I asked him why he had spurned the Wavell plan when he had won his point of parity for the League with the Congress. His reply stunned me for a moment: "Am I a fool to accept this when I am offered Pakistan on a platter?" After painstaking inquiries, I learned from high official and political sources that a member of the Viceroy's Executive Council had sent a secret message to Jinnah through the League contacts he had formed.

While I could not quote Jinnah's off-the-record remark, I made it the background for my story on his Press conference. I said Wavell had asked the Congress leaders whether they would back his plan even if the League decided not to co-operate. The Congress had given that assurance. When Wavell announced the failure of the parleys, I posed the questions: Is the rumour that Whitehall does not want the Viceroy to antagonise Jinnah after all correct? Did the Viceroy receive instructions from above or did he yield to the pressure of certain Civil Servants?

Gandhi did not participate directly in the Simla conference but stayed in the background as "adviser" to those who did. I met him several times, and he told me that the most unfortunate aspect of C.R.'s parleys with Jinnah and Desai's with Liaquat Ali to bring about a Congress–League entente was that they had either misunderstood or misrepresented his approach to the issue. When Desai had approached him with the formula providing for equal Congress–League representation in the proposed interim government, he had readily agreed, but this provision had been distorted in Wavell's proposals.

Again, he had blessed C.R.'s offer to Jinnah not because he accepted the two-nation theory nor because he recognised the League as the sole representative of the Muslims. On the contrary, it was precisely because he rejected both these proposals that he supported elections to a constituent assembly on the basis of adult franchise and separate electorates for the Muslims. He said: "I hold the view that we must accept the verdict of the Muslims so elected on whether they want independence for India as a whole or wish to live separately." Polls held on a narrow franchise would not meet the tests he had laid down.

It was unfortunate, he added, that most of his colleagues had come out of jail tired and dispirited and without the heart to carry on the struggle. They wanted a settlement with Britain and what is more, hungered for power. "I fear," he added, "they may throw to the winds the basic principles for which the Congress has stood. The Hindus are indivisible. India is indivisible. There can be no *Swaraj* without Hindu–Muslim unity. Jinnah objects to the expression Ram Raj, by which I mean not Hindu Raj but divine Raj, Insaf Raj, where justice will prevail between man and man. If God gives me strength, I will fight for these principles with my life."

Chapter 6

WAR CORRESPONDENT

With the victorious Allied forces driving up the Italian peninsula, Sir Claude Auchinleck, Commander-in-Chief of the Indian Army, planned a tour by a delegation of about a dozen editors to the war fronts in the Middle East and in Europe. Our itinerary took us through Iraq, Iran, Syria, Palestine, Egypt, North Africa and thence over to Italy. As most of the Indian soldiers were from the northern regions, the brunt of questioning and addressing them on behalf of the delegation fell on my shoulders.

Our first hair-raising brush with the reality of war came just beyond Florence. We spent a night under tents close to the battle-front. The German guns opened up that particular night. It was a nerve-shattering experience. But what lifted up one's spirits was the answering barrage that the Allied batteries put up—sixty shells to every one of the enemy's screaming overhead. Here was heartening proof of the massive offensive strength the Anglo–Americans had piled up on the Italian front. It was not an uneventful night, however, for a German shell tore into a Nissen hut a few hundred yards away from our tent, killing twenty-nine people.

For me, that was not the end of the adventure. On the way back to Rome, the man driving my jeep halted at a roadside pub and apparently imbibed more alcohol than was good for him. On the road, rendered slippery by rain, he soon lost control of the wheel and sent the jeep skidding into a tree. The vehicle was badly smashed. We were lucky, though, for I escaped unscathed save for the loss of my glasses, and the driver had only a minor leg injury.

At Basrah, on the way home, the Indian members of the delegation decided that an agreed report be published, the preparation of a draft being entrusted to me. So for several hours between Basrah and Karachi I tapped away at my typewriter and produced a bulky document running to some 10,000 words. On landing at Karachi, however, the Editor of *Dawn* backed out of the arrangement. Thus I could use the material exclusively in the columns of my paper but it had to run the gauntlet of censorship. Brigadier Desmond Young told me the censor was not agreeable to its release. It was political censorship, he said, there was not a word that could be objected to on grounds of security. I thereupon sought an interview with Auchinleck, and the Commander-in-Chief, to his credit, stuck to his pledge that political censorship would not be exercised and ordered the unconditional release of my impressions.

The articles created a sensation. I had painted a vivid picture of how Indian soldiers were being discriminated against on grounds of race and colour. What made matters worse was that was done notwithstanding their outstanding gallantry on the battlefield. In the course of our 14,000-mile tour of the fronts, we had met several top-ranking American and British commanders, all of whom said without exception that the Indian soldier was first-rate in every sphere of war activity.

Among the complaints I recorded in talks with Indian other ranks and officers with Viceroy's commissions was that they received no newspapers or magazines except the official *Fauji Akhbar* (Army News) from home although their British counterparts did so. They knew scarcely anything about happenings in India and their general opinion was: "We want home news, not war news, we want amusement, not lectures."

Other troops saw films daily, while they had this opportunity only once a week, and the Indian films they saw were very old. The cigarettes they got from army canteens were inferior to those supplied to British other ranks, and they were denied family allowances. The wheat flour they got as rations was old and infested with weevils, and the *chapatis* made from it were unpalatable.

They could understand being governed by Indian standards of living and pay when they were in India, but when on service overseas they felt they should get the same treatment as their British comrades in arms. We visited an American camp, and found living conditions that verged on the luxurious. A British camp was located in a picturesque setting, with a hill in the background. There were more billiard tables in this camp than I am sure there were in both Delhis at that time. The nearby Indian camp, on the other hand, had the appearance of a *sarai* (resting-place for travellers). The kitchen was dark and smoky, and the facilities in what was called the recreation room were pitifully meagre.

Asked about these disparities, an army welfare officer said that the Indian soldiers' demand for the same treatment as other Allied fighters was "unfair." He added unfeelingly: "They get here more amenities than in barracks in India. How many of them see films in India? How many read newspapers, magazines or books? How many smoke cigarettes?"

My revelations aroused considerable public feeling. T. T. Krishnamachari, who later became Finance Minister in the Nehru Cabinet, and B. Das, a veteran legislator from Orissa, tabled motions of adjournment of the Central Assembly to censure the Government on the Indian soldier's disabilities on the war fronts. After a high-spirited two-hour debate, the Opposition scored a notable victory and the censure motion was carried.

In the lobby of the Council of State, Auchinleck assured me that he was determined to set right the grievances of the Indian soldiers and officers to which I had drawn attention. He had already taken remedial measures for some of them; as for the rest, he had ordered a thorough inquiry. He was outspoken, however, about what was indispensable to the evolution of a truly national army. To promote unity and solidarity, all the troops must learn to conform to the standard army rations. They had taken one big step forward by fashioning Hindustani written in Roman script into the army's lingua franca: it now remained for them to adopt a common diet.

He pointed to one transformation the war had brought about; the Indian soldier had, regardless of religious sentiment, taken to the beret. I contended that the *jawan* at the front had adopted the beret to escape being discriminated against by the local population, who looked down on men sporting a turban. "Well," exclaimed Auchinleck, laughing, "whatever the provocation, the result has been good."

One of the most stimulating experiences I had as a war correspondent accredited to the American and British Army commands in Europe was a visit to the war-devastated areas made soon after the end of the war. It was a ghastly sight. Since the Allied commanders and public relations officials were in Wiesbaden, I made it my headquarters. I first tried to get an idea of the way the American mind was working because everyone realised that, having escaped destruction and geared her economy to massive production, the U.S. alone would have the strength to determine how Europe was to be rehabilitated.

When I asked what future was visualised for Germany, the American spokesman declared that the question was premature because they had first to denazify the German people, and that would take at least a decade. I was shown a number of books and pamphlets prepared to ensure denazification through schools and churches. I next sounded the spokesman of the British headquarters. I was told that it would be a generation before Germany could think of standing on her own feet. That was long enough for the Allied powers to make sure she would never threaten the peace of Europe or of the world again.

The spokesman of the French command was quite positive. The French, he said, would see to it that Germany did not become a power again. The Russian headquarters were very reticent on this question, and when I persisted all I could get out of the spokesman was that the question of Germany's military revival did not arise.

I was not satisfied with these answers for the reason that people with such skill, talent and strength of purpose as the Germans could not be disposed of so summarily. I persuaded the U.S. command to place at my disposal a jeep and an interpreter so that I could find the answer to my question from the Germans themselves. I used to go out daily eighty to 100 miles, visiting villages and small towns to see how the Germans lived after defeat. Once I drove over 200 miles and paid a visit to Nuremberg, where I saw a hall being prepared for the trial of the top Nazi war criminals, including Goering. A fortnight of wanderings revealed to me that, whereas the national and provincial political structure had broken down, life at the grassroots had been unaffected by the war. In fact, villages and small towns had been reinforced by the inflow of skilled workers and intellectuals in search of sustenance in return for the service they could perform.

In the bombed-out Mercedes-Benz plant for manufacturing motor vehicles I found workers labouring twelve hours a day in return for a slice of bread and two cups of tea. They were trying to see what could be salvaged from the wreckage and whether the plant could be restored as a repair or manufacturing unit. Even more significant was the fact that, although political authority had collapsed, the church organisation and basic social institutions were functioning normally. This made me feel that, given the necessary aid for rehabilitation from the U.S. Germany could rebuild herself rapidly. In the series of articles I wrote on war-devastated Europe I conveyed my impression that it would not take more than ten years for the country to recover. In retrospect, this proved correct.

Chapter 7

IN LONDON AGAIN

I was in London not long after Jinnah torpedoed the Wavell proposals. It was the day after the first atom bomb had flattened Hiroshima. A few days later came Japan's unconditional surrender and the end of World War II. It is difficult to describe the mighty whirlpool of emotions into which I found myself sucked as Londoners celebrated VJ-Day with fantastic abandon. My own preoccupation, however, was with the inexorable forces driving India willy-nilly towards freedom. On 26th July, less than three weeks before the Japanese capitulation, Labour had surprisingly worsted the Churchill Government at the polls and assumed office. Churchill had once declared that he had not become the first Minister of the Crown "to preside over the liquidation of the Empire." Happily for India, neither Attlee, the new Prime Minister, nor his Secretary of State for India, Lord Pethick-Lawrence, was committed to this diehard view.

I was staying with Dr. Katial and had a talk with William Whiteley, Chief Whip of the Labour Party in the Commons, at a quiet dinner in my host's apartment. Whiteley agreed to convey to Attlee our plea that Labour could win India's friendship permanently by transferring power immediately and making India a dominion. He suggested that, meanwhile, I should strengthen the Government's hands by putting forward these views in the *Daily Herald*, the Labour Party organ. Accordingly, I contributed an article to the *Herald* of 18th September and among other things urged that in India, as in Britain, the urgent tasks of reconstruction could be tackled "only by the leaders of the masses."

Wavell, summoned to London for discussions towards the end of August, had returned to Delhi and announced on 19th September plans for fresh elections to and for a constitution-making body. Hailing the announcement, the *Herald* commented editorially two

days later: "The key sentence in Lord Wavell's announcement—
and it was underlined by Mr. Attlee when, last night, he broadcast
from London—is that 'India has to play her full part in working
out the new world order'. India can never play her full part until
she is self-governing. . . . A prominent journalistic supporter of the
Congress Party—Mr. Durga Das, Joint Editor of the *Hindustan
Times*—wrote in this paper a few days ago that the day when Labour
was elected to power in Britain was regarded as a V-Day by
Indians. . . . The Labour Government shows itself eager to break
the deadlock which has for so long paralysed Anglo–Indian relations.
It proposes, as soon as the forthcoming elections in India have taken
place, that the Viceroy should seek discussions with representatives
of the new provincial legislatures and of the Indian States, aimed at
establishing a constituent assembly to frame a new constitution. The
Indian representatives will be invited to decide whether they wish to
achieve self-government according to the procedure of the 'Cripps
offer' of 1942 or by some alternative procedure."

Whiteley next arranged for me to meet Attlee for a quiet, informal
talk. Attlee greeted me warmly with the remark: "It is good you
are here, you know the pulse of your politicians." For a minute I
realised it was a different Attlee from the one I knew. Dressed in a
blue suit, he exuded confidence and soon proceeded to give me the
background to the Wavell announcement. On his visit to London,
Wavell, he said, had told him that there were two alternatives
confronting Britain—one, to hold India down by force, for which
purpose he would require thousands of additional British troops, and
the other to pass on the responsibility for government to the representatives of the people. Attlee added that he, for his part, was clear
in his mind that Britain must quit; he firmly believed too that the
transfer of power must not be made conditional on India's remaining
a Dominion of the British Commonwealth. In this matter, he would
leave the decision entirely to the Indians themselves—as envisaged
in setting up a Constituent Assembly.

Attlee did not conceal his deep agitation over the Muslim demand
for Pakistan and agreed with my plea that a minority should not be
allowed to hold up the progress of the majority to self-rule. At the
same time, he frankly contended it was as impossible for the
British to help the majority put down a revolt on the part of the
minority as for it to hold India down by the force of arms. He added
that his intention was to promote in India a structure that would
give her federal unity. Should he be baulked in this attempt, he
would rather transfer power to the provinces and let the Indians
sort out their difficulties among themselves.

He then returned to the theme he had twice earlier propounded to me—that the American presidential system would be more suitable to Indian conditions than British parliamentary democracy. The Constituent Assembly to be set up to formulate a blueprint for the future governance of India, should he felt give serious thought to granting a fixed tenure to the executive, particularly at the Centre. (In the sixties, when Attlee, now an Earl, visited India to deliver the Azad Memorial Lectures, I harked back to this argument. Did he still cling to his preference for the American system for India? The doyen of the Labour Party met the question squarely. The Indians, he admitted, had shown a remarkable democratic temper in conducting elections and forming majority administrations. He was not sure, though, that the strains and stresses likely to follow Nehru's departure would not call for modifications in the light of Indian needs. The country's politics in the post-Nehru years have indeed borne witness to Attlee's profound insight.)

Churchill, his severe electoral reverse notwithstanding, was as pugnacious as ever. Conducted into his presence in the central lobby at Westminster by Whiteley, I found him staring curiously at my army uniform. Somewhat overawed, I explained I was a war correspondent and had visited the Middle Eastern and Italian fronts and seen the famous Tenth Indian Division in action. That set Churchill going. He spoke of how he had started his journalistic career as a war correspondent for *The Pioneer* in India and then remarked: "Indian soldiers are fine fighters, but your politicians are men of straw—not Gandhi and a few others. You are going to be a burden on us. You have to be your own shield, though as I see it you are a continent—not one nation, but many nations. You have poverty and an increasing population." To end the brief interview, he added with a characteristic flourish: "We will play fair by you, if you play fair by us."

I rounded off my visit with a second meeting with Whiteley in Katial's apartment. The Chief Whip made the point that his party and many Tories felt that the Indian Army should remain united in the interest of the security of South-East Asia and the Near East and join other Commonwealth nations in ensuring the security of the Indian Ocean. He considered the Congress the freedom party and the League disruptionist and expressed the hope that in the impending elections the League candidates in Punjab, Sind and North West frontier province would be defeated. That would help preserve the unity of India.

Chapter 8

CABINET MISSION

Wavell's announcement of 19th September, 1945, reinforced by Attlee's broadcast from London the same day, showed that Whitehall's concern now was to determine through negotiation how, and to whom, power was to be handed over.

In India, the feeling that the curtain was now up on the penultimate scene of the political drama released a flurry of activity and counter-activity. The main actors in the domestic power struggle were the Congress and the League. Both sensed the proximity of freedom. It was not Jinnah's superior tactics alone, however, that yielded him victory. There was a group of British civilians in Delhi to bolster the League at every step in this tortuous game of political chess.

In November 1945, the Commander-in-Chief took the fateful decision of committing to trial three officers of Subhas Bose's Indian National Army—a Hindu, a Muslim and a Sikh—before a military court at Red Fort, Delhi. In its unwisdom, this equalled Irwin's proposal for an all-white Simon Commission on reforms. The trial unleashed nationalist forces, Indian sympathies naturally being overwhelmingly on the side of these martyrs to the cause of freedom.

A dramatic turn was given to the proceedings when Nehru appeared before the court wearing the barrister's gown he had discarded twenty-five years earlier. It was a gesture, for the defence of the accused was largely conducted by Bhulabhai Desai. Jinnah too attempted to figure in the affair. He sent word to Shah Nawaz Khan, the Muslim on trial, that he would defend him if he dissociated himself from the other accused. Shah Nawaz Khan flatly declined, remarking: "We have stood shoulder to shoulder in the struggle for freedom. Many comrades have died on the field of battle inspired by our leadership. We stand or fall together." An attempt to drive a communal wedge into the solidarity created by the I.N.A. movement thus failed.

The authorities realised that they had made a blunder and that the men in the dock had become national heroes. Less than two months later, there came the strike in the Indian wing of the Royal Indian Air Force and the menacing mutiny in the ranks of the Royal Indian Navy—both portents of the rapidly mounting popular upheaval.

The prestige of the Congress shot up as a result of the I.N.A. trial. This was reflected in the ensuing elections, in which the Congress captured practically all the general seats, while the League took most of the Muslim ones. Jinnah could claim with some justice that the League by and large represented Muslim interests and that his demand for Pakistan had popular sanction among the Muslim masses. On the other hand, with the ouster of the Conservative Party from office in Britain, the prospect of getting Pakistan "on a platter" faded. Labour, he knew, would not countenance the demand in its prevailing state of mind, and he was now uncertain whether he would be able to get even a "moth-eaten" Pakistan. But he still had allies in the British and Muslim members of the Civil Service, and he told me he counted on Nehru to give him the opening he needed to attain his goal.

I accompanied Wavell and his wife to the Andamans in the last week of December 1945 together with a group of newsmen. Wavell explained to us that the British fleet had assembled in the Andamans for action in the First Burma War. If they had not been occupied by the Japanese in World War II, they would have been used as a major naval base for operations in South and South-East Asia. The object of his visit was to see to what use the islands could be turned in the future.

In the relaxed atmosphere of the Andamans, I found Wavell inclined to be communicative. He said the separation of Burma from India was a mistake. Burma's defence from external foes was an integral part of the defence of India and the Andamans. He said the countries on India's periphery should have a common system of defence. If India was partitioned, Pakistan would have no elbow-room to defend herself. He had tried to solve the deadlock between the Congress and the League, but politics was not his line. The Congress pulled in one direction and the League in the opposite, and the Civil Servants were too partisan to help find an acceptable solution within the framework of an undivided India. He expected Labour to make a fresh effort at a solution in the coming summer and hoped it would be fruitful.

The Cabinet Mission despatched by Attlee landed in Delhi towards the end of March 1946. Its plan envisaged a Union of India, embracing both British India and the States dealing with foreign affairs, defence and communications and having the power to raise the finances required for these subjects. Any question raising a major communal issue in the legislature was to require for its decision a majority of the representatives of each of the two major communities as well as a majority of all the members voting. All the subjects other than the Union subjects and all residuary powers were to vest in the provinces and the states. Provinces were to be free to form groups. The Constitution, to be drawn up by a constituent assembly, was to provide each province, with the right to call for a reconsideration of the constitution at ten-yearly intervals. Briefly, the scheme was rooted in the unity and indivisibility of the country.

To Jinnah, therefore, its labours were anathema. As early as 10th April, he summoned in Delhi a convention of some 400 members of the provincial legislatures elected on the League ticket. The rallying cry at this convention was the demand for an independent Pakistan. The Muslims, Shahid Suhrawardy declared, were straining at the leash, and Noon said even the exploits of Halaku, the Mongol conqueror, would be put in the shade by a bloodbath should their right to a separate state be denied. (Both Suhrawardy and Noon had an inglorious political end as Prime Ministers of Pakistan.)

As I listened to the passionate and blood-curdling oratory at the session, I realised that the recent election, in which the League had scored a signal victory, had been a tactical mistake. The demon of communalism having been let loose, it was little wonder then that the first scheme formulated by the mission should have been repudiated as unacceptable on two grounds; one, that it did not go far enough to satisfy national aspirations; the other, that the concessions to the Muslim clamour went beyond the limits of justice and equity and were inimical to the concept of Indian integrity.

Undaunted by this rebuff, Wavell convened a second conference at Simla. It was a triangular affair. On one side were Azad, the Congress President, Nehru, Patel and Khan Abdul Ghaffar Khan, representing the premier nationalist organisation; on the second were Jinnah, Mohammed Ismail Khan, Liaquat Ali Khan and Abdur Rab Nishtar, the spokesmen of the League; and on the third were the members of the British delegation, striving valiantly to effect a compromise. But the seven-day talks early in May proved abortive.

Gandhi was present in Delhi as well as in Simla while the parleys with the Cabinet Mission proceeded. When I met him, he said there was too much deceit all round and added that Patel and Rajen Babu (Rajendra Prasad) had ceased to be his "yes men." There was too much violence in the hearts of the people. The League Ministers were preaching violence as the final sanction for Pakistan.

On 16th June, hoping against hope, the Cabinet Mission came out with specific proposals for the formation of an interim government at the centre and setting up a constituent assembly to devise a constitution for a self-governing India. That was the signal for another round of tortuous bargaining. The Congress asked for the right to appoint a Muslim of its choice to the interim Cabinet to establish its claim to represent all communities in the country. The Viceroy, however, assured Jinnah that he did not countenance the demand.

Predictably, the Congress Working Committee thereupon turned down the scheme for an interim government, while at the same time signifying its willingness to participate in the deliberations of the constitution-making body. Jinnah's response was not any the less surprising. He was wholly agreeable to the League's joining an interim cabinet; but he chose to be studiously non-committal in the plan for a constituent assembly.

The Congress–League tussle came to a head when Nehru took over the Congress presidentship from Azad on 6th July. In one of his first pronouncements on assuming office, he declared: "We are not bound by a single thing except that we have decided for the moment to go into the Constituent Assembly."

Nehru had for long been Jinnah's *bête noire*. At this particular moment, he was understandably more distasteful to the League champion than ever before. It was Nehru, as Congress President, that the Viceroy would call upon to form an interim government, a prospect that Jinnah was bound to regard with annoyance and deep suspicion. He lost no time, therefore, in condemning Nehru's statement of 6th July as "a complete repudiation of the basic form upon which the long-term scheme rests."

From this posture of hostility it was but a short step to the startling *volte face* of some three weeks later when he prevailed upon the Council of the Muslim League in Bombay to withdraw acceptance of the Cabinet Mission plan in its entirety and to call for the observance of 16th August as Direct Action Day.

In 1945, the Tories had prevented Wavell from honouring his commitment and forming a Cabinet of Congressmen because they did not wish to offend the League, which had served as their Crescent Card. Now, however, Wavell could not redeem his pledge to entrust the formation of an interim government to whichever party accepted the Cabinet Mission proposals. Jinnah got the Council to accept the proposals after learning from his British friends in the Government that the letter Wavell had written him, and which had not yet been delivered to him, withdrew the offer. Wavell had withdrawn it because this time Labour was unwilling to alienate the majority party, the Congress, and hand over power to the League.

In the League Council, Jinnah hit out violently both at the mission and the Congress. The former he accused of bad faith, and in his vituperation of the Congress he was even more unbridled. The League, he thundered, had "no alternative but to adhere once more to the national goal of Pakistan." The session witnessed an emotional outburst as the leading lights of the League, known for their traditional loyalty to the Raj, came to the platform and announced the renunciation of their British titles.

The country thus went to the polls to choose its representatives in the Constituent Assembly on a franchise limited to twenty-six per cent of the adult population in an atmosphere charged with intense communal antagonism. The results emphasised the cleavage between the Congress and the League, for the former won all but nine of the general seats, and the latter all but five of the Muslim seats.

Among the administrative changes which took place at this time was the transfer of H. V. R. Iengar to Delhi from Bombay as Secretary to the newly created Department of Planning. The Department soon set up cells to draft plans for river valley projects, steel mills, cement factories, and machine tool plants, scientific laboratories and the other sinews of industry. The attempt was to put the Government ahead of the economic planning of the Congress and of the Tata–Birla Plan, published with fanfare early in 1944.

But this satisfactory progress did not continue long. One morning, Iengar was stupefied to read in the newspapers that his department had been abolished. He asked his boss how this had happened so suddenly and who was to pay his salary. He was told that Jinnah had gone to Wavell and asked him whether the Department was planning for one country or two. If it was doing so on the assumption that India would stay united after independence, he objected. Wavell did not want to show Jinnah that he opposed partition, and to placate him he ordered the immediate closure of the Department. Iengar was informed that he had been appointed Secretary of the new Department which would manage the affairs of the Constituent Assembly.

In this capacity, he frequently called on V. P. Menon. One day, Menon showed him a secret cable Wavell had sent the Secretary of State saying that law and order had broken down in India and that the administration was on the verge of collapse. Wavell suggested two courses of action: that power be handed over to those who commanded the confidence of the people and could restore faith in the administration; or that large numbers of British troops be rushed in to maintain security and put down the unrest with a heavy hand. Wavell added that as a soldier he abhorred the second choice and preferred the first.

Iengar flew to Bombay, met Sardar Patel and advised him to take charge of the Government without insisting on a formal transfer of power with dominion status as such a move could not be effected technically. Patel told Iengar to see him the next day, when he said he agreed to the suggestion and would do his best to persuade the Working Committee to take the same line. Iengar returned to Delhi and Wavell sent a cable to the Secretary of State saying that he had learned on the most reliable information that the Congress would agree to an invitation to form a government. London gave Wavell the go ahead signal. Nehru, as the Congress President, was sent for and he accepted the proposal.

A pertinent and interesting aspect of the story of the time was the election of Nehru as the Congress President, when the office, in one sense, assumed its highest importance. Patel was the head of the Congress Parliamentary Board and the provincial Congress committees had expressed their preference for him as Azad's successor. But Gandhi felt Nehru would be a better instrument to deal with Englishmen as they would talk in a "common idiom," (a remarkable testimony to this view was afforded by Lord Mountbatten in November 1968 while delivering the Nehru Memorial Lecture in Cambridge. Mountbatten said: "I found myself more attracted by Nehru than anyone else. Having been educated at Harrow and Trinity and having lived so many of his formative years in England I found communication with him particularly easy and pleasant.").

Many years later, I sought Kripalani's explanation of Gandhi's preference for Nehru as against Patel. He said that like all saints and holy people Gandhi wanted "significant men" among his adherents. A legend had grown round the sacrifices made by the Nehrus for national freedom and Gandhi, therefore, preferred them. Insofar as Jawaharlal Nehru's election was concerned, Kripalani added: "All the P.C.C.s sent in the name of Patel by a majority and one or two proposed the names of Rajen Babu in addition, but none that of Jawaharlal. I knew Gandhi wanted Jawaharlal to be President for a year, and I made a proposal myself saying 'some Delhi fellows want Jawaharlal's name'. I circulated it to the members of the Working Committee to get their endorsement. I played this mischief. I am to blame. Patel never forgave me for that. He was a man of will and decision. You saw his face. It grew year by year in power and determination. After fifty years, a face reveals a man's full character. For all his faults, Patel was a great executive, organiser and leader."

Chapter 9

INTERIM GOVERNMENT

The stage was now set for the dénouement of two parallel conflicts. The larger struggle for freedom had reached its climax. The country was on the threshold of a national government at the Centre. Side by side, the fight for a breakaway Muslim state was forging ahead. On 12th August, 1946, Wavell announced he was inviting the Congress President to form a provisional government. Nehru thus inherited the responsibility of office. But most members of the Working Committee were not altogether happy. They preferred Sardar Patel, who his admirers felt, was the "Iron man with his feet firmly planted on earth." He would be able to deal better with Jinnah and, even at this late stage, ensure the integrity and stability of the sub-continent. Critical hours lay ahead and the Sardar's rugged realism, they argued, would provide a safe shield.

I asked Gandhi for his reactions to this feeling among a majority of the Working Committee members. He readily agreed that Patel would have proved a better negotiator and organiser as Congress President, but he felt Nehru should head the Government. When I asked him how he reconciled this with his assessment of Patel's qualities as a leader, he laughed and said: "Jawahar is the only Englishman in my camp." Seeing that he had further roused my curiosity, the Mahatma added: "Jawahar will not take second place. He is better known abroad than Sardar and will make India play a role in international affairs. Sardar will look after the country's affairs. They will be like two oxen yoked to the governmental cart. One will need the other and both will pull together." I mentioned Rajendra Prasad's lament expressed to me that Gandhi had once again sacrificed his trusted lieutenant for the sake of "the glamorous Nehru" and the fear that Nehru would follow British ways. Gandhi replied that he appreciated the views of his colleagues but felt that

Nehru would see reason when confronted with the problem of improving the lot of the masses.

This was idle speculation, however, for Nehru's choice as Prime Minister had become inevitable. Jinnah, his sights trained on Pakistan, promptly spurned Nehru's offer to the League of five seats in his Cabinet of fourteen. Thwarted in his demand that all the Muslims in the Government should be League nominees, he carried his fight into the streets by ordering the observance of Direct Action Day on 16th August. This was the signal for the great killings in Calcutta (about 5,000 killed, 15,000 injured) and for sporadic outbursts of violence and incendiarism elsewhere.

Eight days later, despairing of a Congress–League rapprochement, Wavell proclaimed the installation of the new Government at the Centre, comprising Nehru, Patel, Rajendra Prasad, Rajagopalachari, Asaf Ali, Sarat Chandra Bose, John Matthai, Baldev Singh, Shafeat Ahmed Khan, Jagjivan Ram, Ali Zaheer and C. H. Bhabha. Nehru's plea for abandoning further attempts to appease Jinnah had prevailed.

Jinnah's riposte was immediate. Encouraged by the response to his call for "direct action," he repeated his demand for the division of the country. The Viceroy met Gandhi and Nehru in yet another bid to end the deadlock. He favoured coalition governments in Bengal as well as at the Centre and told the Congress representatives that he could not summon the Constituent Assembly until they submitted to the Cabinet Mission's interpretation of the formula for grouping provinces. This, Nehru replied, was unacceptable.

The storm clouds were thickening as the interim Government took office on 2nd September, 1946. Communal riots broke out afresh in Bombay and Ahmedabad. To the Viceroy this was a challenge to a further effort at bringing the Congress and the League round to a settlement. Even as he wondered on the next move, Sir Sultan Ahmed and the Nawab of Chhatari called on Wavell at the inspiration of Jinnah. They told him that the League would join the Cabinet if the Viceroy directly sent for Jinnah to formalise the deal. Wavell approved of the proposal but felt awkward for he was treating Nehru as his Prime Minister. He, therefore, decided to have a word first with Nehru.

When Wavell consulted Nehru, the latter (according to my informant, V. P. Menon) told him: "How can I stop you from seeing him if you wish to?" In English idiom, it meant that Nehru disfavoured the move. But Wavell took advantage of the political connotation of the remark that Nehru would not make an issue of it and resign. He now proceeded to talk to Jinnah directly and Nehru missed the opportunity of cutting the League leader down to size. (Had Nehru asserted himself as Prime Minister and firmly resisted this move, the events may have taken a different course with Labour in power in London.)

The conventional impropriety having been condoned, Jinnah's ingenuity received all the latitude for manoeuvre and he extracted from Wavell the concessions he was seeking without yielding a single point in return. Wavell told Nehru that the League had agreed to join the Government, but he conveyed to him only vague verbal assurances that the League would participate in the Constituent Assembly. Patel and some others felt that Nehru should insist on written commitments and leave Jinnah no scope for mischief. However, Nehru accepted Wavell's plea that "all will be well." A communiqué was issued on 15th October, announcing that the League would join the interim Cabinet.

Jinnah lost no time in revealing his hand. The ousting of the nationalist Muslims from Nehru's interim Cabinet was not enough. Jinnah himself would not stoop to accept office under one he considered a junior. But he fought dourly to secure Home Affairs for the League. In the tortuous negotiations that followed, Rafi Ahmed Kidwai, for the Congress, suggested that Finance be yielded to the League instead. No League representative, he told me, would have the competence to deal with Finance and failure would bring the League bad odour. But Rafi had not bargained with the League rejoinder. Buttressed by able and experienced Muslim Secretaries like Ghulam Mohammed, Chaudhri Mohammed Ali and Moham-med Shoaib, all destined later to play distinguished roles in Pakistan, Liaquat Ali agreed to accept the challenge. This proved disastrous for the Congress.

More than the victory in bagging vital portfolios was Jinnah's *volte face* on the issue of the Constituent Assembly. The League, it was disclosed, was adamant on boycotting the constitution-making body. Exasperated by this obduracy, the Congress session at Meerut under Kripalani's presidency called upon the League either to accept the Cabinet Mission plan in its entirety and come into the Constituent Assembly or quit the interim Government. The quarrel was pursued amidst mounting communal violence. In the middle of October rivers of blood flowed in Noakhali, in East Bengal. Gandhi went into this ravaged area as a lonely pilgrim of peace, to comfort the stricken, to heal wounds and to assuage the flames of communal passion with his message of love. A chain reaction occurred in Bihar and Calcutta causing terrible riots. Gandhi visited both places and brought peace through moral persuasion.

Foreign observers noted that he achieved what many battalions of troops would have failed to in restoring amity.

The outlook at the close of 1946 was really grim. Sapru, whom I had invited to attend the wedding of my eldest daughter on 3rd December, wrote back that his health had grown worse. Along with a silver tea set as a wedding gift he sent a letter from Allahabad in which he said: "What anxious times are we passing through! Do you see any gleam of hope? I see none."

Nevertheless, the reconstituted Cabinet took office on 26th November. In the early days of December, Wavell, accompanied by Nehru, Jinnah, Liaquat Ali and Baldev Singh, flew to London to resolve the deadlock over the differing interpretations of the Cabinet Mission plan relating to the setting up of the Constituent Assembly. But the effort proved unavailing. The Assembly met on 9th December without the League members and adjourned till 20th January.

The Cabinet, meanwhile, functioned uneasily. Nehru originally felt that all members of the Cabinet should first meet informally in his room and take decisions on the items of the agenda so that the Cabinet meeting under Wavell would become a mere formality. However, an unconscious act of Nehru disrupted this plan. Instead of writing personally to Liaquat Ali to attend the first informal meeting, he asked his personal secretary to send the invitation. This roused the League leader's ire and, in retaliation to this "affront," he called a separate meeting of the League members of the Cabinet and stuck to this practice to the end. The two thereafter met when Wavell presided and the Cabinet functioned only as a house divided.

The budget of March 1947 afforded Liaquat Ali the crowning opportunity to vent his spleen on the Congress. He raised a storm by his tax measures and, what is more, by proposing a commission to inquire into the affairs of about 150 big business houses on the charge of tax evasion. It was a "socialistic budget," he contended blandly, but its true intent was barely concealed. It was designed calculatedly to hit the most powerful supporters of the Congress, namely, the Hindu industrialists and also to latently promote the cause of partition.

When the proposals came to light, there was a feeling of total discomfiture. Nehru had, no doubt, asked Dr. Mathai earlier to scrutinise the Finance Minister's budget speech. But Mathai was unable to discover anything objectionable in the absence of the offending tax proposals. Some in the Cabinet felt that the proposals should not be approved. But by then it was too late to apply the brakes. The Viceroy, moreover, would not permit any frantic last-minute revision and urged Nehru to let Liaquat Ali go ahead. There would be ample opportunity later to make amends, he argued.

The crucial differences between the two wings in the interim Government had in truth come into the open much earlier. Both sides voted *en bloc* and Liaquat Ali, determined to disrupt the Government from within, adopted invariably an obstructive stance. What made matters worse was that Wavell, who had begun extremely well, was showing signs of partiality for the League and acting largely on the advice of pro-League officers. The Congress found this intolerable and discreetly conveyed to Whitehall the need for Wavell's recall.

About that time, Katial was on a visit to India and staying as my guest. On the eve of his return to London on 16th December I gave a dinner at my house at which Patel, Rajagopalachari and Pant were present. Patel told Katial to convey to Attlee his feeling that Wavell should now be recalled. On his return, Katial contacted Whiteley, who stated that Attlee had already decided on his recall and a search was on for a successor.

The situation in the interim Government continued to deteriorate from day to day. By mid-February Nehru's patience gave way and he demanded the resignation of the League members. Close on the heels of this came Patel's threat that the Congress members would withdraw from the Cabinet if the representatives of the League did not quit forthwith.

The provisional Government would indeed have broken up but for a momentous development. On 20th February, Attlee announced in London Britain's firm intention to leave India by June 1948. That was accompanied by the further announcement that Lord Mountbatten had been chosen to succeed Wavell as Viceroy. The feeling that India's moment of destiny was within sight served to keep the Cabinet from falling apart. It was imperative to have a national government functioning in Delhi until the final transfer of power was accomplished.

Chapter 10

THE ASSEMBLY SCENE

Before we move to the final scene in the drama of "Divide and Quit," a salute is due to those who promoted a temper in the country and kept the pot boiling in the Central Legislative forum, which in a sense played as significant a part in transforming the Indian political scene as the non-violent mass struggle outside it. But, Jinnah excepted, the personalities who had a decisive role in fashioning the course of the movement for freedom functioned outside the legislature in the post-Irwin period.

Sir Nripendra Sircar, the Advocate-General of Bengal, succeeded Mitter as Law Member and proved the most effective Leader of the House. He disagreed with the politics of the Congress Party, but would not be a tool of bureaucracy. He explained his attitude to me thus: "The Hindus have been kept down for centuries. We need fifty years of association with the British to learn all they know. Let them raise industries. Everything will be ours one day." His nationalist sentiments brought him into conflict with Finance Member Grigg over the revision of the insurance law to enable the India companies to get business worth Rs. 350 million a year, which was siphoned off by foreign companies. The idea of such a change germinated in Sapru's time, but every Law Member who followed him avoided implementing it. Sircar, however, decided to see it through and secured the support of Bhulabhai Desai, the Opposition Leader.

British insurance interests were lobbying feverishly against the Bill and Grigg exerted his influence to see that the Upper House did not endorse it. Sircar learned of Grigg's plans. He sent for me and showed me a copy of the letter of resignation he had sent the Viceroy. It said: "I understand my own colleague is working against me to get the Bill undone in the Council of State. My Lord, my self-respect does not permit me to stay a minute longer in your Council. I request I may be relieved immediately." Willingdon asked Grigg to remove the misunderstanding. Sircar told me that Grigg had apologised and that he had withdrawn the letter of resignation.

Sir Mohammed Zafrullah Khan, who succeeded Sircar in 1939,

was an effective speaker but was not his predecessor's equal in legal talent. In collaboration with some British bureaucrats, Zafrullah brought a band of Muslim Civil Servants into the Secretariat in New Delhi. These men proved useful to Jinnah at the time of partition because they were instrumental in setting up the administrative machinery for the new State of Pakistan.

Ambedkar was perhaps the most erudite member of the Executive Council and was a powerful speaker. But he was too embittered in his role of Harijan leader to build up a following in the legislature. He was a nationalist to the core. He narrated to me several instances when he had clashed with the superior powers in New Delhi but ultimately got his way. Once, an Indian colleague proposed a Bill to apply economic sanctions against South Africa because of the maltreatment of Indian settlers in that country. The European members opposed the measure. Ambedkar thumped the table in anger and said India's self-respect was at stake. His spirited intervention proved decisive and the Council approved the Bill.

A chief engineer was needed to head the commission to draw up plans for flood control in the Damadar Valley in Bihar. Wavell favoured the choice of a British expert who had been adviser on the Aswan dam project in Egypt. Ambedkar, however, wanted an American who had experience of the development undertaken by the Tennessee Valley Authority. He argued in support of his demand that Britain had no big rivers and its engineers lacked experience in building big dams. He had his way.

For eleven years, the Speaker's seat was occupied by Sir Abdur Rahim. His tenure of this office coincided with a period of acute political unrest, during which India passed from one crisis to another. The struggle between Government and Congress intensified, to a large extent against the grim background of World War II. Elections to the Central Assembly were put off again and again, and the climate for the growth of India's infant parliamentary institutions was anything but healthy.

His rulings, concise and weighty, established sound Parliamentary practices. The most notable of these concerned the Speaker's competence to declare a Bill *ultra vires*. He took nearly two months to arrive at a decision. He felt that the tendency to convert the Assembly, dominated by lawyers, into a legal debating society had to be arrested. The courts, and not the Speaker, should pronounce on the validity of a measure. Mavalankar later reaffirmed this ruling, and it still holds good.

Where he sensed a threat to the supremacy of the Speaker in the House, Sir Abdur was uncompromising. He once told me: "This is a politician's job. I may give a wrong ruling, but, if I fail to maintain discipline I fail completely. Orderliness is the essence of the parliamentary system." This was his guiding principle throughout his term of office. In his chamber, he would study issues in dispute deeply, and when he took the Chair his mind was made up.

He showed me the vast amount of material he had gathered for the book which death prevented him from writing. He opposed partition as well as linguistic provinces. What mattered to him was the strength and unity of the nation in independence, and to sustain this concept of nationhood he favoured the division of the country into four or five provinces or zones. He had planned to present Cripps with a memorandum embodying his views on these and allied subjects, but Jinnah manoeuvred to foil him. Of Jinnah, whom he appeared to hold in contempt, he said to me: "He knows little of Shakespeare and Milton."

G. V. Mavalankar (Dadasaheb to his friends) was the golden bridge between the Central Legislative Assembly of the British era and the Parliament of free India. The story of his election early in 1946 to succeed Sir Abdur is full of drama. The Government backed by Jinnah put up Sir Cowasji Jehangir. Voting took place in a tense atmosphere. When the result was announced, the Treasury benches were shrouded in gloom. But most crestfallen of all was Jinnah, who left the Chamber immediately. Mavalankar soon proved that his hard-won victory was more than deserved. When the Congress decided to boycott the Viceroy's inaugural address to the Assembly, he as a non-party man received Wavell at the entrance and greeted him with the utmost courtesy. Wavell then delivered what was to be the last viceregal address ever to the Assembly.

Mavalankar was the first holder of the office to discard the wig hitherto regarded as mandatory for formal occasions and to preside over the House wearing a Gandhi cap. "Your wig is unsuited to this warm climate," he would say to Britons who queried him on this point. But he confided to me that he had made the change because "the Gandhi cap is symbolic of the new political climate in the country." Yet, in every other respect, he proved himself a stout champion of parliamentary traditions.

Chapter 11

TOWARDS THE TRANSFER OF POWER
MOUNTBATTEN

In the early months of 1947, one sensed a speed-up of the movement towards the transfer of power. The drama was played both in India and at Whitehall. Plans being shaped in London about this time envisaged British exit on the basis of dominion status. Attempts were being made to persuade the Indian leaders to settle for this status and not to stand uncompromisingly for complete independence.

Operation Quit India called for a change of Viceroyalty and the choice of Mountbatten was a happy one. As the Supreme Commander of the Allied operations against the Japanese in South-East Asia, Mountbatten had made many friends in India. Nehru himself had developed a measure of intimacy with both Lord and Lady Mountbatten from the time he visited Singapore during the war and Mountbatten had given him a red carpet treatment by telling his aides to treat him as they would a Prime Minister. The Mountbattens' links with British royalty were another powerful factor in their favour. Sworn in on 24th March, 1947, the new Viceroy lost little time in reassuring Indian opinion that there would be no going back on Britain's promise of freedom.

But fresh political developments precipitated a crisis. The Punjab was the crux of the tussle for Pakistan. Although the League had captured seventy-nine seats in the provincial Legislative Assembly out of a total of 175 in the 1945 elections, it was still in a minority and Khizr Hayat Khan, the Unionist leader, formed a ministry with the support of the Congress and the Sikhs. To intimidate the Government as well as the people of the province, the League organised "national guards" and the Hindus answered by joining the Rashtriya Swayamsewak Sangh (Servants of the Nation) in large numbers. Khizr Hayat Khan outlawed both organisations.

The supporters of the League defied the ban and whipped up mass hysteria against the Ministry. The Hindus avoided counter-demonstrations, thus creating the impression that the administration lacked popular backing. Consequently, after Attlee's announcement on 20th February, 1947, Khizr Hayat Khan resigned. This was the signal for bloody riots in Lahore and Amritsar, where Hindu and Sikh life and property suffered severely. The police remained passive spectators of these happenings, a rehearsal for what was to follow in August.

The Congress Working Committee met on 8th March and charged "some people in high authority" with coercing and toppling the popular Ministry and responsibility for the violence that followed. The Committee said the situation in the province "would necessitate a division of the Punjab into two provinces, so that the predominantly Muslim part may be separated from the predominantly non-Muslim part." This was the only major decision the Congress Working Committee ever took without consulting Gandhi and getting his prior approval. In a letter to Nehru dated 20th March, Gandhi expressed his bitterness that the Committee had suggested the partition of the province on the basis of community and the two-nation theory. For him, this was an hour of great humiliation.

Gandhi arrived in Delhi in the last week of March to meet Mountbatten. He had six meetings with the new Viceroy covering fourteen hours. Devadas and I called on Gandhi twice, and he told us that his followers had let him down badly. Now that power was within their grasp, they seemed to have no further use for him. As neither Nehru nor Jinnah would consent to take second place in a government at the Centre, both had agreed to partition the country, he said. Patel was directing all his energies towards saving India for the Hindus, and Azad was equally obsessed with the plight of the Muslims. Subhas Bose, Gandhi observed, had proved a true patriot by organising the I.N.A. and showing how Hindus and Muslims could work in harmony. Gandhi said he would rather have a blood-bath in a united India after the British quit than agree to partition on a communal basis and give birth to two armed camps, perpetually in conflict.

The Congress, we suggested, had already conceded partition in principle. He replied that he would make one final bid to retrieve the situation. He would suggest that Jinnah be asked to form a national government of his choice. That, he said, would test the *bona fides* of Mountbatten, Nehru and Patel. What if that failed? we asked. He replied that he would summon all the moral authority he possessed to avert the inevitable holocaust and try to undo the evil effects of partition, if this should come about. Bapu was unusually pessimistic. But he had revealed his inmost thoughts for our guidance.

It was my practice to call on Patel at his residence every evening, often immediately after Gandhi's prayer meeting. Our regular contact lasted until his death. I used to give him a brief outline of the day's news and the latest lobby gossip, as well as any comments Gandhi had made. In return, I would get to know inside information about the state of the country and the trends in the inner Cabinet.

As usual, after Devadas and I had met Gandhi, I gave Patel the gist of our conversation, omitting, however, personal references. Patel commented at the end of my recital that Gandhi must bear part of the blame for the unhappy developments. Why did he listen to his *samdhi* (son's father-in-law, namely C.R.) and hold talks with Jinnah? This recognition had "made a hero of Jinnah in Muslim eyes." Had not Gandhi talked of self-determination for the Muslims? Why only for them? "He trusts only Jawahar to bring about Hindu–Muslim unity."

Patel said his principal anxiety was to save India from chaos by countering the Anglo–Muslim moves in the opposite direction. Maulana Azad was only worried about the Muslims. "Jawahar is the only nationalist Muslim today," he remarked. (This is how Patel jocularly described Nehru time and again.) Patel added that Nehru was unduly amenable to Mountbatten's influence. Nehru had "always leaned on someone." He was under Bapu's protective wing and "now he leans on Mountbatten." Patel concluded by saying that he counted on the Hindus and the Sikhs and patriotic Civil Servants and Princes to support him.

In his last desperate gamble to snatch the country from the edge of the precipice, Gandhi appealed to the Viceroy to dismiss the interim Cabinet and summon Jinnah to form an alternate government. Gandhi, who alone among the Congress leaders stood firm as a rock against what he believed was the ultimate disaster, was slowly finding himself isolated from the mainstream of the party. To him, it was a moment of profound mental anguish, and he saw no other way out. Had his counsel, fantastic as it appeared, been accepted, perhaps Jinnah would have abandoned his insistence on a separate Muslim state. The setback to the Congress, in Gandhi's eyes, was a small price to pay for Indian solidarity. But Gandhi's was a voice crying in the wilderness. Already both in India and Britain, plans were being discussed for the division of Bengal and the Punjab.

V. P. Menon gave me details of these prolonged talks. Mountbatten was just flattering the old man, he said: "He is doing business with Sardar and has Nehru in his pocket. Sardar is playing a deep game. He, in turn, is flattering Mountbatten and using him to net the Princes. We must have all of them in the bag before 15th August, with three exceptions—Hyderabad, Kashmir and Junagadh. Sardar is more than a match for the plan of Corfield, Bhopal and C.P. (Ramaswami Aiyer) to carve out independent states which will split up and encircle the Indian Union. You see, Baroda has defied the Princes Chamber and joined the Constituent Assembly. Patiala, Bikaner and Gwalior are coming in. The rest will follow. Our only worry is that Mountbatten is very soft towards the Nizam. We cannot have this cancer in our belly. Jinnah is encouraging the Corfield-Bhopal move to weaken India."

The following letter Mitter, the Dewan (Prime Minister) of Baroda wrote me on 8th March, 1947, throws a revealing light on the currents and cross-currents at work at the time:

My dear Durga Das,

I congratulate you on your ruthless exposures of the dirty tactics in the Princes Chamber. It is a matter of deep regret to me that Sir C.P. (Ramaswami Aiyer) should lend his great talent to destructive instead of constructive endeavour at this critical time of India's destiny. I should like you to pay a deserved compliment to Patiala, Bikaner and Gwalior. It will hearten them to frustrate further attempts at sabotage. Bhopal, with his political adviser and director, both miserable creatures, has been shown up. C.P.'s cloven feet have been exposed. Jam Saheb (the ruler of Nawanagar), Durgapur and Bilaspur have been silenced. From what I gather from the Resident here, Jam Saheb is about to turn his attention to Kathiawar, where the Resident anticipates a dog fight. It would be a good thing if you can make an open appeal to Pattani of Bhavnagar, to the sagacious Ruler of Morvi and the enlightened Rulers of Porbandar and Dhrangadhra and Palitana, warning them against the wiles of the Jam Saheb under the protective wings of the political Department.

I will give you an idea which you can use with good effect on a suitable occasion. Corfield (the Political Secretary) and his minions have been pressing on the Rulers the urgent necessity of "a united front." The answer is that the phrase is used in relation to "enemies." Why should Indian Rulers look upon British Indian leaders as enemies? They should meet not to fight but to discuss and negotiate for the good of the people and the freedom of India from bondage. British India is importing democracy from the West. The Rulers can claim to have preserved, to a large extent, the distinctive and essential culture of India. The two currents

I.F.G.N.

Q

should meet and go forward as a mighty stream for the good of humanity.

God bless you,

Yours sincerely,
B. L. Mitter

V. P. Menon was my oldest friend in the Central Secretariat. I knew him when he was an assistant in the Home Department and we came to be friends when he was promoted Superintendent of the Reforms Section created for the Muddiman Reforms Inquiry Committee in 1923, whose proceedings I reported for A.P.I. From then, he had been in the Reforms Section and risen step by step until he became Reforms Commissioner. He shared his confidence with me throughout his career.

Mountbatten advised the Princes to accede to the Dominion of India or to Pakistan according to geographic compulsion, and he warned them that after 15th August, they would not get any protection from the Crown. (A member of a family which provided hereditary Prime Ministers to a ruling house in Central India, who recently retired from the Indian Foreign Service, explained that the Princes gave in and the princely order finally disappeared for three reasons: "Firstly, the Princes were nationalists; secondly, they were chicken-hearted; thirdly, the majority of them were fools and lost in vice.")

The plan for a "united front" did not succeed because the rulers feared Patel, and because of Mountbatten's pressure. The Bhopal camp envisaged a block of states from Bhopal to Karachi, splitting India in two. Jinnah promised the Princes the use of Karachi as a free port. But a slice of the territory of the ruler of Udaipur cut through this arc. The old Maharana refused to join the conspiracy, remarking: "If my ancestors had joined the Mughals, I would have had today a bigger state than Jaipur or Jodhpur." This action of the oldest ruling dynasty of India upheld the honour of the house of Maharana Pratap and helped fulfil his ancestor's dream of freeing his motherland from the foreign yoke. It was the Maharana of Udaipur who had whispered into the ear of Sir Narasimha Sarma in the twenties that he wished to see the country rid of the foreign "devils."

Mountbatten paid little attention to Gandhi's advice, confident that neither Nehru nor Patel would back it. He was confirmed in this belief when Nehru declared in a public speech on 20th April that the League could have Pakistan "on condition that they do not take away other parts of India which do not wish to join Pakistan." When I asked Nehru whether he had taken into account the effect his statement would have on Gandhi, he said Gandhi had fully supported the objection raised by Gopinath Bardoloi, Congress Chief Minister of Assam, to that state's inclusion in the eastern zone envisaged in the plan of the Cabinet Mission. That was the major difference, Nehru explained, in the Congress and League interpretations of the plan.

The issue was clinched when Prasad, as the President of the Constituent Assembly, read out on 28th April an authoritative statement of the Congress stand, that no constitution would be forced on any part of the country that was unwilling to accept it. "This may mean," the statement ended, "not only a division of India but a division of some provinces. For this, we must be prepared, and the Assembly may have to draw up a constitution based on such division."

This declaration had little effect on the communal situation and as reports of communal clashes poured in, Mountbatten suggested that Gandhi and Jinnah issue a joint appeal. It ran: "We deeply deplore the recent acts of lawlessness and violence that have brought the utmost disgrace on the fair name of India and the greatest misery to innocent people, irrespective of who were the aggressors and who were the victims. We denounce for all time the use of force to achieve political ends, and we call upon all the communities of India, to whatever persuasion they may belong, not only to refrain from all acts of violence and disorder, but also to avoid, both in speech and writing, any words which might be construed as an incitement to such acts."

Jinnah signed in English, the language he knew well, and Gandhi in Hindi, Urdu and English. This appeal vindicated Gandhi's ideals, but it had little effect on Jinnah's followers, for his hold on them was not moral but political and his technique of direct action was based on mob violence. His supporters were particularly busy stirring up hatred to topple the Congress Government in the Frontier Province.

Patel issued a statement on 26th April inviting the Princes to join the Constituent Assembly and declaring that fresh elections would not be held in the Frontier because only a year before one had been fought on the clear issue of Hindustan or Pakistan and the League had been routed. The Congress Ministry in the province would not be intimidated by rowdyism, he added.

Meanwhile, the Constituent Assembly, minus the representatives of the League, met and defined the rights of citizens and drew up a Charter of Equality. Outside the Assembly, Shaheed Suhrawardy, the League Chief Minister of Bengal, created a little diversion by declaring that he wanted an "undivided sovereign Bengal" instead of Pakistan. But his demand made no impact on the Hindus of Bengal and the Punjab because they had been frightened by the riots into accepting the division of their provinces on communal lines. Tension continued to mount as Leaguers worked up popular sentiment in favour of partition.

Mountbatten sent his plan to London on 2nd May for approval and himself went up to Simla, accompanied by Nehru and V. P. Menon, for some rest. He received the revised version of the plan on 10th May and revealed its contents to Nehru. Menon was keeping Patel informed of the developments in Simla, and I was in daily touch with Patel. He told me Nehru had reacted violently to Mountbatten's plan as it had proposed that the British pull out after handing over power to the provinces established under the Government of India Act if the Indian leaders failed to agree among themselves on the new constitutional set-up.

Patel continued: "When I was informed of this by V.P., I suggested that the Congress should throw a bait to Mountbatten, namely that India would be willing to accept dominion status and appoint him as Governor-General. The move worked and Mountbatten got the impression that the Congress was not as hostile to the British as the Tories in London had imagined. Mountbatten thereupon prepared with the help of V.P., a new plan on the basis of partition. Mountbatten thought that he could make Jinnah agree to the plan and that, even if Jinnah did not agree to a united India having dominion status, he would agree to India and Pakistan having him as a joint Governor-General. Mountbatten consulted Jinnah, who gave him the impression that he was agreeable to the latter suggestion."

A letter from Krishna Menon to Katial from Simla, dated 12th May, 1947, shed light on the intense drama taking place there at the time. The letter was from Viceregal Lodge, and Menon, who had accompanied Nehru, was staying at the Lodge with the rest of Nehru's entourage. Katial forwarded the original letter to me for showing to Patel and for my own information. It read: "I am taking advantage of the rest and the time here to write a brief note to you. I am conscious that I have not written but I have done the things that you would expect me to do. It is not possible to write in detail as things change from day to day and yet remain the same. The outlines of it you know from there from your sources which are near enough to facts. In spite of the very good personal impressions created by the Mountbattens, we are yet no nearer solution. The only big change is that people are beginning to realise that the British are quitting, though often people wonder! The Viceroy has been successful in impressing on some of the Governors the hard fact of the change in British policy though on all of them the effect is not the same. But there are improvements at some places.

"The Frontier and the Punjab are in an awful state. The Punjab atrocities are reported to have even made an impression on Jenkins, though one does not know how long it will last. He is not the worst of Governors, they say. Caroe is hated by our people and is said to be at the bottom of the Frontier mischief. It is not possible to draw any conclusion except that the League, by pursuing Hitler's tactics, hopes to win the whole of India for Pakistan. Jinnah will agree to nothing, he has agreed to nothing and what is more is trying to lead the Viceroy up the garden path. What we have to ask, and our friends there have to ask, is even if we agreed to a Pakistan by partitioning Punjab and Bengal, will Jinnah abide by it or will it be only the beginning of fresh demands for 'minorities' inside the rest of India? The same business will go on all over again. Arms are being smuggled in here and the Leaguers mean to create chaos. They don't care what happens to India. Some of the minorities are also playing a tricky game and there is talk of uneasiness, etc.

"The Viceroy has made contacts with all people, but we can't say whether all that helps him to appreciate or to get more nonplussed. He works very hard and makes everybody do the same. There is a lot of feeling about the people around him, particularly Abell & Co. But what can we do about it? I think he keeps the Cabinet together better and gets on with people better, but that would not be independence. Would it? The British have to make up their mind to make Jinnah agree to what at the very outside he can have, and if he does not, they must stick to the Cabinet plan of dominion status and interim government and let that government settle down to business. There is no other way. But instead they are trying to perform major operations in quick time.

"Actual partition in twelve months is an impossibility, which means you must have a common Centre, which, if accepted, means Cabinet plan and all the evils of partition without its benefits. Our people are in no mood to let the League meddle in our defence, if partition is granted. However, situations change. Gandhiji alone stands out with definite views on India's division. But he does not have to deal with practical affairs just now. But it is notable the way he stands out. Panditji is worn out and alone thinks of these things. Sardar Patel has a clear mind and sees all the dangers, but in the present situation he is helpless, as we're not in a fight and the third party is still here. I have had long talks with him usually at five-thirty in the morning. I also see Mountbatten, in an informal way, but all this does not help you more than you know already . . .

"So far people trust the Viceroy's integrity, and the feeling here is that he is not getting enough backing from London, where Cripps and others are making difficulties and using their position to assist disruption. So you see, in spite of all I have said you are in no better position to appreciate the situation. I don't think that the 2nd June statement will represent agreement. Jinnah will agree to nothing."

The letter ended surprisingly with this warning: "Please don't send letters except by bag and don't sign political cables. The League gets everything."

The first reaction in London to Mountbatten's plan for partition was adverse. That was why he was asked to visit London and he left Delhi on 14th May. Attlee was also aware that the Congress leaders were irritated by the activities of certain high British officials, as Katial's cable of 15th May to me indicated. The cable said Mountbatten's proposal for partition was unacceptable to the Labour Government, that Mountbatten was visiting London immediately and that the removal of Caroe, Jenkins and Abell was being pressed.

While reconciled to the transfer of power, many Britons in India were keen on salvaging whatever they could from the wreck of the Empire. They genuinely felt that Pakistan would give them a foothold on the sub-continent and support British presence in the Near and Middle East. Sir Olaf Caroe, a brilliant I.C.S. officer, whom I had often met at the weekly briefings he had given the Press when he was Foreign Secretary, was now Governor of the N.W.F.P. Congress leaders suspected that he wanted to dislodge the Congress Ministry in the province which was backed by the Red Shirts. As soon as Nehru assumed office on 2nd September, 1946, the Frontier authorities started bombing and other reprisals against tribesmen. This seemed like deferred action of a routine nature for tribal raids on the settled areas of the province, but the Red Shirt leaders immediately informed Nehru that it had been deliberately synchronised with his installation in office to discredit his Government and that the Government's agents throughout the province were representing it as the first fruits of Hindu Raj.

Nehru told Wavell that this action must stop immediately and that he would visit the Frontier. The provincial authorities in turn warned the Viceroy that they would not be responsible for Nehru's safety as pro-League and anti-Congress feelings were strong in the province. Nehru would not, however, be deflected fron his resolve, and when he flew into the airfield at Peshawar he was met by large numbers of Leaguers waving black flags. On his tour of the tribal area, snipers' bullets ploughed the air round the car he travelled in and stones struck it, the intention being that, while he should be convinced that he and the Congress lacked popular support, his life should not be endangered. Jinnah seized on the opportunity to demand fresh elections in the province.

Mountbatten left for London on 14th May with the agreement reached with the Congress and League leaders and suggested to Attlee that the date for the transfer of power be advanced from June 1948 to 15th August, 1947. (I was told he chose 15th August because the Japanese had surrendered to the Allies on this date in 1945.) Attlee approved both the agreement and the change of date, and a vastly pleased Mountbatten returned to New Delhi in time to meet the Indian leaders on 2nd June. But a shock was in store for him. Patel told me later the same month that "when it came to finalising the deal, Jinnah backed out. He turned down the proposal for a joint Governor-General and said he himself would become the Governor-General of Pakistan. This change of attitude of Jinnah made Mountbatten friendly to us."

Chapter 12

DIVIDE AND QUIT

The Viceroy's partition plan was unfolded to the Indian leaders on 2nd June. All the provinces were empowered under it to decide on whether their constitution was to be framed by the existing Constituent Assembly or by a new and separate Constituent Assembly. Members of the Punjab and Bengal Assemblies were given the rights to decide whether their provinces were also to be partitioned on a communal basis. The N.W.F.P. was treated as a special case because of geographical consideration and although two of its three representatives were already attending the existing Constituent Assembly it was decided to give the province an opportunity to reconsider its position. This proposal for a referendum in the Frontier was the most distasteful aspect of the plan. Nevertheless, the A.I.C.C. approved the Mountbatten Plan at its meeting on Sunday, 15th June, by 157 votes to twenty-nine.

Gandhi attended the session by special request and spoke in

favour of the resolution for acceptance. I wondered how he would reconcile the conflict between his head and heart. He put the issue in a nutshell. "The fact is," he said, "there are three parties to the settlement—the British, the Congress and the Muslim League. The Congress leaders have signed on your behalf. You can disown them, but you should do so only if you can start a big revolution. I do not think you can do it." As a sop to those who opposed the resolution in spite of Gandhi's speech, Azad said: "There will be reunion before long."

Among the topmost leaders, only Purushottamdas Tandon stood out against partition. He was prepared to suffer British rule a little longer rather than pay this heavy price. He said the Nehru Government had been intimidated by the League. "Let us fight both the British and the League," he ended amidst applause. But Gandhi had sensed the feelings of his followers more accurately. Had the audience roared back that they would follow him to resist partition he might have reflected on his duty to the nation. In advocating approval of the plan, he rose to a great moral height. While accepting defeat at the hands of his lieutenants he used his personal authority to get them a vote of confidence for the new adventure.

Having secured the A.I.C.C.'s favourable verdict for his plan, Mountbatten now tried to blunt the opposition of the Red Shirts to a referendum. He brought Jinnah and Badshah Khan together and, although no agreement resulted from this meeting, the Frontier leader declared he would not oppose joining Pakistan provided the areas inhabited by the Pathans were merged to a form on autonomous Pakhtoonistan and had the right to opt out of the dominion if they wished. This statement seemed to ease the conscience of the Congress leaders, for they were not prepared to cause a deadlock over the Frontier's future.

To help matters further, Mountbatten asked Caroe to go on leave when the referendum was held. In the highly charged atmosphere in the province, the Red Shirts decided not to put up candidates for election, and the League notched a victory with 50.49 per cent of the electorate voting in favour of Pakistan. The pro-League Britons' objective, to keep the Frontier out of the Indian Union or from being reborn after partition as an independent Pakhtoonistan, was thus fulfilled. Azad blamed Nehru for his impetuosity in visiting the Frontier and playing into the hands of the anti-Congress forces. For once Patel agreed with Azad.

Now that partition was a settled fact, tension between the Hindus and the Muslim increased and riots erupted in Lahore and Amritsar. In an editorial on 24th June, I said: "Governor Jenkins is almost earning the title of a modern Nero. Nothing short of martial law can save Lahore and Amritsar from total destruction."

B. L. Sharma, who was for years Special Officer on Kashmir and represented India in that capacity at the U.N., told me he had seen a letter written by a high British official to Jinnah suggesting that Pakistan's security be ensured by not permitting any Hindu or Sikh to live west of Lyallpur in the Punjab. Anyway, the wholesale murder and arson which occurred drove people of these communities out of the region at the time of partition and set off a chain reaction, equally brutal in its intensity, in India.

Indeed, some Sikh leaders decided on the deliberate removal of Muslims in East Punjab to make room for refugees from the western half. They had a political motive for this action, for had the Sikhs been split in roughly equal numbers between India and Pakistan they would not have been an important factor in the politics of either country. Accordingly, the far-sighted among their leaders brought them to East Punjab and settled them in contiguous districts, where they formed the majority. They thus became not only a political entity in India but could also work for a state of their own within the Union.

Both in India and Pakistan, power-hungry politicians were hatching diabolical plots in their self-interest which involved the disruption of the lives of millions of innocent helpless peasants on the greatest and the most tragic movement of refugees in history.

The provisional Governments of India and Pakistan were formed on 20th July and proceeded with the task of partitioning the services and financial assets and demarcating boundaries. The Partition Council achieved the extraordinary feat of dividing the services and assets so speedily that on 15th August both dominions could function as separate sovereign states.

In the days of agonising indecision from June to August, Gandhi proved what a very powerful moral force and educator of the masses he was in his addresses to his daily prayer meetings in New Delhi. His addresses were in the nature of commentaries on current events, and broadcast by All–India Radio, they made a profound impression on his hearers, although they could not change the course of history.

I attended most of these meetings and took note of some of the significant things he said. On 7th July, for instance, he said the Indian and Pakistani Armies were being created not to fight a common danger but to destroy each other. The following day, he said the Englishman was sincere in quitting India but was insincere when he said he was not exposing the country to chaos since he was actually turning it into a cockpit for two organised armies.

He wanted the Congress and the League to leave the Pathans to shape their own internal administration. On 24th June, he said the Congress must change its objective after independence, a hint that it should cease to be a political party. After visiting Kashmir in the first week of August, he said this state was very important strategically and joint discussions between the Maharaja and the representatives of the Kashmiris and of the two dominions would avert trouble over its future.

He said that after partition he would travel between East Bengal, West Punjab and the Frontier to heal the wounds of partition and promote love and harmony between the Hindu and Muslim, but this intention was cruelly cut short by an assassin's bullet on 30th January, 1948.

Gandhi advised the people of the French and Portuguese possessions in India not to revolt against their overlords on 15th August but to trust Nehru to do for his kith and kin what he was doing to assist the Indonesians to become free. Indirectly, Gandhi was voicing the fact that he differed from Patel's view on Goa and Pondicherry and other foreign enclaves and agreed with Nehru's that the question of their liberation could wait for some time.

On 14th August, Sir Claude Auchinleck, who had been appointed Supreme Commander of the armed forces of India and Pakistan, gave a farewell party at his official residence, which Nehru later turned into Prime Minister's House, and I shared a table with General Sir Arthur Smith, the outgoing Commander-in-Chief of the Indian Army.

I asked Smith how he visualised India's future, especially that of its armed forces. He replied bluntly: "I do not give your army six months. It will crack up before that. You see, the *jawans* are like bricks, and the officer provides the mortar that holds them together. The Indian officer will not provide the mortar because his leadership has not been tested and the *jawan* has no respect for him."

I felt some apprehension at this statement in my heart, but replied confidently: "General, patriotism is a great force. It will provide the mortar." Smith snapped back: "No, not with the *jawans*. They have loved their British officers because they took care of them. Your boys are too selfish and snobs." This statement too had an element of truth, and I replied: "I thought the army had iron discipline and moulded character." "It does," Smith said, "but it can be tested only on the battlefield. Life in barracks, too, matters a lot and the atmosphere."

In a way, I believe the war in Kashmir with Pakistan-led tribal raiders soon after independence was a godsend. It provided the mortar to build a cohesive army and it gave the opportunity to the officers belonging to the so-called non-martial races to provide inspiring leadership to their comrades by offering their lives at the altar of patriotism.

I also learned at the party of the pulls behind the scene on the impending Radclyffe Award. The lawyers representing India had made out a very strong case for incorporation in India of Lahore, which had a Hindu and Sikh population with an edge over the Muslim in size and predominant share of the city's wealth. The Hindu leaders of the city were so confident that it would come to India that they had advised the non-Muslims to stay put instead of migrating. Further, Lahore had a sentimental appeal to Indian nationalists, for it was on the banks of the Ravi in December 1929 that the Congress resolved to ask for nothing less than independence. It was also the centre of Ayra Samaj, the Hindu religious and social reform movement, as well as the biggest Hindu educational centre in the Punjab.

Ironically, it was here too that the League had decided in March 1940 to demand Pakistan, and in offering it to Jinnah Radclyffe seems to have felt that it balanced the award of Calcutta, which the League had demanded for East Pakistan, to India. I gathered that British officials advised Jinnah to pick Lahore in preference to a part of Gurdaspur district which would have cut off India from direct overland communication with Kashmir. They are said to have explained to Jinnah that the League leaders had in any event made plans to occupy Kashmir by force. This story sounded rather odd, but I mentioned it to Patel that evening. His reaction was: "This is Nehru's charge. We will wait and watch."

Neither the Congress leaders had visualised the possibility of two sovereign nations existing within the sub-continent, nor had Muslims of the U.P. and Bombay, who had clamoured for a homeland, realised that the creation of an independent Pakistan, separate in all respects, from the Indian Union, would reduce the Muslims of India from a politically significant force to an ineffectual minority and cut them off from their kith and kin across the border. When the holocaust occurred, Gandhi alone stood steadfast while other leaders fumbled and quailed before the storm. But for his superior moral force and martyrdom, which he seemed to have foreseen with his prophetic vision, the whole sub-continent of India would have perished in flames.

Chapter 13

THE FINAL SCENE

The period from 1920 to 1947 was the most significant in the history of British India. Beginning with the Gandhian revolution, it culminated in independence. The crystallisation of the Congress agitation in the Quit India demand brought about the liquidation of alien rule; at the same time the Muslim League's counter-slogan of "Divide and Quit" led inexorably to the colossal tragedy that accompanied the dawn of freedom—the country's vivisection, and the holocaust in which half a million people perished and some ten million were uprooted from their homes.

Independence came to India in 1947 unexpectedly, but inevitably. It was the result of three movements which appeared to run parallel.

First, the Gandhian movement of non-violent non-cooperation, which caused such an unprecedented upsurge among the inarticulate masses that the British Raj could be sustained only at the point of the sword.

Second, the ballot box revolution, which contributed to the awakening of the political consciousness of the people. Its by-products were religious antagonisms and the intensification of class and caste divisions. But the debates in the legislatures, being mostly directed against the Government, provided ammunition to the Gandhians out to rouse mass enthusiasm for freedom.

Third, the two World Wars having debilitated Britain's economic strength to a point at which defence of the far-flung Empire became an impossible burden, the increasing pressure from the United States for the liquidation of colonialism made Britain see the wisdom of cutting her losses and quitting her possessions overseas.

By 1905, when Curzon left, the power struggle had become bipolar, the Congress projecting itself as the alternative power. This phase was intensified with the introduction of the first instalment of responsible government in 1920. It ended with Irwin's viceroyalty in 1931. The Simon Commission's activities and the pressures developed during three successive Round Table Conferences rendered the power struggle pentangular, the British, the Congress, the Muslims, the Hindu depressed classes and the Princes constituting the rival claimants to power.

The power struggle, however, became triangular in 1940, when Linlithgow, acting under Amery's instructions, placed a veto on a constitutional settlement in the hands of the leader of the Muslim League. As inner Tory circles put it, this was Britain's Crescent Card.

The fortunes of war and Japan's threat to India made London realise that India was a lost dominion. The Crescent Card, instead of being a trump in British hands, served to make the struggle once again bipolar in 1945 during the regime of Wavell. The contenders were the Congress and the League, the British having decided to quit.

Who conceded Pakistan? Some name one person, some the other. But, in point of fact, there is no simple, straight answer.

Both the Congress and the Raj for their own reasons were keen on maintaining a united India, but both were walking the slippery path of winning the support of the third side of India's power triangle: Muslims. Whitehall unconsciously first planted the seed of partition by conceding separate electorate and communal representation, in Minto's words, to the Muslim "nation."

Following the outbreak of World War II, which caught the Congress unprepared for its political repercussions, Gandhi was the first to concede to the Muslims at the Ramgarh Congress session in 1940 the right of separation as in a Hindu joint family. He suggested the setting up of a Constituent Assembly based on adult franchise and proposed that the Muslim members be allowed to decide whether they wished to live separately or as members of a joint family. Gandhi's offer was essentially a move in the political game of outbidding and outwitting the British.

The British outbid Gandhi in August 1940 when Leopold Amery, through Linlithgow, placed in Jinnah's hands a veto on advance to self-government. This was done both to ride over the period of war and checkmate the Congress. But it had the effect of fixing a pointer to the road to partition.

When Japan entered the war towards the close of 1941 and its warships appeared in the Bay of Bengal, C.R. got his followers in Madras to pass a resolution formally conceding the claim for Pakistan made by the League in its Lahore resolution of March 1940. Although adopted to enable the formation of a national government to resist the Japanese, the resolution was repudiated promptly by the A.I.C.C., which reaffirmed its faith in a united India.

Nehru came next, when American pressure made Churchill despatch Cripps to India with a proposal that envisaged partition as a possibility and gave political content to the veto placed in Jinnah's hand. The Congress Working Committee rejected the Cripps offer but, in a resolution drafted by Nehru, it formally conceded for the first time the principle that it did not believe in keeping within the Union any area against its expressed wish.

The drift towards partition thereafter received inadvertently a push when Bhulabhai Desai and Liaquat Ali entered into an agreement providing for equal representation to the Congress and the League in the reconstituted Cabinet. Gandhi blessed the proposal but Wavell transformed it into an equality between Muslims and caste Hindus—as against equality between two political entities. Gandhi then disowned the pact, but the damage was done.

Rajagopalachari now intervened with Gandhi's blessings to resolve the deadlock by offering the matter of partition to be settled by a referendum. In essence, this gave concrete shape to Gandhi's plan vaguely enunciated at the Ramgarh session as a tactical move.

Wavell almost succeeded in preserving the unity of India in co-operation with the Congress with his plan for a wartime coalition. But his effort was frustrated at the eleventh hour when Jinnah received the secret offer of "Pakistan on a platter" from his friends in Whitehall and in Delhi.

Nehru, Patel and Prasad next acknowledged and endorsed Jinnah's two-nation theory in March 1947, by advocating in a resolution adopted by the Congress Working Committee the division of the Punjab into Muslim-majority and Hindu-majority areas. This was done by the three without consulting Gandhi, who reacted sharply and considered this to be an hour of great humiliation.

When Mountbatten found himself running into a blind alley around May 1947, he came up with his partition plan and informally consulted Nehru, who gave his consent to it. As Mountbatten himself stated in his Nehru Memorial Lecture: ". . . Nehru realised that this would mean a much earlier transfer of power even though it were to two Governments and left a good chance for the essential unity of India to be maintained."

Patel was the first to accept the partition plan at the formal conference of national leaders convened by Mountbatten on 2nd June. Indeed, he gave it his wholehearted support. As Home Minister, Patel had realised that the drift towards partition had gone beyond the point of no return and chaos could be prevented only by conceding Pakistan. If this meant a break with Bapu, he was willing to pay the price—as indicated by him to me in his candid talk referred to earlier.

In the final analysis, the Congress leaders and the party as a whole were too weary to carry on the struggle any further and were, in their heart of hearts, anxious to grasp power and enjoy its fruits without further delay. As Badshah Khan told me in Kabul in 1967 in so many words: "Some of my colleagues in the High Command did toy with the idea of going ahead with the fight. But the majority accepted the view that they might then miss the bus. In the next elections in Britain, it was feared, the Labour might be thrown out of office and the diehard Tories voted back to power . . ."

Unknown at the time, Churchill played a key role in the creation of Pakistan. Following the outbreak of the war, he realised that India could not be held indefinitely and, as revealed by King George VI in his book, *His Life and Reign*, decided "to give up India to the Indians after the war." Churchill and his colleagues decided, at the same time, to save what they could out of the wreckage and it was this conviction that lay behind the offer to Jinnah of "Pakistan on a platter." Pakistan was expected to give them a foothold in the sub-continent.

Attlee and his colleagues in the Labour Party did not agree with this policy and earnestly attempted to maintain a united India, however fragile its federal structure. But the compulsion of events went beyond the control of the main British and Congress actors in the final scene of the freedom drama. And, destiny helped Jinnah.

Chapter 14

THE AUSPICIOUS HOUR

An interesting hitch arose over the exact timing of the transfer of power. Mountbatten had proposed and Attlee had agreed to 15th August. However, leading astrologers in Delhi suggested that 14th August was more auspicious. Nehru then hit upon an interesting compromise. He called the Constituent Assembly in the afternoon of 14th August and continued its sitting till midnight when, according to Western practice, 15th August took birth and the zero hour was within the auspicious period envisaged by the Hindu calendar. The Constituent Assembly, as the Provisional Parliament, assumed sovereign power at midnight on 14th/15th August.

Calling upon its members to pledge themselves to serve India and her people, Nehru said: "We end today a period of ill fortune and India discovers herself again." Earlier, its President, Prasad, said: "To all we give the assurance that it will be our endeavour to end poverty and squalor and its companions, hunger and disease, to abolish distinctions and exploitation and to ensure decent conditions of living." Prasad was cheered twice, once when he referred to Gandhi as "our beacon light, our guide and philosopher," and again when he, while expressing sorrow at the separation, sent his good wishes to the people of Pakistan.

Conches were blown on the last stroke of midnight and a cry of "Mahatma Gandhi ki jai" (long live Mahatma Gandhi) echoed throughout the Central Hall of the Council House. In that emotionally charged atmosphere, tears of joy swelled up as I watched the fulfilment of a dream. Nehru moved the adoption of the pledge, and this was seconded by the League Leader Khaliq-uz-Zaman. Supporting the motion, Dr. Radhakrishnan contrasted the British action in quitting India with that of the French in Indo-China and the Dutch in Indonesia and expressed admiration, amidst cheers, for the political sagacity and courage of the British people.

The Assembly endorsed Mountbatten's appointment as Governor-General and adjourned after Mrs. Sucheta Kripalani, who in the sixties became India's first woman Chief Minister in the U.P., had sung Iqbal's *Hindustan Hamara* and the first verse of *Jana Gana Mana*, Rabindranath Tagore's composition which was later adopted as the National Anthem, while Nehru and Prasad went to Government House to give Mountbatten an account of the proceedings.

On the morning of Independence Day, Nehru unfurled the tricolour at Red Fort, watched by nearly a million people. They reserved their loudest cheers for a reference to Subhas Bose, who Nehru said, had raised the flag of independence abroad. Men of the Indian National Army and their band participated in the ceremony, and they had the added joy of knowing that the first act of the Nehru Government was to announce the release of I.N.A. prisoners as well as those held for political offences.

As I listened to Nehru, my thoughts went back to my last meeting with Bose—some seventeen years earlier to Lucknow, before his final incarceration by the British and his secret escape to Berlin via Kabul. Bose, young and dynamic, was then very angry and poured out his wrath against Gandhi, whom he said had deliberately backed Nehru to keep him out of the Congress hierarchy. The war, he added, had given him an opportunity to show that action, and not talk, would get freedom. (He later joined the Axis powers and organised the Indian National Army.)

There is no doubt that had Bose not died in an air crash, he would have proved a most formidable rival to Nehru and influenced for the better the course of Indian history after independence. Nehru paid him a compliment by adopting "Jai Hind" (Long live India), the salute of Bose's I.N.A., as the national salutation and by unfurling the national flag on the Red Fort. Bose's slogan to his freedom fighters was "Delhi Chalo" (On to Delhi) and he had vowed to plant the tricolour on the Red Fort to the cry of "Jai Hind." Gandhi for his part, described Bose as a true patriot. But it was too late . . .

I wrote in the *Hindustan Times*: "Pandit Nehru as the first Prime Minister and Lord Mountbatten as the first Governor-General were the heroes of the drama. They got receptions which any monarch or President would have envied. The outburst of popular joy was like the burst of a dam and the mighty torrent breaking through all barriers."

Addressing the Constituent Assembly on Independence morning, Mountbatten said, "At this historic moment, let us not forget all that India owes to Mahatma Gandhi—the architect of her freedom through non-violence. We miss his presence here today, and we would have him know how much he is in our thoughts."

Where indeed was the Mahatma, instead of sharing the joy of his newly liberated countrymen? While the Constituent Assembly was holding its epoch-making midnight session, he was sleeping peacefully in Calcutta after bringing about the miracle of Hindu–Muslim fraternisation in that hate-maddened metropolis. When the Calcutta correspondent of All–India Radio approached Gandhi earlier that night for an Independence Day message, he meaningfully observed: "I have run dry."

I published in the *Hindustan Times* a 5,000-word review headed "Journey's End—Beginning of Another" and carried a box with a quotation from Gandhi and the picture of Nehru shaking hands with Attlee at their meeting in London the previous December. The quotation from Gandhi was headed "The Dharma of Every Indian" and quoted what Gandhi said during the Salt Satyagraha: "British rule in India has brought about moral, material and spiritual ruination of this great country. I regard this rule as a curse. I am out to destroy this system of Government. I have sung the tune of 'God save the King' and have taught others to sing it. I was a believer in the policy of petitions, deputations and friendly negotiations. But all these have gone to the dogs. I know that these are not the ways to bring this Government round. Sedition has become my religion. Ours is a non-violent battle. We are not out to kill anybody but it is our 'Dharma' to see that the curse of this Government is blotted out."

Diplomats and other foreigners who were present in New Delhi expressed astonishment at the fact that tens of thousands of joyous Indians, celebrating the end of British rule, should have lustily shouted "Mountbatten ki jai" in honour of the last pro-consul of the departing order. This was a genuine tribute, personally to the glamorous Viceroy and his consort but also to the British as a race, with whom the Hindus had developed a love-hate relationship. The Hindu admired the Briton for his efficiency, business integrity, punctuality, strength of character and parliamentary system of government. But he detested him as an imperial overlord.

When Cripps came to India with his plan in 1942, he told me that he laid the blame for poisoning Indo–British relations over the years on the Britons and Anglo–Indians who represented the British Press and gave their reports an anti-Congress and anti-Hindu and pro-Muslim or pro-League slant. There was an element of truth in this remark, but after independence I expected the Briton's business acumen to come out on top and teach him that in close friendship with India lay his best chance of sustaining his economic strength and influence in international diplomacy.

I even dreamed of a commonwealth revolving on a London–Delhi axis and constituting a third force in world affairs. The Mount-battens, Edwina even more than Dicky, were to Nehru and most other Indian intellectuals the idealised image of this new relationship. But Indian well-wishers of Britain counted without the Blimps of the Foreign Office and the Commonwealth Relations Office, and the Indo–British honeymoon therefore lasted only six months officially, although unofficially it lasted longer between Nehru and the Mountbattens.

I was a witness at very close quarters of this pulsating drama, the ebb and flow of the struggle for freedom. I knew intimately the men and women who shared its hazards and rewards. Twas bliss to be alive in those stirring times.

1947–64
THE NEHRU ERA

INDIA ON THE DAY
OF PARTITION,
15 August 1947

Chapter 1

TRYST WITH DESTINY

(a) THE BRITISH LEGACY

With Nehru's words about India's tryst with destiny ringing in my ears, as in those of millions of my countrymen, I pondered over the shape of things to come. I had written in my enthusiasm that "on 15th August, 1947, Delhi, the capital of several empires, became for the first time the seat of Lok Raj—government of the people, by the people, for the people." It seemed clear on that historic day that Indian nationalism was an all-pervasive force, that we had inherited a going concern and that we were endowed with the leadership that would take the nation along the path that led to the promised land. But beneath the surface were strong under-currents, communal, caste, linguistic, parochial, social and economic, all of which may be summed up in the phrase "rising expectations."

One of Gandhi's remarks haunted me. He had said to me, describing his differences with Nehru: "Jawahar wants Englishmen to go but *Angreziat* (English ways and culture) to stay. I want *Angreziat* to go and Englishmen to stay as our friends." Gandhi wanted to rid India of the Western culture which had been imposed on the country and had stifled the older and more natural Indian cultural and social traditions. Nehru, although the idol of the masses, was aloof from them mentally. He was an Englishman in Indian skin. After independence, the conflict between these diametrically opposed approaches was swept under the carpet to meet the upheaval caused by the partition. Gandhi, as moral force and mentor, stood rocklike amid the raging storm of patriotic emotions and communal rivalries. Mountbatten was the symbol of captaincy, beaming a confidence which was infectious and imparting a dynamism which almost moved mountains. There was Jawaharlal, the darling of the nation, the new ruler and the refuge of the minorities. The Iron Man, Patel, inspired trust in those days of uncertainty. He drew to himself the elements that would, under his leadership, hold the country together and weld it into a nation. Rajendra Prasad was the embodiment of Gandhian humility and the spirit of selfless service.

How did people at various social levels react to the dawn of *Swaraj*? Two hundred thousand people had swirled round Council House when the Constituent Assembly assumed power. A million-throated cry of "Jai Hind" had gone up when Nehru unfurled the national flag on the ramparts of Red Fort, built by the same Mughal Emperor Shah Jahan who fashioned the Taj Mahal as his wife's mausoleum. Half a million people milled round India Gate when the flag was broken and Mountbatten and Nehru saluted it. I went among people in various walks of life to find out what freedom meant to them to get an idea of the vision of the future they had and the hopes that swelled in their breasts. Everybody said Gandhi was the architect of India's freedom. "We will now have Ram Raj," the common man said. Among the thousands of village folk who had come to Delhi for the *mela* (celebration), I asked one why he had done so and he replied: "To have the *darshan* (sight of a venerated person) of Raja Jawaharlal."

(b) DOUBTS AND FEARS

The reaction of officers of the all-India services, especially the ICS, was very significant. This was the only category of people who put a question mark on the shape of things to come. One group told me they would happily change over to the Gandhi cap and resort to simple living and adjust their habits accordingly.

The other group said the service tradition and code of conduct must be maintained as before in the interest of stability and good government. They asserted that the pivot of British parliamentary institutions was the Civil Service and that political bosses could come and go without making much difference so long as the civilians were honest, efficient and had the incentive to work well. In short, they felt that the "steel frame" character of the administration should be retained intact. The politician in charge could depend on them to execute his policy so long as he did not meddle with the administrative machine.

But from their experience of the interim Government they were not sure that things would turn out as they wanted. Already, the element of *durbar* (paying court to one's superior) was creeping in and some Civil Servants were becoming too closely associated with their bosses and ignoring the rules of the game.

The politicians I tapped for their views were of three categories. The giants were loyal to Gandhi to a man, but they felt a growing estrangement from the Mahatma in that the business of government had made them abandon their Gandhian ideals both under political and administrative compulsions as well as under their own personal craving to wield power as the British had done and to live like the "White Sahibs (Master)." They could not resolve this conflict, and the more Gandhi spelled out his views at his daily prayer meetings on how they should conduct themselves the more they shrank from his commandments. In fact, they charged him in private with attempting to exercise power without responsibility. Those in the second rank openly exhibited their itch for power and pelf, and those at the bottom rungs of the political hierarchy also saw in the advent of freedom the long-awaited opportunity to cash in on their sacrifices for the cause.

Businessmen too were divided in their reactions to the new order. A majority of traders and bankers had the traditional outlook: "Our forefathers have told us a *bania* is not made to be a ruler. He buys security by buying the ruler." Sophisticated businessmen put it thus: "Politicians need funds for elections and they want jobs for their relatives. They have ambitions. We cater for them. We have already learned during the war how to get things done at the lower and higher echelons of the Secretariat." The younger executives felt differently. They said: "Democracy in the West is run by men drawn from business and the professions. Modern government is too complex a machine to be left to the mercy of ignoramuses, be they saints or political charlatans. We must jump into the arena to make sure the Government is well run."

(c) EXODUS

My preoccupation with these matters seemed, however, academic, for hardly had the echoes of "Jai Hind" died in the capital than the nation was plunged in sorrow as reports came in hourly of millions of refugees on the march and of dreadful carnage on both sides of the India–Pakistan border. About ten million people were uprooted from their homes and another half a million massacred. Thousands of women and girls were kidnapped and raped on both sides.

Within fifteen days of independence, Nehru and Liaquat Ali decided to fly to Lyallpur and Lahore, in West Punjab, to study the refugee problem. A small Press party accompanied them. We took off from Amritsar and landed at Lyallpur, where half a million Hindus and Sikhs begged for safe passage to India. It was the day of *Rakhi*, when a Hindu sister ties a thread round her brother's wrist, thus committing him to defend her honour. A dozen women came to the Circuit House, where we had made our headquarters, and tied the symbolic thread on Nehru. The act brought tears to our eyes, and

Nehru was visibly moved. He responded to their plea that he fly over Jhaṅg and Chiniot to lift up the thousands of refugees who had gathered there from the despair in which they had been plunged. As our Dakota passed over these places, we saw huge crowds looking up at the aircraft and we could almost feel a vast sigh rise upward to meet it.

This trip delayed our arrival at Lahore airfield by ninety minutes. There I met the Governor, Sir Francis Mudie, who had been Home Member under Wavell, and Giani Kartar Singh. "What the devil are you doing here?" Mudie asked me in a voice betraying panic. "To see what the Frankenstein monster you and we all have let loose has done to innocent people," I retorted. He snapped back: "You wanted independence. Now you have it." The deputation who met the two Prime Ministers said this was the refrain of many British officers to whom they had appealed for protection. Giani Kartar Singh was in tears and appealed to Nehru to save the hundreds of thousands of Hindus and Sikhs who had gathered in various towns in West Punjab, seeking protection in numbers. He seemed repentant for the part he had played in working up communal passions.

Most touching were the replies of the refugees whom we spoke to when we came across a long caravan on the way to India along the road through Sheikhupura, where the worst slaughter had occurred. An old peasant said: "This country has seen many changes of rulers. They have come and gone. But this is the first time that with a change of rulers the *riyaya* (subjects) is also being forced to change—and flee their homes." An elderly woman, not aware she was addressing Nehru but judging him an important personage from his dress and demeanour, said: "Partitions take place in all families. Property changes hands, but it is all arranged peacefully. Why this butchery, loot and abductions? Could you not do it the sensible way families divided?"

I talked to politicians, Civil Servants and military officers on both sides and came to the conclusion, as I wrote in the *Hindustan Times*, "that while the communal orgy of March 1947 was the result of the Muslim League's preaching of violence and hatred the holocaust of the past three weeks is the work of the civil officials and the police and military." I added that, "there was little to choose between West Punjab and East Punjab. By dividing the Army, the police and the Civil Service on communal lines, they let loose a Frankenstein." I concluded my report by stating that Mountbatten had hurried through with partition without making sure that the Boundary Force would be able to maintain peace.

The Hindu and Sikh officials who had migrated from West Punjab after witnessing the orgy of murder and destruction in that region had permitted it to be avenged in the eastern part. The state of affairs can well be imagined from the fact that because of the communal break-up of the provincial services the police force in East Punjab had dwindled from 17,000 to 3,000. The magnitude of the tragedy struck me with full force when I visited the camp at Kurukshetra, a few miles from Delhi, where 270,000 refugees from West Punjab had been sheltered in tents and makeshift dwellings, and saw the fifteen-mile-long caravan of the displaced and dispossessed moving towards India from Montgomery district.

An intelligence official, Rai Bahadur Bakshi Badri Nath, who was in charge of Muslim League activities, gave me an account of a conspiracy to extend Pakistan's boundary up to the river Jumna. When the administrative changeover took place, every East Punjab district had a predominantly Muslim·constabulary, and the Leaguers decided that they should capture the police armouries between 12th and 14th August, kill the Hindu and Sikh officers and declare the area independent of India. This information leaked out. The Hindu officers met and decided to station more of their number wherever British and Muslim officers predominated. By 5th August, these postings had been made and the Muslim constables, except for some who fled with their rifles, were disarmed. The result of this action was that the Muslims in East Punjab became demoralised. They felt they could not save themselves from mob violence. In Amritsar Fort police lines, a hundred bombs were found in the possession of a Muslim police officer, who revealed on questioning the plan to revolt and seize the territory up to the river Jumna. That was why Sardar Patel said he had evidence that the Muslims were preparing to kill the Hindus and Sikhs in the Punjab. One letter conveying these instructions to the Muslim Leaguers in Montgomery was intercepted. It said that the League leaders would appeal for stopping the killing, but such appeals should be ignored unless they received a message on a secret telephone which had been installed for this purpose.

V. Vishwanathan, who was in Geneva with the Palestine Commission, was appointed Deputy High Commissioner in Pakistan. Relations between the two countries deteriorated so badly that there was no air service between them and he had to fly in Mountbatten's special plane with Lord Listowel. In Karachi, he found such enthusiasm for Pakistan that every taxi carried a national flag on its bonnet. Karachi was seething with anti-India hysteria, but he managed to organise the movement of 900,000 Hindus and Sikhs out of West Pakistan. On his own initiative, he requisitioned ships belonging to Indian lines, saying he was doing so on the authority of the Indian Government. The greater problem he faced was the fact that the very presence of Sikhs provoked riots and murder. There were 600 Sikhs in a regiment in Maler Cantonment under a British officer, who proposed to disarm them and send them by train to India. Vishwanathan knew they would all be slaughtered on the way. So he chartered a ship, smuggled the Sikhs on board when it was dark and sent them to Dwarka in Gujarat. From there they were taken to Ahmedabad and Delhi.

(d) PULLING IN DIFFERENT WAYS

Four special articles I wrote in the last week of September 1947, comparing political conditions in India and Pakistan, said that the manner in which the two countries were reacting politically and emotionally suggested that before long Pakistan would become another Iran and India would go the way of Chiang's China. I envisioned government by politicians for politicians in India, and in Pakistan rule by Civil Servants, army officers and the landed aristocracy for themselves. The sanction behind the Indian politician was the people's trust in him and the mass base of the Congress Party, which spread its roots to the remotest village. The Muslim masses had played no part in the manoeuvres and haggling for Pakistan, nor had the Muslim politicians who jumped on Jinnah's bandwagon when they learned that their British patrons were quitting and were, furthermore, encouraged to do so by these same patrons.

Jinnah set the pattern of thinking at the top in Pakistan by making Mountbatten agree to a vital change in the law extending the Indian Independence Act to Pakistan by providing that in choosing and summoning Ministers the Governor of a province "shall be under the general control of and comply with such particular direction, if any, as may from time to time be given to him by the Governor-General." This was personal dictatorship assumed by the progenitor of Pakistan.

A factor, invisibly at work, was the purpose that Britons in both dominions wanted them to serve. Those in Pakistan wanted her to look towards West Asia and to assume, with her superior intellectual development, her greater social advance, modernised administrative set-up and better-trained army, leadership of an Islamic bloc under the aegis of the British Commonwealth. So every move that helped loosen the ties between India and Pakistan was welcomed, even devised by Britons who headed the majority of departments of the Government of Pakistan.

Mountbatten, on the other hand, personified the broader objective of Whitehall of nourishing India's strength so that she would become the balancing factor in the Indian Ocean area, particularly in South-East Asia. Thus the vengeful' attitude of some British officials who stayed on in the sub-continent to see it dissolve in chaos did not reflect the thinking of the British Government.

Foreign observers, surveying Indian developments with trained and generally detached outlook, found before 1947 was out that Gandhi, Patel and Prasad stood for one policy in domestic and international affairs, Nehru for another. The rank and file Congressmen sided with the trio, the Communists and Socialists with Nehru. But to the unsophisticated masses, newcomers to the political arena, Nehru's denunciation of affluence did not seem to conflict with Gandhi's identification of himself with the poor and the downtrodden and his belief in social and economic advance through *Sarvodaya*, which sought to convert the haves into selfless trustees and benefactors of the have-nots.

Chapter 2

RESETTLING THE REFUGEES

I sponsored the cause of the refugees, whose sufferings I knew as one providing refuge to two families, those of my wife's sister and of my own sister. Prominent refugees met at the *Hindustan Times* office and decided to organise the Punjab Reconstruction Committee with Bakshi Tek Chand, former Chief Justice of Lahore High Court, as its chairman and me as its convener. We arranged interviews with the Prime Minister, the Deputy Prime Minister, the Finance Minister, the Defence Minister, the Minister for Public Works and the Minister for Relief and Rehabilitation.

Our main contention was that whereas the refugees who arrived up to the middle of September brought personal effects like cash and jewellery those who followed had been stripped of everything they possessed. We feared that while the agriculturists among the refugees would be compensated with land left behind by Muslim evacuees to the extent of their assets, the non-agriculturists would not be able to get even a tenth of their losses from the Muslim property left behind in the towns. We therefore pressed for fulfilment of the agreement reached by Nehru and Liaquat Ali Khan for the exchange in military trucks and under armed escort of the movable assets left on both sides.

We waited in deputation on Nehru at 4 p.m. on Saturday, 20th September, 1947, in his room in the External Affairs Ministry. The following extract from the minutes I drew up of the meeting are significant in the light of later developments:

"Mr. Yodhraj, Chairman of the Punjab National Bank, began by explaining the need for an area of several hundred acres to be set apart for a residential colony at a distance of about seven miles from Delhi. Pandit Nehru's immediate reaction was one of opposition. 'I won't let you come within 700 miles of Delhi,' he interjected angrily because of his grievance against the Punjabis, who, he thought, were responsible for the disturbances in Delhi. He mentioned that these disorders had brought the Government a very bad name all over the world and upset their programme with regard to certain Princely States. Bakshi Tek Chand explained the vital bearing of the question of a residential colony and an industrial area on the settlement of refugees. The question of an early decision in regard to the capital of East Punjab was also raised. Pandit Nehru thereupon realised that a good case had been made and began to take notes.

"Pandit Nehru was firmly of the opinion that the new capital for East Punjab should not be Delhi or any place in close proximity to Delhi. If near Delhi, it would not have the chance of healthy growth as the centre of an autonomous provincial government. He said it was really a matter for the people of East Punjab to decide, but he appreciated the urgent need of settling it. He personally favoured the establishment of a capital on a new site instead of selecting an existing town. That would, he said, give a chance for the capital to be developed on modern lines. (His views prevailed in the end and led to the birth of Chandigarh.)

"Mr. Durga Das mentioned the problem of Sikhs and said that steps should be taken now to make sure that this problem did not take a serious form later. The Sikhs should be asked to state categorically whether they wished to have a small province of their own in which they would have a majority. If so, the refugees should from now be settled in such a manner as would fulfil this desire of the Sikhs. If the Sikhs wished to live as citizens of India, it should be made clear to them that they would not have any special privileges, legislative, administrative, or by convention. They must sink or swim with the Hindus under a system of joint electorates.

"Pandit Nehru, replying, said that Master Tara Singh had met him the previous day and that he had asked the Sikh leader whether his community wanted Khalistan (a Sikh State). Pandit Nehru said he had never seen Master Tara Singh so crestfallen as on that day. The Sikh leader vehemently protested against any idea of Khalistan and said that the Sikhs, being a very small section of the people of India, would not pick any quarrel with them. They wished to remain citizens of India and live with the Hindus as brothers."

(Although the deputation pleaded for facilities to settle 50,000 families, ultimately half a million families found refuge in Delhi. Indeed, the city's expansion to embrace an area far exceeding the seven capitals of the old empires is largely the result of the enterprise of these refugees from the Punjab.)

A deputation of the committee had met Patel a day earlier. The meeting, which began at 8.30 p.m. at Patel's residence, lasted an hour. The main issue discussed was protection of the Indian border. The following extract reveals the mind and methods of the Iron Man:

"Sardar Patel gave a full picture of the situation and the measures taken by the Government. He said that the Pakistan Prime Minister had that day met him and Pandit Nehru. It was clear, he said, that Pakistan was not in a position either to declare war on India or to organise raids on our border. Nevertheless, the Government of India had taken measures to be ready for all contingencies. He had ordered all the ordnance factories to work twenty-four hours a day and produce arms and ammunition.

"Sardar Patel further informed the committee that he had told the Pakistan Prime Minister to declare his policy regarding the property of Hindus and Sikhs left behind. If Pakistan wanted to write off all such property, India would then be free to do the same in respect of Muslim property. Otherwise, Pakistan must take the responsibility for compensation. He also made it clear to Mr. Liaquat Ali Khan that if no Hindus and Sikhs remained in Pakistan, it was difficult to see how Muslims could remain in India. In a word, the policy of the Indian Government was to pay the Pakistan Government in the same coin."

Another interesting meeting was with the Defence Minister Baldev Singh, at 8 a.m. on Friday, 26th September, at his residence. He admitted that law and order had broken down in the countryside in East Punjab, due to lack of armed forces. He mentioned with regret that public leaders, magistrates and the military and police had all made common cause on both sides in promoting the holocaust.

To add to the agony of partition came the Pakistani-inspired attack on Kashmir by tribal hordes from the North-West Frontier area. The meagre forces of Maharaja Hari Singh withered under the surprise onslaught and he fled from Srinagar to Jammu. He appealed to Nehru for help and, shedding the earlier policy of fence-sitting, offered the accession of his state to the Indian Dominion. Nehru hurriedly consulted Mountbatten and Patel and it was decided with Gandhi's consent to accept accession and fly out troops in Dakotas across the treacherous Banihal Pass to save Srinagar and the Valley. It was touch and go. The marauders had reached the outskirts of Srinagar and were heading for the airport. However, luck was on India's side and a near-impossible situation was miraculously saved by the troops. Sheikh Abdullah's endorsement of the accession in his capacity as the leader of Kashmir's principal political party, the National Conference, lent moral weight to India's deed. (It was this role of the Sheikh that Jinnah had dreaded most. He had made a vain bid to win over Abdullah before Independence. He was manifestly sore on his return from Srinagar. Asked what he thought of the Sheikh, he contemptuously remarked: "Oh, that tall man who sings the Koran and exploits the people?")

Simultaneously, India approached the U.N. Security Council for action against Pakistan, little realising then that the simple and straight-forward issue of aggression would get bogged down in world power politics. Who precisely originated the idea that India should take the Kashmir question to the Security Council (described by Patel as "Insecurity Council") is not clear. Some at the time mentioned the name of Mountbatten and others that of Nehru and his key official advisers. The British wanted the state to go to Pakistan. Mountbatten advised the Maharaja to accede to either of the dominions and added, on the authority of Patel, that if he chose to join Pakistan, India would not object.

Jinnah's British advisers and fanatical followers were determined to get Kashmir for Pakistan. This was more than evident from the way they conducted themselves. The Army, for instance, had ordered prior to independence a large number of maps of Kashmir from the Survey of India. At the time of partition, these were quietly handed over by British officers to Pakistan. Worse still, Indian officials discovered at the time of taking over that all the records of Military Intelligence and most of those of the Central Intelligence Bureau relating to the state were also missing. Equally significantly, Gilgit, which was under two British officers, "revolted" against the Maharaja and declared itself independent. Today, Gilgit is a part of the Kashmir territory now under Pakistan's illegal occupation.

Chapter 3

CONSTITUTION MAKING

A ticklish constitutional problem arose on 15th August, 1947, and Nehru put it jokingly to me in Parliament's lobby: "Mavalankar has vanished into thin air." He was referring to the provision in the Indian Independence Act under which the Legislative Assembly, of which G. V. Mavalankar was President, automatically dissolved on Independence Day and the Constituent Assembly became the supreme sovereign and legislative body. The question arose how Rajendra Prasad, a member of the Cabinet as well as the President of the Constituent Assembly, could preside over the deliberations of that body when it functioned as a legislature.

Both Nehru and Patel felt that Prasad should continue in the Cabinet and another President should be chosen for the Constituent Assembly. When Nehru took the stand that it would be intolerable in a democracy for a Minister to preside, Benegal Narsing Rau proposed that a Deputy Speaker be elected to preside over the Assembly in the name of the President of the Constituent Assembly. This led to tension between Patel and Prasad and resulted in a sharp exchange in the Cabinet. A Civil Servant who attended the meeting told me: "These men whom we adored as giants quarrelled like children." The dispute was referred to Gandhi, a bare week before his assassination. Prasad wanted to make a statement in the Constituent Assembly; Gandhi sent for it and modified it. Prasad accepted the changes, saying: "I stand for harmony and therefore do not press my point." Gandhi's terse comment, conveyed to me by Devadas, was: "Even Rajen Babu is lured by power. I feel disillusioned."

At this point, another issue was raised: "What would be Prasad's position on the legislative side and Mavalankar's as Speaker? Reluctantly, Prasad agreed to the election of another Speaker, provided he was subordinate to the President of the Constituent Assembly. Mavalankar demanded equality of status and full control over his Secretariat. Prasad yielded after a hard struggle, retaining the Presidentship of the Constituent Assembly, and Mavalankar took over as Speaker of the Legislative Assembly.

But the squabble did not end there. At the instance of Gandhi, Nehru suggested that Prasad become President of the Congress Party. Prasad objected strongly to what appeared to him an attempt to push him out of the Cabinet and Presidentship of the Constituent Assembly. For some time it appeared as though he would repudiate the agreement over Mavalankar's appointment. When Nehru dropped the proposal and Prasad's ruffled feelings had been soothed, still more difficulties were encountered. Rau took away the Legislative Assembly Secretariat, and Prasad ruled that the new staff could not be appointed without his sanction. The matter was referred to Nehru who then got Prasad to delegate to Mavalankar the authority to appoint staff. Later, a provision was written into the Constitution making the Parliament Secretariat independent of the Government.

Meanwhile, I watched, analysed and commented on the progress of the Constituent Assembly in fashioning the instrument of government and the tense drama over six issues of a delicate and controversial nature.

Should adult franchise be introduced, involving an increase in the electorate from 35 million to 170 million? Maulana Azad advocated its deferment for fifteen years. Prasad and Nehru plumped for adult franchise as an act of faith. The vote favouring it was carried amidst acclamation.

Nehru favoured incorporation of a section establishing a special relationship with the State of Jammu and Kashmir, thus inferentially recognising the state's right to frame its own constitution within the Indian Union. Patel wanted the State to be fully integrated with the Union. The Cabinet was divided on the issue and the trend of opinion in the Constituent Assembly favoured the Sardar's stand. But when the matter came before the Assembly, Patel put the unity and solidarity of the Government before everything else and backed the Nehru formula.

The most delicate issue related to safeguards for minorities. Azad wanted reservation of seats for the Muslims and other minorities within the framework of general electorates. Patel opposed such

Sardar Patel (right) with the Nizam of Hyderabad after the integration
of his state

ABOVE The author meets President Johnson at the White House on his
world tour in 1967

BELOW Nehru takes his daughter Indira Gandhi, then politically unknown,
to receive the Freedom of the City of London in July 1956

safeguards. Nehru left it to Patel to jump the hurdle as Chairman of the Advisory Committee on Minorities. Two women members played a key role in this high-strung drama. Amrit Kaur, speaking for the Indian Christians, said that reservation of seats and weightage based on religion or sect would lead to fragmentation of the Indian Union. The Sikhs demanded the same treatment as given to the Muslims.

After the Committee had wrestled with the problem for weeks, Patel decided to clinch the issue at its final meeting. He called on Begum Aizaz Rasul of Lucknow to state the Muslim view. She was a zealous Muslim Leaguer before partition and had even gone to the length of giving up saree and adopting the costume worn by the Begums of Oudh. The Muslims left behind in India, she said nervously, were an integral part of the nation and needed no safeguards. Patel seized this crucial moment to declare that the Muslims were unanimously in favour of joint electorates and adjourned the meeting.

Much heat was generated on whether the President of the Republic and Governors of the constituent states should be elected by popular vote and whether they should have discretionary powers. Legal luminaries and constitutional pundits had a field day, but Nehru and Patel brought a practical approach to bear on the issue. They opposed popularly elected heads. Indeed, Nehru as Prime Minister took steps to see that the Union President even though chosen by an electoral college consisting of all the members of the Central and State Legislatures, would be a constitutional figurehead. Patel as Home Minister made sure that Governor of a state was the nominee of the Union Government and had enough discretionary powers to act as the executive agent of the Centre in an emergency.

The question of a national link language posed the most difficult hurdle. Swami Dayananda and Mahatma Gandhi, both from Gujarat, and Tilak and Savarkar, from Maharashtra, had zealously pleaded for Hindi as the symbol of nationhood. Prasad and Patel strongly supported Hindi, while Nehru left it to the Hindi lobby to work out a formula acceptable to the non-Hindi regions, especially Madras and Bengal. Finally, the formula providing for replacement of English by Hindi in fifteen years was embodied in the Constitution, although each side did it with mental reservation.

A great deal of excitement was caused over the issue: Should the Fundamental Right to be embodied in the Constitution guarantee fair payment for private property acquired by the State and should the right be made justiciable? Nehru was against making the right justiciable. Patel stood rocklike for the Fundamental Rights adopted by the Congress Party under his Presidentship in 1931 in Karachi. After a prolonged tug-of-war Patel won because he had the backing of the distinguished lawyers, who were fashioning the Constitution, and of the overwhelming majority of members of the Constituent Assembly. (This right was somewhat diluted by an amendment of the Constitution after Patel's death in order to facilitate land reforms involving abolition of the feudal system of landlordism.)

The Constitution-makers swept under the carpet the important matter relating to the scheduled tribes in the Assam hills in the north-east. They adopted a formula virtually placing the region outside the pale of normal Union laws and administrative apparatus. Nehru did this on the advice of Christian missionaries. His colleagues in the top echelons let it pass, treating the matter, in the words of Azad, as "a Nehru fad."

Chapter 4

THE PASSING OF THE MAHATMA

Gandhi had his own ideas of how Congressmen should live and behave after freedom had been achieved. He was in Calcutta on Independence Day, when the huge crowd celebrating the occasion around Chowringhee burst through the gates of Raj Bhavan, the official residence of the Governor, and took whatever they could lay their hands on. Gandhi seized on the opportunity to read a sermon to Rajagopalachari, the Governor of West Bengal, and his counterparts in the other provinces. He wanted them to abandon the gubernatorial mansions associated with foreign rule and reside simply in cottages, inexpensively furnished, spin yarn by hand, abstain from liquor and speak only Hindustani and the language of the province.

Communal trouble flared up in Calcutta again in September, and Gandhi resorted to another fast, which had the required effect. C.R., who had at first ridiculed the idea of Gandhi fasting to deter *goondas* (hoodlums), admitted that this method of protest had produced truly wonderful results. By now, Delhi was in the throes of the upheaval caused by the incoming refugees from West Punjab and their local sympathisers to push out the Muslims to make room for the newcomers. The Muslim policemen of the city having gone to Pakistan, the Hindu and Sikh members of the force and the magistracy found themselves facing a situation where their sympathies lay with the refugees. Mass murder and destruction of property was launched to terrorise the Muslims to leave the city. Gandhi resolved to rush to Delhi, which he described as a city of the dead where he must make a supreme effort to restore sanity. His sermons at his daily prayer meetings had a powerful effect, but every fresh wave of refugees which poured in, bereft of their possesions and with blood-chilling tales of atrocities committed on them, caused further upheavals.

Patel urged the Pakistanis to change their ways. He pointed out that Jinnah used to call Gandhi the greatest enemy of the Muslims, but now Pakistanis were acclaiming Gandhi their sole protector and benefactor. Anxious to restore confidence in the minorities, Patel had earlier accepted Wavell's advice and agreed to have a Muslim Chief Commissioner, a Christian Inspector-General of Police and a Sikh Deputy Commissioner for Delhi. But when trouble erupted in a big way, Patel confessed to me that he had made a mistake in accepting the advice. This balance was all right in normal times, but once the communal holocaust occurred the Chief Commissioner and the head of the police became ineffective.

A crisis occurred around New Year. The Partition Council had arrived at several decisions regarding the division of assets. A financial agreement between India and Pakistan had also been reached and it had been further decided that all the outstanding disputes which eluded settlement be referred to an arbitration tribunal. Accord was subsequently reached on all points, including the withdrawal of Pakistani raiders from Kashmir, and Patel made a statement in Parliament that the agreement would have to be implemented fully. The Pakistani leaders changed their mind on Kashmir, insisting at the same time that India honour the financial clauses of the agreement, which included the payment of cash balances amounting to Rs. 550 million to Pakistan. Patel took a firm stand against turning over this sum to Pakistan until the other provisions of the pact were honoured and the Finance Minister, Shammukham Chetty, strongly backed him.

When Pakistan's Prime Minister said this was an attempt to "strangulate" his country, C. D. Deshmukh, the Governor of the Reserve Bank of India and Pakistan, saw Gandhi and pointed out that Pakistan had been provided with the required ways and means. Liaquat Ali's charge, he added, was a political stunt. But Gandhi, who had made the restoration of peace and harmony in Delhi an issue on which he staked his life, announced an indefinite fast at this stage. Word went round that the fast was directed against Patel's decision to withhold the cash balances. Mountbatten and Nehru were, in fact, known to have told Gandhi that India was morally bound to transfer the balances to Pakistan and that, as both Patel and Chetty had adopted an unbending position on the issue, he alone could save the situation. Patel finally yielded and Gandhi broke his fast at the behest of leaders of all communities.

Gandhi had felt obliged to stay at Birla House rather than at Bhangi (Sweepers) Colony because Muslims could approach him there with greater safety. He said it was a shame that Dr. Ansari's daughter and son-in-law (now Governor of Orissa) had to seek shelter in a hotel and men like Zakir Husain (now President of the Republic) could not move about freely in the capital. Before long, Gandhi's presence in the capital had its sobering effect and as the situation progressively improved, he told me one day that he had decided to visit Pakistan accompanied by General Shah Nawaz Khan of the I.N.A. They had planned to leave in mid-February. He wanted the Hindus and Sikhs and Muslims restored to their homes.

But it was not only the communal situation that troubled Gandhi in those months following independence. He was also deeply concerned about the rot that was setting into the Congress Party. He had received information that some Congress legislators were taking money from businessmen to get them licences, that they were indulging in blackmarketing and subverting the judiciary and intimidating top officials to secure transfers and promotions for their protégés in the administration. Gandhi thought of a remedy for this alarming state of affairs. He called together representatives of such autonomous organisations as the All–India Spinners Association, the Harijan Sevek Sangh (Society for service to the Untouchables) the Village Industries Association, the Goseva Sangh (Cow Protection Society) and the Nai Talimi Sangh (New Education Society), all of which he had either founded or with which he was closely connected, for a conference in Delhi. Among those who attended were Zakir Husain and Kripalani.

Gandhi told the conference that he wanted to organise a co-ordinating committee on which all these bodies would be represented to screen candidates for election to Parliament and the provincial legislatures and certify their integrity and selfless spirit of service to the community. This would guide voters in their choice of suitable persons to speak on their behalf in the nation's political forums. The members of these organisations, which were engaged in constructive social work among the masses, were to keep out of politics themselves. But Gandhi's proposals did not appeal to the conference, as most of the participants thought they should remain politically inactive and some felt they should put themselves up for election.

After this conference, Gandhi felt more isolated than ever from the men who claimed to follow him and practise his precepts. He felt like one exploited by his comrades for their political ends and therefore hit on a revolutionary plan. The Congress must dissolve and a Lok Seva Sangh (Servants of the People Society) take its place. He drew up a constitution for the Sangh and decided to place it before the Congress overlords. But the assassin's bullet ended Gandhi's life with both tasks to which he had dedicated himself unfinished. He could neither restore peace and goodwill between India and Pakistan nor could he purge Indian politics of its corrupting influences.

By a cruel stroke of luck, I missed the prayer meeting where Gandhi was assassinated. I rarely missed these evening meetings and occasionally followed them up with a brief chat with Bapu as he took his evening stroll. But on that day my mind was preoccupied with a bigger story, in fact the biggest and the most important politically after independence.

Two days earlier I had met Azad and learned from him that tension between Nehru and Patel had mounted to a point where the Prime Minister had angrily thumped the table at a Cabinet meeting and said: "Patel, you do what you like. I will not have it." Patel, according to Azad, did not react and remained quiet. But all the Ministers around the table and the senior officials in the room clearly saw that a crisis had developed.

Nehru's outburst was basically sparked by the feeling, fed by his courtiers and hangers-on, that Patel was taking the country to the Right. Time and again, it was whispered into the Prime Minister's ears that Muslims were being harassed by Civil Servants who enjoyed the Sardar's protection, and that Princes and capitalists were basking in the sunshine of the Iron Man's patronage. In other words, Nehru was accused by his courtiers of permitting communal and reactionary forces to be on the ascendant under his very nose.

When I called on Patel the following day, he told me that Nehru had "lost his head" and he, for his part, had made up his mind not to stand "the nonsense any more." He said he was going to see Gandhi and tell him he was quitting. I said Bapu would never agree to let him go and recalled how he had referred to him and Nehru as the two oxen that must pull the governmental cart. Patel quietly replied: "The old man has gone senile. He wants Mountbatten to bring Jawahar and me together."

Accordingly, Patel called on Gandhi on the fateful day and was
closetted with Bapu longer than scheduled and even caused him
to delay his attendance at the prayer meeting. To chase the story, I
left my office for Patel's residence instead of going to Birla House
and told Devadas to meet Bapu and get his version in case I was
held up. When I arrived there, I learned that Bapu had been shot
and that the Sardar had left for Birla House.

When I reached Birla House, Gandhi was dead. I went into the
room where he lay and touched his feet. Devadas was already there,
and I sped back to the office to bring out a supplement carrying the
tragic, nation-shattering news which shocked the whole world. It
was almost time for the next day's edition to be despatched by rail
to outstation centres and it was impossible to change the editorial.
I, therefore, wrote a 500-word bylined article on Gandhi for the
front page under terrific emotional strain and with but a few minutes
to the deadline for copy. I said: Gandhi's weapon of soul force
which had proved stronger than the atom bomb was the only hope
of the world.

The Gandhian era ended on 30th January, 1948, leaving a
vacuum that nothing could fill. He was the High Command, the
soul force on which the party had built and sustained its hold on
the masses. Its leaders depended on him as the court of final appeal
and the powerful sanction behind their actions. As with the prophets,
each of Gandhi's chosen disciples took Gandhiism to mean what he
had imbibed from the fountainhead of the nationalist movement
and could articulate.

To Nehru, it meant crusading for peace and non-violence in the
international arena and propagating secularism at home. To Patel,
it meant mobilising the nation's will to preserve its integrity and
improve its lot through hard work and harmonious relations
between capital and labour. To Prasad and Tandon, Gandhism
meant the inculcation of Sanskrit culture, the most important
instrument of which was the adoption of Hindi as the national
language, and the ascetic Indian way of life. To Vinoba Bhave and
Jayaprakash Narayan, it meant *Sarvodaya*, a social philosophy
according to which one works for the good of others and shares the
rewards of one's labour in a corporate life.

Gandhi's ashes were immersed at *Triveni*, the confluence of the
Ganges, the Jumna and the underground Saraswati at Allahabad,
because the ashes of his wife, Kasturba, had been deposited there.
Nehru, Patel and Prasad participated in the final rites along with
Gandhi's sons, Ramdas and Devadas. I watched the moving scene
closely from a boat carrying newsmen as the holiest of Indian rivers

took to its bosom the remains of the man who had liberated Bharat Mata from a thousand years of foreign domination. After the ceremony, Nehru and other Congress leaders addressed a mass meeting on the river bank. As the meeting ended, Rafi Ahmed Kidwai whispered to me: "Jawaharlal has performed the last rites not only of Gandhi but of Gandhiism as well. Now that the master has gone, there will be no one to discipline the crowd. The High Command is dead."

Chapter 5

MEETING CHALLENGES

(a) RUTHLESS ACTION

Gandhi's death wrought a miracle. The country reacted to the foul deed with the determination to preserve the patrimony he left. The people responded as one to the appeals for unity broadcast by Nehru and Patel in the face of the great calamity that hit the nation with cyclonic force. The overwhelming grief expressed throughout the world and the tributes the Pakistani leaders paid Gandhi turned the tragedy into a triumphant assertion of his conviction that all Indians, be they Hindus, Muslims, Sikhs or Christians, were brothers and must live in peace so that the country which had mothered them might grow in greatness.

At one stage, there was fear of fresh outbreaks of violence and Mountbatten ordered the guard of Viceregal House to patrol the city. The Governor-General considered this necessary in view of a strong rumour that those who had assassinated Gandhi were not alone. They were suspected of being implicated in the alleged plot of some rulers of the Jat States surrounding Delhi to overrun the capital and bring off a political coup. Gandhi had said: "If Delhi is lost, India is lost." He was, no doubt, referring to the fight against communalism. Now, if Delhi was captured by troops from the neighbouring states, this could be the signal for a general uprising stirred up by the princely houses. But, happily, nothing happened.

Gandhi's martyrdom brought Nehru and Patel together. Two days after Bapu's death, Patel himself told me that Nehru and he had instinctively felt that they must come together in the face of the crisis. "We owed it to the country," he added. And, true enough, they were soon pulling the governmental cart again like two oxen under one yoke, as Gandhi had envisaged and wished for even minutes before his assassination. Both directed their renewed attention to the problem of protecting the hard-won freedom from external and internal threats. Nehru took overall charge of defence matters because of Pakistan's attack on Kashmir. Patel got down to ensuring internal stability through the liquidation of the forces of disruption and the integration of the Princely States.

Patel launched a powerful attack on the disruptionists; both of the Left and the Right. He ruthlessly crushed the Communist revolt in Telengana in Hyderabad State with the help of hand-picked officials. He ordered the police to shoot at sight and kill as many rebels as was necessary to break the back of the uprising. As a result of the directive, over a thousand persons were shot dead and the Communist extremists were so demoralised that for the next two decades they eschewed armed action and took to constitutional means. Patel, equally, dealt a severe blow to the militantly Hindu R.S.S. Hundreds of its workers were thrown into prisons with the result that the R.S.S. leaders reverted to their programme of social regeneration, putting their political ambitions into cold storage.

The Sikh extremists raised the most delicate issue. Conveniently forgetting Master Tara Singh's pledge to Nehru, they started talking in terms of a Sikh state and, if that was not possible, a Sikh-majority State where they could establish their separate identity and function as a religio-political entity by making Punjabi in Gurmukhi script its official language. Tara Singh and his brains trust in the Akali Dal decided to try conclusions with Patel first. They demanded separate representation for the Sikhs in the Central Services on the basis of their population. Sardar readily agreed, but meaningfully added that the population formula would also apply to the Army. Since the Sikhs constituted a large proportion in the Army, Tara Singh saw through the implication and dropped the request.

Later, Tara Singh decided to organise a demonstration in Delhi in a bid to project the Akalis as a major political force. He called upon a hundred thousand of his followers to swarm into the capital for a march demanding Punjabi Suba, a Sikh state. But Patel was not to be awed. He got Tara Singh arrested before he could reach Delhi, held up the lorries and trains bringing in his followers and broke up the various camps that were being organised to receive and feed the demonstrators. At this point, Tara Singh and his aides realised that they could not intimidate or blackmail the Iron Man and decided to suspend the fight and take their chance after Patel left the scene.

Patel told me that he had been helped by three factors in dealing with Tara Singh's challenge. Intelligence kept him posted on the divisions in the Akali camp and this helped him to play one against the other with the support of Defence Minister Baldev Singh, a financier of Tara Singh. Secondly, his Regional Commissioner, M. R. Bhide, a Punjab civilian, gave him a detailed assessment of the main personalities among the former Sikh rulers and the Sikh politicians and their manoeuvres. He also drew attention to the influence that the Communists were building up in the Punjab countryside with a view to repeating Telenlgana. Thirdly, Patel had brought to Delhi from Ajmer as Chief Commissioner a Civil Servant, Shankar Prasad, who was very experienced in handling problems of law and order and troublesome politicians.

As Home Minister, Patel pushed through Parliament in one day all three readings of the Preventive Detention Bill designed to safeguard internal security. When the Nehru–Liaquat Pact regarding safeguards for the religious minorities was negotiated in 1950, Shyama Prasad Mookerjee and K. C. Neogy, both Bengalis, resigned from the Nehru Cabinet in protest at what they considered a betrayal of the eleven million Hindus in East Pakistan. The Government was in a state of crisis. Patel was unhappy about the agreement, and he realised that the large majority of Congress and opposition M.P.s shared his feelings. Nonetheless, he stood by the Prime Minister and his speech in Parliament fully supporting Nehru helped the Government to weather the storm. Patel was so conscious of his responsibilities that when Parliament was in session he used to ring up the Chief Whip of the Congress Parliamentary Party every night before retiring to inquire about both the business in the Lok Sabha the following day and the prospects for lobbying.

(b) MERGER OF STATES

The integration of the Princely States with the rest of India was not planned in advance. Patel told me it was the result of fortuitous circumstances which were helped by the wave of nationalism in which the Princes were caught up. To this, however, may be added the prestige and authority of Patel himself. The merger of the smaller States began in Orissa by accident and the process spread from there to other areas.

Narrating the story of the first merger, Patel told me that the idea had originated with Hare Krushna Mahatab, who formed in 1938 the State Praja Mandal, an organisation of the people living in the States of Orissa. This Orissa Congress leader proposed that the small States be merged with the provinces under British administration, and the States Peoples Conference appointed a committee with Mahatab as its chairman to study the proposal in relation to Orissa. The committee recommended that the States be brought under the provincial Government as reforms in them, while they maintained their separateness, would have no value. Mahatab took up this matter with Cripps when he came to India in 1942. The Political Department agreed that this was the only feasible solution of the problem but did nothing about it. When India became independent, the British departed leaving the States as they were. Mahatab convinced Gandhi and Patel of the soundness of his scheme, and he suggested to Patel in November 1947 that he should set the process in motion in Orissa.

V. P. Menon, on the contrary, proposed to Patel that a system of joint control, leaving some administrative powers in the hands of the Princes, should be evolved. Mahatab objected, saying this would only cause confusion and insisted that complete merger was the only solution. Patel agreed, and when the two leaders met in Cuttack and Bhubaneshwar the entire memorandum relating to the merger of States was redrafted with the help of the Chief Secretary of the provincial Government and, what is more, reprinted overnight.

The next day, when the rulers of Orissa conferred with Patel and Mahatab, they referred to the earlier memorandum of association which had been sent to them. Patel and Mahatab disowned knowledge of it. Patel then told the rulers: "If you do not accept our proposal, I do not take responsibility for law and order in your State. You take care of yourself." As the Praja Mandal leaders were ready to overthrow the Princes and effect merger by force, the rulers accepted the new scheme. Thus the first merger of States went through without a single incident in Orissa, to be followed in Chattisgarh, where the States were merged with the Central Provinces.

The Congress leaders were prepared to consider eighteen States viable and permit them to continue as autonomous units under the Instrument of Accession. These included Alwar and Bharatpur, but Gandhi's assassination set in motion the second wave of integration. The pistol which fired the fatal shot was alleged to have belonged to the Maharaja of Alwar's collection of firearms, and volunteers belonging to the R.S.S. were said to have been trained in the use of arms in the State. Dr. N. B. Khare was then the Chief Minister of

Alwar and the suspicion that the ruler had a hand in the shooting grew stronger because Khare was known to bear Gandhi a grudge for getting him ousted from the chief ministership of the Central Provinces.

K. B. Lall, Special Administrator for Alwar, meanwhile, sent to the Home Ministry a report on the basis of available evidence which showed that the rulers of Alwar and Bharatpur were implicated in a plot to topple the Government. Patel decided that the two Princes should be tried by their peers and five of the leading rulers were summoned to Delhi.

As soon as the Princes arrived, they anxiously sought the reason for the call. They were told that the summons was in connection with Gandhi's assassination. This disclosure caused them much alarm. They were taken to Mountbatten, who told them to their great relief that they were personally not suspected of complicity. They had been called to judge the role of Alwar and Bharatpur. The evidence collected was placed before them and they readily agreed that the two Princes should be punished by depriving them of their powers. Matsya Union thus came to be formed and states considered viable were merged for the first time. Then followed other mergers.

The Maharajas of Alwar and Bharatpur might not have been stripped of their powers and Matsya Union created but for the allegations that they had taken part in the massacre and forcible eviction from their lands of Meos, Muslim peasants. This greatly angered Nehru and he was not willing to show any sympathy to the two rulers. In fact, Patel told me that had Nehru not reacted angrily, Mountbatten might not have been as helpful as he was in depriving the Princes of their powers and in effecting the changes.

That, however, was not the end of the story. Later the rulers in the Matsya Union planned a secret meeting to consider joint action to regain their powers. As soon as Lall received the news, he rang up the Maharaja of Dholpur, at whose headquarters the meeting was to be held, and said he would like to join him in a hunt for big game. The Prince invited him over at once and Lall reached Dholpur on the day fixed for the secret meeting. His presence acted as a damper to the princely plotters and rung the curtain on further conspiracy. Incidentally, Congress leaders of the area complained to Delhi that Lall was too fond of the company of the former rulers, with whom he ate and drank frequently. They did not realise, however, that by approaching the Princes at the social level Lall had not only got them to do the things the Government wanted but scotched a major plot.

The Sardar also used the proverbial carrot to persuade the rulers of the larger States to sign instruments transferring their powers to the Union Government. He offered them the prospect of becoming a Raj Pramukh, an office similar to that of Governor and the move worked. Rulers like Jamnagar and Patiala, for instance, saw in this an opportunity to become leaders among the Princes and to extend their authority over larger territories than their own hereditary princedoms. The rulers saw from the fate of Alwar and Bharatpur that the new Government would intervene effectively when law and order were threatened and would encourage the growth of democracy. At the same time, they realised that their best bet for retaining personal status, palaces and privy purses lay in giving up their powers as rulers.

(c) HYDERABAD AND JINNAH

Hyderabad provided Patel his biggest challenge. Mountbatten's Indian Press Attaché told me that the Governor-General wanted to depart from India in a blaze of glory by negotiating a settlement between Delhi and the Nizam. Nehru, too, was keen on a speedy settlement and backed Mountbatten in his effort. But the Nizam proved difficult, encouraged and inspired by Pakistan and his own pro-Pakistani advisers. Mountbatten finally left India on 21st June, 1948, handing over charge to C. R., who earned the distinction of becoming the first Indian Governor-General.

An attempt was made earlier to bring the Nizam to agree to accession through an informal economic blockade. But the stoppage of trade with the state proved ineffective and Patel sent K. M. Munshi to Hyderabad as the representative of the Indian Government to keep Delhi informed about developments in the state. Munshi did his job well but, in the meantime, the failure of the blockade resulted in heavy pressure on Patel to distribute arms to the people of Hyderabad so that they could rise against the Nizam. Significantly, Patel refused to countenance the proposal, throwing light on his method of work. If force was to be used, he ruled, it must be done by the Government and not by indisciplined volunteers.

A few weeks after the departure of Mountbatten New Delhi received a report that the Nizam was trying to buy Goa from Portugal so that his landlocked State would have access to the sea. The Nizam was also said to have loaned a large sum of money (about Rs. 200 million) to Pakistan as part of his effort to win Jinnah's support. Nehru took counsel with Patel, who advised him to send troops to garrison Secunderabad Cantonment and take police action against the Nizam if he resisted. Nehru announced this move on 10th September and troops moved into Hyderabad three days later with the command: "March on, protect all, crush resistance."

The police action in Hyderabad was preceded in New Delhi by days of tenseness and high drama. Twice the zero hour was fixed by Patel, who as Home Minister was to authorise the police action, and on each occasion he was compelled to cancel it under heavy political pressure. The zero hour was then fixed for the third time and Patel was determined to see it through. Once again a hitch developed at the eleventh hour. The Nizam appealed personally to C. R., who conferred with Nehru and they both decided to call off action again. Patel was informed and the question of drafting a suitable reply to the Nizam arose.

The Defence Secretary, H. M. Patel, and V. P. Menon were summoned and they exhausted three hours in consultation and formulating a reply. When the reply was finally ready, Patel coolly announced that the Army had already moved into Hyderabad and nothing could be done to halt it. Defence Minister Baldev Singh and Patel were of one mind and had resolved to bring the Nizam to his senses and not yield to any further counsel of weakness. I kept a tab on this midnight drama from my house through telephonic contact with Patel's residence. Not unexpectedly, Nehru and C. R. were at once agitated and worried about whether it would provoke retaliation by Pakistan. But, within twenty-four hours, the action was successfully underway and there were smiles all round.

A relevant aside was Pakistan's unexpected success in raising the Hyderabad issue in the Security Council. Eight members of the Council voted for considering the matter, while the Soviet Union, the Ukraine and China remained neutral. The Nizam surrendered on 17th September. Pakistan and its supporters looked small when India's representative at Lake Success did not appear at the next meeting of the Council and Pakistan's complaint was automatically dropped.

Nehru declared on 19th September that the future of the state would be decided according to the wishes of its people. The following day, Jinnah died of cancer that had afflicted him for years, and, in its preoccupation with ensuring stability and continuity after his departure from the political scene, the Pakistani Government decided not to pursue a militant line on Hyderabad.

Hyderabad symbolised the last of Jinnah's failures in the post-1947 period. Strangely enough, Jinnah, who was so successful a strategist and tactician when he was fighting for Pakistan, failed to achieve any of the objectives he set himself as head of the new state that he won on "a platter." Jinnah's military adventure in Kashmir failed both when he sent in the tribal hordes and subsequently when he unsuccessfully ordered his British Commander-in-Chief, Sir Douglas Gracey, to march troops in. His manoeuvre to get some Princes to form a separate bloc and ally with Pakistan as a counterweight to India too failed to pay off. His attempt to detach Junagadh from India did not succeed. The reason for these failures was not difficult to see. Jinnah was left to his own devices and there was no third party to help him in his efforts to bully Nehru—and India.

(d) ARMY REFASHIONED

General Smith's gloomy forecast on 14th August that the army would break up within six months rang in my ears. World War I had proved that the Indian soldier was valiant and could fight in any terrain or climate. World War II showed that given proper training the *jawan* could use modern weapons skilfully and Indian officers could lead their men ably in battle. But partition found India's army faced with unprecedented problems. The units were divided between the two new dominions and there was a large-scale change of officers and men as a result of the option offered to them to choose between India and Pakistan. The Army required to be given fresh cohesion and refashioned into an efficient fighting force.

This was no small task and Nehru decided to take advantage of the British experience. General Bucher was invited to continue as the Commander-in-Chief and so also the British officers heading the Navy and the Air Force. But the scope of the C.-in-C.'s job underwent a sea change with the dawn of independence. In the British days, the C.-in-C. enjoyed prerogatives and powers next only to the Viceroy as the Empire ultimately depended for its survival on the Army. He resided in the large imposing mansion on Roberts Road (later occupied by Nehru as Prime Minister) a few hundred yards to the south of Viceroy's House. Now, he was only the head of the Army, taking his orders from Free India's first Defence Minister, Sardar Baldev Singh.

The Defence Minister, tall and well-built, was an impressive personality. For all the anecdotes fabricated around his person about his knowledge of English idiom, he succeeded remarkably in promoting consolidation of the armed forces. He had sharp intelligence, personal courage and freedom from communal bias. He realised the high stakes involved in giving India a fine army and was firm on matters involving principle. His first task was to establish once and for all the supremacy of the civil power in matters governing the armed forces and, towards this end, he laid down that all appointments to the rank of colonel and above would be approved by the Defence Minister.

The Defence Secretary, H. M. Patel, for his part, made a major contribution to this evolution by ordering the Defence Ministry to maintain its own records of files. Till then, the Army Department merely rubber-stamped every file because the C.-in-C. was also the Army member of the Viceroy's Executive Council. Today the Defence Ministry is the custodian of all files, symbolising the supremacy of the civil authority.

Pakistan's attack on Kashmir posed the hastily regrouped Army its biggest test. The Pakistani raiders were on the outskirts of Srinagar by the time India went into action and troops were flown into the Valley. However, our troops not only halted the advance but rolled back the marauders. Baldev Singh as Defence Minister played no small part in the success of the operation by his air dash to the Front, together with Patel. Our forces in the Valley were not only inadequate but ill-equipped. As Baldev Singh later told me, there was not enough ammunition, and our aircraft lacked bombs, were even starved of fuel to keep them airborne. Snap decisions and their prompt implementation turned the tide in our favour.

Following his return from Kashmir, Baldev Singh decided to relieve Bucher of his command. Nehru backed him and turned his face against Bucher's suggestion that he continue as military adviser to the Government. The choice of successor lay mainly between Géneral K. M. Cariappa and General Rajendrasinhji. Patel favoured the latter, but Cariappa was chosen as the next C.-in-C. in view of the strong views expressed in his favour by Baldev Singh and the Defence Secretariat. Rajendrasinhji, a kinsman of the Jam Saheb of Nawanagar, had his innings when he was chosen as successor to Cariappa.

Cariappa was a stickler for discipline and believed in the British tradition of spit and polish. He forged the Indian Army on the old British style. The transition to the new pattern in regard to the highly important question of the relations between the Defence Secretary and the Army Chief was not easy. However, Cariappa eventually adjusted himself to the new situation.

The warfare in Kashmir proved a blessing in disguise from the national point of view. It not only trained our officers and *jawans* to plan operations and work in cohesion but also threw up men like

Shrinagesh, Thimayya and Kalwant Singh whose daring and exploits marked them for future leadership. The blood shed by the officers and men in the state did not go in vain. If the Army gave India Kashmir, Kashmir gave India its Army.

Chapter 6

TALKS WITH NEHRU

(a) MORAL LEADER OF MANKIND

Once stability and security had been assured by the strong-arm methods of Patel, Nehru concentrated attention on projecting his ideology at home and abroad. Internally, he declared war on feudalism, capitalism and ignorance to give economic and social content to freedom and to take India into the modern age. He had earlier named the communalists as the main enemy. He now turned on the *bania*, the wealthy and the capitalist as the villains of the piece. Externally, with his unrivalled zeal, he became the torch-bearer for the freedom of Asians and Africans from colonial bondage and for peaceful coexistence between the democratic and Communist worlds.

Patel, on the other hand, got down to building up a new Indian Administrative Service and to integrating and raising to the level of administration in the provinces of erstwhile British India the administrative structure in the Princely States, which had first formed separate Unions and were later absorbed in the various states under the new Constitution. He also set about creating confidence in the regime so that when the first general election enfranchising all the 170 million adults was held, the operation, the biggest among democracies, might be carried out peacefully and in freedom. He set up the Election Commission having the same independent status as the Supreme Court and the Auditor General.

Of course, an administrative machinery was already in existence when India became independent. But the steel frame had been split into two with the creation of Pakistan and, moreover, a yawning gap was left with the wholesale departure of the British officials. New foundations had to be laid and a whole new cadre of Indians had to be entrusted with functions few of them had performed

ABOVE Left to right: Radhakrishnan, Nehru and Shastri

BELOW Jinnah speaking into the microphone at a reception given at India House
In December 1946. Nehru, wearing the European dress for which
he had been criticised, is second from jinnah's right

Gandhi with Lord and Lady Mountbatten in the spring of 1947

before and the administrative services had to be oriented to the role of working for the nation and not for a foreign ruler. Patel's instinctive judgment of men helped and he soon won the respect and confidence of the steel frame and the other services. Nationalist feeling was particularly strong against the Indian members of the ICS But Patel silenced the critics and saved the situation by declaring: "They served the British well; they will now serve the nationalist Government even better."

A tangible asset India enjoyed was the goodwill of almost all nations and their admiration at the orderly manner she had gained freedom. India became the beacon for other nations struggling to break the shackles of colonialism. Among the first tasks Nehru had to perform was to select Ambassadors to the U.S. and the Soviet Union and a High Commissioner for Britain. Attlee made it known that he would be happy to have John Matthai or Radhakrishnan accredited to the Court of St. James's. He did this, Patel told me, with the aim of hinting broadly to Nehru that Krishna Menon would not fill the bill. But Menon had already succeeded in working Nehru round to getting Mountbatten to propose him for the post.

While India's diplomatic representatives made little impact on the three centres of power, Washington, Moscow and London, Nehru captured the world stage and assumed the moral leadership of mankind as Gandhi's heir. The accent in which he spoke made the war-weary nations listen to him as they would to a crusader. Nehru made world headlines when he sponsored a conference of eighteen Asian nations in Delhi in January 1949 and fixed a deadline for Indonesia to be freed from Dutch rule. The U.N. backed him, and Indonesia became independent on 1st January, 1950. Nehru also inspired the conference of five member-nations of the Commonwealth to discuss the disturbed state of Burma and back its democratically-elected Government headed by U Nu.

Nehru was clearly on top, and strode the national and world stage like a colossus. His success showed up pointedly when I visited Karachi as a member of the Inter-Dominion Press Consultative Committee in March 1949. That was the time when Delhi was hoping for better relations with Pakistan and was trying to bring about a customs union. I remember Khwaja Nazimuddin, the Governor-General of Pakistan, telling me on the occasion that the people of the two countries had identical characteristics—the same strength and the same weaknesses. But India, he added, had "one plus—Nehru." Because they had no charismatic personality to look up to, the Pakistanis had to whip up Islam to provide a cementing force.

By the middle of 1949, Indo–Pakistani relations, however, deteriorated. India was prepared for an immediate plebiscite in Kashmir but Liaquat Ali, knowing it would go against Pakistan, shirked the challenge. Karachi then sent up a balloon suggesting that the state's partition on the ceasefire line could solve the problem. This time, Delhi rejected the feeler, confident that it would win the whole state in a free vote. Indo–Pakistani relations were further strained by Karachi's refusal to devalue her rupee when Delhi devalued hers at the same time as the sterling. The proposal for a customs union went by the board. Instead, India and Pakistan found themselves pitted against each other in an economic war.

Pakistan's position on Kashmir hardened when Liaquat Ali, according to what Nehru told me, successfully blackmailed Washington and London into making a political deal with Karachi by accepting an invitation to visit Moscow. Under the bargain, Pakistan agreed to join the Anglo–American military bloc in return for support on Kashmir. Accordingly, reviewing the second year of independence on 15th August, 1949, I wrote in the *Hindustan Times*: "Each party will continue to hold what it has in Kashmir." I further wrote that the new Commonwealth formula would not help since India and Pakistan were enmeshed in an intense cold war. Pakistan's view was made brutally clear by Khaliq-uz-Zaman when, addressing an Islamic Economic Conference in Karachi on 10th December he plumped for an Islamic bloc in the Middle East as a counterpoise.

(b) NATIONAL LANGUAGE

I had four meaningful off-the-record interviews with Nehru in 1949. They aimed at ascertaining his views on certain basic issues which I felt had a bearing on the evolution of democracy in India and India's place in the world.

I first took up the question of a national language, on which Tilak and Gandhi had laid much emphasis as the most unifying factor. I told him I was present at a meeting addressed by Gandhi at Birla House when he expressed his views on decontrol of food, sugar and clothing. Gandhi spoke in Hindustani, and when some officers said that they were unable to follow, he replied sharply: "Now we are independent, I shall not speak in English. You have to understand *rashtrabhasha* (the language of the country) if you wish to serve the people."

I also recalled an incident when Gandhi addressed a conference of Food Ministers in Hindi. At the end of the meeting, the Minister from Madras requested Gandhi to say a few words in English as he had not been able to understand the Hindi speech. Gandhi angrily told the Minister: "In that case, you had better resign." The Minister apologised with folded hands and promised to learn Hindi in six months.

Nehru replied: "Of course, Hindi will be the national language. It cannot be English. How many people understand English? In any case, we cannot communicate with the masses in English. You know, we gave Sarup (Mrs. Pandit) her credentials in Hindi for presentation in Moscow. That is good enough to indicate our stand and our determination. But I am not a fanatic. It must be done gradually and with due regard to regional sentiment."

I mentioned that parents all over the country were deeply interested in this issue and the fact that he preferred those educated in Britain or in Anglo–Indian schools in India in making diplomatic appointments had created the impression that the future rested with pupils of public schools, convents and similar institutions. When independence came these institutions were thinking of selling off their property and closing down. But this had been followed by a sudden spurt in their enrolment and they had long lists of applicants for admission. It was only fair that parents should know the future as he envisaged it. Nehru said he must send abroad persons who could speak English "decently" and were familiar with foreign ways. Japan, he said, took special care to train and orient its diplomats.

Since I understood that Nehru favoured Hindi as the national language, I suggested that he would make a nationwide impact if he merely laid down the rule that any Indian who talked to him at his residence must speak Hindi-Hindustani. Otherwise, he should see him in his office. That would be a signal to all who wished to see him at home to learn Hindi. Nehru laughed at the idea that he should talk "to my own people through interpreters" and added: "I can have no worthwhile dialogue with foreign visitors or diplomats who do not talk English and I have to have an interpreter." He continued: "Anyway, we are making provision in the Constitution. Everyone will have to fall in line with that."

I inquired whether the Congress leaders had given thought to the social aspect of living and whether they proposed to lay down a yardstick for the Ministers in regard to their way of life and dress. Gandhi had suggested that Nehru should stay in the quarters meant for members of Parliament, but he had shifted to the stately mansion formerly occupied by the British Commander-in-Chief. His Ministers had followed suit by occupying the large houses meant for Executive Councillors. Again, several Ministers who used to squat on the floor and eat off brass plates or plantain leaves in their homes were now trying to ape Western ways. They contended that Nehru considered only Westernised people modern. I asked whether he would indicate his ideas about the pattern of living the Ministers should adopt. He replied that these things would get sorted out as time went by.

In my talks with Civil Servants I found they looked down on the average politician as a crude and semi-civilised person. The politician, on his part, considered the civilians Brown Sahibs who wallowed in drink and vice and had no sense of patriotism. Since democracy was nurtured on the cross-fertilisation of ideas between politicians and Civil Servants, it was important that these two groups should develop respect for each other and meet socially. Nehru, for his part, felt that every Minister and Civil Servant would live and learn.

Salaries and perquisites, I said, must be so fixed that politicians in office and Civil Servants did not feel the temptation to be corrupt. The British had observed certain principles in governing their Empire. They gave a sense of security to their officers and a salary and perquisites which would not tempt them to depend on the richer elements in society to meet their needs. But already some politicians were getting attached to business houses which were providing them with various perquisites, some secretly and some indiscreetly.

I next inquired if he had taken note of the growing trend towards parochialism and nepotism. Ministers, I said, were choosing their staff, whether personal or ministerial, largely from among those who belonged to their region and spoke the same language. Some went so far as to give preference to their caste and community. This type of nepotism could be checked only if a new norm was laid down and practised universally. He had the power and the emotional appeal to apply correctives and take the people into the modern age. Nehru remained silent and I sensed that he had set a limit on his power to take the people with him.

What about a national opposition for the healthy growth of democracy? At the back of my mind was the series of talks I had had on the subject with Kidwai, who was trying to force Nehru to break away from the "reactionaries," as he described Patel and his followers, and form a Socialist Party. "You cannot create an opposition artificially," Nehru replied. Kidwai, I said, was confident that if he formed a new party they would win a majority in the first general election and implement a Socialist programme without inhibitions.

Nehru replied that Kidwai had a lot of "hare-brained" schemes and forgot that the overall need was to consolidate freedom. They

could not overnight create a political machine which reached down
to the village. Elections could not be won by an appeal to emotion
in the countryside. A mass organisation which had contact with the
people was needed to get votes. Only the Congress, with its revolutionary past, had such a base and men dedicated to its creed and
programme. The differences between the two groups were not
intelligible to the masses. It would be disastrous to break up the
Congress just to create an opposition. He thought that as people
developed their political awareness and economic and social problems showed a clear dividing line, an organised opposition would
grow. So far as he could see, that was not to be expected for at least
a decade.

(c) ECONOMIC POLICY

What about Nehru's outlook on economic matters? He agreed that
the production of food and other essentials must be increased to
fight inflation and put the economy on a sound footing. He had
planned a food drive and saw no reason why the country should not
become self-sufficient in food in two years. But he was more concerned with building a broad industrial base even if it meant
austerity in regard to consumer goods.

Gandhi, I said, wanted an integrated economy in which the
villager and the townsman shared equally. He had hoped to do this
through small-scale and cottage industries as he was thinking in
terms of work for the unemployed and underemployed. Would he
not first build agriculture and light industries and then build an
industrial base out of the national savings they generated? Nehru
accepted the need to encourage cottage industries, but side by side
the nation must undertake to build heavy industry. In the final
analysis a country's military strength depended on its industrial
sinews. He wanted to take advantage of the period of peace, which
he expected would last ten to fifteen years, to create a strong industrial base.

Who were the enemies he had in mind? It was obvious, he replied,
that Pakistan was on the warpath. Whether it would attempt another
military conclusion or not, India must be prepared to meet the
threat. There was no other external danger. China would never think
of invading India. At any rate, it would be a couple of decades
before it would settle down to an ordered life.

Would nationalisation of the means of production achieve what
he had in mind? Nehru was emphatic that the Government could
not undertake such a colossal task. That would be a move towards an

authoritarian state. He was thinking of the parallel growth of the public sector and the private sector, with the Government acting as the watchdog of the national interests and safeguarding them through laws, regulations and administrative acts.

Did he consider a bureaucrat a better instrument than a capitalist to bring about the social changes he had in mind? No, they were equally bad. Only, the bureaucrat could be held answerable, the capitalist was elusive. Anyway, he added, it was for the Planning Commission to work these matters out and for the Labour Minister to undertake practical schemes. He could only give broad policy directives and indicate the goals he had in mind.

But I said his refrain about *sarmai dari* (capitalism) being the enemy of the people was not producing the proper climate for co-operation between management and labour. The real enemy was poverty, lethargy, corruption and incompetence. Capitalism and communalism merely exploited the people's backwardness. Nehru retorted: "Mine is an all-out war on all evils. I count on the people rising against them and cleaning up this centuries-old muck."

(d) FOREIGN POLICY

Nehru considered India's foreign policy his main concern. The country needed peace to build up its economic strength and a new social order. This could happen only if another world war was avoided and imperialism and colonialism liquidated. Having achieved her freedom, India must spearhead the movement for the freedom of all the subject peoples of Asia and Africa. India's voice must be firm and loud on their behalf. He had returned disappointed from his visit to the U.S. in 1949. The Americans were so scared of Communism that they were underwriting colonialism and reactionary regimes. He sensed the arrogance of power in Washington and the arrogance of money in New York.

Nehru spoke at length and it was clear the key note of his foreign policy was that, China and Russia being India's neighbours, India should be friendly with both. Moreover, Indian military power should never be permitted to serve the political ends of the Western powers in Asia or anywhere else in the world. But even as he spoke of friendship with the northern neighbour, big things were happening in China. K. M. Panikkar, India's Ambassador to the Chiang Kai-shek regime in Nanking, had reported victories for the Communists on the battlefield and advised Nehru to recognise them as the rulers of China.

In September, the Communist radio asserted that Tibet was a

part of China and that "the British and American imperialists and
their running dog Nehru are now plotting a coup in Lhasa for the
annexation of Tibet." I asked Nehru for his comments and he told
me this was the Communist Chinese reaction to his permitting a
Kuomintang mission to pass through India. He said he would not
quarrel with China over Tibet. He would not take over Curzon's
role and establish Indian influence in Lhasa. Patel and Prasad, to
whom I spoke later, reacted differently. They felt Tibet was India's
northernmost outpost in the Himalayas and that the Communist
radio comment was a danger signal which New Delhi must heed.

Chapter 7

TO THE NEW WORLD

(a) NEHRU A "COMMIE"

How did the world outside look at Independent India? I got my
first opportunity of studying this in the summer of 1950, when I
attended the seventh Imperial Press Conference in Ottawa as one
of the six Indian representatives. India had, at long last, arrived and
one was thrilled to discover that Indian opinion now received due
consideration. C. R. Srinivasan, Publisher-Editor of *Swadesamitran*
of Madras, and I, for instance, made it known soon after our arrival
that we wanted the organisation to be renamed the Commonwealth
Press Conference. Some British delegates, led by the Editor of
Beaverbrook's *Daily Express*, strongly plumped for the Churchillian
phrase "Commonwealth and Empire." But our proposal was
carried unanimously (without any lobbying on our part) when the
leader of the Australian delegation, Sir Keith Murdoch, powerfully
supported us.

I recall an interesting aside at the outset—my meeting with
Altaf Hussain, Editor of *Dawn*, who was the sole delegate from
Pakistan. Altaf had played no small part in spearheading the demand
for Pakistan on the basis of the two-nation theory, but he said to me
in the lounge of the Hotel Château Fontenac in Quebec: "Here we
realise we are one and we flock together. We have little in common
with the other delegates." However, we were of them also because
we stood for the freedom of the Press and freedom of information.

The comradeship created at the conference was an invaluable asset to me later. To mention a few, the friendships I formed with Colonel (now Lord) Astor, Roy (now Lord) Thomson, R. P. T. Gibson of the Westminster Press Provincial Newspapers, John Grigg (formerly Lord Altrincham) have grown stronger with the passage of time.

Indeed, we were able to persuade the Conference to arrange for training journalists from our countries and for exchanges of staff to promote better understanding among the members of the Commonwealth. The need for this was brought home to me when a Canadian journalist, who was also a member of the national Senate, asked whether I was a Brahmin or a Hindu and the charming wife of a newsprint magnate wanted to know whether New Delhi was the capital of Pakistan. But while there was ignorance about India among average Canadians, my talks with St. Laurent, the Prime Minister, and his predecessor Mackenzie King were heartwarming. They seemed to be happy at Nehru standing up to the U.S. Both of them assured me they were more in tune with New Delhi than with London on anti-colonial issues.

Canada was otherwise preoccupied with internal matters and appeared at that time a question mark. I said in the series of articles I wrote entitled *Report on America*: "The British and the French elements in Canada stand apart nursing age-old linguistic, religious and cultural differences (even more deeprooted than the so-called Hindu–Muslim differences in our country), and in that respect are even more reactionary than people in England and France." The Mayor of Toronto called his city "the centre of Britain" at a banquet in honour of the delegates. A top banker said to me: "We hold the purse strings. The French will starve without us."

I mentioned in my articles that the demand of the French-speaking Canadians for a new national flag (conceded in 1966) and a new national anthem was born out of racial conflict. I ended my piece on Canada by stating that Canada's geographical boundaries and politics could not be said to be stable, while "some (mostly French Canadians) think that partitioning of the country into two separate republics within the Commonwealth or merger with the U.S.A. is her ultimate destiny." I presume Canada is still a question mark.

The impact of the U.S. was even more dream-shattering. The State Department official who gave me a brief orientation talk said: "The U.S.A. is like a child just emerging into manhood and not knowing how to use its new strength." A journalist accredited to the White House told me at a cocktail party: "No one knows what the country's policy is on a given subject. I spoke one day to five officers of the State Department and each gave a different answer on the same question." American opinion was, however, almost unanimous on two matters. They told me "Nehru is a Commie," and that domestically their main headache was where to park their cars.

They also reacted emotionally rather than rationally to events. I found, for example, that a leading journal which had castigated Nehru's "pro-Marxist politics" one morning, lauded him frenziedly the next when the news came through that the Indian Cabinet had endorsed the U.S. Security Council resolution on Korea. A leading newspaperman wrote to me at the time: "Nehru can have ten Damodar Valley projects on a platter."

Vijayalakshmi Pandit, who was our first Ambassador in Washington to sell India to the U.S., had for lunch at her residence Walter Lippman, Herbert Elliston, Marquis Childs and James Reston. She left us together after we had eaten to discuss relations between India and the U.S., and our talk centred largely on the American commitment in Indo-China. Had their Government acted rightly? Why hadn't India recognised the Bao Dai regime? Did not India see the danger inherent in her attitude of neutrality? Communism was on the march in Asia and unless it was checked in Indo-China, would not India be its next victim? (Curiously I was confronted seventeen years later with similar posers when I met President Johnson and his principal aides in June 1967.)

I wrote in my travel diary in 1950 that the developments in Indo-China would have taken a different shape if Nehru had been allowed to handle it the way he did Indonesia. Had that been done, I wrote, "Ho Chi-minh would have reacted differently. He is a nationalist. The whole of South-East Asia is surging with the spirit of nationalism." The various countries in the region "would hate nothing more than Chinese suzerainty," but if they were driven into the Communist camp they would have no alternative but to accept Chinese hegemony under Communist colours. I added that communism could not be contained by military or economic aid "rendered through colonial powers or directly to puppets." Lippman had remarked: "The British have led us into this (Indo-China) business. They told us Bao Dai is the man to back."

I met another group of writers and commentators at a luncheon given by the Editor of the *Washington Post*. They included Ferdinand Kuhn, André Visson of *Reader's Digest*, Stewart Alsop, Eric Stevareid of Columbia Broadcasting System, James Reston, Edward Weintal of *Newsweek* and George McGhee, Assistant Secretary of State for South-East Asian Affairs. Indo-China figured again in the talk, and also Kashmir on which one sensed blind prejudice. It was apparent that on the Kashmir issue the Americans had accepted the British view that because the state had a Muslim majority it should go to Pakistan. In general, the attitude of the average American publicist and politician was that "those who are not with us are against us."

Nehru had returned disappointed from his visit to the U.S., as he told me. How did the U.S., for its part, take him? Nehru, I learnt, had failed to hit off with both White House and Wall Street. His ideas and outlook did not click with theirs. When Nehru was entertained to lunch in New York and was told that the guests represented so many billions of dollars, he took it as a crude attempt to overawe him—and not as a compliment, as intended by the host. The American attitude at the time was best reflected by President Truman when I was introduced to him after his weekly Press Conference. When I suggested he should visit India, he smilingly replied: "Are you sure Nehru would welcome it?"

A luncheon with some Wall Street tycoons in the company of the Indian Consul-General in New York a few days after was a revealing experience. I recalled how a Vice-President and treasurer of Westinghouse had said in a speech at the India–America conference in Delhi in 1949 that "for business, tomorrow rested with Asia." But, judging by the questions fired at me at the lunch, I could see that foreign bankers and businessmen operating in India had created in my fellow-guests the feeling that "caution rather than enterprise" should be their watchword in India.

I visited the Negro ghettoes of New York and Chicago as well as of other cities, and came to the conclusion that these underdogs of the affluent society were exploited alike by well-to-do blacks and whites. A visit to Warner Studios in Hollywood, showed how Pakistan was scoring over India in propaganda. Warner's manager asked why India was not putting out material of the type Pakistan was supplying the studios. "We are a nation of salesmen," he added. I found throughout the tour that our embassies were selling Nehru, not India, unlike our neighbour's which were selling Pakistan.

(b) A WINDOW ON THE WORLD

I met Nehru and the Secretary General of the External Affairs Ministry after my tour of the New World to give them my impressions and get to know their attitude towards Russia and China. I had told Americans that they were wrong in describing Nehru as a "Commie" and that the Russians wanted the support of India as a counterweight to China. I had learned in New Delhi earlier that soon after the successful climax of the Chinese revolution, a Russian feeler was put out through its Mission in Peking for a treaty of non-aggression and friendship between New Delhi and Moscow. Panikkar who was Ambassador in Peking, ignored the suggestion. When it was repeated at the ambassadorial level, he wrote to Nehru that the suggestion was not to be taken seriously. Nehru therefore did not pursue the matter as he felt that India and China had coexisted peacefully for centuries and there had never been a clash of arms. He did wonder if this happy state would continue after Mao took over in Peking. Nevertheless, he decided that India should cultivate the goodwill of the Chinese Communist leaders and seek peaceful relations.

Nehru realised that India had a long border with China and indirectly sought a guarantee of its frontier. Consequently, whenever there were diplomatic parleys in those early days between Indian and Chinese officials, the Indians repeatedly suggested that Peking should, in the interest of its international image, create confidence among its smaller neighbours by declaring categorically that it accepted the existing international boundaries. This was an indirect attempt to get confirmation of India's border with China. Nehru told me he was against taking up the issue directly with Peking as that might give the Chinese an impression that New Delhi had doubts about the exact location of the border. Peking's reply to Indian hints was invariably that no public declaration of the kind suggested was necessary, and in any event the question of revising maps could wait.

I returned from the New World convinced that India must establish direct communication with the outside world to fulfil the role India through Nehru was assuming in foreign affairs. A few months later, I had two meetings with the Prime Minister and suggested the need for an Indian news agency with a worldwide system of gathering and disseminating news. I told him how Reuter men, like trade, had followed the Union Jack to all parts of the globe. As a former Reuter man myself, I also explained how this agency gave the British Government a big pull in international affairs by the way it functioned.

I was convinced that India was in a position to organise a world news agency. We had a larger number of embassies and legations abroad than any other non-European country. Secondly, Nehru was taking a leading part in international affairs, and whatever he said in India or the stand his representatives took at the U.N. commanded worldwide attention. All that was required was to station an Indian newsman in every country where we had a diplomatic mission.

These men would be taken into confidence by our diplomats so as to enable them to be the first with the news.

How was this to be done? Nehru asked. I told him it was possible to achieve what I had in mind without much expense or dislocation of the administration. The journalists his Ministry had recruited as Press Officers could be transferred to the newly-created foreign cadre of the Press Trust of India and assured as attractive terms of service as the Ministry had promised them. The additional expenditure could be met by the Government subscribing to the P.T.I. service on commercial terms and thus compensating it in the manner done by other Governments.

"I am all for it," said Nehru, and asked me to prepare a note. But I urged him to dictate the note himself as that would give the impression that the scheme had come from him. It would then be treated with the respect it deserved.

A fortnight later he summoned me and said he had not been able to find time to dictate the note and asked me to write it and leave it with him unsigned. India and Nehru, I again emphasised, were riding the crest of a wave of worldwide interest and esteem, and a global news service could be built at a modest cost. A decade later, when other nations had gained importance and the world was attuned differently, this opportunity would be lost and the monopoly of the Western news agencies would continue.

Nehru assured me he would take a personal interest in the project. He sent the note to the Ministry, but nothing happened. A decade later, P.T.I. was helped to open offices in a few foreign countries. The amount sanctioned for the purpose was not less than what I had recommended for a worldwide set-up. But what the Government then secured was not a world agency, projecting the image of India and of the coloured world, but the feeding of the Indian Press with the doings of our Embassies abroad.

Chapter 8

CLASH OF PERSONALITIES

(a) PRASAD FIRST PRESIDENT

An important aspect of the post-independence scene was the clash of ideals and personalities that marked the initial three years—and determined to a large extent the events in the first two decades. Gandhi's assassination in January 1948 brought Nehru and Patel together and on Nehru's sixtieth birthday on 14th November one saw heartwarming evidence of their reunion. Patel praised Nehru for leading the nation safely out of the crisis that faced India during the year and enhancing its prestige abroad. Nehru responded by describing Patel as a tower of strength. He said he did not know what would have happened to India had Patel not been present to advise and act firmly. But by the time the new Constitution came into force on 26th January, 1950, the situation on the Congress front had deteriorated. I wrote in my annual review: "There is no doubt that the Congress is split in two main camps. Perhaps the path of wisdom lies in acknowledging that and allowing a strong opposition to grow so that democracy may have a chance of healthy development."

At our daily conferences, Devadas and I often exchanged notes on the state of the two "power blocs" in the Nehru Cabinet. His regular contact with C.R., his father-in-law and the Governor-General, kept him in touch with the doings in the Nehru camp, while my daily contact with Patel and G. D. Birla enabled me to gather gossip in the opposite camp. Devadas and I agreed on two points: there was a retreat from the Gandhian path one way or other; it was clear that in the economic and social spheres Nehru took the Marxist line and Patel the Gandhian. On the other hand, in foreign affairs Nehru pursued the Gandhian ideology while Patel believed in the Curzonian concept of Indian security and the maintenance of a firm hold on Nepal and Tibet.

The relations between Nehru and Patel got noticeably strained over the choice of the first President of the Republic of India. Nehru had by then come to lean on C.R. and, therefore, decided to bestow on him the signal honour. In fact, he even persuaded Prasad to let C.R. be the President, to the great chagrin of the former's supporters. Saddened by this news, Prasad's sponsors repaired to Patel for advice knowing that the Iron Man himself favoured their candidate in preference to C.R. Laughingly, Patel told them in my presence with his typical dry humour: "But the bridegroom has fled. How can the *barat* (wedding party) move?" When the sponsors pleaded that some way must be found, it was decided to force Nehru's hands in favour of Prasad and against C.R. when the matter was formally taken up.

A meeting of the party was called by Nehru for formal approval of his choice. He spoke at length about C.R.'s virtues, especially his quality as a window on foreign lands and the profound impression he had made on foreign dignitaries and Ambassadors. However, one backbencher after another denounced C.R. for resigning from the party when the Quit India movement was launched by Gandhi in 1942 and for giving the demand for Pakistan respectability by his "sporting offer" to Jinnah. In vain did Nehru plead for C.R. Finally, to save the leader's face, the party left the decision to Nehru and Patel in the light of the feelings expressed at the meeting. The party's will prevailed and, much to Nehru's annoyance, Prasad was elected President.

Devadas had the particularly delicate task of maintaining a balance between his pro-Nehru father-in-law and pro-Patel proprietors, the Birlas. But the fact that we exchanged notes enabled us to steer clear of the political shoals. The situation changed when Nehru failed to get C.R. elected President and, about this time, I found C.R. rather critical of Government in private conversation. The rift at the top was widening and a delicate question that arose was how our paper should serve the national cause by exposing the happenings behind the scenes without damaging the cause we stood for, namely Congress policies and programmes.

I offered to write a weekly column in the *Hindustan Times* on the understanding that it would be published under my pen-name Insaf and that I would have the columnist's freedom to write what I felt without inhibitions imposed by our editorial policy. My idea, I added, was to apply the Gandhian yardstick to the Government's acts of omission or commission. I added that to dissent and to debunk was the key role of a columnist in a democracy. So was my *Political Diary* born. (Some years later the brilliant correspondent of the *New York Times* in New Delhi, Abe Rosenthal, wrote me a letter saying that if I would produce the column twice weekly it would greatly help foreign correspondents in analysing and interpreting India.)

Hardly had the *Diary* appeared for a few weeks than Azad sent me word that he would like me to meet him. Azad came straight to the point. Nehru and he felt that the *Diary* was "inspired by Patel and Birla." I asked him whether he or Nehru really felt that way. He replied: "You know the woman who has been carrying tales to Nehru." I told Azad that Nehru was not usually accessible to newsmen and gave time more readily to foreign correspondents than to Indian. As a rule, I checked all the information I gathered about Nehru with Kidwai, whom I met frequently, and also with the P.M.'s top civilian aides, who were my personal friends. Anyway, I suggested that Nehru or he should give me a weekly appointment and that I would check facts directly with him before writing my column. Azad welcomed my suggestion and I added that I found my normal practice more rewarding, namely seeking an interview with the Prime Minister periodically and making momentary contacts in the lobby to get his reactions on matters of topical interest. I had found Nehru very courteous and stimulating on such occasions.

A day later Azad sent for me and said he had talked with Nehru and that they had agreed that I should meet Azad every Sunday. I expressed happiness at this decision because I had had a close understanding with Azad since 1924, when he presided over a special Congress session in Delhi. Thus the Sunday morning meeting over coffee became a habit and one that proved most stimulating and rewarding. We would discuss politics and personalities without inhibition. Azad would tell me in confidence all that happened in the Cabinet and the Working Committee meetings and I would keep him up to date on happenings elsewhere at home and abroad. The last of these meetings took place four days before his death.

(b) THE IRON MAN PASSES

The conflict between the Nehruites and the Patelites came to a head in August 1950 when Kidwai secured Nehru's support for his proposal to put up Kripalani for the Congress presidentship as against Tandon for the party's annual session at Nasik. Within a fortnight of this decision, Kidwai arranged the publication of a letter declaring that Nehru would refuse to serve on the Working Committee if Tandon was elected. Patel backed Tandon and Kripalani was defeated in the most exciting contest since Subhas Bose clashed with Gandhi. Tandon retaliated by refusing to appoint Kidwai to the Working Committee. Kidwai, in turn, organised a Democratic Front which came to be known as the "KK (Kidwai-

Kripalani) Group." Tandon considered the creation of a group within the party to be wrong. But he found it difficult to take disciplinary action against the Front because of Nehru's sympathy for the policies it stood for. This development marked the beginning of splinter groups in the ruling party.

A crisis was caused by Nehru's resignation of the membership of the Congress Working Committee formed by Tandon. The Kidwai group had made Nehru resign from the Committee by telling him that the "reactionaries" in the party would use him to win the elections and then throw him overboard. Tandon told me he did not want the Congress to split on a personal issue at a time when so much needed to be done. He would not cross swords with Nehru but would make way for him by resigning his office of Congress President. Tandon knew he had the full backing of Patel. His decision to step down was, therefore, not only graceful but highly patriotic.

The man who emerged quietly to a place of prominence out of the drama of Nehru–Tandon differences was the Police Minister in U.P., Lal Bahadur Shastri. He was a trusted lieutenant of Tandon and he figured behind the scenes in avoiding an open clash between them. Nehru sensed in Shastri the qualities of an unostentatious and solid worker with a genius for compromise. Before long Nehru drafted Shastri to the Centre particularly to help him in organising the party for its first battle of the hustings in the general election of 1952.

Not long afterwards, the situation across the northern border took a turn for the worse, resulting in what was perhaps the last clash between Patel and Nehru in the Cabinet. Red China invaded Tibet and Nepal was in the grip of internal turmoil. It was well known that Patel and Prasad differed from Nehru on Tibet. They had urged him to ensure that Tibet continued as an independent buffer between China and India. Now their fears had proved correct. Nehru felt upset because Peking had disregarded his counsel. Patel, whose heart ailment had become more marked, declared emphatically that India's relations with China should be readjusted. Azad told me that though his head was with the Sardar, he had supported Nehru.

Delhi's trouble across the border stemmed mainly from a Himalayan blunder committed by the Government in describing China's position vis-à-vis Tibet in its first communication with the Chinese Communist Government. Britain had recognised Chinese "suzerainty" over Tibet. But Delhi's communication unfortunately employed the word "sovereignty" for suzerainty. The Chinese Government took full advantage of the mistake and when India raised the question of Tibet's invasion, Peking assured that it respected Tibetan autonomy. It further stated that it would not press for religious, political and social changes in Tibet and that it was aware that it would take Tibet and its people at least twenty-five years to emerge from their cocoon of feudalism. Many in Delhi considered the assurance to be an eyewash. But there was little that could be done.

At the last talk I had with him, a few days before his death in Bombay on 15th December, 1950, Patel showed me a letter dated 7th November, 1950, he had written to Nehru. (The letter was published by K. M. Munshi in *Bhavan's Journal* in its issue of 26th February, 1967; because of its historic importance its text is given as Appendix II.) After I finished reading it he said: "I have loved Nehru but he has not reciprocated. I have been eating my heart out because I have not been able to make him see the dangers ahead. China wants to establish its hegemony over South-East Asia. We cannot shut our eyes to this because imperialism is appearing in a new garb. He does not realise that people work only when they have the employment motive or the profit motive. He is being misled by his courtiers. I have grave apprehensions about the future."

Patel's death plunged the nation into grief. Prasad flew to Bombay to attend the funeral, overruling Nehru's objection; the President refused to regard the Prime Minister's advice binding on him in this matter. Nehru took the stand that it would be a bad precedent for the Head of the Union attending the funeral of a Minister. Prasad felt that Nehru was trying to denigrate the stature of Patel. Tributes to the Iron Man came from far and near. Pakistan's Prime Minister, Liaquat Ali succinctly stated: "Sardar Patel always said what he meant and meant it." All were agreed on one thing: While Gandhi was the architect of India's freedom, Sardar was the architect of India's unity.

Chapter 9

FIRST GENERAL ELECTION

(a) NEHRU PARTY BOSS

With Patel gone and Prasad elevated to presidentship, Nehru became all-powerful and felt free to shape domestic policies. He had learned two lessons from his brushes with Patel and Tandon. He must have as Home Minister and Defence Minister only those unquestionably loyal to him and as Congress Party President one subservient to his will. As the country was getting ready for its first general election in 1952, he simultaneously took overall command of the Congress Party to personally fashion the poll strategy and choose the new rulers. The Congress dominated the political scene, despite the decision of Kripalani and some others to break away and form the Kisan Majdoor Praja (Peasants and Workers) Party. There was hardly any organised challenge worth the name. The Communist Party had limited appeal and the Jana Sangh (Peoples Party) started by Shyama Prasad Mookerji following his resignation from the Nehru Ministry, was newly founded.

Two decisions taken about this time influenced the elections significantly although they were not inspired by this motive. Nehru did not think it proper to travel for his election campaign in the aeroplane he used for official purposes as Prime Minister. At the same time, neither he nor the Congress Party could afford to charter a plane for the purpose. An obliging Auditor-General salved Nehru's conscience by devising a convenient formula. The Prime Minister's life, he said, must be secured against all risks, and this could be assured best if he travelled by air. Air transport would avoid the need for the large security staff required if he travelled by rail. Since it was the nation's responsibility to see to his security the nation must pay for it.

So a rule was framed that Nehru would pay the Government only the normal fare chargeable by civil airlines for transporting a passenger. The fares of the security staff accompanying him would be paid from Government funds, and any Congressman accompanying Nehru would pay his own way. Thus, by contributing a bare fraction of the total expenses, Nehru was able to acquire a mobility which multiplied a hundredfold his effectiveness as a campaigner and vote-catcher. As Prime Minister, Nehru received top priority in all communication media, particularly the Press and the Government-controlled radio. Day after day, Nehru's picture and speeches would crowd out anything said by his rivals and the opposing political parties.

Another decision, too, helped this process considerably. Nehru did not like the presence of policemen in uniform at his meetings. But here again, the Civil Servants round him proved very resourceful—and obliging. The official who devised a compromise which was acceptable to Nehru and at the same time ensured his safety described it to me thus: "Nehru in the beginning showed great annoyance at having policemen round him. Once he said that he wanted all policemen to be withdrawn. They must not be seen anywhere when he went about his business. The Principal Private Secretary and the Cabinet Secretary held consultations. They knew how to tackle Nehru. Next day they met him and said: 'We have found a solution. We have decided that the Prime Minister's security is not the Prime Minister's business and that we will have to make adequate arrangements whether the Prime Minister likes it or not.' We promised him, however, that whatever arrangements we would make, the policemen would not be visible. Nehru was quite satisfied with that solution."

The extensive security arrangements for Nehru wherever he went were a sort of advance notice to the locality of a momentous event, and when this was followed by the announcement that Nehru was coming crowds would gather in thousands from far and near. Nehru, too, profited from these devices personally. The large crowds that collected to hear him made all other Congressmen feel that he was their biggest vote-getter and they, therefore, willingly submitted to his authority.

There was a great rush for Congress tickets because of the general feeling that "even a lamp post carrying the Congress ticket will win." As was natural, many candidates made allegations of corruption, immorality and blackmarketing against their rivals. A committee was appointed to screen applications and its slogan was: "Let us give Nehru the 500 men he wants and five years—and leave the rest to him." Gandhi's wishes that deserving men from various professions and spheres of activity be inducted into public life was quietly forgotten.

The Congress won the general election, and that gave birth to a new phase in India's political life, namely the emergence on top of

courtiers, sycophants and hangers-on. When I asked Azad to comment on this development, he said: "We are still feudal, but what
has distressed me is that many good persons have been denied
tickets because the trusted courtiers had labelled them as anti-
Nehru."

(b) INTO ELECTORAL BATTLE

I, too, had personal experience of the din and dust of the electoral
battle by standing for Parliament (House of the People) from New
Delhi. Three factors were mainly responsible for my decision. First,
at the back of my mind was the wish expressed by Vithalbhai Patel
in Vienna in the thirties that I should seek election to India's
Parliament after freedom. Secondly, my friends among the refugees
felt I would best represent their views because of the keen interest
taken by me in their welfare following partition. Thirdly, my visit
to the U.S. in 1950 showed that a large number of public men had
practised journalism in their early life. Also contributing to some
extent was the fact that I was one of the oldest residents of New
Delhi (from 1919 onwards) and among the pioneer builders of a
home in the federal capital.

Patel welcomed my intention to stand for Parliament when I
mentioned it to him. I, thereupon, proceeded to canvas the support
of the leading citizens of New Delhi and of a large number of
inarticulate government officials who had twice helped me to get
elected to the Municipal Committee of Simla in the late twenties.
Everyone that I met welcomed the idea of having a non-party man
to represent the cosmopolitan capital in Parliament. I drew up a
manifesto and several leading citizens endorsed it. But Patel's
death was a damper and altered the situation.

Meanwhile, Nehru and Kripalani fell out. Kripalani and his wife,
Sucheta, left the Congress Party. Sucheta, who had done much
political and social work as the wife of the then Congress Party
President and had played a notable role in refugee relief, announced
that she would stand as a K.M.P.P. candidate from New Delhi.
Nehru could not tolerate the idea of Kripalani challenging him in
his own stronghold and retorted by nominating one of his woman
relatives as the Congress candidate. I selected a bicycle—the
commoner's transport—as my election symbol. But the K.M.P.P.
seized on this symbol to project me as representing the Birlas since
they owned a well-known cycle factory. Such propaganda was,
however, in the game and I was not unduly worried.

The fight had now become triangular and my friends thought I stood a good chance. In fact, as a top Congress leader told me later, the local bosses too were worried, but what I had not reckoned with happened. Nehru threw himself personally into the campaign, addressing a record number of meetings in any one constituency. I lost but the votes polled for me made all the difference between success and defeat for the Congress candidate. Sucheta won and Nehru's cousin lost. The campaign cost me much, but I had no regrets. Indeed, I gained invaluable experience of the working of a crucial aspect of our parliamentary democracy. I realised that a candidate could not depend solely on his own resources. The backing of a party machine and propaganda were essential to fight parliamentary elections.

Chapter 10

PLANNED DEVELOPMENT

(a) POWER BEFORE FOOD

To Nehru must go the credit of bringing economic planning within the realm of practicability. There can be no two opinions that planning over the last two decades or so has benefited the national economy and brought India a long way towards the modern age. At the same time, however, first things have not been done first. In the days of the British rule, the national budget was just a gamble on the monsoon. The severe drought in 1967 and the consequent food crisis showed that twenty years after freedom, the national economy was still dependent mainly on the monsoon—because the vast underground water resources had remained largely untapped.

Following independence, Nehru talked boldly about becoming self-sufficient in food in two years. But both he and his colleagues failed to fathom the magnitude of the food problem. A Fabian and an admirer of Lenin, Nehru thought more in terms of electricity, the symbol of industrialisation, than of food and agriculture. The gigantic river valley projects were basically intended to generate power. Irrigation was incidental. Water was denied to farmers because the electrical engineers did not want to reduce the power load. Where water was made available, the rates initially demanded from the agriculturists were often exorbitant. India could have

built up buffer stocks of food, but a false sense of confidence made
New Delhi reject offers from Washington of food grain supplies to
build up a stockpile.

The food portfolio in the Indian Cabinet proved a graveyard of
political reputations, with the exception of Rafi Ahmed Kidwai,
who had luck and the monsoon gods on his side. Moreover, he
understood well the psychology of the trader, small *bania* and the
wholesaler. I recall seeing big headlines one morning in the newspapers announcing the Government's decision to import a large
quantity of rice. When I saw Kidwai a day later I said to him: "You
told me that we have enough rice now." He smiled and replied:
"Yes, that is so, but this news is the only language that our *bama*
understands." Kidwai was right. The report had its impact and rice
prices came down. The emphasis, however, was mainly on food
procurement and very little on agriculture.

It was only years later that C. Subramaniam brought a sense of
realism to the portfolio by introducing science and technology in the
production of food and helping India to move towards an agricultural breakthrough. Most Indian farmers, including those totally
illiterate in the general sense of the term, are today receptive to the
idea of using quality seed, fertilisers and insecticides. However, he
was unable to get the Government to evolve a clear policy on
fertilisers and push forward vigorously. Some twelve years ago,
Government's agricultural advisers strongly urged the use of synthetic
fertilisers for stepping up food output. But the Planning Commission
successfully resisted the proposal. It preferred to go by the advice
of a South-Indian expert that green manure and compost would do
the job cheaper and more effectively.

(b) T.T.K. AND STEEL

A major achievement in the post-independence period has been the
growth of the steel industry, which at once provides an interesting
and rewarding study of Government at work. Indian steel in 1947
was the cheapest in the world and there was a demand on all sides
that the capacity for steel making be rapidly expanded. But nobody
conceived of plants with a capacity exceeding half a million to one
million tons. George Woods came to India as the World Bank's
special adviser on steel after two American and one British con-
sultancy firms had visited the country to draw up a blueprint for
the development of the steel industry. He advised expansion of the
existing private sector plants and Government loans were given to
Tatas and the Indian Iron and Steel Company.

When T. T. Krishnamachari became Minister for Commerce and Industry in 1951, he recast the nation's steel policy with imagination and, in due course, planned and established three steel mills in the public sector with a total capacity of six million ingot tons yearly. The Government first sounded Britain and West Germany in connection with this programme and both countries expressed their willingness to collaborate in achieving it. Then came the Soviet Union with an offer to set up a plant. The common belief that the Russians made the first offer and the British and Germans came in as a result of this is not true. What, however, is true is that the Russians clinched the agreement on Bhilai more speedily. There is also no doubt that Soviet economic aid acted as a spur to the U.S., Britain and the other Western countries. As Khruschev told Manubhai Shah, Minister of Industry during his visit to India: "We have little to spare. However, we will help you rob the robber. Every rouble we give you will bring you five dollars!"

The story of the projected steel plant at Bokaro throws interesting light on U.S.–Soviet rivalry in winning friends among the developing nations through economic aid. New Delhi had received a hint from Moscow that the Soviet Government was ready to put up a plant at Bokaro, which lies in the coal belt of south-eastern Bihar and forms a part of the area under the Damodar Valley Authority, a body established on the lines of the Tennessee Valley Authority. Nehru and other members of the Cabinet were, however, keen on persuading the U.S. Government to underwrite this project, partly because they wanted to give the Americans a feeling of participation in the development of the industry and partly because they wished to acquire modern steel technology.

At this point, the different approaches of the Americans and the Russians to propositions of this nature became evident. The Russians as usual, did not ask too many questions. They said "yes" and offered to go ahead with a project. But the Americans, as usual, wanted first to go into the entire economics of the Bokaro scheme, the availability of raw materials, the potential market, construction schedules and other details. Bokaro had been included in the Third Five-Year Plan and was supposed to go into production by 1966. Indian officials calculated that it would take the Americans two to three years to investigate the feasibility of the project, and they would therefore never be able to complete the plant in time, whereas the Russians could.

Accordingly, the Russian proposal was put up to the Cabinet for approval. Meanwhile, a cable arrived from the Indian Embassy in Washington saying that the Kennedy Administration was sympathetic to India and should be given a chance to help in the Bokaro project. The Russian offer was pigeonholed and negotiations started anew with the Americans. They took about two years to prepare a preliminary report and then started talking about giving the plant's management freedom to fix its own prices and stipulated that Americans should manage the plant for the first ten years.

A fresh snag developed when New Delhi discovered that Kennedy's chances of getting the concurrence of the U.S. Congress for the venture were doubtful because of his slender majority. Therefore, to spare him embarrassment, it was decided to withdraw the request for aid and turn once more to the Russians. At first, Moscow showed pique because New Delhi had shelved its proposal unceremoniously and gone to the rival American camp. But political considerations later prevailed and the Russians agreed to collaborate.

I took a special interest in finding out how the public sector steel plants were working soon after they were installed. The Minister for Steel at the time was Swaran Singh and I accompanied him on a tour of the three plants at Rourkela, Durgapur and Bhilai. It was obvious that the British and the German experts were stand offish in their social relations but were keen to train Indians in the techniques in which they were understudying them. The Russians, on the other hand, made a special effort to talk to their Indian colleagues in Hindi and also lived in the same manner as they— creating a good impression at the social level.

Conditions had changed, however, when I visited Bhilai later to spend a brief vacation with my second son Vikrama Jit, a member of an all-India service for managing State enterprises. The Russian Chief Engineer, who had spent five years in Bhilai and spoke English told me frankly in an informal chat following a dinner at the house of the General Manager, Indarjit Singh, that the labour welfare laws and the attitude of the workers stood in the way of getting the best results. The rivalry between the trade unions created tension between the management and the workers. While young Indian technicians were very keen to learn and were proving an asset, the worker's attitude was not good. He felt that public enterprises would not make good unless productivity became the main objective. As matters stood, there were too many surplus hands in the plant and nobody was getting rid of them. (I heard an echo of this in Moscow in 1967, when I was told by various Russians I met that the public sector could prove itself only if the anti-work and anti-productivity attitude of the workers was eliminated.)

(c) NON-CONVERTIBLE RUPEE TRADE

Was T.T.K. guilty of frittering away India's sterling balances? The truth is that he looked far ahead and realised that India could build up its industrial base only if it produced plentiful steel cement and soda ash. He sanctioned the import of capital goods for two reasons: to introduce the competitive element into production and thereby improve Indian manufactures and to create a demand for certain types of goods so that the industries which produced them would expand or new ones develop. These were national objectives, well-conceived and well-executed, and as a policy, unexceptionable. But trouble arose because of T.T.K.'s weakness in tending to view his action and policy decision in terms of its effects on the fortunes of individual business houses, some his favourites and some not so. The first foreign exchange crisis was thus not the result of T.T.K.'s alleged prodigality but of the ambitious programmes of industrialisation.

Morarji Desai, who took over Commerce and Industry when T.T.K. moved to Finance, brought with him a breath of fresh air by looking at proposals in terms of policy and fair play. His handling of this portfolio created great confidence in business circles and led to a boom in the share markets. Unfortunately, he, like T.T.K., paid insufficient attention to developing domestic sources of industrial raw materials—a lapse which continued after Desai switched over to Finance and for which the country is still paying heavily.

A development of far-reaching consequence occurred when trade on the basis of payment in non-convertible rupees was initiated with the Socialist bloc in Europe. I gathered that K. B. Lall (now the Commerce Secretary) after consultations with the Secretaries of various departments at the Centre on the desirability of negotiating pacts with these countries on this basis, went to Moscow for talks. The first reaction of the Russians was hostile; but Lall did not give up. He requested the Indian Ambassador, K. P. S. Menon, to pursue the matter and convince the Russians that one way of enlarging trade between the two countries was to adopt the system he had suggested. From Moscow, Lall went to Berlin, where he found the East Germans eager to establish trade relations with India. On his own initiative, he signed an agreement providing for payment for imports from East Germany in non-convertible rupees.

He then went on to Warsaw and negotiated a similar agreement. but before he signed it he received a message from New Delhi saying the deal was unacceptable. This was followed by a cable from Nehru himself, giving arguments against signing but adding that Lall was free to act as he thought fit. Politics was at play here. Nehru favoured diversifying India's foreign trade and a larger exchange of goods with the Socialist countries, but apparently there was some roadblock at the secretarial level. Lall did not wish to go openly against his colleagues in the Civil Service and so, in spite of Nehru showing him the green light, he spoke to some of the Secretaries concerned on the phone from Warsaw and told them he would not sign the agreement with the Poles.

Meanwhile, a message came from Menon in Moscow that the Russians were prepared to sign a non-convertible rupee agreement. Lall explained his difficulty to Menon because of the opposition of his colleagues in Delhi. Menon said he would sign the pact and take the full responsibility for it. But that would not have solved Lall's problem, because no matter who signed, his colleagues would pin the responsibility on him. He, therefore, exchanged letters with the Russians stipulating that the five-year agreement could be revised or revoked in the light of its working for a few months. Before Lall reached India, the Press had splashed the agreement as a five-year deal.

When the first pact on trade in rupees was signed, Morarji Desai as Finance Minister expressed his disapproval on the ground that the Russians and their East European allies could use the Indian currency they accumulated to finance their agents and propaganda machine in this country. (Charges that this had happened have been heard frequently since the third general election.) But the results have proved beneficial. The rupee trade has helped India in her foreign exchange crisis and, at the same time, led to a big increase in her business with the Socialist bloc.

The Russians always insisted on inserting a clause in their trade agreements with India to the effect that the rupee would be valued on the basis of parity with gold. But as private Indian traders made export contracts with the Russians, the Indian Government did not insist on a similar condition on its side. When it was suggested that this be done, the Government's financial brains objected on the plea that this might cast doubts on the stability of the rupee. How mistaken this policy was came to light when the rupee was devalued in June, 1966. The Commerce Minister at the time, Manubhai Shah, had to fly posthaste to Moscow to persuade the Russians to add forty-seven per cent to the prices of Indian exports although India would have to pay fifty-seven per cent more for imports from Russia. This was the best he could get the Russians to agree to.

(d) THE SILENT REVOLUTION

One day in 1955, Nehru suggested that Indian newspapermen were too urban-minded and that insufficient attention had been paid to the silent revolution in the countryside, the result of the community development programme and the agricultural extension service which now embraced the entire country. He was right, and wishing to meet his challenge I planned a tour of 8,000 miles by road covering eight states. I persuaded my wife to join me since I was anxious to know the outlook of the rural folk to family planning and village women would be willing to share their inner feelings only with a motherly person. The tour began in December and after every week of travelling we returned to Delhi for a week to rest and attend to normal chores. I wrote twelve articles on the basis of my observations which were published in the *Hindustan Times* with the title: "Ram Rajya in Action."

The idea of community development had been sold to Nehru by Chester Bowles, U.S. Ambassador, and it embraced not only the development of the countryside but also the creation of small towns as centres of rural, cultural and commercial life. By and large the programme failed to achieve practical results, and no attempt was made to develop the agro-towns Bowles had proposed. There was no doubt, however, that it planted in the head of the villager a desire to improve his methods of cultivation and living conditions. In a way, this also helped them to vote intelligently, conscious of what they should ask for and work for.

My wife gathered much valuable information in her talks with village women. Almost all of them, whether in villages up north or in the heart of the undeveloped areas in the central region, gave the same answer when asked about family planning. They wanted fewer children; they all said their husbands were unconcerned about the matter and would not use or pay for contraceptives. In fact, they confided that mating could never be planned in the way they lived. They suggested they should be supplied with pills which they could keep in their head covers for instant use. So I wrote, the villagers' hope and salvation was the pill. Family planning would not encounter resistance in the village, I later told Nehru, who felt immensely pleased.

We were struck by the fact that one village had been wholly reconstructed and that this project had provided employment to about 600 hands for two years. I suggested that all the villages of India be rebuilt in twenty-five years and linked by road. No foreign

aid was needed for this work, and what was more, it would enable
workers in towns to live in villages nearby and cycle to and from their
work places. The countryside would be enriched and the multiplica-
tion of slums in towns checked. Each villager would not only own a
house but would also let out a portion to workers in towns. I wrote
that in my view, this was the only genuine answer to the evils
of urbanisation and the problem of providing urban amenities to the
countryside. (Perhaps the official planners will turn their attention
to this question now that the leverage in elections is held by the
farmer.)

(e) F.I.C.C.I.

One of the most interesting phenomena on the economic front
since independence is the eclipse of the Federation of Indian
Chambers of Commerce and Industry. Under the British, the
Federation was the economic wing of the Congress. Business leaders
supported the freedom movement with money and moral backing
and the Congress leaders supported the business community in the
legislatures. In fact, the comments of the Federation on the Central
Budget were awaited by Congress and other legislators to decide
what line to take in the general discussion on it. F.I.C.C.I. also had
a powerful lobby in the Central Assembly and successive Finance
Members invariably consulted it before initiating action on important matters for fear that the Opposition would otherwise charge
them with acting arbitrarily and promoting British business interests.

The situation changed radically after independence. On coming
out of Almora Jail in 1945, Nehru addressed a meeting at Ranikhet
in which he declared: "Blackmarketeers and profiteers have
flourished at the cost of the nation. All such persons will be hanged
from the nearest lamp post when the Congress comes to power and
the country becomes independent." The Congress Party adopted
this declaration as one of its key talking points after independence.
Although it has not succeeded in punishing such men or stopping
these evils, the Congress has by this attitude put itself and the business community in opposite camps. The role of the business community since independence has therefore been defensive.

What mainly derailed businessmen politically was the action the
Government took against firms suspected of evading taxes. Liaquat
Ali had proposed a commission of inquiry and drawn up a list of
about 150 business houses under suspicion. This action paralysed
business leaders and most of them never recovered from the shock.
Sardar Patel told me that businessmen offered to settle their dues

collectively by depositing Rs. 500 million in the exchequer. This would have enabled them to bring out their black money and use it legitimately. Patel favoured the deal because he wanted business to play its full role in activating the country's economy. But Nehru, for reasons of ideology, would not listen to him. The result was that not only did black market money not come out but it kept multiplying.

Perhaps the most objective view of the business community on the economic and political health of our nation was given to me by a self-made leading industrialist of Bombay, K. C. Mahindra, who headed India's Purchasing Mission in the U.S. during World War II, and took keen interest in national affairs. Writing to me on 15th July, 1963, he stated that "the lapses in the economic determinants have become acute, and unless a drastic revision of the instruments of policy is made, there may rapidly be drift to chaos." He added: "I feel it is becoming more relevant that the execution of policy should be left to technocrats. Social and economic objectives have been spelt out in great detail, but failure is writ large on the methods and procedures followed in implementing that policy. But who would listen? The P.M. is strongly entrenched in the party's forums; likewise in the affections of the people. It is, therefore, a personal decision alone which could bring about healthy changes. If he shies away from a drastic proposed revolutionary change, one may have to wait until events and circumstances force his hands. I do not otherwise see any other light."

Chapter 11

INDIA AND THE BIG POWERS

(a) SUCCESSION OF VISITORS

The five years between the first and second general elections saw marked activity on the international front. The Big Powers made moves and counter moves to woo (or, whenever necessary, to browbeat) India. A succession of dignitaries visited India. Some came to understand how this country, without military or industrial strength, had come to acquire a powerful voice in world affairs. Others came to seek Nehru's views and to check their own assessment of events. Nehru, for his part, forged ahead with his policy of non-alignment. He actively sought the friendship of China and Russia and played a leading role in bringing Afro–Asian nations together at Bandung.

America's relations with India were not very happy when John Foster Dulles visited India in May 1953. Henry Grady as the first U.S. Ambassador had helped to lay the foundations of economic and technical co-operation between the two countries. But Loy Henderson, who succeeded, caused a setback when his wife made contact with Sheikh Abdullah and dabbled in Kashmir's affairs. Chester Bowles came next and applied the healing touch. He made Indians feel that the U.S. was really their friend. However, the Bowles left after a stay of one and a half years. George Allen, who followed, caused eyebrows to raise when, speaking at the presentation of credentials, he referred to himself as "directing the activities" of the U.S. in India.

On the eve of the visit of Dulles, a balloon was sent up. It was said that India could have a Monroe Doctrine which would embrace Burma and Thailand as a protection against Communist expansionism. New Delhi reacted adversely to the suggestion, to Washington's disappointment. India did not want to establish her hegemony over South-East Asia. About the same time, New Delhi received another report according to which a military pact was to be signed between Turkey, Iran and Pakistan underwritten by the U.S. Dulles tried to use this to bring India into his scheme of encircling Russia. However, Nehru made it clear that he would consider such a pact as unfriendly as, according to him, its sole purpose was to arm Pakistan, a "pact friend," to enable it to try conclusions with India.

Richard Nixon followed in December. He met C.R. in Madras. Allen introduced me to Nixon and, after meeting him, I wrote: "Extremist Republicans think that they can kick the world into shape with their dollar-studded boots." Nixon was told by me about India's objection to the U.S. military pact with Pakistan and that "Kashmir will have to be put into cold storage, since Pakistan's sole object in seeking military aid and economic aid was to prepare herself better to try military conclusions with India." The American attitude to Pakistan, I gathered from Nixon, was: "Here is a little chap who is prepared to stand up and fight this Moscow bully. Shall we not applaud him and give him all the help and encouragement we can?" Nixon did not accept the theory that Pakistan would not fight Communist Russia but would attack democratic India.

The day after Nixon's arrival in Delhi the first Indo–Soviet trade agreement was signed. This was a rebuff to Washington. It meant that the U.S. would lose India and Asia if it followed a policy of divide and rule and tried to build up feudal Pakistan against democratic India.

Canada's Prime Minister, Louis St. Laurent, came in February 1954 and received a warm welcome. He made it clear soon after arrival that "North America does not mean the United States. Canada attaches great importance to India's role in world affairs." I renewed contact with him and said: "Please tell Washington that by isolating India it will weaken the democratic forces." "Be assured," he responded. "They take from us what they will not take from anyone else."

Tito came in December and was the first head of state to visit India. He travelled like a monarch and the ceremonial platform in New Delhi was found inadequate for the purpose. No protocol was possible, for nothing had been rehearsed. Tito was then isolated and Nehru had attained the status of a world leader. The two found much in common in their outlook and views and the friendship struck between them became a force in global politics. Anxious to develop relations with India, Tito had earlier sent a high-power delegation headed by Vice-President Colakovic. During Tito's visit, Yugoslavia agreed to enter into a trade agreement with India on the basis of payment in rupees.

A ten-week visit to Europe in the summer of 1954, accompanied by my wife and my third son, Satya Jit, then a fighter pilot in the Indian Air Force, enabled me to study the European outlook on India. Nehru, I discovered, was considered pro-Communist and anti-U.S. Some Europeans, especially the French, showed a sneaking admiration for Nehru as the man who had ticked off the Americans. They added: "We cannot afford to differ with America."

The only statesman in Europe who appreciated Nehru's constructive role was Chancellor Adenauer. He told me that Nehru alone was in a position to create confidence between Russia and America. He felt that German reunification and the future of Berlin were tied up with the cold war. It was only when both sides accepted coexistence that tension would relax. India and Nehru, he said, were a great factor for peace. I rather got the impression that being a Catholic, he was not particularly keen to welcome reunion with the predominantly Protestant East Germany until West Germany had consolidated itself.

I also visited London and Cairo before returning home. It was interesting to find the British take the view that "once again, Germany had won the war." She had rebuilt her economic strength with American aid and was now leaving Britain behind in several spheres, especially shipbuilding. In Cairo, I had a talk lasting over two hours with Nasser, whose enthusiastic friendship for India and regard for Nehru was most heartwarming. He candidly recognised that Israel had come to stay but felt there was a genuine fear that with the backing of the Jewish wealth Israel might become a danger to the security of the Arabs.

(b) NEHRU GOES TO PEKING

At this stage, the country was thrilled with the news that Nehru would visit Peking in response to a pressing invitation by Chou En-lai, who broke journey in New Delhi in June 1954 on his way back from the Geneva Conference on Indo-China. Since Chou had gone to the Geneva Conference in a Chinese-owned Dakota, Nehru decided to fly to Peking in an Indian Dakota. But before he left, Nehru was rattled by a report from Korea that the Chinese had told our representative there that India had not shed her slavery because even the Army commands were given in English. So, Nehru ordered the commands to be given in Hindi. Tyagi was then the Minister of Defence Organisation. With his army background and sound knowledge of popular Hindi, he undertook the task and did it competently and expeditiously.

Azad mentioned to me at our Sunday meeting over coffee that Peking was making great preparations to receive Nehru as the leader of 360 million people. But he had told Nehru to find answers to two questions: Is China Communist first and Asian next? Will it guarantee the safety of the smaller Asian states?

Nehru's trip to China was marked by an enthusiastic welcome wherever he went. But Nehru was not deceived by this show of goodwill. He told me that for all their Communism the Chinese had not changed their traditional outlook. Their country was still the Middle Kingdom. He sensed in the protocol observed during his visit that he was treated as a visitor from an important state which paid tribute to China. That had put him on his guard. The Chinese, he added, talked little and depended on poetic allusions to drive their point home politely. "Time is on our side. They will take long to be a strong, industrial power," was Nehru's consoling conclusion.

Writing on 2nd November, 1954, I said: "Small nations would want India to develop strength to maintain the balance of power in Asia, meaning that India should hold China to her word." The way newspaper reports portrayed the trip, showing Nehru had been idolised, swelled India's pride and strengthened the "Hindi–Chini bhai bhai" (Indians and Chinese are brothers) psychology. I contributed my bit to this atmosphere by writing that the Chinese had made Nehru feel a world figure, whereas the U.S. had treated him only as Prime Minister of India in their "motorcade protocol."

Nehru told officers of the External Affairs Ministry that the Chinese were proud of being Chinese and that one language had given them national cohesion. He tried to speak to the officers in Hindi, but desisted when he met with a chilling response.

After getting Nehru's impressions and talking to Ministry officials, I wrote that "unless India is industrially strong and politically and socially well-knit she cannot maintain the balance of power in Asia and the Middle East. Political life will not progress unless there are 300,000 Nehrus to work at all levels; collective leadership is the way to strengthen a people's government."

We had a feeling of deflation when we found that the *New York Times*, in listing the fifty most important events in 1954, omitted Nehru's visit to China and Tito's to India and gave credit to Britain for the Geneva agreement on Indo-China. Indeed, India did not figure at all in *The Times* of London, which published 237 items of global interest. Even the fact that Mrs. Pandit was the first woman diplomat at the Court of St. James's was not mentioned.

The year ended with another blow. Peking republished old maps showing large chunks of Indian territory as Chinese. When New Delhi protested, Peking replied that the maps had not yet been revised.

(c) INDIA AND RUSSIA

The greatest factor in India's foreign relations and internal development has been her close ties with the Soviet Union. Their origin and growth were largely the handiwork of Nehru and Khrushchev. Mrs. Pandit's appointment as the first Indian Ambassador in Moscow pleased the Russians much as she was Nehru's sister. She was given a standing ovation at the Bolshoi Theatre. But this feeling did not last long. In her private talks with the American and British Ambassadors, she expressed her personal views and as the Russians had bugged all the diplomatic missions they got to know of this and dropped her altogether.

Radhakrishnan, who followed Mrs. Pandit, was liked initially by the Russians because of his reputation as a philosopher and scholar. He retained his Oxford professorship and shuttled between Moscow and London. Since he kept aloof, Stalin thought well of him and granted him two interviews. This pushed up Radhakrishnan in

Nehru's estimation. During his tenure, New Delhi's role in bringing about a cease-fire in Korea and in Indo-China opened Moscow's eyes to its growing influence. Before these developments, the Russian attitude could be summed up in Vyshinsky's remark at the U.N. when India moved her resolution on Korea: "At best, you are idealists and dreamers; at worst, you are stooges of the U.S."

In the early years of independence the Russians persisted in believing that India was bound hand and foot to Britain and was incapable of independent action. They described Gandhi in an official encyclopedia as a reactionary and mountebank who exploited the religious sentiments of superstitious folk. The references to Nehru were also uncomplimentary. Indeed the Kremlin considered Nehru India's Chiang Kai-shek.

On taking over in Moscow, K. P. S. Menon received a summons to call on Stalin. He cabled Nehru for instruction. He was told to explain India's stand on Korea. I learned from Nehru that Stalin showed no interest in the explanation. He wanted the fighting to continue, for it suited him to have a direct confrontation between the U.S. and China. On one occasion when Ambassador Menon called on Stalin in his office, the master of the Kremlin did a doodle of wolves fighting. He explained to Menon: "Our peasant is simple and wise. When he sees a wolf, he shoots and kills. He does not give a lecture on morality." Menon wrote to Nehru telling him that the time had passed when teaching philosophy could be combined with diplomacy.

The climate in Moscow towards India changed considerably after Nehru visited China in 1954 and was well received there, as films and television recordings showed. The Soviet Foreign Office immediately asked our Ambassador to get in touch with Nehru in Peking and ask him to visit Moscow on his way back to New Delhi. Nehru replied that he would visit Moscow separately and not incidentally. This pleased Moscow.

Nehru visited the Soviet Union in June 1955 and the reception he received on arrival in Moscow was unprecedented—something no visiting head of State or Government has received after him. The Russians went all out to fête Nehru. Before his arrival a special study was made of his diets and habit. Nehru travelled in an open car, something unheard of in the Soviet Union, and Bulganin and Khrushchev had to sit or stand with him in it. Thousands of roses were showered on them by the onlookers. The entire Politbureau of the Soviet Communist Party came to dine with Nehru at the Embassy. Proposing a toast, Khruschev said: "Some say Nehru is a Communist. I do not want him to be a Communist. I want Nehru to be Nehru. So I propose a toast to Nehru." Before the Prime Minister's visit only a Deputy Minister attended the 15th August celebrations at the Embassy.

This visit to Russia made the West feel that it would result in relaxing tension. The feeling in India was one of exultation over the triumphant tour of their national hero. Swept along by the wave, President Prasad decided to bestow the highest honour, *Bharat Ratna* (Jewel of India), on the Prime Minister. This caused much surprise in diplomatic circles and among sophisticated Indians. Convention was disregarded and the decoration was awarded at a banquet without a citation. Some felt it was an exhibition of subservience; others thought it was degrading to national pride that a visit to a foreign country, however successful, should be so rewarded.

Prasad's explanation to me was straightforward. He said: "Jawahar is literally a *Bharat Ratna*. Why not formally make him one? He has laid the foundation for peace and you will see the visit will prove of historic significance." (Not long afterwards, Nehru appeared at an official reception wearing the insignia round his neck.)

There was much excitement when it was announced that Bulganin and Khrushchev would return the visit in November. India was the first democratic state B. and K. visited. Nehru took a keen personal interest in giving the Russians a very warm welcome—and in putting India's best foot forward. The names of the main thoroughfares in the capital were changed in a bid to remove the symbols of colonialism. Kingsway was renamed Rajpath and Queensway Janpath. Khrushchev, driving down Rajpath, however, spotted the statue of King George V facing India Gate and asked why this relic was still there. The Chief of Protocol replied that this was "a part of our history," but Khrushchev was unimpressed. (Queen Elizabeth, who visited India in 1961, was, however, greatly pleased to see her grandfather honoured. The statue was removed by Indira Gandhi in 1968 in response to popular demand.)

Indian protocol placed Bulganin above Khrushchev. This order of precedence annoyed Khrushchev who exhibited his feelings publicly by loudly remarking in Russian when Bulganin spoke at any function: "He is talking nonsense. He does not know the facts." He would also whisper with embarrassing loudness to his colleague to stop speaking. This experience of having to play second fiddle to a figure-head seems to have taught Khrushchev a political lesson. For, after returning to Moscow he pushed Bulganin out of office and combined in himself the post of Chairman of the Council of Ministers and Secretary of the Communist Party.

B and K got receptions in Delhi and Calcutta exceeding anything before for a foreign visitor. Foreign newsmen called them
Government-promoted, but the crowds which assembled at the
Ramlila Grounds in New Delhi to see the visitors did not do so at
the behest of the Government. There was a quiet dinner for the
Russians at Nehru's house, and according to Azad, Khrushchev said
to Nehru: "We want you to be our friends, but we do not want
you to give up your old friends. We are like children. We want to
be friends, but if we are hated or hit we hit back." He spoke for
only five minutes, but what he said made a deep impact on his
hearers.

When they visited Kashmir, Khrushchev was struck by the fact
that in looks and dress the Kashmiris resembled the people of
Tadzhikistan in Soviet Asia. This gave him a feeling of oneness with
the Kashmiris, and in one of his not uncommon emotional outbursts
he declared that if the people of Kashmir were ever in trouble all
they had to do was to whistle and the Russians would come to their
aid. This was interpreted in India and the world beyond as a Soviet
pledge to help India militarily if Kashmir was attacked.

Dulles, with his penchant for doing the wrong thing, signed a
statement with Portugal's Foreign Minister acknowledging Goa as
part of metropolitan Portugal. Sherman Cooper, who was nearest
to Nehru of all the diplomats in New Delhi at the time, felt very
embarrassed. He told me that Dulles had reacted unfavourably to
Khrushchev's backing of India on Kashmir and Goa. I replied that
"India is not inviting the bear's hug, but geography places Russia
at shouting distance from Delhi and makes Kashmir the connecting
door."

The lessons B and K learned on their tour of India were seen at
the twentieth Congress of the C.S.P.U. in Moscow at which Khrushchev said war was not inevitable, that revolution could take place
without violence and that coexistence rather than subversion would
be the keystone of the party's international policy. Khrushchev saw to
it that the Soviet encyclopedia described Gandhi as a great liberator.
The Luxembourg Ambassador congratulated our Ambassador in
Moscow on Nehru having transformed the Russian Communists.
When B and K went to Geneva to meet Ike, the Russians travelled
in an open car while Eisenhower moved in a bullet-proof closed car
with helicopters flying overhead for added security.

China did not like the way the Russian leaders had been hailed in
India and sent Madam Soong Ching Ling, the widow of Sun Yat
Sen, with pledges of Chinese support against attacks on Indian
sovereignty.

In a review of 1955, I described it as "India's year." Besides B and K, India had high-ranking State visitors from Yugoslavia, Egypt, Saudi Arabia, Afghanistan, Burma and Indonesia. I mentioned that while Anthony Eden was personally keen to use India as a bridge with China, the British Press and diplomats were anti-Indian. The U.N. had ceased to be the handmaid of the Anglo–Americans and the Soviet had offered India massive aid for the second plan unasked.

(d) SUEZ CRISIS

Following the Franco–British attack on the Suez, the Soviet Ambassador delivered a letter from Khrushchev to Nehru saying that he was issuing an ultimatum to Britain that unless there was a cease-fire by a stipulated time he would attack that country. The threat was not taken seriously in London but Nehru was upset. He quickly drafted a reply to Khrushchev, observing that a second and bigger war was not the way to stop the first and he feared Khrushchev would precipitate a universal conflagration by his action. The letter was delivered to the Soviet Embassy, which at that time occupied Travancore House.

Around midnight, the British High Commissioner, Malcolm MacDonald, wished to see Nehru. But Nehru was infuriated at what he considered the British Government's provocative and irresponsible action in attacking Egypt and refused to see MacDonald, turning him over to N. R. Pillai, the Secretary-General for External Affairs. MacDonald handed Pillai a message from London saying that the British troops engaged in the operations had been asked to cease fire. This was a great relief to the Indian Government, because Nehru had convinced himself that a major clash of arms could not be averted. Nehru backed Nasser to the hilt and Nasser, in turn, accepted the formula prepared by Krishna Menon regarding the Suez Canal. But the British rejected it.

Ali Yavar Jung was India's Ambassador in Cairo at the time of the Suez crisis. His role was to support Nasser in public but restrain him in private. He found the Egyptian President a man of intelligence and common sense; but those around him indulged in bravado and bluff. The question of U.S. economic aid was under consideration. Dulles was very angry with Nasser for recognising China. He also did not like Nasser approaching the Russians for arms. U.S. Congress was against granting much economic aid to the UAR and undertaking the Aswan High Dam project.

Dulles said that Egypt, having pledged its cotton crop to Russia

for armaments, was not in a position to pay interest on U.S. investment on the dam and that Washington had decided to drop the
project. At that time, Nehru halted at Cairo on his way to Brioni.
Jung mentioned this matter to Nehru, who advised Nasser to avoid
hasty or drastic action. Nasser promised to do so, but soon after
Nehru reached India he announced nationalisation of the Suez
Canal. Jung, who had gone to Beirut on holiday, rushed back to
Cairo and told Nasser that this would have grave consequences and
that Indian public opinion would not favour this step. Nasser did
not agree. That very day Jung received a cable from Nehru asking
him to tell Nasser that he had acted hastily and that public opinion
in India was likely to be unfriendly. Nasser thought Jung had
inspired the message!

Chapter 12

LINGUISTIC STATES

Linguistic states? Have they strengthened national unity or
weakened it? These and many other questions repeatedly asked over
the past many years may not perhaps have arisen but for the fact
that Rajagopalachari's Ministry in Madras after the first general
election was not a happy family. His differences with T. Prakasam,
popularly known as Andhra Kesari (Lion of Andhra), accentuated
the clash between the Tamils and the Telegu-speaking Andhras.
The Andhras now revived their demand that the Madras State, as
formed by the British, be carved into two separate Tamil and Telegu-
speaking states. This movement got a big fillip when a respected
leader, Potti Sriramulu, undertook a fast unto death. Nehru told
his Cabinet colleagues he would not be intimidated by these tactics.
But when the fasting leader died and the tragedy was followed by
widespread riots and destruction, Nehru yielded.

The creation of Andhra State was the signal for a demand for a
Kannada-speaking state comprising old Mysore State and including
areas then part of erstwhile Bombay and Hyderabad States. Nehru
and his Cabinet and the Congress High Command decided to resist
all attempts at further division of the states according to language.

However, when Nehru was greeted with black flags at Belgaum he sensed the danger to his position as the idol of the people and announced the formation of a Commission to study the question of reorganisation of states on a linguistic basis under the chairmanship of Fazli Ali, a judge of the Supreme Court. The inquiry created a nationwide ferment. It gave a stimulus to parochial tendencies and created fear among the nationalist-minded that the end-product would be Balkanisation of the country.

When the Fazli Ali Report was published, we expected it to be treated as an award. In fact, Devadas and I decided to make journalistic history by publishing overnight the full text of the voluminous report. Pandit Hriday Nath Kunzru, who was a member of the Commission, had told me that he agreed to join it only after extracting a promise from Nehru that its recommendations would be treated as an award. However, this was not to be. Nehru took counsel with Pant and Krishna Menon. Pant advised he should declare that the Government would form its own conclusions, which meant that the report would not be treated as an award. Menon told Nehru to shelve the report by circulating it for the opinion of the State Governments. Everywhere, nationalist-minded Congressmen who were opposed to linguistic states waited for word that the report would be treated as an award. They felt the country could be saved from disintegration if Nehru did this.

Nehru went by Pant's advice. However, as Pant told me the morning after Nehru had gone on the air to broadcast his decision, Nehru had overtalked in expressing "surprise at some of the recommendations of the commission." Menon, who knew Nehru's mind, told me that the Prime Minister had only expressed his true feelings. He did not like the break-up of Hyderabad, which he thought was a model composite state. Pant, on the other hand, welcomed this recommendation, for it would remove Hyderabad as "a focus of Muslim power." Pant told me he wanted to give a "decent burial" to linguism as an active political force. But Nehru and he were not operating on the same wavelength.

Pant and Azad sensed the dangers in the expectations roused by Nehru's radio talk. Azad condemned it outright. In the light of my talk with both of them, I wrote on 25th October: "The danger is the High Command may encourage linguism up to a point where various groups begin to think and function as sub-nationalities. Such a situation would transfer the scene of regional tug-of-war to the Centre. It is only composite states that provide a safe base for a composite Union."

The country was now in the grip of the controversy over the

Fazli Ali report. I wrote that the debate on it in Parliament had revealed "how skin-deep is the loyalty to the Congress ideology when it clashes with a regional outlook or comes in the way of personal ambition." And, as days passed, the controversy gathered momentum. C.R. asked Nehru to shelve the report for twenty-five years and our paper advised Nehru to "debunk the one language, one state" proposal. The Chief Ministers of Bengal and Bihar offered to amalgamate their states in a bid to check "linguistic madness." Proposals for the merger of a few other states were also mooted and it was even suggested that the country be carved out into five or six zonal administrative units. But all these remained a pious wish as the Centre did not respond favourably.

Nehru's own attitude to implementing the recommendations in the report weakened, and when he declared that "no decision is irrevocable in democracy" he gave an opportunity to every linguistic group to get what it wanted if it could amount the necessary political pressure. Encouraged by Nehru's attitude, the people of Maharashtra gave a keen edge to the controversy over Bombay State. They demanded that the composite state be split into separate states of Maharashtra and Gujarat. But the question arose about the future of Bombay city. I visited Bombay at the suggestion of Pant, and after talking to many prominent citizens I returned to Delhi and informed Pant that the general feeling was that Bombay should remain a composite state with the city as its capital. But if Maharashtra and Gujarat were to be separated, Bombay, which had a majority of non-Maharashtrians, should be made a Union Territory.

Pant agreed with this view and invited me to give my impressions at an informal meeting of the Congress High Command at which Nehru and Azad were present. Everyone agreed with the desire to keep Bombay a composite state and this is what the Nehru Government finally decided despite strong pressure from C. D. Deshmukh, then Finance Minister, who quit the Cabinet in protest. The Congress High Command formulated its views on other aspects of the report of the States Reorganisation Commission but did not stand up to Nehru when he kept modifying them under political pressure.

Krishna Menon told me he advised Nehru not to redraw state boundaries on the basis of language as this would lead to national disintegration. But if Nehru decided to do so, Menon advised him to divide the country into about fifty provinces or counties, as in Britain, with a central government at the apex. Alternatively, Menon suggested the creation of five presidencies. Of interest is Menon's claim that it was he who first put forward the three-language formula in education to ensure national unity. Under the formula, every student is expected to learn his regional mother tongue, Hindi and English; if Hindi is his mother tongue, he learns another modern Indian language in addition.

Menon later told me that he had put forward the theorem that the more administrative power was decentralised the stronger the Centre would be. The Centre should look after defence, external affairs, communications, international trade and currency and leave the rest to the states. The Centre should collect all taxes and distribute them to the states on the basis of population, or the states could collect taxes and give a part of the collections to the Centre. The residuary powers should remain with the Centre. Menon added that he wished he had stood up to Nehru on the numerous occasions when this would have helped. To explain his failure to do so, he said: "It is an Indian trait that when you respect a man you do not stand up to him." These reactions were given when he was a free man. He had suffered electoral defeat twice for his seat in the Lok Sabha from Bombay in 1957–60. He looked forward to his return to Parliament, if possible, with the help of Leftists in West Bengal or Kerata.

Not long afterwards, C.R. started a campaign against making Hindi the official language. Pant was disturbed because C.R. had been a strong supporter of Hindi and had even incurred unpopularity in the South by making it compulsory in schools. The *volte face* sounded ominous. He suggested I speak to Azad, who as Education Minister was concerned with the matter and could take it up with Nehru. Azad said at our weekly dialogue that he had already spoken to Nehru and that both of them felt that C.R. was venting his spleen at the polite rejection of the idea that C.R. be used as Government's envoy at large. Nehru was of the opinion that Radhakrishnan was already fulfilling that role informally.

Nehru, Azad and Pant decided not to yield on the issue of making Hindi the official language. Any concession, as Azad said to me, would have been disastrous against the background of their decision to go in for linguistic states. But an unexpected controversy erupted in the Cabinet in regard to Urdu after the statutory commission on official language provided for under the Constitution had made its report and the parliamentary committee which examined the report had made its recommendations. Pant had deliberated very carefully over the report of the commission and had made four or five different drafts for every contentious paragraph in his anxiety to see that the report was accepted fully by Nehru and the rest of the Cabinet.

Nehru suddenly insisted that Urdu was the language of the people of Delhi and due recognition should be accorded. Pant disagreed and maintained that only six per cent of the Delhiwalas claimed

Urdu as their language. When Nehru retorted that Pant's statistics were incorrect and suggested a presidential order laying down the official purposes for which Urdu should be used, Pant replied that such an order would create problems in the future, for it would be like the institution of communal electorates. These electorates were justified for the first time as a temporary measure, but they not only became permanent but led to reservations for the Muslims in the services and in other spheres. Ultimately, the principle of communal electorates ended in the country's partition, Pant said. The use of Urdu could be very easily safeguarded by an executive order based on instructions sent by the Prime Minister to the Chief Ministers of the states concerned.

Although Nehru did not agree with this view, he did not press his own and the idea of a presidential order was dropped and a circular sent out on the subject. But Pant was most unhappy by Nehru's exhibition of annoyance at the way in which he had handled the matter. Soon thereafter Pant suffered a heart attack. Some thought that the attack was caused by Pant's verbal bout with Nehru. At any rate, Pant hinted to B. N. Jha, Home Secretary, that it had been caused by the strain of the work on the language issue. Officials who had worked in close co-operation with Pant on the report remarked they had never seen the Minister so visibly upset.

Pant assured me he was not against Urdu. In fact, he was "prepared to give it official recognition in Delhi and U.P. if it could be written in the Devanagari script." He felt it would be suicidal, however, for the Muslims to keep out of the main current of Hindi and concentrate on Urdu. Since Hindi was the official language of U.P., Bihar and Delhi, it was best for the Muslims to learn it and, if they wished, Urdu too in the same script. But since Arabic, the script in which Urdu was written, was associated with religion, influential Muslim divines insisted on its use instead of Devanagari.

(If the efforts to make Hindi the national link language in practice have failed, the main blame, according to Jha, is that of Nehru and his colleagues. Two big opportunities for doing this presented themselves, the first of which was the Chief Ministers' Conference in June 1961 attended by all the Union Cabinet Ministers. A note from President Prasad recommending the Devanagari script for all the Indian languages had been circulated and Jha suggested that Jivraj Mehta, the Chief Minister of Gujarat, propose its acceptance at the conference, but Pattom Thanu Pillai from Kerala offered to do it instead. The only dissenting voice was that of Humayun Kabir, the Education Minister, who favoured the Roman script. But the decision on Devanagari was not implemented. The second opportunity came at a Cabinet meeting at which proposals based on the parliamentary committee's report were put up by Pant. Nehru reacted violently saying: "What is all this nonsense? It is not possible to have scientific and technological terms in Hindi." The proposal did not refer to this subject at all, but Nehru was expressing his dislike of Hindi.)

Chapter 13

PRESIDENT AND PRIME MINISTER

(a) CONSTANT FRICTION

The Constitution has defined the powers of the President of the Republic as head of State and in relation to the Prime Minister. But the written word is not enough to ensure harmony in thought and deed between the two. Mutual sympathy and understanding and a sense of comradeship are required. Between President Rajendra Prasad and Prime Minister Nehru, who had shared the sufferings and the glory of fighting for freedom under Gandhi, one sensed constant friction. Fortunately, this was not permitted to erupt into the open. The President, for his part, was not sure whether he could successfully make a public issue of their differences. As for Nehru, his concern for the proprieties of public conduct inclined him to a similar course.

Nevertheless, it was no secret to knowledgeable people in Delhi that Nehru looked upon Prasad as a "revivalist." Nehru's rift with Prasad began in the mid-thirties, when he, along with Patel, C.R. and Kripalani disowned Nehru's creed of Socialism. It took a sharp edge when in 1950 Prasad decided to visit Kutch for the ceremonies connected with the reconstruction of the historic Somnath temple, destroyed and looted in tenth century A.D. by Mahmud of Ghazni, a northern invader from across the Khyber Pass. Nehru opposed the visit on the ground that it was not politic for the head of a secular state to associate himself with "religious revivalism" of this kind. Prasad did not agree and pointed to the significance of Somnath as the symbol of national resistance to an invader. "I believe in my religion," he added, "and I cannot cut myself away from it." I watched the impressive ceremony in the company of Patel and the

Jam Saheb of Nawanagar. In his anger at Prasad's "defiance" of his wishes, Nehru told the Information Ministry not to issue the speech Prasad made at the ceremony as an official handout.

Prasad had legal talents of a high order and would have been a judge of a High Court in the early twenties if he had not joined Gandhi's movement. He presided over the Constituent Assembly with marked ability, invariably bending his energies towards giving India a sound, workable Constitution. Soon after assuming the presidentship of the Republic, he raised three points of constitutional importance in relation to his powers and those of the State Governors. Prasad said he had power to withhold assent to Bills in his discretion, dismiss a Ministry or Minister and order a general election and as the Supreme Commander of the Defence Forces send for the military chiefs and ask for information about defence matters.

Nehru sought the advice of the Attorney-General, M. C. Setalvad, who held that the President could not withhold assent to Bills but, like a constitutional monarch, he could exert his influence in other ways. Secondly, he could not dismiss a Minister but he could get rid of a Ministry and order elections. The power to hold elections in his own discretion was not according to the letter of the law but could be exercised as a reserve power if the President felt strongly that Parliament did not reflect the political balance in the country. The President could not send for the Service Chiefs but he could send for the Defence Minister and direct him to make inquiries.

Setalvad further held that the President, being a constitutional head, should avoid speeches which ran counter to Government policy and might embarrass the Ministry. Of course, when the Ministry was mismanaging affairs there was some justification for public expressions of presidential disapproval. (Presumably, Radhakrishnan's Republic Day broadcast in 1967, which Congressmen described as a parting kick, fell within this category. He said: "The feeling should not be encouraged that no change can be brought about, except by violent disorders. We make the prospect of revolution inescapable by acquiescing in such conduct. As dishonesty creeps into every side of public life, we should beware and bring about suitable alterations in our life.")

Then came the clash over the Hindu Code Bill. Prasad did not oppose the measure but argued that it should not be enacted and his assent sought until the issues involved had been submitted to the verdict of the people. He said he had discussed the Bill threadbare with more than half the M.P.'s and had discovered that the majority of them supported his views. Nehru was riled; he appeared to agree with Law Minister Ambedkar, who had fathered the Bill, that the President was "reactionary," but there was nothing he could do in the face of Prasad's determined stand. When the Bill came before Parliament after the general election, Prasad supported the measure, examined its draft and made no attempt to tone it down.

Nehru resented Prasad's decision to go to Bombay for Patel's funeral. But he reacted more strongly when late in 1952 Prasad washed the feet of pundits as a token of homage on a visit to Banaras. To Nehru's angry protest, Prasad's rejoinder was that even the highest in the land was lowly in the presence of a scholar. As between the two, the general sentiment among Hindus supported the President's stand. However, all these incidents, coming one after the other, cooled relations between the two to a point where the Prime Minister's contact with the President got limited to the bare requirements of protocol and propriety and Nehru started leaning more and more towards Radhakrishnan, the then Vice-President.

(b) PRASAD'S SECOND TERM

There was high drama behind the scenes before Prasad got his second term as President. Nineteen fifty-six was drawing to a close when suddenly three of my rival columnists, two in Delhi and the third in Calcutta, started advocating out of the blue a case for a South Indian as President. Suspecting some deeper design, I sought from Home Minister Pant his comment on the writings. Pant replied that Nehru did not want Prasad for a second term and had Radhakrishnan in mind for the job. Radhakrishnan himself was getting old as was not interested in a second term as Vice-President. Nehru, he added, had had a word with Prasad but the latter had replied that he was in the hands of the party.

I called on Azad for our usual get-together on Sunday morning and told him about what had appeared in the newspapers and Pant's comments on it. I asked him his own view and he warmly replied: "Of course, I want Rajenbabu to continue for a second term. But, what is his own feeling? Is Prasad willing to continue?" Azad then suggested that I call on Prasad and find out. When I asked Prasad whether he had agreed to retire or whether he would be available for another term he replied he would be guided in the matter by the wishes of the High Command, meaning that he would go by whatever Nehru and Azad wanted.

I told Azad what Prasad had said to me and it was decided that he should take the earliest opportunity to call on him. Azad did

this a couple of days later and informally obtained his consent for
a second term during a walk in the famous Mughal Gardens of the
President's House. I announced this in my next Political Diary
which appeared on 18th December, 1956. In fact, I opened the
weekly column with the words: "Dr. Rajendra Prasad has agreed
to seek re-election as Union President. This puts an end to speculation on the subject. The Congress High Command, it is said,
conveyed its wishes some time ago through Maulana Azad. . . ."

The disclosure came as a bombshell to those that were trying to
build up Radhakrishnan for Presidentship. A telephone call followed
from the Prime Minister's house. Nehru wanted to see me. When I
called Nehru inquired how I had come to say that the High Command had decided on Prasad. I told him frankly that Azad had told
me he had spoken to Prasad and that the latter had agreed. "You
know Panditji, I see him regularly, every Sunday," I added. Nehru
replied: "Yes, I know," and I took leave.

The story did not, however, end at that. Now it became a battle
of the columnists, my rivals plugging in the view that the High
Command had not yet decided finally on the question. Nehru
could not take this line in view of Azad's firm stand and the enthusiastic approval with which leading M.P.'s and other members
of the electoral college hailed the disclosure in my *Diary*. Nehru
then called on Prasad and suggested that he could retire after doing
half the term and added that Azad had persuaded Radhakrishnan
to continue as Vice-President with great difficulty. Prasad replied
he would go by his health and might not do the full term. Nehru's
expectations were, however, not fulfilled and Radhakrishnan had
to wait five full years before he could occupy *Rashtrapati Bhavan*
as had been promised.

After Prasad was re-elected for the second term, I learnt that
Nehru had spared no effort to get Radhakrishnan as President. He
had had a private meeting with the Chief Ministers of the four
southern states and told them informally that he would prefer a
South Indian as President because a North Indian had held the
post for a whole term. The Chief Ministers, as one of them confided
to me, told Nehru that they were not concerned with regional
considerations and were of the view that Prasad should be re-elected
if he was available. They also did not accept the view that Prasad
had already had "more than one term" in view of his election as
President in 1950.

Although Pant enjoyed Nehru's confidence and was utterly loyal
to him, he and Prasad thought alike on national language and culture. Indeed, Prasad often shared with Pant his inner feelings on

matters on which he differed with Nehru. It was my practice to call on Pant twice a week and share morning tea with him. He was happy, he told me at one of these meetings, at the turn of events which had led to another term of presidentship for Prasad. I asked him why Nehru had attempted to dislodge Prasad. Pant replied that a group of "courtiers" had been poisoning Nehru's mind about the possibility of Prasad staging a coup with the help of the R.S.S. and the Jana Sangh. Nehru wanted both the President and the Vice-President to be "colourless" politically but (like Radhakrishnan) to command respect by their erudition and standing in the community.

(c) THE GAP WIDENS

Nehru seemed to treat every proposal for a presidential tour abroad with reserve, apparently feeling that Prasad did not project the image of a modern secular India. In the first term, he agreed to his visiting only the Hindu Kingdom of Nepal in 1955. Reluctantly, Nehru agreed to Prasad's visit to Japan in 1958 and thereafter to some South-East Asian countries. The visit was a grand success everywhere. In Japan, at the Emperor's banquet only vegetarian dishes were served "as a symbol of the reverence in which we hold President Prasad." At lunch in Hanoi on the day of the Indian festival of Holi, to celebrate Spring, Ho Chi-minh suddenly rose, smeared Prasad's face with *gulal* (coloured powder) and embraced him warmly, exclaiming: "We do not differentiate: we follow India." In Ceylon, Prime Minister Bandaranaike told him: "India is our mother country; there can be no dispute between brothers."

Soon after his return from a visit to India in 1959, Eisenhower sent a pressing invitation to Prasad to visit the U.S. before he laid his office. He had described Prasad in Delhi as "God's good man" and was keen to take him personally around the country. But between Nehru and the External Affairs Ministry, the proposal was killed. While the Ministry felt the time was not opportune, Nehru went on record to observe: "So many of us have been to America that it does not seem necessary for you to visit the U.S. immediately." The President replied: "I will choose my own time." It was not much different when Queen Elizabeth, during her State visit to India in 1961, urged Prasad to visit Britain in return.

Prasad told me that Nehru studiously excluded foreign affairs from the scope of his talks with him, and even discouraged him from serious discussions with foreign dignitaries visiting India. Prasad's visit to the Soviet Union in 1960 demonstrated, however, that his presence abroad could benefit India. Prasad avoided talks on foreign policy, but made an intensive and fruitful study of the Soviet educational system, of the country's agricultural development and of the manner in which the Russians had resolved the problem of a national language. He produced a twenty-page note for the Cabinet on language based on the lessons he had gleaned from his Russian visit.

The President was a man of erudition and had a firm grasp of national problems. He often showed me letters and notes he had written to Nehru on a wide variety of subjects, political, social and economic. He did this because he could not speak freely in Nehru's presence. He avoided a dialogue. He appeared to suffer from an inferiority, even fear, complex in the presence of Nehru. Whenever I urged him to convert his meetings with Nehru into a dialogue, he would say that would inevitably lead to disagreement and passionate argument.

The note to Nehru on corruption was perhaps the strongest Prasad ever penned. Corruption, he said, "will verily prove a nail in the coffin of the Congress." Prasad strongly supported C. D. Deshmukh's proposal for a tribunal or an Ombudsman, directly under the President or as an independent authority to inquire into charges of corruption and maladministration. Nehru did not reply to the note in writing; instead, he complained to Prasad personally about what he called "an unfriendly suggestion." Prasad told me he was deeply hurt at this misinterpretation of his motives and abjured Nehru to look into the future and see whether such measures were not necessary.

Prasad told me soon after the publication of the report of the States Reorganisation Commission that it should have been accepted as an award and faithfully implemented. But when the report was modified he felt that the State of Bombay could not be preserved for long as a bilingual unit. He was far from happy at the creation of Kerala; he felt it was much too small to exist separately. On Kashmir Prasad was all for the full integration of the state in the Indian Union. In his eyes, the special status accorded to Kashmir was hardly in tune with the realities of the situation.

Prasad was particularly concerned about Centre-states relations. "Do not interfere needlessly with the affairs of the states," he told the Prime Minister. "Learn to leave them to their own devices." Of his opposition to the agitation to suppress the Communist regime in Kerala in 1960, he made no secret. He said he had tried to dissuade Indira Gandhi, the Congress President, from heading the liberation movement. "Do not act in this way," he told her. "It will set a bad precedent." Asked later about this admonition, Mrs. Gandhi said she did not remember having had a talk with Prasad on this subject.

Prasad felt very strongly that India's diplomatic approach to China was riddled with weaknesses and a proneness to wishful thinking. The "Hindi–Chini bhai bhai (Indians and Chinese are brothers) honeymoon," he told me, did not blind him to Peking's ultimate aims and real feelings towards India. He was greatly upset at the Indian Government's impassivity when Tibet was occupied by the Chinese Reds. His words of caution to Nehru, he said, had fallen on deaf ears. The Prime Minister had been misled by his Ambassador in Peking, Panikkar. With his eyes moistened, Prasad observed: "I hope I am not seeing ghosts and phantoms, but I see the murder of Tibet recoiling on India."

I recall with interest my talk with the President after Sanjiva Reddy, (now Speaker of Lok Sabha) presiding at the Bhavanagar session of the Congress, suggested that those who had held office for ten years should voluntarily retire. When I asked Prasad for his reaction to this proposal, he remarked: "It is very interesting, I am all for it. But what will Nehru do?" He confided that had Nehru resigned in fact, he would have grown in stature and helped the nation grow in the same manner. (Those close to Nehru, in turn, asked: "What will Prasad do?")

(d) NEW IDEAS

The President had strong grounds for complaint against the Prime Minister, for he often read of appointments of Ambassadors and Governors in the Press and was officially informed only afterwards. As a result of Prasad's spirited protest against being overlooked, an order was passed by the Cabinet stipulating that all the papers relating to the appointment of Governors, Ambassadors, the Chairman of the Union Public Service Commission, the Auditor-General, and Secretaries to the Ministries be submitted to him before orders were issued.

Prasad took umbrage at being kept in the dark about the crisis precipitated by the resignation of General Thimayya, the Chief of Army Staff. This, he held, was a violation of his authority as Supreme Commander of the Defence Services. Krishna Menon, reprimanded for the lapse, had to apologise. Later, Prasad remonstrated with Nehru: "You are laying down bad precedents. A President who did not like you could have given you a lot of trouble." The President was getting new ideas about his constitutional role and powers.

Nehru's fears seemed to be strengthened when in an address to the Law Institute on the eve of quitting his office, Prasad suggested that legal experts study the presidential powers under the Constitution. Underlying the proposal was the President's reluctance to equate his position with that of the British monarchy and his anxiety that, as a matter of courtesy, wholesome conventions should be established in this regard.

Prasad told me that Nehru had met him and complained that his remarks at the Law Institute were not calculated to promote the national interest and that he had apparently been misled by K. M. Munshi. Prasad explained that Munshi had no hand in the affair, that the kind of study he had in mind was essential "while we are still a young republic," and that he could think of no better body than the Law Institute to undertake it. One result of Nehru's reaction was that Prasad's speech was not issued to the Press. But the Constitutional issue became alive in 1969 with the possibility of an unstable Centre judging by the trend of the mid-term poll.

Ten months before Prasad retired from the presidentship of the Republic on 13th May, 1962, he fell gravely ill and was moved to a private nursing home. Nehru feared he would not survive and ordered arrangements for a State funeral and for swearing in his temporary successor. While this was being rehearsed, Nehru's mind was exercised about where Prasad was to be cremated. He did not want the ceremony to be performed next to Rajghat, Gandhi's cremation ground, but he feared that M.P.s from Bihar, Prasad's home state, would insist that this site be chosen. He accordingly asked Home Minister Shastri to find a place as far from Rajghat as possible. This was a very delicate mission and had to be performed secretly. Shastri, accompanied by the Chief Commissioner of Delhi, Bhagwan Sahay, was driven by the Deputy Commissioner, Sushital Banerji, along the banks of Jumna, and chose a spot a couple of furlongs from Rajghat for the cremation.

Fortunately, Prasad survived the illness. The spot Shastri selected for the President's cremation was used to cremate Shastri in 1966 and became known as Vijayghat (Victory Mausoleum). Nehru was cremated on the plot of land adjacent to Rajghat, and is called Shantivan (Abode of Peace).

After his retirement, Prasad was preparing material for a book covering the period of his presidentship. But it could not be completed before death struck him down. He died in Patna on 28th February, 1963, in the special cottage built for him next to Sadaqat Ashram (Abode of Truth) on the banks of the Ganga. The Ashram was his headquarters during the freedom struggle. When the news came to Delhi, Nehru told Radhakrishnan that he was going to Rajasthan to collect money for the Prime Minister's Relief Fund and would not be able to attend the former President's funeral in Patna. He added: "I do not see any reason for you to go." Radhakrishnan replied: "No, I think I must go and attend the funeral. That respect is due to him and must be paid. I think you should give up your tour and come with me." But Nehru stuck to his programme.

Chapter 14

ROUND THE WORLD

(a) EDITOR-IN-CHIEF

Early in August 1957, I had just checked out of a hotel in Vienna and my baggage had been put in a car to take me to the airport to catch a flight to Budapest. As I was entering the car, a hotel page rushed out saying there was a long-distance call for me. I went back to the hotel, and to my great surprise I found my eldest son, Inder Jit, at the other end. For an instant I felt shaken, for I guessed there would only be bad news. He apprised me of Devadas Gandhi's sudden death of heart failure in Bombay. His voice was so distinct that I could hardly believe I was talking to Delhi. I told him the news was too shocking for words and that I would cancel my tour and return home by the fastest route.

It took me six hours to cancel the flight, explain to Hungarian and Russian officials in Vienna why I had to change my plans, and find a seat on a plane to London. I was received there by Gunther Stein, our London correspondent, who took me to his house. I put through a call to Delhi and I gathered that the juniormost assistant editor had been made acting editor, superseding four others. I could not divine the meaning of this development, except that this particular person might have been recommended by C.R. or by T.T.K. as he enjoyed their confidence.

Anyway, speculation was beside the point. It seemed like a palace coup, and I had to sort things out back at home without delay. I decided to fly to Bombay and meet the paper's proprietor, G. D. Birla. I landed in Bombay and went straight to Birla House, which had always hosted me over the years. I first called on R. D. Birla,

G.D.'s elder brother, and found C.R. having an intimate talk with him. Apparently, he was concerned with financial support for Devadas's widow and the education of her children. It was probably at this meeting that the Birlas generously agreed to provide free quarters and other perquisites for a decade.

I then proceeded to G.D's room. He was very cordial, and as was his wont came straight to the point. We had a heart to heart talk. I returned to Delhi, and three days later came a call from Birla House. When I drove there, I was handed a letter of appointment as Editor-in-Chief. The appointment was duly announced in the paper the following morning. I took counsel with the Birlas and decided to resume my tour, for it had been planned very carefully to have a close-up of the two Super Powers and to assess the views in world capitals of developments in India. The series of articles I wrote after the tour were published as a book by the *Hindustan Times* with the title *India and the World* with a foreword by President Prasad.

The trip lasted 100 days from August to November and enabled me to see Vienna, Prague, Moscow, Leningrad, Tiflis, Paris, London, New York, Washington, Puerto Rico, Columbus, Chicago, Minneapolis, Los Angeles, San Francisco, Honolulu, Tokyo, Hongkong, Manila and Bangkok. Earlier, for thirty-one days in April and May, I had covered Australia, Malaya, Singapore and Ceylon, and gathered interesting impressions.

As I entered Hotel Australia in Sydney, I found a large world map on the wall of the entrance hall displaying clocks showing the time in Rome, Paris, London and New York. This was proof enough of Australia's material and spiritual links. The ruling Liberal–Country Party coalition with Menzies at its head was pro-Pakistan, but its Minister for External Affairs, Richard Casey, later Governor-General, was not only sympathetic to India but had the singular distinction among members of the Government of believing that Australia's future was tied to Asia's. The Labour Party leader also told me that his party "understands Nehru's policy and will make friends with Asian countries."

(b) HARK BACK TO BANDUNG

Premier Bolte of Victoria urged young Australian men and women to "marry young and rear larger families." Here was a paradox: overpopulated Asia trying to curb births while underpopulated Australia—with some twelve million people spread over more than two million square miles—encouraging them. Asians think, I said at a gathering, that the Australian continent could hold 1,000 million people. This frightened my audience, for the Australians traditionally sense danger from "the people up north." I left Australia with the feeling that it was standing at the crossroads and that its empty spaces were a challenge to the conscience of man.

India's relations with Indonesia since independence had undergone some strange changes by 1957. They began with effusive demonstrations of gratitude for India's help in winning freedom for Indonesia. Sukarno did not make a speech without referring to Gandhi and Nehru. By 1957, Sukarno had begun to dream he was Nehru's equal, or even his superior as the hero of Bandung. The board outside the Prime Minister's office in Jakarta read "Pradhan Mantri"—what we call our Prime Minister in India—and I was happy at the living proof of the cultural ties between India and Indonesia. In my talks with Sukarno, however, I sensed a tenseness in his reference to India and the economic stranglehold of the Chinese on his country.

I gathered some interesting details of the happenings at the Bandung Conference, the highwater-mark of relations between India and Indonesia. At it, Sukarno described India as his country's "window on the world." A member of the Indian delegation wrote the speech with which Sukarno inaugurated the conference. Nehru, playing the role of master of ceremonies, introduced Chou-En-lai on the Afro–Asian stage at Bandung. He made Chou acceptable to Nasser and the other leaders of the emergent world. The Turkish delegate would not, however, attend a banquet to Chou. Nehru had a trunk call put through to Ankara to ensure that he did so. In spite of all these efforts, Chou exhibited displeasure because he felt that Nehru was patronising him. From Bandung, the Chinese made special efforts to cultivate Indonesia and flattered Sukarno lavishly. India's Ambassadors could not counter this development, and relations between New Delhi and Jakarta deteriorated in direct proportion to the improvement of those between Jakarta and Peking. The seeds of China's subsequent friendship with Pakistan were also sown at Bandung.

Malaya, I found a nation in the making, Ceylon a nation in ferment and Singapore with a big question mark over its future. The only difference between the pre-independence scene in India and Malaya was that whereas British Civil Servants had treated their exit from India as a scuttling operation, those in Malaya were co-operating heartily in helping the country stand on its own feet. This was under the inspiration of Malcolm MacDonald, the British Commissioner for the area.

A talk with the Prime Minister of Thailand was very revealing. He complained that Nehru had characterised the Thai Government as corrupt and said the country had a "Coca-Cola economy." Thailand, the Prime Minister explained to me, had a long tradition of independence, and if she had taken shelter under the U.S. umbrella it had done so to safeguard her independence. If Nehru was willing to underwrite their security, the Thais would prefer to be with India since Thai culture was predominantly Indian. When I suggested that a visit by the King and the Prime Minister to India would improve matters, he replied that their very experienced Ambassador in New Delhi had warned them against inviting an insult by undertaking such a visit. They treated their ruler as a demi-god, and he would not go to India unless assured of a cordial welcome.

(c) STATE WITHOUT TENSION

My first visit to Russia gave me a pleasant surprise. The Russians had achieved social and economic equilibrium. Their main thoughts were of better housing and more consumer goods. The first successful test of an intercontinental ballistic missile, news of which came as a flash when I was talking to the Editor-in-Chief of *Pravda*, seemed to make every Russian feel they had arrived militarily. "We can relax now," said the Editor. "War is ruled out. Now we join issue in the race in science and technology." I did not realise the significance of this remark until the first Sputnik went up into space when I was in the U.S. later in the year.

Accidentally, the most rewarding moment I had in Moscow took place at a diplomatic reception at which I was introduced by our Minister to Khrushchev, who recalled having answered my questions at a Press conference in Delhi. "We have a common enemy, sir," I said. Taken by surprise, he responded: "That is a profound observation." I added: "We total 700 million." He advanced his hand and shook mine warmly. I knew then that Khrushchev considered China the real enemy and that the Kremlin's interest in India was more an insurance against China than a factor in the cold war.

On further inquiry, I found that Moscow and Peking had quarrelled over Outer Mongolia. China wanted to divide the territory, but the Russians would not agree. The Russians sensed the Chinese intentions when they published old maps showing large chunks of Russian territory as their own. I wanted to check on this, and accordingly raised the issue at a dinner my host, the Editor-in-Chief of *Izvestia*, gave me. I told him Nehru had said after his visit to Peking that he had failed to reach Mao's heart and did not know what Mao was thinking. Nehru had added: "It is not the same with the-Russians. You meet them and you know they are like you. But not Mao, and I suppose Chinese generally." My host's face lit up when he heard this, and he poured another drink to Indo–Soviet friendship. That was more eloquent than words.

A short stay in Prague made me feel that the Czechs were not quite happy with their fate but realised the need for remaining under the Russian umbrella for security. Their spokesmen complained that India had not shown interest in their offer to supply arms when Defence Organisation Minister Mahavir Tyagi visited Prague. "You will need them one day," they said. The Czechs were even prepared to establish factories for manufacturing arms. India did not take advantage of the offer because Indian military officers were accustomed to British weapons. Nehru too was pro-British in this matter and considered Mountbatten a guide.

My wife joined me in London. My visit to Britain was aimed at discovering whether Britain was interested in the Commonwealth developing and functioning as a positive world force. I met Premier Macmillan at 10 Downing Street and started the conversation by saying that India was looking forward to a visit by the Queen. He said he had not heard from Nehru on this matter. I had met Nehru before I set out on my travels and had asked him about it. He had replied: "I would like to invite her, but I cannot take the risk of some Communist creating trouble. The monarchy is held sacrosanct in Britain and I have to make sure that nothing unpleasant will happen. I suppose it will come about in due course."

I told Macmillan that Nehru had joined the Commonwealth because he believed it could develop as a force for peace—a cushion between the two giants engaged in the cold war. We in India, I added, thought Britain was falling between two stools, the Commonwealth and the European Common Market. Macmillan replied that the Commonwealth concept would be invested with reality by setting up consultative machinery. I mentioned that I had learned in my talks with British bankers and industrialists that they were willing to invest in India, but the politicians got in the way. Macmillan expressed surprise at this statement and promised to look into the matter.

Hugh Gaitskell, the Leader of the Opposition, was more forthright. He said the Conservatives were "congenitally anti-India" and only Labour could give meaning to the new Commonwealth concept. But I took Macmillan at his word and wrote in my articles on

the tour: "Maybe that in turning to the wider vision of the Commonwealth Mr. Macmillan is trying to assess the chances of the Commonwealth developing into a positive force for peace."

Many Britons asked me: "After Nehru, what? Why does Nehru
moralise? Isn't your five-year plan over-ambitious?" Somehow, the
question of the Commonwealth did not register either with politicians
or journalists. I told them that Russia was a union of nations of
different races, colour and languages. So was the Commonwealth.
Russia was building up the economies of all her component units.
She would match the economic strength of the West in ten years.
The stock answer I got was that Russia could exploit people and
impose sacrifices on them while democratic Britons were engaged
in a spending spree.

(d) MEETING WITH IKE

I arrived in the U.S. in September and met President Eisenhower.
A problem I had not anticipated was created by the fact that my
stay in Washington coincided with the visit of Queen Elizabeth and
Eisenhower was not free to receive other visitors. After the Queen
left, he had many other urgent matters to attend to, and Governor
Sherman Adams had said I should visit San Francisco and fly back
after a few days for an interview with the President. This was not
possible because my schedule of appointments included one with
the Japanese Prime Minister. On the last day of my stay in Washington, I had a flash of inspiration. Sherman Cooper had a pull with
Eisenhower and I spoke to him about an interview. He drove
straight to the White House and I had my meeting.

Apparently, the appointment was so unexpected that the White
House Press corps reported it, and my youngest son, Brahma Jeet,
undergoing training in business management in Los Angeles, heard
about it in a radio news bulletin. I gave Eisenhower my impressions
of the Russian scene. I told him that in my view the Russians were
interested in peaceful coexistence, that they would not attempt to
subvert non-Communist regimes and were thinking of peaceful
competition in science and technology. I told him that the real state
of affairs in Russia was not reflected in the U.S. Press. He said that
in the U.S. any idea must be sold to the Press and to the Congress.
He suggested that I write an article on my Russian impressions for
the *New York Herald Tribune*, which published it on 20th October,
1967.

I was happy that my visit to Washington took place at the same
time as that of the Queen because this enabled me to attend the

National Press Club reception to her. More than a thousand guests queued up to be introduced to her. I was the only Indian, and, baffled by my presence, the club president introduced me with these words: "Your Majesty, this is one of your subjects." Prince Philip, who was standing nearby, realised the gaffe and tried to make amends by asking: "How are Delhi and Prime Minister Nehru?" I replied: "All of us are looking forward to Her Majesty's visit." Overhearing my remark, the Queen gave a charming smile.

The Russian Sputnik went up and I felt the wave of fear that swept ordinary American citizens. It seemed that the American fortress had become vulnerable even more than to the I.C.B.M. But my talks with General Maxwell Taylor and General Powell at Fort Benning showed that they took the Russian achievement in their stride. The American striking power, they said to me, was "overwhelming." The Soviet Foreign Minister, Andrei Gromyko, whom I met in New York in October, tersely remarked that the satellite's release "could help to put the brains of some people right."

The visit to Japan was of the greatest interest because I had worked out in my mind a security arch with Tokyo as a peg at one end and Delhi at the other with Canberra in between. This was not the whole picture so far as India was concerned, for, as I hinted in my talk with Khrushchev, I considered a Delhi–Moscow axis as the continuation of this arch. But in my talks with leading Americans I had emphasised the gravitational pull Tokyo–Canberra–Delhi could provide to counter that of the Communist world.

When I sent a printed copy of my articles to Hubert Humphrey, then a Senator, he wrote back: "Your views are refreshing and stimulating to me. I wish some other people I know who fly round the world—including our Secretary of State—were as observing and sensitive to what they see and hear as you have been. I was particularly impressed with your description of what you called the 'gravitational pull' which the Soviet Union and China are exerting. I like this phrase, and I remember it from our conversation. I think it expresses a concept which, more often than not, is simply missed in public understanding here in the United States."

I discovered from my talks with Prime Minister Kishi, Foreign Minister Fujiyama, our Ambassador in Japan, C. S. Jha and Japanese businessmen and journalists that Indo–Japanese relations had been stabilised as a result of Nehru's visit, which had preceded mine. Until 1957, there had been no dialogue between Delhi and Tokyo because Nehru treated Japan as a "lackey" of the U.S. Nehru's visit was the first by a foreign head of government after the end of the Second World War and it revived among Japanese citizens the memory of Justice Radhe Binod Pal's judgment absolving their leaders of war crimes and of Nehru's double gesture in waiving war reparations and not signing the San Francisco treaty.

Nehru's talk with Kishi resulted in the Japanese Government instructing its representatives at the U.N. to work in harmony with the Indian representative and in an offer of a yen credit worth fifty million dollars in response to Nehru's remark that there was no reason why the economies of India and Japan should not be dovetailed. The proposed collaboration at the U.N., however, did not come through. The Japanese representative Matsushima went to Krishna Menon and told him that he had received instructions from Tokyo to collaborate with India. Matsushima said Menon "shooed me off," remarking that the policies of India and Japan were so different that collaboration was out of the question.

Chapter 15

X-RAYING THE NATION

In the early part of 1958, when India had completed a decade of independence, I invited articles for the editorial page of the *Hindustan Times* on the political health of the nation. This was more than the annual stocktaking to which Indian newspapers are accustomed. Individuals, each distinguished in his own sphere, analysed social, economic, political and cultural affairs to discover whether India had grown in strength since freedom or had developed symptoms of some serious illness.

The new feature was called "X-raying the Nation" and the response was rewarding. Rajagopalachari provided the curtain-raiser. He wrote: "Instead of traditional loyalties and bonds of duty to one another, we have ill-will and unwillingness to co-operate, a feeling that work is tyranny and idleness is happiness. Political emancipation and democracy, instead of cultivating a sense of humility and responsibility, have been allowed to intoxicate majority caste groups with a thirst for power and tyranny and electoral corruption of the unprivileged classes."

The views expressed by contributors to the series on our economic policies were no less harsh. Of planning, John Matthai said he saw "intractable proof of the growing gulf between resources and targets" and the spirit of individual initiative and enterprise "kept in check by ill-conceived fiscal and executive measures." Matthai went on to say: "The momentum created in the earlier years of independence is subsiding and giving way to a spirit of passive acceptance of the inevitable. We seem to be at the beginning of a period of mental stagnation and lack of purposeful activity. Respect for law is gradually diminishing, and the sense of unity which filled us in the first flush of fulfilled nationalism is disappearing."

On the psychological plane, Mrs. Lakshmi Menon, Minister of State for External Affairs and a former President of All–India Women's Conference, wrote with wit and vigour. She exposed the Indian weakness for moral posturing and false thinking, particularly in relation to the rest of the world. Her basic theme was: "We fail to realise that our external influence depends steadily on our internal strength." She remarked ruefully: "Often in our anxiety to go forward by taking long strides to help others, we fail to notice how slippery the ground under our feet is."

"An Old Stager" and "a Civil Servant," both administrators of very high calibre, were at pains to study the administrative machine since the advent of freedom. The former saw a "drift towards administrative chaos" and traced it to the lack of inner discipline and of moral and civic consciousness. The latter's stress was all on the need for an independent, efficient and fearless Civil Service to buttress a democratic society. The blame for the present state of affairs, he felt, rested with the ruling politicians who did not scruple to abuse the administrative machinery.

In retrospect, this exercise in self-analysis yielded much that was worthwhile. Many of the conclusions are valid even today. Certain evils then dimly foreseen have now assumed frightening proportions. Men endowed with perspicacity saw even further ahead, to the eclipse of the Congress in more than half the states of the Indian Union. Writing in the *Hindustan Times* of 1st January, 1959, on Where and How We Go?, I observed that "India, having had the advantage of Gandhiji's leadership and the influence and authority of Nehru and of the Congress Party, has fared better than Pakistan. However, this country, too, is showing historic tensions. Tribalism, by whatever name it may be called—communalism, linguism, regionalism, clanism, casteism—is trying to assert itself against the forces of nationalism. . . . The alternative of nationalism is not tribalism but disintegration followed by totalitarianism, whether of the fascist or communist brand."

Contrasting the varying attitudes of the U.S., the Soviet Union and Pakistan to India, I said: "America's own security and economic prosperity depend, in the long run, on the uplift of the under-developed and undeveloped peoples and a political alliance with their governments. Washington is thus prepared to underwrite India's economic plans and help her with knowhow to enable her to become a reservoir from which the smaller nations of Asia and Africa can draw guidance and help. . . . Moscow is in equally desperate need of partnership with India in stabilising communist economy and polity. It calculates that 400 million Indians, combined with 200 million Russians, would balance 600 million Chinese and prevent the Communist world from going under Peking's hegemony. . . . Karachi calculates that the Indian leadership is suffering from so many inhibitions and complexes that it will not choose its side and cash in on the advantage which the cold war has created for her and that the Pakistanis should keep their powder dry for their opportunity when Mr. Nehru is no more on the scene."

Discussing the various remedies prescribed for India's ills, I wrote: "On the political plane there are advocates of the American presidential system as the most suited to Indian conditions, and of a benevolent dictatorship as the system more suited to the Indian genius. The fact is that no remedy is worth considering while the patient refuses to take any medicine. The people of India are as fit as those of any country for democratic self-government, but the Congress rulers have allowed themselves to be mesmerised by the ballot box. Their thinking has been paralysed by fear of the voters' reaction. . . . The obvious remedy is that a brains trust should make up its mind to rule the country in a purposeful way and tone up the administration to make it perform its legitimate functions. The Centre's authority, which has been continuously weakened by placing increasing reliance on *subedars* (provincial Chief Ministers), must be restored and corruption and inefficiency, which have set in because of the lapses of the people at the top, eliminated."

Next to the Army, the Railways used to be the most disciplined entity in India. Their management by a board comprising experts is subject to the control and direction of the Union Minister for Railways. A very senior official's experience of how this Ministry was run and how demoralisation had set in illustrates what has happened in other Ministries as well in the past two decades.

The first Railway Minister was John Matthai. He did a remarkable job in two respects. With the backing of Patel, he told the British Chief Commissioner of Railways that his services were no longer required. The Britons in the ICS and other services had left, but those in the railways had stayed on. Matthai thus gave a chance to

Indian officers to fill posts of responsibility. He had to restore order in the railway organisation after the chaos of partition. The drivers and firemen and mechanics were mostly Muslim and the guards and station staff mostly Hindu. Thus there was a shortage of staff in one sphere and an excess in the other which had to be balanced. There was also the problem of moving tens of thousands of refugees. Matthai's time as Railway Minister was devoted mainly to restoring order and making the railways work like a machine.

One of Matthai's most striking characteristics was that he was utterly non-communal. People used to write to him describing him as the leader of the Indian Christians and saying they were proud of him and that they expected him to safeguard their interests. Matthai would tear up such letters and throw them into the wastepaper basket.

Gopalaswamy Ayyangar, who succeeded Matthai, rationalised the railway organisation and divided it into six zones. These zones had to be further split later as the total volume of traffic continued to increase and is now three times what it was in Ayyangar's time. Then came Lal Bahadur Shastri. He was the first Railway Minister to make a political approach to his duties. Freight constitutes two-thirds to three-fourths of railway operations, and the railway staff are freight-oriented in their outlook. Shastri wanted to provide more comforts for the third class passenger. He improved railway platforms, waiting rooms, introduced *Janata* (people's) trains and air-conditioned coaches for the third class, and increased the space for passengers and introduced sleeping berths and fans for the same class.

Shastri's lack of punctuality and odd hours of work created headaches for the railway headquarters staff. He would give ear to the complaints of all and sundry and was inclined to accept their word against that of the higher staff. All this caused demoralisation at the time, but ten years later it was clear that Shastri was only a forerunner of the shape of things to come.

Jagjivan Ram, who succeeded Shastri, destroyed the chain of command in another way. He ordered promotions for *Harijan* (depressed class) employees out of turn. Officers do not mind reservations for persons belonging to the minorities, but they are disheartened when juniors are promoted above them because they belong to a particular caste or religion. This is what caused trouble in the Punjab after the Montford reforms and started chain reaction of communal riots. Railway employees were now demoralised because an officer could not tell whether a junior would be above him the following year.

Neither Shastri nor Jagjivan Ram really cared to understand railway economics or tried to comprehend operational and other problems. Shastri thought mostly in terms of the third class traveller and low-paid railway employee. Jagjivan Ram spent most of his time trying to give a better deal to members of the depressed classes. This phase of his career cast a shadow on his reputation as an efficient Minister whom successive senior Civil Servants had regarded as a model political boss. Fortunately for the railways, their administration had been built on a firm foundation by Matthai and Ayyangar and it was thus able to withstand the shocks it was subjected to by their successors.

In 1957, there was an outcry that there were transport bottlenecks. This led to massive investment on new lines and rolling stock in the next five years. By 1962, the railways were able to cope with the demands of the increased goods traffic which followed the growth of economic activity. Everything went off well until 1965, when there was a succession of crop failures because of drought.

The Curzonian phrase that the budget is a gamble on the monsoon ceased to apply for a few decades, but its validity was revived because of the increase in population and the need for more food. Our economy is still based on agriculture. The current excess of railways freight capacity is a passing phase. It is better to have the capacity to deal with the inevitable growth in traffic that will follow the rise in production.

S. K. Patil as Railway Minister showed a quick grasp of essentials. He was conversant with railway economics and took quick decisions. The Railway Board functioned efficiently under him. Patil did not always adhere to his brief when speaking in Parliament and even got away with unverified statements because he was a powerful speaker and skilful parliamentarian.

Patil rightly thought that a Minister should not resign because a train was involved in an accident. Shastri resigned ostensibly on this issue, but really because Nehru wanted him to do so to function more effectively as his aide in organising the Congress campaign in the 1957 elections. In fact, this assignment resulted in Shastri becoming Nehru's confidant in a way and paved the way for Shastri succeeding him as Prime Minister.

Today, the Indian Railways are paying the penalty for breaking the chain of command and putting inferior men in offices of responsibility. This accounts for the series of serious rail accidents which have taken hundreds of lives in the last few years, the cause of which, according to official findings, is "human failure."

Chapter 16

THE SHRUNKEN IMAGE

(a) JAPAN ADVANCES

My second trip around the world in 1957 had begun in Russia and
ended in Thailand. I reversed the order in 1959, for I had heard
from some of our Ambassadors that India's stature had shrunk in
Asian eyes. I met Nehru on 25th May, 1959, before setting out. He
said he had decided to invite the Queen early in 1961 and that he
wanted Eisenhower to visit India before that. This would enable
him to perfect the arrangements for the Queen's visit. Nehru said
he had succeeded in getting the U.S. and Russia closer and to
accept coexistence. He wanted those two powers to co-operate in
providing economic aid to the Afro–Asian world.

China's shadow had begun to fall on her smaller neighbours and
the U.S. and Russia were trying to establish their presence in Asia.
Having established rapport with Hanoi and Jakarta through
massive military aid, Moscow resented the American presence in
South Vietnam and Thailand. Peking was flirting with Sukarno
and plotting subversion in Burma, Thailand and Cambodia. The
period of moral posturing was over, and as India could supply
neither military hardware nor financial aid it had ceased to count.
Indeed, Japan had overshadowed India as an Asian power, for she
had built enough economic strength to make Australia a captive
market and the non-Communist area from Korea to Burma her
trading partner.

It was not surprising in the circumstances that Premier Kishi
and other leaders in the political and business world whom I met in
Japan showed lack of interest in Indian attitudes. In fact, the
Japanese were beginning to come out of their shell and were talking
of changes in their constitution to enable them to undertake the
defence of their country. I found the Americans encouraging them
in their effort to multiply and expand their para-military forces
and develop military muscles in the name of self-defence. The
Governor of the Bank of Tokyo told me, however, that the Japanese

were in no hurry to go in for their own defence set-up, for they needed further investment to catch up with the West in scientific and technological development. Already, they had outmatched the West in the manufacture of cameras, transistors, TV sets and watches and had made great headway in electronics.

The highlights of my stay in the U.S. were my meetings with President Eisenhower, John F. Kennedy, George Kennan, Robert Anderson, Douglas Dillon, Sherman Cooper, Dean Rusk and Paul Hoffman. (The last two had visited my house in Delhi the same year and had sought my views on the desirability of financing International Press Institute by the Rockefeller Foundation.) In my talk with Treasury Secretary Anderson and his Under-Secretary Dillon, I raised three points. I said the U.S. should set aside one per cent of its gross national product for economic aid and get all the rich nations to follow suit. Secondly, they should form a pool and administer the fund on a regional basis through the U.N. so that integrated economic development could take place. Thirdly, they should try and join hands with Russia in drafting a joint programme to help the advance of the poor nations, whose population totalled 2,000 million.

Sherman Cooper and Kennedy had jointly sponsored a resolution in the Senate favouring massive economic aid to India, and as Kennedy was a candidate for the U.S. Presidency I was keen to meet him. Our country stood the best chance of getting friendly treatment from Washington if Kennedy occupied the White House. As the Senator entered his room in the Capitol, where I was awaiting him, I was struck by his youthful appearance. He welcomed me by saying, "Sherman has told me you are the James Reston of India." He then made flattering references to Nehru and expressed deep interest in India as the country that had held free elections and had full-fledged democracy. He said his brother, Robert, and he had visited India in 1952 and met Nehru. The Prime Minister paid little attention to them, thinking they were just two young Americans. Nevertheless, he had since developed admiration for Nehru by reading his books and speeches. That this was not a casual statement is shown by the fact that Kennedy referred to Nehru in complimentary terms in his inaugural address as U.S. President.

I explained how Russia was building up its Asian republics and taking them into the modern age and how the West, with twenty times Russia's economic strength, did not have either a philosophy or a plan to aid the underdeveloped nations. As I was arguing the case for economic uplift of the underdeveloped world, Kennedy kept nodding his head or said: "I stand for it." He finally said that what I had said represented the challenge of the age and that he for one would meet it. I got a sense of fulfilment from this dialogue. I talked fast and crowded into the time I got with Kennedy as much as I could. I did not know then that he was a very fast reader and thinker. When I finished he said: "Will you join me and write my speeches?"

Since Hubert Humphrey had expressed the same wish after I had concluded my talk with him in 1957, I presumed this was only a courteous remark. I grasped its significance only when I met Edward Henley, President of a steel corporation, at a dinner given in Pittsburgh by my youngest daughter, Karuna Rani, and my son-in-law, Dr. Ram Tarneja, then Director of Graduate Studies in Business Administration in Duquesne University. Ghost writers, he explained, were very highly valued in the U.S. Kennedy had, therefore, meant what he said. Anyway, Kennedy fulfilled his promise, for he put through the Congress a five-year programme of economic aid to India when he became President.

I had a forty-minute interview with Eisenhower, who told me of the difficulties he was facing in the Congress. But he added that he would press again for the integrated economic development of the underdeveloped. The President asked me whether newspapers in India were as massive as those in the U.S. He said the Sunday edition of the *New York Times* was so heavy that he read only the editorial section. I told him our leading papers published eight to twelve pages on weekdays and sixteen on Sundays. He said that was sensible. I explained that this was because we were starved of newsprint. I asked him whether it was fair that in a year the *New York Times* consumed twice as much newsprint as the entire Indian Press. Since democracy was sustained by freedom of expression, I added, the low circulation of Indian dailies (five million copies and 200 million voters) was not good for democracy. He told his Press Secretary to look into the matter.

After a brief visit to Canada, where I met Premier Diefenbaker in Ottawa and R. M. Fowler, President of the Canadian Pulp and Paper Association, in Montreal, I pushed on to London armed with a message which Macmillan would be happy to receive. I met the Prime Minister on 20th July with the help of Mrs. Pandit, our High Commissioner, at Downing Street and opened our conversation by saying that Nehru had decided to invite the Queen at her convenience. I added that I had met Nehru before leaving Delhi and recalled my talk with Macmillan in 1957. Macmillan was very pleased at the news I brought and became informal. He told me he was confident India would set an example to other Asian and African countries in working democratic institutions. He said his rise to the Prime Ministership proved that in a democracy even the poorest had a chance to aspire to the highest post. He took me to his apartment and showed me a picture on the mantelpiece of the cottage in Scotland where his grandfather had lived and from where he walked barefoot to earn his living.

I told Macmillan of the feeling in India that his personal friendliness was not reflected in Whitehall's attitude to Indo–Pakistani affairs. He said Britain had got tied up with military pacts and cold war politics. Nehru and he were hoping to end the cold war between Moscow and Washington. This would have a beneficial effect on the Indian sub-continent (Earl of Home expressed similar hopes). I mentioned to him the grave handicap from which the Indian Press suffered for want of newsprint. He too promised to help. In fact, on returning home, I was pleasantly surprised to learn from Nehru that Macmillan had written to him about my talk offering help, but that the Government of India were unable to give higher priority to the product.

(b) INTEGRATED BID

I passed through some European capitals whose interest in India had shrunk because this country appeared to them more in the role of a client for aid than the leader of a new force in world affairs. The exception was West Germany, the only Western nation which shows deep respect for Indian culture. German Indologists study Sanskrit, whereas their British counterparts confine themselves to the Indo–Muslim period. This was impressed on me by Kurt Kiesinger in 1954 when he met a delegation of Indian Editors in Dusseldorf as the spokesman of Indo–German Friendship Society. (When I met him again in Delhi after he had become Federal Chancellor in the winter of 1968, he recalled our earlier meeting and said he was very interested in friendship with India.) My talk with Chancellor Adenauer and his Finance Minister gave me the feeling that they despaired of developing economic relations with India because of the many restrictions in this country, but they appreciated Nehru's role in bringing the two Super Powers closer.

When I reached Moscow, I had a novel experience. Khrushchev held a Press Conference in a room where a couple of hundred newsmen were present. Anybody could shoot a question at him. I asked just one to show that India too figured. At that time, no Indian correspondent had been assigned to Moscow. In fact, this was the main grouse the Kremlin conveyed to our Embassy. I told our

Ambassador my paper would gladly assign a correspondent provided the Russians agreed to sell him a car at the export price and give him a house at the rent they charged Russian journalists. The authorities were sounded, but they did not agree to make these concessions.

Eisenhower, at a Press Conference, had stated that five basic points for discussion in his forthcoming talk with Khrushchev would include the following: "To suggest that together they explore ways and means to advance the living standards of the almost 2,000 million people of the newly developing or underdeveloped countries."

I raised this issue with Mr. Khrushchev at the Press Conference he gave at the Kremlin following the announcement of his projected visit to the States. I reproduce the question and answer as issued by the Soviet Information Bureau, Moscow:

"Durga Das (*Hindustan Times*)—Is it planned that Mr. Khrushchev will discuss with President Eisenhower the question of aid to the underdeveloped countries of Asia and Africa?

"N. S. Khrushchev—The programme of my meeting with the President of the United States has not been planned. And I cannot say now on what questions we shall exchange views. I think we shall exchange views on all questions that will arise during our meeting, including the question of aid to economically underdeveloped countries. This is a serious question and it deserves attention."

Dillon writing to me on 1st October, 1959, appreciated my comments on the economic aid programmes of the U.S. and thanking me for quoting Khrushchev's reply to my question, added: "We are also pleased by the support being voiced at the current World Bank meeting for our proposal for the creation of an International Development Association. Through the creation of such an institution we hope to introduce further flexibility, on a multilateral basis, in development loan assistance."

However, Eisenhower failed to make Khrushchev discuss economic aid when they met at Camp David, presumably because the Russians were averse to meshing their aid programme with those of the U.S.

Writing to Sherman Cooper on 21st August, I stated: "I met Mr. Nehru on 19th August and gave him a review of the world situation as I had gathered in my conversations with leaders of various nations. I also reported to him my conversation with President Eisenhower. Mr. Nehru expressed a strong hope that President Eisenhower would visit India. I think the time has come for President

Eisenhower to have a heart-to-heart talk with Mr. Nehru on problems of Asia and Africa. The plan of integrated economic development which I mentioned to you at your house, and which I think is the key to the solution of our problems, can be discussed threadbare in India. A meeting of hearts between Mr. Nehru and American leaders has not taken place yet. I feel that with proper understanding Mr. Nehru can play a very big role in consolidating the situation in non-communist Asia and Africa."

During my visit to New York, Franklin Lindsay, a leading management consultant, had given a lunch at his house where I met George Kennan and had a discussion with him on the Soviet Union. I then promised to tell them of my assessment of Russia. Writing to Lindsay on 16th August, 1959, I said: "The Russians want an understanding with the U.S.A. so that they may divert their attention to the production of more consumer goods. They also want a larger output for distribution in the form of trade and aid to the underdeveloped countries of Asia and Africa. This makes it all the more necessary for the West, especially the U.S.A., to have clearly defined objectives and pursue them relentlessly."

A memorable aspect of my visit to Moscow was a brief meeting with Boris Pasternak, author of *Dr. Zhivago*. Pasternak was very warm and friendly and was glad that I had managed to find his place. He autographed my diary and asked me to convey his thanks and greetings to his numerous friends in India who had written to him and to whom he was not able to send a reply. He feelingly said: "I can only meet them in my dreams."

One of the objects of my global tour was to study the working of parliamentary institutions as I was Chairman of the Press Gallery Committee of Parliament. I was particularly interested in the rules regarding admission to the Press Gallery and to the lobby. On my return home, I wrote to the Speaker of the Lok Sabha telling him that I found the practice in London and Paris of special interest to India. Lobby tickets were issued in Britain to newspapers and news agencies and their editors sent in the names of persons who would hold such tickets.

Another question in which I was interested was the relation of a newspaper editor to his publisher. I had talks with the presidents of the Society of Newspaper Editors and of the Publishers Association in the U.S. and also with individual publishers and editors in the U.S., Britain and Japan. I gathered that in the U.S. about a third of the publishers took an active part in the production and in framing policy directives. Another third gave the editor freedom to pursue the policy he thought best but scrutinised closely what was published.

Last came the category of editors who had the freedom to run the paper as they willed so long as they produced the dividends the publisher wanted.

The Press in Britain was by and large aligned to political parties even though newspapers were not party-owned. Perhaps the most unorthodox opinion was expressed by Roy Thomson, now Lord Thomson of Fleet. He said he considered the newspaper business an instrument for making money and his instructions to his editors were that they must sell whatever would bring in larger earnings. Newspapermen in Japan told me that their tradition was to be anti-Government in their editorial columns. They felt more papers were sold that way and made for healthy public life.

Chapter 17

INFA IS BORN

On 16th October, 1959, I took six months leave preparatory to retirement from the *Hindustan Times*. In a signed farewell editorial, I said I proposed to use my retirement from the paper to fill in some gaps in Indian journalism. These gaps were the absence of a syndicated news and feature service and of a reference book on Press and advertising media. As President of the All–India Newspapers Editors' Conference, I had made a special study of the state of the Press during my tour of the various parts of the country. I had come to the conclusion that a large number of medium and small newspapers could not afford to buy quality editorial material in competition with the dozen giant metropolitan newspapers. Moreover, many papers often resorted to scandal mongering or turned to free material dished out by publicity officials or foreign missions to fill space.

During my world tour of 1959, I studied syndication in the U.S., Britain, Russia and Japan and countries in West Asia and South-East Asia. The fact that I was President of A.I.N.E.C. and Editor-in-Chief of the *Hindustan Times* helped to make the trip rewarding both professionally and from the point of view of my plans for the future. Of particular interest was my talk with Walter Lippmann and the advice he offered to make syndicated columns a success in India.

358 The Nehru Era

Early in November 1959 I met Nehru to explain to him my plan for a news and feature syndicate. I was with him for forty-five minutes and ended my remarks with the request that he inaugurate India News and Feature Alliance (I.N.F.A.) on his birthday, 14th November, 1959. I added that the date was doubly auspicious as it was also the day of worship of Goddess Durga, after whom I had been named. Nehru looked up his diary and said he would be out of town on that date and that I should approach Pant or Morarji Desai to inaugurate the function.

I asked Nehru whether the scheme had appealed to him on merit. He smiled and said: "You want to test me?" Then he added after a moment's thought: "Well, I understand it will help to cut across the proprietorial and editorial monopoly of the capitalist Press by supplying quality material to smaller newspapers. It will promote national integration and inter-state communication and it will help project India's image abroad." I felt swept off my feet with the way he had articulated in those few words all that I had laboriously tried to explain in forty-five minutes.

I then told Nehru that I had consulted two others, Pant and an old friend, K. C. Mahindra. Pant had blessed the venture with the proviso that I must arrange to produce the service in the regional languages as soon as possible as the best way of securing communication among the states. K.C., as we called him, had said that it would be a success if I could guarantee to live a year.

The inaugural message Nehru gave I.N.F.A. ran: "I am interested in your new journalistic project which will provide a new and specialised news service and syndicated columns. I send you my good wishes for it."

Morarji Desai was the chief guest at the inauguration. For the first anniversary, attended by Pant, Nehru sent another message almost suggesting he remembered my fears and was happy to see the service had made good. This is what he wrote: "I am glad to learn that your India News and Feature Alliance has made good progress. I send you my good wishes for it."

I consider two persons co-founders of the Syndicate. K.C. made it possible to give it a start by sparing some accommodation for it in his office in Parliament Street, the most central and exclusive business locality in New Delhi. Trevor Drieberg, whom I had brought into the *Hindustan Times* as Deputy News Editor, volunteered to join me, and his zeal and professional competence provided a sound base for the organisation we built up.

Luck helped in another way. My third son, Satya Jit, who was in the Indian Air Force, developed trouble in his spine which made the

Medical Board ground him. He had a passion for flying and not for a desk job. So he resigned, and since I.N.F.A's operations had grown to the point where it needed a wholetime business manager, his acceptance of my offer that he work with me was very welcome.

A week after he joined the organisation and had been given the power of attorney, I got a fairly severe heart attack while flying in a Dakota from Ahmedabad to Bombay in December 1960. That grounded me in Bombay for three months. Although I had survived the one year K.C. had prescribed, the organisation was kept going by Drieberg and Satya Jit. In fact, my illness provided a stern test for the organisation. Inder Jit joined I.N.F.A. as Editor in mid-1962, after ten years with the *Times of India*: earlier, he spent two years in Britain on attachment with the *Westminster Press* Provincial Newspapers, the *Daily Telegraph* and *The Times*.

Over the years, it has grown in strength. Its succeeding anniversaries were presided over in turn by B. P. Sinha, Chief Justice of India, Lal Bahadur Shastri, when he was Home Minister, Lok Sabha Speaker Hukam Singh, and Zakir Husain at the time he was Vice-President. Prominent among those who blessed it at birth, and attended every anniversary were Morarji Desai and Mehr Chand Mahajan, former Chief Justice of India.

I am more than ever convinced that the healthy development of the Press in India depends on syndication, both on a national and regional scale, and I consider the trail-blazing success of I.N.F.A. the most rewarding achievement of my journalistic career.

Chapter 18

CHINA BETRAYS NEHRU

(a) N.E.F.A. DEBACLE

Twenty-first October, 1962 marked a turning-point in the Nehru era. That was the day China launched its wanton aggression against India. Not many days afterwards, our Armed Forces in N.E.F.A. were routed and India's national pride suffered its worst humiliation since independence. What went wrong? How did our officers and jawans, who had earned fame in World Wars I and II as one of the finest fighting men, suddenly come a cropper? Who were the guilty men and did they get their deserts? These and other questions have been asked again and again and sought to be answered by

Government leaders, retired generals, military experts and journalists. The story of the debacle has been told only partially. Not all the guilty men have been named.

Nehru decided to cultivate Peking after the revolution in 1949 not in a spirit of romanticism but because he realised India's security demanded this, although Peking had branded his Government a "running dog of U.S. imperialism." Peking responded eagerly: it wanted an influential friend who would provide a bridge to the non-Communist world.

Proof of this is an incident which took place when the Nepalese Prime Minister, Tanka Prasad Acharya, visited Peking. At a reception in his honour, he raised the slogan of Nepal–China friendship. Mao, who was present, quickly corrected him, saying it was Nepal–China–India friendship. Acharya's mission, to cultivate Peking at the expense of Kathmandu's ties with New Delhi, did not pay off.

Nehru also foresaw that China and Russia would clash one day, because these two countries had too many border disputes to avoid clashes and that their common Communist ideology was by itself no guarantee against differences.

India and China had drifted apart towards a point of no return by April 1960 when Chou came to Delhi for further talks on the border question. Nehru was anxious to get China to accept the MacMahon Line as the northern boundary of N.E.F.A. and Chou was willing to do so. But in return, the Chinese Prime Minister asked for India's acceptance of Chinese presence in Aksai Chin. Nehru was not interested in Aksai Chin (where, as he told Parliament later, "not a blade of grass grows") and at one stage was quite agreeable to strike a deal. But premature leakage in the Press of what was going on between him and Chou and its description of the proposed announcement as a "sell-out" on Aksai Chin blocked the agreement. The Opposition in Parliament pounced on the report and extracted from an embarassed Nehru the undertaking that "not an inch of Indian territory" would be ceded or bartered away without the approval of the House.

Nehru still favoured the deal personally, as he indicated to Bhagwan Sahay who as India's Ambassador in Nepal had had an exceptional opportunity for a long talk with Chou when the Chinese Prime Minister visited Kathmandu after Karachi, Kabul and Delhi in 1959. Why then did Nehru not accept Chou's offer of April 1960? Nehru replied to Sahay that Parliament and public opinion had been roused to such a pitch by the slanted Press reports that he could not persuade them to approve of the deal. Even his

Cabinet colleagues, Morarji Desai and others, had strongly opposed it.

The unpreparedness for the sudden Chinese onslaught across the Himalayas was as much political as military, if not more. In the face of mounting evidence to the contrary, Nehru and Menon clung overlong to the delusion that the Chinese would not attack. Menon invariably flaunted Chen Yi's "assurance" to him in Geneva that China would "never resort to the use of force to settle the border dispute" as though it was a talisman that ruled out the need for armed vigilance. (M. J. Desai, the Foreign Secretary, told me he had received a similar assurance on behalf of China from Russia in 1959.) If Menon was guilty of hugging the illusion, so was Nehru, perhaps to a greater degree. (He openly ticked off General Thimmaya, Chief of Army Staff at a Governor's Conference months earlier for even suggesting the possibility of an attack by China.) Many others in the Cabinet were not innocent. Either through ignorance or fear of going contrary to the Prime Minister, they endorsed his complacent attitude.

While the menace from Peking mushroomed, even at the highest level one encountered not positive action but only wishful thinking joined to a sense of helplessness. Man the entire frontier with China was the first frantic call; but the response was to throw up a thin line of defensive posts, inadequately manned, along the long border. In vain did experienced officers like Lieutenant-General S. P .P. Thorat plead for defence in depth. We had only to parade our resolve to oppose aggression and Peking would stay its hand, it was argued instead. A foray or two in Aksai Chin was believed to have effectively checked Chinese truculence, and it was contended that we had only to announce our intention to throw them out of Thag La for the Chinese to retreat. The absurdity of this reasoning was established when the enemy thrust deep into Indian territory and inflicted upon us a defeat whose psychological wounds have yet to heal fully.

The disarray in political thinking is just half the story of this disaster. Militarily, our unpreparedness was no less woeful. Here again, though Menon cannot absolve himself of a larger part of the guilt, there are others who must bear it as well. From the Army's point of view, the order to hurl the Chinese back to the point where their attack originated and to clear the last inch of Indian territory of the aggressor was ill-judged, ill-timed and suicidal. It ran flatly counter to the exigencies of defensive strategy, for no experienced officer would have ordered the enemy to be opposed at heights to which our troops were not acclimatised. After a subsequent visit to Se La, Sir Edmund Hillary said it required at least a week's acclimatisation for soldiers to become operationally effective at such heights.

(b) HALF-TOLD STORY

According to one of the protagonists in the drama played out so disastrously for India, in July 1962, three months before the first large-scale Chinese attack, Morarji Desai agreed to give additional allowances to troops stationed at camps 10,000 feet above sea level. General P. N. Trhapar, the Army Chief of Staff, at the same time, approached Desai for Rs. 4,970 million, including Rs. 1,970 million in foreign exchange, for meeting deficiencies in equipment and the requirements of modernisation. Desai assured he would do everything to strengthen the defences but said that since such a large expenditure would have far-reaching economic repercussions, Cabinet sanction would be necessary. It was, therefore, for the Defence Minister to sponsor the proposal. When the matter was taken up with Nehru, the Prime Minister replied that China would not resort to force. He also said he had been told that the ordnance factories were helping meet the deficiencies in equipment.

Menon turned a deaf ear to repeated requests from Army Headquarters for action to meet the serious shortage of modern equipment. A.H.Q. said the Army was out-gunned and out-tanked by the Chinese. In June 1962, it addressed a seventh letter on the subject to Menon, enumerating the deficiencies listed in previous letters sent from October 1961 onward and warning him of the danger inherent in failing to take prompt action. Headquarters did not receive even an acknowledgement of the letter. When this matter of lack of equipment was raised in talks, Menon, once again, flaunted Chen Yi's "assurance" to him. External Affairs supported Menon's view.

At a meeting of the Defence Council in September 1962, a bare month before the Chinese struck, the Army Commander in Ladakh said: "If China attacks massively, we shall be annihilated." The head of Eastern Command said at the same meeting: "If China decides to come down in a big way, we are in no position to hold it anywhere in N.E.F.A." It was thus evident that the Army chiefs were against any action that the aggressive Chinese might seize on as an excuse for striking hard. They also pointed out that the Chinese had more than a brigade at Dho La, with a division not far behind. Apart from a decided edge over our men in arms, the Chinese had in all four divisions in proximity to N.E.F.A. and two facing

Ladakh. In contrast, India had altogether two divisions in N.E.F.A and Ladakh.

Lieutenant-General "Biji" Kaul was appointed Corps Commander in N.E.F.A. on 5th October after Menon agreed to split the existing corps in the north-eastern region in two—one to operate in N.E.F.A. and the other in Nagaland and along the East Pakistan border. A.H.Q. had recommended another name for the region, and on its asking Menon to speed up a decision after three months of inaction, he replied: "You can't push me. If a Minister likes, he can sit on a file for six months or as long as he wants." Later, at an emergency meeting of Army chiefs and civilian officers of the Defence Ministry on 4th October, Menon said the Government "would like" Kaul to be appointed Commander of the new N.E.F.A. corps.

Kaul came to Delhi from N.E.F.A. on 11th October to report to a top-level meeting which the Prime Minister and the Defence Minister attended that the Chinese could not be evicted from Dho La as the men and equipment he had at his disposal were inadequate for the purpose. The two Ministers accepted Kaul's assessment, although some weeks earlier they had rejected an identical statement of views by the Chief of Staff and the G.O.C. Eastern Command. The meeting decided to stay "Operation Eviction" until the following spring. The Chief of Staff issued formal orders to this effect on 12th October and called for details of the requirements of materials and other resources for this purpose.

On 13th October came Nehru's statement in Madras on his way to Ceylon that the Army had been ordered "to throw out the Chinese." A.H.Q. was dumbfounded. Thapar at once went to see Menon, and I am told, said: "This is contrary to the decision of two days ago which said we were not to attack or engage the Chinese." Menon replied: "This is a political statement. It means action can be taken in ten days or a hundred days or a thousand days." Eight days after Nehru's statement, the Chinese attacked. Of course, they could not have done so in such force unless they had been preparing for quite some time. Nehru's remarks were apparently only a contributory factor in provoking the Chinese. The main cause seems to have been the creation of a new command and the appointment of Kaul, who had direct access to the Defence Minister and the Prime Minister. The Chinese took this to mean that India was preparing to attack.

Kaul was in New Delhi, where his doctors had ordered him to go because he had strained his heart, and his successor, Lieutenant-General Harbaksh Singh, was on his way to N.E.F.A. when the

Chinese attacked on 21st October. After the action had started, Thapar saw Menon, who said: "How could I know the Chinese would act like this?" A few days later, Kaul wanted the N.E.F.A. command back to show that he had not run away from his post. Thapar refused requests from Menon and him on the ground that corps commanders should not be changed so quickly. Thapar agreed, however, when Nehru intervened, saying: "Why don't you send Kaul back? Why are you being adamant?" Kaul was posted back to N.E.F.A. towards the end of October.

The withdrawal of the poorly-equipped Indian forces was inevitable in the face of the massive Chinese attack. The "penny packet" border defences proved a broken reed in N.E.F.A. But the debacle was partly brought about by blunders, among them the premature withdrawal from Se La. (The mountain brigades fighting on the Ladakh front, however, acquitted themselves creditably.) Several military reputations also crumbled before the Chinese onslaught. Kaul, whose half-told "Untold Story" roused much controversy on its publication about five years after these events, was one of the casualties. Thapar conveyed his resignation orally to Nehru personally on his return from N.E.F.A. after the fall of Bomdi La. Nehru appreciated Thapar's gesture but hoped it would not be necessary to accept the resignation. Later, on receiving news that the Chinese were racing towards foothills south of which lay the Brahmaputra Valley, Nehru sent for Thapar and asked for his resignation. This, he said, might prove helpful in the difficult situation facing the Government.

(c) MENON FALLS

The debacle could not be explained away as an accident. Behind it lay failures at the political and military levels. The country's mood was reflected in Parliament, when members of all parties demanded somebody's head. It had to be either Menon's or Nehru's. The people were willing to overlook Nehru's part if he gave up Menon. The Prime Minister realised, however, that if the party and Parliament tasted blood they would not stop with Menon. They might even ask for his. In fact, two days before a crucial meeting of the Executive Committee of the Congress Parliamentary Party, Nehru told Chavan, who had come to Delhi to attend a meeting of the Chief Ministers: "You see, they want Menon's blood. If I agree, tomorrow they will ask for my blood."

But whichever way Nehru turned he found pressure on him to throw Menon out. What made him do this finally? Hare Krushna

Mahatab, Deputy Leader of the party, and Mahavir Tyagi claim that the fatal blow was struck by the Executive Committee, whose actions they had carefully planned and rehearsed. Nehru shouted at the Committee members at the meeting and threatened to dismiss them all, but the solid phalanx was not intimidated and the Committee made it clear that no one was bigger than the country. Menon must go or . . .

Satya Narayan Sinha, Chief Whip and Minister for Parliamentary Affairs, told me that a private meeting he had with Nehru that night at the Prime Minister's residence clinched the issue. He told Nehru point-blank that if he did not drop Menon his leadership was in danger. Lal Bahadur Shastri confided he too met Nehru privately and convinced him that unless he dropped Menon his own position would be endangered. Indira Gandhi, worried for her father's sake, went to Vice-President Zakir Husain and asked him to tell Nehru that Menon's dismissal alone would appease the Congress Party and the country.

Nehru himself is reported to have approached President Radhakrishnan with a suggestion that he might write to Nehru advising him to drop Menon. Radhakrishnan is said to have jocularly remarked that that would reverse the relations between President and Prime Minister. It was the duty of the Prime Minister to advise the President, and in any event it would be a bad example for the President to suggest a Minister's dismissal. So, Nehru wrote to Radhakrishnan recommending acceptance of Menon's resignation, which some said had been predated, and others that Menon had submitted voluntarily.

Could Menon have survived the disaster? His failures as Defence Minister are not enough to explain the political calamity that overtook him. Had he been less brusque and truculent, he might not have been afflicted with so many enemies, both within the Congress and outside. Instead, confident of Nehru's unfailing friendship and trust, he appeared to set out deliberately to antagonise his colleagues. In his relations with Nehru himself, he betrayed uncertainty; at one moment, he was proud and overbearing, sure of gaining his purpose; at the next, he would exhibit fear and servility. All that seemed to matter to him was that his public image as Nehru's confidant should not be impaired.

Menon was obsessed with the fear of a military coup. When B. N. Jha was Cabinet Secretary, he received oral report from a Home Ministry intelligence official that General Thimayya and a group of officers were planning a coup. His informant mentioned the movement of some Army units in support of his claim. The official said this information was based on reports from military sources. The official suggested to Jha that jeeps and other vehicles be requisitioned to keep a watch on troops movements and that Thimayya and other suspected officers be sent compulsorily on leave or retired.

Jha replied that it was not proper to take such action without concrete proof. But if proof was available, the suspects should be arrested immediately. He added that from his experience he judged that the shift of troops was probably a routine exercise. As the official refused to make a report in writing, Jha merely passed on the information to Pant. The Home Minister in turn conveyed it to Nehru, but Jha heard nothing more about it from higher quarters.

Menon had many solid virtues. Endowed with both intellect and imagination, he remodelled the whole structure of the Defence production wing, boosting the value of defence production to Rs. 500 million and setting the country on the road to self-sufficiency. But the trouble with Menon was that he was too ambitious and hoped to move higher on the strength of his achievements as Defence Minister. At the same time, he did not trust anyone implicitly, interfered with appointments and transfers. The price he had to pay for this was truly heavy. At the crucial moment China struck, discontent was rife in the higher echelons of the army.

Menon, it might be said, had found the cards well stacked in his favour, but he played them so recklessly that when it came to a showdown he had no trumps left. Nehru jettisoned Menon only when he discovered that all the forces inside the Cabinet and in the Congress Parliamentary Party were ranged against his favourite and he had no choice. But Nehru did this not without an agonising inner conflict. Menon was his blind spot and at least three times in his talks with me Nehru had praised him for his "colossal intellect." The fact of the matter is that Nehru felt gnawings of conscience throughout this episode. He knew that the blame for the disaster was more his than that of his loyal friend.

(d) CHANGING IMAGE

My wife and I visited Japan in 1963 and toured the country extensively. I made contacts with governmental and business leaders and newspapermen, and of them perhaps the most fruitful was the talk with Prime Minister Ikeda. He had said on an earlier visit to Delhi that Japan and India had a common destiny, and I was keen on getting him to spell out his ideas on this subject. He recalled the

Anglo–Japanese military alliance at the turn of the century which was directed against Russia. It had been formed because Britain had at its disposal an efficient army in India. India's manpower, besides British naval strength, provided the basis of the alliance. Ikeda declared that the situation had altered only to the extent that China, instead of Russia, might be the power against which a balance would have to be established. Thus Tokyo and Delhi were the natural pegs of a system of security. He did not think Japanese trade with China would reach serious proportions.

But what aroused his concern was India's failure to make good on the economic front. Japan's economic regeneration had been undertaken step by step. Education was first made universal; agriculture was then modernised and good road, rail and telephone communications provided to link every village. Thereafter, light industries were created, then heavy industries and finally chemical industries. India had, however, tried to reverse the process. He said Japan believed that without economic strength India could not play an effective role in Asian and world affairs. The crusade against colonialism was over. He did not think Australia could win the confidence of the Asians without radically altering her White Australia policy and insular outlook.

My talks with Japanese bankers and industrialists showed that they considered China a growing danger, while merchants and traders and the student community considered her a natural market and an ally. India, the birthplace of Buddhism, was to them too distant, whereas their cultural and geographical affinity was with China.

My wife got a headline in the mass circulation *Mainichi* when she said in reply to a question that when she visited Japan in 1957 it was Japanese, and six years later it had become America. The Japanese took her remark as a compliment, for they have modelled their progress in science and technology as well as their way of life on that of the U.S.

The following year, I visited Britain for a month as a member of a delegation of editors. I used the occasion to pose a very awkward question. I said the time had come for Britain to choose between India and Pakistan; these two countries had taken up irreconcilable positions and were drifting towards an armed clash. By and large, the politicians supported Pakistan and the economists and businessmen India.

The most forthright answer came from Duncan Sandys, Minister for Commonwealth Relations. Nehru, he said, had led the movement for the liquidation of British influence and power in Africa. Why did he poke his nose into their affairs? What did he expect Britain to do? How could the British be friends with India, which had shown nothing but hostility to them and had been the cause of their downfall? John Freeman, who was editing the *New Statesman*, put the case differently. The old India hands had sold the idea that the Hindu was a crafty *bania* and the Muslim a loyal friend. That generation was dying out, but the prejudice they had created would take time to solve.

Chapter 19

FATHER AND DAUGHTER

(a) AFTER NEHRU, WHO?

Nehru doted on his sister Vijayalakshmi Pandit, whom he affectionately called Nan. She mothered him, and was his friend and companion in the lonely years of his widowerhood. This relationship suffered, however, when M. O. Mathai came on the scene as his personal assistant after Nehru became Prime Minister. This aide had the knack of gauging Nehru's feelings and wishes, and he strove to fulfil them. He thus gained his confidence and began gradually to influence Nehru's thoughts and decisions without appearing to do so. One of his qualities which impressed Nehru greatly was his deftness in drafting letters and notes, and in looking after Nehru's personal finances.

Gradually, the aide became the most powerful member of Nehru's staff and was designated Special Assistant to the Prime Minister. As he was a bachelor, Nehru provided Mathai with a room in his large house so that he was available almost round the clock. This enabled the aide to acquire more power and dictate orders to the other members of the household. Indeed a stage was reached when he even interposed himself between Nehru and everybody else, including his daughter and sisters and even those in whom he placed his trust in the Government. In fact, barring Azad and one or two others none could think of walking directly into Nehru's room without going through the aide's.

Nehru was told over the years of instances of Mrs. Pandit's

extravagance as India's Ambassador in the Soviet Union and the United States and High Commissioner in Britain. Audit officials and diplomats who had served under her abroad retailed stories of her "wasteful" expenditure of the taxpayers' money and how his image was being tarnished by the sister. But as head of the Ministry of External Affairs, he generally sanctioned her bills; on an occasion or two when audit raised objections, he even offered to pay from his pocket. Nevertheless, his feelings towards her did undergo a change to some extent.

Around 1956, the tide began to turn against the aide when Indira Gandhi decided to assert herself. She began to take control of the running of the Nehru ménage and discuss matters directly with Nehru. When the aide resigned following allegations in Parliament that he had abused his connection with Nehru, Indira advised her father to accept his resignation. Nehru did so. The aide was cleared of the charge but the incident tarnished Nehru's public image somewhat, for the Indian saying that "there is darkness beneath the lamp" was on everybody's lips as they read detailed Press accounts of the proceedings in Parliament.

Nehru had his own plans for his daughter—plans which some of us clearly discerned. That was the time when people at home and abroad had started asking: "After Nehru, who?" All manner of guesses were being made. However, few realised then that Nehru was, in point of fact, building up Indu, as he affectionately called her, to carry forward the Nehru legend for the third successive generation. It was not without reason that he had welcomed her idea of retaining use of her maiden name after marriage to Feroz Gandhi and calling herself Indira Nehru-Gandhi.

In fact, I disclosed Nehru's succession plan in my weekly *Diary* in the *Hindustan Times* as early as 18th June, 1957. I wrote: "It is wrong to suggest that Mr. Nehru is trying to build up Mr. Menon, or anyone else, as his successor. If Mr. Nehru is consciously building up anyone, he is building up his daughter." That was shortly after Nehru had gone to London for the Commonwealth Prime Minister's Conference and taken Menon along. Menon was then a member of the Cabinet and the fact that a Minister was accompanying the Prime Minister for the first time to the Conference had encouraged talk that Nehru was building up Menon for succession.

Before writing my column, I checked my impression with Azad the previous Sunday morning. To my welcome surprise, he had independently reached the same conclusion. That was enough for me and I put it down in cold print. Of course, I had good reasons for my surmise on the succession question. A few years earlier, when

Dhebar as Congress President made Indira Gandhi a member of the Congress Working Committee, I had begun to sense what was coming. I described the nomination as very significant and I said that this was so because she had been brought into the higher circles of the party from the top like her grandfather and her father.

Nehru did not relish my comment and sent for me. He said that Tandon as Congress President had made Patel's daughter, Maniben, a member of the Working Committee but I had had nothing to say about it. I replied that Maniben had been an active Congress worker since 1920, when she commanded the women's corps at the Ahmedabad session of the Congress. She had gone through the mill, whereas Indira had been given a place in the High Command without any experience of the organisation. Nehru said Indira had refused a ticket for Parliament. We, however, parted smiling as I said that the publicity she had received through my column would stand her in good stead for a public career.

Nehru was upset by the publication about the paragraph on succession. He again sent for me and inquired about my basis for writing it. I recalled the previous talk I had with him and said this impression was shared by those who were in very close contact with him. Nehru said my comment might hurt his daughter. But I again replied that this might, on the contrary, prove useful as a seed sown in the popular mind. I also pointed out that Nehru might find one day that I had unconsciously done his daughter a good turn. This made him relax. I did not tell him that the paragraph was based on the impression given me by Azad and Pant, his closest associates.

My *Diary* caused sharp reaction in other quarters also. Some of the aspirants were surprised, while others were angry. One was wild and went to the length of accusing me of having "lost" my head. "We are not dead yet," he angrily thundered. But a year later, the situation had changed materially. Dhebar resigned from Congress Presidentship after the Nagpur Session and Indira succeeded him, to the great astonishment of all, after an intense drama behind the scenes. But, thereby, hangs another story, told to me by those present and confirmed by Pant, Kamaraj and other friends.

All the leaders present had agreed that S. Nijalingappa be appointed President. At various functions held in connection with the Session, Nijalingappa was thereafter the centre of attention, as the delegates vied with one another to felicitate him. A large crowd even collected at the station to give him a hearty send-off when he left for Bangalore. The same evening, Dhebar called an unscheduled meeting of the Working Committee. When it met, Kamaraj asked what it was about. Dhebar replied that it was about the next President. Kamaraj said: "But the matter has been settled." Thereupon, Shastri quietly suggested that Indira might be asked to become President.

Pant, unaware of the background moves, was surprised by Shastri's proposal and said: "But Indiraji is not keeping good health. She must first . . ." Before he could complete the sentence, Nehru agitatedly interrupted to say: "There is nothing wrong with Indu's health. She will feel better once she has work to keep herself busy." That ended the argument and attention was next turned to the tricky question of communicating the decision to Nijalingappa. Nehru entrusted Pant with the job. Pant, in turn, asked Kamaraj to talk to Nijalingappa. Kamaraj suggested that in the circumstances it would be better if Nijalingappa, Sanjiva Reddy and he issued a joint statement proposing Mrs. Gandhi. He then flew to Madras where the three met and issued the statement.

Even before Indira Gandhi became Congress President, Nehru started building her up as a public personality. Whenever he invited a distinguished Indian or visitor from abroad to lunch or dine with him, he would tell Indira to invite such guests to an entertainment of her own. Thus, when Nehru had a formal luncheon for the Nelson Rockefellers and Eleanor Roosevelt, Indira played host to them at an informal coffee party. The aim of this policy was twofold: to give Indira the confidence she lacked in meeting outsiders and to establish her as a hostess in her own right.

Once she became a member of the Congress Working Committee, other members on the body began to utilise her as a channel of communication with her father, treating her as a means of conveying their ideas and wishes on particular matters to him. This function gave her a position of great importance in the eyes of others as well as in her own. When she became Congress President in 1959, Nehru planned her tours, and saw to it they proved rewarding. Later, under his patient and watchful guidance Indira grew into an important figure on the national scene, particularly after the Chinese attack, when he appointed her the Chairman of the Citizens' Central Council.

Discerning readers saw in Nehru's publication towards the end of 1958 of *A Bunch of Letters* a subconscious attempt to identify his family with the nation. These letters, written to Nehru or by him, are given in chronological order except for the opening letter "written on the birth of my daughter Indira (now Indira Gandhi)" by Sarojini Naidu from Madras on 17th December, 1917. It congratulated him on the birth of "my new niece" and ended with "a kiss to the new Soul of India."

(b) THE KAMARAJ PLAN

The Kamaraj Plan cleared the line of succession for India by eliminating Morarji Desai, who after Pant's death was "number two" in the Government. I, therefore, sought Kamaraj's own explanation of the plan named after him. What Kamaraj told me confirmed the information gathered by me from other members of the Congress High Command. This is what he said: The D.M.K. had won only fifteen seats in the Madras Legislative Assembly in 1957, while it won fifty in 1962 and about twenty-seven per cent of the votes cast. This was a danger signal and Kamaraj decided to devote himself fully to countering the D.M.K. and strengthening the Congress organisation in Madras. He suggested to Nehru that he resign the Chief Ministership for this purpose. The Prime Minister asked Kamaraj to let him think over the matter. This was soon after the 1962 elections.

Then came the Chinese attack and the defeat of the Congress in three by-elections to Parliament which were won by Kripalani standing as an independent, the Samyukta Socialist leader Ram Manohar Lohia and the Swatantra spokesman Minoo Masani respectively. At the time, Biju Patnaik, Chief Minister of Orissa, met Kamaraj and said he would like to join the Central Cabinet and strengthen it. Others too should do the same, he said. Kamaraj told him it was more important to strengthen the party organisation by resigning office and working among the people. Patnaik fell in line with this view and expressed readiness to give up the chief ministership of Orissa. Nehru was in Kashmir and Patnaik went there and discussed the matter with him.

Nehru came to Hyderabad for a week and sent for Kamaraj and asked him for details of his proposal. Kamaraj replied that it was meant only for Madras, but Nehru said it should be applied to other states where the Congress was not strong. He gave the impression that he was worried by the by-election results and the effect on public opinion of the Chinese invasion and the controversy over Menon. Subramaniam was with Nehru and Sanjiva Reddy was also in Hyderabad. After consultations, it was agreed that attention should be paid to organisational work. Nehru suggested that Kamaraj raise the issue in the Working Committee, which was to meet shortly. He did not know what was in Nehru's mind but did as he was bid.

There was general agreement on it in the Committee. Nehru said the principle should apply to leaders in the states as well as at the Centre. He christened it the Kamaraj Plan and had it endorsed by the A.I.C.C. It was decided that all Ministers at the Centre and the Chief Ministers should place their resignation in Nehru's hands and he would decide who should work for the organisation. Kamaraj's own idea was that it would be enough if as a symbol of the new resolve two Chief Ministers and one or two Central Ministers vacated office and took up organisational work. Until then, he did not suspect that Nehru had a deeper motive. But he realised this when Nehru said he had decided to relieve several Chief Ministers and top leaders, including Morarji Desai.

(c) NEHRU'S CRITICS

There were only three effective spokesmen of the Opposition during the Nehru era. They were S. P. Mookerjee, Kripalani and Lohia. The first was a real leader because he spoke for the largest group which opposed Nehru's policies. In oratory and debating skill, he excelled all others who have followed him. Kripalani was always the dissenter and a lone performer. He would have been more effective had he led an Opposition bloc. Lohia was the debunker. He ruthlessly attacked Nehru at every opportunity, repeatedly accusing him of spending Rs. 25,000 a day on himself as Prime Minister in maintaining a large retinue of assistants and bodyguards and a "luxurious" standard of living. He called Mrs. Gandhi a "dumb doll."

Mookerjee used to tell me that the only way to create an alternative to the Congress was to demolish Nehru's image. He died while in detention in Srinagar in 1953, and a promising political career was thus cut short. Kripalani too believed the evils in the country emanated from the top and that Nehru was the pace-setter in abusing patronage and power. Lohia believed that the Nehru family's identification with the nation was not only undemocratic but harmful and that Nehru's acceptance of Anglo–Indian cultural values led to his opposing anything that would give the nation a sense of Indianness.

Lohia told me several times that the North, especially the U.P., had remained backward because the Prime Minister had always been chosen from this region. This made the holder of the office lean over backward to please the South in planning economic development and the allocation of important portfolios in the Cabinet. He reinforced this by saying that whereas the revenue from income tax had gone down in the U.P. in a period of ten years it had

trebled in Madras. He wanted a South Indian Prime Minister so
that the North might get its fair share of economic growth.

The Congress Government at the Centre has been unlucky so
far as its Finance Ministers are concerned. None served his full term;
most of them resigned, while Desai was purged under the Kamaraj
Plan and brought back into Mrs. Gandhi's second Cabinet. But
every Finance Minister was a successful parliamentarian.

Chapter 20

ENTER THE SOOTHSAYER

The community of astrologers did not merely influence the hour
when independence of India should dawn. It shadowed most men
in top echelons—and continues to do so. In some cases, the "Royal
Astrologers," as they came to be called, became all powerful. I
found Satya Narayan Sinha, for several years Minister for Parliamentary Affairs and now Minister for Information and Broadcasting
a delightful storehouse of anecdotes in such matters. One who has a
parliamentary record longer than most other active Indian politicians
Sinha is a gay, debonair soul, with a passion for Hindi literature,
a belief in esoteric lore like astrology. Of the Nehru anecdotes that
Sinha recounted to me, many relate to his closing years.

Sinha told me how he himself came to acquire faith in astrology.
A certain reader of horoscopes, derisively known as a *patriwala*, had
forecast Patel's death nine months before it happened. The Sardar
himself was sceptical, and one night, during his accustomed telephone conversation with Sinha about parliamentary matters,
chaffed him asking: "What does your *patriwala* say?" The seer,
however, proved right to the exact day and we were all completely
taken aback, said Sinha to me.

When T.T.K. seemed to be at the peak of his power in 1958,
came another pundit to assert that he was riding for a fall. Sinha
ridiculed him, saying: "You are talking through your turban."
But the undaunted man made a still more dire prophecy. "On the
very day that Mr. Krishnamachari quits the Government, Maulana
Azad will suffer a fall in his bathroom and die four days later."

When Azad met with an accident, B. C. Roy was summoned from Calcutta. His verdict was that there was no cause for anxiety. Sinha met Nehru in the lobby of Parliament and told him of the prediction. Nehru exploded angrily: "What rot are you talking? Bidhan (Dr. Roy) is certain that Azad is in no danger." Four days later, the Education Minister passed away. Sinha recalled how shaken Nehru was after this.

Nehru's first serious illness was in March 1962, when he returned to Delhi from Poona running a high temperature. His doctors thought this was merely the aftermath of an exhausting election campaign, but it turned out to be a grave ailment which confined him to bed for more than a month and compelled him to keep away from the meeting of the Congress Parliamentary Party at which he was re-elected leader.

To Sinha's first suggestion that his horoscope be shown to a *jyotishi* (astrologer), Nehru turned a deaf ear. Gulzari Lal Nanda, the Planning Minister, prevailed upon him, however, to relent. There was an explosion when the man, well-known in Delhi, told Nehru he would be betrayed by his "best friend" and would have to face an attack from China that very year. Nehru flared up and shouted: "This can never happen. You are talking bilge." The *jyotishi* folded the horoscope, handed it back and retreated.

Not many weeks after the Chinese launched their aggression. Nehru was in a mood to listen to the astrologer. But the pundit's words were hardly comforting. Nehru's life span was over, he pronounced. Only *puja* (ritual worship) could prolong it. What followed was shrouded in the utmost secrecy. Fifty learned priests were engaged by his admirers to perform the prescribed rites at a temple in Kalkaji, a suburb of Delhi. At the end of the daily ceremonies, the Brahmin pundits repaired to the Prime Minister's residence to place an auspicious *tilak* mark on his forehead.

The astrologer had predicted that Nehru would have a second and more serious illness in January 1964 and that he would not survive beyond May 27th. Sinha tried without success to dissuade Nehru from attending the Bhubaneshwar session of the Congress. Nehru left New Delhi on 4th January and became very ill two or three days later. He never recovered fully from the stroke he had at this time. At the A.I.C.C. session on 14th May, Sinha warned some of his Cabinet colleagues that the Prime Minister was likely to die in about ten days as a *jyotishi* from Bombay had predicted. Nehru passed away on 27th May.

A high official close to Nehru revealed to me later something that lent weight to Sinha's story of Nehru's gradual drift to queer beliefs. For instance, he considered Ayurveda, the ancient Hindu system of therapy, unscientific, but he yielded in his last years to the ministrations of one of its noted practitioners.

It is a peculiar Oriental trait, this faith in soothsayers. Nehru the iconoclast fell prey to it in his last years. Ayub Khan the fallen dictator of Pakistan consulted crystal-gazers. Firoze Khan Noon, when he was Governor of East Pakistan told me that all that a Brahmin had forecast about his political career had come true. Sir Chimanlal Setalvad, a modern man and a leading lawyer of Bombay in the twenties and thirties and Sampurnanand who rose to Chief Minister of U.P. and later Governor of Rajasthan practised astrology as a hobby.

Chapter 21

NEHRU, MAN AND PRIME MINISTER

(a) IN THE POLITICAL MIRROR

We live too close to the epoch straddled by Nehru's charismatic personality to assess him as a man or as the undisputed leader of the world's largest democracy. People still speak of him with a feeling not far short of idolatry; many still utter his name like a *mantra*. But few saw beyond the trappings of greatness and power to his frailties.

Radhakrishnan, who laid down the office of President in 1967, was closely associated with Nehru for seventeen years or more. His last homage to Nehru was a panegyric. Yet, to those very near him, Radhakrishnan once confided that Jawaharlal was a "poor judge of men" and often extended his confidence and protection to unworthy persons. He had in mind Pratap Singh Kairon and Dharma Teja. Kairon was the "strong man" and Chief Minister of Punjab who had to quit when a Commission of Inquiry pronounced him guilty of some of the numerous charges of corruption and maladministration levelled against him. Dr. Teja caught Nehru's fancy as a "dynamic figure" and was able to wheedle out of the Government a loan of Rs. 200 million to finance a shipping company he floated. It was not long before the company was in difficulties and Teja and his wife fled the country to avoid arrest.

Morarji Desai, now Deputy Prime Minister under Indira Gandhi, might justifiably have had harsh things to say of Nehru, for after being reckoned heir apparent he was dropped from the Cabinet in a purge euphemistically labelled the "Kamaraj Plan." But Desai spoke of Nehru's failings without a trace of rancour. He would not agree that Nehru was a bad judge of men. When Nehru sketched the character of a man, he sized him up pretty shrewdly, Desai said. "He once gave me an analysis of Krishna Menon's personality that no one else could improve upon," he added. Nehru utilised the men around him for his own purposes and they in return exploited him fully.

When Gopalaswamy Ayyangar died, Nehru inducted Pant, the Chief Minister of Uttar Pradesh, into the Central Government. Pant, incidentally, was loth to quit Lucknow ·and face the political hazards of Delhi. I undertook a self-imposed mission to Lucknow to persuade him to accept his new assignment. He listened to me patiently, and then, after a great deal of humming and hawing, explained: "You see, here I hold Cabinet meetings in my drawing-room at any hour of the day or night of my choosing. In Delhi, though, I shall be subjected to a discipline. . . ." After much further argument, he blurted out: "I don't like this move. It is a Rafian (an expression used to describe Rafi Kidwai's political methods and followers) manoeuvre to get me out of U.P."

In any event, Kidwai's death ended the feud between the two and it did not take Pant long to ingratiate himself with Nehru. He had a capacious mind: he was a super Civil Servant in administrative affairs, and a suberb parliamentarian as well. In the Cabinet, he stood head and shoulders above his colleagues, and had he been younger he might well have stepped into Nehru's shoes. Nehru became very fond of him. Pant, for his part, treated Nehru like a god and was happy to serve the master even to the point of compounding misdemeanours in the case of Nehru's blind spots.

Nehru and Azad were intellectually and emotionally very close. Their friendship was based on two factors. First, they found themselves in agreement on most of the political issues that came before the Congress Working Committee. Secondly, Azad believed Nehru was an idealist with intellectual integrity, a progressive outlook and above all free from religious bigotry. At the same time, Azad was not unaware of Nehru's weaknesses. He blamed him for giving Jinnah the opportunity to win the leadership of the Muslims.

But Azad revised his opinion of Nehru in the last two years of his life. Indeed, he went to the extent of expressing regret for being unfair to Patel and asserting that he was sure that the country would have been better off if Patel had been Prime Minister. What motivated this change? Towards the end of his life, Azad realised that the best protection for the Muslims was the goodwill of the Hindus and a strong government. He told me he had come to the conclusion that Nehru's policies had weakened the adminis-tration and that his economic theories had failed to improve the living conditions of the people, especially the Muslims.

"You know, my attitude towards him is one of complete adora-tion," Mrs. Pandit once said of her brother Nehru. Nevertheless, her assessment of him was outspoken. "I used to think, as many others seem to do, that he was a bad judge of men. But I am sure now that he was not. Of course, some people did fail to measure up to the jobs assigned to them. But Nehru was tolerant to a fault: he was anxious to give everyone a fair deal, every reasonable chance to make good. I agree, though, that no leader should abdicate his authority completely. If my brother had asserted himself, Sheikh Abdullah would not have developed ideas of grandeur. Neither would Bakshi Ghulam Mohammed have strayed from the strait and narrow path had Bhai (brother) retained firm control in his own hands."

Shastri, who succeeded Nehru as Prime Minister, was a man of few words. One day, when I told him that with his rapport with Nehru he should be able to speak to him frankly, he confessed: "I know Panditji is wrong. He is not practical. He has strong likes and dislikes. He has little contact with the people; he mistakes the worship in their eyes for a complete endorsement of his policies. He has never known what poverty or human suffering is. Yet his heart is in the right place. He wants to see people happy and prosperous."

Shastri was critical of Nehru's plans and projects. "They only serve to strengthen the bureaucracy. When you take too much on hand, you do too little. Look at me. I have my limitations, both educational and administrative. I do not go for grandiose schemes." Shastri candidly admitted: "We have to submit to all he says and does. My loyalty to him therefore is unqualified. I keep my counsel to myself and carry out his wishes. I look for the greatest common denominator in all political and party disputes entrusted to my care by the leader. He has developed confidence in me, for he knows I am utterly loyal to him, and useful too."

Kidwai first came into prominence as a whip of Motilal Nehru's Swaraj Party in the Central Legislative Assembly. Next he made his mark as Revenue and Home Minister in the Pant Cabinet in U.P. Later, drafted by Nehru to the Centre, as a counterweight to Sardar Patel, he held in succession the portfolios of Communications and Food, acquitting himself in both posts with remarkable success, and died in 1954. Had Kidwai outlived Nehru, he might have been a powerful contender for the succession. He was one of the few Muslim politicians who derived their strength from Hindu followers and financiers. All through his life, he yielded Nehru unquestioning friendship and loyalty: but his last spell of office at the Centre seems to have started a process of disenchantment with his leader.

"You know, I never go to Nehru to seek advice or guidance," Kidwai, who was looked upon as the Patel of the Nehru camp, was in the habit of saying. "I take a decision and just present it to him as a *fait accompli*. Nehru's mind is too complex to wrestle with the intricacies of a problem. Those who go to him for advice rarely get a lead—and that only serves to delay matters."

On another occasion, Kidwai lamented Nehru's "obsession" with foreign affairs. "Does he not realise that the economic strength of a nation is the sole basis of its influence? Nehru does not understand economics, and is led by the nose by 'professors' and 'experts' who pander to his whims and fancies." Kidwai did not see eye to eye with Nehru on matters of high policy either. "I found a solution for Kashmir. I got him to agree to throw Sheikh Abdullah out. Unfortunately, however, there was no follow-up action. We should have absorbed Kashmir for good and all." Most poignant of all that Kidwai had to say was: "I do not know where we are going. The country needs a man like Patel."

At an international round table on Nehru's role in the modern world held in New Delhi in 1966, Krishna Menon had this to say of his friend and patron:

"I think it is no reflection on Panditji to say that so long as Gandhiji lived, or perhaps till about a year afterwards, he reigned and he was India. There was no question of Panditji or anybody else deviating from that. Everybody came under that umbrella."

According to Menon, Nehru was, in spite of all his internationalism, a nationalist because nationalism was a liberating force in India. Nehru's approach to all issues was "inductive." He solved each problem as it arose.

I met Chester Bowles on 22nd November, 1966, and asked him how he would sum up the Nehru era. He said, "Nehru held the country together because of his hold on the people and the supreme authority he wielded. But he had no idea of economics. He talked of Socialism, but did not know how to define it. He talked of social justice, but I told him he could have this only when there was an increase in production. He did not grasp that. So you need a leader who understands economic issues and will invigorate your economy."

According to what Walt Rostow told me in Washington "Nehru's contributions to the development of post-independent India have been three. He converted the Congress Party, which had fought for independence, into a political party with a platform where compromises were reached. He made the Congress take the responsibility for running the Government. He directed the people's attention to the domestic economy and the need for development. But his manner of doing it was not successful."

(b) CIVILIAN VIEWS

M. N. Kaul, Secretary of the Lok Sabha throughout Nehru's prime ministership and now a nominated member of the Rajya Sabha, was an admirer and close observer of Nehru. Kaul told me that Nehru's will, in which he had asked that his ashes be scattered all over India, was symbolic of his life. Throughout it, he had scattered ideas by the thousand. He was full of ideas, and it was for others to work on them. There was no aspect of human activity which he did not touch or provide for. In the last years of his life, he was left to carry the burden of statecraft alone and the politicians failed him.

How did the politicians fail Nehru? Kaul explained that Nehru used to stay on in Parliament for all important debates to set an example to his Ministers. He disposed of his daily work without delay. But the Ministers did not copy him in either of these things. Nehru did not pull his Ministers up when they deserved this treatment. In fact, he was very soft to them. Nehru could not master the administrative machine. He never rebuked any wrong doer. He never cut short procedure to take decisions. He bowed before challenges like the language issue and his troubles multiplied. He could never pick out an administrator who could put his ideas into effect.

A very able and experienced official of the Ministry of External Affairs gave me his frank assessment of India's foreign policy under Nehru. He ended his narrative with this remark: "I have never spoken like this to anyone. I have shared my innermost thoughts with you." I told him that many of his colleagues had said to me that they learned of our policy on any given subject from Nehru's speeches in Parliament. The official observed: "There was no policy, no direction. It was all drift and improvisation. This was partly the fault of Nehru and partly of the political and administrative machine. We got our freedom too cheaply and did not realise its value. We should have had 'rectification,' purged people and adopted a firm and clear policy. We did nothing of the kind. . . . Each Secretary went to Nehru, talked to him, got his consent for what he wanted and went his way."

A senior I.C.S. officer who worked closely with Nehru for 16 years said that nothing was so revealing of his outlook and philosophy as his fortnightly letters to the Chief Ministers. They were exceedingly well-written, but what was their theme? He lectured to them on the evils of regionalism, communalism and linguism. Yet he failed to remove any of them. In fact, they became so aggravated that he had to call a national integration conference. His failure to accept the report of the States Reorganisation Commission caused the failure of his campaign for integration.

The second theme of his letters was emphasis on planning. Nehru repeatedly described big industrial plants and dams as modern temples and held them up as proof of India's progress. He would give his impressions of his own tours of such work and also refer to what foreigners told him after they saw them. His letters never referred to such matters as exports, imports, balance of payments, food, prices and inflation. Giganticism seemed to act on him like a dose of opium, inuring him to the effects of economic laws. His eggheads fed his ego by preaching bigger and bigger plans.

Basically, Nehru was allergic to Americans, my informant said, and narrated an interesting incident. When Dulles visited Delhi in 1954 some people wished to hold a hostile demonstration in front of the U.S. Embassy. Nehru came to know of this and sent for the Chief Commissioner, who told him that popular feeling against Dulles was strong and that a demonstration may prove a safety valve. Nehru said: "I know this fellow Dulles is conscientiously stupid. But I do not want any hostile demonstration."

Two senior I.C.S. officers who worked as Nehru's Principal Private Secretaries found Nehru accomplished in his public relations. Once the correspondent of an American newspaper asked for an interview. The Principal Private Secretary put up with his letter clippings of the man's writings from Karachi which wholly supported Pakistan and criticised India violently. Nehru turned down the request, but a little later, as the Secretary was drafting a refusal, Nehru came into his room and said: "We are going to Kashmir tomorrow. Ask this man to join us on the flight." Nehru hardly devoted ten minutes to the correspondent in the plane, but that he should have had the privilege of flying with Nehru completely changed his attitude. After that, he wrote in glowing terms about Nehru and also wrote a life of Gandhi.

As Prime Minister, Nehru was methodical and punctual and ordered his life carefully. He took notes of conversations with important visitors and filed them for reference. He was extremely hostile to certain countries and was accordingly curt to their diplomatic representatives in New Delhi. He had no stomach for administrative details and niceties. He was satisfied with issuing broad directives and expected his subordinates to put them into practice. However, he went into details on particular problems of foreign affairs when they interested him.

In the early stages of his prime ministership, he was firm against corruption of any kind. He used to come down heavily on anybody, whether an official or a politician, if any charge of dishonesty or misdemeanour was brought to his notice against the person concerned. This was the pattern from 1947 to 1951, but he gradually began to acquire a tolerance for the malpractices of politicians. He thereupon substituted political expediency for principle in dealing with his ministerial colleagues. Unhesitatingly, he turned a blind eye to a demand by C. D. Deshmukh for the appointment of a high-power Tribunal to eradicate corruption when one of the cases listed by him related to the son of a close colleague.

It was not difficult for a Civil Servant to get Nehru to do what he wanted. There was the instance of an officer, whom Girija Shankar Bajpai, the Secretary-General to the Ministry of External Affairs, wanted appointed Ambassador in Europe. When the papers proposing the appointment were taken to Nehru, he hurled them to the floor saying he would never sign them. Next morning, his Private Secretary told him the man might make good in this post. Nehru, however, still refused to sign. A day or two later, the Private Secretary brought up the matter again and Nehru said: "Are you sure he will make good? All right, I shall sign the papers." The man was not a success, but his sponsor was pleased that the appointment had been approved.

(c) SUPERB PERFORMER

Nehru was a superb performer and the people loved him. He always dramatised his role and was so sensitive to the reactions of his audience that he would change his act if even a few voices booed.

He could not stand dissent or disapproval. When some people waved black flags at him in Belgaum, demanding reorganisation of the states on a linguistic basis, he yielded without a fight. If he stuck tenaciously to his stand on Kashmir, it was because he knew that the whole nation stood behind him.

Nehru enjoyed the company of intellectuals and picked Krishna Menon's brains. Menon served as his Alsatian and Nehru threw him to the wolves when, following the debacle in N.E.F.A., he realised that his own leadership was in grave danger. He liquidated every politician, Morarji Desai in particular, who he felt might destroy the Nehru legend. He knew India was still feudal and needed to identify itself with a leader and a family. He used his British-oriented education for intellectual flights based on Fabian Socialism; he used his social upbringing to play the gentleman, the nobleman and the humanist; he used his inborn talent as a Kashmiri Brahmin to outmanoeuvre his detractors and rivals. He excelled his contemporaries in statecraft.

Nehru was an aristocrat at heart. Like royalty in the feudal days, he was not averse at times to the company of jesters, and there were those among the top circles of the Government who fulfilled this role. But he had little communication with ordinary Congressmen or with the people. In general, too, his contact with his Cabinet colleagues did not extend beyond official routine. Kidwai was the only member of his Cabinet who was free with him, but Nehru ceased to lean on Kidwai after Patel's death.

One of Nehru's far-seeing moves was to organise the Himalayan Mountaineering Institute, which he opened on 4th November, 1954. He took counsel with Chief Minister Roy of Bengal soon after Hillary and Tenzing had conquered Everest in 1953 and put Tenzing in charge of the institute. The gratifying outcome of this move is that teams of Indians organised by the armed services have. established a record in the frequency of conquest of Everest and that civilians, especially women, have scaled many difficult Himalayan peaks.

The entire equipment for mountain climbing is now manufactured in India by defence installations. The institute has proved its utility in helping organise national defence in the light of the lessons learnt in the war with China. The Secretary of the Defence Ministry, Harish Sarin, the president of the Indian Mountaineering Foundation was instrumental in employing climbers trained at it to instruct troops in scaling heights as a preparation for combat in mountainous regions. The feeling among the people, in the words of Sarin, is "that the Himalayas, which have protected us through the ages must be protected by us now against the onslaught of any aggressor."

Indeed, India has come a long way in mountaineering in the last ten years. Some eighty expeditions have been organised to peaks of 18,000 or 19,000 feet or more. There have been ten all-women Himalayan expeditions and about fifty mountaineering clubs and associations functioning.

Nehru had few personal friends. Prominent among these was Padmaja, the daughter of Sarojini Naidu and later Governor of West Bengal, who always brought him good cheer. She laughed and joked with him and affectionately called him a "bald-headed old man." Her elder sister, Leelamani, told me more than once that Nehru would have married Padmaja after he lost his wife but for considerations of political expediency.

To Nehru, his image as a democrat and secular being was of the highest importance. Once M. C. Chagla, who was Education Minister in Nehru's Cabinet, and Ali Yavar Jung, now Ambassador in the U.S., conveyed to me their concern and chagrin over the fact that whereas Nehru backed progressive Muslims among the Arabs he lent his ear to Conservative Muslims in India. They saw no reason, for instance, why there should not be a common civil code applicable to all citizens alike. When I asked Nehru why he seemed to have adopted double standards, he replied his friendship with Nasser and other progressive Arab leaders was designed to counter-balance the Conservative Muslim bloc, which stretched from Pakistan to Jordan and posed a threat to India's security and its secularism. But he was hesitant to attempt reforms in the domestic sphere for fear that Muslim obscurantists would raise the cry "Islam in danger."

Gandhi's outlook on life was based on economics. Patel understood that money was a very powerful motivating force. He encouraged capital and bent it to his purpose. Gandhi created an organisational alternative before he started to destroy what existed. Patel mastered the organisation and used whatever instrument was available and reshaped it to suit the need of the hour. Nehru had no experience of organisation. He did not understand economics, nor did he bother to face facts. He wove fantasies round his ideals and believed that somehow his preachings would make the people do the things he wanted.

The Indian people made a hero of Nehru. For ten years, he made them feel as the chosen people whose leader was the moral leader of the world. Indeed, they began to think that India had come full circle to the Vedic age, in which all wisdom was the privilege of the seers of India. Much of the charisma had worn thin towards the closing years of his life. The Chinese attack rudely awakened the people to the harsh reality that they had been living in a world of make-believe. Nevertheless when Nehru passed away, he still enjoyed in the minds and hearts of the Indian people a place which few before him have had—and few ever will.

Book V

1964–69

AFTER NEHRU, WHAT?

INDIA
in
1969

JAMMU and
Srinagar •Leh•
KASHMIR
Jammy
Amritsar• HIMACHAL
•Simla
HARYANA PUNJAB
•Chandigarh
Delhi •Nainital
•Bikaner UTTAR
RAJASTHAN Mathura
•Jaipur Agra Lucknow •Darjeeling
PRADESH SIKKIM BHUTAN
Chitorgarh Allahabad •Patna
Khajuraho Banaras •Gaya
Ahmedabad MADHYA BIHAR Asanol
Rajkot• Bhopal• W.
GUJARAT •Jabalpur Jamshedpur BENGAL
Baroda PRADESH •Calcutta
Diu• Indore
(G.D.and D.) Ajanta •Nagpur •Sambalpur
Daman •Ellora Wardha ORISSA •Bhubaneswar
MAHARASHTRA •Puri
Bombay• Poona
ANDHRA •Visakhapatnam
GOA •Hyderabad
(Goa, Daman PRADESH
and Diu) •Kurnool
N.E.F.A.
ASSAM
•Gauhati NAGALAND
Shillong
MANIPUR
TRIPURA

MYSORE
Bangalore •Madras
Mysore• •Mahabalipuram
LACCADIVE, •Pondicherry
MINICOY and TAMIL NADU
AMINDIVE ISLANDS •Tiruchirapalli
KERALA •Madurai
Thivandrum•

CEYLON

ANDAMAN
and
NICOBAR
ISLANDS

Chapter 1

"BIG LITTLE MAN"

After Nehru what? When Gandhi died, there were at least half a dozen men who could ably lead the party—and the country. But when Nehru passed away, he left behind no second line of command, much less an obvious successor. The Congress confounded the Cassandras, of whom there were not a few. In its hour of greatest trial since 1947, the party closed its ranks to a man, and successfully met the challenge.

In the days of Nehru's declining health, some fostered the legend that Lal Bahadur Shastri was being groomed for succession since the Prime Minister had brought him back into the Government after suffering a stroke at Bhubaneshwar. Others said in the whispering galleries of Delhi politics that the only person Nehru really favoured was his own daughter. Besides, Gulzari Lal Nanda, Home Minister and No. 2 in the Union Cabinet, would not relinquish his pre-emptive right without a struggle. And there was also Morarji Desai, waiting in the wings. His removal from the direct line of succession under the so-called Kamaraj Plan had not dampened his spirits.

Desai, for all his "rigidity," had many loyal adherents in the Congress Parliamentary Party because of his reputation for integrity and administrative ability. Shastri's personal following, on the other hand, was somewhat negative. Few of his supporters were as passionately committed as Desai's were. But Shastri had one big advantage over Desai. Congress President Kamaraj and some of the senior members of the High Command favoured Shastri because they had good relations with him and, what is more, considered him easy to get on with. They considered Desai the stubborn type who would prove difficult as a colleague and might even try to become the all-powerful boss. Desai's views on Hindi were also an obstacle to close co-operation in Kamaraj's opinion. Shastri's views on Hindi were, in fact, stronger than Desai's. However, he had wisely not trodden on any non-Hindi corns.

Indira Gandhi, who was in mourning, was not in the running and

Nanda had hardly any support. Kamaraj played his cards dexterously and, in consultation with like-minded colleagues, evolved the concept of consensus. Under the formula, Kamaraj was to assess the broad opinion in the party and name the candidate enjoying the largest support for unanimous election. Desai was aware of Kamaraj's own views and expressed himself against the formula when the matter came up for discussion at a meeting of the Working Committee and the Congress Chief Ministers. But he was heavily outnumbered. Kamaraj now went ahead with his plan, ascertained the consensus informally on an *ad hoc* basis and named Shastri as the winner. Desai was greatly chagrined and many of his supporters urged him to challenge the consensus and press it to a vote. However, Desai, as a disciplined Gandhian, bowed to the verdict and the party was saved from a threatened split.

Shastri—now the "Big Little Man"—stepped into Nehru's shoes somewhat diffidently. Born in a village and brought up in poverty he typified the common man who had come up the hard way. To be accepted as a compromise candidate was not flattering to his ego. Moreover, he was painfully aware that he lacked Nehru's overpowering personality and the Nehru legend was, as he himself confessed, no easy burden to live with. Among the many handicaps he had to contend with was his feeling that Mrs. Gandhi had been inclined to favour Nanda for the prime ministership. But questioned by me on this point, she explained she was in sympathy only with Nanda's plea that he be allowed to act as Prime Minister a little longer.

Shastri was in broad agreement with Nehru's basic policies. But he wanted to chart a different course, especially in economic matters, without being accused of scuttling the democratic Socialist pattern and non-alignment Nehru had stood for. He was convinced that he understood the people better than Nehru. He had a sense of belonging to the masses, but, doubtful of his own strength, he imposed a large measure of restraint on himself. When Mrs. Pandit castigated him in Parliament for being a "prisoner of indecision," Shastri said to me: "People do not realise that I am up against the Nehru legend."

It was no small matter to shift the emphasis in India's foreign policy. Shastri felt that India's neighbours like Afghanistan, Ceylon, Nepal and Burma had not received the attention they deserved in New Delhi and he set out resolutely to atone for the lapse. Not long after he assumed office, broadcasting from the ramparts of Red Fort on Independence Day, he gave an indication of the inflexible spirit behind his mild exterior. Force would be met with force, he warned Pakistan, whose tone was rapidly acquiring a dangerous belligerency. To its cost, Rawalpindi ignored the warning.

Shastri's style was cramped by the fact that he had for several reasons refrained from making sweeping changes in his Cabinet. One aspect of Cabinet formation that gave Shastri uneasy moments was the question of inducting Indira Gandhi into it. He sounded her through Zakir Husain and discovered that her own choice was the image-building Information and Broadcasting portfolio. He entrusted External Affairs to Swaran Singh, of whose loyalty he had formed a high opinion. For the rest, he was content to go along as best he could.

The Prime Minister's approach to economic problems was pragmatic; he could not reconcile himself to the rigid controls that prevailed. T.T.K., on the contrary, seemed stubbornly opposed to a major liberalisation of policy in commerce and industry. Despite their latent hostility, Shastri kept him in the Cabinet until the eve of his departure for Tashkent when T.T.K. offered his resignation on the ground that his personal integrity had been impugned. Shastri seized the opportunity, refused to accede to T.T.K.'s terms for continuing in the Cabinet and accepted his resignation. It was a bold step, taken despite President Radhakrishnan's advice that he stay his hand until his return from the Tashkent negotiations.

When he became Prime Minister, Shastri suffered from a sense of inadequacy. He was anxious to avoid criticism, and in his desire not to make mistakes he used to assume the responsibility for more than he was capable of handling. Some of the Civil Servants who worked with him found him ill-organised. However, he had a gift for improvisation, of which there is ample evidence. One of his earliest measures was to reorganise the Prime Minister's Secretariat. He did not merely change its staff but invested the men he had carefully picked himself with a much larger degree of responsibility than their predecessors held under Nehru. Shastri, for all his apparent lack of skill in the art of administration, thus created an instrument on which he could rely completely.

Nehru was a demon for work. He took upon himself a workload under which more robust men would have broken down. Shastri, on the other hand, was a man of few words, shy of writing. The large part of the routine he delegated to his lieutenants in the Secretariat. It was apparent he was not attempting to build himself on the Nehru pattern and set out to overcome his limitations in his characteristic way. His powers of observation and gift for absorption stood him in good stead.

It did not take him long to find his feet in Parliament. His speech was somewhat faltering, but his lucidity of mind and outspokenness more than made up for this disability. He impressed on his colleagues the need to be present in Parliament and defend themselves against the assaults of the Opposition. He held himself in reserve to cope with larger conflicts. Nehru's assessment of his Ministers was often faulty and distorted by emotional reflexes. Shastri's, on the other hand, was rooted in down-to-earth realism.

Realism, indeed, was the keynote of his policies. His Socialism was no dogma; it was a faith he was not afraid to adapt to India's peculiar needs. The country's economy was in sore need of revitalisation. To impart to it a new buoyancy and vigour, he intended making the economy freer. Decontrol of cement was his first move in that direction. At the time of his premature death at Tashkent, he had directed his Secretariat to prepare a scheme to reduce public expenditure and taxation and to remove most of the shackles on the economy. He brought to the dialogue with the private sector a refreshing note of cordiality.

Shastri had little understanding of international affairs but this was to a large extent compensated for by his innate shrewdness and common sense. He understood people and the forces that motivated them. He was liked in Washington not merely because he presented the image of a little man standing up resolutely to India's vast problems but even more because he was a realist and his economic and political thinking was acceptable to the Johnson Administration. He knew India needed the economic support of the U.S., and he did not let ideology stand in the way of getting it.

Shastri had a "Privy Council" of his own, but he did his own thinking. He always chewed over his problems and thought a lot before coming to a conclusion. But he devoted attention only to the most urgent ones and neglected others. He was weak in English, but he had a flair for choosing the right expression. He would not accept secretarial drafts using clichés. The changes he made in such drafts had significance and were an improvement on the original. He sensed what the people wanted and he knew how to give it to them.

Here, then, was a man who had begun somewhat shakily but was finding his feet and stretching out with increasing self-confidence towards stability and greatness. The initial misgivings among senior Civil Servants about his capabilities were transformed into warm respect. In Congress parliamentary circles he was being hailed as a man of destiny. His relations with the Congress President too had undergone a subtle change. Owing his success in the leadership contest primarily to Kamaraj, he had initially shown a certain deference to him. But as his stature as Prime Minister grew he established his equality with Kamaraj. The bond between the two did not weaken, but Shastri no longer hesitated to think and act independently. He had definitely arrived.

Shastri's finest hour was, however, yet to come. The soft-spoken man of peace had his greatest political test in the flaming crucible of war. Hostilities with Pakistan, much as he abhorred them, swept him on to an abiding place in the history of our times.

Chapter 2

THE TWENTY-ONE-DAY WAR

(a) INDIA STRIKES BACK

By the time Pakistan forced the twenty-one-day war on us in 1965, India had fortunately learnt the bitter lesson of its military humiliation at the hands of China three years earlier. In October 1961, Army Headquarters had bemoaned the state of our unpreparedness for defence against a large-scale attack. India, it had warned the Government, was in a position to hold neither the Chinese in N.E.F.A. or in Ladakh nor the Pakistanis in the Punjab. We were both out-gunned and out-tanked. But by the middle of 1965 the Army had been nearly doubled and re-equipped with the right type of hardware—thanks to the new overall awareness in the country of defence requirements and the leadership provided by Yeshwantrao Chavan as Defence Minister and General J. N. Chaudhuri, who succeeded General Thapar as Chief of the Army Staff.

In fact, the armed forces had been refashioned into a well-trained force ready to go into action at a moment's notice. This was more than proved when Pakistani armour suddenly erupted in Chhamb–Jaurian sector of Jammu in a calculated move to cut off India's road link with the Kashmir Valley, precipitating an unprecedented crisis. When Chaudhuri reported that the Pakistanis had broken through in strength and that air cover was vital to stop the enemy, Chavan took the advice of Air-Marshal Arjan Singh, Chief of the Air Staff, and immediately ordered the Air Force into action. Within a matter of twenty minutes, our Vampires, intended for the scrap heap, took off for swift retaliation and a catastrophe was averted.

Pakistan, nevertheless, continued its pressure on the sector. Two days before India struck back at the aggressive Pakistanis, I met Shastri at his residence in the evening and expressed the view that the grave military situation called for an immediate counter-attack along the West Pakistan border. He replied in strict confidence that a decision to do so had been taken that very day and an attack on Sialkot and Lahore would follow. The decision followed consultations with senior Civil Servants, who counselled Shastri that there was no alternative if overland communications with Jammu were to be maintained and Kashmir saved from Pakistan conquest. They advised Shastri that Pakistan must be diverted from Kashmir to the defence of Lahore and Sialkot.

Shastri also confided to me that he had encountered unexpected opposition to this course of action from the Minister for External Affairs, Swaran Singh, at a meeting of the Emergency Committee of the Cabinet. While Chavan strongly supported his proposal for a counter-attack, Swaran Singh was worried about the adverse reactions abroad. As the External Affairs Minister remained adamant in spite of the arguments advanced in favour of an offensive, the Cabinet Secretary, Dharma Vira, whispered to Shastri that the meeting be adjourned so that the officials could discuss the issue privately with Swaran Singh. They then told Swaran Singh that if Kashmir fell to the invaders and the Indian troops trapped in the state were compelled to surrender, the Government would be thrown out. This had the required effect. When the Committee met next morning, the Foreign Minister kept silent and a decision was taken without further discussion.

Shastri told me that Chaudhuri, too, did not at first favour attacking Pakistan in reprisal for the infiltration in Kashmir. But when the Pakistani Army started operations along the international border, the military experts took the view that the situation now justified a massive counter-attack. The General Staff did not expect a major Pakistani attack in the Chhamb–Jaurian sector. This was a clear, calculated act of aggression to catch India unawares. Intelligence reports revealed that the Pakistani strategy was to go down the Beas, penetrate the Ferozepur area in the Punjab, capture the road leading northward from Delhi and thus choke the lifeline to Kashmir. Having achieved this, the Pakistanis felt sure they would be able to impose a dictated peace.

The war seemed to prove the common belief in defence circles that Chaudhuri was a lucky general. Pakistan's Pattons could have wiped out the Indian tanks in a confrontation, but the height of the standing crops in the Khem Karan area completely screened our smaller armour, and when the Pattons came within their firing range they proved a sitting target. In many cases, the Pattons got bogged in fields which had been heavily watered. Luck again saved India on the Ferozepur front. The only explanation for the Pakistani Army's failure to make a forward thrust in force there, is that the enemy was either demoralised by the tank disaster at Khem Karan or was poorly served by its intelligence network. For India had no defences worth the name in the region.

Why did the Indian Army fail to take Lahore or Sialkot when these prizes were within its grasp? Civilian intelligence sources had conveyed to New Delhi full information in advance about the fortifications along the Ichhogil canal, built between the border and Lahore. Apparently, military intelligence did not realise the significance of these installations in relation to a counter-thrust. Shastri and Chavan led Parliament to believe that Sialkot and Lahore would be taken, but Shastri told me that when Chaudhuri was asked to take action he replied: "We must move with the caution and wisdom of an elephant. We will take them in God's good time."

Chaudhuri is reckoned in many quarters to have betrayed a measure of hesitancy in the conduct of the hostilities, if not lack of military daring. Indeed, members of the Cabinet's Emergency Committee felt that Chaudhuri had to be egged on to fight. There is an impression that he erred in not marching our armed forces into Sialkot when it was known that all communications from the Pakistan side with this vital stronghold had been cut, and it was believed that the enemy had pulled out of the city. The failure to occupy Sialkot was significant against the background of pronouncements at the highest level.

Defence Minister Chavan had confided to many that he had instructed the Army to press forward and capture both Lahore and Sialkot, and Shastri had expressly stated that he favoured the occupation of Sialkot, though he would be satisfied if Lahore was merely encircled. Why then did Chaudhuri show a seeming reluctance to capture Sialkot and encircle Lahore? His own explanation reportedly was: "I know these politicians. The U.N. will intervene and they will agree to give up all our gains. Why then should I sacrifice my manpower to this end or that? My policy is to inch forward, not to gallop."

There were critics who did not hesitate to say that in similar circumstances General Thimayya would have acted differently. They argued that as a military leader Chaudhuri could not have been unaware of the humiliation and demoralisation that Pakistan

would have suffered had we taken Sialkot. "Timmy" had displayed
courage and dash amidst bursting shells in Kashmir in 1948, and
he had driven the Pakistanis out of Chad Bet, in Kutch, in 1956 by
a bold stroke even while the Cabinet was debating schemes to
accomplish this. Chaudhuri's plans for clearing Kanjarkot in the
same area of Pakistani intruders early in 1965 had, on the other
hand, remained just paper schemes.

(b) THE TASHKENT MEETING

Our troops nevertheless, did well in the Kashmir sector and strategic
Haji Pir, a vital pass across the cease-fire line, was captured. But
before Pakistan could be rolled back farther, U.N. had decisively
intervened. U Thant flew into Pindi and New Delhi and a cease-fire
was brought about. Russia, which by now was anxious to make its
presence felt in the sub-continent, offered its good offices to bring
the two warring countries together and suggested Tashkent as the
venue for talks between Shastri and Ayub. Shastri's first reaction
to the proposal was not favourable and he did not want to go to
Tashkent, as I was told by L. K. Jha, who was then Secretary to
the Prime Minister. But he was finally persuaded to accept Kosygin's
invitation.

At Tashkent, Kosygin argued his case convincingly. He knew the
whole history of the Kashmir affair and was surprisingly well posted
on connected developments, as the Indian delegation found. The
Soviet approach to the Kashmir problem was broadly as follows:
half of Kashmir, containing a fourth of her population, is in the
illegal possession of Pakistan and China. India has three-fourths of
the population with the other half of the state. How could India be
asked in fairness to give up more territory? Pakistan, having tried
all methods, including war, and having failed must accept the *status
quo*. No other basis would produce the conditions for peace and
stability in the sub-continent. Neighbouring China stood for peace
at home and chaos abroad, particularly among her neighbours.
Unless India and Pakistan settled their differences amicably on the
existing *status quo* they would expose themselves to Chinese
machinations or blandishments.

Kosygin wanted both India and Pakistan to renounce war and
seek a solution of the Kashmir problem and other questions across
the conference table. At the same time, he proposed that in accordance with the Security Council's resolution both countries should
withdraw to the positions prior to the conflict. While Ayub was
unwilling to renounce the use of force on the Kashmir issue, Shastri

was unwilling to give up Haji Pir, having categorically told Parliament that "we shall not withdraw from it" since the whole of Kashmir lawfully belonged to India. Under the insistence of the Soviet Premier and having regard to the terms of the U.N. Charter, Ayub after much hesitation agreed to reaffirm the obligation under the Charter and to settle the question only through peaceful means. This change of attitude on Ayub's part made it possible for Shastri, out of deference to world opinion, to agree to withdraw to the pre-conflict positions.

Draft conclusions were then exchanged between Shastri and Ayub at the suggestion of Kosygin. India proposed a no-war pact. Pakistan summarily returned the paper and instead proposed a brief communiqué regarding troop withdrawals only. Two more drafts were exchanged, but neither side found them acceptable as both refused to budge from their respective positions. On the night of 8th January the deadlock was complete. All seemed to be over except the final rites. In fact, Shastri said so in an off-the-record talk with Indian newsmen, including Inder Jit who had accompanied him on behalf of I.N.F.A.

The Soviet Premier was dismayed at the failure of India and Pakistan to agree on a draft since, sitting through the discussions, they had noticed a great deal of common ground between the two sides. But he was not prepared to accept defeat and now asked his Foreign Minister Gromyko to try his hand. Gromyko called on Swaran Singh, his opposite number, at 11 p.m. the same night to plead: "The eyes of the whole world are on us. Some solution must be found." Swaran Singh suggested that it was now up to the Russians to try their hand at producing a neutral draft. The Russians then worked through the night and at 10.30 the following morning, Kosygin called on Shastri and presented to him his first draft incorporating the common ground between the two sides and the principles to which they subscribed. The talks were resurrected and Kosygin went back and forth six times during the day between the villas occupied by Shastri and Ayub and, more or less, finalised the Declaration. One or two small spaces in the draft were left blank. These were filled in at the lunch Ayub had with Shastri on the final day, 10th January, a few hours before the Declaration was signed.

Kosygin shrewdly crossed the principal hurdles presented by India and Pakistan. He persuaded Shastri to agree to India's withdrawal from Haji Pir by arguing that the renunciation of force by Pakistan, which would be underwritten by the U.S.S.R. and the U.N., would facilitate the maintenance of the cease-fire line and contribute to a settlement on a realistic basis. India's refusal to withdraw could create a precedent which Pakistan might exploit to annex some Indian territory at a later date. Ayub was told that as a member of the U.N., Pakistan was already pledged to resolving disputes through peaceful means. He was now only being asked to reaffirm and respect the principles enshrined in the U.N. Charter. At any rate, there could be no Indian withdrawal unless Pakistan renounced the use of force since Shastri had firmly refused to "live from one cease-fire to another cease-fire."

Foreign Minister Bhutto tried to sabotage the agreement by raising all kinds of objections to the Soviet draft. Even after Ayub had, in his own handwriting, agreed to include "non-use of force" in the draft declaration, Bhutto omitted these words from the fair draft sent back by the Pakistanis to the Russians. The Soviets were indignant and decided not to let Bhutto, whom by now they were describing as a "gariachi glava" (hothead), to get away with it. They successfully poured cold water on him by going back directly to Ayub and holding him to his earlier commitment. Bhutto, thereafter, cut a sullen figure at Tashkent. At the glittering ceremony at which the Declaration was signed, those present saw Bhutto quietly rapped by Ayub for blowing smoke rings and conducting himself in a manner which was not in keeping with the dignity demanded by the occasion.

What about Kashmir? Shastri and Ayub met separately more than once in Tashkent. They discussed various matters arising out of the conflict and their talk also turned to Kashmir. But the merits of the issue were not discussed. Each merely explained to the other his difficulties on the question. Kosygin was known to have tried to persuade Ayub to settle for the *status quo* with minor adjustments along the cease-fire line. Ayub referred to this in his talk with Shastri but said that he would not be able to sell the deal to his people. Of interest in this context was his reported plea: "I am not a dictator, as I am made out to be!"

Shastri accepted Kosygin's draft declaration only after he was personally convinced that it was fair and that it constituted a virtual charter for peace between India and Pakistan, and that it was an honourable basis for peaceful coexistence between the two neighbours. He had secured not only the approval of Chavan and Swaran Singh accompanying him but, as was his wont, also confidentially sounded the reaction of some of the Indian newsmen. Shastri, the Little Man of Steel, was not one who could be pressurised. I gathered from Inder Jit, who covered the meet, that at one stage, when Kosygin initially put to Shastri the suggestion of Ayub for a plebiscite in Kashmir, Shastri firmly told him: "Mr. Chairman, you will have to talk to some other Prime Minister, not me." The sudden relaxation that followed several days of strain and high tension, and the emotional reaction to his long-distance talk by telephone with his wife and son brought on Shastri a severe and unexpected heart attack.

In retrospect, India appears to have made one mistake. She should not have taken for granted that Ayub would honour the agreement. She should have delayed the withdrawal of troops until he had normalised relations and returned the Indian property he had seized. Having got the Indian troops out and having got the right for Pakistani planes to fly over India, he refused to fulfil the other clauses of the agreement unless India discussed Kashmir. The plain fact was that the Pakistani leaders feared that Pakistan would cease to exist if she normalised relations with India.

The Nawab of Kalabagh was Governor of West Pakistan when war with India was discussed at a Cabinet meeting. According to the account given to me by our High Commissioner in Pakistan the Nawab told the President: "Ayub, do not listen to Bhutto. His father and grandfather did not handle a sword or gun. I warn you that if you attack India you will face reverse." Kalabagh did not agree with Ayub's policy. He did not accept the view that if there was peace with India Pakistan would lose her justification for existing. He believed that both countries would benefit if they got together. He was removed from the governorship not long after and later shot dead by his son.

Just before the war, Bhutto told India's High Commissioner, who had called on him: "You know, we are not afraid of India. It is a dying nation. Its internal tentacles are now spreading and the country will break up and have chaos. India has no stability." The High Commissioner replied: "Mr. Foreign Minister, if India were to base its policy on the assumption that Pakistan was breaking up it would be foolish, and vice versa." The Bhutto group had planned the infiltration of Kashmir over a long period. They were confident that by this method they would ultimately succeed in annexing the Valley. When things went wrong Bhutto lost face and had to go.

The news of Shastri's premature death stunned the nation. The courage with which he had hit back at Pakistan had made the Little Man India's biggest hero overnight. Fate was cruel. Barely twenty months after Nehru passed away, India found itself, once again, forced to look for another leader.

Chapter 3

A WOMAN LEADS

(a) NOVITIATE

When Indira took the oath of office as Prime Minister after Shastri, she did so as Indira Nehru-Gandhi. In a tradition-bound society, she was not deliberately making a gesture of unusual daring. She was only being correct in taking her full name as registered in the electoral list. But to many present it reflected in India's feudal world an instinctive acceptance of the fact that she owed her exalted position to being Jawaharlal Nehru's only child. To say so is not by any means to belittle her own very considerable talents. Yet few will deny that had it not been for her paternity, she would hardly have prevailed in the struggle for power.

Up to the mid-fifties, Indira had little experience of party work. But once U.N. Dhebar Congress President nominated her to the Working Committee, she started functioning energetically. She visited the South and Bombay to assess the reactions to the Ali Report on states reorganisation and, in the course of speeches, took a highly unorthodox line on party matters. An individual might rise to towering heights, she said, but he was essentially built through the party. In Russia, she added, the Communist Party kept a close watch on the Government and sacked Ministers if they failed. "The sooner we do so in India the better."

This view ran counter to Nehru's theory of parliamentary government under which the parliamentary wing of the party must be free from the control of the organisational wing. Kripalani resigned from the Congress presidentship on this issue in 1947 and later, made the famous statement in which he said: "Corruption, nepotism and favouritism start from the top and not from the bottom. Nehru is not a model of selflessness but on occasions he gives evidence of the spell cast on him by Gandhian ideas." But Indira's speeches caused few political ripples.

Nehru, no doubt, was grooming her for succession. This became an open secret when at Nagpur she was suddenly named the next Congress President after S. Nijalingappa had already been informally chosen for the honour. I asked Indira to recall the happenings at Nagpur. She said she did not know that the presidentship had been offered to Nijalingappa. She had told her father she did not want the post, but she accepted it when Dhebar told her that her refusal would amount to a confession she could not make a success of it. Her term as Congress President, political circles recognised, was a prelude to greater honours. As the party leader, she persuaded her father to split composite Bombay into separate linguistic States of Maharashtra and Gujarat. Moreover, she got the Centre to dismiss the first Communist Ministry in Kerala for its anti-democratic and unconstitutional policies.

There was more to Nehru's grooming of his daughter than these promotions in the Congress hierarchy. When following the Chinese attack he found himself absorbed in handling the political crisis, he told Union Ministers and Chief Ministers to talk to Indira to relay their problems to him. Indira told him about these things at mealtime or when he retired to his room at night. Most Central and State leaders, especially the aspirants to the "throne," resented this and privately attacked Nehru for forcing them to pay court to his daughter. "We have made sacrifices and worked our way up; who is she?" they bitterly complained. But Nehru was all-powerful and there was nothing they could do about it.

Lal Bahadur Shastri was quick to see the opportunities this arrangement presented. Sometimes, he sat patiently in an anteroom on the ground floor of the Prime Minister's house for as much as an hour until Indira was ready to see him. He was prompt in answering her summons and mostly depended on her to transmit whatever he had to sell to Nehru. Indira, on her side, was not slow to appreciate Shastri's worth and exhibition of devotion to her father. She told me it was at her suggestion that Nehru recalled him to the Cabinet as Minister Without Portfolio. Indeed, when Nehru suffered the stroke which led to his death, the first person Indira called to his side was Shastri.

Nehru, for his part, had his own reasons for bringing back Shastri into the Government. When he suddenly fell ill after having earlier remarked that his health was "disgustingly good," Nehru realised that the task of building up Indira politically could not be completed in his lifetime. Therefore, he wanted a successor whom he trusted and who would treat Indira well. Shastri fitted the role eminently by his general conduct and his attitude towards Indira. As a person very close to Nehru at the time told me: "That is why he brought in the Kamaraj Plan and later built up Shastri."

Whether Indira was politically ripe enough to succeed her father

at the time of his death is beside the point. She herself disclaims that
she had ambitions in that direction and considered Shastri the best
man for the job. Anyway, nobody offered Indira the prime ministership at that time although Shastri did call on her. D. P. Mishra,
the Madhya Pradesh Chief Minister who eighteen months later
was to play a notable part in her elevation as head of Government,
alone urged her to bid for the office, enlisting Morarji Desai's
support with the inducement of the post of Deputy Prime Minister.
Desai was sounded, but would not go along with it. He told Mishra he
had no reason to prefer Indira to Shastri. However, on becoming Prime
Minister, Shastri persuaded her to join his Cabinet. He told me he did
it as a tribute to Nehru's memory. Asked by me she said she had
agreed believing that her presence would give stability to the Ministry.

Shastri's attitude towards Indira changed before long. Indira
had hoped that he would consult her on matters of State. But he
was cold to her. Indeed, when Shastri fell ill just before the Common-
weath Prime Ministers' Conference in 1965 and had to postpone his
departure for London, Indira called on him to inquire about his
health, but like others she was not allowed to see him. In fact, her
meetings with Shastri were so few and far between that she got the
impression that he was deliberately avoiding her. He was frank
enough to indicate to me that he had developed a feeling of inferiority in relation to her. He felt he could build up his public
image effectively only if he showed he was not dependent on her.
Before Shastri went to Tashkent, it was even whispered among the
informed people that Indira might be offered High Commissioner-
ship in Britain, where her two sons were then studying.

(b) TESTING TIME

When Shastri died, the struggle for succession, averted in 1964 by
Kamaraj's "consensus" formula, was not to be similarly warded off.
Desai, fitted by experience and standing in the party hierarchy for
the prime ministership was determined to resist all attempts to get
him to withdraw from a contest. The Congress President flew to Delhi
from Madras with Indira Gandhi's name in his pocket; he preferred
her to Desai for the same reasons as Shastri. Indira's willingness to
contest was hedged in by reservations in the early stages. But, as
the other likely candidates faded into the background, she was not
averse to a trial of strength. To have Kamaraj on her side was a
decisive advantage and when a majority of Chief Ministers entered
the lists in her favour everything was over except the counting of
votes.

The controversy over whether the Congress President and the Chief Ministers should have been allowed to influence a choice that by rights was exclusively that of the Congress Parliamentary Party has never been satisfactorily resolved. It has been argued that had the choice of the Congress M.P.s been unfettered Desai might have had an edge over his rival. As things turned out, Mrs. Gandhi climbed to power on the broad shoulders of Kamaraj, Chavan and Mishra. Jagjivan Ram, himself a candidate at one time, and then reckoned to favour Desai, swung his considerable following to the side of Mrs. Gandhi once her victory seemed certain. Desai's showing in the party poll was not unimpressive (169 votes as against 355) and, unbowed in defeat, he pledged support to the new leader. Efforts to persuade him to join the Cabinet proved unavailing. Mrs. Gandhi, on her side, was far from enthusiastic about offering him a position in it.

Mrs. Gandhi's first term as Prime Minister proved a bed of thorns. The economy was slithering downward, our foreign exchange resources were dwindling rapidly, the import of essential goods had to be severely restricted and the export programme was beginning to show alarming signs of sluggishness. In international affairs, the aftermath of the Indo–Pakistani conflict was not conducive to tranquillity. Peking's hostility towards India acquired a sharper edge following its new understanding with Pakistan. The Western powers were not averse to rearming Pindi even as they turned their faces against our request for similar help. And as though these difficulties were not enough, there was the spectre of famine in Bihar, eastern Uttar Pradesh and several other areas of the country where a second successive year of drought had played havoc.

Early in her stewardship, Mrs. Gandhi appeared resolved to establish her capacity for independent thinking and quick decisions. But she might have made a better start had she shown greater wisdom in the selection of her Cabinet colleagues. Obviously, she did not think highly of Nanda, but was loth to ease him out of office. What made matters worse was the feeling that the Prime Minister was leaning somewhat too heavily on a small group around her—the "Kitchen Cabinet" as it came to be known. Prominent in this circle of the select were Food Minister Subramaniam, Asoka Mehta and Dinesh Singh, an old family friend. Though Chavan enjoyed Mrs. Gandhi's confidence, he was not actively associated with the "inner confabulations."

One unfortunate consequence of the line Indira adopted was her growing estrangement from Kamaraj. True, Shastri had gradually asserted a certain degree of independence in relation to the Congress

President, but Kamaraj found little to take exception to because he recognised the basic soundness of Shastri's policies. But insofar as Indira was concerned Kamaraj, before long, started expressing his disillusionment with her performance. The gulf between the two suddenly widened when the Government decided to devalue the rupee. The rights and wrongs of devaluation apart, the impression gained ground that this step had been taken under pressure from Washinton. Kamaraj was unhappy and so also some of Indira's Cabinet colleagues and a few senior Congress M.P.s, among them Commerce Minister Manubhai Shah and Morarji Desai.

With the approach of the general election, Mrs. Gandhi might have had reason to view her prospects for a second term of office with misgivings. Nevertheless, she appeared to hold one strong trump—the general belief that as Nehru's daughter she was a vote-catcher. She and her principal supporters also played on this theme by stating that the people wanted her.

(c) A COMPROMISE

The near-debacle that overtook the Congress in the general election of February 1967, the defeat of party candidates in Delhi and its poor showing in U.P., her home state, showed that she lacked her father's charisma. The party's rout in Kerala and Madras was complete. In Bengal, it stood little chance of being able to form a government, in Orissa even less. Bihar had been as good as lost to a combined Opposition. The situation in Rajasthan was precarious; the Punjab was lost. The only states that the Congress had retained firmly in its grasp were Assam, Maharashtra, Andhra Pradesh, Mysore, Himachal Pradesh and, for the time being, Haryana and Madhya Pradesh.

The parliamentary elections were less unflattering to the Congress, but the sharp drop in its majority in the Lok Sabha from 369 in a House of 502 to 285 in a House of 520 caused a flutter in the higher echelons of the party. The situation had changed vastly in a year when the Congress Parliamentary Party again addressed itself to the business of electing a leader. The Congress President, who had himself bitten the dust in his home state of Madras, was not in a position to exert the same decisive influence as in January 1966. Nor were the State Chief Ministers and party bosses better off. Moreover, the pattern of post-election defections in the states was a portent that could not be ignored. Should this be repeated at the Centre, the stability of the Union Government would be in jeopardy.

Mrs. Gandhi made no secret of her firm determination to stand for re-election and, on the other side, Desai was strongly backed. The contest this time seemed to be more evenly balanced. Kamaraj was disillusioned with Indira and, privately, even described himself "a sinner" for having helped her to reach the summit. His former antipathy to Desai had been largely overcome and one heard talk of a "meeting of minds." Among other senior Congress leaders, too, one sensed disenchantment with Indira. It was freely said that Civil Servants and competent political observers favoured a change not because of hostility to Mrs. Gandhi as a person but because of the mounting desire for a strong leader in the country's hour of crisis.

Kamaraj and his colleagues now toyed with the idea of making Desai the new Prime Minister. The Congress President felt that if he and his colleagues, including Atulya Ghosh and S. K. Patil, came out openly for Desai they could get him a majority in a straight contest. They counted on Mysore, Madras, Kerala and Rajasthan to go with them, and so also C. B. Gupta, party boss in U.P., and D. P. Mishra. The Andhra votes would have been split. Soon, however, Kamaraj gave up this line as he feared that a contest for prime ministership might weaken the organisation, which was already reeling from the effects of its electoral reverses. Added to this was the rumour that some forty of Indira's "solid supporters" might cross the floor in case she was not re-elected.

The Congress President felt that that might precipitate· a crisis and force a premature general election. He wanted the Congress to rule for at least two years and produce some tangible gains before going back to the electorate. It was, therefore, decided that the solidarity of the party must be preserved and the only solution that appeared feasible was to bring Mrs. Gandhi and Desai together. As Mishra saw it, Desai, for all his "rigidity," might be won over by a promise of deputy prime ministership. He was too loyal a Congressman to want to break up the party. Mishra's counsel found ready acceptance. Kamaraj thought likewise, and so did other senior Congressmen when it was argued that they should not hesitate to subordinate their own feelings to the country's paramount interests.

Eleventh-hour negotiations were now set in train to resolve the stalemate. Mrs. Gandhi's "allergy" to Desai was overcome, and equally Desai's unyielding refusal to accept her as his leader. Desai had to be content with Finance, much as he might have preferred Home as more in keeping with the official status accorded to him under the compromise. But Mrs. Gandhi would not hear of moving Chavan, who was the first among the top leaders to come out for

Indira's re-election. Desai conceded that he could enjoy only such rights as the Prime Minister allowed him. Mrs. Gandhi did not take long to find her feet in the new equilibrium of forces.

Indira had three choices when she became Prime Minister, as I ventured to suggest to her at a meeting. She could have made peace with the Old Guard, following the Indian saying: "If the ruler is old, he should have young counsellors; if he is young, he should have wise counsellors." She could follow the footsteps of her father and act as the tribune of the people, above party and above all else. She could have made herself the leader of the new generation and, appealing to the youth, she could have worked for social transformation to take India into the modern age.

She chose the second course—as a chip of the old block and because she had received her training in politics directly from her father. Once re-elected leader, she started ignoring the Old Guard in the belief that her strength lay in keeping the political reins tightly in her hands and operating the party machine with the power and prestige that prime ministership gave her. In selecting her Council of Ministers, she exercised a measure of independence. Again, at an early date, she clearly indicated that she would look to her "Kitchen Cabinet" and special secretariat for guidance in matters of high policy and distribution of patronage. This brought her into clash with the Old Guard and even her strong supporter Home Minister Chavan, who felt unhappy about her style of work.

By the middle of 1967, Indira set out to cut the Old Guard to size with a view to eliminating its members one by one. Kamaraj's second term as Congress President was coming to a close and it was whispered that she was flirting with the idea of following in her father's footsteps and combining the prime ministership with the leadership of the Congress for a time. But the proposal was dropped when all except those very close to her frowned upon it. Indira instead decided to get somebody more friendly to head the organisation. She first thought of Dhebar, who had helped her up the political ladder, and then plumped for Nanda. When the Old Guard backed Bombay's S. K. Patil and seemed poised to win a decisive victory. Nanda was dropped and an unwilling Nijalingappa, Chief Minister of Mysore and a friend of Kamaraj, was pushed on to the *gaddi* as a "compromise" candidate.

Nijalingappa started well in his new prestigious post, which came to him a decade after he had been almost chosen for the honour at the Nagpur Congress. As a Gandhian, he was clear about his role and responsibility. Much needed to be done to consolidate freedom and bring economic emancipation to people. He realised that the country could not afford the luxury of a divided Congress leadership and decided to bring Indira and the Old Guard together. However, he, too, found himself ignored by the Prime Minister and within a few weeks the struggle for power in the higher echelon was again on. At the Hyderabad session of the Congress in January 1968, the Old Guard successfully outmanoeuvred and isolated her by bagging six of the seven elected seats in the Working Committee. The seventh went to her supporter, C. Subramaniam, but only after he had secured the blessing of Kamaraj.

Indira is fighting on two fronts. The Old Guard would if it could, dislodge her. The tradition-bound common people keep questioning the capacity of "a mere woman" to run a government, which they feel is "a man's job." Indira has so far managed to stay afloat. She has a tremendous knack for playing politics ("in fact, better than her father," as a prominent member of the Old Guard said to me). But in the bargain most of the time of the Congress leadership is taken up in political manoeuvres and counter manoeuvres. By the end of 1968, the spirit of sacrifice and service which was the hallmark of Congressmen before independence had given place to a naked struggle for power. India's vast problems of stability and progress took a back seat.

Chapter 4

DEMOCRACY ON TRIAL

(a) HUSAIN PRESIDENT

The general election of 1967 marked a new phase in the development of the democratic system in India. There was a wave of disillusionment throughout the country over the mismanagement of affairs by the Congress Party. This anti-Congress sentiment was so strong that if another all–India party with a proper organisation and a clear-cut platform had been in the field it would have easily cashed in on it. The people wanted to "throw out the scoundrels."

I met Jaya Prakash Narayan well ahead of the elections and recalled Gandhi's idea of establishing an organisation of respected public men who would certify the integrity and ability of all candidates for election and thus help cleanse public life of the corruption born of the spoils system. I suggested that Vinoba Bhave and he, with their Shanti Sena (Peace Corps) and Sarvodaya workers, had enough manpower at their command to organise an alternative to the Congress. J.P. suggested that I also talk to Bhave, but I replied that if the idea appealed to him he should sell it to Bhave. Nothing came of it. J.P. told me later that electioneering required much money and it was not possible for Bhave and him to organise an electoral front.

The Congress entered the election battle in the winter of 1967 against parties which claimed to be national but were really regional. The result was that whereas the Congress received a battering in half the sixteen states it emerged with a reduced but safe majority at the Centre. The electorate showed maturity by asking the anti-Congress forces to show results in the states before entrusting them with the management of the country's affairs at the Centre. This was clear from the fact that many voters who supported non-Congress candidates for the State Assemblies, cast their votes for the Lok Sabha in favour of the Congress.

The Congress High Command decided to let non-Congress United Fronts form governments in those states where the Congress had emerged as the single largest party and could have retained power by forming coalitions. This caused much heartburning among the State Congress legislators who apprehended that power might be exploited by their opponents to weaken the party by tempting members to defect and join them. Defections of two types occurred. In Haryana, U.P. and Madhya Pradesh, Congress defections led to the fall of the Ministries, while in West Bengal and Bihar, where the Congress was in Opposition, they caused disarray among the ruling party members.

Although marked by a great deal of political confusion, the post-election scene saw at least one of Gandhi's many wishes fulfilled. Bapu had looked forward to the day when a predominantly Hindu India would elect a Muslim or a Harijan as its President. This dream came true when Zakir Husain, sponsored by the Congress, was voted President after defeating K. Subba Rao, the candidate of the combined Opposition. But Husain was not chosen on the basis of communal considerations. He was chosen because of the distinction and success with which he had held the office of Vice-President and the patriotic and non-partisan way in which he had conducted himself. Mrs. Gandhi had felt uncomfortable with Radhakrishnan who, she feared, might one day exercise the inherent and undefined powers of the President to dismiss the Ministry and assume control of the nation's affairs. She did not favour a second term for Radhakrishnan and in consultation with Desai boldly sponsored Husain's candidature. The move received moral strength when Desai insisted that the Congress show its disapproval of the manner in which Subba Rao had made the office of Chief Justice of India a subject of controversy by agreeing to resign and stand for election.

Husain had gone through the apprenticeship the office required. As Vice-Chancellor of the Muslim University at Aligarh, he had handled for a decade the very difficult and delicate task of introducing a whiff of nationalism into its stifling communal atmosphere. He had grasped the significance of the new order as a member of the advisory committee of the Chief Commissioner of Delhi when the capital was settling down to ordered life after its post-partition bloodbath. The governorship of Bihar was offered to him by Nehru while he was travelling in Europe and he accepted it. The vice-presidentship, too, came to him unexpectedly. Only a day before he was sounded by Nehru, he had returned from the Prime Minister's confidante, Padmaja Naidu, that Mrs. Pandit would be put up for the post.

How did the top Congress leaders otherwise discharge their responsibilities in the face of the electoral rebuff in 1967? After her election as Prime Minister in 1966, Mrs. Gandhi wanted to do better than her father and her predecessor. She remembered her aunt's barbed shaft that Shastri was "a prisoner of indecision" and the charge against her father of sweeping difficult issues under the carpet. Her first important political moves were the further partitioning of the Punjab to create a state with a Sikh majority and devaluation of the rupee.

But she did these things without adequate planning. She failed to cash in on devaluation because the necessary follow-up measures were not taken and the substantial help promised by Washington as a "reward" was not pressed for. She could have extracted a price from Sant Fateh Singh who had threatened self-immolation and whose followers were only too keen to save him from this fate. Instead, he got his state on a platter and asked for more at the cost of Haryana and Himachal Pradesh, the two other parties directly concerned.

The devaluation debacle caused two results: first, the question of an official link language was put in deep freeze; secondly, the size of the Fourth Plan was not finalised even by April 1969—three years after it was scheduled to be launched. Mrs. Gandhi showed commendable firmness, however, in dealing with Sheikh Abdullah and on the vital question of signing the nuclear Non-Proliferation Treaty. She released Abdullah from jail in a bid to normalise the

situation in Kashmir and strongly backed Chief Minister Sadiq in
the ensuing confrontation. She has refused to sign the N.P.T. and
defied thereby both Moscow and Washington.

Before many months had elapsed, the United Front Governments
toppled under the weight of their internal contradiction and six
states came under President's rule. As a tour of West Bengal, Bihar
and U.P. in July–August, 1968 showed the people wanted good,
stable government. This may not be possible so long as India is
plagued with a multiplicity of parties. As matters stand, the polarisation of political forces seems a distant cry and the fragmentation
that is taking place gives rise to the fear that democracy is on the
way out. Whether this is the fault of the Constitution in not providing
for an irremovable executive on a fixed tenure or due to the failure
of the politician to develop the required sense of responsibility, the
fact is that the parliamentary system patterned on Westminster has
lost its original shape and acquired a certain Indianness.

(b) CRUCIAL ISSUES

In the final analysis, any government at the Centre will, as of today,
be judged in terms of how it tackles the two issues on whose solution
depends the stability of the Indian Union. These are: the Centre-
State relations and Kashmir.

Sheikh Abdullah has been hoping that somehow New Delhi will
be constrained to make Kashmir independent. But this is a pipe
dream. Twice India has shed blood for the defence of Kashmir and
no government that alters the existing status of the state can
survive the political upheaval such a decision would cause. History
cannot be unwritten or the good work done in regard to the Kashmir
issue by three politicians and one Civil Servant wished away. Of the
politicians the most notable was Rafi Ahmed Kidwai, who took
courage in both hands and ousted Abdullah from power. New Delhi
had learned from its intelligence sources that the Sheikh was preparing to declare for independence. I was taken into confidence by
Rafi, who planned the coup and asked me to leave by a plane that
would take me into Srinagar to report on the event. But when Rafi
learned that Mridula Sarabhai, a friend of the Sheikh and a confidante of Nehru, was also booked by the same plane the flight was
cancelled on the pretext that the airfield in Srinagar was red. I
reached it a day later and gathered from an American that the secret
talks between Abdullah and some intermediaries from the U.S. had
broken down because he wanted to be a "hereditary sultan" while

the negotiators maintained that they could sell to the U.S. Congress only life presidency, not a sultanate!

Pant and Gulzari Lal Nanda gave the next two crucial turns to history. Pant visited Srinagar and declared at a public meeting that India was no longer committed to a plebiscite in view of the changed circumstances. Nanda put through the scheme for further integration of the state with the Union.

Nehru had told the people of Kashmir that Section 370 of the Constitution, which provided for special relations with Kashmir, would be gradually eroded. But it was given to a Civil Servant, Shankar Prasad, who was Secretary for Kashmir Affairs for nearly a decade, to erode it effectively. He did this adroitly in the crisis that erupted following the removal of the sacred hair of the Holy Prophet from a Srinagar mosque. The then State Government fell and G. M. Sadiq, one of Abdullah's principal aides at one time and the President of the Constituent Assembly of Kashmir when Abdullah was Prime Minister, was called upon to form the Government. Bakshi Ghulam Mohd, who stepped down from prime ministership under the Kamaraj Plan, was at loggerheads with Sadiq and set about canvassing a motion of no confidence. The situation was too delicate to permit politicking and Bakshi was arrested at night and the move quashed.

The Sadiq Ministry thereafter unanimously decided to request the Government of India to extend to Jammu and Kashmir the provisions of the Indian Constitution relating to the appointment of governors and the establishment of President's Rule in case the administration broke down. Earlier, the Sadr-i-Riyasat (Head of State) could take over the state's administration but his action was subject to approval by the legislature. These provisions put Kashmir on a par with the other states. Although Home Minister Nanda was annoyed that Shastri had, in approving Shankar Prasad's quick move, by-passed him, he pushed the matter with zeal and got the President's order sanctioning the amendment through within a month. (The Pakistanis contend that they unleashed the war with India in 1965 because of these changes, which cut the ground under the feet of Abdullah and strengthened India's plea that Kashmir was a domestic problem.)

Abdullah must now either wait on events or take to the barricades. But neither alternative seems feasible in the circumstances. Abdullah knows Kashmir can retain her personality in India, where the existence of several other sub-nationalities will safeguard their identity. If he joins Pakistan, his people will be swallowed by the Punjabi Muslims. I had talks spreading over six hours with him and his principal lieutenant, Mirza Afzal Beg, in May 1968 and these led me to the conclusion that he wants an honourable way of re-entry into India, if possible through special relations in which the Valley would enjoy more autonomy than the other parts of India.

The Sheikh is not alone in entertaining this desire. The late E. N Annadurai, then DMK Chief Minister of Madras, and Namboodiri-pad, the Marxist Chief Minister of Kerala, expressed similar opinions. My talks with them in the last quarter of 1967 threw interesting light on the issue of Centre-state relations. Both wanted the Centre to shed many of its powers and to confine itself to external affairs, defence, communications and international commerce. Annadurai wanted the Lok Sabha to be an indirectly elected Council of States in which each state would be equally represented. He said Nehru had the stature and the authority to make Hindi the link language but did not do it. After him the Congress had no leader of stature to make Hindi replace English.

Centre-state relations came under increasing strain, following the mid-term poll of February 1969 and the landslide victory of the Marxists in West Bengal. The Congress-governed states, too, started protesting against having to run for sanction of even small projects to a "bureaucratic and ineffective Centre," as a young Chief Minister complained. But the Marxists have raised basic issues: they have questioned even the right of the Union Government to post its Central Reserve Police in West Bengal and its own Security force to protect Central plants and establishments. Earlier, they demanded the withdrawal of the Governor and suggested a panel of names to the Centre for its selection of a successor, which the latter ignored. Indira Gandhi has agreed to have a fresh look at the Centre-state relations, but as she told a group of Editors in March 1969: "The Marxists may clamour for greater autonomy for the states today. Should they come to power at the Centre, there would be no scope for such demands. The Centre has clearly to be strong."

Of interest in this context is the remarkable fact that three Chief Justices of the Supreme Court felt it necessary to express themselves strongly in favour of a unitary form of Government as best suited to Indian conditions. Mehr Chand Mahajan virtually carried on a crusade in this regard after his term as Chief Justice. S. R. Das expressed a similar view following his retirement. The present Chief Justice, M. Hidayatullah, also pleaded in favour of a unitary form of Government in a Feroze Gandhi Memorial lecture. Echoing the growing feelings of the intelligentsia, he said that a unitary

Government at the Centre was essential to prevent disintegration and Balkanisation of the country through regional pulls and pressures.

Chapter 5

INDIA COUNTS

How did the world view India after Nehru? I girdled the globe again in the summer of 1967, accompanied by my wife, after a gap of about eight years. My visit took me this time to fourteen capitals—Bangkok, Saigon, Manila, Tokyo, Mexico, Washington, Ottawa, London, Paris, Bonn, Rome, Vienna, Moscow, and Kabul. Luck was on my side and I was able to meet almost all the heads of Government including President Johnson and Prime Minister Sato. I also met U Thant and Robert McNamara, the U.S. Secretary for Defence and now President of the World Bank, and other top people. Chairman Kosygin was away on a holiday when I arrived in Moscow. However, I got an unexpected opportunity of a brief talk with him at the banquet given by Mrs. Gandhi in his honour in New Delhi on 25th January, 1968.

Although there was unqualified admiration for the way we had smoothly resolved the question of succession after Nehru and again after Shastri, India's image had shrunk further. Nevertheless, I returned home with the clear impression that India counts and the world at large is keenly interested in our welfare and progress. India matters to the world because she holds the balance between the two Super Powers, America and Russia, between the Soviet Union and China, between China and America, between Asia and the West, between the haves and the have-nots and between peace and orderly progress on the one hand and war and disruption on the other. At the same time, the future of the Indian sub-continent is of the greatest consequence to the stability of Asia.

The world wants to see India make good economically and keep politically stable. The fourteen capitals were not concerned with ideological issues. They would like to see our people get down to business and give up their anti-work and anti-productivity attitude. Food production must get priority and the population stabilised by the end of the century at 750 million against 550 million at present. India was considered pivotal to the security of Asia. New Delhi, it was felt, must build up relations with South-East Asia and especially with Japan. By a curious coincidence Washington, Moscow and Tokyo expressed the common view that India would take fifteen years to make good and count in world and regional affairs.

The first halt was at Bangkok, which had become a miniature Tokyo since our last visit. A talk with tne Deputy Prime Minister and with Prince Dani, an elder statesman, and with leading journalists made it clear that the military junta ran the country and that the aristocracy did not quite relish Thailand's total commitment to the U.S. The country's economy was sound and its élite was waiting on events, deeply concerned about the outcome of the conflict in Vietnam.

My visit to Saigon was very revealing. I inquired there how we had lost our standing in Hanoi, for our first Consul-General had been very well received by the North Vietnamese leaders and had been entertained by President Ho Chi-minh and had called on him several times. I learned that the climate changed when the Chairman of the International Control Commission, G. Parthasarthi, reported that there had been infiltrations from North Vietnam to South Vietnam to subvert the regime. Ho protested to New Delhi that the Vietnamese were one people and there could not be infiltration within their own territory. Nehru's reply to Ho's letter was stiff and added that he had to state the truth even if it was unpleasant or irritating to a friend. From then on Ho thought India unfriendly.

There was, of course, a very definite clash of views between the Americans, South Vietnamese and the diplomatic colony. I met General Nguyen Van Thieu, now the Chief of State. He was quite definite that there would be no military victory and that one could not win a guerrilla war with conventional weapons. The real fight was on the political and economic fronts. He opposed Japan trading with China and having the best of both worlds. Diplomats who surveyed the South Vietnamese scene objectively felt that the people did not have their heart in the war. The people of the North were more industrious, brainy and hardy, while those of the South were pleasure-loving and indolent.

President Marcos of the Philippines is a very intelligent man full of ideas about laying the groundwork for his country's progress and for a balance of power which would protect the region from Chinese attempts at domination. But the President's close associates and Filipino newspapermen told me in Manila that he was not good at implementing his ideas. When I met him, about fifty of his supporters were in the room cashing in on their support in his election.

Ex-President Garcia said Philippine relations with India were at first friendly. But they soon began to cool. The first cause of irritation was when Krishna Menon referred to General Carlos Romulo, the Philippines representative in the U.N., as an "American boy." The second incident was when our Ambassador in Manila, M. R. A. Baig, told a Western journalist that the Philippines were under American domination. The Philippines Press attacked Baig and the Philippines Government demanded his recall. The third incident occurred at Bandung, when Indian spokesmen described the Philippines as a camp follower of the U.S. and Romulo was called an "American spy."

The Filipinos believe that the non-Communist nations of Asia should get together to prevent Chinese domination of the continent. This implies co-operation among them, but at the same time they do not want another taste of Japanese "co-prosperity."

The impression I formed by talking to diplomats of other countries posted in Manila was that the realities of life in the Philippines were very different from the picture painted by leading politicians. The country reeked with corruption and there was no proper administration, they said. Americans and people of Spanish descent form the richer classes. The middle rung is filled by Chinese traders. The real Filipino only runs eating houses and small stores or is a labourer or peasant.

In Tokyo, I had talks with Premier Sato, Foreign Minister Miki and Foreign Vice-Minister Ushiba. We reviewed Indo–Japanese relations since 1947. They recognised that India had a great potential, but as matters stood Japanese security depended on the pact with the U.S. This situation would continue for the foreseeable future. They understood that China wanted to isolate India and tempt Japan with trade, but the security of Asia lay in the smaller nations being politically stable and economically viable and India and Japan being industrially strong.

Japanese bankers and industrialists whom I met felt that India had over-industrialised herself and must build up agriculture first. I met Dr. Matsudaira, a former Ambassador to India, and newspapermen who spoke without inhibitions. Some of them confessed that their countrymen were again becoming arrogant and treating other Asians with contempt. They had revived the idea of glory through co-prosperity and thought they could trade with China and be under the U.S. umbrella at the same time and make the best of both worlds.

I was told by the Editor of the *Japan Times* that the image of India had shrunk since Nehru's death and that India did not count today in Asian affairs. Japan would consider India an important factor in Asia when it stood on its own feet. At the back of the mind of most Japanese was the hope that India and Japan would be strong enough to fill the power vacuum in Asia in fifteen years.

A friendly ex-Ambassador of Japan said Nehru had "ruined India" by following policies which created an oversize image of India on the world stage which could not be sustained by internal realities. The Japanese bureaucrat who runs the country as does his French counterpart in France thinks India is a bottomless pit where aid is wasted until she puts her economy right.

Sato told me that Japan and India, two principal nations of Asia, must work together. The balance of power in Asia, other Japanese leaders said, would have to be found by Asians, and Japan and India were important countries for this purpose. The idea of a South-East Asian pact was only preparatory to total regional co-operation and there was no intention of keeping India out. Japan did not have enough resources to help the other states of the region to the extent they required. India, I told them, would join the South-East Asian community as a donor and not as a recipient.

I visited Mexico after Japan and met the Foreign Minister and the head of the Foreign Department and men in public life and in the universities. The impression I got was that just as Asia had a resurgence after the First World War and Africa after the second, there would be a Latin American resurgence by the end of the century. Mexicans expect India to cultivate close ties with this region. The Foreign Minister of Brazil, whom I met in Delhi early in 1968, said that what India was to Asia, Brazil was to Latin America.

The Mexicans are very sensitive about their relations with the U.S. They want the Latin Americans to stand on their own legs and are accordingly promoting a common economic market in Central America. Mexican intellectuals respect India's civilisation.

The official Mexican view of India is that it is a land of spiritual values. Gandhi and Nehru symbolised that. It is recognised that the Indian stand on non-violence had to be modified when China attacked and military preparedness had to be undertaken at the cost of economic development. India is also recognised as a great force for peace. India's basic image remains what it was and her current economic difficulties are regarded as a passing phase.

Chapter 6

INDIA AND THE UNITED STATES

(a) RELATIONS IN RETROSPECT

One of the more exhilarating experiences on my visit to Washington in June 1967 was to observe the sudden change towards India after the Johnson–Kosygin meeting at Glassboro. I met Robert McNamara and Averell Harriman after the meeting and felt the difference in the tone of the talks compared with those I had with Johnson and Walt Rostow two days before Glassboro.

Before the Glassboro meeting, Washington had assumed that the Arab–Israeli war had been precipitated by India withdrawing her forces under the U.N. Command in the Gaza strip and had done this under pressure from Moscow and Nasser and that U Thant was a party to the. "conspiracy." Johnson and his colleagues were pleasantly surprised to learn that Kosygin had been unaware of the Arab moves as much as he and that Kosygin thoroughly disapproved of the brinkmanship that had disturbed the peace in the sensitive area.

After that, Johnson and Kosygin found it easy to establish an understanding on the basis of each power agreeing to the other's presence in West Asia as an insurance against a fresh outbreak of fighting. I had an exceptional opportunity to sense the thinking of top columnists and editorial writers at a dinner given me by Russ Wiggins, then Editor of the *Washington Post*, and at a guest dinner in New York with Vermont Royster, Editor of the *Wall Street Journal*. It was obvious that most newspapermen had lost the zeal for championing larger causes and were more concerned with local problems and newspaper economics. They were tired of preaching sermons and thought the U.S. must first set her own house in order. Politicians, and members of the U.S. Congress in particular, had not become more insular but were irritated by the pinpricks of de Gaulle and his supporters in France and the drain of American resources and manpower by the war in Vietnam. They were not decided whether the President was right in going the way he was. Bankers and businessmen on the other hand took a different view. They were looking far ahead, not thinking like newspaper publishers only of sales tomorrow, nor like politicians only of the next election. They sensed the likely impact of the technological revolution on them. They felt that even with all its manpower and vastness the U.S. was a restricted market and that production of goods must be in terms of world markets and that management must be an amalgam of all talents.

At luncheons with executives of the Bank of America and the Chase Manhattan Bank and in a very rewarding talk with Eugene Black, I learned that American bankers and industrialists were not thinking in terms of investment and returns according to the classical ideas of capitalism. They were thinking of meeting the challenge of the space age, of removing human want and promoting human welfare. They realised the world was becoming one and was being united in a universal common market. They wanted to work for the goal progressively, region by region and hemisphere by hemisphere. To begin with they aimed at a market of two billion embracing the non-Communist world.

My visit to Washington helped me review Indo–U.S. ties from only of sales tomorrow, nor like politicians only of the next election. They sensed the likely impact of the technological revolution on the time Gagan Mehta took over the ambassadorship to the term of Brij Kumar Nehru. Mehta was not a social success, but he sold the commercial and business community the idea that India was a good risk and that her economic plans should be supported by Wall Street. He did not fare well, however, at the political level because Krishna Menon queered his pitch with his posturings at the U.N. Mehta's successor Mohammed Currim Chagla sat on his high chair and expected Americans to come to him. He made public speeches which got much play in the Indian press, but they did little good in the U.S. because they were loaded with fusillades against Pakistan over Kashmir.

When B. K. Nehru landed at Idlewild Airport on his way to Washington to succeed Chagla, he was asked about the conclusions of the Belgrade Conference of non-aligned nations. This was followed by a television interview at which he was asked why Menon was anti-American. Menon had said that underground nuclear tests were more dangerous than those of the surface obviously in defence of Russia, which had broken the agreement on halting tests and blasted an atom bomb in the air, when the Belgrade conference was in session. Ambassador Nehru was asked on TV whether Menon had scientific evidence to sustain his contention. Of course Menon's blast was politically motivated.

Bijju Nehru's period of office affected Indo–U.S. relations in several respects. Its highlights were the war between India and China and between India and Pakistan, the issue of increasing economic aid and the prolonged drought which threatened to cripple the Indian economy. Nehru held the post longer than any of his predecessors, and he was able to establish good personal relations with Kennedy and Johnson. This meant an upgrading of the Indian Embassy. The Indian Minister would talk officially with the Assistant Secretary of State and not with the Deputy Assistant Secretary. The State Department knew Nehru had ready access to the White House and took care to see there was no occasion for complaint.

A story was told to me about Jacqueline Kennedy. Pakistan felt aggrieved that Galbraith, a confidant of her husband, had been appointed Ambassador in India while an orthodox diplomat had been posted to Pakistan. The State Department requested Mrs. Kennedy to give their man in Pakistan a boost on her Asian tour. So when she landed in Karachi and shook hands with President Ayub she said that the Ambassador to Pakistan and his wife were the personal friends of the Kennedys and had eaten at the White House several times and enjoyed a special status with the American President. Thereupon, the Ambassador remarked: "Mrs. Kennedy is joking, sir, I have never had a meal with them and I have met the President only once, and that also at a large party at the White House."

Washington held clear cut views on the ability and performance of its various representatives in New Delhi. Chester Bowles was considered to have been very successful in selling the U.S. to India in his first term. He removed the prejudices created by his predecessor, Loy Henderson. But the most successful U.S. diplomats were Ellsworth Bunker and Sherman Cooper. Bunker was a cross between the British and the American schools of diplomacy. His assessment of India was accepted by the U.S. Congress Foreign Affairs Committee and he got the aid Bill through. He created confidence in Prime Minister Nehru and persuaded him to be less aggressively anti-American. He tried to remedy the damage done by his predecessor Allen. Cooper was the best of them. He had great pull with Eisenhower and his wife was a socialite. Kenneth Galbraith was successful in making Nehru's plan for a welfare State acceptable to John Kennedy, although in fact J.F.K. was already in sympathy with these plans, but he could not sell them to Wall Street. He helped reopen talks on Kashmir with his proposal to divide the Valley by drawing a line which would give Pakistan a small portion of it to connect Gilgit by road with the rest of West Pakistan. But Rawalpindi torpedoed his effort.

Galbraith's greatest service to India was to get Washington to recognise the McMahon Line as the India–China border. I played some part in this. After the Ambassador had concluded his informal monthly talks with senior newsmen and columnists in New Delhi, I stayed behind and mentioned to him that if he could get Washington to accept the McMahon Line this would morally align the U.S. with India against China. He liked the idea, got in touch with Washington and rang me up two days later to say it was through. He then announced the decision to the Press. I could have scooped other newsmen, but refrained from doing so in the national interest. I wanted the news to be flashed all over India and the world through the normal news channels.

Bowles was very close to Kennedy and wrote his platform when he stood for election in 1960. There was talk of his being made Secretary of State, but when Kennedy talked to Bowles his answers to the issues Kennedy raised were said to have lacked precision. His mind did not move fast enough for Kennedy, who was a very fast reader and thinker. Accordingly, Bowles fell in Kennedy's estimation and was given second position in the State Department. He was later sent to India for a second spell. This time, Bowles found himself selling India to Indians, who had by then become disillusioned with Nehru's giganticism.

(b) WASHINGTON ON KASHMIR

The U.S. attitude on Kashmir has been generally pro-Pakistan, although from time to time it has put forward different proposals for a solution, including handing over the Valley to Pakistan, making it independent, handing it over to the U.N., forming a condominium, or dividing it between India and Pakistan. To begin with, Washington took its cue from the British, but later it took the line recommended by the U.N.-appointed American mediator on Kashmir, Graham, and from Galbraith.

Two months after the war with Pakistan, Johnson's aide told our Ambassador to ask New Delhi to settle the Kashmir issue, but the aide was told firmly that Pakistan was out of court for resorting to arms. It was pointed out that India had withdrawn from the sitting of the Security Council, stating that Kashmir was a domestic issue. This withdrawal helped India's cause more than Menon's nine-hour oration on a previous occasion.

I was keen on finding out how Kennedy and Black had reacted to Nehru's refusal to allow Black to try to bring about a settlement on Kashmir. Our Ambassador pressed Nehru to agree because India was not bound to accept Black's proposals. While Kennedy was pro-

Pakistan on Kashmir like all Americans, he was pro-India generally and would be convinced of the strength of the Indian case if Black failed to find a solution, our Ambassador argued. But Menon advised the Prime Minister that this was a matter for India and Pakistan to settle among themselves.

Nehru's letter to Kennedy turning down the suggestion that Black mediate was sent to our Ambassador for personal delivery to the President. But M. J. Desai, Foreign Secretary, also simultaneously handed over a copy of it to the U.S. Ambassador in Delhi. The result was Kennedy saw the rejection before our Ambassador delivered it to him. After making a pretence of reading it, he said: "I do not like this. What is the harm in letting Black make a try? It is not mediation nor arbitration. I want you to take this letter away and change it."

Kennedy then added angrily: "Well, this letter has already been seen by thirty-five people in India and in Washington. I can't even say now that it should be taken back and changed." Obviously he felt hurt that a personal letter did not reach him first. Fortunately, Kennedy did not take this to heart and no damage was caused to India–U.S. relations. Black took the rebuff with a laugh. He said he had told Kennedy that he did not expect the Prime Minister to agree.

Nehru, as everybody knew in Delhi, lost his nerve at the time of the Chinese aggression. His appeal to Kennedy for immediate help included a sentence which said that parting with some territory here or there did not matter in the face of the crisis. That was how Harriman and Sandys were successful in making him reopen the Kashmir question. The situation was retrieved later when Nehru sent them to Morarji Desai, the hard-liner on Kashmir, who spoke to them sharply and thereby made an enemy of Galbraith.

Johnson was also pro-Pakistan to begin with, but he changed his attitude after Ayub started flirting with China. Johnson told Ayub when they met in Washington a folksy story the purport of which was: "You are free to abuse me and America, but I am also free not to help." He was particularly annoyed at the personal abuse showered on him in the Pakistani Press. Ayub promised to set matters right and shook hands.

When I sought the American version of aid to India, this is what I learned. A start was made with technical aid. Both technical and financial aid rose gradually, but in 1958, when the sterling balances were exhausted, it became massive. India wanted more than a 1,000 million dollars a year. Black was approached by B. K. Nehru and helped organise the Aid India Consortium. India got more than she expected. Our plans looked good and our performance in the First and Second Plans was impressive; and so the Third Plan was underwritten. But our performance in this Plan was very poor, the rate of economic growth falling below two per cent against the targeted five per cent. The World Bank sent the Bell Mission to find out what was wrong, and the mission proposed a package deal of which devaluation of the rupee was a part. But it made the mistake of wording its recommendation on devaluation in such a manner that it appeared to be interfering with the internal affairs of India. If it had mentioned that India had suggested this course, the financial adviser of the Government would have accepted it. As matters stood, T.T.K. reacted violently and resisted the proposal. But Prime Minister Shastri was agreeable. Ashoka Mehta felt the only way to get it through was to get Shastri to throw out T.T.K. Sachin Chaudhury, a flourishing company lawyer of Calcutta, succeeded T.T.K. but he seemed unaware of the concession he should extract from Washington as the price for devaluation. Finally, the responsibility for taking the fateful decision to devalue devolved on Mrs. Gandhi who did not seem fully aware of its consequences.

Kennedy was the first President to put aid to India on a long-term basis of five years. He was able to get Congress to endorse his policy. Johnson knew on the other hand that Congress was not favourable to foreign aid and asked for annual grant linked to performance. I learned that Johnson was a man with a golden heart, but moody and whimsical.

There was much excitement in the Kennedy camp when Nehru agreed to visit Washington in 1961. But his first meeting with Kennedy was a flop. Nehru did not respond to what Kennedy said and it was left to Bijju Nehru to carry on the dialogue. The Prime Minister was fatigued, probably by his heavy schedule of engagements. The same thing happened when he flew to Kennedy's holiday resort. There too, as they went sailing, Nehru would not react to Kennedy's conversational gambits and Kennedy again felt disappointed. They did not talk politics. This happened in 1961. Nehru was apparently a tired man. Finally, they had a quiet talk, mostly on Vietnam. Here again, Nehru would not state his view; he asked M. J. Desai to tell the Americans that they should not go into South Vietnam as they would get bogged down there. Kennedy was really worried about Vietnam and wanted to know Nehru's mind to help him determine his own policy.

It was arranged that Kennedy's eggheads should meet Nehru for an hour. There was a great demand for inclusion in the meeting and many applicants had to be shut out. The meeting started late, because Nehru, usually very punctual, arrived fifteen minutes after schedule. The very first question put to Nehru was: "What is the place of intellectuals in the life of India?" Nehru gave a rambling reply. Other questions too got similar replies. The meeting lasted forty-five minutes. At the end of it, Kennedy and the eggheads concluded that he had grown old and lost his grip. Perhaps Nehru did not feel spiritually akin to them. He apparently felt that the talks would inevitably lead to the issue of private sector versus public sector. The political climate in Washington was against public enterprise and so he clammed up.

(c) JOHNSON'S VIEWS

I also got the facts about the cancellation of Shastri's visit to the U.S. in 1965, which it was believed in India at that time had been dropped because Johnson was annoyed with Ayub Khan for his too fervent display of affection for China. Ayub was to have visited Washington a little after Shastri, and it was said that Johnson had cancelled both visits as he wanted to equate India with Pakistan. I found there was no basis for this belief. The real facts were that Michael Stewart had visited Washington and made a speech at the National Press Club quoting Jefferson on the need to pay attention to world opinion. Johnson took offence at the remark, thinking it was aimed at him. He was also annoyed at Lester Pearson's criticism of his policy on Vietnam in a speech in Philadelphia. Johnson rang up Pearson to tell him to keep out of American politics and not criticise him on American soil.

Johnson sent for Dean Rusk after Stewart's speech and said that foreign politicians came to Washington to build up their image in their own country. He did not want them to exploit their meetings with him in this manner and told Rusk to cancel the projected visits of all foreign dignitaries. The Secretary of State thought it was a momentary outburst and took no action. When the Pearson incident occurred, Johnson asked why the visits had not been cancelled and insisted that this be done immediately.

When B. K. Nehru contacted the White House to find out why Shastri's visit had been cancelled, Johnson said "all these people" were coming for aid and he could not tell them anything until Congress had passed the Foreign Aid Bill. Nehru explained that Shastri was not coming on an aid-seeking mission. Johnson relaxed and agreed to speak with him by phone when Shastri visited Ottawa. But the call was never made as Paul Martin said he did not want

Indo–American politics to be projected into Canada. This was obviously a reprisal for Johnson's curt remarks to Pearson. At that time, Indira Gandhi was on a lecture tour of the U.S. and wanted to make a courtesy call on Johnson, but days passed and there was no response from the White House to the request. Phillips Talbot told the Indian Embassy that the State Department was helpless, but McGeorge Bundy was told that if Johnson refused to meet Mrs. Gandhi she would not visit Washington. He promised to fix an appointment, but when the time came for it Johnson tried to transfer Mrs. Gandhi to Mrs. Johnson. Nehru protested, and Johnson finally saw her. The meeting lasted fifteen minutes and was devoted to desultory talk on inconsequential matters.

But things were vastly different when Mrs. Gandhi visited Washington again as Prime Minister. The moment the helicopter carrying her touched down on the White House lawn, Johnson was there to greet her warmly. At subsequent meetings, he expressed his willingness to do whatever she wanted.

Presidential protocol in Washington prescribed that the President entertain foreign dignitaries at the White House but not accept a banquet in his honour in return. He only attends a reception, and that too for a brief fifteen minutes. On Mrs. Gandhi's visit, Johnson agreed to attend a reception at the Indian Embassy to which only a select few had been invited, and the idea was that he would leave by 7 p.m. The Ambassador had fixed a dinner party the same evening for 8.30, but Johnson was in an amiable mood and continued to stay long after the time for his departure. The dinner guests had arrived and the clock showed nine but Johnson showed no sign of leaving. Mrs. Nehru went up to him and invited him to join the dinner party. Johnson said: "You want me to join you? You invite me to dinner? All right, I will join you." An Indian diplomat helped by dropping out. At dinner Johnson said loudly, referring to Mrs. Gandhi: "I want her to be elected. Tell me what I can do. I can make a speech criticising her, if that will help. I will do what will help her. I want her elected. You, Mr. Ambassador, I want you to meet me every week." These remarks clearly indicated that Mrs. Gandhi had gone down well with the President.

Another subject I was interested in was to assess the effect of Krishna Menon on Indo–U.S. relations. I gathered that the general impression in Washington was that he was anti-American and caused irritation to the Administration whenever the opportunity presented. I was told that the good work Mehta had done as Ambassador in a year was undone by Menon in one TV appearance or speech at the U.N. The worst incident occurred at New York Airport, when a reporter put him a question and Menon raised his walking-stick and chased him. This incident was screened on TV three times and made a very bad impression on the millions of Americans who viewed it. I recalled that Prime Minister Nehru told me once that Menon was his answer to Dulles. He told me on another occasion that Menon was not India's Ambassador to the U.S. but to the U.N., to which I replied that as the U.N. was in New York what Menon said there had an impact on American public opinion. Furthermore, there was his frequent appearances on TV, undertaken apparently under the impression that they were good publicity for India but actually producing the contrary effect.

I met President Johnson on the understanding that he would not be quoted. I began by offering him hearty contratulations on the birth of a grandson that day, and as a grandfather welcomed him into our club.

He was glad, he said, to join Grandpa's Club, and his flattering words of welcome put me at ease. I told him that Asians believed that he felt towards the coloured people the same way as for the white, and that with his global outlook he was fighting to preserve for the people of Asia their freedom to grow and to live peacefully.

The President said that his critics would protect the white and not care for the coloured. That was why they wanted his head cut off. He stood for all alike, for the coloured who are two-thirds of the people of the world, and wanted them to feel secure, to have food, education and the opportunity to grow as the white had. His critics stood for Little Rock. At heart he was convinced that the richer nations must put a ceiling on their urges as consumer societies and direct their surplus resources to the have-nots of the world.

I had had talks in Delhi with Food Minister C. Subramaniam and L. K. Jha, Special Secretary to the Prime Minister, who had earlier met Johnson. The U.S. President had told one of them that Mrs. Gandhi should not bother about her reduced majority in Parliament and had remarked: "My majority is also reduced. This is in the day's game." He had added: "We should have a code among politicians not to talk too much and too often when it embarrasses a friendly government. Take Vietnam, I understand your stand. You are entitled to make it, but why keep on repeating it and give my critics a chance to play it up?" Since the Israeli–Arab issue was very hot and Mrs. Gandhi had spoken, according to Washington, out of turn, the President's talk with me dramatised this issue even more passionately when he pulled out a penknife from his pocket and, holding it up, asked whether it was right to place it in the hands of his enemies. The lively man-to-man dialogue lasted over half an hour. I left his room with the impression that the Indian sub-continent would count in any balance of power that may emerge in Asia.

Soon after I met Johnson, I went on TV with columnist Rowland Evans. "India has been a dirty word for the past week here," he cautioned me as we entered the studio. The TV programme gave me the opportunity of explaining the domestic compulsions which had made Mrs. Gandhi take the stand she did on the Arab–Israeli issue and India's firm belief that peace in Vietnam could be had only by the U.S. and the Soviet Union jointly guaranteeing the territorial integrity of all the states in our region.

I met McNamara, Harriman, Walt, Rostow, William Bundy and Sherman Cooper, among others, in an attempt to gauge the minds of those who influenced thinking in the White House, the State Department and the Pentagon, the three major centres of power in the U.S. I found in Harriman the greatest understanding of India's role in Asia. McNamara had the most comprehending mind on Asia in the context of world security and Bundy was well posted on affairs in East and South-East Asia. From these talks, I gathered that American mothers would not agree to sacrifice their sons on the Asian mainland indefinitely. The U.S. could commit its manpower to this region for five years at the most. Japan was living in a fool's paradise if she thought she could have a protective American umbrella for many years to come.

Two opposite views, one friendly and the other critical, were expressed in these talks. I was told: "India cannot fight on three fronts—China, Pakistan and poverty. You are as big in relation to Pakistan as we are in relation to Mexico. You as the bigger power have to settle this question of Kashmir."

India's foreign policy, I was told, was very parochial and had to change to be effective. It had been determined by Kashmir. I was asked why New Delhi did not settle with Pakistan and free itself from its present obligations to Russia. "You cannot run your foreign policy on clichés," they said to me. "You must not take America for granted. Why should we keep on paying a billion dollars and giving you all the food you want and let you kick us all the time?"

On the credit side, they noted that our democratic institutions were firm. They were impressed by the manner in which the general election had been run. They noted approvingly that our younger farmers and businessmen had vitality. They said: "You can be a great country if you put your economy right. But you and Pakistan should join hands and make the sub-continent one force."

They realised that there could be no peace and stability in Asia unless India was stable and strong, but we had to make a bigger effort. Pakistan was doing better than India, and we had to let younger people use their vitality to speed up the country's progress. One of these experts said: "You know that in Vietnam we are defending your backyard. Has any Indian politician the guts to say that? Look at my President. He wants to fight poverty everywhere. He does so much for your country, and what does he get in return? He gets through to you aid and grain, which is more valuable than gold today, and you behave as you do.

"You have no relations with South-East Asia. You should care more for these neighbours. You should develop your trade with Japan. That will do you a lot of good. I know China and Pakistan want your dismemberment, but it is only your people who can dismember your country. I do not think you will dismember. I believe you will hold together. But your foreign policy has been all wrong."

For my part I was disappointed with the attitude of the average American to the world at large. He could not become insular because of his global responsibility, but he was becoming inward looking. I was invited by the Editor of the *Wall Street Journal* to give my impressions of his country, and he published them as centre piece on the editorial page of the paper in its issue of 16th October, 1967. I concluded my impressions thus:

"The average American may feel it is not his duty to police the globe. He may want to devote his resources to eradicating poverty at home, improving education, fighting crime, rebuilding decaying cities and purifying air and water. But the thinking element does not subscribe to this philosophy of the 'American fortress.' Delhi, Saigon and the U.N. Secretariat are agreed on the way out. The U.S. and Russia must agree to provide the U.N. with the power and the tools to do the job of uplifting the backward segment of humanity and of putting down aggression and keeping the peace.

"No one that I met in the U.S. is yet thinking on these lines. The Press is concerned with reporting on yesterday's events, the politician with today's developments bearing on his electoral chances and the businessman is worrying about what tomorrow will unfold.

"The U.S. is the laboratory in which answers to race relations, economic well-being, social fulfilment, human happiness and security from aggression can be found. But one senses all round the nation an atmosphere of stalemate—a desire to drug oneself with the complacent belief that you can allow the world to pass by."

A very learned professor of a Japanese university told me at a dinner party given by our Minister in Tokyo in June 1967 that he was confident the twenty-first century would be Asia's, with India, Japan and China forming the points of a power triangle.

In his column in the *New York Times* of Sunday, 1st October, 1967, on "Johnson's personal approach to history," James Reston wrote: "The President is being told by his shrinking company of intimates that the Communist aggression in Vietnam is the same as the Nazi aggression in the Rhineland, Austria and Czechoslovakia, and he is holding the line; as Churchill defended freedom in Europe, so Johnson is holding the bridge in Asia until Japan and India, the two potential anchors of free Asia, finally take over responsibility for creating order in that part of the world."

(d) INDIA'S NEW ROLE

I discussed three issues with C. V. Narasimhan, U. Thant's Indian Chef de Mission and with the Secretary General. This was to understand the views held in U.N. quarters on India, China and the Middle East. Our well wishers, I gathered, wanted our country to change its economic policy. There was too much industrialisation and State-owned business, and private enterprise must get a larger share. The population must be stabilised at 750 million. Food production must get priority. Mrs. Gandhi must gather "forward-looking" people round her.

The question of balance of power depended on what came out of China. The next two years were crucial. If Mao's revolutionary plan of the countryside encircling the town succeeded, the U.S. and Russia would pull together and thus stabilise the world. This would involve a package deal, including the Middle East and Vietnam.

If, on the other hand, China went the way Russia did in the last thirteen years, there would be peace in Asia and the U.S. was likely to make friends with China. That development may make Russia feel insecure and thus attempt to cause trouble in sensitive areas.

The role India had to play in all this depended on what she made of herself. If she was overtaken by chaos and went Left, she would become a satellite of China. That would only increase the chances of Mao's theory coming true. The countries of the Middle East would not join hands with India. This was because in the short run Panislamic ideas would dominate the scene. In any event, Pakistan would never agree to work with India. Her rulers had a vested interest in keeping up the war of nerves with India as a guarantee of the continuance of their regime. Thinkers in U.N.

rejected the view that the division of the world would be on religious or racial lines, it would be according to geographical continuity. The general view at the U.N. was: "You in India do not act. You only react. India lacks leadership."

I had two meetings with U Thant, one in Delhi, when he received the Nehru Award, and the other in New York a day after the U.N. General Assembly had concluded its debate on the Israeli–Arab conflict. U Thant told me India was pivotal to the security of Asia. It was feared in U.N. quarters that China would continue to develop its atomic power and would use it astutely to blackmail India. The answer was that India, Australia and Japan should get together. The real solution to present-day world problems was a package deal between the U.S. and Russia; otherwise, the U.N. was lost.

When I reached Ottawa, I was cautioned by our High Commissioner that I would be asked why India went out of its way to back the Arabs, but I had a ready answer. My main task was to find out what the Canadians thought of India, as Canada was the friendliest of the Commonwealth countries. I met Paul Martin and other spokesmen of the Government and exchanged views with the editors of leading newspapers in Toronto, Ottawa and Montreal. The Government view was India's image had suffered recently. If Nasser practised brinkmanship, he should have been ready to go over the brink and should not shout when he got clubbed. India's attitude on the Arab–Israeli issue, I was told, "has hurt us all, it was one sided." The Canadian people did not know enough about India, but they thought India and Pakistan were brothers and should act as such. Canada would not break up but would have some type of confederation with the U.S. She was resisting the overflow of American friendship, but she could not resist the economic invasion of the U.S. She would, however, control and regulate it. The U.S. was to the American hemisphere what China was to Asia. India should play its role in resisting China and act as a bridge between Asia and America. The editors I met told me that the image they had of India was that of a country which had too many problems. The reports they got of India, mainly about famine and similar difficulties, showed that India was not faring well.

The main purpose of my talks with representative Britons in London was to see how far their country was prepared to help India develop her own technological base and what kind of leadership Britain had. Almost every journalist and politician I met told me that Wilson had gone "insular" and was a very unpopular Prime Minister. I think my most rewarding talks were with Cecil King and

Roy Thomson, and their chief editorial aides, with David Astor of *The Observer*, Alistair Burnett, Editor of *The Economist*, the columnist John Grigg, Sir Maurice Parsons of the Bank of England and Sir Jeremy Raisman of Lloyds Bank. I had a dull session with Ted Heath, but of the politicians I met Sir Edward Boyle impressed me most with his live mind. I learned from them that both Britain and India originally had mixed economies, but India's had become a "mixed-up" economy. Public enterprise, they said, must be judged by its efficiency, and it was not lack of skill in management but the appointment of the wrong men that caused inefficiency.

They considered India a good economic risk and felt that Britain and India should co-operate in technological development. But India must be realistic in her foreign policy. What was the point in lending substantial sums of money to the U.A.R. when India herself was in difficulties? This was not realism but misguided sentiment. India must count in establishing a balance of power in Asia, and any attempt to keep her out would damage the cause of peace and security.

They envisaged the emergence of a power pattern in which Canada, Central and South America would form a single economic unit with the U.S. while Africa would have similar relations with Western Europe. West Asia would fall within a triangle whose three points would be the Soviet Union, the U.S. and Britain. The Russians should be encouraged to establish a foothold in the U.A.R. as this would give them a stake in maintaining peace in West Asia. Because of their mutual rivalries, the Russians and Americans would probably like the British to stay in West Asia as a third party, friendly with both sides.

The U.S. would have to pull out of Asia, and leave it to India, Japan and Australia to fill the power vacuum. China would not be in a position for some years to exercise its economic strength. India had to play a pivotal role in Asia, and her economy had to be strengthened accordingly. India must first of all solve her food problem. Nehru went wrong when he neglected agriculture and overdid heavy industry and thereby created an economic imbalance.

There were two schools of thought among newspapermen. One considered that by the end of the century Europe would be under Russian hegemony, Asia under the Chinese and the Americas under the U.S., leaving Africa free for all. The other view was that Britain must either join the Common Market or merge with the Atlantic Community for her survival. India would not count as a world force for the next fifteen years. Pakistan had become a West

Asian power. India should pull her weight in South and South-East Asia.

On this tour, I fulfilled a very worthwhile engagement by participating in the study conference on the partition of India organised by Professor C. H. Philips, Director of the School of Oriental and African Studies in the University of London. The conference brought together men who had played a significant part in those exciting times or were keen observers of the scene. The effort was very praiseworthy and the Britons and Indians who participated in it made a valuable contribution. But the conference was not as successful as its sponsors hoped because the delegates from Pakistan united in projecting their political views and not in helping to unravel, in the spirit of scientific research, tangled facts of partition. The conference laid the groundwork for future historians.

Since de Gaulle had gone to the Montreal Exposition, I met the acting Prime Minister Joxe and exchanged views with a spokesman of the Foreign Office, the Deputy Governor of the Bank of France and leading French journalists. They were interested in developing economic and cultural ties with India but felt that since the French could not use English and Indians knew only English it was difficult to establish communication.

The visit threw light, however, on how de Gaulle had reacted to China's attack on India. At the time Jung was our Ambassador in Paris and he had a talk with the President on the subject. De Gaulle said he was very disappointed with the performance of the Indian Army, which he said had been frostbitten and had retreated in disorder. When the British withdrew from India, he had thought that the Indian Army would fill the vacuum because the British Empire was founded on it. The performance of the Army against China showed it was not the same organisation he had known.

When the Ambassador explained that Nehru had believed that the Himalayas were an impenetrable frontier, he replied that Nehru had no business to take that view, knowing the recent advances in military science and weaponry. When a country chose to be non-aligned, it must proceed in the belief that it was capable of defending its frontiers without the aid of allies. Apparently, India had not prepared herself in that way and had therefore suffered because it had no allies. He offered all possible help in arms against China and gave spare parts for fighter aircraft, but he said the defeat had lowered India's prestige so much that it would take much time to recover the lost ground.

The impression de Gaulle gave Jung was that the Indian sub-continent could play an effective international role if India and

Pakistan came to terms. Since this did not seem to be likely in our lifetime, the only course left for India was to strengthen her economy and build up her military strength.

An important role Indian diplomacy played in Paris was to encourage de Gaulle in his efforts to settle the Algerian issue peacefully. He was the only man in a position to defy the French generals and the Rightists who wanted to continue the fight. Jung advised Nehru that India should not recognise the Algerian provisional government functioning in Cairo as such recognition would weaken de Gaulle. Once India recognised it, the other countries of Asia and Africa would follow. Nehru accepted this advice.

Again, after the plebiscite in Algeria went in favour of independence, there was pressure on New Delhi to recognise the provisional government. Again Jung was successful in preventing its recognition until a similar referendum had been held in France and the French had agreed to independence. His argument on this occasion was that if India accepted the provisional government it would be setting a bad precedent and paving the way for our enemies recognising similar bodies for Nagaland and Kashmir. Moreover, he argued that it was not certain that the provisional set-up would be the actual government of Algeria when independence was established.

A visit to Bonn revealed two distinct views on the future of Europe. These were prevalent as much among politicians and journalists as within the Kiesinger Cabinet. Among others, I met the Foreign Minister, Willy Brandt and the Finance Minister, Franz-Josef Straus, the Defence Secretary, the Leader of the Opposition and the President of the Indo–German Friendship Society. One view was that Europe could survive in competition with the U.S. if Europe up to the Urals pulled together. The other was that Russia should be left to stew in her own juice but the East-European states be drawn into the Common Market and that a free flow of capital and goods within the Atlantic Community be established.

I visited Rome primarily to assess the role of the Pope in influencing world opinion. Besides a brief audience with Pope Paul, I had an interesting talk with the Editor of the official organ of the Vatican, the *Osservatore Romano*. The Vatican finds that the younger generation does not care for church and religion, and governments are too slow to act on the Pope's appeal that more attention be given to social welfare.

I met a high-level spokesman of the Italian Foreign Office as the holiday season was on and the President and the Prime Minister were away from Rome. I also exchanged views with newspapermen including the Editor-in-Chief of *Il Tempo*, who is also a Senator. The impression I gathered from these meetings was that political conditions in Western Europe were confused because of de Gaulle's policies, but in ten years Western Europe would be drawn into the American sphere of influence and Eastern Europe would in turn be drawn towards Western Europe. The U.S. would try to make friends with China and this would isolate Russia, whose survival as a major power would depend on its own technological and industrial strength and not on power groupings like the Warsaw Pact. China was out to dominate Asia, but India was a roadblock and should be helped economically. But there was no prospect for the next five years of the nations of Western Europe doing the right thing by India in the matter of economic aid.

A dinner at the residence of our Ambassador in Austria provided an opportunity for a dialogue with a Foreign Office spokesman and top journalists. The idea was to project our minds to the end of the century and foresee events. The outcome of this exercise was agreement that Eastern Europe would remain Communist but would draw closer to the rest of Europe. The U.S. and Russia would avoid a clash of arms and come to terms with China. Russia would maintain a balance of power with Europe on the one hand and China on the other on the basis of her friendship with and support of a strong India. One journalist forecast that South America would go Communist, and so would the whole of Asia. But conditions in Africa would be chaotic for a long time.

Chapter 7

MOSCOW LOOKS AT DELHI

(a) KOSYGIN'S PLEDGE

I looked forward to my visit to Moscow because of the growing feeling in India that the friendship of the Russians could not be taken for granted. I met a spokesman of the Foreign Office, the Health Minister and the Chief Editors of *Pravda, Izvestia, Tass* and *Novosti* in Moscow. For the first time, I found Russian journalists expressing divergent views on issues of vital importance to their Government. One view was that the war in Vietnam had proved that a great power could not crush a small people determined to be free. The best guarantee of world peace was the U.N. Charter, and not a package deal between the U.S. and Russia. The relations of the Soviet Union with India were like those of friends who walked shoulder to shoulder and helped each other. The Russians would not make a deal with Pakistan, Iran or any other country at the cost of their friendship with India.

Russia could not be isolated and it was strong enough to meet any challenge from anywhere. De Gaulle was the one man who saw that Europe must be saved from another military catastrophe. If the U.S. were to withdraw from Asia there would be peace on the continent. China would take long to build herself and clear the mess created by Mao.

The contrary view on world affairs asserted that China would come round and behave herself and that the Socialist forces would join hands again. Germany was going fascist. The Russians were ready for a settlement of the German question on the lines of the Potsdam Agreement. Germany must, however, denazify itself first and end monopoly control of industry. Today, former Nazis were holding the highest offices and war criminals had been allowed to move about freely. Neither Russia nor France could let Germany be a danger again. If the Pakistanis insisted on self-determination for Kashmir, they would be faced with similar demands, from the Sindhis, the Baluchis, the Pakhtoons and the Bengalis. A forecast borne out by the events leading to Ayub's exit.

The relaxation in Russia whose beginnings I had noticed in 1957 had now reached the stage where a puppet show I attended was a satire on Russian politicians. Perhaps the most rewarding experience was the renewal of my friendship with Kovnej Chukovsky, the sale of whose books for children in many languages totalled millions of copies. He received a doctorate from Oxford University and the Lenin Prize. He was 83, and this is how I summed up to him my impressions of his people:

"The younger people in Russia want a free Press and free political discussion in a parliament. They want a wide range of consumer goods like other people. You are a very rich nation. The people are better off than ever before, but they can be twenty times richer and better off if there was no bureaucracy and the laws of supply and demand operated freely. These young people will be in a majority in ten years and will change your system and outlook. The Russians have got rid of their inferiority complex to a large extent and visualise a common market for the whole of Europe, including Russia.

Integration will start in the economic sphere. Only a Europe including Russia will be a match for the U.S."

Chukovsky nodded and then remarked: "India is a great country with great traditions. Its image here is not that of a starving people but of a people who have life."

At a luncheon at the Indian Embassy, the Soviet Health Minister told me there were 3,000 centenarians in Russia. The Russians were the longest-living people in the world. He recalled how it was found in Paris in the First World War that Russian food was more nutritious than that of any other nation. This conclusion was drawn from the fact that wounded Russian soldiers recovered faster than others. The Russians no longer subsisted on bread and potatoes. They had proteins and vitamins in a non-fatty diet. It was not milk that made people grow taller but a balanced diet.

My talks in Moscow with Russian leaders, various diplomats and the Chief Editors of *Pravda* and *Izvestia* may be summed up thus: Kosygin is a great realist and the Russians admire him greatly. He has discovered that the basic defect of Russian industry is the absence of cost accounting. He found that the American economy was doing better and felt that the Russian factory manager should be given a free hand. The party boss is being eliminated from industry. Kosygin says that the old order must change. Every child has to have the best education and every individual should have enough to meet his requirements. The people's wishes should be respected. He believes that economic planning should be liberalized and that leadership should be collective instead of individualistic. The Soviet people are in a confident mood because of three factors. Militarily, they are convinced that they are as powerful as the U.S. They are not therefore on the defensive so far as the U.S. is concerned. Secondly, the Soviet economy is self-sufficient and self-generating. Thirdly, Russia has now got a generation of producers who, instead of brooding over the restrictions imposed by a tyrannical dictatorship are getting rewards for their work.

Kosygin, unlike Mao and Castro, does not want to export Communism. He has repeatedly said that he wants a détente in Europe. He has called for a conference on European security and spoken so much on this theme that it is difficult for the West Europeans to say that Russians have any evil intentions towards them. The Russians say: "Let us live as neighbours and brothers. Then the question of East Germany and West Germany will solve itself. Let us have cultural exchanges, scientific exchanges. Even if the German problem was there, why should it come in the way?" They take the same attitude on Kashmir.

Khrushchev was mercurial, but he put Russia on the world map. The present Soviet leadership of Brezhnev and Kosygin is more cautious and conservative. They are sincerely anxious to help India, and the proof of this is the ever-growing flow of trade and aid and the supply of sophisticated weapons for India's defence machine. (This policy underwent a change in 1968–69 with the supply of such weapons to Pakistan.)

One compelling reason why the Russians wish to keep India happy is that they live in constant dread of a coming together of the U.S. and China. When Stalin died, the Russians felt that Mao was trying to succeed him as the head of the international Communist movement. This was the beginning of the Russian suspicion of the intentions of the Chinese in Asia and elsewhere.

India is at present a liability to the Russians, economically, politically and militarily, and this inhibits Moscow from making positive gestures of friendship. Until a firm leadership is thrown up in New Delhi and makes a serious attempt to solve the food problem and insulate itself from external diplomatic pressures and internal disruptional forces, the Soviet Union will not feel certain about India's future policy nor entertain sufficient confidence to consider it in the role of an ally instead of a client.

In the Soviet Union, I had the welcome surprise of being invited to attend the celebrations of the twentieth anniversary of India's independence at Tashkent. Russia was the only country to celebrate the occasion and the functions in Tashkent were followed up by those in Moscow and Leningrad. This was partly to emphasise Indo–Soviet friendship, which was beginning to come under a cloud because of Moscow's overtures to Pakistan, and partly to stimulate a reciprocal gesture by India on the fiftieth anniversary of the Russian revolution the following November. (Mrs. Gandhi attended the celebrations in Moscow.) We stayed at Tashkent at the Government guest house, close to the villa where Shastri died. Kosygin, whom I met in New Delhi the following year, was glad to hear about the visit and, recalling Tashkent talks, said: "It was a great occasion. Shastri proved a statesman. He was a great patriot. . . . The Tashkent agreement must be observed in the sub-continent."

(b) TASHKENT AND KABUL

I met the President and Acting Prime Minister of the Republic of Uzbekistan. I expressed surprise at the fact that huge multi-storied flats had gone up in less than a year after earthquakes had caused much destruction to the city. They said to me: "We are an Oriental people. We are different from Westerners. We say our house is yours, our children are yours. We share what we have. We say that if our enemy comes to our house he is as welcome as a friend. After he leaves the house, he is an enemy again. In the last war, more than two million people came from Ukraine and other areas. We had them in our homes. We shared our all. Now, when we have an earthquake, all the republics have come to our aid to reconstruct our town. We like Indians. Our cotton fields provide four-fifths of Russia's needs. We get twenty times more cotton per hectare than India because of fertilisers and irrigation. We don't have rains like you have, but we have rivers and we use their waters."

A Friendship Society official who took my wife and me round the new city and also the new ten-mile-long Shastri Avenue confessed that the older people do not wish to live in flats. They liked houses with open yards and space for growing grapes and peaches.

A visit to Kabul served the dual purpose of enabling me to learn in a two-hour talk with the Prime Minister of Afghanistan how the two super-powers were co-operating in the country's economic development and whether he favoured putting the issue of Pakhtoonistan in cold storage. It gave me an opportunity for two long sessions with the "Frontier Gandhi," Khan Abdul Ghaffar Khan, and he explained how he had been "let down" first by India and later by Afghanistan in the matter of getting an autonomous state for the Pahktoons. He said he was the victim of partition and of Nehru's consent, under Mountbatten's advice, to accept the Durand Line as the international border between Pakistan and Afghanistan.

At the end of the tour, I felt de Gaulle had become the Nehru of the sixties. Nehru was an irritant to the Western powers in the fifties because he took a moral stand on issues impinging on colonialism and neo-colonialism. Rebuffed by the Anglo–Saxons in his attempt to establish special relations with the U.S. of the type Britain had, de Gaulle proceeded to undermine first the position of Britain and then of the U.S. in Europe. Thus, I found that he was denounced everywhere in the Anglo–Saxon world but was the hero of the Europeans, including Russians, in that he had restored Europe's image and financial standing.

Naturally, wherever I went I was asked about the state of India, especially about the threatened famine because of the failure of two successive monsoons, a calamity which occurred once in seventy to a hundred years. In all sincerity, I assured them that India was well set for a breakthrough in agriculture in five years, in economic development as a whole in ten years, and in family planning in twenty years. I asserted this because without such an advance India could not survive as a viable state. It was only in the sphere of political stability that India might take two to five years to attain an equilibrium in national politics and in Centre-state relations.

Chapter 8

THE CRYSTAL BALL

During the trip, I also tried to assess thinking about the future and posed two questions to heads of State and Government, leading politicians, thinkers and writers and businessmen and bankers. My questions were:

(1) An uneasy peace prevailed in the world because of the balance of terror. Permanent peace could be based on a balance of power. What would be the state of the world by the end of the century?

(2) Peace was unthinkable unless the gap between the rich and poor nations narrowed. As matters stood, two-thirds of the world was poor, and by the end of the century four-fifths would be poor. How could this growing imbalance be remedied?

My questions provoked answers of great variety. Broadly, they fell into three categories.

The first view was that U.S. hegemony would extend to the whole American continent. European hegemony, with the Soviet Union playing the dominant role, would extend to Africa and the Middle-East. The rest of Asia would be a Chinese sphere of influence.

The second forecast was based on racial division. The Aryans would form one bloc embracing the Americas, Europe and an eastward projection from southern Europe in a straight line up to Singapore, the Mongoloids would form the second bloc, and the Negroid races the third.

The third guess was that Communism and Islam, two fanatical religions, would join hands against the three liberal religions of the world—Christianity, Buddhism and Hinduism.

Nobody subscribed to Mao's theory of the coloured have-nots of the world laying siege to the white haves. All these forecasts seemed, however, based on fear. They did not take note of the revolution science and technology are about to unleash.

The developing and underdeveloped world would have to leap

over the transitional period of the industrial revolution, for the technological revolution would eliminate the transition. The conquest of space symbolised by landing on the moon and the creation of earth satellites had made the world one. Science had invented gadgets which had destroyed individual privacy. It had invented machines, which would dispense with people going to polling booths to record their votes or waiting for a newspaper to be delivered at home.

Women would cease to be subservient to men. They would be able to go to a store and buy a tube which would give them a child of the colour and pedigree they wanted. There would be free love and sex would be relegated to personal relaxation because the pill would induce or neutralise its procreative potential.

The point of this analysis was that the coming revolution was catching the human race napping. The old and the middle-aged were totally oblivious of its onslaught. The young, on the other hand, felt the change and were releasing themselves from the inhibitions and complexes of the way of life and the code of behaviour they had inherited. What was little realised was that in the new age man would survive only if he was equipped to handle the new machines and master the new technology.

Will the world split on the basis of colour or race? My hunch is it will not; economic compulsions forbid such a division. The human mind will revolt against it, for the trend is towards breaking down the barriers, created in a world in which security depends on the cohesion of linguistic or ethnic groups. Colour, race or language do not change the basic character of man. There should before long be a United States of Europe and similar combinations in Africa, Latin America and in West and East Asia.

Human thinking has simultaneously undergone a revolution. Religion as a dogma has ceased to be a force, just as national boundaries are ceasing to inspire people to lay down their lives in battle. When religion had its grip on the people, their savings were invested in buildings dedicated to the worship of God. Next came the phase of tribalism, which led to investment in fortifications. Then came the urge for glorification, which found expression in prestige-building and in extending empires. Now the world is committed to investing savings in social welfare and creating an egalitarian society. Because the present order has led to concentration of power in a few hands, there is a revolt against the establishment everywhere.

Science and technology will take care of the world's resources. But the disparities between the haves and the have-nots must be reduced and ultimately eliminated. The present trend would further widen the gulf and leave four-fifths of the world poor by the end of the twentieth century. Human ingenuity must now find political institutions based on free expression and produce a social order that will ensure the people both purposeful participation in government and a fair share in the fruits of new discoveries.

The world has to fulfil three conditions for survival. It must adopt the Gandhian creed of non-violence to eliminate wars and passive resistance to redress wrongs. It must accept peaceful co-existence as the only form of civilised behaviour. Finally, it must create a reservoir of the world's achievements through science and technology and see that human society as a whole benefits from them.

The end of the century would then see the emergence of the new man and the new age. The pattern of life of the twentieth century would look to our successors in the twenty-first as distant and as remote as life in the Stone Age seems to us.

Chapter 9

CHALLENGING ISSUES

A journalist is ever on the move, the whole world is his home. This saying was fulfilled, as if by some hidden design when I took off for Cairo, Geneva and London on 25th November, 1968, the day marking the golden jubilee of my entry into the profession. It was an apter way of celebrating it than through dining and wining.

The trip was in response to a challenging symposium held in Geneva from 5th to 7th December on how to make parliaments come to terms with the mass media, especially radio and TV. On my way to Geneva I spent eight days in Cairo assessing the situation in the Middle East and ended the tour with a twenty-day stay in London, where I watched the American-manned Apollo 8 take off for a trip round the moon and live pictures of this fantastic adventure ending in the reception of the astronauts on board the U.S.S. Yorktown on 27th December. I also heard about forecasts of landing on Venus and Mars before the end of the century, helped by an observatory planted on the moon.

The symposium in Geneva was held by the International Centre for Parliamentary Documentation under the auspices of Inter-Parliamentary Union. It was attended by representatives of parliaments and the Press. I was the only delegate from India.

Britain sent a strong delegation headed by the Leader of the House of Commons, Frederick Peart. The day before he spoke in Geneva, he tabled a motion in the Commons which legitimised the presence of the Press in the Parliament's gallery. It ran "That notwithstanding the Resolution of the House of 3rd March, 1762, and other such Resolutions, this House will not entertain any complaint of breach of privilege in respect of the publication of the debates or proceedings of the House, except when any such debates or proceedings shall have been conducted within closed doors, or when such publication shall have been expressly prohibited by the House."

It was quite clear from the three-day debate in Geneva that Parliaments have to open their door to radio and TV. Indeed, radio and TV may prove to be the greatest instruments for the spread of education and culture in backward societies because heavy investment in newspaper industry was a handicap against this media reaching the masses with the speed enjoined by the fast moving world.

The year 1968 was significant for India because it marked a turning-point in thinking prompted by the centenary of Gandhi's birth and the revival of faith in his message of non-violence and passive resistance to evil. The West German Parliament met on 2nd October, 1968, which marked the beginning of a year-long celebration of the Centenary, and Mrs. Indira Gandhi acclaimed the Mahatma in a broadcast as the greatest son of India since Buddha. The world turned to Gandhi, shocked by the assassination of Martin Luther King Jr. and Robert Kennedy, the student revolt in France and elsewhere and the passive resistance of the Czechs to Russian and Warsaw Pact troops. Indeed the young people in the West finding themselves rootless were in search of peace of mind. They turned to the mystic East—the guru and coined such names for the new culture as the "Swami Circuit" and the "Nehru Jacket."

My first engagement in London in December was a meeting with Lord Mountbatten. He had succeeded in making Indian Princes accede to the Indian Union and was happy that Nehru and Patel had enshrined their covenant with the Princes in the Constitution Act. Reports had reached him that the Congress Party had decided to amend the Constitution and omit the provisions guaranteeing the Princely privy purse and privileges. Naturally, some of the Princes

whom he as Viceroy had persuaded to sign the Instrument of
Accession had approached him for intervention. He felt that repudiation of the agreement would not only damage India's credit in
the world but would affect Indira Gandhi's reputation for fair play.
It was apparent that he was doing his best to prevent this development.

My talk with Lord Mountbatten led to an invitation to a preview
of the film on *The Life and Times of Lord Mountbatten.* The Indian
episode was the main piece for the preview. It was a great event.
I felt, however, that in its attempt to prove that partition of the
country was unavoidable the film perforce gave excessive notice to
the final phase at which Jinnah emerged as the rival force to the
Congress and overshadowed the basic fact that freedom was won by
Gandhi and his lieutenants, especially Nehru and Patel, and that
Jinnah was only the by-product of the Congress–Raj struggle for
power.

I wound up my survey of the scene in London with a revealing
talk with Sir Paul Gore-Booth, head of the British Foreign Office.
I noticed for the first time that the twenty-year-old British attitude
of promoting friendly relations with Russia had given way to the
type of bogey which haunted London during the Czarist regime.
Russia's military intervention in Czechoslovakia and her growing
naval presence in the Mediterannean and in the Indian and Pacific
Oceans was considered indicative of a new phase of imperialism
based on the centuries-old dream of the Czars. So far as India was
concerned, Whitehall had now decided, I gathered, to adopt an
attitude of genuine neutrality on the Kashmir issue and Indo–
Pakistan disputes generally.

Back in India at the turn of the year, I found the country in the
throes of the mini-general election scheduled for mid-February.
About 102 million voters were wooed in the States of Uttar Pradesh,
Bihar, West Bengal and Punjab to reconsider their verdict of 1967,
which had failed to provide stable governments. The Congress
claimed that it alone could provide stability. Mrs. Gandhi undertook
a whirlwind tour of these states, addressing as many as forty meetings
in three days, thanks to the privilege available to the Prime Minister
of using Air Force jets and helicopters on a token payment. She made
a plea of "strengthen my hands" in the belief that the people trusted
her even if they did not love the Congress leadership. Huge crowds,
often as large as those drawn by her father, thronged her poll
meetings, rousing hopes among Congressmen that their party would,
after all, win back the confidence of the people and enable it to
forget the 1967 elections as a bad dream.

In the first three general elections, the Congress, as a national front, worsted every other party—Praja Socialists, Jana Sangh, Swatantra and the Communists—which tried to stand up as an alternative to its monolithic rule. But the situation altered radically in the fourth general election of 1967 when the Opposition, at the instance and inspiration of the Rightist C.R. in Madras and the Marxist Namboodiripad in Kerala, realised that the Congress, which was a front of diverse interests, could be defeated only by another front. Consequently, united fronts comprising such mutually contradictory elements as the Communists and the Muslim League were forged, and yielded rich dividends. This tactic also paid off well in Punjab, where the Akalis and the Jana Sangh, reflecting orthodox Sikh and Hindu sentiment, joined hands to oust the Congress from power.

The same strategy was adopted by the Opposition more zealously and successfully in the second week of February. While the Congress confidently hoped to win majorities in West Bengal and U.P., the party was severely trounced in West Bengal and failed to get even a bare majority in U.P. At the end, the United Fronts successfully installed coalition governments in Punjab and West Bengal. In U.P. and Bihar, where no such fronts were formed, the Congress emerged as the largest single party and formed coalitions.

Nagaland also went to the polls early in February for its second general election. Its results were of special importance as successive Indian governments had been blowing hot and cold on the thorny issue of dealing with the Naga insurgents. As a top Army officer once confided to me: "We were asked to deal with the rebels, but before we could really go into action our hands were securely tied as someone in New Delhi sold the Government the idea of 'winning' them over." Only after Biju Nehru took over as Governor of Assam and Nagaland did New Delhi harden its policy towards the rebels and treat them for what they were—outlaws. The military authorities, on their side, were clear that if India ever conceded the rebel demand of independence, Nagaland would be eventually swallowed up by China. India's security would then be greatly endangered. This, in essence, is what I gathered from separate conversations with Chief Minister Chaliha of Assam and Lt. Gen. Sam Manekshaw, now named Chief of Army Staff.

Governor Nehru's policy has paid dividends. The elections held in Nagaland in February 1969 resulted in a decisive victory for the pro-India Naga National Organisation over the United Front, whose candidates were backed by the underground rebel group. The first elections held in 1964 had been boycotted by the underground and the NNO Ministry was denounced as a puppet regime. But in the 1969 elections, 80 per cent of the Naga electorate went to the polls, establishing a record for the whole of India. The result meant that the Naga people voted for the party that stood for peace and identity within the Indian Union. There is no doubt that this transformation was brought about largely by the firm stand of the Governor and partly by the recently growing conviction of the Baptist Church leaders that an independent Nagaland would be swallowed up by "godless Red China."

The mid-term poll proved two things. First, the voters have become sophisticated and mature. They attended all the election meetings organised both by the Congress and the Opposition in large numbers, but voted according to their own predilections. Secondly, although the Congress hold on the electorate was sustained, it met with catastrophic defeat in West Bengal and Punjab because the very factors which gave it supremacy in the past now operated against it. In the general elections of 1952, 1957 and 1962, the Congress annexed about 70 per cent of the seats on a 45 per cent vote because the other parties were divided. In 1967, it won only about 54 per cent seats at the Centre although it secured 41 per cent of the votes cast. Election by a simple majority now encourages unity among contestants and discourages splinter groups.

The February poll has, at the same time, put a question mark over the future of parliamentary democracy in India. The Marxists have no doubt fought the elections and been swept back into office, this time as the single largest party, in Bengal. But do they really accept the parliamentary system? Earlier doubts continue. The party's secretary in Bengal, Mr. Promode Das Gupta, told a victory celebration: "We firmly believe that we will not be able to reach our goal through parliamentary democracy. Our goal is socialism, and for that is required a bloody revolution. We want to reach a state of clash between the Centre and the State through the path of parliamentary democracy to such a level as would spark off a bloody revolution."

The poll has moreover ushered in an era of coalition governments. Top leaders no doubt agree that the two-party system is ideal— something to hope for and work for. But they realise that this system does not easily obtain and many countries have had to learn to live with more than two parties. Consequently, a debate has begun on coalitions. More and more politicians are now sorting out answers to the twin questions: coalitions for what and with whom? The Congress Working Committee has agreed in principle to accept the fact that coalitions are inescapable and should therefore be formed with likeminded parties. However, the Congress needs first to know its own mind before picking likeminded allies.

Three questions relating to the functioning of parliamentary institutions have remained unresolved: first, the question of political defections in legislatures; secondly, that of the powers of the Speaker, and, thirdly, the power of a Governor in regard to the dissolution of the State Assembly. Are defections to be permitted to plunge the country into political turmoil? Are presiding officers to be allowed to run the legislatures as their lords and masters? Who is to determine the legality of a government, the Speaker, the legislature or the Governor? Is the Governor to be bound by the advice of a Chief Minister and dissolve the Assembly or can he exercise his individual judgment and explore the possibility of forming an alternative ministry? Should a Governor have the benefit of some guidelines in regard to his functioning in the style of the Instrument of Instructions in pre-independence days?

The verdict of the ballot box administered a shock to the Congress, confirming the result of the last general election. It has clearly indicated to the party that it will lose its hold on the Centre unless it puts its house in order and corrects its image. It may have successfully stolen the thunder of the Leftists over the last twenty years by liberal use of progressive slogans. However, the people seek action and results and will no longer be led up the garden path by the mere mouthing of pious platitudes. They demand good government, active participation in democratic functioning at all levels and solutions to mounting problems. A top Communist leader from West Bengal confided to me: "The younger generation has voted in a big way for us, thinking that we have answers to offer. Have we?"

I exchanged views with eleven persons of eminence who reviewed the post-election scene in the light of the likely developments in the future and the remedial measures they envisaged in the interest of the healthy growth of democracy. These were S. Nijalingappa, Congress President; K. Kamaraj, Sanjiva Reddy and U. N. Dhebar, three former Presidents of the Congress Party; Sachin Chaudhury, Humayun Kabir and K. D. Malaviya, all former Union Ministers; B. K. Nehru, Governor of Assam and Nagaland; Dharma Vira, Governor of West Bengal; V. Vishwanathan, Governor of Kerala; and G. S. Pathak, Governor of Mysore. All agreed that political stability and unity depended on how the Central leadership acted in the governmental sphere and in managing the affairs of the ruling party. They differed, however, on how the situation should be handled by the Prime Minister and the Congress High Command.

There was a distinct cleavage among Congressmen. One view

was that the Congress could be saved from defeat at the polls in 1972 only if the High Command and the Union Cabinet acted on the principle of collective leadership. This would ensure that State Ministries would not be allowed to exert pressure on the Centre and erode its authority in relation to the states. Secondly, it would enable the High Command to revamp the party organisation at all levels and develop the party's appeal on the basis of the problems which various states and regions faced and not on the basis of an all-India platform.

The second view was that the Congress Party was on the way out and that democracy would be saved only if Mrs. Gandhi decided to split the party into Right and Left, thus causing a polarisation of forces. The proponents of this view contended that the Right Communists and the Leftists in splinter groups and in regional parties would all join hands to form a united front. Such a decision would isolate the Marxists and prevent them from swallowing the other Leftists who had joined hands with them on the anti-Congress plank. This section felt that the Old Guard should be dropped and Mrs. Gandhi should take the Leftists and progressives together under her wing. This means that both in the states and at the Centre polarisation would come through election strategy and that simple majority rule would promote the evolution of a two-party system.

A third view was that the Congress Party could revive the people's faith in it only if it provided them with an administration at the base which was clean and efficient and attended to the needs and grievances of the masses. Failing such a transformation, the country would drift to chaos and pave the way for a take-over by the Communists.

Those who left the Congress because of its flirtation with the Communists and the power-hungry manner in which its leadership had acted felt that the general election of 1967 and the mid-term elections of February 1969 had proved that the voters were not influenced by either ideological appeals or by slogans based on religion. The most powerful influence was a candidate's caste and the stand he took on regional issues. Thus casteism and regionalism have come to identify the individual and group interests of voters. This development was a reaction to the manner in which the politicians had exploited power for personal ends. The remedy lay in creating a united front of the forces which stood for democratic freedom and Gandhian values in public life.

Those who did not practise politics confessed that they saw no silver lining to the cloud that hung over Indian democracy. They thought that the remedy might lie in a presidential coup which might give the country a period of good government and make it economically strong by carrying forward the "green revolution" in agriculture and accelerating industrial growth—the kind of job President Ayub Khan did in the first five years of his authoritarian regime in Pakistan. But this school of thought is puzzled by the way the Ayub regime collapsed in four brief months in the face of an upsurge largely staged by students and townsfolk in West Pakistan and by politicians in East Pakistan who led a crusade against the exploitation of the Bengalis by the Punjabis and industrialists of West Pakistan.

But do the powers-that-be really care about the way things are shaping in our land? A clash of personalities and unbridled ambitions led to the partition of India. Now, at a much lower level, a similar clash is paralysing government and destroying the people's faith in democracy and the integrity of the administration. Top thinkers have been crying their hearts out about the state of the nation. But the politician is too engrossed in the pursuit of power and misuse of patronage to look ahead and be forewarned. Alas, the public too seems to have developed apathy in this respect.

In a front-page article headed "Collective Responsibility," Frank Moraes, Editor-in-Chief of the *Indian Express*, said in the issue of 19th March, 1969, and in his weekly column on 24th March headed "Country and Congress" that "if the Congress breaks up, it will be calamitous for the country." He deplored that "Mrs. Gandhi is at times prone to ruffle her colleagues by her speech. More often she is apt to startle them by her studied silence. . . . This habit of mind and approach does not make for happy individual relations or for the smooth conduct of public affairs. . . . Collective Cabinet responsibility is the cornerstone of the British Constitution. It is also the cornerstone of our Constitution. . . . Lapses from the principle account for much of the misunderstandings and controversies generated in recent weeks. . . . A closer understanding between the Congress Party President and the Prime Minister is overdue."

In his weekly column, the National Scene, Sham Lal, Editor of the oldest English daily in the country, the *Times of India*, wrote on 25th March: "There are only two ways of advancement, according to a Chinese saying: 'One is to build your own reputation, like a mountain and stand on it, and the other is to dig pits for everyone else to fall into, so as to appear the only one without fault.' So widespread is the moral rot in the Congress by now that few in the party are even aware of the first choice. Everyone opts for the second as a matter of course. . . . The worst of it is that in all this vicious back-biting there is not the least trace of any concern over policies. . . . The Congress' leaders will soon lose even such little moral authority as they have today if they do not give up this vicious game of digging pits for one another."

Two other commentators, Nirad Chaudhuri, representing the older generation, and Inder Jit, representing the younger columnist, had the following to say. Author and columnist Chaudhuri wrote in his column in the *Hindusthan Standard* of Calcutta on 16th March, 1969, in a tone of despair, that "parliamentary democracy as worked by means of the party system has totally failed in India, and therefore, we must now think of an alternative method by which the Government of the country may be carried on. . . . There is no doubt that the Congress must be held responsible for the unsatisfactory working of the party system in India." Inder Jit, in his nationally syndicated column, wrote on 31st December, 1968, that "masterly inactivity cannot be a substitute for positive moves in search of agreed solutions . . . basic issues must be pulled out of the deep freeze and courageously tackled in 1969. Unless we take active interest in national affairs, tomorrow may have to be postponed."

Chapter 10

BREAK-UP OR BREAK-THROUGH

(a) VANISHING VALUES

In 1900, the year of my birth, the British Empire was the richest political organisation in the world and the greatest military power. India was the "brightest jewel" in the British Crown. Peace and "pathetic contentment" reigned in my country.

The turn of the century marked the birth of the nationalist movement, the first challenge to the Raj and the culmination of the renaissance inspired by Raja Ram Mohan Roy and invigorated by Swami Vivekananda and Swami Dayanand. The death of Queen Victoria and the outbreak of the Boer War in South Africa, which shook the traditional concept of Empire to its foundations, marked too the beginning of the decline, from its zenith, of imperial glory.

In 1969, without its empire and only loosely associated with the countries of the Commonwealth, Britain is groping for a new basis of stability and security. After twenty-two years of independence, India reveals a vast restlessness. Today, my generation finds few traces of the life and values into which it was born.

Life for me has been worth living—one unending thrill. This may be because journalism is the most interesting game of life. Maybe the restless spirit, keen to live intensely, contributed materially to it. Maybe a sense of inadequacy urged me on in the desire to fulfil myself. Perhaps the urge was provided by the outlook in life I had imbibed from my parents and the godmother who held a daily session on the Ramayana or the Bhagwad Gita—that, however poor or lowly born a person may be he had the power to mould, remould or change his destiny by the manner in which he thought, felt and acted.

As I look back, I feel that being a Hindu I did not find myself a stranger in any country and among any people in my several journeys around the world. A Hindu's concept of the universe is that of oneness with all things, animate and inanimate, and of the whole world being one's home. He also believes that each person is free to seek spiritual evolution along the path he considers best. In this sense a Hindu, holding to no rigid dogma, is the most tolerant of all beings. He believes that a person born in India may be born in his next life in Russia or America or anywhere else in the world. He fills the vacuum according to the evolution of his spirit. When a Hindu therefore enters a church, a mosque, a synagogue or vihara he has a feeling of reverence, not of revulsion.

One test of a civilisation is the nature of punishment for crime. Judged by this test, the period of Ram Raj and that of the Pathans and the Mughals was partly barbarous, but one feels nostalgia for the spirit of sacrifice and renunciation, for justice to the lowly and the underdog, they propagated. There is, similarly, nostalgia for British rule. While the Raj lasted, the normal reaction of the common folk to anybody who was overbearing or cruel was: "Don't forget we are under British Raj." Even at the height of Gandhi's rebellion, when the overzealous Briton and the subordinate Indian official indulged in ruthless repression, condemnation took the form: "This is un-British. It is against the code." What was condemned was the aberration. Indeed, Gandhi reflected popular sentiment when he said: "I love Englishmen but fight imperialism."

As I look back over the past, many ifs of history strike me. If the British had at the turn of the century thought of modernising Indian ociety by introducing scientific methods of agriculture and promoting industry, would not the country have been a great asset to humanity and to the Commonwealth? The explanation for the fact the British behaved as they did was that their rulers had lost the perspective of history and were content to perpetuate the *status quo* that had yielded them rich dividends in the past. They had no leader in the twentieth century with a vision to mould the empire into a Commonwealth of free nations. Churchill, the greatest of them, was a *status quo-er*.

All through the last twenty-two years, the average Indian has judged the performance of his new rulers by the yardstick of British rule. The question he puts is: Would such a thing have happened under the British? There is a longing for certain values the average Indian came to associate with good rulers in the three main phases of Indian history. He has not fully understood the complexities of present-day life, the population explosion, the rising economic, social and political expectations, the military confrontation with two enemies on our border after the British shield was withdrawn, and the replacement of the code which enjoined one to work for the good of his family and of the commune with the attitude "each for himself."

There is a general sense of frustration and disillusion at the way our own people have governed the country. During the British rule, it was said that good government was no substitute for self-government. After independence it is realised that the reverse is equally true. The basic fact about the India of today is that this mass of humanity, which may touch 1,000 million by the end of the century, is engaged, because of the revolution of the ballot box, in breaking out of the constricting walls created by caste divisions and the roof representing layer upon layer of imposed authority.

Ram Raj meant the benevolent rule of an individual. It was basically an insurance against marauding bands and famine. The Pathan and Mughal periods created and multiplied a class of agricultural parasites—the landlords. The layer thickened by the time the Mughal Empire disintegrated. The British rulers accepted the prevailing social order and imposed on it a bureaucratic layer to administer justice between man and man and the landlord and his serfs. This was a vertical relationship between the ruler and the ruled. Whoever occupied the seat of authority was the master, and his orders had to be obeyed and his favour sought or bought. The Gandhian revolution did not change this mentality; in fact, it was strengthened during World War II, when the Government presses worked overtime to print currency notes galore to pay for defence orders.

Independence was not the product of a social revolution. So it meant continuance of the bureaucratic system and its expansion.

Thus, the evils of the system multiplied, and so also its beneficiaries who successfully exploited the vast new opportunities for social and material advancement in urban and rural life. The politician, the bureaucrat, the businessman, the farmer, the tenant and the worker have all exploited in their own sphere and in their own way the opportunities opened up by the increased economic activity resulting from the investment of thousands of millions of rupees under the five-year plans. None can cast a stone at the other, for all have participated in this game of sharing spoils and black-marketing and profiteering.

It is a tribute to the genius of our people for survival that the administrative machine, inept, over-extended and feudal in its outlook, functions. It saved millions from dying in the 1967–68 famine and ensured free and fair polls both at the time of the general and mid-term elections. Law and order have not broken down either in the sense that authority has been superseded anywhere or has failed to assert itself, except of course in the hill areas in the north-eastern region where political authority has wavered between a soft line and a hard line in dealing with Naga and Mizo rebels. The Army, the ultimate sanction of governments, has not only been maintained in a state of preparedness for war but has functioned as a standby for civil authority in handling periodic riots. It has grown as an integrated patriotic force.

The big politician has messed up politics, the Civil Servant has clogged the administration, the businessman has indulged in sharp practices and increased the imbalance in the social order, the worker has let down the country by his stance against higher productivity, the farmer has upset the normal channels of trade by hoarding and blackmarketing his produce, the petty official and petty politician have organised rackets to defraud the State and the people. The calibre of the ruling class has weakened, and so has that of the judiciary at large. The Supreme Court, independent under the Constitution, has fulfilled the hopes and expectations of the Founding Fathers. But the same cannot be said of the High Courts, where appointments have not always been made on merit and have been influenced by the Chief Ministers.

However, the people are wide awake as never before; they value the right to elect their rulers. They fall a prey to caste, parochial, religious and regional appeals, yet they have a vision of Mother India, and will give their all to defend it. Successive Parliaments since independence have willingly voted without question whatever funds the Government wanted for defence. The politicians who year in and year out crusaded against military spending in the British

days because it was Rs. 500 million now vote thirty times as much
without demur, indeed with cheers. No sacrifice is considered too
great to defend the nation.

(b) SURGE OF REVOLT

What is really happening in India is not religious revival but a
revolt against the established order. Naturally, people seek shelter
under a religious or caste or regional umbrella or escape from
challenges by clubbing with likeminded and identifiable elements.
But the challenge of modernism is all pervasive, and the churning
of the social order will produce a viable human order. For the first
time since the dawn of history, the Hindu (this term includes all
Indians) has begun to give up taboos and live in harmony not only
with the world in abstract but in form and practice, in dress and
food habits, in his attitude towards morality and sex and his ideas of
sociability. Endowed with a nimble mind and perhaps an extra-
sensitive intelligence, he will play a constructive role in giving
reality to the Gandhian concept of non-violence as the sheet-anchor
of the human race and Nehru's creed of coexistence of various
political and economic beliefs as the basis of international relations
in a dynamic society.

Change is the law of life, and the Western nations have progressed
faster than the Eastern because they have believed in experiment
and in survival through ordeals. The struggle for existence motivated them originally to explore the secrets of nature. The easier
way of life in the tropics has induced people to simple living and
high thinking. Now everybody's survival depends on hard work and
on extracting the best from Mother Earth with the help of science
and technology, and the Indian will not only get into the race but
will contribute his genius to winning it.

The Gandhi era caused the country to stagnate intellectually.
Till his coming, its talent had found an outlet mainly in the legal
and teaching professions. These were paralysed by his triple boycott
of the legislatures, law courts and educational institutions. Moreover,
he reduced politics to a simple formula which even the unlettered
peasant could comprehend. Nehru opened many institutions of
higher learning and established Art academics. However, he did not
encourage intellectuals. He had use only for such as would or could
advance his purpose. Shastri shied away from talent because it
exposed his shortcomings. Indira Gandhi has a modern mind but
she is still a question mark.

Parliament and a government reflect the standard of intelligence of people at various social levels and the general level of intellectual attainment of a nation. In that sense, our Parliament may claim to be a true representative of the people but modern government is a very complex mechanism and administration a huge business operation. Can the Government be run by Civil Servants, who learn as they operate the machine, and by elected representatives who have not learned the lessons of life through hard work and personal endeavour? In other words, is the professional politician any good? The answer is that a wholetime politician can be a salesman provided he has goods to sell. And this means that every political party must have a hard core of members well versed in economics, the humanities, science and technical knowledge who can evolve ideas and plan fresh solutions.

The weakness of the political set-up in India is partly due to the fact that the system of Cabinet government has been brought into disrepute. Nehru did not consult his Cabinet colleagues on foreign affairs and encouraged the practice of each Minister clearing his policy decisions with him, thus converting the Ministries into so many sub-empires of his own empire. Shastri organised a committee of secretaries of key Government departments to advise him, and the Cabinet generally rubberstamped the decisions of this body. Mrs. Gandhi has combined the practices of her predecessors with this difference—that Ministers generally take decisions without consulting her and are happy that the Cabinet is ineffective.

The great mistake Nehru made was that he decided to build up defence and the development programme simultaneously after the Sino–Indian war. His refusal to scale down development resulted in heavy deficit financing. Inflation had already started as a result of the long gestation of public sector investment. To add to the misfortunes of the country, there came two successive years of drought. The only way to rescue the national economy is by linking labour productivity with incentives. India has already become industrially self-reliant to the extent of fifty to sixty per cent. This should rise to eighty per cent in the next five years. The country is on the verge of an economic breakthrough if only it has a good administration.

The only two civilisations that have survived the ravages of time are those of India and China. Through the centuries, there was cultural unity in India because of the all-pervading influence of Sanskrit, the Hindu classics written in that language and the existence of an intellectual élite represented by the Brahmins. Thus the absence of political unity did not affect cultural unity. For the first time, political unity was achieved under the republican Constitution adopted by the Constituent Assembly in 1950. That unity is now threatened by divisive forces working at the cultural level. This is because for the first time the inert mass which was quiet under Sanskritic culture has become politically conscious and socially active.

Democracy has been weakened by the manner in which the Communist Party has functioned in India. It has exploited every divisive factor. It has championed the cause of linguistic provinces and of tribal separateness. Unfortunately, the Congress Party tried to counteract the influence of the Communists by adopting measures which in a way conceded what the Communists were demanding. Only economic forces are working for integration. India is a natural common market and economic compulsions, combined with science and technology, make it clear to the people that they can survive and raise their standard of living only if they pool their resources. The Press has not played the expected role in the building of a new India. During the struggle for freedom, the pen of the journalist, particularly of the politician-journalist, played a mighty part. Journalism was a mission in which one felt more than rewarded with the services one was able to render to the motherland. Today, the missionary spirit is gone and journalism has become a mere vocation. As matters stand, Indian democracy lacks the base which competent mass media, especially the Press, provide in other countries. Today the total circulation of the 600 dailies in existence does not exceed seven million, and eighty per cent of the newspaper readers are in the metropolitan areas and big towns. Hardly two per cent of the total newspaper circulation reaches half a million villages, which hold eighty per cent of the population. The control of the Government over the supply of newsprint and import of printing machinery acts as a damper to the production of journals more alive to the needs of the common man. But there is also a lack of enterprise on the part of the proprietors and journalists.

The Press of India, like its politicians and parties, has run out of ideas. Again, like the legislators, it is content with running down individuals and institutions rather than facing the challenges of the space era and the age of dissent. The Press has to alter its outlook and technique, partly because of the competition of the radio and television and partly because the new reader wants to know the causes of developments before they burst into news and the rulers bow to pressures.

The greatest role of the Press is to report on social forces and analyse events in depth. The Press Council of India, constituted in 1967, can be the guardian of the freedom of the Press, judging by my experience of its membership for three years. But the Press has to use its freedom to dissent and debunk those whose powers in this nuclear age can be ruthless. We have at present a compliant Press. What is needed is a barrage of fire based on facts and analysis.

(c) HOPE OF NEW DAWN

India has today two enemies, China and Pakistan. Confrontation with China will last twenty-five years, maybe fifty. It is a long-term problem, and India has to live with it. The only chance of establishing peace and security in Asia is for Russia and the Indian sub-continent to present a united front on land and for Russian and American naval power to ensure peace in the surrounding seas. Confrontation with Pakistan cannot last long. It has to end within the next five years or so, either through a political settlement or through a clash of arms. If the two countries wish to ensure the security and stability of the sub-continent and provide their people with full employment and better standards of living, they have to get together. Both political and economic obligations tend towards a solution because of the growing menace of China and the pressure from Moscow and Washington for a settlement.

Will India meet the challenge? True, it today faces not one but many formidable problems. All these can be tackled one by one provided we resolve the basic crisis of character. Gandhi, the Father of the Nation, helped India to regain something of its lost character. But we have been quick to lose whatever we gained under his leadership, notwithstanding all the ritualistic tributes paid to him especially in the year of Gandhi Jayanh. India has spent hundreds of millions of rupees under the Plans to build what Nehru described as modern temples. But the Indian for whom these have been built feels sadly neglected. There has been little, if any, investment in man. Nevertheless the Indian genius for survival and improvisation will come to the rescue.

I have been asked over and over again in world capitals in the past two years whether India will break up or register a break-through. I have faith in the future of my country and its destiny. I hope I shall see the beginning of the new dawn in my own lifetime. I consider myself a strategic optimist and a tactical pessimist (a phrase borrowed from Malcolm Muggeridge, with whom I had a stimulating talk on the terrace of Hotel Imperial, New Delhi, on 6th April, 1969). The world is moving inexorably towards a four-tier federation in which its resources will be allocated at the United Nations on a geopolitical basis so that regional reservoirs could canalise them to nations, while the constituent nations will distribute them to the participating democracies at the base. But before that stage is reached various countries, democratic and communist, will have military dictatorships. The goal, which looks so dim and distant, should be reached by the end of the twentieth century. Without this consummation there is no hope of survival for civilisation.

In November 1969, I will complete fifty years of journalism and married life. I hope that the story unfolded in these pages, which I have greatly enjoyed writing, has been worth telling and will provide a fitting climax to a career my wife and our children have helped to make purposeful—and worthwhile.

EPILOGUE

Little did Inder Jit and I realise, when we were handed over by Dr. Zakir Hussain, the third President of the Republic, his foreword to my memoirs on 20 March, 1969, that he would die in two months and that the event would prove a catalyst in churning domestic politics and transforming its character. Indeed, momentous events have taken place in the international sphere as well, what with the US making friends with China and Russia; West Germany recognizing East Germany: Pakistan breaking up into two independent States; and India concluding a 20-year Treaty of Friendship with Russia and a 25-year Treaty with Bangladesh!

My publishers requested that the narrative which covers the period ending 7 April 1969 may be brought up to the end of 1972. My first reaction was one of disinclination for two reasons. First, I felt that the intervening period was too short to be assessed in the perspective of history. Secondly, the forces now operating both above and below the surface would need a decade and more to yield calculable results. However, I agreed to write this epilogue as it is possible to note the trends in the manner indicated in the closing chapters of these memoirs.

It is mentioned there, for instance, that in viewing the prospects for a second term as Prime Minister, Indira Gandhi held "one strong trump-the general belief that as Nehru's daughter she was a vote-catcher." It is further stated: "One re-elected leader, she (Indira Gandhi) started ignoring the Old Guard in the belief that her strength lay in keeping the political reins tightly in her hands and operating the party machine with the power and prestige that Prime Ministership gave her. By the middle of 1967, Indira set out to cut the Old Guard to size with a view to eliminating its members one by one ..... Indira has so far managed to stay afloat. She has a tremendous knack for playing politics ("in fact, better than her father," as a prominent member of the Old Guard said to me). But in the bargain most of the time of the Congress leadership is taken up in political manouevres and counter manoeuvres. By the end of 1968, the spirit of sacrifice and service which was the hallmark of Congressmen before independence had given place to a naked struggle for power. India's vast problems of stability and progress took a back seat."

These evils which persist are in a sense endemic. They existed even during the days when Gandhi and other giants manned the top echelons of the Congress. I had just completed editing ten volumes of Sardar

Patel's Correspondence during the crucial years 1945 to 1950. Each volume covering between 450 to 600 pages is replete with instances of power struggle and pulls and pressures. But the leading figures were possessed of overriding patriotism. As recalled in Volume I, Sardar Patel in "a word to Congressmen" stated: "Humility is a Congressman's first requisite because that is the badge of service. Our proper place is not at vantage points of power but at vantage points of service. Who shall be ministers, and where shall State capitals and other things be located are matters for small people to talk and write about. Congressmen will be forced and pushed into seats of power if they are true Congressmen."

The review of Volume II in the *Sunday Statesman* of 2 July 1972 observed: "The picture that emerges from the correspondence is that the Congress as a political party was never nearly so united as it appeared even before the birth and rise of the Congress (R) and the decline of the Congress (O). The man of action that Sardar Patel was, he rarely dithered. His decisions, which were prompt and occasionally unpleasant, are reflected in the style of his letters."

The Times of India reviewing the same volume remarked: "More interesting in some ways is the evidence that the unsavoury practices that are derided so much today were far from unknown even on the eve of independence."

Of particular interest at a time when toppling of ministries is considered a worthy pastime is the injunction Sardar Patel laid down in sharply rebuking Congress leaders' plan of toppling the Muslim League Ministry in Sind. He wrote to the leader of the Congress party in Sind (Volume III): "It is futile to depend upon internal quarrels of the League for building up the strength of the Opposition. They must lay out a programme for steady work among the masses who will be convinced only by honest hard work in their cause. The Hindus in Sind will have to adopt the only honourable course of a dignified Opposition which must be of a constructive nature ..... The Ministry, if it breaks, must break through its inherent weakness and not through our efforts."

I have mentioned in the section of my memoirs headed "After Nehru, What?" that I exchanged views with eleven persons of eminence on the post-election scene in 1967-69. I stated that one view was "that democracy would be saved only if Mrs. Gandhi decided to split the (Congress) party into Right and Left, thus causing a polarisation of forces. The proponents of this view contended that the Right Communists and the Leftists in splinter groups and in regional parties would all join hands to form a united front. Such a decision would isolate the Marxists and prevent them from swallowing the other Leftists who had joined hands with them on the anti-Congress plank. This section felt that the Old Guard should be dropped and Mrs. Gandhi should take the Leftists and progressives together under her wing. This means that both in the States and at the Centre polarisation would come through election strategy and that simple majority rule would promote the evolution of a two-party system."

Indira Gandhi's ideas percolated to me through an inner circle nicknamed "the Kitchen Cabinet." The question of the choice of a new President of the Republic following Dr Zakir Hussain's death slowly gathered political significance and ultimately became one of confrontation between the Prime Minister and the Old Guard. There was the hidden hand of fate in this because neither the PM nor her colleagues of the High Command had originally given it political importance. In fact, Dr Zakir Hussain's death upset the calculations of the Old Guard. I had been told both by the Congress President, S. Nijalingappa, and the Deputy Prime Minister, Morarji Desai, that they had chosen V. V. Giri as Vice President because they felt that he would be too old to be considered for Presidentship at the end of Dr Zakir Hussain's term of office. They had hoped that one of the members of the High Command would fill the top post.

There were murmurs about the role of the President, and some high-ups did mention as political gossip that the President should be a person to whom the Prime Minister should turn for advice. As one of them put it to me: "After all she has just walked from the drawing room of her father's house to the Prime Minister's chair." There was an occasional suggestion that a competent and experienced President could fill the power vacuum in a crisis as the Constitution did not specifically bar such a contingency. Whispering galleries blew these casual talks into a deep laid plot of the Old Guard to have as President their nominee who would cut the Prime Minister to size and even dismiss her!

Indira Gandhi took counsel with her colleagues regarding a suitable candidate and after considering the names of V. V. Giri, Jagjivan Ram and Swaran Singh, fixed on Sanjiva Reddy, who had efficiently done Speakership of the Lok Sabha and had held offices of the Congress President and of the Chief Minister of Andhra Pradesh. Mrs. Gandhi even endorsed the nomination paper of Reddy. From what I knew of the mind of the Old Guard, they had no intention of dislodging Indira Gandhi or of prompting the President to create a crisis. But the political climate at the time got surcharged with intrigues and Mrs Gandhi's camp got convinced that they must defeat the Old Guard's candidate. This became possible as V. V. Giri resigned from his office and stood as a candidate independently.

The split at the Bangalore session of the AICC, which caused Indira

Gandhi to denigrate Morarji Desai, was the outcome of the suspicion that the Old Guard was out to dislodge her and also the result of her political intuition that if she struck a radical posture, she would carry the country and the Congress with her.

To test the reaction to the split among the people and the rank and file of Congressmen, Inder Jit attended the annual session of the Old Congress at Gandhinagar near Ahmedabad in December 1969 and I attended the New Congress's session in Bombay a few days later. Since Bombay was the scene of the first session of the Indian National Congress, the decision to mark the rebirth of the Congress in Bombay was imaginative. As one who had watched, reported and analysed Congress sessions since 1918, I was extended the privilege of sitting on the dais where I spent considerable time by the side of Chief Minister V.P. Naik of Maharashtra and Shankar Dayal Sharma, then General Secretary of the ruling Congress. The Bombay session at Azad Maidan left no doubt in my mind about its impact. The crowd was unprecedented and Indira Gandhi was heard in pin drop silence. Hardly anyone else, except Y.B. Chavan, got the ear of the vast audience.

When the split occurred, the common people labelled the rival Congress organisations in common parlance as Syndicate (the Old Guard) and Indicate (the new Congress). Mrs Gandhi reacted sharply when a speaker from Mysore called the new Congress Indicate, meaning Indira Congress. The term Congi and Congo, again meaning the Indira Congress and the Old Congress, gained currency instead. The mid-term election for the Lok Sabha in 1970-71 giving Mrs Gandhi's party a two-thirds majority in the popular chamber and the General Election in 1972 placing power in all the States, except Tamil Nadu, in the hands of the ruling Congress, finally sealed the fate of the Old Congress and of all opposition parties.

It may be said that in sweeping the poll in 1972, Indira Gandhi's party reaped rich political dividends from the crisis in Pakistan which led to a revolt in East Pakistan under the banner of an independent Bangladesh. India got involved in the crisis because ten million refugees from East Pakistan poured into our country when the Yahya Khan regime unleashed the most brutal attack on their people by the army. The situation in East Pakistan became desperate and Islamabad in its attempt to internationalise it made its air force attack India in the West on 3 December 1971. This precipitated a war in the West and in the East, resulting in the defeat of Pakistan and the emergence of Bangladesh as an independent state. On 17 December a ceasefire was unilaterally ordered by India in the West and the Pak forces surrendered in the east to the joint Indo-Bangladesh Command.

As a result of the war, Mr Bhutto replaced President Yahya Khan and later concluded an agreement with Prime Minister Indira Gandhi known as the Simla Agreement. It has resulted in establishing a new line of control in Jammu and Kashmir and in commiting both countries to settle all disputes bilaterally and peacefully.

The fact, however, is that what Mrs Gandhi effectively cashed in on was the *Garibi Hatao* slogan — a slogan which came to her as a reaction to the one-point 'Indira Hatao' programme of the so-called grand alliance of the opposition parties. "The Grand Alliance," she said, "urges 'Indira Hatao.' But I say 'Garibi Hatao' and ask you to judge." The spontaneous applause that followed her juxtaposition of the rival slogans made her feel that she had hit upon a winner. Thereafter, she successfully sold and got for herself the supreme authority she needed for political stability and for implementing her radical programme as exemplified by nationalization of major banks and abolition of princely purses and privileges.

Not only was the domestic scene thus transformed but momentous events took place in the international sphere. I explained in the concluding chapters that India mattered to the world because of its huge population and potentiality as an industrial power. But I added that the various world capitals I visited in 1967 wanted to see "our people get down to business and give up their anti-work and anti-productivity attitude." I further stated that the US would try to make friends with China and that this would isolate Russia. I added: "India has today two enemies, China and Pakistan. Confrontation with China will last twenty-five years, may be fifty. It is a long-term problem, and India has to live with it. The only chance of establishing peace and security in Asia is for Russia and the Indian sub-continent to present a united front on land and for Russian and American naval power to ensure peace in the surrounding seas. Confrontation with Pakistan cannot last long. It has to end within the next five years or so, either through a political settlement or through a clash of arms."

Now that the euphoria of election victory and of the success of Indian arms in the 14-day war from December 3 to December 17 in 1971 which resulted in the emergence of Bangladesh as an independent republic is over, the elite and the common people are beginning to judge the rulers by their performance.

Significantly the first anniversary of the Indo-Pak war has been marked by realistic assessment of the state of the nation in quarters which may be described as either friendly or not unfriendly to the Indira regime. *The Hindustan Times* in its editorial of 7 December 1972 stated: "The state of the Congress party, which is at a new zenith of power, must cause serious concern as it directly affects the ability and will to act of the Central and State Governments at a time of critical importance. The party continues to lack clear purpose other than the pursuit of power in furtherance of which it has not hesitated to try and topple non-Congress Governments and win over defectors. Quite evidently the split in 1969 had little to do with any ideological cleavage, which was only incidental. The polarisation was primarily around personalities and partly represented a generational change. The Congress today, however, reflects the same spectrum of confused ideologies, factions and wayward principles as it did prior to 1969. The party is almost back at square one."

The Times of India in its editorial of 15 December remarked: "The Prime Minister is no doubt fully aware of the infighting but has, for some curious reason, chosen to play down the danger. She has asked the party members to prepare for 'the challenges on every front', without asking whether engaged in factional intrigues, they are in a fit state of mind to do so. The whole point of forcing a split in the party in 1969 was to give it a new sense of direction and a greater cohesion than before. The irony of it is that the party is more hag-ridden by factionalism than ever before. It can hardly serve as a political instrument for banishing poverty from the land. A party that took itself seriously would not allow its members, old or new, to fight, with means more foul than fair, for positions of vantage in the organisation."

Shankar's Weekly's editorial of 17 December stated: "Indian left radicalism which revived for a time during the last elections to State assemblies has lost itself in petty phrase mongering. The great leap towards establishing an egalitarian society has turned out to be an empty gesture. For all practical purposes we are back in square one ..... The large mass of people are not so much impressed by the unity of the ruling party as by stable prices for easily available essential commodities and reasonable opportunities for employment. This is noticeably lacking in the country and it would be self-delusion to think that these failures can be swept under the carpet until another election comes up when the old slogans can be raised again. It is perverse folly to think that patience, if sufficiently extended, will convert itself to resignation."

The political columnist of the *Sunday Standard* of Delhi, had this to say in its issue of 17 December: "At this time last year India had passed through a difficult but glorious period in its history. Dacca had fallen with the capitulation of the 90,000-strong Pakistani army. On the west India's Prime Minister had made the magnanimous gesture of a unilateral cease-fire. The economy had withstood the strain of the 15-day war and the burden of 10-million refugees for nine months. There was a new sense of confidence in the leadership of Mrs Gandhi. Things have radically changed since ..... There is a general mood of sullen disillusionment among the people which is being fully exploited by the Opposition ..... No one now seriously believes that the split of 1969 has brought about any fundamental change in the functioning of the Congress. The only change is that the old bosses have been replaced by new ones, more ambitious and more ruthless, because they have no firm base of their own. Naturally the new political leaders imposed by Mrs Gandhi in the States find themselves ineffective and unable to function ..... These and such other developments are the first storm signals to Mrs Gandhi. If she succumbs, much of her power and authority would get eroded, although she may continue as the Prime Minister for the full term till 1976. Her achievements on the international front cannot sustain her unless she shows equal determination and courage in solving domestic problems both on the economic and political fronts."

Nayantara Sahgal, a talented author and niece of Jawaharlal Nehru in her review of 1972 in the same issue of (*Sunday Standard*) has said: "From elation at the beginning of the year, today there is disillusionment and tension, a feeling that the year has ebbed away leaving stark economic facts lying before us like driftwood on a beach without even the beginnings of a solution ..... The year's end sees this whole issue highlighted in the debate on fundamental rights in the Supreme Court ..... In the economic sphere confusion reigns, perhaps of design, with the frontier between socialism and communism blurring, and the main lines of policy no longer clear ..... In the past year the class war has been intensified bringing its inevitable consequences of unrest, gathering violence and sporadic upheaval. There is talk of expropriatory and confiscatory legislation ..... Will my life's savings be there when I need them? Will the future I sacrificed for in the hope that my children would be better off than I come about? Will business, or the land into which I put years of work and investment, stay mine? This is the basic insecurity, not of the rich, but of the struggling middle class, worse off today than at any time before, paying more and more for fewer and fewer goods, with no reprieve in sight, and threatened regularly with further erosions of income and prospects ..... With political mischief and in the background, the cynicism, that hard work gets one nowhere, is it any wonder that the students, and that sorely tried and troubled tribe, their teachers, are caught in the massive unease that now has hold of us? ..... There is gross miscalculation somewhere if the war that should have been declared on poverty has been declared instead on achievement — on anyone who has achieved a measure of success in agriculture or industry or in his profession. Strip these gains, and it is assumed equality will result ..... The politician, fortunately for him, is a nationalised individual, with many of his expenses taken care of by the state. He can have no conception of the difficulties of the ordinary man ..... Political morality, never high, is at its lowest ebb, and money is the great scandal tossed about in talk. The blatancy of its collection and the vulgarity of its use are a public secret."

The National Herald of December 30, 1972 reacting to the 74th session of the Congress which concluded in Calcutta the previous day, wrote an editorial headed: Congress Paradoxes. The paper was founded by Jawaharlal Nehru and its Editor, Chalapati Rau, has been generally accepted as an authentic interpreter of Nehru's politics.

The editorial, commenting that even after several years of the party system since independence, the Congress is struggling to be a party, stated: "Gandhi preached the close connection between means and ends; yet most Congress socialists think that any means, are good enough for socialist ends. The people are asked to tighten their belts, but Congressmen do not." It pointed out: "Lenin said that most of his followers were not desirable people. Yet, no true leader can blame his instruments. Gandhi did not, Nehru did not, Indira Gandhi cannot." The editorial concluded with the following injunction: "The Congress cannot do much to redeem its pledges without returning to its pre-independence standards of sacrifice and austerity."

Almost in tune with this judgment was the assessment made by Indira Gandhi herself in the article she wrote for the Congress souvenir to mark the party's Calcutta session. With unerring intuition she diagnosed the malady and bemoaned: "Despite 25 years of political independence as a nation we continue to be intellectually diffident and culturally imitative." This is an indictment of the elite and even more of our leaders.

As matters stand the national scene and mood may be summed up thus:

The revolution started by Raja Ram Mohan Roy and given a thrust by Tilak found culmination through the Gandhian revolution in the attainment of independence on 15 August 1947 and through the absorption of all Princely territories into the Indian Union at the hands of Vallabhbhai Patel. The integration of the country was sanctified by the Indian Constitution and endorsed by the people at five general elections held since 1952.

The modernization started by the British rulers through the introduction of science and technology was given a big thrust by Jawaharlal Nehru. The conquest of the moon through manned missions which cost the US 25 billion dollars to secure 7000 man-hours in space and over 300 lbs of lunar rocks and Russia's adventures in space have in any case pushed India into the modern age. This revolutionary process should find culmination by the year 2,000.

The ballot box introduced by the British in 1920 and given a big thrust by Vallabhbhai Patel, Jawaharlal Nehru and Indira Gandhi has had the effect of politicizing the country in both its urban and rural sectors.

Since the disappearance from the scene of the national heroes of the freedom movement, the people have not had the advantage of being governed by leaders who could sustain confidence in their professions. India is the most populous democracy in the world, but democracy is only a means to an end. We have a Government with a massive parliamentary majority and popular support ensured by a spell-binder. Naturally, the world expects stability and rapid growth. These are not there because politicians by and large are engaged in the game of self-preservation and have little time to divine answers to pressing socio-economic problems. The traditional pulls and historical tensions are below the surface, and they are by no means dormant. They erupt off and on like a volcano. Witness the Telengana and Andhra explosion and the language riots in Assam.

It is in resolving historic tensions that a contribution is made by the elite — the class that cherishes values and culture and propagates them. This class is at a discount because communication has broken down for various reasons — regional and linguistic fanaticism, for instance — and the fact that the ruling class is semi-literate or illiterate. What India is suffering from is not a generation gap, but a gap between the elite and the illiterate. Perhaps the ruling class feels comfort in the fact that it is intellectually in tune with the masses. Speaking at India International Centre on November 2, 1972, Professor V.V. John, Adviser, University of Delhi, observed that conflict of ideas and opinion could advance human welfare provided there was a will to accept that which served the interest of a larger section of society. But the existing situation, he said, was very different — brilliant ideas turned out to be mere slogans. This situation existed because most of our leaders were devoid of intellectual resources, and when they ran short of arguments they resorted to physical violence.

Reacting to the upheaval caused by the judgment of the Supreme Court in upholding the Mulki Rules in Andhra Pradesh and their repercussion on Indian Polity, I wrote in my weekly Political Diary which appeared in the *Tribune* of Chandigarh and several dailies all over the country as a syndicated column on 19 December 1972: "India cannot be held together by the charisma of a national leader, nor by physical ties. It has to be held together by an elite that has shared values and the common yardstick of patriotism. In the past, it was provided successively by the Brahmin elite, Pathan, Iranian and Moghul rulers and the British ICS. After independence, it was provided by national heroes and the all-India Services. Now a new elite has to be created which will override linguistic and regional divisions and loyalties."

Our people's blind faith in the leaders of the freedom struggle has been partly replaced by reversion to faith in soothsayers. This is because the giants of yesterday have not been succeeded by persons of high calibre and burning patriotism. Such a relapse is not unusual in countries that emerge after a long night of darkness.

The Guardian of London carried on its editorial page in its issue of 12 December 1972 the following by an African contributor. Sam Uba, in explaining President Idi Amin's action in expelling Asians from Uganda: "Juju men, witch-doctors, soothsayers and fortune-tellers are potent influences in the life of many African politicians, military leaders, intellectuals and academics. Conversely, almost every Head of State in Africa is believed to have powerful Juju-men and witch-doctors to protect him. Dr. Kaunda of Zambia is the only African Statesman I have not heard associated with juju or witchcraft, although they are widely practised in his country. It was an open secret in Accra that Dr. Nkrumah had three witch-doctors and "a big Juju-man" whom he consulted before he did anything. One was a woman in her 80s. She was installed in Flag Staff House, Nkrumah's official residence. She inspected all food before Nkrumah touched it, and was said also to arrange the bed, for she alone decided in which room he would sleep after she had consulted the oracle."

The Indian masses and even the so-called intelligentsia have a soft corner in their heart for soothsayers. But performance and not blind faith will hereafter determine the people's choice of their rulers. Until now the people wanted security of life and property; hereafter they will demand bread and butter through gainful employment.

India has to reach great heights of economic growth with social justice for sheer survival, but whether this will be achieved peacefully or through an upheaval will depend on how our rulers act and react to the challenges which are built in the system of a poor country.

A fragment of our people are holding the rest of the community to ransom. These consist largely of organised labour, organised industry, government officials and the tribe of self-seeking politicians.

A clear line has not been drawn as to where a politician's function ends and that of the civil servant begins. As matters stand we seem to be drifting towards a semi-democratic authoritarian system without any rules of the game.

The Indian ethos is not against possession or acquisition of wealth. It expects top leaders to set an example of discipline and integrity. When Gandhi advised Nehru to live in a house meant for every MP, he was cautioning against setting living standards far beyond the means of the Indian people. The ruling class has to˙ observe austerity either of the Gandhian or the Communist type, if it wishes to get the people organised under a viable system and have a conscience. It has to set an example in patriotism.

The much-needed reforms, if practised, should release the energies of our people and revive their belief in righteous conduct and the integrity of the administrator and the politician. Today the evil is growing because all means, fair and foul, are used in the single-minded pursuit of power.

The fact is that social changes and economic growth are very much dependent on the ethos of our people. Life in villages is undergoing a change but its positive phase may begin to reveal itself only in the eighties.

Gandhi and Patel carved out a destiny for themselves and the country; Jawaharlal Nehru was the child of destiny; Lal Bahadur Shastri was thrown up by destiny; Indira Gandhi is an instrument of destiny. What that destiny is the late seventies may reveal.

APPENDIX I

The Gandhi–Irwin Agreement, 5th March, 1931

1. Consequent on the conversations that have taken place between His Excellency the Viceroy and Mr. Gandhi, it has been arranged that the civil disobedience movement be discontinued, and that, with the approval of His Majesty's Government, certain action be taken by the Government of India and local Governments.

2. As regards constitutional questions, the scope of future discussion is stated, with the assent of His Majesty's Government, to be with the object of considering further the scheme for the constitutional Government of India discussed at the Round Table Conference. Of the scheme there outlined, Federation is an essential part; so also are Indian responsibility and reservations or safeguards in the interests of India, for such matters as, for instance, defence; external affairs; the position of minorities; the financial credit of India, and the discharge of obligations.

3. In pursuance of the statement made by the Prime Minister in his announcement of the 19th of January 1931, steps will be taken for the participation of the representatives of the Congress in the further discussions that are to take place on the scheme of constitutional reform.

4. The settlement relates to activities directly connected with the civil disobedience movement.

5. Civil disobedience will be effectively discontinued and reciprocal action will be taken by Government. The effective discontinuance of the civil disobedience movement means the effective discontinuance of all activities in furtherance thereof, by whatever methods pursued and, in particular, the following:
(a) The organised defiance of the provisions of any law.
(b) The movement for the non-payment of land revenue and other legal dues.
(c) The publication of news-sheets in support of the civil disobedience movement.
(d) Attempts to influence civil and military servants or village officials against Government or to persuade them to resign their posts.

6. As regards the boycott of foreign goods, there are two issues involved, firstly, the character of the boycott and secondly, the methods employed in giving effect to it. The position of Government is as follows. They approve of the encouragement of Indian industries as part of the economic and industrial movement designed to improve the material

conditions of India, and they have no desire to discourage methods of propaganda, persuasion or advertisement pursued with this object in view, which do not interfere with the freedom of action of individuals, or are not prejudicial to the maintenance of law and order. But the boycott on non-Indian goods (except of cloth which has been applied to all foreign cloth) has been directed during the civil disobedience movement chiefly, if not exclusively, against British goods, and in regard to these it has been admittedly employed in order to exert pressure for political ends.

It is accepted that a boycott of this character, and organised for this purpose, will not be consistent with the participation of representatives of the Congress in a frank and friendly discussion of constitutional questions between representatives of British India, of the Indian States, and of His Majesty's Government and political parties in England, which the settlement is intended to secure. It is, therefore, agreed that the discontinuance of the civil disobedience movement connotes the definite discontinuance of the employment of the boycott of British commodities as a political weapon and that, in consequence, those who have given up, during a time of political excitement, the sale or purchase of British goods must be left free without any form of restraint to change their attitude if they so desire . . .

8. Mr. Gandhi has drawn the attention of Government to specific allegations against the conduct of the police, and represented the desirability of a public enquiry into them. In present circumstances Government see great difficulty in this course and feel that it must inevitably lead to charges and counter-charges, and so militate against the re-establishment of peace. Having regard to these considerations, Mr. Gandhi agreed not to press the matter.

[*India's Ambassador in Peking
at the time was K. M. Passikkar*]

APPENDIX II

Sardar Patel's letter to Jawaharlal Nehru on 7 November, 1950

D.O. No. 821–DPM/50
New Delhi, 7th Nov. 1950

My dear Jawaharlal,

Ever since my return from Ahmedabad and after the Cabinet meeting the same day which I had to attend at practically fifteen minutes' notice and for which I regret I was not able to read all the papers, I have been anxiously thinking over the problem of Tibet and I thought I should share with you what is passing through my mind.

2. I have carefully gone through the correspondence between the External Affairs Ministry and our Ambassador in Peking and through him the Chinese Government. I have tried to peruse this correspondence as favourably to our Ambassador and the Chinese Government as possible, but, I regret to say that neither of them comes out well as a result of this study. The Chinese Government have tried to delude us by professions of peaceful intentions. My own feeling is that at a crucial period they managed to instil into our Ambassador a false sense of confidence in their so-called desire to settle the Tibetan problem by peaceful means. There can be no doubt that, during the period covered by this correspondence, the Chinese must have been concentrating for an onslaught on Tibet. The final action of the Chinese, in my judgment, is little short of perfidy. The tragedy of it is that the Tibetans put faith in us; they chose to be guided by us; and we have been unable to get them out of the meshes of Chinese diplomacy or Chinese malevolence. From the latest position, it appears that we shall not be able to rescue the Dalai Lama. Our Ambassador has been at great pains to find an explanation or justification for Chinese policy and actions. As the External Affairs Ministry remarked in one of their telegrams, there was a lack of firmness and unnecessary apology in one or two representations that he made to the Chinese Government on our behalf. It is impossible to imagine any sensible person believing in the so-called threat to China from Anglo-American machinations in Tibet. Therefore, if the Chinese put faith in this, they must have distrusted us so completely as to have taken us as tools or stooges of Anglo-American diplomacy or strategy. This feeling, if genuinely entertained by the Chinese in spite of your direct approaches to them, indicates that, even though we regard ourselves as the friends of China, the Chinese

do not regard us as their friends. With the Communist mentality of "Whoever is not with them being against them," this is a significant pointer, of which we have to take due note. During the last several months, outside the Russian Camp, we have practically been alone in championing the cause of Chinese entry into the U.N.O. and in securing from the Americans assurances on the question of Formosa. We have done everything we could to assuage Chinese feelings, to allay its apprehensions and to defend its legitimate claims, in our discussions and correspondence with America and Britain and in the U.N.O. In spite of this, China is not convinced about our disinterestedness; it continues to regard us with suspicion and the whole psychology is one, at least outwardly, of scepticism, perhaps mixed with a little hostility. I doubt if we can go any further than we have done already to convince China of our good intentions, friendliness and goodwill. In Peking we have an Ambassador who is eminently suitable for putting across the friendly point of view. Even he seems to have failed to convert the Chinese. Their last telegram to us is an act of gross discourtesy not only in the summary way it disposes of our protest against the entry of Chinese forces into Tibet but also in wild insinuation that our attitude is determined by foreign influences. It looks as though it is not a friend speaking in that language but a potential enemy.

3. In the background of this, we have to consider what new situation now faces us as a result of the disappearance of Tibet, as we know it, and the expansion of China almost up to our gates. Throughout history, we have seldom been worried about our north-east frontier. The Himalaya has been regarded as an impenetrable barrier against any threat from the north. We had a friendly Tibet which gave us no trouble. The Chinese were divided. They had their own domestic problems and never bothered us about our frontiers. In 1914, we entered into a convention with Tibet which was not endorsed by the Chinese. We seem to have regarded Tibetan autonomy as extending to independent treaty relationship. Presumably, all that we required was Chinese counter-signature. The Chinese interpretation of suzerainty seems to be different. We can, therefore, safely assume that very soon they will disown all the stipulations which Tibet has entered into with us in the past. That throws into the melting pot all frontier and commercial settlements with Tibet on which we have been functioning and acting during the last half a century. China is no longer divided. It is united and strong. All along the Himalayas in the north and north-east, we have, on our side of the frontier, a population ethnologically and culturally not different from Tibetans or Mongoloids. The undefined state of the frontier and the existence on our side of a population with its affinities to Tibetans or Chinese have all the elements of potential trouble between China and ourselves. Recent and bitter history also tells us that Communism is no shield against imperialism and that Communists are as good or as bad as imperialists as any other. Chinese ambitions in this respect not only cover the Himalayan slopes on our side but also include important parts of Assam. They have their

ambitions in Burma also. Burma has the added difficulty that it has no McMahon Line round which to build up even the semblance of an agreement. Chinese irredentism and Communist imperialism are different from the expansionism or imperialism of the Western Powers. The former has a cloak of ideology which makes it ten times more dangerous. In the guise of ideological expansion lie concealed racial, national and historical claims. The danger from the north and north-east, therefore, becomes both communist and imperialist. While our western and north-eastern threats to security are still as prominent as before, a new threat has developed from the north and north-east. Thus, for the first time, after centuries, India's defence has to concentrate itself on two fronts simultaneously. Our defence measures have so far been based on the calculations of a superiority over Pakistan. In our calculations we shall now have to reckon with Communist China in the north and north-east—a Communist China which has definite ambitions and aims and which does not, in any way, seem friendlily disposed towards us.

4. Let me also consider the political considerations on this potentially troublesome frontier. Our northern or north-eastern approaches consist of Nepal, Bhutan, Sikkim, Darjeeling and the Tribal Areas in Assam. From the point of view of communications they are weak spots. Continuous defensive lines do not exist. There is almost an unlimited scope for infiltration. Police protection is limited to a very small number of passes. There too, our outposts do not seem to be fully manned. The contact of these areas with us, is, by no means, close and intimate. The people inhabiting these portions have no established loyalty or devotion to India. Even Darjeeling and Kalimpong areas are not free from pro-Mongoloid prejudices. During the last three years, we have not been able to make any appreciable approaches to the Nagas and other hill tribes in Assam. European missionaries and other visitors had been in touch with them, but their influence was, in no way, friendly to India or Indians. In Sikkim, there was political ferment some time ago. It is quite possible that discontent is smouldering there. Bhutan is comparatively quiet, but its affinity with Tibetans would be a handicap. Nepal has a weak oligarchic regime based almost entirely on force; it is in conflict with a turbulent element of the population as well as with enlightened ideas of the modern age. In these circumstances, to make people alive to the new danger or to make them defensively strong is a very difficult task indeed, and that difficulty can be got over only by enlightened firmness, strength and a clear line of policy. I am sure the Chinese and their source of inspiration, Soviet Russia, would not miss any opportunity of exploiting these weak spots, partly in support of their ideology and partly in support of their ambitions. In my judgment, therefore, the situation is one in which we cannot afford either to be complacent or to be vacillating. We must have a clear idea of what we wish to achieve and also of the methods by which we should achieve it. Any faltering or lack of decisiveness in formulating our objectives or in pursuing our policy to attain those objectives is bound to weaken us and increase the threats which are so evident.

5. Side by side with these external dangers we shall now have to face serious internal problems as well. I have already asked Iengar to send to the External Affairs Ministry a copy of the Intelligence Bureau's appreciation of these matters. Hitherto, the Communist Party of India has found some difficulty in contacting Communists abroad, or in getting supplies of arms, literature, etc., from them. They had to contend with difficult Burmese and Pakistan frontiers on the east or with the long seaboard. They shall now have a comparatively easy means of access to Chinese Communists, and through them to other foreign Communists. Infiltration of spies, fifth columnists and Communists would now be easier. Instead of having to deal with isolated Communist pockets in Telengana and Warrangal we may have to deal with Communist threats to our security along our northern and north-eastern frontiers where, for supplies of arms and ammunition, they can safely depend on Communist arsenals in China. The whole situation thus raises a number of problems on which we must come to an early decision so that we can, as said earlier, formulate the objectives of our policy and decide the methods by which those actions will have to be fairly comprehensive involving not only our defence strategy and state of preparation but also problems of internal security to deal with which we have not a moment to lose. We shall also have to deal with administrative and political problems in the weak spots along the frontier to which I have already referred.

6. It is, of course, impossible for me to be exhaustive in setting out all these problems. I am, however, giving below some of the problems, which in my opinion, require early solution and round which we have to build our administrative or military policies and measures to implement them:

(a) A military and intelligence appreciation of the Chinese threat to India both on the frontier and to internal security.

(b) An examination of our military position and such redisposition of our forces as might be necessary, particularly with the idea of guarding important routes or areas which are likely to be the subject of dispute.

(c) An appraisement of the strength of our forces and, if necessary, reconsideration of our retrenchment plans for the Army in the light of these new threats.

(d) A long-term consideration of our defence needs. My own feeling is that, unless we assure our supplies of arms, ammunition and armour, we would be making our defence position perpetually weak and we would not be able to stand up to the double threat of difficulties both from the west and north-west, and north and north-east.

(e) The question of Chinese entry into U.N.O. In view of the rebuff which China has given us and the method which it has followed in dealing with Tibet, I am doubtful whether we can advocate its claims any longer. There would probably be a threat in the U.N.O. virtually to outlaw China, in view of its active participation in the Korean War. We must determine our attitude on this question also.

(f) The political and administrative steps which we should take to strengthen our northern and north-eastern frontiers. This would include the whole of the border i.e. Nepal, Bhutan, Sikkim, Darjeeling and the Tribal territory in Assam.

(g) Measures of internal security in the border areas as well as the States flanking those areas such as U.P., Bihar, Bengal and Assam.

(h) Improvement of our communications, road, rail, air and wireless in these areas, and with the frontier outposts.

(i) Policing and intelligence of frontier posts.

(j) The future of our mission at Lhasa and the trade posts at Gyangtse and Yatung and the forces which we have in operation in Tibet to guard the trade routes.

(k) The policy in regard to McMahon Line.

7. These are some of the questions which occur to my mind. It is possible that a consideration of these matters may lead us into wider questions of our relationship with China, Russia, America, Britain and Burma. This, however, would be of a general nature, though some might be basically very important, e.g., we might have to consider whether we should not enter into closer association with Burma in order to strengthen the latter in its dealings with China. I do not rule out the possibility that, before applying pressure on us, China might apply pressure on Burma. With Burma, the frontier is entirely undefined and the Chinese territorial claims are more substantial. In its present position, Burma might offer an easier problem for China, and therefore, might claim its first attention.

8. I suggest that we meet early to have a general discussion on these problems and decide on such steps as we might think to be immediately necessary and direct quick examination of other problems with a view to taking early measures to deal with them.

Yours
(sd.) Vallabhbhai Patel

The Hon'ble Pt. Jawaharlal Nehru,
Prime Minister of India,
New Delhi.

India's Ambassador in Peking at the time was K. M. Passikkar

ACKNOWLEDGMENTS

This book is the result of prodigious effort by colleagues and aides who inspired the project and helped in the fulfilment of a common objective: narrating the story of a most revolutionary period from the inside.

John Grigg and Richard Ollard guided me with their comments and suggestions on the manuscript as it got ready in five instalments. Bhaskar Rao, Trevor Drieberg and Inder Jit helped in processing, editing and revising the material to tailor it to the required length and the broad objective.

C. S. Venkatachar, Shankar Prasad, Bhagwan Sahay, three good friends, who reached the top of the ladder as members of the ICS, Uggar Sain, A. R. Vyas and Ram Tarneja went through the text and made valuable suggestions.

The enormous material consisting of clippings of my writings, numerous letters and notes on men and events, including off-the-record talks, was handled by three research aides, Amrit Kakaria, S. P. Gulati and Harinder Anand.

Scores of men and women who figure in the memoirs or whose talks formed the basis of notes were met during 1966–69. This helped to check on records about events to which they and others were related. These included Zakir Husain, S. Radhakrishnan, V. V. Giri, Indira Gandhi, Morarji Desai, Y. B. Chaven, Jagjivan Ram, S. Nijalingappa, K. Kamaraj, Sri Prakasa, Mrs. V. L. Pandit, T. T. Krishnamachari, Satya Narain Sinha, Krishna Menon, G. S. Pathak, Khandubhai Desai, C. D. Deshmukh, U. Thant, H. P. Mody, M. C. Setalvad, Mahavir Tyagi, K. D. Malaviya, Mehr Chand Mahajan, D. P. Mishra, Humayun Kabir, C. Subramaniam, Manubhai Shah, Sushila Nayyar, Fakhruddin Ali Ahmed, C. N. Annadurai, E. M. S. Namboodiripad, Ram Subhag Singh, K. K. Shah, Karan Singh, B. P. Chaliha, C. B. Gupta, Kamlapati Tripathi, Charan Singh, Jyoti Basu, T. N. Singh, S. G. Barve, Ujjal Singh, P. V. Cherian, C. D. Pande, R. K. Hegde, P. N. Sapru, N. Raghavan Pillai, K. P. S. Menon, H. V. R. Iengar, H. M. Patel, B. N. Jha, S. S. Khera, Dharma Vira, V. Vishwanathan, S. Boothalingam, S. Jagannathan, L. K. Jha, D. L. Mazumdar, V. Shankar, B. K. Nehru, A. N. Jha, P. N. Haksar, K. B. Lall, T. N. Kaul, Azim Husain, Arshad Husain, H. C. Sarin, Kewal Singh, Ali Yawar Jung, Rashid Ali Baig, Generals Shrinagesh, P. N. Thapar, Kumaramangalam, Maneckshaw and Bahadur Singh, Chester Bowles, Ronald Michener, Sherman Cooper, John Freeman, Arthur Tange, J. R. Mudholkar, K. Srinivasan, S. P. Jain, Keshub

Mahindra, Harish Mahindra, G. L. Bansal, I. J. Bahadur Singh, R. Jaipal, Jamal Kidwai, Mohd. Uunus, Ranjit Singh, P. L. Sondhi, R. R. Gupta, Joginder Singh, Duni Chand Sikka, Hans Raj Gupta, R. L. Handa, A. G. Sheorey, Pothan Joseph, Narain Das, Tulsi Ram and A. P. Dube.

Index

Printed in Great Britain
by Amazon

83093200R00294